PENGUIN BOOKS

BREAKING ICE

Terry McMillan is the critically acclaimed
author of *Mama, Disappearing Acts,* and *Waiting to Exhale.* She lives outside San Francisco.

BREAKING ICE

An Anthology of Contemporary
African-American Fiction

EDITED BY
Terry McMillan

PENGUIN BOOKS

PENGUIN BOOKS
Published by the Penguin Group
Penguin Books USA Inc.,
375 Hudson Street, New York, New York 10014, U.S.A.
Penguin Books Ltd, 27 Wrights Lane,
London W8 5TZ, England
Penguin Books Australia Ltd, Ringwood,
Victoria, Australia
Penguin Books Canada Ltd, 10 Alcorn Avenue,
Toronto, Ontario, Canada M4V 3B2
Penguin Books (N.Z.) Ltd, 182–190 Wairau Road,
Auckland 10, New Zealand

Penguin Books Ltd, Registered Offices:
Harmondsworth, Middlesex, England

First published in 1990 in simultaneous hardcover and paperback
editions by Viking Penguin, a division of Penguin Books USA Inc.

13 15 14 12

Copyright © Terry McMillan, 1990
Preface copyright © John Edgar Wideman, 1990
All rights reserved

Pages 691–693 constitute an extension of this copyright page.

LIBRARY OF CONGRESS CATALOGING IN PUBLICATION DATA
Breaking ice : an anthology of contemporary American Black fiction /
edited by Terry McMillan.
p.   cm.
ISBN 0 14 01.1697 4
1. American fiction—Afro-American authors.   2. American
fiction—20th century.   3. Afro-Americans—Fiction.   I. McMillan,
Terry.
PS647.A35B58   1990
813'.5080896073—dc20   89-72191

Printed in the United States of America
Set in Electra and Novarese Book
Designed by Kathryn Parise

PREFACE

Dear Terry,

Congratulations. It's time we had a new anthology of African-American fiction. I don't know what you've gathered, but I'm sure your sample will be enjoyable and instructive. The notes that follow are wishes, cautions, play with the issues and ideas that could/should, in my view, surface in a collection of contemporary Afro-American writing.

> The African artist allows wide scope to his fantasy in the mask. . . . With colors, feathers, and horns he accomplishes some astonishingly lively effects. In a slow creative process he brings to life a work which constitutes a new unit, a new being. If the sculpture proves to be a success, a helpful medium, the tribe adheres to this form and passes it on from generation to generation. . . . Thus we have a style, a firmly established formal canon, which may not be lightly discarded. . . . For this reason a style retains its specific character for decades, even centuries. It stands and falls with the faith to which it is linked.
>
> —*The Art of Black Africa.* Elsy Leuzinger

Since we're seen as marginal politically, economically, and culturally, African-American writers have a special, vexing stake in reforming, revitalizing the American imagination. History is a cage, a conundrum we must escape or resolve before our art can go freely about its business. As has always been the case, in order to break into print we must be prepared to deal with the extra-literary forces that have conspired to keep us silent, or our stories, novels, and poems will continue to be treated as marginally as our lives, unhinged, unattached to the everyday reality of "mainstream," majority readers. Magazine editors know that their jobs depend upon purveying images the public recognizes and approves, so they seldom include our fictions, and almost never choose those which transcend stereotypes and threaten to expose the fantasies of superiority, the bedrock lies and brute force that sustain the majority's power over the *other*. Framed in foreign, inimical contexts, minority stories appear at best as exotic slices of life and local color, at worst as ghettorized irrelevancies.

However, as the assumptions of the mono-culture are challenged, overrun, defrock themselves daily in full view of the shameless media, more and more of the best fiction gravitates toward the category of "minority." The truth that each of us starts out alone, a minority of one, each in a slightly different place (no place), resides somewhere in the lower frequencies of our communal consciousness. New worlds, alternative versions of reality are burgeoning. In spite of enormous, overwhelming societal pressures to conform, to standardize the shape and meaning of individual lives, voices like Ralph Ellison's reach us, impelling us to attend to the *chaos which lives within the pattern* of our certainties.

Good stories transport us to these extraordinarily diverse regions where individual lives are enacted. For a few minutes we can climb inside another's skin. Mysteriously, the dissolution of ego also sharpens the sense of self, reinforces independence and relativity of point of view. People's lives resist a simple telling, cannot be understood safely, reductively from some static still point, some universally acknowledged center around which all other lives orbit. Narrative is a reciprocal process, regressive and progressive, dynamic. When a culture hardens into heliocentricity, fancies itself the star of creation, when otherness is imagined as a great darkness except for what the star illuminates, it's only a matter of time until the center collapses in upon itself, imploding with sigh and whimper.

Minority writers hold certain peculiar advantages in circumstances of cultural breakdown, reorientation, transition. We've accumulated centuries of experience dealing with problems of marginality, problems that are suddenly on center stage for the whole society: inadequacy of language, failure of institutions, a disintegrating metropolitan vision that denies us or swallows us, that attracts and repels, that promises salvation and extinction. We've always been outsiders, orphans, bastard children, hard-pressed to make our claims heard. In order to endure slavery and oppression it's been necessary to cultivate the double-consciousness of sere, artist, mother. Beaten down by countless assertions of the inadequacy, the repugnance of our own skin, we've been forced to enter the skins of others, to see, as a condition of survival, the world and ourselves through the eyes of others. Our stories can place us back at the center, at the controls; they can offer alternative realities, access to the sanctuary we carry around inside our skulls. The African-American imagination has evolved as discipline, defense, coping mechanism, counterweight to the galling facts of life. We've learned to confer upon ourselves the power of making up our lives, changing them as we go along.

Marginality has also refined our awareness, our proficiency in nonliterary modes of storytelling. Folk culture preserves and expresses an identity, a history, a self-evaluation apart from those destructive, incarcerating images proliferated by the mainline culture. Consciously and unconsciously we've integrated these resources of folk culture into our writing. Our songs, dreams, dances, styles of walk and talk, dressing, cooking, sport, our heroes and heroines provide a record of how a particular group has lived in the world, in it, but not of it. A record so distinctive and abiding that its origins in culture have been misconstrued as rooted in biology. A long-tested view of history is incorporated in the art of African-American people, and our history can be derived from careful study of forms and influences that enter our cultural performances and rituals. In spite of and because of marginal status, a powerful, indigenous vernacular tradition has survived, not unbroken, but unbowed, a magnet, a focused energy, something with its own logic, rules, and integrity connecting current developments to the past. An articulate, syncretizing force our best artists have drawn upon, a force sustaining both individual talent and tradition. Though minstrel shows were popularized as a parody of black life, these musical reviews were also a vehicle for preserving authentic African-derived elements of black American culture. Today rap, for all its excesses and commercialization, reasserts the African core of black music: polyrhythmic dance beat, improvisational spontaneity, incantatory use of the word to name, blame, shame, and summon power, the obligation of ritual to instruct and enthuse. It's no coincidence that rap exploded as the big business of music was luring many black artists into "crossing over." Huge sums were paid to black recording artists; then a kind of lobotomy was performed on their work, homogenizing, commodifying, pacifying it by removing large portions of what made the music think and be. Like angry ancestral spirits, the imperatives of tradition rose up, reanimated themselves, mounted the corner chanters and hip hoppers. As soul diminished to a category on the pop charts, the beat from the street said no-no-no, you're too sweet. Try some of this instead. Stomp your feet. Don't admit defeat.

Put your hands together. Hit it. Hit. Boom. Crank up the volume. Bare bones percussion and chant holler scream. Our loud selves, our angry selves. Our flying feet and words and raunchy dreams. Instruments not possessed mimicked by our voices. Electronics appropriated. Recording tricknology explored and deconstructed, techniques reversed, foregrounded, parodied. Chaboom. Boom. Sounds of city, of machines of inner space and outer space merge. Boom boxes. Doom boxes. Call the roll of the ancestors. Every god from Jah, Isis, Jehovah, Allah, and Shango to James Brown and the Famous Flames. Say the names. Let them strut the earth again. Get right, children. Rap burst forth precisely where it did, when it did because that's where the long, long night of poverty and discrimination, of violent marginality remained a hurting truth nobody else was telling. That's where the creative energies of a subject people were being choked and channeled into self-destruction.

When an aesthetic tradition remembers its roots, the social conditions (slavery, oppression, marginality) and the expressive resources it employed to cope with these conditions, the counter version of these conditions it elaborated through art, when it doesn't allow itself to be distracted, that is, keeps telling the truth which brought it into being—the necessity of remaining human, defining human in its own terms, resisting those destructive definitions in the Master's tongue, attitudes and art—then that tradition remains alive, a referent, a repository of value, money we can take to the bank. Afro-American traditions contain the memory of a hard, unclean break. This partially accounts for key postures that are subversive, disruptive, disjunctive. To the brutality that once ripped us away and now tries to rip us apart, we turn a stylized mask of indifference, of malleability, a core of iron, silent refusal. Boom. Chaboom. Boom. While our feet, feet, feet, dance to another beat.

I look for, cherish this in our fiction.

On the other hand—or should I say other face, since the shield I'm raising has two sides and one cannot be lifted without the other—what about the future? Is there any difference between sitting in at an all-white lunch counter and a minority writer composing a story in English? What's the fate of a black story in a white world of white stories? What can we accomplish with our *colors, feathers, and horns*, how can we fruitfully extend our tradition? How do we break out of the circle of majority-controlled publishing houses, distributors, critics, editors, readers? Vernacular language is not enough. Integration is not enough, unless one views mathematical, proportional representation as a goal instead of a step. If what a writer wants is freedom of expression, then somehow that larger goal must be addressed implicitly/explicitly in our fictions. A story should somehow contain clues that align it with tradition and critique tradition, establish the new space it requires, demands, appropriates, hint at how it may bring forth other things like itself, where these others have, will, and are coming from. This does not mean defining criteria for admitting stories into some ideologically sound, privileged category, but seeking conditions, mining territory that maximizes the possibility of free, original expression. We must continue inventing our stories, sustaining, not sacrificing, the double consciousness that is a necessity for any writing with the ambition of forging its own place.

Black music again illuminates glories and pitfalls, the possibility of integrity, how artists nourished by shared cultural roots can prove again and again that, even though they are moving through raindrops, they don't have to get soaked. Their art signifies they are in the storm but not of it. black music is a movable feast, fluid in time, space, modality, exhibiting in theme and variations multiple relationships with the politically, socially, aesthetically dominant order, the fullest possible range of relationships, including the power and independence to change places, reverse the hierarchy, *be* the dominant order.

What lessons are transferable to the realm of literature? Is musical language freer, less inscribed with the historical baggage of European hegemony, exploitation, racism? Is it practical within the forms and frequencies of this instrument (written English) to roll back history, those negative accretions, those iron bars and "White Only" signs that steal one's voice, one's breath away?

Are there ways fiction can express the dialectic, the tension, the conversation, the warfare of competing versions of reality English contains? One crucial first step may be recognizing that black/white, either/or perceptions of the tensions within language are woefully inadequate. Start by taking nothing for granted, giving nothing away. Study the language. The way we've begun to comb the past. Rehistoricize. Contest. Contest. Return junk mail to sender. Call into question the language's complacencies about itself. At the level of spelling, grammar, how it's taught, but also deeper, its sounds, their mamas, its coded pretensions to legitimacy, gentility, exclusivity, seniority, logic. Unveil chaos within the patterns of certainty. Restate issues and paradigms so they are not simply the old race problem relexified. Whose language is it, anyway?

Martin Bernal in *Black Athena* has traced the link between European theories of race and language. How nineteenth-century theories of language development parallel, buttress, and reinforce hierarchical concepts of race and culture. How social "sciences," the soft core posing as the hard core of academic humanities curricula, were tainted at their inception by racist assumptions and agendas. How romantic linguistic theory was used as a tool to prove the superiority of the West. How uncritical absorption of certain hallowed tenets of Western thought is like participating in your own lynching. Be prepared to critique any call for "back to basics" in light of the research Bernal gathers and summarizes. The great lie that systems of thought are pure, universal, uncontaminated by cultural bias is once more being gussied up for public consumption. Whose Great Books in whose interest must be read? Whose stories should be told? By whom? To what ends?

How does language grow, change? What are the dynamics that allow individual speakers to learn a language, adapt it to the infinite geography of their inner imaginative worlds, the outer social play, the constant intercourse of both? Can the writer love language and also keep it at arm's length as material, a medium, foregrounding its arbitrariness, its treacherousness, never calling it his/her own, never completely identifying with it but making intimate claims by exploring what it can do, what it could do if the writer has patience, luck, skill, and practices, practices, practices?

In it, but not of it. And that stance produces bodies of enabling legislation, a grammar of nuanced tensions, incompatibilities, doors and windows that not only dramatize the stance itself but implicate the medium. A reciprocal unraveling below whose surface is always the unquiet recognition that this language we're using constantly pulls many directions at once and unless we keep alert, keep fighting the undertow, acknowledge the currents going our way and every other damned way, we drown. We are not alone but not separate either; any voice we accomplish is really many voices, and the most powerful voices are always steeped in unutterable silences. A story is a formula for extracting meaning from chaos, a handful of water we scoop up to recall an ocean. Nothing really stands still for this reduction, this abstraction. We need readers who are willing to be coconspirators. It's at this level of primal encounter that we must operate in order to reclaim the language for our expressive purposes. The hidden subject remains: what is our situation with respect to this language? Where does it come from? Where do I come from? Where do we meet and how shall I name this meeting place? What is *food?* What is *eating?* Why do people go to lunch counters? Black music offers a counter integrative model because it poses this species of question about music and fills us with the thrill of knowing yes, yes, the answers, if there are any, and it probably doesn't matter whether there are or not, yay or nay, the answers and the questions are still up for grabs.

—John Edgar Wideman

CONTENTS

Contents

INTRODUCTION

As a child, I didn't know that African-American people wrote books. I grew up in a small town in northern Michigan, where the only books I came across were the Bible and required reading for school. I did not read for pleasure, and it wasn't until I was sixteen when I got a job shelving books at the public library that I got lost in a book. It was a biography of Louisa May Alcott. I was excited because I had not really read about poor white folks before; her father was so eccentric and idealistic that at the time I just thought he was crazy. I related to Louisa because she had to help support her family at a young age, which was what I was doing at the library.

Then one day I went to put a book away, and saw James Baldwin's face staring up at me. "Who in the world is this?" I wondered. I remember feeling embarrassed and did not read his book because I was too afraid. I couldn't imagine that he'd have anything better or different to say than Thomas Mann, Henry Thoreau, Ralph Waldo Emerson, Nathaniel Hawthorne, Ernest Hemingway, William Faulkner, etc. and a horde of other mostly white male writers that I'd been introduced to in Literature 101 in high school. I mean, not only had there not been any African-American authors included in any of those textbooks, but I'd never been given a clue that if we did have anything important to say that somebody would actually publish it. Needless to say, I was not just naïve, but had not yet acquired an ounce of black pride. I never once questioned why there were no representative works by us in any of those textbooks. After all, I had never heard of any African-American writers, and no one I knew hardly read *any* books.

And then things changed.

It wasn't until after Malcolm X had been assassinated that I found out who he was. I know I should be embarrassed about this, but I'm not. I read Alex Haley's biography of him and it literally changed my life. First and foremost, I realized that there was no reason to be ashamed of being black, that it was ridiculous. That we had a history, and much to be proud of. I began to notice how we had actually been treated as less than human; began to see our strength as a people whereas I'd only been made aware of our inferiorities. I started thinking about my role in the world and not just on my street. I started *thinking*. Thinking about things I'd never thought about before, and the thinking turned into questions. But I had more questions than answers.

So I went to college. When I looked through the catalog and saw a class called Afro-American Literature, I signed up and couldn't wait for the first day of class. Did *we* really have enough writers to warrant an entire class? I remember the textbook was called *Dark Symphony: Negro Literature in America* because I still have it. I couldn't believe the rush I felt over and over once I discovered Countee Cullen, Langston Hughes, Ann Petry, Zora Neale Hurston, Ralph Ellison, Jean Toomer, Richard Wright, and rediscovered and read James Baldwin, to name just a few. I'm surprised I didn't need glasses by the end of the semester. My world opened up. I accumulated and gained a totally new insight about, and perception of, our lives as "black" people, as if I had been an outsider and was finally let in. To discover that our lives held as much significance and importance as our white counterparts was more than gratifying, it was exhilarating. Not only had we lived diverse, interesting, provocative, and relentless lives, but during, through, and as a result of all these painful experiences, some folks had taken the time to write it down.

Not once, throughout my entire four years as an undergraduate, did it occur to me that I might one day *be* a writer. I mean, these folks had genuine knowledge and insight. They also had a fascination with the truth. They had something to write about. Their work was bold, not flamboyant. They learned how to exploit the language so that readers would be affected by what they said and how they said it. And they had talent.

I never considered myself to be in possession of much of the above, and yet when I was twenty years old, the first man I fell in love with broke my heart. I was so devastated and felt so helpless that my reaction manifested itself in a poem. I did not sit down and say, "I'm going to write a poem about this." It was more like magic. I didn't even know I was writing a poem until I had written it. Afterward, I felt lighter, as if something had happened to lessen the pain. And when I read this "thing" I was shocked because I didn't know where the words came from. I was scared, to say the least, about what I had just experienced, because I didn't understand what had happened.

For the next few days, I read that poem over and over in disbelief because I had written it. One day, a colleague saw it lying on the kitchen table and read it. I was embarrassed and shocked when he said he liked it, then went on to tell me that he had just started a black literary magazine at the college and he wanted to publish it. Publish it? He was serious and it found its way onto a typeset page.

Seeing my name in print excited me. And from that point on, if a leaf moved on a tree, I wrote a poem about it. If a crack in the sidewalk glistened, surely there was a poem in that. Some of these verbose things actually got published in various campus newspapers that were obviously desperate to fill up space. I did not call myself a poet; I told people I wrote poems.

Years passed.

Those poems started turning into sentences and I started getting nervous. What the hell did I think I was doing? Writing these little go-nowhere vignettes. All these beginnings. And who did I think I was, trying to tell a story? And who cared? Even though I had no idea what I was doing, all I knew was that I was beginning to realize that a lot of things mattered to me, things disturbed me, things that I couldn't change. Writing became an outlet for my dissatisfactions, distaste, and my way of trying to make sense of what I saw happening around me. It was my way of trying to fix what I thought was broken. It later became the only way to explore personally what I didn't understand. The problem, however, was that I was writing more about ideas than people. Everything was so "large," and eventually I had to find a common denominator. I ended up asking myself what I really cared about: it was people, and particularly African-American people.

The whole idea of taking myself seriously as a writer was terrifying. I didn't know any writers. Didn't know how you knew if you "had" it or not. Didn't know if I was or would ever be good enough. I didn't know how you went about the business of writing, and besides, I sincerely wanted to make a decent living. (I had read the horror stories of how so few writers were able to live off of their writing alone, many having lived like bohemians.) At first, I thought being a social worker was the right thing to do, since I was bent on saving the world (I was an idealistic twenty-two years old), but when I found out I couldn't do it that way, I had to figure out another way to make an impact on folks. A positive impact. I ended up majoring in journalism because writing was "easy" for me, but it didn't take long for me to learn that I did not like answering the "who, what, when, where, and why" of anything. I then—upon the urging of my mother and friends who had graduated and gotten "normal" jobs—decided to try something that would still allow me to "express myself" but was relatively safer, though still risky: I went to film school. Of course what was inherent in my quest to find my "spot" in the world was this whole notion of affecting people on some grand scale. Malcolm and Martin caused me to think like this. Writing for me, as it's turned out, is philanthropy. It didn't take years for me to realize the impact that other writers' work had had on me, and if I was going to write, I did not want to write inconsequential, mediocre stories that didn't conjure up or arouse much in a reader. So I had to start by exciting myself and paying special attention to what I cared about, what mattered to me.

Film school didn't work out. Besides, I never could stop writing, which ultimately forced me to stop fighting it. It took even longer to realize that writing was not something you aspired to, it was something you did because you had to.

I did not want this introduction to be a defense, but I must let you know how the whole idea for this anthology came about.

In 1987, I was teaching at the University of Wyoming. In my fiction workshop, since most of the students didn't read much serious fiction, I wanted to introduce them to what I thought were quality contemporary fiction writers. Since I keep abreast of just about every annual anthology of contemporary writers that's published (from *Pushcart*, to *Editor's Choice*, *Prize Stories: The O. Henry Awards*, and *The Best American Short Stories*, to name a few), I combed through the last seven years' collections, and it became quite apparent that something was wrong. There was rarely an African-American writer among the "best" of these stories that had supposedly gone through much deliberation and scrutiny. The editors had attested to reading hundreds of stories that had appeared in magazines ranging from *The New Yorker*, *The Atlantic* on down to the smallest of the literary quarterlies. The few African-American quarterlies (*Callaloo*, *Catalyst*, *Sage*, *Hambone*), and *Essence* magazine, were not among those considered. I was appalled as I snatched every last one of these anthologies off my bookshelf, and could literally count on one hand the number of African-American writers who were in the table of contents.

I sat at my desk and fumed. My heart pounded with anger. How dare they! Then, in the next breath, I found myself standing in front of my "black" shelves, and I pulled out all the recent anthologies of fiction I had: *Black Voices* and *New Black Voices* (both edited by Abraham Chapman), *Black Short Story Anthology* (edited by Woodie King), *19 Necromancers From Now* (edited by Ishmael Reed), and *The Best Short Stories by Negroes* (edited by Langston Hughes). There were others, but most of them had either been published prior to the sixties, and they concentrated on fiction, drama, poetry, essays, playwriting, and literary criticism. What became apparent almost immediately was that I couldn't recall any recent anthologies in which contemporary African-American fiction—writers who'd been published from the early seventies to now—had been published. Not sure that I was right, I went to the campus library that afternoon, got a computer printout of everything that fell under the heading of "black . . . fiction, literature, anthology, short story." The list itself was long, mostly because the same books kept reappearing as they were cross-referenced under "black literature." As I continued to go through this list, I realized most of the books were in fact historical, segregated by gender or geography, and I learned quickly that there hadn't been an anthology comprised of fiction in over seventeen years. There were a number of critical (scholarly) texts "about" twentieth century "black" fiction, even an annotated index of "The Afro-American Short Story" compiled by Preston M. Yancy in 1986. By the time I finished going through the computerized tear sheets, I picked up the phone and called a number of knowledgeable folks and asked them: "What's the most recent anthology you know about that has nothing but black fiction writers in it?" Many of them paused, and had to think about it. Some of them couldn't remember at all. Many reported the same few.

Shortly afterward, on a snowy morning I sat in my study and looked out the window. Surely there were enough contemporary African-American fiction writers out there to warrant an anthology. At least thirty of them popped into my mind. Then I thought about all the ones I wasn't aware of. Those who'd probably been trying to get published, but couldn't. Those who'd had one novel or story collection published by a major publisher or small press that went unnoticed in *The New York Times*, by the publisher itself or other critical places. I came to the conclusion that there was a void here, and someone needed to fill it.

Without thinking for a minute of the work that a project like this would entail, I dashed off a letter to my publisher and told them about this "problem," stating my case and backing it up with examples or lack of them. Would they be interested? After several days of "checking into the matter" they agreed with me. There was a void here.

I knew that I wanted an anthology that reflected how our lives have changed on a personal level since the 1960s. Although "protest literature"

had its rightful place in time, I knew our work had gone through a series of
metamorphoses. It wasn't that race was no longer important, it's just that in
much of the work I've read from the seventies to now, race wasn't always
the focus. There has been an understanding that many African-American
writers write out of our Africaness. To say it differently, our only frame of
reference is as African-Americans, so we write about what our experiences
mean to us, what concerns us as African-Americans.

However, our visions, voices, outlooks, and even our experiences have
changed and/or grown in myriad ways over the last two decades. Much of
our work is more intimate, personal, reflects a diversity of styles and approaches to storytelling, and it was this new energy that I hoped to acquire
for this anthology. This is exactly what I got.

This is not to say that I for one minute negate the value and significance
of writers who made a contribution to African-American literature up through
the sixties whose work may have fallen under the heading of "protest" literature. But how much sense would it make in the nineties if folks were still
writing "we hate whitey" stories or, say, slave narratives or why we should
be proud of our heritage (we've known it for a long time now—our children
know it, too). It would be incongruent. And it is for this reason that many
of the writers whose work follows on these pages reflect a wide range of
experiences that are indicative of the times we live in now. Our backgrounds
as African-Americans are not all the same. Neither are our perceptions,
values, and morals. The following stories are not filled with anger. Some
are warmhearted, some zingy, some have a sting and a bite, some will break
your heart, or cause you to laugh out loud, sit back and remember, or think
ahead. You may very well see yourself, a member of your family, a loved
one, or a friend on these pages, and that is one thing good fiction should
do: let you see some aspect of yourself.

Trey Ellis has coined a phrase which he calls "The New Black Aesthetic,"
a kind of *glasnost*. He believes that all contemporary African-American artists
now create art where race is not the only source of conflict. We are a new
breed, free to write as we please, in part because of our predecessors, and
because of the way life has changed. "For the first time in our history we
are producing a critical mass of college graduates who are children of college
graduates themselves. Like most artistic booms, the NBA is a post-bourgeois
movement; driven by a second generation of [the] middle class. Having
scraped their way to relative wealth and, too often, crass materialism, our
parents have freed (or compelled) us to bite those hands that fed us and sent
us to college. We now feel secure enough to attend art school instead of
medical school."

Ellis believes, and I support his position, that "new black artists [are no longer] shocked by racism as were those of the Harlem Renaissance, nor are we preoccupied with it as were those of the Black Arts Movement. For us, racism is a hard and little-changing constant that neither surprises nor enrages."

We now comment on ourselves in our work. We can poke fun, laugh at, and pinpoint ourselves as we see fit. Sometimes there is a price for this. From the production of *For Colored Girls Who Have Considered Suicide, When the Rainbow Is Enuf,* by Ntozake Shange, and then Alice Walker's *The Color Purple,* on to Gloria Naylor's *The Women of Brewster Place,* members of the African-American community began criticizing these writers because of their negative depiction of African-American men. "We" had no right to "air our dirty laundry" in front of the white world.

In a recent article appearing in *The Washington Post,* staff writer and *Book World* reviewer, David Nicholson's, "Painting It Black: African American Artists, In Search of a New Aesthetic," states: "True artists often travel lonely roads, but black artists are in the unenviable position of having too much company on their journeys—everybody wants to tell them what to do and how to do it. . . . black literature, films by black filmmakers, black music and black art . . . are expected to carry the weight of politics and sociology. They are subject to the conflicting imperatives—too seldom aesthetic—of various movements and ideologies. They must present a positive image, and they must never, ever reveal unpleasant truths (dissension among blacks, color and caste prejudice) to outside (read "white") eyes."

Most of the literature by African-Americans appearing from the thirties through the early sixties appeared to be aimed at white audiences. We were telling them who we were and what they'd done wrong. Times have changed. We do not feel the need to create and justify our existence anymore. We are here. We are proud. And most of us no longer feel the need to prove anything to white folks. If anything, we're trying to make sense of ourselves to ourselves.

Needless to say, good fiction is not preaching. If a writer is trying hard to convince you of something, then he or she should stick to nonfiction. These days, our work is often as entertaining as it is informative, thought-provoking as it is uplifting. Some of us would like to think that the experiences of our characters are "universal," and yet sometimes a situation could only happen if the color of your character's skin is black. When a writer sits down to tell a story, staring at a blank page, it amazes me how some people are so naïve as to believe that when we invent a character, that we've got the entire race of African-Americans in mind; that these characters are supposed to be representative of the whole instead of the character we originally had in mind. Let's face it, there are some trifling men and women that some of us have come across, so much so that we *have* to write down the effect they had on us. On the other hand, there are also some kind, loving, tender, gentle, successful, and supportive folks in our lives, who also find their way into our work.

But good fiction is filled with conflict, drama, and tension. If we were to spend our time writing lackluster, adult fairy tales, only to please our readers and critics, I know I would be bored to death. I read enough uneventful stories about dull people who live dull lives, and everything that happens to them is dull. As writers, we have a right to choose our own particular focus.

Without a doubt, writing fiction requires passion and compassion. A sense of urgency. Excitement. Intensity. Stillness. For many of us, writing is our reaction to injustices, absurdities, beauty. It's our way of registering our complaints or affirmations. The best are not didactic. They do not scream out "message," nor are they abstractions. Our stories are our personal response. What we want to specify. What we see. What we feel. Our wide angle lens—our close-up look. And even if the story doesn't quite pinpoint the solution or the answer, it is the exploration itself that is often worth the trip.

It didn't take long to gather a list of potential submissions, and word traveled fast and far about this anthology. I received close to three hundred submissions, and it was hard to narrow it down to the fifty-seven writers who appear here. There are what I have deemed three categories of writers: seasoned, emerging, and unpublished. In order to be democratic, the authors appear alphabetically. There are no stories grouped by themes. These pieces stand on their own. Many are excerpts from novels; there apparently aren't as many short story writers as I thought. Some, however, have been discouraged from writing in that form and were encouraged to write novels if they ever wanted to "make it" or be taken seriously. Of course I disagree with this notion, but it is for this reason that I think we have more novelists than short story writers. How many African-American stories have you ever seen in *The New Yorker? The Atlantic Monthly? Grand Street? Q? Redbook?* And even many of the prestigious literary quarterlies?

I've been teaching writing on the university level now for three years, and much to my dismay, rarely have I ever had an African-American student. I wish there were more ways to encourage young people to give writing a shot. Many of them still seem to be intimidated by the English language, and think of writing as "hard"—as in Composition 101-hard. So many of them are set on "making it" (solely in material terms) that we find many of our students majoring in the "guaranteed" professions: the biological sciences, law, engineering, business, etc. If I can make an appeal to those who will read this anthology, I would like to say this to them: if for whatever reason you do not derive a genuine sense of excitement or satisfaction from your chosen field, if you are majoring in these disciplines because of a parent's insistence, if you are dissatisfied with the world to any extent and find yourself "secretly" jotting it down whenever or wherever you can; if you don't understand why people (yourself included) do the things that they do and it plagues you like an itch—consider taking a fiction writing course. Find out if there are African-American writing groups or *any* workshops that are available in your area. Then write. Read as much "serious" fiction as you can—and not just African-American authors. Then, keep writing. "Push it," says Annie Dillard. "Examine all things intensely and relentlessly. Probe and search . . . do not leave it, do not course over it, as if it were understood, but instead follow it down until you see it in the mystery of its own specificity and strength."

Persist.

Acknowledge your bewilderment.

Remember. Writing is personal. Try to write the kind of stories you'd like to read. Do not write to impress. Do not write to prove to a reader how much you know, but instead write in order *to know*. At the same time, you want to snatch readers' attention, pull them away from what they're doing and keep them right next to your characters. You want them to feel what your characters feel, experience it with them so the readers are just as concerned about their outcome as the character is. Perhaps, if you do your job well and you're lucky, readers may recognize something until it clicks.

Everyone has a different opinion about what a good story should do and here are a few that I love:

"A story is a war. It is sustained and immediate combat."

"Your character should want something and want it intensely. It need not be melodramatic, earth-shattering or tangible. But it should be important to them whether or not they get it."

"A good story is a power struggle between equal forces. Something keeps getting in the way of the protagonist from achieving whatever they desire."

I like to think of what happens to characters in good novels and stories as knots—things keep knotting up. And by the end of the story—readers see an "unknotting" of sorts. Not what they expect, not the easy answers you get on TV, not wash-and-wear philosophies, but a reproduction of believable emotional experiences. All I want my readers to do is care about what's going to happen to these folks in the story. First, I have to care, and I don't waste my time writing about folks I don't care about. Once I've done this, I hope by delivering an exciting and convincing story with a satisfying ending, I can exhale, and think about what itch I must scratch next. Every story and excerpt in this anthology fits this description.

As for the title, I was living in Wyoming when I was trying to coin a phrase that would suggest what African-American writers have been doing for some time. I was looking out my window at the snow piled up, the thick icicles hanging off the house, and I thought about how hard life is in general, and further, as African-American writers how we have literally been breaking ice not only in getting published, but getting the respect and attention our work deserves. It's often been cold and hard, but we're chipping away, watching it slowly melt.

There is indeed a new generation of African-American writers emerging, and what we have in this collection are a fine group who have strong voices, who have each seen the world from a different stair. Our experiences as African-American women and men are undoubtedly distinctive, and in some cases unconventional. And just like the color of our skin varies in shades of black, so does our vision. The stories here reflect fifty-seven versions of them. If there appear to be omissions of certain authors, it is not out of disrespect, but because their work didn't fall into the time frame that I wanted to capture.

Needless to say, I wish there hadn't been a need to *separate* our work from others, and perhaps, as Dr. Martin Luther King expressed, one day this dream may come true, where all of our work is considered equal, and not measured by its color content, but its literary merit. Notwithstanding, I'm sure there are more of us "out there" just waiting to be discovered. We need as many voices, as many stories as are willing to come forth. And although we are not in the strict sense of the word historians, we are in fact making history. We are capturing and making permanent and indelible, reactions to, and impressions of, our most intimate observations, dreams, and nightmares, experiences and feelings about what it felt like for "us" to be African-Americans from the seventies until now—the nineties.

Terry McMillan
Tucson, Arizona
January 1990

SARAH

Tina McElroy Ansa

When Lena ran onto the side screen porch she was too excited about her new friend Sarah to remember not to let the screen door slam. But her grandmother only smiled absentmindedly when she ran into the sewing room chattering away about the little girl across the street.

"Lena, baby, be careful 'round that hot iron," she said as Lena nearly collided with the ironing board that was always set up in the room while her grandmother and mother sewed. Then she made the girl stand straight and still while she held a green-and-red plaid pleated skirt with matching suspenders up to the child's waist. The entire woolen skirt was only about half a foot long.

"Hmmm-huh," the old lady muttered with a few straight pins still in her mouth as Lena wove the story about magic fruit made out of red jewels and a little girl named Puddin'.

Her mother, when Lena found her sitting in the living room in her favorite rose-colored chair reading a thick book without any pictures in it, was no more receptive.

"Lena, baby, sit still for just a minute so Mama can finish this one last page. You've been such a good girl all afternoon. As soon as I finish this one last page, I'll put on some music for you. Some Billie Holiday or some Sarah Vaughan, how about that? Then you can help me bake a cake. What kind do you want? A chocolate or a coconut?"

Nellie's voice was as seductive as the thought of a homemade cake.

"Chocolate, chocolate, chocolate," Lena screamed as she jumped down from the arm of her mother's chair and ran over to the sofa to sit quietly until her mother finished her reading. The thought of a moist yellow cake covered with warm smooth brown icing pushed the image of Sarah right out of her head.

But the next morning, with the sun barely breaking through the trees and the boys still stumbling into each other half-asleep in the bathroom as they got ready for school, the household seemed to rock with the sound of banging at the front door.

At first everyone but Nellie, who knew she had left him snoring in the bed next to her, thought it was Jonah again firing off shots from the pistol he always carried with him—*bam, bam, bam, bam, bam*—the way he had done late one night when he came home and found that Nellie had locked and barred all the doors against him. Weary from a long night of poker and carousing, he hadn't yelled and he hadn't cussed. He had just pulled the gun out of his back pocket and fired into the roof of the side porch, and the doors of the house had magically opened to him.

The five small holes that the gunshots made were still in the porch's forest-green ceiling. Lena giggled whenever she looked up and saw them. Her father's brashness frightened most people, but it didn't scare her one bit. She knew she was immune.

The gunshots had not only opened the locked door for her father, they also had held in check all the talk Nellie had said she had for him about him staying out as late as he wanted and not expecting anybody to say anything about it. About what did he think she was, anyway? About how sick and tired she was of him and his whores.

Overhearing Nellie's mutterings, Lena, sitting on the toilet, had wondered what a whore was, since it didn't exactly sound like the thing her grandmama used to turn the dirt over in her garden. A simple garden tool couldn't have made her mother as mad as this whore seemed to. And Lena didn't think anything that sounded as bad as her mama made the word sound could be so harmless. The way her mama said it, "whore" sounded like it was covered with spikes and prickly barbs.

So, as she pulled up her panties, she asked her mother for a definition. Nellie just snapped, "Go back to bed, Lena."

The early-morning banging at the door was loud and insistent. Lena's grandmother strode down the stairs with Lena beside her. Lena was walking so close to her grandmother that she almost got tangled up in the length of chenille robe flapping between the old lady's legs and tumbled down the steps head over heels. Grandmama scratched the side of her nose again and marched down the downstairs hall on her way to the front door muttering to herself, "Who the hell is this come to our door this time of morning banging like the goddamn police? If it's one of Jonah's half-witted flunkies, they'll be sorry they were ever born. Yes, if it's one of those fanatical fools from The Place come here this time of morning to borrow a couple of dollars to throw away on some foolishness, they'll be sorry they ever learned how to count pennies when I finish with 'em. Knocking on this door like they the damn police or something."

Lena had to walk fast to keep up with her grandmother. Despite the threatening banging at the door, she wasn't a bit afraid. She thought nothing could befall her as long as the older lady stood between her and the world.

Grandmama was out of breath and still cussing out "that fool out there" when they reached the door. She didn't even peep out of one of the panes of glass that edged the big door first. She just flung it open and stood there with her arms folded over her flat breasts as Lena peered around her legs.

At first all Grandmama and Lena could see in the breaking morning light was a wide smile and a pink blouse. Then Lena recognized her friend.

"Sarah!" Lena screamed as she dashed past her grandmother's legs and ran up to the door, pressing her face against the screen.

Grandmama, still annoyed at the early-morning visit, looked down at Lena with a confused expression.

"It's Sarah, Grandmama, Puddin' Tame. I told you all 'bout her yesterday. She's my friend. Don't you remember?"

Grandmama was still puzzled. It had never occurred to her that Lena could have anything to do with this early-morning commotion at their front door. On top of that she was having a hard time believing that Lena, her baby, had made a friend without her grandmama knowing about it. And what a friend!

The dark little girl who stood on the front porch smiling for all she was worth looked to Grandmama like a little piece of street trash who had tried to doll herself up.

Grandmama was halfway right. Sarah had stayed up nearly all night preparing for her first visit to Lena's big house. It felt like the most important event of her short life, and she knew if she didn't prepare for it, nobody would.

Everyone in Sarah's family was used to her doing things on her own. So the night before, when her mother had heard her bumping around in the nearly darkened house, the woman had just smacked her lips a couple of times sleepily, turned over against the warm body of her husband, and gone back to sleep.

Sarah had stopped rummaging through a cluttered drawer and stood perfectly still when she heard her mother stir. She knew she had her work cut out for her, and she didn't need anybody asking a lot of questions and getting in the way while she tried her best to piece together some kind of outfit.

Sarah wanted so much to look nice when she met Lena's people. But she had so little to work with. When she thought she couldn't find a decent pair of matching socks in the whole house, Sarah sat in the middle of the cold bathroom floor and wept.

The only matching set was the tiny pair of faded lacy pink baby socks she found stuck in the back of a drawer, which her mother had bought for one of the children but had never had a fancy enough occasion to use. Sarah brightened when she found a dark blue sock and a dark brown one that belonged to her younger brother. If she didn't fold down the cuffs of the socks, they almost looked like they were bought for her. And in the light thrown off by the lone lamp with the broken shade in the front room, the brown and blue socks looked like a perfect match. Sarah didn't realize until she was standing in Lena's mama's big bright kitchen that she was wearing mismatched socks. By then she was too happy to care.

There was no shoe polish of any color in the house, so Sarah just took a damp rag and wiped the red dust from her lace-up brown oxfords. They looked fine as long as the leather remained wet, but as soon as the shoes began to dry, they reverted to the smoky hue they had been for months.

At least, Sarah thought, I don't have to worry that much about my underwear. If I keep my dress down and don't flounce around too much, it won't matter if I got holes in my drawers or not. As luck would have it, she found a pair of her own panties that were still white and didn't even have a pin hole in them in a pile of clean laundry someone had taken off the line and left on the swayback chair in the kitchen.

Then her main concern became finding a dress without a hole in it. Because she was usually as raggedy or neat as anyone else in her house, Sarah rarely gave any thought to her attire. She woke in the morning, put on something to cover her body, and went on with her day. But the way Lena had been dressed that day, and the size of the house Lena lived in, had made Sarah look at herself for a long time in the wavy mirror of the old hall dresser and decide she wanted to wear something special to her new friend's house.

With tiny lines of concentration creasing her forehead, she picked up and discarded nearly every piece of clothing she found in two chests of drawers, stuck down between the frayed cushions of the couch, or lying under the cot where she and two of her sisters slept. She had long ago outgrown the only "nice" Easter dress she had ever owned. It had been passed down to her next sister, who despoiled it right away by putting it on and playing in the mud.

The search seemed hopeless. Then she remembered the cardboard box full of old clothes that a white woman her mother had once worked for had dropped off at their house the Christmas before instead of coming up with the five dollars she owed for almost a week's work. Her mother was so disgusted that she had thrown the box into a corner of the porch and dared anybody to go near it.

At the time, Sarah had shared her mother's anger and disappointment and wouldn't touch the box of old clothes for anything in the world. She had even stopped her sisters and brother from messing with it. But that was then. Now Sarah needed something that wasn't ripped and torn and soiled beyond repair, so she broke down and dragged the box into the kitchen from the back porch.

She pulled out dozens of old men's shirts and plaid housedresses and faded pastel dusters before she came to anything that looked like it might fit her. At the bottom of the box, under a piece of a yellowed sheet, she found a layer of children's clothes. She lifted them all out and laid them on the kitchen table. Then she threw everything else back into the box.

The bare light bulb hanging from the cord in the ceiling was one of the brightest ones in the house, so Sarah stayed in the kitchen to examine her discovery.

"Too little, too little, too big, too little, too big," Sarah muttered to herself as she held up each piece to examine it briefly and then dropped it into one of two piles on the table. When she had gone through all the children's clothes on the table, she realized she hadn't once said "My size." So she picked up the small pile of "too little" clothes, dropped them back into the cardboard box, and pushed it back onto the porch. Then she returned to the "too big" pile on the table to see what she could use.

First Sarah went through the pile to check for pants and dresses and blouses that had no holes or rips in them. Earlier, while Lena had been engrossed in the piles of rocks and sand they had been building to dam up the flow of the stream cascading beside the street, Sarah had examined her new friend close up. She had been struck with the vivid red of Lena's frock, which was unlike anything she owned.

But later, going over the afternoon meeting in her mind, the thing that stood out about Lena's dress was not only its bright color but also its neatness. No rips or tears at the seams, no threads hanging down—none of the hem of the wide skirt dipping like a shelf below the rest of the dress. Sarah was sharp enough to see that the collar was hand sewn and the sleeves were eased into the armholes so they didn't pucker. And she just somehow felt that the hem of the skirt had been turned under, ironed flat, and stitched before the final edge was expertly measured and hemmed. That's the kind of dress she was looking for in the pile of "too big" items on the kitchen table.

In what was left of her childish hopes, Sarah fully expected to find it there. But there was no hand-made red dress to fit her in the pile of children's apparel on the kitchen table. The closest she came to it was a long-sleeved pink blouse with stitching on the cuff and around the buttonholes that was only slightly frayed at the collar, and a navy-blue pleated skirt with elastic at the waist that some little girl had worn as part of her school uniform.

The blouse's long sleeves hung below her knuckles and the armholes sagged beneath her shoulders, but when she tucked the hem of the blouse down into the elastic waistband of the blue skirt, it settled into neat little pleats all around her rib cage and looked kind of cute, Sarah thought. The skirt was longer than she would have liked, but it made a pretty umbrella-like display when she twirled around, and since she had a clean white pair of panties to wear that weren't holey, she figured she could twirl around a few times and remind everyone who thought the skirt was a sad little sack that it was really quite attractive on her.

She planned to hit the skirt and blouse a few times with the ancient iron her mama kept on a kitchen shelf under the sink. But when she plugged it in, the iron shot golden sparks from the raw copper coils exposed beneath the ragged black covering on the cord. Sarah jumped back and yanked the plug from the wall socket for fear of going up in flames before she got the chance to see inside Lena's house. She spread the outfit on the kitchen table and tried to press out the wrinkles by running the palm of her hand over and over the material. But she gave up after a few tries.

"I'll just walk fast and whip them wrinkles out, like Mama say to do," Sarah told herself as she went into the bathroom and started running warm water into the sink.

It was much too cold in the small bathroom for Sarah to think about stripping naked and getting into a tub full of tepid water—the only kind that came out of their hot-water faucets. And besides, if she had run water into the tub, everybody in the house would have awakened to find out what was going on that deserved a full bath. Instead, Sarah took the bar of rough gray soap from the wire dish above the sink, held it under the warm running water, and rubbed up enough suds on a rag she took from hanging on the side of the tub to run over the trunk of her body and leave a light trail of suds behind on her skin. It was the type of bath her mother took when she was late running out to work or going downtown to a juke joint. "I don't have time to bathe," she'd mutter to herself as she undressed. "I'll just take a wipe-off."

The toilette was what most women in Pleasant Hill, regardless of where they lived, called a "whore's bath," but Sarah didn't know what a whore was any more than Lena did.

After she rinsed the suds off with the wet rag, she dried off with a stiff towel hanging on a nail behind the door and quickly slipped into the pair of panties and undershirt she had found in the laundry. As she walked around the house in her bare feet turning off lights, she shivered a bit as the air seeping through gaps in the thin walls hit her damp skin. When she finally settled in for the night, she was grateful for the warm spots her sisters, asleep in their narrow cot, made for her to snuggle into.

The walls of her house were so thin and holey that in winter the wind whistled through the small rooms like a prairie storm through a log cabin. The floors, buckled and rough in unexpected places, creaked each time someone in the house shifted, let alone walked across them. And the whole place smelled of dried and fresh urine that seemed to have soaked into the very wood of the structure so long ago that its residents no longer even noticed the scent.

When Sarah awoke the next morning, she didn't feel as if she had slept a bit that night. She had dozed off a little, but the excitement of her visit to her new friend's house woke her before daylight and before anyone else got up. She put on her socks and shoes in the dark room, turned on the light in the bathroom only long enough to find the hair brush and rake it over her head one time, then switched the light off and headed for the kitchen.

Her new pink blouse and blue skirt were still lying on the table, wrinkled as they had been the night before, but Sarah didn't pay the wrinkles any attention as she quickly buttoned up the blouse and pulled the skirt over her head.

She twirled one time to make sure the skirt still ballooned prettily the way it had the night before and headed out the door to Lena's house without waking anyone—not even her father who woke early to get a spot on the day-worker's truck that drove through the neighborhood. By the time she got halfway down the driveway leading to Lena's house, she couldn't keep from grinning.

Before Sarah knew anything, she and Lena were standing on opposite sides of the screen door beaming at each other in the glow of their new friendship. But Lena soon grew impatient with her grandmama's dazed gaping from one to the other of the two little girls and pulled a handful of chenille robe.

"Grandmama, open the door. Let Sarah in. She came to visit me."

"Okay, baby," her grandmother answered vaguely as she flipped the metal hook from its eye and pushed the door just wide enough for Sarah to squeeze through.

Sarah bounded into the hall and stood beneath the overhead light, excitement and awe written all over her ashy face. It was like a palace to Sarah: the highly polished hardwood floors, the pictures hanging on the wall near the door, the simple chandelier over the dining-room table in the next room, the dining room itself with its big oval table and six high-backed matching chairs pulled up to it, the mouth-watering bowl of fruit sitting in the middle of the table were like something in her dreams.

Grandmama thought just what Lena knew she would when she got a good look at Sarah: I sure would like to scrub that little rusty neck and grease her down with Vaseline. And when the old woman got a whiff of Sarah's mildewed clothes, she thought, I bet she hasn't ever had a real good hot soapy bath in a tub in her life.

"So you're our baby's new friend?" Grandmama said out loud.

"Yeah," Sarah answered, her voice gravelly from getting up so early but so respectful that her short answer didn't imply rudeness, even to Grandmama.

"Say, 'yes, ma'am,' " Grandmama instructed Sarah gently.

"Yes, ma'am," Sarah said carefully, repeating Grandmama's gentle inflection.

"Well, next time wait till the sun has come up good before you come visiting," Grandmama said pointedly. Then, "I guess ya'll want something to eat. You had breakfast yet, Sarah?"

"Bre'fast?" Sarah was puzzled.

"Have you eaten this morning?" the old lady rephrased her question as she headed for the kitchen.

"Oh, no," Sarah answered with her eyes caressing the fruit on the dining-room table as they passed by.

All three of them had to blink a few times as they entered the black-and-white kitchen situated at the eastern corner of the house. The early-morning sun flooded the spacious room with shafts of startlingly bright light that hadn't reached the other parts of the house yet. Sarah felt as though she were walking out onto a stage: it didn't seem real. She had seen kitchens similar to Lena's when she accompanied her mother to her occasional day-work jobs in the white neighborhood behind their house. But those kitchens didn't smell like Lena's. In fact there had been no smell at all except the ones she and her mother brought there.

But even first thing in the morning, Lena's kitchen smelled wonderful. And it wasn't just the fresh aroma of coffee brewing on the stove and buttery grits and sausage grease and cinnamon and sugar dusted lightly on buttered slices of toast. It was the layers of smells that had settled on the walls and floor and worked their way into the fiber of the room that made Sarah come to a halt near the threshold. Sarah could smell the vegetable soup Nellie had made the week before when the weather first turned chilly. She smelled the fish dinner they had had that Friday. She smelled the chocolate layer cake even before she saw it sitting in a glass-covered cake dish on the top of the refrigerator. She came close to bursting into tears with the yearning that the room called up in her swelling heart.

Lena grabbed her friend's dry hand and pulled her into the kitchen and over to the white enamel table to sit down.

"Nellie," Grandmama said to Lena's mother who stood by the sink looking out the window in the direction of the woods. "Look who was making all that noise at our front door this time of morning."

Nellie turned around with her thin eyebrows raised. They shot up even higher when she saw Sarah.

"Well, I be damned," she said. "Now, who is this?"

Lena giggled and so did Sarah.

"This is a new friend of Lena's," Grandmama said with a strange lilt to her voice on the word "friend" that made both little girls stop laughing and look into the old woman's face.

Lena kicked Sarah under the table to encourage her to speak.

"Girl, what you kicked me for?" Sarah asked in her gruff, raspy voice.

"This my mama, Sarah," Lena said as she reached under the table and patted the spot on Sarah's leg that she had kicked.

"Where do you live?" Grandmama asked Sarah as she placed a small glass decorated with circus animals and filled full with orange juice in front of each girl.

"She lives across the street in those houses next to Mrs. Willback's house. Next to that big tree. What kind of tree is that?" Lena asked Sarah.

Sarah couldn't answer at first because she had picked up her glass of juice and was drinking down the fresh tart drink in small continuous swallows, allowing the citrus tang to coat the inside of her mouth and throat. With one last gulp and a loud smack of her lips, she put the glass back on the table and answered.

"Chinaberry."

"And just how did the two of you get together?" Grandmama asked as she walked over to the table with more orange juice and poured another stream into Sarah's glass that made the child's eyes light up even more.

But before Sarah had a chance to answer, Nellie jumped in and said

nervously, "Oh, with our little girl, it's no telling, but I assume that you
didn't cross that street out there, Lena."

"No, Mama, Sarah did. You ought to see her dodge those cars," Lena
said proudly.

Nellie laughed softly. "I bet she can."

After that, Sarah would show up on their doorstep regularly to join Lena
and the boys for breakfast. Some days she had to run home after eating to
"do something." Other times she stayed all day until Grandmama made her
go home. When anyone asked her why she didn't go to school, she'd say,
"We going up there any day now, soon as Mama gets a chance to 'roll me."
But for more than a year she never attended any school other than the one
she found in her own backyard.

"Lena, what are you and old Rough-and-Ready doing today?" Grandmama would ask as the two girls came into the kitchen and took seats next
to where she sat making peach puffs or carefully cutting the seams away
from a pile of pole beans covering the table. Lena's father said he had gagged
and nearly choked on strings Nellie had left on the beans soon after they
got married. From that time on, Grandmama always prepared the pole beans
in their house.

"Don't know yet," Sarah would answer for both of them, not minding
the old lady's all too appropriate nickname for her. Grandmama made a
point of always having something healthful for Sarah whenever she came
into the kitchen—a piece of fruit, a sandwich with extra slices of tomato, a
pile of raisins—and she always gave the bigger portion to Sarah.

But whatever their plans were, everyone knew that they would involve
pretend. It was their favorite game. Everything they played hinged on the
basic unit of Let's Pretend. These games sometimes involved props and
background and sometimes they didn't, and that was fine, too. At Lena's
house, where her attic, filled to bursting, yielded all kinds of costumes and
paraphernalia to fill in the chinks of the stories, their games were elaborate
and staged. But Grandmama or Nellie or one of the boys always had to go
up the steps and drag down boxes or armloads of stuff because Lena still
refused to go into the attic as long as she knew the portrait of her dead infant
aunt was stored up there.

For the few days each winter when it was too cold to play out-of-doors,
Sarah came to Lena's house and they played and danced in the big upstairs
hall in front of the wide floor-length mirror so they could see every movement they made. In the daytime, with her friend by her side, Lena was
never frightened of the big mirror, as she was during the nights on her
bathroom runs.

At Sarah's it was bare-bones pretending under the chinaberry tree, which
was the only place they were allowed to play at her house year-round, but

that didn't bother the girls. Despite the house's deficiencies—glaringly obvious to the adults in the neighborhood—Sarah had two things in her yard that Lena and every other child in Pleasant Hill envied her for: a mature and flourishing pomegranate tree and the ancient chinaberry whose broad sturdy limbs swooped down to the ground and back to the sky to form natural nooks and dens. Lena and Sarah called it their "house."

The year Sarah and Lena discovered each other, the two of them planned all winter that, when the warm weather came, they would both move into the chinaberry tree by themselves and live off the fruits of the pomegranate.

"You'll have a room, and I'll have a room," Lena assured Sarah. Sarah's two sisters still wet the cot she shared with them in the front room of her house. "We'll make two beds out of pine straw and Grandmama's flowers, and it'll smell so good in our house, we won't never have to clean up." It was hard for Lena to believe, considering the number of babies and toddlers that roamed the house and yard all day long, but Sarah was the eldest child in the Stanley household. She had responsibilities that Lena never knew about.

They were best friends, sharing games and secrets, special words and questions. But the first time Lena remembered seeing Sarah's world clearly, it was winter and raining very hard, too hard for Lena to head out the door into the cold sheets of water. Lena was stuck at Sarah's for dinner, even though her mother had told her not to accept dinner invitations because Sarah's family had enough trouble feeding their own members without having guests' mouths as well.

"Just say, 'No thank you, I already ate' or 'I'm going to eat when I get home,'" Nellie instructed Lena.

By the time Raymond came running up on the porch with her yellow raincoat and an umbrella, Lena had seen Sarah's family at home for dinner. It was a revelation.

Sarah's mother stood in the tiny kitchen, moving quickly from the sink to the tiny white stove, opening cans, stirring, and chopping. She worked quietly, not saying a word to Lena and the other children assembled on the floor and sitting in the room's one swaybacked chair. When she was finished, Sarah's mother laid down the big metal spoon with holes in it, turned to the children, and announced, "Catch as catch can." Then she walked out onto the lean-to porch to light up a cigarette, blowing long furls of white smoke out into the driving rain.

The other children rose quickly and lined up behind Sarah with small plates and bowls in their hands. Lena could tell what was cooking in the big blue pot even before Sarah lifted the lid off and steam roiled up to the cracking ceiling.

It was neckbones. The distinctive pork scent mixed with tomatoes from the two big yellow-labeled cans sitting on the kitchen table had wrapped itself around the very hairs in Lena's nose. She didn't dare look in the pot for fear of going against her mother's orders and succumbing to the temptation to share the meal, but she guessed that Sarah's mother had put in lots of onions and pungent bell peppers and fistfuls of spaghetti that she broke in half first. Neckbones was one of Lena's favorite dinners. They had them two ways at her house. If her mother cooked, they were made the way Sarah's mother did, with tomatoes and spaghetti. If her grandmother was in charge of cooking the meal, the bony meat was always prepared with potatoes and thick brown gravy.

Although Lena knew both her mother and grandmama wanted her to lean one way or the other in her preference for neckbones, prepared red or brown, she never made a choice. She could never bear the thought of life without neckbones both ways.

When Sarah had filled all the children's bowls and plates, she filled her own plate, broke off a piece of bread from the charred hoecake in the black skillet, and sat on the floor with the others who were already wolfing down their food. Not a word was said until every plate was clean. When Lena asked why everybody was so quiet while they ate, Sarah looked at her as if she had just pointed out the holes in her sisters' drawers, and Lena was sorry she had said anything.

One warm murky day in their second summer, Lena found her friend sitting beneath the protected wings of the chinaberry tree, playing with mounds of dirt between her opened legs. Sarah's house seemed strangely quiet, free of the noises and traffic that usually encircled the house.

The dirt in Sarah's yard was gray and dusty and didn't look as tempting to Lena as the rich brown loam under the pine trees in her own yard. But she had to fight the urge to reach down and put a handful of it into her mouth anyway. Lena understood perfectly why Estelle, who came from time to time to help clean the house, kept chunks of stark white laundry starch in her apron pockets and munched on it throughout the day.

But Lena had promised her mother that she would stop eating dirt. And it seemed no matter how hard she wiped her mouth, Nellie could always tell when she had been eating the stuff. So, instead of picking up a palmful, holding her head back, and letting the grains of dirt trickle into her open mouth from the fist of her hand, she just sat down next to Sarah and started building her own pile of earth into a hill.

"What's your name?" Lena asked playfully, in their customary greeting.

Sarah looked up from the sandhill of earth at her knees and smiled at Lena. "Puddin' Tame," she answered.

"What do you want to play?" she asked Sarah after a while.

"Let's play like we married," Sarah said without hesitation.

"Okay," Lena agreed.

"I'll be the man and you be the woman," Sarah said as she pushed aside the top of the pile of dirt.

"You sit at the table and I'll cook us some breakfast," suggested Lena as she looked around the yard for the few pieces of plastic and china plates and cups they used for serving pieces of sticks for bread; rocks for meat; mounds of dirt for rice, mashed potatoes, and grits; and dark green leaves from the trees around them for collard and turnip greens.

It was a careful game of pretend eating they played. Lena treated it with as much reverence as the real thing was accorded in her own household. She always got a pan of water and washed the rock of "meat" well before putting it in an old dented pot or shoebox "oven" to cook. And she washed and fingered the chinaberry leaves carefully and tenderly, just the way her mother and grandmother did before shredding them and putting them in a pot with a rock for seasoning.

She had been in the kitchen once and seen her grandmother stand at the sink for the longest time examining each leaf in a pile of collards she had just picked from her garden, where they grew year-round. Lena had thought at first that the old lady was looking for worms until she beckoned her over to stand on a chair at the drain beside her.

"Look at this, baby, all these little roads in a single leaf," Grandmama said softly as she traced the separate pale veins in the dark verdant leaf with her wrinkled index finger. "And listen, just listen to this music." Then she had run the soft pad of her thumb over the dark green surface of a leaf, and the thing let out a little baby squeak. They both just smiled in wonder.

Sarah sat near her pile of dirt and thought a while. Then she shook her head as she watched Lena begin to gather the plates. "No, not like that. You want me to show you how to really play house? I know. I seen it plenty of times."

"Okay," Lena agreed easily, even though she knew she had watched her family all her life and knew how to play house just as well as Sarah. But she figured she and her friend enjoyed each other too much to waste time disagreeing over something that didn't matter all that much.

"We just need one thing," Sarah said. "I'll go get it."

And she hurried off to the empty front porch of her house and returned right away with a copy of the *Mulberry Clarion* in her hand. It looked so stiff and clean, Lena knew it had to be that day's copy of the newspaper. Besides, it was Friday and Lena knew that most people in Pleasant Hill, even those who didn't read the newspaper every day, took the *Clarion* on Fridays because that was the day the paper included the page that Rowana

Jordan wrote and edited. Stretched across the top of that inside page, just before the want ads, was the standard heading "News of Our Colored Community."

When Mulberry's one colored newspaper had gone out of business at the beginning of the fifties, Miss Rowana, as everyone called her, persuaded the *Clarion* to insert black folks' news once a week by promising to sell ads, take photographs, and write all the stories herself. And she was true to her word, rushing all over town in her too-fancy dresses and outrageous hats collecting news, church notices, wedding and birth announcements, and gossip, along with receipts and ads from funeral homes, barbershops, grocery stores, and the Burghart Theatre. She already had a tiny storefront office on Cherry Street, far enough away from the newspaper's building to please both her and her employers. So she just changed the sign from the *Mulberry Crier* to the *Mulberry Clarion* and continued working.

The newspaper Sarah carried was still rolled up the way it had been thrown. And the little girl held it out in front of her like a magic wand. As soon as she got back to their spot under the tree, she plopped down in the dust and began unrolling the paper.

"Sarah," Lena said, "your daddy read that paper yet?"

"Uh-uh," Sarah answered as she continued to spread the paper out in her hands.

"Then you better leave it alone till they do read it. Nothing makes my daddy madder than for somebody to come and tear up the paper before he gets a chance to read it. He says it shows a goddamn lack of consideration."

Sarah sucked her teeth derisively as she separated one big broadsheet from the others and laid it up on the elbow of a limb of the chinaberry tree they sat under. "Shoot, nobody'll even notice it's gone. If I didn't move it, it woulda sat there forever."

Lena still wasn't convinced, but she was too intrigued with what Sarah was going to do with the paper to press her argument.

When Sarah had all the sheets separated from one another, she divided them evenly, giving Lena four double wide sheets and keeping the others for herself.

"What we gonna do with these?" Lena wanted to know.

Sarah looked around the base of the tree that was their "house" and picked a corner where the limbs touched the ground.

"We need to go over to our bedroom. It's nighttime," Sarah said as she picked up her sheets of newsprint and stepped into another part of the "house."

Lena followed her.

Sarah sat down and pointed to the spot next to her for Lena to join her in the dust. Lena sat down. She was beginning to realize that this was a private, ritualized game they were about to play. And when Sarah said, "Our children 'sleep so we gotta be quiet," Lena knew she had been right, and she was excited. As many times as she had been frightened by some apparition or discovery, she couldn't keep herself from loving a mystery, especially when she was with someone in her family or Sarah and felt safe.

"This what you got to do," Sarah explained as she crumpled a sheet of the newspaper up into a ball, lifted up her skirts, and stuck the paper down into the front of her panties. She leaned back against the stump of the tree and looked down at her crotch, appraising the difference the addition made. Lena sat next to her staring at it, too.

Lena couldn't take her eyes off Sarah's dingy panties, now bulging at the crotch as Sarah added another ball of newspaper, then another. The news-paper balled up like it was and nestled inside Sarah's drawers didn't look like anything other than what it was. But Sarah continued to fool with it, ar-ranging the rounded part against her body and making one end of the clump of paper into a pointed edge, which she aimed at the pad of her panties.

Lena knew she was supposed to keep quiet because the ritual had begun, but she just had to ask. "Sarah," she whispered, "what's that sup-posed to be?"

"I'm the man," Sarah said authoritatively. "That's my thing, my johnson. I'm supposed to have it."

She patted her newspaper growth one last time, then grabbed one of Lena's sheets of paper and scooted over to her spot in the dust.

"Here," Sarah said as she handed Lena a ball of the newspaper. "You do the same thing. That'll be your thing, you a grown 'oman, so that'll be your pussy."

"I already got one," Lena said as she started to pull down her panties to show Sarah. "We call it a matchbox at our house. It just ain't as big as a grown woman."

"I know you got a thing," Sarah said, with a touch of exasperation creeping into her voice. "All girls do, but you right, it ain't big enough. So, go on, put the paper down in your panties like me."

And Lena complied, shoving the stiff paper into the front of her white panties, now rapidly turning gray in the dust. "Ouch, that's scratchy," she complained as she moved the paper around trying to find a more comfortable place against her skin.

"That's okay," Sarah said as she scooted over to Lena to sit facing her between her opened legs. "I think it's supposed to hurt some. That's what my daddy make it sound like. He say, 'Oooo, baby, yeah, that hurt so good, do it some more, uh, yeah, that hurt just right.' "

Sarah had moved in so close to Lena that their two panty fronts, both bulging out in front of them, were now touching. Without any further explanation, she started moving her body around, rubbing her paper penis against Lena's panties and making short sucking sounds as she pulled air between her clenched teeth. She threw her head back and closed her eyes, imitating her father, the whole time repeating, "Uh, yeah, uh, yeah, right there, uh-huh."

Lena watched in fascination as her friend continued to rub up against her in the dust and to suck her teeth as if she were in pain.

Sarah's face was a picture of pleasure glazed over with a thin icing of pain, like the faces of women at The Place who danced and ground their hips to the beat of a saxophone solo played on the jukebox. She seemed to pay Lena no attention, so Lena figured she was supposed to imitate her friend.

She threw her own head back and closed her eyes like Sarah and began rotating the bottom of her body, the part in her panties stuffed with stiff newspaper, up against Sarah. Lena felt a little silly at first and couldn't stop thinking about how dirty the seat of her panties was getting from being ground into the fine gray dust under the big chinaberry tree. But since Sarah, with her eyes still closed and her raspy voice still spitting out the litany of "Yeah, ooh, yeah, ooh, yeah, do it," seemed intent on playing this game, she closed her eyes and gave herself over to the pretending.

"Oh, baby," Lena mimicked her friend in earnest and scooted her bottom a little closer to Sarah's. The movement forward suddenly pressed an edge of the newspaper in her panties into the split of her vagina and across her clitoris. "Uh," she yiped in surprise, and the prick of pleasure shot through her pelvis and slowly melted in her stomach.

Her elbows, resting on the crook of a low limb of the chinaberry behind her to prop her back up off the ground, suddenly lost their gristle and slipped off the edge. Her shoulders landed on the ground with a dull plop, raising a dry dust storm around her ears. But Lena didn't stop to give the fall a thought. She was lost in the exquisite wet feeling that was spreading through her hips and rolling down her thighs. Letting the ball of newspaper lead her, she rose up on her elbows and pushed her bottom back toward Sarah, brushing her stuffed panties back up against her friend in search of more of that quick warm feeling.

She opened her eyes briefly to stare into Sarah's face to see if it mirrored what she imagined her own must look like. Satisfied that it did, she closed her eyes again and continued gyrating her little body against her friend's, sucking air between her teeth the way she had done automatically when the quick warm thing inside her had melted before.

Suddenly she felt the large strong grasp of a fist clutch her upper arm just below the sleeve of her dress and pull her roughly away from Sarah. At first Lena thought it was the strong arms of the chinaberry tree come to life to grab her. Her eyes flew open.

Sarah's mama's face was a mask of rage. She had just been weary when she came looking for Sarah, calling her name over and over to ask what had happened to the newspaper, but when she found her with Lena pressed together, rubbing against each other in the dust, their panties protruding with the turgescence of her Friday newspaper, she turned furious.

"What are ya'll doing!" she screamed as she loomed over the two girls. "What are ya'll doing over here?"

But she didn't wait for an answer. She just screamed at Lena. "Don't be trying to hide from me. I see you. I see what you doing. You little nasty girl. I shoulda known better than to let Sarah play with you."

Sarah and Lena didn't know what to say. Sarah's mama still had Lena's arm in her grasp and lifted her away from her daughter like a rag doll. "Think you so damn fine with your little red dresses and your hair ribbons and your big house. Well, you ain't so fine, is you? Just another dirty little girl, trying to do nasty when you think ain't nobody looking."

Sarah, seeing the attack on her friend, tried to jump in with an explanation.

"It was me, Mama, it wasn't Lena. It was my game."

But the woman didn't want to hear any of that. "Shut up, Sarah. I know what I see with my own eyes. You go on up to the house. I'll deal with your butt later. You know better than this." But Sarah didn't move.

Then, turning back to Lena, who was trying to wrench herself away from the woman's grasp, "I got a good mind to go across the street and tell your fine-ass ma just what I caught her precious baby doing. Yeah, I oughta go tell her what her precious daughter was doing with my little girl."

Then she turned on Sarah again. "Sarah, if you don't get your ass in that house, you better, girl."

With her attention wandering from Lena, her grasp on the child loosened, too, and Lena, suddenly free, started to dash away from the screaming woman. But Sarah's mama looked back in time and caught Lena's skirt tail in her fist.

"Yeah, but she probably wouldn't believe me. Yeah, probably put it off on Sarah. That's right, little girl, you better run on home, get on out my yard. You don't own everything, you know." Sarah's mother was about to release her grip on Lena's skirt. Then she had a thought. She flipped the girl's skirt tail and grabbed the elastic band of Lena's panties and reached inside.

"And gimme back my newspaper," she said with a snarl as she yanked the crumpled paper from Lena's drawers. "I ain't read it yet."

Lena ran all the way home and sat quietly on the side porch steps getting her breath until her mama called her in to dinner.

The last thing Lena thought before she fell into a dreamless sleep that night was that she and Sarah would be friends forever, no matter how her mama had acted earlier that day. Nothing could change that.

Sarah had always been there when Lena called her. Usually, when Lena's household got busy midmorning, she would just go to the end of her driveway and yell for Sarah, and Sarah would emerge from her house or the chinaberry tree and lead Lena safely across the street or just come over to Lena's house to play. Lena could count on Sarah's consistency. Consistency of any kind pleased and reassured Lena in her world of apparitions and uncertainties.

So she couldn't understand it when, late in the afternoon, three days after Sarah's mother had found them rubbing their bodies together, she went to the end of her driveway as usual and shouted for her friend and no one appeared in the yard across the street. No one. Lena didn't think she had ever seen Sarah's house when there wasn't someone playing in the yard or sitting on the porch or standing in the doorway. Whenever she and her family drove past, she always threw up her hand in greeting before she even looked over that way good, as her grandmother said, because she was so sure there would be someone there to return her greeting.

Lena called for Sarah a couple more times, and when she still didn't get a response, she looked both ways up and down Forest Avenue then dashed across the street by herself. She giggled with pride at having made it safely across the street, but as soon as she stepped into Sarah's yard she felt something was different. It was so quiet and still.

Not only was no member of Sarah's family visible, there was no sign that any of them were even there. The front door, usually standing wide open except on the few bitterly cold winter days, was shut tight. No light burned in the front room or the kitchen window on the side. The radio that was turned on every time Lena had ever been there was gone from its spot on the front-room windowsill and the window itself was tightly shut.

"Sarah! Sarah!" She called as she headed around the side of the house past the low limbs of the chinaberry tree that looked as deserted as the house did. But there was no answer. When Lena got around to the back of the house she saw that even the raggedy curtains that had hung at the kitchen window in back were no longer there.

Maybe they're doing spring cleaning like at my house, Lena said to herself. She headed up the plank steps leading to the back porch with the

idea in mind of looking through the low kitchen window and rapping on it
to stir someone inside. With each step she took, the tiny porch made a
mournful squeak that sent small shivers up her legs. But even before she
made it to the window, Lena had a strong feeling that she wouldn't like
what she saw. So the kitchen with its dirty linoleum floor bare of its few
pieces of furniture and the hall without its old dresser and mirror and what
she could see of the empty front room didn't surprise her. It just left her
very sad. As if she had lost the delicate pearl necklace her grandmama had
given her.

At first Lena tried to tell herself that Sarah would probably show up soon,
laughing in her familiar raspy way, her brother and sisters in tow. But even
as she thought of her friend, Lena realized with a start that she couldn't
even remember what her friend's voice sounded like, and her sadness turned
to fear.

A sudden cool breeze raised goose bumps on her arms and she looked
up and noticed that dark clouds were gathering in the western sky. When
the smell of rain blew in on the next gust of wind, Lena knew it was time
to go back home. There didn't seem to be anything else to do. She couldn't
wait any longer.

As she hurried back through the empty yard in front of Sarah's house,
big drops of rain began hitting the ground, raising tiny clouds of gray dust
like puffs of smoke. Suddenly, going through Sarah's yard felt like a walk
through a graveyard. As a sense of loss enveloped her, Lena began to feel
as if her friend Sarah were dead.

Not bothering to look either way, Lena dashed across the street toward
her house as the rain started coming down in pellets. She didn't stop running
until she had reached the kitchen, where she found her mama and grandmama cleaning out the pantry.

"Mama, Mama," she cried as she ran into the first pair of arms she came
to, knocking her mother to the floor. "Sarah's gone, Sarah's gone!"

"What, baby? What in God's name is wrong?" Nellie asked, becoming
frantic at the sight of Lena's tears.

"Sarah, she's gone—nothing there. I think she's dead!" Lena sobbed.

"Oh, sugar," Grandmama said as she stooped beside Lena and Nellie
sitting on the floor. "I forgot all about it. I shoulda told you, baby."

"Told her what, Miss Lizzie?" Nellie demanded.

"It's Rough-and-Ready, Lena's little friend Sarah. She and her family
moved away. Moved on the other side of town, to East Mulberry. You know,
Nellie, Yamacraw, you know that neighborhood. Miss Willback 'cross the
street told me. Sarah and her people got put out over there. Miss Willback
saw their pitiful little few sticks of furniture out in the yard yesterday."

"Sarah's gone, Sarah's gone," was all Lena could say.

"Oh, don't worry, baby, you and your friend can still visit each other," Grandmama tried to reassure her. She would say anything to make Lena feel better.

"Oh no she won't, not in that neighborhood she won't," Nellie said.

"See, I told you Sarah was gone, she's gone for good," Lena cried, her sobs turning into hiccups.

"Lord," Nellie said to Miss Lizzie as she kissed the top of Lena's head and rocked her in the salty, sweaty valley between her breasts. "My baby is getting to be so high-strung. Just like I was when I was her age."

Nellie's ministration finally calmed Lena down, but it did nothing to ease the knot of pain Lena felt at the loss of her friend. The following fall when she went to grade school for the first time, she stood around in the yard searching for a little girl who looked like Sarah. There was none. All these girls were shined, polished, and pressed, their hair neatly snatched back into braids and barrettes. None had Sarah's rusty beauty. Then one of her first-grade classmates, a chubby girl who stood alone with her blouse already creeping out of her skirt first thing in the morning, caught Lena's attention. Her eyes didn't sparkle like Sarah's, but they did seem to be full of as much mischief. And when Lena sidled up to her, she smiled and slipped her hand into Lena's.

The gesture reminded Lena of Sarah.

When the first bell clanged, Lena and her new friend Gwen marched bravely into the strange schoolhouse side by side.

Still, on her way home from school that day, Lena felt a tug at her heart when she passed Sarah's house and missed her all over again. From time to time down at The Place, Lena saw Sarah's mother, but when the girl tried to speak and ask about Sarah, the woman pretended she hadn't heard and kept walking from the back door on out the front.

LOOKING FOR HOME

Doris Jean Austin

Orelia Jeter climbed the porch steps and stared in numb surprise into the heavy fog from which she had literally just emerged. She didn't exactly remember leaving the bar but figured that must be where she was coming from. Where she was coming from was not her main concern now, however. All she wanted to do right now was find her keys and get to her room in the attic without waking Miz James and the boy. She opened her pocketbook and began searching methodically for the keys that hid from her every Friday night God sent. Tears of frustration filled her eyes as she stood swaying in the key-searching ritual. She sat down on the top step and began taking items out of the bulging handbag: cigarettes, comb, change purse, wallet—no keys. She turned the bag upside down close to the floor of the porch and shook out an assortment of lint-covered objects and loose tobacco. None of them resembled her keys. She was panting with the effort not to cry.

Orelia had been living in the large front attic room at Elzina's house for two years now. She had no future plans, no dreams, and since she seldom hoped, she had few disappointments. Her only friends were those who stopped in the bars with her on Fridays after work at the lamp factory. And even though they had to be back at work Saturday morning, they all observed the beginning of the weekend on Friday nights. Some stayed longer than others. Orelia seldom left the bar until it closed.

Orelia was a small, dark-brown knot of a woman who seldom met anyone's eyes when speaking. She was satisfied to be remembered once in a while by the boisterous rascals who tolerated her presence on Friday and Saturday nights. Everything about her apologized. A lack of love had, at some crucial point in Orelia's life, retarded her unfoldment. Even her memories were as colorless as the washed-out blue sweater she now hugged to her, sitting there on the damp porch, trying to find a warmth that had eluded her all her days. Tears trickled down her cheeks to meet under her chin as she leaned her head forward on her knees in rare self-pity. She remembered her one shining victory: Dawkins!

Dawkins Jeter was a retired custodian of sixty-six when he met Orelia. She was thirty-two. She had just gotten the job at the lamp factory and was going to start Monday. Dawkins took Orelia home with him from the bar where they met Saturday afternoon. Actually, they met in the back of the bar where food was served. A single hot plate where hot dogs were boiled and served qualified the establishment where Dawkins met Orelia. After two hot dogs, he took her home and they finished his pint of Calvert's. She had not minded later when he removed his teeth and put them in the jar of liquid by the bed. In a fit of generosity, Dawkins married Orelia three months to the day after she came into his life. Her gratitude to the old man was to him a public embarrassment and a secret delight. Under Dawkins' ministrations, not-being became unacceptable to Orelia. Her coworkers were puzzled at the change. Some were offended at the turning of the worm who now did only her own work. Even those who at first felt betrayed, however, shortly accepted this new Orelia as the only one who had ever been. Acceptance of today, whatever it turned out to be, was easier on the mind. They had a reverence for weekend banquets at house parties that boasted fried chicken and chitlins, collard greens, and potato salad, twenty-four-hour bid whist and poker. No behavior was socially unacceptable enough to ban offenders. Hard times. Monday through Friday times. "Johnnie Mae cut Meat's ass so bad last week he still up in the Medical Center." But Johnnie Mae still came to the party the next Friday night after she left the hospital seeing Meat. "She took that mean nigger, Eddie Boy, home Sunday morning, too. She be lucky if Meat don't kill her when he get out." But Friday night was a time of no rejection. Fights won and lost; men and women, loud cussing and laughing, loving, crying, fucking—"What the hell! See you next Friday night if I don't see you 'fore then."

Orelia sat on the porch steps remembering the fire that turned her into another something lonesome—a widow—and tears squeezed from under her tightly closed eyes. She fell asleep leaning on the banister, snored gently, and smiled at memories that warmed her although she still shivered. Her bag lay open on the porch, its contents scattered.

When the bartender announced, "Last call!" Jesse ordered two more double shots of scotch. "And a nip, man," he added in slightly slurred afterthought.

Red, as usual, was the soberest one in the bar at closing. He brought the beer and picked up a bill from Jesse's money from the bar. When he brought Jesse's change, he urged, "Take it easy, my man. Go on home and get some sleep."

Jesse stood unsteadily as the bright lights went on. Taking a deep breath, he threw down the second shot of Johnnie Walker and chased it with the rest of the beer straight from the bottle.

"You ain't gotta go home but you gotta get the hell outta here."

Jesse started toward the door, smiling at the familiar phrase that was closing bars all over town about this time. The men leaving the bar in front of him called back to Red at the door, "See ya later, man. You comin' down Charlie's?"

Red assured them, "In about a half hour, man."

So it was that Jesse followed the two men he didn't know down to Charlie's, a well-concealed after-hours place in a garage on Sackett Street that the police department knew was there. When it became obvious to the men that the fool behind them talking to himself had been at it for the last three blocks, the shorter of the two challenged Jesse with, "Hey, where you on *your* way to, man?"

Jesse answered with easy confidence, "Down to Charlie's, baby."

The three of them continued as before with Jesse now five or six feet in back of the more relaxed duo. A heavy fog replaced the earlier rain, and Jesse strained his eyes to keep the two men in sight. They walked for about eight blocks before turning off the avenue onto Sackett Street and into the garage. Jesse caught up with them as a small side door opened and filled the silent night air with the muffled sound of music. The man at the door smiled Jesse's leaders inside. Standing there in the dim light, appraising Jesse coolly, the bouncer said, "Sorry, buddy, members only," and slammed the door in his face.

Jesse couldn't help laughing at the bouncer, at himself, at homecomings and goings, before and after hours. At this time, that time, and all time. Motherfuckers! Should've been able to tell he was a member by the color of his skin. What the hell was getting into folks, anyway?

"What the hell is it, man? Am I too black or ain't I black enough? Make up your minds!" He pressed his face against the door. "Fuck you!" he yelled mightily. "Fuck you," he mumbled repeatedly as he traced his steps to the bar, only remembering it was closed after trying the door.

Now, headed for Astor Place once more, he was again deep in conversation with himself. He stumbled through the fog as though he were out for an afternoon stroll. He stopped obediently at red lights, waited patiently until the signal changed from amber, to red, to green. Few cars passed as he stopped to light another cigarette from the one he was smoking, throwing the butt away only to repeat the process a few blocks later. As he drew closer to home, his pace quickened. Scotch-logged deductions finally revealed in brilliant light the exact nature of his problem. He was close to tears in toxic gratitude.

He was crazy! Musta lost his mind in Rahway!

He kept repeating, "So that's it. So that's it."

He burst out laughing as he turned on Astor Place. He could just see Elzina's face when he explained the problem to her. He'd wake her up the minute—

Jesse stopped dead in front of the house. He looked at his watch and back to the body half lying on the top step of the porch. He climbed the steps and stood looking down curiously at—

Whatever it was, it didn't have no damn business sleeping on his porch at three o'clock in the morning. He shook the woman's shoulder.

"Hey, wake up! Wake up, I said! What you doing sleeping on my porch?"

Orelia opened her eyes, preparing her apologies even as she tried to focus on the figure before her. And suddenly Jesse was overcome by the pitifulness of the creature before him. Lord, she was so pitiful! "Poor baby, you ain't got nowhere to go?" He swayed in compassion.

With the help of the banister, Orelia raised herself until she was standing on the second step down from him. She picked up her pocketbook, shoving things back in as she spoke. "I lost my keys. I was just sitting down a minute until I figured what to do," she mumbled as she closed her bag, stood up straight, looked up into Jesse's face for the first time, and repeated, "I lost my keys."

Suddenly Jesse knew the answer to both their problems. "I know just what you need, little lady. You need a drink." He took her arm and ushered her back down the steps, steadying himself with one hand on the banister. "I know where there's a party. That's what we need—a party! My mama give the best parties in Jersey City."

"I can't go to no party looking like I look." She tried to pull away and succeeded only in stumbling into Jesse's arms.

"Shhh," he silenced her. "You wanna wake up your landlady?" He examined her stricken face and added, "You done already scared her husband half to death." He stifled his laughter as he guided her back down the street.

It was almost 4:00 A.M. when they turned onto Kearny Avenue. Jesse wondered who was at his mama's tonight. His baby sister, Cissy, he hoped; maybe, Nappy. Napoleon B. James (even the teachers had taken to calling him Nappy) had been everywhere the railroad could send him. Always came back to Jersey City—said it was his God-given duty to keep coming back until he gave every female here a chance to know what the good Lord put 'em here for in the first place. Nappy's good looks could be found in the face of many Jersey City youngsters who were mistakenly calling another man daddy. "I was gonna be just like my brother, Nappy," Jesse confided to Orelia. "Ya gotta always follow your first mind. Shoulda been just me and Nappy," he informed her. He thought of Elzina and quickly directed his attention back to his family—all those brothers and sisters, some of whom he hadn't seen since that day in court, almost five years ago.

He walked faster now as they neared Truselle's house. Orelia trotted beside him in silence. He held her arm as they entered the gate and climbed the porch steps to his mama's house. He stood a minute, grinning at the familiar sounds and smells coming through the screen and the open window. Closing his eyes, he allowed his mind to describe for him the scene inside. The living room was where the music came from. Full of people dancing, sitting, standing—all of them talking loud. Paper plates of his mama's cooking all around the room in various stages of destruction. The little side room that used to be his bedroom had a card table and chairs in the center where the poker game was going on. He wondered who was cutting the game tonight. The bed, dismantled, stood leaning against the wall as if temporarily. But Jesse knew the bed hadn't been set up in at least twelve years. When any of his brothers and sisters came home they stayed in one of the bedrooms upstairs. Folks was in the kitchen playing bid whist, lying in rapid, machine-gun fashion. Lord, some of the most beautiful lies. Make you laugh yourself sick. He recognized a laugh and chuckled to himself. Nobody in the world he ever met had a laugh as big and healthy as his mama's.

Orelia shivered. Her hair was standing a bit higher, encouraged by the damp night air. He raised his hand to knock just as the door opened from inside. The tall, skinny man stood silhouetted in the doorway against the light from inside the house. He squinted, peering into Jesse's face.

"Yeah? Who you, man?"

"Hey, L.D., what's happening, man?"

"Jesse, thatchu?" cautiously. Then, "My ma-a-a-a-n."

L.D. was grinning and breathless, having held onto his last word until his lungs refused to cooperate. Gold teeth gleamed in an ear-reaching smile.

"Come on i-i-i-i-in," he bellowed, hitting several notes not suggested for the baritone he was naturally. Jesse put both hands over his ears to muffle the volume. L.D. was wiping unashamed tears from his cheeks with one hand, pumping Jesse's hand with the other, and somehow trying to hug the younger man at the same time. Jesse's own eyes were glassy at this greeting from this man who meant more to him than other men. It was fitting that L.D. should be the first to welcome him into this house. L.D. had paced the living room floor the night Truselle delivered the boy upstairs in this very house. And he'd hung around for all those years after with the nickels, dimes, and quarters—and later when Jesse was in high school, the dollars. He bought Jesse his first raggedy car for fifty dollars—it never did run. And now he stood with glad tears in his eyes bellowing back into the house, "It's the return a Jesse James, y'all. Goddamn me, it's the return a Jesse James!" L.D. raised his voice, "Truselle, it's Jesse. Jesse home!"

Truselle rushed into the living room from the kitchen and stood breathing hard with her efforts to run through wall-to-wall party. "Baby! Lord Jesus, my baby home, y'all." She burst into tears as Jesse lifted her short bulk to kiss the top of her head, her cheeks. There were tears on his own face.

"Hey, Mama, I'm home." He choked on emotions that were in reality the homecoming he'd expected to find on Astor Place.

Orelia, forgotten in the greetings, stood nappy-headed and quiet just inside the door, trying not to be noticed—and succeeding. Sticking her hands deep into the pockets of the blue cardigan, she came across the keys that she had looked for so hard on the porch. She stood, feeling no more awkward than usual, running her fingers back and forth over the edge of first one key and then the other. Somebody in the little side room cracked the door wide enough to demand, "A li'l less fucking noise out there." Truselle rushed over to the door forcing it wide open, dragging Jesse behind her.

"Hey, y'all, my baby home! Drinks on the house," she hollered above the music, by now her only competition. A blur of color, hoop earrings flashing, high heels galloping, alerted Jesse to turn just in time to catch Ollie Mae as she threw herself into his arms. Jesse hugged her to him, still holding Truselle's hand. Turning to L.D. without lowering her volume one decibel, Truselle bellowed instructions. "L.D., go get that case of Martins out the closet on the back porch. Everybody got to get drunk tonight. My baby home." And two minutes later, "L.D., hurry up. Ain'tchu back yet?"

Everybody was moving out the side room with faces showing anger, relief, indifference—but they all came to share Truselle's triumph. She still held Jesse's hand, patting it with her free hand that doubled as a wiper for the stream-tears that contradicted the wide smile on her face. Ollie Mae stood hugged on his other side, her head on his shoulder, occasionally lifting her head to plant a noisome kiss on his cheek. Jesse spotted Orelia looking so painfully out of place and bedraggled, and finally pulled Truselle over to the door. "Mama, Ollie, I want you to meet . again, baby?"

"Orelia," she replied hoarsely, looking at Trus

"Come on in, Reba, and get yourself a glas enthusiastically kissed Orelia's cheek. "You respons. home? You the parole officer?" Truselle laughed uproariously, Orelia smiled her watered-down smile—timidly, in case she had to withdra. it. She accepted the glass Truselle handed her and did not correct her name. Let it stand as Reba. For all the days Truselle knew the lady, Orelia would never correct her, personally.

L.D. was pouring scotch fast as he could. Handing glasses to Truselle who handed them to the first outstretched hand she met. "L.D., you better go back and get that rum, and the vodka. This ain't gonna last long, and I want everybody to get drunk as bigger fool than they already is." Again she laughed until tears were streaming.

When Truselle waved Ollie Mae away and pulled Jesse into the hall, took him upstairs to her bedroom to talk, the party resumed gradually. He waved to Orelia from the stairs. "I'll be back in a minute, just drink up." He winked and was gone.

Sitting in his mother's flounced, ruffled bedroom, Jesse grimly stared at the red carpet, sorting and filing indigestible facts.

"You know how busy the child been with that big old house and the boy and all." Truselle was defending Elzina. Her eyes closed a moment as she thought of Charles—the boy's very goodness struck her as strange. She opened her eyes to stare at her son. She was so glad Jesse was home to see about Charles. Ain't no boy-child got no business to be that good all the time, she thought. "They need you home, Jesse," she said, smiling brightly. Then changing the subject, "Elzina and Cissy thick as thieves. I tell you Cissy home?" When Jesse nodded, she continued, "Lord, you got to see that baby she got. Jesse, he prettier'n Cissy was. You remember what a pretty baby Cissy was? Well, Clinton—that's what she named him, Clinton—Clinton as pretty as five times Cissy." She grinned triumphantly.

He smiled in spite of himself. But his thoughts returned to Elzina. Why hadn't she been to see his mama but four or five times in that many years? He knew by what Truselle didn't tell him that she hadn't been invited to that house on Astor Place in a long time, if ever, since he'd been gone.

Truselle dropped by now and then to see the boy, she confessed. And she knew how hard Elzina worked "to have everything just right when you came home," she added appeasingly. She got up and freshened Jesse's drink from her private stock.

And they talked.

hen they reached a lull that threatened to keep stretching out, Jesse both Truselle's hands into his and studied the contrasting shades. "It's ice Pop was the one to let me in tonight. He's a good old dude, ain't he?" He spoke the words impulsively, finally giving in to this years' old desire to boast his knowledge of their relationship. Truselle's startled eyes met her son's and immediately fell to stare at the spot where her hands disappeared into his. She shook her head and shoulders as if just remembering who she was and who he was. She glared at him with mock fierceness. "Jesse James, you been a burden to me all your days with your nosiness. Yes, you have! Lord knows you been sneakin' and snoopin' in my business—"

"Mama, that secret been my pride and joy a whole lot of years. A man would have to be a fool not to be proud to have L.D. for his daddy, wouldn't he?"

They were quiet. The hysteria of L.D.'s invalid wife had reminded the family more than one time that Kearny Avenue was not really L.D.'s home. Her calls had interrupted many of Truselle's parties, and Truselle suspected that some of the visits from the police had come from way across town, rather than from any of her own neighbors. But a man had to find a way to sustain his life. And Truselle had helped a few of them over the years, asking nothing in return that they didn't give freely. Their pictures were in frames along the back of her dresser. The children knew each of them by name, but none of them, to Truselle's knowledge, knew the relation they bore to the photographs. Jesse looked at L.D.'s picture, sitting farther front than all the others, and guessed its significance and smiled. His mama was the spunkiest Christian he knew as far as he was concerned. He approved of her unreservedly. He looked around at the familiar, ugly beauty of the bedroom, grateful to be there again. When he began to speak, he chose his topics carefully . . . excluding now, excluding why he was at Truselle's with Orelia. He talked about before he went to jail. He talked about how Charles had grown. He talked about his hopes for the future, but he did not talk about now. And his face forbade Truselle's many questions. And she saw all the tender places and did not test them lest in her clumsiness she unwittingly open up some buried sore spot or add to the pain he couldn't hide from her.

When they finally started back down the stairs to the party, it was well after 5:00 A.M. The bid whist game had resumed. The records accompanied dancers who knew the music better than they knew their own names. Molded against one another, eyes closed, impossibly, they danced. And their feet did not move as they swayed and rocked together in a rhythm as old as steam. As natural to them as breathing. They did not see their hostess return. The door to the poker room was closed once again. That quiet little room was a dormant volcano. If the police or an ambulance arrived at this Friday night celebration, five would get you ten, if there was trouble, it would be found in the poker room where Truselle once more went silently in and out selling whiskey and beer. The noise in the kitchen was again at a comfortable level—no louder than any air-raid siren or train wreck. The wall of voices blended in one clear note. There was music here truer than the record player in the living room. The records became only background—muted accompaniment. The concert proper was in the kitchen.

Ollie Mae had struggled with Truselle's squinch-eyed demand and reluctantly allowed Jesse's freedom to consort with whatever kind of woman he'd come straggling home with. It wasn't in the James nature to hold hard judgment too long. She'd gone on back to the kitchen and now held court at the head of the kitchen table dealing yet another hand of whist. Her long tan fingers handled the cards expertly. "White folks," she was saying as she dealt the cards, her earrings catching the light and throwing slivers at each player as her head moved in the circle of cards issued, "live academically."

"Academically? Whatchu mean, they live academically?" defensively, from L.D. L.D. maintained he never knew what the hell Ollie Mae was talking about anyhow. He claimed it proudly.

"Well, see, it's like this." Finished dealing now, Ollie Mae picked up her own cards one at a time, sliding each one in its proper place in the growing fan of cards in her hand. "It's like this," she continued. "They consider life an intellectual endeavor." Ollie Mae was enjoying her usual spotlight, enjoying the laughter. Her face was damp with sweat as she continued telling it like it was.

"White folks never, never screw. Niggers screw! Niggers are not intellectual as white folks. White folks make intellectual love . . . once a week . . . in the dark . . . by which means only the highest level of intellectual babies are born . . . who, needless to say, never, never screw."

The laughter became a roar. Folks left the living room to come find out what was going on in the kitchen.

"Hey, Ruby, pay attention to that chicken 'fore you be done burned it up."

L.D., "Bid, woman. Ain't it your bid?"

Ollie Mae motioned for somebody to get her another beer from the refrigerator and drank deep and long when it arrived. At a knowing look from L.D., she reached into her pocket and handed him the money for the beer. "Damn, you don't miss nothing, do you? This my mama's house, you know." She rolled her eyes at L.D. "Well . . . like I was saying"—she turned back to her audience—"white folks have somehow found out how extremely personal we take life. And . . . they ain't never gonna forgive us for it."

More laughter.

"Shit! Whose bid is it, anyway?"

Ruby removed golden pieces of chicken from bubbling oil in a black iron skillet, shaking her head in profound agreement. Ruby always shook her head in profound agreement when Ollie Mae spoke.

Orelia sat alone in the living room near the record player listening to Percy Mayfield's latest hit, "Please Send Me Someone to Love." She tapped out the rhythm with sturdy fingers. Her other hand lifted her glass to her lips, punctuating the beat that filled the room. She was free and flying high in that place alcohol often took her to rest from too much reality. Too much woman-loneliness. She sat, eyes closed, in grateful relief for her freedom. She always got here accidentally, and not often lately, since you never could tell which drink would shoot you into slurring, stumbling too-soon drunkenness.

Jesse stood in the doorway watching her through the smoke-filled room, through his own inebriated haze. She really wasn't ugly, he decided. The comedian in his head shot back a swift, *She just as good as ugly, man. That's a fact!* Going over her body with calculating eyes as he poured scotch from one of the open bottles on the coffee table, Jesse appraised Orelia from the neck down, recognized the pure quality there, and made his decision to be comforted by the evidence in her favor.

They left Truselle's around six-thirty Saturday morning, both far from sober. Truselle stood in the doorway extracting Orelia's promise: "Be sure to be here next Friday night, Reba. You ain't got to wait for Jesse. Child, you got to learn to play some cards. Ain't no sense in not knowing how to play. You got to do something with yourself." Truselle shook her head sorrowfully, watching the two of them amble unsteadily toward the corner. Then she turned back into the house to give Saturday morning eviction notice.

Jesse and Orelia made their first trip to the Matawan Hotel, right across the street from Mount Sinai Baptist Church. With Truselle's compliments, they had an almost full bottle of scotch that would last them all day. Orelia did not go to work and she did not call in. She didn't even mention the problem to Jesse for fear he'd tell her she ought to go.

From years of experience, the factory expected only half of their workers to show up on Saturday morning. The foreman was never disappointed.

Orelia and Jesse drank. Orelia talked. She spoke of her mother, who'd always been old—an old woman when Orelia was born, an old woman when she died. Orelia's greatest asset in her mother's eyes had been her ability to *"shut the fuck up immediately"* when told. By the time Orelia was nine years old she was a quiet shadow turned in on herself, trying to nurture her own self with inadequate tools.

Jesse listened to her uneventful life story with his mind on Astor Place. When his thoughts threatened his intentions, he poured himself a drink and chased it with first one erect black nipple, then the other. Orelia's body became quiet with waiting. With a life of their own, her impatient fingers crept down his chest and, in mild surprise, encountered his unreadiness. She bent her head in encouragement until her cheek rested on the taut muscles of his stomach. Her lips nibbled, then began a slow, sensuous massage. Suddenly, violently, Jesse hated where he was and what he was doing. The shame of it clutched at him, made him limp and sober when the moment called for him to be hard and good-time-high. He raised himself on one elbow and poked clean through the thin mattress to the springs. He poured himself a generous stimulant as the first sun reached the hotel room and sprayed the shadow of Orelia's bobbing head against the wall. He gulped his scotch and felt pity for them both—for a moment—before he raised his hips to meet the dancing shadow of Orelia's bobbing head. He felt a vicious anger at her. He pulled her up by her armpits and pushed her roughly onto her back. With his first thrust their bodies came together with a sound like a butcher's mallet pounding a side of meat. The same impact to her head would have undoubtedly caused concussion. The creaking springs were demented violins that sang to the drums of their flesh. *If I could dance real fast,* Orelia thought with head-snapping humor, *I could dance to the music. The Charleston! The huck-a-buck! Mama, look, I'm dancing.* Buffeted about with the force of the attack, her teeth clicked sharply together as she slammed against the mattress. The springs etched their geography on her buttocks. At first she struggled to keep up with the pace he set, but she could only run behind him gasping. Finally she slowed down, then stopped altogether, realizing that she was not personally involved in Jesse's race. She looked up into his face once, and quickly shut her eyes. It was a long, savage tune he played in and out of his anger. At last he reached the solitary victory he'd been chasing—left her trembling with relief—and fell over her body, breathing noisily. He snored. They slept on a damp rope of sheets, each safely hidden in the other.

Aided by Truselle's scotch, Jesse and Orelia played their sad game until early evening when another hunger drove them out. When Orelia declined his invitation for something to eat, he was relieved. Smiling gratitude at his bare feet, she left the hotel room before he finished dressing. She really did understand why they had to be careful, she addressed the closing door. She stopped at the liquor store on her way home—just in case. You had to be prepared for anything in an attic room alone on Saturday night. Even after miracles like Jesse, you couldn't keep your guard down too long. She was much too smart today to be fooled. Still, she smiled as she headed back to Astor Place.

Jesse opened a fresh pack of Lucky Strikes from the machine in the lobby and lit one before heading back to his mama's house. He had no plans. No explanation crossed his mind. He thought about all that had happened these past two days, and his mind felt like confetti in a windstorm. How the hell had he managed to get from Rahway to here in just two days? Lord, how he needed to lay down. Alone!

He walked away from the Matawan Hotel and Orelia, putting one foot in front of the other, looking neither left nor right. Tired, hung over, with a stomach that growled, Jesse hadn't felt this near death in the five years in the penitentiary. He didn't even remember feeling this bad in all the twenty-four years before he went to jail. Maybe that Orelia was a witch—put a voodoo curse on him. Maybe he was still in Cellblock #14, dreaming he'd come home and screwed one of Elzina's tenants all day his first Saturday home. Each step he took was a thundering miracle that brought Jesse closer to the God of his childhood. Only a little way now and he'd be at his mama's house and he could sit down and rest. Just keep putting one foot in front of the other and he'd make it. He'd "understand it better by and by." The words of the old hymn rose from his mind and loomed at him in three-dimensional, living color accompanied by a host of angels, "coming for to carry me home." He sang out loud now. Lord, he'd humble appreciate if some kind spirit would "throw out the life line." He took his last step. Then another.

MY MAN BOVANNE

Toni Cade Bambara

Blind people got a hummin' jones if you notice. Which is understandable completely once you been around one and notice what no eyes will force you into to see people, and you get past the first time, which seems to come out of nowhere, and it's like you in church again with fat-chest ladies and old gents gruntin' a hum low in the throat to whatever the preacher be saying. Shakey Bee bottom lip all swole up with Sweet Peach and me explainin' how come the sweet-potato bread was a dollar-quarter this time stead of dollar regular and he say uh-hunh he understand, then he break into this *thizzin* kind of hum which is quiet, but fiercesome just the same, if you ain't ready for it. Which I wasn't. But I got used to it and the onliest time I had to say somethin' bout it was when he was playin' checkers on the stoop one time and he commenst to hummin' quite churchy seem to me. So I says, "Look here Shakey Bee, I can't beat you and Jesus, too." He stop.

So that's how come I asked My Man Bovanne to dance. He ain't my man mind you, just a nice ole gent from the block that we all know 'cause he fixes things and the kids like him. Or used to 'fore black power got hold their minds and mess 'em around till they can't be civil to ole folks. So we at this benefit for my niece's cousin who's runnin' for somethin' with this black party somethin' or other behind her. And I press up close to dance with Bovanne who blind and I'm hummin' and he hummin', chest to chest like talkin'. Not jammin' my breasts into the man. Wasn't 'bout tits. Was 'bout vibrations. And he dug it and asked me what color dress I had on and how my hair was fixed and how I was doin' without a man, not nosy but nice-like, and who was at this affair and was the canapés dainty-stingy or healthy enough to get hold of proper. Comfy and cheery is what I'm tryin' to get across. Touch talkin' like the heel of the hand on the tambourine or on a drum.

But right away Joe Lee come up on us and frown for dancin' so close to the man. My own son who knows what kind of warm I am about; and don't grown men call me long distance and in the middle of the night for a little Mama comfort? But he frown. Which ain't right since Bovanne can't see and defend himself. Just a nice old man who fixes toasters and busted irons and bicycles and things and changes the lock on my door when my men friends get messy. Nice man. Which is not why they invited him. Grass roots you see. Me and Sister Taylor and the woman who does heads at Mamies and the man from the barber shop, we all there on account of we grass roots. And I ain't never been souther than Brooklyn Battery and no more country than the window box on my fire escape. And just yesterday my kids tellin' me to take them countrified rags off my head and be cool. And now can't get black enough to suit 'em. So everybody passin' sayin' My Man Bovanne. Big deal, keep steppin' and don't even stop a minute to get the man a drink or one of them cute sandwiches or tell him what's goin' on. And him standin' there with a smile ready case someone do speak he want to be ready. So that's how come I pull him on the dance floor and we dance squeezin' past the tables and chairs and all them coats and people standin' 'round up in each other face talkin' 'bout this and that but got no use for this blind man who mostly fixed skates and skooters for all these folks when they was just kids. So I'm pressed up close and we touch talkin' with the hum. And here come my daughter cuttin' her eye at me like she do when she tell me about my "apolitical" self like I got hoof and mouf disease and there ain't no hope at all. And I don't pay her no mind and just look up in Bovanne shadow face and tell him his stomach like a drum and he laugh. Laugh real loud. And here come my youngest, Task, with a tap on my elbow like he the third grade monitor and I'm cuttin' up on the line to assembly.

"I was just talkin' on the drums," I explained when they hauled me into the kitchen. I figured drums was my best defense. They can get ready for drums what with all this heritage business. And Bovanne stomach just like that drum Task give me when he come back from Africa. You just touch it and it hum thizzm, thizzm. So I stuck to the drum story. "Just drummin' that's all."

"Mama, what are you talkin' about?"

"She had too much to drink," say Elo to Task cause she don't hardly say nuthin' to me direct no more since that ugly argument about my wigs.

"Look here Mama," say Task, the gentle one. "We just tryin' to pull your coat. You were makin' a spectacle of yourself out there dancing like that."

"Dancin' like what?"

Task run a hand over his left ear like his father for the world and his father before that.

"Like a bitch in heat," say Elo.

"Well uhh, I was goin' to say like one of them sex-starved ladies gettin' on in years and not too discriminating. Know what I mean?"

I don't answer 'cause I'll cry. Terrible thing when your own children talk to you like that. Pullin' me out the party and hustlin' me into some stranger's kitchen in the back of a bar just like the damn police. And ain't like I'm old old. I can still wear me some sleeveless dresses without the meat hangin' off my arm. And I keep up with some thangs through my kids. Who ain't kids no more. To hear them tell it. So I don't say nuthin'.

"Dancin' with that tom," say Elo to Joe Lee, who leanin' on the folks' freezer. "His feet can smell a cracker a mile away and go into their shuffle number post haste. And them eyes. He could be a little considerate and put on some shades. Who wants to look into them blown-out fuses that—"

"Is this what they call the generation gap?" I say.

"Generation gap," spits Elo, like I suggested castor oil and fricassee possum in the milk shakes or somethin'. "That's a white concept for a white phenomenon. There's no generation gap among black people. We are a col—"

"Yeh, well never mind," says Joe Lee. "The point is Mama . . . well, it's pride. You embarrass yourself and us, too, dancin' like that."

"I wasn't shame." Then nobody say nuthin'. Them standin' there in they pretty clothes with drinks in they hands and gangin' up on me, and me in the third-degree chair and nary a olive to my name. Felt just like the police got hold to me.

"First of all," Task say, holdin' up his hand and tickin' off the offenses, "the dress. Now that dress is too short, Mama, and too low-cut for a woman your age. And Tamu's going to make a speech tonight to kick off the campaign and will be introducin' you and expecting you to organize the council of elders—"

"Me? Didn' nobody ask me nuthin'. You mean Nisi? She change her name?"

"Well, Norton was supposed to tell you about it. Nisi wants to introduce you and then encourage the older folks to form a Council of the Elders to act as an advisory—"

"And you going to be standing there with your boobs out and that wig on your head and that hem up to your ass. And people'll say, 'Ain't that the horny bitch that was grindin' with the blind dude?' "

"Elo, be cool a minute," say Task, gettin' to the next finger. "And then there's the drinkin'. Mama, you know you can't drink 'cause next thing you know you be laughin' loud and carryin' on," and he grab another finger for the loudness. "And then there's the dancin'. You been tattooed on the man for four records straight and slow draggin' even on the fast number. How you think that look for a woman your age?"

"What's my age?"

"What?"

"I'm axin' you all a simple question. You keep talkin' 'bout what's proper for a woman my age. How old am I anyhow?" And Joe Lee slams his eyes shut and squinches up his face to figure. And Task run a hand over his ear and stare into his glass like the ice cubes goin' calculate for him. And Elo just starin' at the top of my head like she goin' rip the wig off any minute now.

"Is your hair braided up under that thing? If so, why don't you take it off? You always did do a neat cornroll."

"Uh huh," 'cause I'm thinkin' how she couldn't undo her hair fast enough talking 'bout cornroll so countrified. None of which was the subject. "How old, I say?"

"Sixtee-one or—"

"You a damn lie Joe Lee Peoples."

"And that's another thing," say Task on the fingers.

"You know what you all can kiss," I say, gettin' up and brushin' the wrinkles out my lap.

"Oh, Mama," Elo say, puttin' a hand on my shoulder like she hasn't done since she left home and the hand landin' light and not sure it supposed to be there. Which hurt me to my heart. 'Cause this was the child in our happiness 'fore Mr. Peoples die. And I carried that child strapped to my chest till she was nearly two. We was close is what I'm tryin' to tell you. 'Cause it was more me in the child than the others. And even after Task it was the girlchild I covered in the night and wept over for no reason at all 'less it was she was a chub-chub like me and not very pretty, but a warm child. And how did things get to this, that she can't put a sure hand on me and say Mama we love you and care about you and you entitled to enjoy yourself 'cause you a good woman?

"And then there's Reverend Trent," say Task, glancin' from left to right like they hatchin' a plot and just now lettin' me in on it. "You were suppose to be talking with him tonight, Mama, about giving us his basement for campaign headquarters and—"

"Didn' nobody tell me nuthin'. If grass roots mean you kept in the dark I can't use it. I really can't. And Reven Trent a fool anyway the way he tore into the window man up there on Edgecomb 'cause he wouldn't take in three of them foster children and the woman not even comfy in the ground yet and the man's mind messed up and—"

"Look here," say Task. "What we need is a family conference so we can get all this stuff cleared up and laid out on the table. In the meantime I think we better get back into the other room and tend to business. And in the meantime, Mama, see if you can't get to Reverend Trent and—"

"You want me to belly rub with the Reven, that it?"

"Oh damn," Elo say and go through the swingin' door.

"We'll talk about all this at dinner. How's tomorrow night, Joe Lee?" While Joe Lee being self-important I'm wonderin' who's doin' the cookin' and how come nobody ax me if I'm free and do I get a corsage and things like that. Then Joe nod that it's okay and he go through the swingin' door and just a little hubbub come through from the other room. Then Task smile his smile, lookin' just like his daddy and he leave. And it just me in this stranger's kitchen, which was a mess I wouldn't never let my kitchen look like. Poison you just to look at the pots. Then the door swing the other way and it's My Man Bovanne standin' there sayin' Miss Hazel but lookin' at the deep fry and then at the steam table, and most surprised when I come up on him from the other direction and take him on out of there. Pass the folks pushin' up toward the stage where Nisi and some other people settin' and ready to talk, and folks gettin' to the last of the sandwiches and the booze 'fore they settle down in one spot and listen serious. And I'm thinkin' 'bout tellin' Bovanne what a lovely long dress Nisi got on and the earrings and her hair piled up in a cone and the people 'bout to hear how we all gettin' screwed and gotta form our own party and everybody there listenin' and lookin'. But instead I just haul the man on out of there, and Joe Lee and his wife look at me like I'm terrible, but they ain't said boo to the man yet. 'Cause he blind and old and don't nobody there need him since they grown up and don't need they skates fixed no more.

"Where we goin', Miss Hazel?" Him knowin' all the time.

"First we gonna buy you some dark sunglasses. Then you comin' with me to the supermarket so I can pick up tomorrow's dinner, which is goin' to be a grand thing proper and you invited. Then we goin' to my house."

"That be fine. I surely would like to rest my feet." Bein' cute, but you got to let men play out they little show, blind or not. So he chat on 'bout how tired he is and how he appreciate me takin' him in hand this way. And I'm thinkin' I'll have him change the lock on my door first thing. Then I'll give the man a nice warm bath with jasmine leaves in the water and a little Epsom salt on the sponge to do his back. And then a good rubdown with rose water and olive oil. Then a cup of lemon tea with a taste in it. And a little talcum, some of that fancy stuff Nisi mother sent over last Christmas. And then a massage, a good face massage 'round the forehead which is the worryin' part. 'Cause you gots to take care of the older folks. And let them know they still needed to run the mimeo machine and keep the spark plugs clean and fix the mailboxes for folks who might help us get the breakfast program goin', and the school for the little kids and the campaign and all. 'Cause old folks is the nation. That what Nisi was sayin' and I mean to do my part.

"I imagine you are a very pretty woman, Miss Hazel."

"I surely am," I say just like the hussy my daughter always say I was.

MONDONGO

Amiri Baraka

"You never go anywhere, Ray, believe me. I know where you go. And you don't go anywhere. Not around here. I mean where everybody can see." Irv Laffawiss pushed his "cunt cap" back on his head so he looked like the posters of how the sloppy airmen looked in the slides shown at Character Guidance lectures on Saturdays. He should have had a red X painted across him to fully resemble the classic well-advertised "Sad Sack" of U.S. military tradition. And it was the U.S. military, the Air Force, in which he and his good friend, Ray Johns, were now entrapped.

Johns was reading, it looked like. But he had on dark glasses, and the lights in the room were low. So how he was accomplishing this reading was vague. But Laffy knew from past and repeated encounters not to get involved with any conversation with Ray about how was it he could read in the near dark with dark sunglasses.

To the comment about "never go anywhere," Ray Johns merely peeped up over the book and stared at Laffy. "Hey, man . . . why I got to go off the base? I ain't lost nothin' out there."

"You're too weird, Johns." Laffawiss sounded mildly annoyed. "Don't you believe in R & R?"

Ray Johns turned over on the bed where he was half sprawled. He knew
Laffy was going on with the conversation, so he wanted to see how he looked
when he said this shit. "R & R? Shit, man. I wanna go home. Naw, I wanna
go to fuckin' Greenwich Village. R & R?"

"Don't you believe in girls, then?" Laffy was pressing it. He was leaning
now against one of the walls, smoking a bent cigarette and flicking the ashes
like Groucho Marx. Groucho was Laffy's alter ego. He enraged the noncoms
and officers by coming into their offices or his own room when there might
be an inspection or something, bent at the waist, holding his cigarette like
Groucho's cigar, and striding in crazy-looking and rolling his eyes like a
roulette wheel.

"Yeah, Laffawiss, I believe in girls. Why, you got any?"

Laffy pointed over his shoulder and imitated Groucho. "They went
thataway." He pointed in the general direction of town. In this case, Aquadilla, a nasty little dot at the tip of Puerto Rico's shore. Laffawiss and Johns,
together with five thousand other airmen, were stationed just outside Aquadilla at the SAC base, Ramey. They, along with the others, commanded by
a thirty-eight-year-old nutty general who wanted to clean up venereal disease,
were busy with the task of keeping the free world free and intimidating any
sonsofbitches who wanted to maybe make wise remarks, or rape freckle-faced
girls, or live too close, or talk in funny languages, or smell or look funny,
or communize the country—any of that stuff. They were doing this by means
of the B-36 bomber. Laffawiss was a radio operator without a crew, and
Johns a weather gunner on the worst crew on the base.

Every weekend and maybe more, Laffawiss would "roar into town" as
the airmen described it, get drunk, pay for some pussy, then stagger back to
the base with a head as big as a propeller. Johns and Laffawiss were pretty
good friends, Johns from a large town in Jersey close to Manhattan and
Laffawiss from the Lower East Side. Not the Lower East Side of boutiques
and poetry readings, but the old East Side of Mike Gold's heroes and heroines,
of herrings and kosher pickles and pushcarts and poverty.

Johns was a college boy, a dropout from a black college, trying to find
himself. Mostly by reading everything that would sit still long enough to be
read. Including gruesome adventures like reading the whole of the *Times*
best-seller list in a month. The complete works of Marcel Proust, James
Joyce, Ernest Hemingway, etc. Hours and hours of guard duty pulled by
Johns had turned reading from an informative pastime to physical and psychological addiction. He got so he could read anything—no, not could, had
to. The sight of words on paper inflamed him, turned him on in a way
nothing else could. Sometimes when he slept, uneasily under the Puerto
Rican moon, he dreamed of reading; pages flowed effortlessly through his
sleep.

And now his barracks room, which he shared with a giant country boy from Long Island, now, thank God, on leave, had, despite the pressures of would-be military s.o.p.s, begun to take on the look of a secondhand bookstore.

Every week Johns had to hear something from one of the noncoms about the room and its unmilitary look. You were only supposed to have "pictures of loved ones," and as many books as the dresser top would allow to sit "in a military manner." But then he had to hear about the weak little fuzz he had sprouting out the edge of his chin, which the "war cats" insisted was a beard, or "the boot salute," which many of the black troops threw in lieu of the war one, viz., this was where the head was bent down to meet the reluctant right hand, producing a bent head "blood" salute. Especially not them Southern white officers did they dig it. Johns once had to stand and salute about forty times in the hot sun, "until he got it right." And he did, "by God," as the game started to tire him and the hot sun had gotten all in the young blond lieutenant's uniform, wetting him to the skin.

Between Laffawiss, the scrawny humped-back Groucho "Jew bastard," as some of the quainter Southern boys called him, and Johns, "a fuckin' nigger snob," many, many incorrect and backward dudes did they light up with their wild antics. Both were young men sufficiently turned around by their younger lives and what they were learning now in "this war shit" (although it was peacetime, right between the Korean and the Vietnam wars). Both had the feelings and the beginning of the stiff self-identification of themselves as . . . what? "Intellectuals," whatever that meant fully to them. And it didn't mean too much, except that both liked to read, both were mostly quiet and inner directed, and they both hated most of the assholes that passed for noncoms and officers in the error farce, plus a whole lot of "them farmer motherfuckers" who would batter at their sanity with endless hours of "I'm in the Jailhouse Now," which was the top country and western hit of the period. Either that or Patti Page singing "We'll Be Together Again."

They were dragged away from civilian life by their own confusion, Johns being tossed out of school for making his "studies" secondary to his social education, and Laffawiss because he didn't realize (either) that school did have some merit—even though you couldn't learn a hell of a lot around those people. But shit, Laffy found out he was learning a hell of a lot less around Curtis LeMay's (SAC CO) relatives and friends.

Both hung around a larger group of full, semi, and closet intellectuals, all now lamenting being trapped and martyred in the Air Force, when, hell, all had joined voluntarily. They figured they were escaping the "malaise" of postadolescence, but now they were in the real fucking malaise with not a hell of a lot of white bread either.

A few nights a week Johns worked as the evening librarian, and the old career special services librarian, seeing Ray was a book nut, let him have the run of the place, including being in charge of ordering books and records. So a few nights a week Ray, Laffy, and the rest of the crowd would ease into the library, draw the blinds, break out the cheap rum and vodka, and play music most of the night—in luxury and in captivity at the same time.

But Johns almost never left the base. Only sometimes, by himself, he would catch the "gua gua" and end up in San Juan, preferably *viejo* San Juan, to wander around the wild and pretty streets, lamenting his fate. And Laffawiss, though not altogether gregarious, still occasionally wanted his on-base walkin' buddy to dare the wilds of the island with him. Shit, at least Aquadilla.

But Ray, most times, just turned over and turned a page, or maybe he'd just turn up the "box" and check what Beethoven or Bird might have to say. Or maybe just wonder what Monk was thinking behind those blue weird glasses.

"Johns, are you masturbating?" Laffy could get rude like that. Matter of fact, that was his standard tone.

"Why, you bottlin' jerk-off come?" Neither laughed, though they were amused.

"Naw, I just wanna find out how come you don't have to go into town and release your tension." Laffy made a lurid leer with his Groucho face on, swiveling his hips.

"Why you think my tension needs to be released? Shit, my tension can do anything it fuckin' want to. Can't you, tension?" He looked down at his fly, but there was no immediate answer.

Laffy did snicker at this, picking up a water glass as if it were a microscope, "Aha, now we are entering the area of microbiology," as he squinted at the same area Ray Johns made believe he was talking to. A perfect comedy team, though a trifle too avant garde and abstruse for some of their buddies and anti-buddies.

Now they stalked the streets of Aquadilla, in which each evening, thousands of restless, sex-starved, largely ignorant troops were released. And there were always incidents, always unpleasantness (which included drunkeness, fighting, sometimes cutting and shooting). And of course, most of the people of Aquadilla just tried the best they could to do the shit they had to do to survive. But just imagine being just outside the gate, to be invaded each evening by about five thousand screaming crazed American airmen. Jeez, what about releasing them this evening into Darien? What about Scarsdale or Palo Alto or Basking Ridge? Yeah, yeah. I'd like to film that, boy. Or hire somebody to film the shit. Like a military/suburban *Animal House*, if you catch my drift.

This Friday evening it was already a little late, since it had taken Laffy an hour or so to convince Ray Johns to come on in and play cowboy. Assorted airmen of all shapes, sizes, and colors were staggering, dragging, heaving, spinning past them. The number increasing each half hour or so as that Friday wound its way out. Most of the troops were in little groups with their buddies, some staggered alone, the lucky ones were with some of the local women. As the ones with women floated by, Laffawiss swiveled his head around on his neck, leering his Groucho leer.

"That's one, Johns. That's one. A woman, ya see?"

"Yeah, I see. Very interesting."

"There's another one. You see they got different features and all."

"Very interesting. So what happens now? My tension ain't been released. Not a bit. Is this all you have to do, twist your head off at the neck? Somehow I thought it was more complicated than this."

"Wow. First you don't even wanna leave the base and stop your meat pullin'. Now you wanna turn into the original flesh fiend."

"Yeah, yeah." Johns whooped a little weakly, in celebration of some of those "farmer motherfuckers" who could be heard, even now, up and down the street, whooping cowboy and confederate war cries.

Walking down the street the way they were headed brought them face to face with The American, the first of the near-base bars for mainly white soldiers. Harry Truman had already desegregated the armed forces, all right, but just as in the rest of American life, the separation still existed. So there were white bars and colored bars and a few fairly mixed. But most, even there in Puerto Rico, were mostly one or the other.

The American was notorious anyway. Black and white soldiers had frequently locked asses inside its doors. And a few times the place had been closed and "Off Limits" signs put up. Laffy got to the door first and pushed it open, peering in.

"Why you come to this joint, Laffawiss? You gotta meet some ol' Klan buddies in there? Jeez, Laffy, let's not get into no abstract shit."

Laffawiss looked over his shoulder. "Hey, we're stalking our prey, man. I thought you were trying to release your tension."

"In The American? Ain't nothin' in there but them farmhouse motherfuckers. And they got all them bitches in there sick as them." Johns meant that the more backward of the white soldiers would try as quickly as possible to infect the local women with their own anti-black views. First, because they, themselves, had been long shaped by the sickness of racism, but also, more practically, they were trying to protect their choice pieces of *choce* from

getting "pulled" by the aggressive black troops. Hence, fights in and around
The American and a lot of other places, in this "neutral zone" outside the
U.S. mainland, where the "bitch pullin' " competition was conducted by a
slightly different set of rules.

"I ain't goin' in that lousy joint." Johns stepped back away from the
doorway as two obvious "farmer cats" just about stumbled by, tossing him
a death look. They also pushed past Laffawiss, who was still peeping in the
door, seeing what he could see, and talking to Ray over his shoulder.

"Hey, they're all dogs in here anyway." Then, in response to being slightly
shoved by the drunken duo, "Creeps . . . you'll probably die with claps of
the mouth."

"Laffawiss, let's go. I ain't in no goddamn boxin' mood, man. You don't
want to release tension, you want to build the shit up." Johns turned now
as if he were going to leave Laffawiss in front of the bar.

"Hey, Ray, shit. Shit, Ray. Look who's in this joint." The sight of
whoever was cracking Laffy up. "Hey, look. Come on, it'll do you good,
come on. Look!"

Reluctantly, Johns crept up toward the pushed-open bar door and peered
in. There were white airmen in uniform, or mostly in uniform, their "cunt
caps" or other class-A visored caps slid all the way to the back of their heads.
Or else there were those in what were supposed to be "civilian clothes,"
which naturally included "Hawaiian"-inspired obscenities as shirts, loud
trousers, jeans, some pants high-styled with contrasting "pistol pockets" and
seams. Bottles, mostly beer, being raised. Loud profane talk and shouting,
confederate whoops, and spaced appropriately throughout the joint, on the
stools and at the tables, different sizes, shapes, and colors of Puerto Rican
women, some prostitutes, some not. The soldiers in the bar didn't care too
much one way or the other, as long as they got over. If they could still get
it up after falling down and throwing up on each other.

But Laffawiss was pointing now, almost frantically, at a fat, stoop-
shouldered, white, red-faced Airman Second with his "cunt cap" cocked
way over on the side of his head. But not far over enough to hide the
screaming red knife scar dug into a white valley down his cheek. Laffawiss
could not contain himself; he was laughing out loud and jiggling from one
foot to the other.

"What?" Ray Johns stared into the now fully lighted bar. "Oh, it's that
goddamn farmer that Grego cut. Wowee, first time I seen that sucker since
Jack the Ripper got his ass."

Grego was a Mexican–American airman who hung with Laffy and Ray
and the others in their little lightweight intellectual gang. Grego was blond
and you couldn't tell he was Chicano until he opened his mouth. Or unless

you spotted the tiny cross tattooed between his thumb and forefinger, which marked him Pachuco, and a member of one of the hardass Chicano youth gangs that littered the Southwest as well as L.A.

The fat farmer had made the mistake of saying something about "spics," and lickety-split, before you knew it, light caught for an instant in a blue blade passing through the air on the way to slash my man's puss, and unless he got plastic surgery it remains so slashed even until this moment.

Johns now howled, too, a little cooler. But at least Laffy hadn't started pointing at the dude and hollering, "Cut that motherfucker too short to shit . . . !"

The "farm boy" apparently was sitting with friends, and Laffy and Ray were all there was of their group, so after another second or two of acid kibitzing, including, "You should thank Grego, motherfucker . . . that scar makes your face at least interesting . . . shit," there was an abrupt about-face by the two laughers, as First Sergeant Barfell called our two heroes, and they swiftly got in the wind.

They cut around the corner, and then across a vacant lot, and presto!— they were standing close by the Estrella Negra (the "Negra" had been added by the black and white troops). Actually, it was simply Estrella, "Star," The Star Bar, and it was the big hangout for the black troops and the Latins and white soldiers who swung out with the blood soldiers.

White (who was not), Perkins (who was), and Yodo, who was from outer space, were sitting and standing at the bar arguing whether Fats Navvaro or Miles Davis played the most shit, to the background music of Lloyd Price singing "Lawdy, Lawdy, Miss Clawdy." This place was also jammed up tight with uniformed and civilian slick airmen, also shouting and laughing at the top of their voices. And while La Estrella was a predominantly black bar, there were more white and Latin troops hollering with the bloods, insulting each other, bullshitting each other, sympathizing with each other, trying to make it and do their various hitches.

"How the fuck you get Ray to come in town, Laffy?" White was standing tall and dour as usual, slightly tipsy and bending slightly toward the new arrivals. "How the fuck you get . . ." He trailed off, giggling. "Yodo, buy Ray a drink for coming off the base."

Yodofus T. Syllieabla (Carl Lawson's chosen moniker to evade the constant depression of being an Air Force medic for seven years of his life and having still only one stripe) was a very yellow colored fellow anyway, and with the booze in him he had colored slightly red, blinking his eyes. "You want Yodofus T. Syllieabla, the high priest of Swahili and the Czar of Yap, to do what?"

"Buy them a drink, silly nigger!"

"Yeah, Ray, why're you out here in this dirty town? And in this dirty bar?" This was Bill Perkins, an aspiring photographer from a suburb of Boston. His name wasn't really Perkins, but his parents had changed it in order to get in the suburb, and Perkins felt guilty about that when he got loaded. So he tried not to get loaded, but it didn't stop him. He got loaded, then guilty, all the goddamn time. "You said you didn't need to come into Aquadilla. But here you are. And with that goddamned Groucho Marx-lookin' cat. Stand up straight, Laffawiss, goddamn it. You're standin' in a hole."

Laffy half turned immediately. "Hey, Johns, let's get the fuck outta here. I'm not gonna be insulted by guys named Perkins whose names ain't really Perkins. Hey, I wouldn't sell you a pickle on the Lower East Side, my friend. Not even a herring. Perkins, shit!"

"Shut up, Laffawiss, I wasn't talking to you. Johns, why are you in town with this guy?"

"Ahaaaaa!" Yodo was pointing the umbrella stick he always carried. "Ahaaaaa! I know. And Anachronobienoid knows, too." Anachronobienoid was the name Yodo had given to his stick. His "all-purpose stick," he called it. The stick had once cursed out a warrant officer, who had been staring too long and hard at Yodo. The stick leaped to the fray, making horrible nigger curses that sent the WO scrambling down the dusty road outside the BX at Ramey.

"I know, I know . . . you two are on a secret pussy mission. That's all this Groucho Marx sucker is roaming around these streets for. What?" Yodo held his stick up as if it were talking. "Yes, yes, Anachronobienoid says he's surprised at you, Airman Johns. Didn't know you was into those SPMs. Ahaaaaaaa!" Yodo's humor always cracked Yodo up the most, and he howled.

"Shut up and buy 'em a drink, Yodo, godamnit!" White persisted.

"Why're you guys concerned about what I'm doing? You're the kinda guys that give SAC a bad name. That's why Ramey's got the highest venereal disease rate in SAC, too. Hey, man, even my AC got the claps."

"In his ear, probably." Laffy was pacing back and forth without moving, Groucho Marx style. "Hey, Ray, I think we got to go before these creeps influence you against sin!"

"These motherfuckers gettin' ready to sin. I knew it. Lemme in on that shit or I'll squeal!" White had to steady himself on Perkins, who was no more sober, but since he was normally stiffer, he could play sober better than White.

Pulling Ray Johns by the arm and exchanging putdowns, jokes, and repeated laments, Laffawiss turned and grunted at the weight of dragging Johns out of the bar. But now with wobbly White in less than hot pursuit,

Yodo waving his "all-purpose stick," White was saying, "Hey, if you guys are gonna start sinning, shit, don't leave me out, you greedy motherfuckers. Don't leave me out, goddamnit."

"Anachronobienoid knows. He will see what you do, no matter where you go," Yodo shouted as Laffawiss and Johns hotfooted it out of the Black Star and up the narrow alley street deeper toward the section known as Mondongo. This was the heavy whore area, and was, of course, strictly off limits. But in reality about as off limits as the dayroom candy machine.

It was night now, and although the low, starry skies over the enchanted island were bright and clear, still the lights of Aquadilla did not make for very much illumination, and so the streets as they wound also got darker, it seemed, the deeper into Mondongo the two adventurers got.

Johns had on a pair of khaki pants that could have been the pants to his class-A khakis, but also a blue striped Ivy League button-down shirt with the sleeves rolled up, plus the usual dark glasses. Laffy had on his class-A khakis with the cap tipped on the back of his head. Ray questioned, "Why you wanna wear your goddamn uniform if we gonna go off limits, asshole? You just wanna get arrested."

"Why should I disguise myself? What am I gonna do—pass for Puerto Rican? Hey, man, people can look at me and tell I'm a Jew from the Lower East Side. I'm telling you."

"Look, man, you got me to leave the perfectly comfortable barracks for some kind of flesh chase. Now you wanna get me busted. Laffawiss, I do not want to get busted. I do not want no Article 15. I don't want no extra duty, no k.p., no double guard duty shit. Why did I go for this bullshit is what I want to know."

And while all this was being said, the two wound farther and farther away from the USAF-sanctioned center of Aquadilla, back down into the center of the off-limits prostitution and gambling sector, Mondongo. Laffawiss was an old hand at winding through these dark, semilit, sometimes unlit streets in search of a little distraction, from the day-to-day (and night-to-night) madness of the "war cats."

For Ray Johns, it was a little too exciting, though no one unfamiliar with his generally calm, even, taciturn manner would know anything out of the ordinary was happening. He could drive polygraph interpreters crazy. But his heart was actually step-stepping a little faster, the darker and narrower the streets got. The farther away from military tourist unreality they got, another Aquadilla emerged, with even fewer stone and clay houses and more and more low tin-roofed wooden shacks.

It was darker, but probably not as dark as Ray Johns's souped-up senses

had it. The streets at first seemed strangely empty, but then as the two soldiers'
eyes adjusted to the tightening light, they could see occasional figures sweep
past them or just beyond them. They could see people sitting on steps or
porches. They could see one or two people stop and turn to regard them as
they passed.

"Come on, come . . . don't get scared, Johns. It's just people walking
up and down like they do all over the world. No need to get psyched out!"
This was Irv Laffawiss, AF 133 75 9011, Airman 2nd Class, radio operator,
73rd Strategic Bombing Command, unassigned, speaking. He was urging
Airman 2nd Class Ray Johns, AF 125 60 8040, weather-gunner, 73rd Strategic Bombing Command, Crew N45, to keep marching through the menacing night toward the Golden Bowl.

"No need to get psyched out? I'm not psyched out, I just don't feel I
need to get busted. Release tension, he says. Hey, and I didn't even go for
it. I was just humoring you, old man. I just thought you needed company
down here in the boonies."

Laffawiss kept on trucking, head poked forward and tilted a little downward, a modified street Groucho. "Oh, man, you can lie. Don't panic. Just
don't panic." And they kept moving into darker Mondongo.

"You mean you have so little self-discipline . . ." A few people scattered
out of their way as they pushed on. They saw a couple of tall, red-faced,
obvious GIs in loud "civilian" clothes poke their heads from behind a shack
and wave at them. Though if they'd stopped to talk to those two troops the
four of them would have been rolling in the dust after exchanging a few
paragraphs as to the nature of reality in general.

"You mean you have such little control over your pecker," Johns picked
up, "that it can demand that you trail around back alleys all night?"

"I know, I know," Laffawiss shot out. "You prefer Merry Fist. You keep
pullin' on that thing, Johns, it's gonna fall off."

"You keep messin' with these nasty whores, yours is gonna turn green
and rot off." The two GIs laughed, too loud for their own purposes. "And
I'm speaking," Johns added quickly, "as a noted microbiologist!"

"Don't make so much noise." Laffawiss slowed a bit. It seemed there
was no light at all. Some flickering matches, muffled laughter close and
fading, unknown movement, overhead the moon and the stars and some
scattered clouds, and somewhere the hint of ocean.

Laffawiss came to a full stop with Johns bumping into him in the dark
like a Charlie Chaplin film. Laffy stood stockstill for a few seconds, till Johns
pulled at his sleeve, whispering sweatily, "What the fuck is going on? Do
you have any idea where we are?"

"Hey, I know this routine cold, Johns. Don't worry. It's okay."

"Okay, my ass. What the fuck's going on?"

In another few seconds a man appeared, in Johns's eye, who was already talking in hurried whispers to Laffawiss. Johns jumped inadvertently as the image came in, but he poked his head toward the two to try to hear what was going on. Laffawiss reached back for his friend, smacking him on the shoulder. "Come on, this guy's taking us to the women. See how quick that happened?"

"Who's this guy, Laffy?" Johns tried to look in all directions, but it was all black and quiet except for indistinguishable shapes and noises. "What's he—a pimp or something?"

"Yeah, yeah, now shaddup before you scare the flesh away."

The three men walked perhaps one hundred yards, up one alley and down another. In a minute or so Laffawiss was leading Johns up three steps and across the short porch of one of the wooden tin-roofed shacks, completely sheathed in darkness. Laffawiss knocked at the door and almost immediately it swung open.

There was a candle or oil lamp lit, and it amazed Johns how much light was in the room, yet it could not be seen from the street. He could not be sure that there were windows; the walls were pasted up with pinups from various Puerto Rican rotogravure sections. But it looked like the *Daily News*, with open-legged blonds, etc., though modest by today's standards.

In the room were a table and chairs, a few notches below your local corner ghetto "furniture" store. A woman had opened the door. And she stood now, in some hopeless colorless cotton housecoat-like garment, without shoes. As Johns's eyes adjusted to the dim light, the hairs on his neck rose and shivered in stiff formation. The woman was old and hideous. She was like some . . . "Witch," the word slid uneasily out of Johns's mouth and punched his comrade in the back. This was followed by Johns's actual hand poking Laffawiss in the small of his back as he leaned forward to half whisper in half Spanish pidgin the desired relationship.

"What?" Laffawiss was showing fingers to the woman, indicating the market value of the *choce*. He was trying to complete the deal, in a fairly circumspect way. He did not need to be bothered by his stuttering friend. So at the next poke he half wheeled around. "What?"

"That witch is ugly as shit, Laffy."

"Two dollars, short time." Laffawiss was talking to the old woman again. "Three dollars, long time." The woman was nodding her head vigorously and making the two- and three-finger signals back to Laffy.

"Hey, Laffawiss." Johns was still trying to whisper, but not really succeeding. "You bring me all the way down here through the goddamn APs for this . . . you fuckin' pervert . . ."

"That ain't the women, Johns. Jeezus H. Christ . . . you think I'm sick?!"

"Yeah. I think that."

The old woman now had her hand extended. She was speaking most of the English she knew. "Two dollar, short time, Three dollar, long time."

"Short time, long time?" Johns looked at the woman and shuddered very openly.

"*Mi amigo no comprende. Que es corto vez?*" Laffawiss felt he was speaking much Spanish, but he sounded as illiterate to the woman as she sounded to him. "*Y . . . largo vez?*"

The woman squinted, trying to understand the Lower East Side gibberish. Then she said, "Short time, very short. Long time . . . is till you come." She laughed at the idea; there was nothing in her mouth but memory.

"Laffy, I don't like this a hell of a lot. Where are the goddamned women? If this ain't the one we s'posed to lay with."

"Okay, okay, unbeliever, good *choce* coming up." Laffawiss was grinning. But the old woman simply stood her ground with her crippled hand extended in the traditional collection position.

"Hey, look, we gotta get the *choce* first," Laffawiss said. "Let us get the women first, then we pay." He winked over his shoulder at Ray.

"Short time? Long time?" The old woman took a step back and turned toward what now seemed another door at the back of the shack, still squinting cynically.

"Long time . . . yeah. You know me. You remember me—Irv?"

"Whatta you—a fuckin' nut, Laffy, tellin' this bitch your name?"

"Hey, I'm an old customer. I gotta see the merchandise before I shell out big bucks."

The old woman repeated Laffawiss's first name. "Irv? *Si, si,* you here before. Okay, okay, come on." She beckoned for the two to follow, and the gesture made Ray Johns think even more of witches.

On the other side of the back door was a smaller room with one bed in it. The room was almost completely dark, but there was a smaller candle stuck in a bottle. On the wall was a gold-and-ivory plastic reproduction of Christ on the Cross bleeding down into the bed. Because even in the dark, the spotted bed sheets, if they could be called sheets, could be perceived.

Sitting on both sides of the bed were two women. They seemed younger than the old woman. But it was going to take a few seconds for the GIs' eyes to adjust. The old woman still had her hand out, but Laffawiss's determination seemed to influence her. "Here, see," the old woman said. "Beautiful!"

Johns's squinting eyes began to see the two women as more than vague shapes in the darkness. And no, they were not beautiful. As they became clearer, Johns was trying to clear his throat so words could come out. "Laffy!" It was like a low but sharply rising moan. "Laffy, Jeezus Christ, man." Johns was pretending to whisper. "Are you that hard up, man?"

Laffawiss had succeeded in cooling the old woman out. The prey was near. Why was this bastard, Ray, trying to queer the deal? "What? Hey, Ray, it's about to happen, man. Don't fuck it up."

"About to happen, hey, man . . . they're . . ." Johns wanted to say "ugly" but he couldn't bear to.

"What's the matter, Johns? You choosy? Goddamn, man, once you get it in you won't know the difference. So they're not bathing beauties. What the fuck you want for three dollars man—Lena fuckin' Horne?"

"Jeezus Christ, Laffy . . . Jeezus Christ." In reality, the women were not as ugly as the old woman, but they were a few years younger.

"Don't worry, Ray. Don't worry. It ain't the looks, it's the movement." Laffy thought this was funny, and bent a little, Groucho style, one arm hung at his side like he had a cigar. "It'll be great, man, great . . . don't worry. I bet you anything you fall in love." And at this Laffawiss almost fell down laughing.

"Okay?" the old woman was saying, and she started to go out of the room.

"Say, man, there's another room back here? Which woman you got and where's the other room?" Johns turned beseechingly to the old woman and babbled the pidgin Spanish he knew. "*Otra cuartro, por favor?*"

The old woman shook her head, about to back out of the room. "No, no." Still shaking her head, she pointed at the single nasty bed that straddled the shadows.

"Hey, man, only one bed?" Johns howled. "How we gonna do that, Laffawiss? Shit, one bed? Man, you crazy!"

"Oh, come on, just lay on the bed sideways. You'll have to let your legs dangle off."

"Let your legs dangle off? Goddamn, you ain't even got the normal positions, and shit happening. I didn't know people from New York were some kind of freaks. Same bed, and let your legs dangle off? Man, how we gonna do anything in the same bed? Don't you even want no privacy?"

This would have cracked Laffawiss up, but he blew the air through his teeth, moving slowly toward one of the women; they were still seated.

"How you get that one?" Their eyes had now fully adjusted, and it did seem in the dark that Laffawiss was getting the better of the deal, but only by a whisker.

"Okay, okay, Ray, you goddamn pest, you take this one. Gimme the other one. It don't make too much difference in the goddamn dark, you know."

"It does to me." They crisscrossed in front of the bed. Laffawiss was already unbuckling his belt as he moved forward, a wide shit-eating grin growing where his face had been.

"Goddamn. Goddamn," was all Ray Johns kept mumbling as he approached the woman who looked like she was in her hard thirties, but who was actually only twenty-seven. Johns was twenty-two, Laffawiss twenty-four. "Goddamn. Goddamn."

For some reason Johns was determined to go through with it, but the whole deal had cooled him out as far as raging animal passion that had to be pulled off by any anonymous *choce*. Laffawiss, on the other hand (and on the other side of the bed) quickly pulled his pants down and without the least adieu got to righteous work, pumping away sometimes at speeds approaching the sound barrier.

Johns was still fumbling and trying to maneuver the woman in some kind of way. And at the same time trying to remain oblivious of his partner three inches away heaving and wheezing like a small white Groucho Marx gorilla on loan from the Lower East Side.

Not long after, Laffawiss's "long time" was gotten to in a relatively short time. But at this point Johns was just beginning to feel that in a little while he might actually begin to feel something. At least he was a little more comfortable. And the woman was not giving much help. Instead of going through a few of Scheherazade's thousand and one sexual variations, the way the old soldiers said it was done for them at bases all over the universe, this less than plain woman lay back in the shadows and scowled. After a while of Johns's aimless pushing, she ventured, "You finished? It's long time."

Ray was raising his head to make some comment to the babe when he could see Laffawiss's narrow butt raising up—what a sight that must have been, Johns thought, a black and white butt flagging away in unison—shit, it's what civil rights is all about, goddammit. But then Laffy started sounding like the babe Johns was supposed to be banging. "Hey, Ray, you finished yet? Huh?"

"What . . . am I finished . . . goddamnit, Laffy, nobody told you to be so goddamn quick. You like a kid, wham, bam, thank you, ma'am." All that to hide the fact that in that surrounding there was nothing going to happen with Ray Johns. In fact, he was lying there mostly embarrassed in the near dark, wondering how the fuck he'd gotten talked into this madness.

"You finished yet, Johns? We can't stay here all night, you know. Not only are we off limits, but we only got about forty-five minutes to get back to the base."

"Aw, fuck that." Johns had his head cocked to one side to talk to Laffy, who had now raised up completely away from the woman. "Ya bastard, I don't care about all that shit. Ain't nothin' happened with me yet, goddamnit."

"Hey, you finish, now," the woman puffing under Johns called out. "You pay for long time, but not for all night. You finish now."

"Goddamnit, I ain't finished. Laffy, look, you got this bitch throwing me on the floor, and shit, I ain't got my money's worth yet."

Laffawiss looked at him and tried to make a suggestive face. But in the half dark Ray couldn't tell what he was making faces about. So Laffawiss whispered, "Hey, we didn't pay, ya creep. We'll get our clothes on, then lam outta here. See, you get a little free stuff."

"I didn't get nothin' in the first goddamn place."

"You finish," the woman repeated again. "Your long time is over."

Laffawiss was pulling up his pants now. Johns had been put off the woman as she made to rise. Laffy was making faces, urging Johns to get his pants on and make ready to dash out of the joint. But Johns was still reluctant, feeling cheated, even though he and his buddy were getting ready to cheat these women (and their pimp). But then the woman Johns had been riding stood all the way up and began to talk to her companion, who had also risen. Ray Johns could see her now more clearly, and in near profile he saw that the woman was a cripple. She had a large hump on her back. Johns's skin felt like pins and needles, and all he could think to do was shout at his buddy, who was about to break out the front door. "Laffy, you dirty sonofabitch. Goddamn you. Goddamn you."

As he was answering Johns, Laffy was already pulling his buddy's arm to get him to move. "Come on, Ray, let's get the fuck outta here."

Johns did not really believe Laffy would run away after fucking the women. It never occurred to him that you weren't supposed to pay, even if nothing happened. But now, after being jerked by Laffawiss, he found himself staggering out into the front room and past the startled old woman, who now had her broom raised to stop the two retreating thieves.

The two women in the back room burst out, too, the three of them screaming, "My money . . . *mi dinero, mi dinero* . . . *maricon* . . . *cholito negro!*"

Then the old lady started calling a man's name. "Miguel . . . *cabron* . . . Miguel!" Laffy and Ray plunged headlong into the darkness. Laffawiss knew generally the direction he was heading in. Johns knew nothing except that it was dark and now three women and soon some crazed pimp were chasing them.

Running, as they were, headlong down the off-limits black streets of Aquadilla—no, Mondongo—made Ray Johns feel absurd. As if he had been shanghaied into a Tom and Jerry cartoon. Laffy, on the other hand, felt exhilarated; the sweaty air laughed around him like his sweaty skin and sweat-soaked uniform; he had his cap in his hand, running in his squatty Groucho Marx gait. The three women had fallen quickly into the far rear, and the

pimp was only a step or two ahead of them. The cries of "*Mi dinero . . .*
maricon, cabron . . ." and other untranslatable obscenities sailed along closer
to the feverishly retreating GIs. But suddenly, out of the darkness, there were
other figures on the side of them, closer.

"Oh, shit!" Johns called out, trying to raise his velocity still higher.
Laffawiss was actually chuckling, and the sight of this made Ray very, very
angry, but there was no time to do anything but hotfoot it.

The Air Force physical fitness programs kept Laffawiss and Johns relatively close in their flight, except Laffy was beginning to breathe a little more
heavily. Johns had run track and cross-country in high school and college,
and actually was running easily. If he had been sitting still, he might have
been more frightened, but during the chase he saw it as an emotion-tinged
physics problem. The bottom line of this was: "You'll never catch me,
motherfucker. . . ."

Then, it seemed, several more dudes leaped out of an alley ahead of
them, and all at once they were just about surrounded. A hand scraped Ray
Johns's face, seeking to grab his clothes or whatever. Laffy was being reached
for, and then both of them were trying to break free from many hands and
the blood-seeking Puerto Rican Spanish.

Johns twisted, flailing his arms, and put his head down, twisting and
diving for freedom, and as he began to receive several glancing blows, he
broke free and then accelerated to light speed. In the darkness it was almost
impossible to see clearly the faces of the seemingly young men who flailed
at them. As he moved away around a dark corner, he caught a glimpse, still
moving, but with someone's hands grasping for him as he tried to round
another corner.

Speeding through the dark, Johns careened blindly into a stack of garbage,
knocking over boxes, cans, bags. As he regained his balance, he grabbed the
lid from one of the cans and bashed at threatening shadows as he ran. He
was trying to get away, number one, but he thought he should try to circle
back behind where they were jumped to see what was going on with Laffy.
But it was not merely one block he had to circle but several, in the blind
hit-and-miss fashion his running enforced. And it seemed a long time and
a long journey, with the voices behind him. Once, he had to swing the
garbage can cover at a couple of dudes moving near the edge of an alley.
As he passed them, he wasn't even sure they were chasing him. But now
they were, for sure. He ran and ran, hoping he still had the right direction.

Turning the corner to what looked like the narrow little street where the
citizens had cornered them, Johns's heart leaped again as he saw the blue
jeep of the Air Police, the red light blinking threateningly from its hood.
He could see two air policemen, one black and one white, talking to what

looked like a huddle of screaming young locals, and at one side of the group the wrinkled old woman stood, adding her two and three cents to the general roar.

Laffy lay up against one of the buildings, turning his head slowly from one side to the other. Somebody or bodies had popped him good. Johns froze for a second, figuring if he showed he blowed . . . but, fuck it, it didn't mean that much. Who cared? A fuckin' Article 15 . . . what the hell? He thought this as he came striding out of the shadows. His appearance set the little crowd on "Vaya!", and for some reason the old woman wanted to spit at him.

Looking up wearily, all Laffawiss could offer was, "Hey, do any of you sad sonsofbitches got a cigarette?" He even gestured at the crowd that strained to ice him. "Mira, dame un cigarillo, por favor." They howled blood.

At Johns, Laffawiss merely tried unsuccessfully to grin. "Hey, Airman, what the fuck happened to you?"

As the APs closed on Johns, particularly because of his ability to move the assembled crowd, Ray answered, "I went home to jerk off. That was the worst pussy I ever had." And they tried to laugh again.

The two buddies did get an Article 15 as punishment, and the First Sergeant made them paint the exterior of both of the large cement barracks that housed the flying personnel of the Seventy-third Strategic Bombing Squadron.

Ray and Laffy renewed their friendship after both got out of the service. Johns had gotten out early because someone had written an anonymous letter to his Squadron Commander that he was a Communist. He didn't even protest. Laffy got out a few months early on a hardship discharge he had phonied up.

Ironically, the last time the two were together was in New York City, the fond and flying apple of their Air Force daydreams. Coming down Ninth Avenue together, crossing into the Village, they were jumped by a screaming bottle-throwing mob of young white boys. Again, Johns with his fabled foot speed, got away, circling a few corners, and picking up a garbage can cover as he ran, laughing at the déjà vu of the whole thing. But this time as he rounded the corner, Laffy had already been taken away in an ambulance. Two guys, who said they were related to Laffy, came by Johns's house a few days later and left an odd message that they were there. They had also asked the superintendent "what color" Johns was, for some reason. But he never saw them again, nor did he ever see his old comrade in arms.

SPILLED SALT

Barbara Neely

"I'm home, Ma."

Myrna pressed down hard on the doorknob and stared blankly up into Kenny's large brown eyes and freckled face so much like her own he was nearly her twin. But he was taller than she remembered. Denser.

He'd written to say he was getting out. She hadn't answered his letter, hoping her lack of response would keep him away.

"You're here." She stepped back from the door, pretending not to see him reach out and try to touch her.

But a part of her had leaped to life at the sight of him. No matter what, she was glad he hadn't been maimed or murdered in prison. He at least looked whole and healthy of body. She hoped it was a sign that he was all right inside, too.

She tried to think of something to say as they stood staring at each other in the middle of the living room. A fly buzzed against the window screen in a desperate attempt to get out.

"Well, Ma, how've you—"

"I'll fix you something to eat," Myrna interrupted. "I know you must be starved for decent cooking." She rushed from the room as though a meal were already in the process of burning.

For a moment she was lost in her own kitchen. The table, with its dented metal legs, the green-and-white cotton curtains, and the badly battered coffeepot were all familiar-looking strangers. She took a deep breath and leaned against the back of a chair.

In the beginning she'd flinched from the very word. She couldn't even think it, let alone say it. Assault, attack, molest, anything but rape. Anyone but her son, her bright and funny boy, her high school graduate.

At the time, she'd been sure it was a frame-up on the part of the police. They did things like that. It was in the newspapers every day. Or the girl was trying to get revenge because he hadn't shown any interest in her. Kenny's confession put paid to all those speculations.

She'd have liked to believe that remorse had made him confess. But she knew better. He'd simply told the wrong lie. If he'd said he'd been with the girl but it hadn't been rape, he might have built a case that someone would have believed—although she didn't know how he could have explained away the wound on her neck where he'd held his knife against her throat to keep her docile. Instead, he'd claimed not to have offered her a ride home from the bar where she worked, never to have had her in his car. He'd convinced Myrna. So thoroughly convinced her that she'd fainted dead away when confronted with the semen, fiber, and hair evidence the police quickly collected from his car, and the word of the woman who reluctantly came forth to say she'd seen Kenny ushering Crystal Roberts into his car on the night Crystal was raped.

Only then had Kenny confessed. He'd said he'd been doing the girl a favor by offering her a ride home. In return, she'd teased and then refused him, he'd said. "I lost my head," he'd said.

"I can't sleep. I'm afraid to sleep." The girl had spoken in barely a whisper. The whole courtroom had seemed to tilt as everyone leaned toward her. "Every night he's there in my mind, making me go through it all over again, and again, and again."

Was she free now that Kenny had done his time? Or was she flinching from hands with short, square fingers, and crying when the first of September came near? Myrna moved around the kitchen like an old, old woman with bad feet.

After Kenny had confessed, Myrna spent days that ran into weeks rifling through memories of the past she shared with him, searching for some incident, some trait or series of events that would explain why he'd done such a thing. She'd tried to rationalize his actions with circumstances: Kenny had seen his father beat her. They'd been poorer than dirt. And when Kenny had just turned six, she'd finally found the courage to leave Buddy to raise their son alone. What had she really known about raising a child? What harm might she have done out of ignorance, out of impatience and concentration on warding off the pains of her own life?

Still, she kept stumbling over the knowledge of other boys, from far worse circumstances, with mothers too tired and worried to do more than strike out at them. Yet those boys had managed to grow up and not do the kind of harm Kenny had done. The phrases "I lost my head," and "doing the girl a favor," reverberated through her brain, mocking her, making her groan out loud and startle people around her.

Myrna dragged herself around the room, turning eggs, bacon, milk, and margarine into a meal. In the beginning the why of Kenny's crime was like a tapeworm in her belly, consuming all her strength and sustenance, all her attention. In the first few months of his imprisonment she'd religiously paid a neighbor to drive her the long distance to the prison each visiting day. The visits were as much for her benefit as for his.

"But why?" she'd kept asking him, just as she'd asked him practically every day since he'd confessed.

He would only say that he knew he'd done wrong. As the weeks passed, silence became his only response—a silence that had remained intact despite questions like: "Would you have left that girl alone if I'd bought a shotgun and blown your daddy's brains out after the first time he hit me in front of you?" and, "Is there a special thrill you feel when you make a woman ashamed of her sex?" and, "Was this the first time? The second? The last?"

Perhaps silence was best, now, after so long. Anything could happen if she let those five-year-old questions come rolling out of her mouth. Kenny might begin to question her, might ask her what there was about her mothering that made him want to treat a woman like a piece of toilet paper. And what would she say to that?

It was illness that had finally put an end to her visits with him. She'd written the first letter—a note really—to say she was laid up with the flu. A hacking cough had lingered. She hadn't gotten her strength back for nearly two months. By that time their correspondence was established. Letters full of: How are you? I'm fine. . . . The weather is . . . The print shop is . . . The dress I made for Mrs. Rothstein was . . . were so much more manageable than those silence-laden visits. And she didn't have to worry about making eye contact with Kenny in a letter.

Now Myrna stood staring out the kitchen window while Kenny ate his bacon and eggs. The crisp everydayness of clothes flapping on the line surprised her. A leaf floated into her small cemented yard and landed on a potted pansy. Outside, nothing had changed; the world was still in spring.

"I can't go through this again," she mouthed soundlessly to the breeze.

"Come talk to me, Ma," her son called softly around a mouthful of food.

Myrna turned to look at him. He smiled an egg-flecked smile she couldn't return. She wanted to ask him what he would do now, whether he had a job lined up, whether he planned to stay long. But she was afraid of his answers, afraid of how she might respond if he said he had no job, no plans, no place to stay except with her and that he hadn't changed in any important way.

"I'm always gonna live with you, Mommy," he'd told her when he was a child, "Always." At the time, she'd wished it was true, that they could always be together, she and her sweet, chubby boy. Now the thought frightened her.

"Be right back," she mumbled, and scurried down the hall to the bathroom. She eased the lock over so that it made barely a sound.

"He's my son!" she hissed at the drawn woman in the mirror. Perspiration dotted her upper lip and glistened around her hair line.

"My son!" she repeated pleadingly. But the words were not as powerful as the memory of Crystal Roberts sitting in the courtroom, her shoulders hunched and her head hung down, as though she were the one who ought to be ashamed. Myrna wished him never born, before she flushed the toilet and unlocked the door.

In the kitchen Kenny had moved to take her place by the window. His dishes littered the table. He'd spilled the salt, and there were crumbs on the floor.

"It sure is good to look out the window and see something besides guard towers and cons." Kenny stretched, rubbed his belly, and turned to face her.

"It's good to see you, Ma." His eyes were soft and shiny.

Oh, Lord! Myrna moaned to herself. She turned her back to him and began carrying his dirty dishes to the sink: first the plate, then the cup, the knife, fork, and spoon, drawing out the chore.

"This place ain't got as much room as the old place," she told him while she made dishwater in the sink.

"It's fine, Ma, just fine."

Oh, Lord, Myrna prayed.

Kenny came to lean against the stove to her right. She dropped a knife and made the dishwater too cold.

"Seen Dad?"

"Where and why would I see *him*?" She tried to put ice in her voice. It trembled.

"Just thought you might know where he is." Kenny moved back to the window.

Myrna remembered the crippling shock of Buddy's fist in her groin and scoured Kenny's plate and cup with a piece of steel wool before rinsing them in scalding water.

"Maybe I'll hop a bus over to the old neighborhood. See some of the guys, how things have changed."

He paced the floor behind her. Myrna sensed his uneasiness and was startled by a wave of pleasure at his discomfort.

After he'd gone, she fixed herself a large gin and orange juice and carried it into the living room. She flicked on the TV and sat down to stare at it. After two minutes of frenetic, over-bright commercials, she got up and turned it off again. Outside, children screamed each other to the finish line of a footrace. She remembered that Kenny had always liked to run. So had she. But he'd had more childhood than she'd had. She'd been hired out as a mother's helper by the time she was twelve, and pregnant and married at sixteen. She didn't begrudge him his childhood fun. It just seemed so wasted now.

Tears slid down her face and salted her drink. Tears for the young Myrna who hadn't understood that she was raising a boy who needed special handling to keep him from becoming a man she didn't care to know. Tears for Kenny who was so twisted around inside that he could rape a woman. Myrna drained her gin, left Kenny a note reminding him to leave her door key on the kitchen table, and went to bed.

Of course, she was still awake when he came in. He bumped into the coffee table, ran water in the bathroom sink for a long time, then quiet. Myrna lay awake in the dark blue-gray night listening to the groan of the refrigerator, the hiss of the hot-water heater, and the rumble of large trucks on a distant street. *He* made no sound where he lay on the opened-out sofa, surrounded by her sewing machine, dress dummy, marking tape, and pins.

When sleep finally came, it brought dreams of walking down brilliantly lit streets, hand in hand with a boy about twelve who looked, acted, and talked like Kenny but who she knew with certainty was not her son, at the same time she also knew he could be no one else.

She woke to a cacophony of church bells. It was late. Too late to make it to church service. She turned her head to look at the crucifix hanging by her bed and tried to pray, to summon up that feeling of near weightlessness that came over her in those moments when she was able to free her mind of all else and give herself over to prayer. Now nothing came but a dull ache in the back of her throat.

She had begun attending church regularly after she stopped visiting Kenny. His refusal to respond to her questions made it clear she'd have to seek answers elsewhere. She'd decided to talk to Father Giles. He'd been at

St. Mark's, in their old neighborhood, before she and Kenny had moved there. He'd seen Kenny growing up. Perhaps he'd noticed something, understood something about the boy, about her, that would explain what she could not understand.

"It's God's will, my child—put it in His hands," he'd urged, awkwardly patting her arm and averting his eyes.

Myrna took his advice wholeheartedly. She became quite adept at quieting the questions boiling in her belly with, "His will," or "My cross to bear." Many nights she'd "Our Fathered" herself to sleep. Acceptance of Kenny's inexplicable act became a test God had given her. One she passed by visiting the sick, along with other women from the church; working on the neighborhood cleanup committee; avoiding all social contact with men. With sex. She put "widowed" on job applications and never mentioned a son to new people she met. Once she'd moved away from the silent accusation of their old apartment, prayer and good works became a protective shield separating her from the past.

Kenny's tap on her door startled her back to the present. She cleared her throat and straightened the covers before calling to him to come in.

A rich, aromatic steam rose from the coffee he'd brought her. The toast was just the right shade of brown, and she was sure that when she cracked the poached egg it would be cooked exactly to her liking. Not only was everything perfectly prepared, it was the first time she'd had breakfast in bed since he'd been arrested. Myrna couldn't hold back the tears or the flood of memories of many mornings, just so: him bending over her with a breakfast tray.

"You wait on people in the restaurant all day and sit up all night making other people's clothes. You need some waiting on, too."

Had he actually said that, this man as a boy? Could this man have been such a boy? Myrna nearly tilted the tray in her confusion.

"I need to brush my teeth." She averted her face and reached for her bathrobe.

But she couldn't avoid her eyes in the medicine cabinet mirror, eyes that reminded her that despite what Kenny had done, she hadn't stopped loving him. But her love didn't need his company. It thrived only on memories of him that were more than four years old. It was as much a love remembered as a living thing. But it was love, nonetheless. Myrna pressed her clenched fist against her lips and wondered if love was enough. She stayed in the bathroom until she heard him leave her bedroom and turn on the TV in the living room.

When he came back for the tray, she told him she had a sick headache and had decided to stay in bed. He was immediately sympathetic, fetching aspirin and a cool compress for her forehead, offering to massage her neck and temples, to lower the blinds and block out the bright morning sun. Myrna told him she wanted only to rest.

All afternoon she lay on her unmade bed, her eyes on the ceiling or idly roaming the room, her mind moving across the surface of her life, poking at old wounds, so amazingly raw after all these years. First there'd been Buddy. He'd laughed at her country ways and punched her around until he'd driven her and their child into the streets. But at least she was rid of him. Then there was his son. Her baby. He'd tricked a young woman into getting into his car where he proceeded to ruin a great portion of her life. Now he'd come back to spill salt in her kitchen.

I'm home, Ma, homema, homema. His words echoed in her inner ear and made her heart flutter. Her neighbors would want to know where he'd been all this time and why. Fear and disgust would creep into their faces and voices. Her nights would be full of listening. Waiting.

And she would have to live with the unblanketed reality that whatever anger and meanness her son held toward the world, he had chosen a woman to take it out on.

A woman.

Someone like me, she thought, like Great Aunt Faye, or Valerie, her eight-year-old niece; like Lucille, her oldest friend, or Dr. Ramsey, her dentist. A woman like all the women who'd helped feed, clothe, and care for Kenny; who'd tried their damnedest to protect him from as much of the ugly and awful in life as they could; who'd taught him to ride a bike and cross the street. All women. From the day she'd left Buddy, not one man had done a damned thing for Kenny. Not one.

And he might do it again, she thought. The idea sent Myrna rolling back and forth across the bed as though she could actually escape her thoughts. She'd allowed herself to believe she was done with such thoughts. Once she accepted Kenny's crime as the will of God, she immediately saw that it wouldn't have made any difference how she'd raised him if this was God's unfathomable plan for him. It was a comforting idea, one that answered her question of why and how her much-loved son could be a rapist. One that answered the question of the degree of her responsibility for Kenny's crime by clearing her of all possible blame. One that allowed her to forgive him. Or so she'd thought.

Now she realized all her prayers, all her studied efforts to accept and forgive were like blankets thrown on a forest fire. All it took was the small breeze created by her opening the door to her only child to burn those blankets to cinders and release her rage—as wild and fierce as the day he'd confessed.

She closed her eyes and saw her outraged self dash wildly into the living room to scream imprecations in his face until her voice failed. Specks of froth gathered at the corners of her mouth. Her flying spit peppered his face. He cringed before her, his eyes full of shame as he tore at his own face and chest in self-loathing.

Yet, even as she fantasized, she knew Kenny could no more be screamed into contrition than Crystal or any woman could be bullied into willing sex. And what, in fact, was there for him to say or do that would satisfy her? The response she really wanted from him was not available: there was no way he could become the boy he'd been before that night four years ago.

No more than I can treat him as if he were that boy, she thought.

And the thought stilled her. She lay motionless, considering.

When she rose from her bed, she dragged her old green Samsonite suitcase out from the back of the closet. She moved with the easy, effortless grace of someone who knows what she is doing and feels good about it. Without even wiping off the dust, she plopped the suitcase on the bed. When she lifted the lid, the smell of leaving and good-bye flooded the room and quickened her pulse. For the first time in two days, her mouth moved in the direction of a smile.

She hurried from dresser drawer to closet, choosing her favorites: the black two-piece silk knit dress she'd bought on sale, her comfortable gray shoes, the lavender sweater she'd knitted as a birthday present to herself but had never worn, both her blue and her black slacks, the red crepe blouse she'd made to go with them, and the best of her underwear. She packed in a rush, as though her bus or train were even now pulling out of the station.

When she'd packed her clothes, Myrna looked around the room for other necessary items. She gathered up her comb and brush and the picture of her mother from the top of her bureau, then walked to the wall on the left side of her bed and lifted down the shiny metal and wooden crucifix that hung there. She ran her finger down the slim, muscular body. The Aryan plaster-of-Paris Christ seemed to writhe in bittersweet agony. Myrna stared at the crucifix for a few moments, then gently hung it back on the wall.

When she'd finished dressing, she sat down in the hard, straight-backed chair near the window to think through her plan. Kenny tapped at her door a number of times until she was able to convince him that she was best left alone and would be fine in the morning. When dark came, she waited for the silence of sleep, then quietly left her room. She set her suitcase by the front door, tiptoed by Kenny, where he slept on the sofa, and went into the kitchen. By the glow from the back alley streetlight, she wrote him a note and propped it against the sugar bowl:

Dear Kenny,
    I'm sorry. I just can't be your mother right now. I will be back in one
week. Please be gone. Much love, Myrna.

Kenny flinched and frowned in his sleep as the front door clicked shut.

Don Belton

Come on up . . . my castle's rockin'

—*Blues*

The night exhales a treasury of stars. You are in the blacked-out backseat of a limousine floating along Upper East Side Manhattan. There is a crowd of reporters with a camera crew outside your building. You fan out your hair and draw it into a knot at your neck. You wrap your face and head in a tulle black veil. Then you put on the dark glasses. The car stops at the canopied entrance to the building. You are a shimmery blur as you are swept into the glass-and-marble lobby and sent floating up in the special elevator. All the while, your teeth flash inside the veil.

You drank too much vodka on the *Concorde*.

The living room is a jack-in-the-box. Statuary, paintings, plates, and mirrors jump out at you. You come and sit on the sofa, stepping from satiny shoes. You lay back your head, closing your eyes. It feels good to relax. You feel the muscles around your eyes relax. Your perfect teeth unclench. In another room a telephone rings, and then you hear the whir of paper passing automatically through a fax machine. You stand and pace the living room and then the entire apartment.

You have not slept here for years. It is hard to believe: when you bought the apartment a decade ago, you imagined yourself, in its peaceable library, reading books in the shine of the lighted fireplace. You dreamed of Sunday mornings in the desert-vast bedroom, spreading the sheets of *The New York Times* across the bed, sipping coffee drawn from a machine, listening to the jazz albums you collected in your early twenties. You said you craved a life filled with books, your own cooking, and other people's music. You believed there might be a man in time whose qualities would enhance your own, who would admire your secret face—who would stay.

But now the apartment houses a six-person staff managing your career in the United States. It still amazes you how easily your home has become a headquarters. How easily you ceased to be the "I" you fought so hard to achieve and began manifesting as "we." The apartment is a prop, a part of the machinery that throws your outsize image at the world.

Here you meet with reporters when your albums are released. Business meetings are conducted in the dining room among gilt mirrors and Venetian glassware. Bodyguards double as waiters. Journalists sip champagne in an atmosphere of chintz and Ming-dynasty horses. You have a private suite of rooms with a king-sized bed, remote-control television sets and stereo systems; there is a mirrored dressing room crammed with unfamiliar clothes. Computerized telephones, bedside, by the couch, desk, and in the bathroom, blink relentlessly. The bathroom offers bone-handled toothbrushes, horn combs, exotic toothpastes and headache cures. The bathtub has a whirlpool and a twenty-four-karat gold grab bar. Lying in the deep tub, in an aura of flowers, you push the loofah sponge from your thighs.

You feel sick and longing.

At exactly seven-thirty, abandoning spilled boxes, belts, powder, and shoes, you emerge from your rooms wearing a short black tasseled dress. Makeup sparkles on your face like blossom dust.

The cook has arrived and filled the apartment with the smells of grilled salmon and beef Peregourdine. In the living room you pour yourself a glass of wine. Fresh flowers have started arriving in profusion, massive bouquets of lilies, camellias, and roses, forty to a bunch.

You pause between worlds, discarnate somehow, unmanifest, waiting for your transformation. You haven't fully arrived. You still feel the motion of the plane. It seems you are always on a plane these days. You break a Valium in half and wash it down with wine.

More than twenty years ago your name exploded into celebrity. Twenty years ago you were still the lead singer of the Jewelettes, four gawky Cinderellas singing with ghetto wistfulness and spurious sighs. Soon you looked more like sepia-toned debutantes than ghetto girls, as coolly mannered as Snow White princesses from Shaker Heights or Grosse Pointe. The Jewelettes: Frances Deal, Marie LaBerth, Lucinda Blood, and Beryl Hopkins.

You think, Where are those other girls? Gone like the fur coats, glamour wigs, dream houses, and big Cadillac convertibles bought on fast new money. Those other girls were like sparks from the flash paper used to herald the acts in the old rhythm and soul revues.

But you still fascinate, riding success like a smooth glissando. You are the fire that burns up everything in your way. You surpass everything and everybody. You surpass your music, as much a model as a singer, as much a face as a sound. The sound is a soul/pop seduction with a built-in cry. In the 1960s it was the sound of a woman crying for freedom that transfixed the world. Later it became the sound of a woman crying for a vision. Your devouring voice still stalks the world looking for a home.

A test pressing of your new album arrived by messenger while you were in the bath. You put the disc on the turntable. Soon the rumbling music vibrates you to your bone. You listen to the jungling mix of horns, drumbeats, and guitars. Then you hear your own voice soaring over the top, stretching out the rhythm, snaking and twisting the time.

You look out your high windows at a panorama of New York City. You light a cigarette. You feel a chill at the small of your back and gradually become present. You are here.

New York has changed since you were last in this room. A new feeling has entered the city. This knowledge reaches you beneath the blaring music, and a muscle around your left eye twitches. You read the change in the mute suspended panorama. The city has a different look, new people. You sense trip wires have been laid for you by your enemies.

The living room with its wraparound windows facing all of New York and the world becomes your stage. You consider the drama of your public life—your magazine covers, industry awards, record-breaking sales, your marriages and remarriages and the lovers who turn into soul-murderers in the dark.

And now this new album and a seventeen-city concert tour, product endorsements, hotel rooms, private jets, parties. Oblivion.

You are always scheming to steal back the limelight and steal it back again and again. Your prayer is: *Let me not be forsaken until I have shown strength to this generation and power to every one that is to come.* And your prayer is: *Bring me up again from the depths of the earth.*

You remove the record from the turntable. You hate the whole sound of the new album. The entire album has the sound of mockery with something ugly howling in the mix.

When the production contracts were drawn up for the album, you told the record producer, "Give me a hit. That's all."

You weren't joking.

You record music you no longer love. Your music no longer expresses your spirit. You've become a simulator. You rehearse every whisper and moan you deliver with letter-perfection. Your early music was structured around voices. You *had* to sing in those days because all you had was the sound your soul made in your body to reach an audience. You couldn't hide behind arrangements, haute couture costumes, and special effects. It would have cost your life to stand on the stage of the Apollo or the Uptown trying to sing something you didn't understand. Those black audiences would have torn you apart.

You came out on those stages, scratching up the floor with your two-dollar high heels, trying to dance in a too-tight gown made from a Simplicity pattern. They weren't studying your smile or the bend of your bright auburn wig. They were waiting. You were naked to them. They were close enough to look right into your eyes, and they were willing to carry you, but you had to show them your heart. You would have wrenched it from the center of your breasts if need be to work up a feeling. They were shriving for your soul while you were up there. You messed up your face with the depth of pain and love pouring through you. You kept up your ragged shuffling and chanting until you were fused with a power that rocks the ceaselessly coming waves of the ocean. Until the tears streamed down your face and your hands gave benedictions of release and blood pardon.

You wish you could cry those tears again. Perhaps they would wash away the years that have pushed you further and further from your audience and from your song. Now you play the big money venues. Most of your audience watches you perform on the giant video monitors set up around the arena or through binoculars or as a diffused light at the center of a dark stadium.

You have become a radiant source of light.

As for your records, your voice now comes clothed in jarring hooks and computer-programmed crashes to penetrate even the mind centered on the ghoulish flame of a drug pipe.

Your voice strains under the burden of cigarettes and isolation. Your voice is blocked up with your own anger and wonderment. You are at a loss to express what you have lived and seen in a pop song. Still your records sell as if imbued with a diabolical charm.

Something stings your hand. The cigarette has burned away to the space between your fingers. You fling it from you as if it were a wasp. It is a moment before you realize it is only a burning cigarette end and retrieve it from the carpet.

Kneeling on the floor for the cigarette, you feel a stealing stroke of nausea, then exhaustion. You hit your arm against the coffee table and, moaning, fall back on your side. Your hair sweeps your face, flipping back. You stretch out on your back, holding your stomach, then your head. You feel hot. You feel as though your head were about to blow apart. Your prayer is: *I can't die here. Not now. Not here alone without anyone who loves me and knows me. Don't let me die before I reach my safe harbor.* Your eyes roll back, watching the ceiling. The ceiling looks so remote—a mute blazing-white world above your head.

You tell yourself to breathe. You try to concentrate on your breath. You breathe soundly and resolutely, listening to the air enter and leave through your mouth until you become all breath, all air. Fire and brimstone fall from the walls and ceiling. The fire catches first in your brain. Next your skin catches. You cry and sweat. Your head throbs, breaking into burning cinders. You are so hot you cannot stand it. Your clothes catch fire from your skin.

Your body burns and rolls on the floor.

You keep on breathing. Through the time on the floor your soul keeps on breathing and watching.

You remember yourself, as the fire disappears. You are supreme, self-existent, single and self-producing.

No one has pierced your mystery.

Next the waters of your spirit begin to break. You walk down a terraced mountain to greet the waves. You are the sea-witch, the mirror of heaven.

The wind refreshes you, anoints your shoulders, neck and face. The wind brings fragrances of Africa and the Caribbean, Newark, Haiti, New Orleans—everywhere your people rush in the move of life with their smells and voices. Even the voice of their laughter and the smell of their fear. Smells of their fiery food and the fucking-dance of their regeneration. The wind is filled with their voices whispering together. Their whispers are like kisses imprinting your whole body with information. Telling you a vocabulary of feelings.

When the waters break, they leap the boundaries of the sea. They overtake the shore. And with them break the glamorous waters of your pain. The waters toss you like a reeling ship. You rock and reel. You toss. You go down. You drown in emerald water. There are emeralds and rare rubies in the sea's foam. The emeralds are your blood pride and the rubies your blood guiltiness. You fall to the sea's floor.

The impact of the fall stuns your mind and knocks the breath out your soul. You are hours on the watery floor, unconscious, angels and demons fighting to bear you away.

Suddenly breath returns to your body with the whir of electricity returning to a whole city after a power failure.

You simply rise.

Slowly you build yourself up from the floor and realize you are back in the living room. You have been in this room the whole time. You rise. As infallible as the daystar. Your movements as gracefully linked as a dragon's.

You turn, hearing the special elevator open in a farther room as your first dinner guests arrive.

JOHNNIERUTH

Becky Birtha

Summertime. Nighttime. Talk about steam heat. This whole city get like the bathroom when somebody in there taking a shower with the door shut. Nights like that, can't nobody sleep. Everybody be outside, sitting on they steps or else dragging half they furniture out on the sidewalk—kitchen chairs, card tables—even bringing TVs outside.

Womenfolks, mostly. All the grown women around my way look just the same. They all big—stout. They got big bosoms and big hips and fat legs, and they always wearing runover house shoes and them shapeless, flowered numbers with the buttons down the front. 'Cept on Sunday. Sunday morning they all turn into glamour girls, in them big hats and long gloves, with they skinny high heels and they skinny selves in them tight girdles—wouldn't nobody ever know what they look like the rest of the time.

When I was a little kid, I didn't wanna grow up, 'cause I never wanted to look like them ladies. I heard Miz Jenkins down the street one time say she don't mind being fat 'cause that way her husband don't get so jealous. She say it's more than one way to keep a man. Me, I don't have me no intentions of keeping no man. I never understood why they was in so much demand anyway, when it seem like all a woman can depend on 'em for is making sure she keep on having babies.

We got enough children in my neighborhood. In the summertime even the little kids allowed to stay up till eleven or twelve o'clock at night—playing in the street and hollering and carrying on—don't never seem to get tired. Don't nobody care, long as they don't fight.

Me—I don't hang around no front steps no more. Hot nights like that, I get out my ten-speed and I be gone.

That's what I like to do more than anything else in the whole world. Feel that wind in my face keeping me cool as a air conditioner, shooting along like a snowball. My bike light as a kite. I can really get up some speed.

All the guys around my way got ten-speed bikes. Some of the girls got 'em, too, but they don't ride 'em at night. They pedal around during the day, but at nighttime they just hang around out front, watching babies and running they mouth. I didn't get my Peugeot to be no conversation piece.

My mama don't like me to ride at night. I tried to point out to her that she ain't never said nothing to my brothers, and Vincent a year younger than me. (And Langston two years older, in case "old" is the problem.) She say, "That's different, Johnnieruth. You're a girl." Now I wanna know how is anybody gonna know that. I'm skinny as a knifeblade turned sideways, and all I ever wear is blue jeans and a Wrangler jacket. But if I bring that up, she liable to get started in on how come I can't be more of a young lady, and fourteen is old enough to start taking more pride in my appearance, and she gonna be ashamed to admit I'm her daughter.

I just tell her that my bike be moving so fast can't nobody hardly see me, and couldn't catch me if they did. Mama complain to her friends how I'm wild and she can't do nothing with me. She know I'm gonna do what I want no matter what she say. But she know I ain't getting in no trouble, neither.

Like some of the boys I know stole they bikes, but I didn't do nothing like that. I'd been saving my money ever since I can remember, every time I could get a nickel or a dime outta anybody.

When I was a little kid, it was hard to get money. Seem like the only time they ever give you any was on Sunday morning, and then you had to put it in the offering. I used to hate to do that. In fact, I used to hate everything about Sunday morning. I had to wear all them ruffly dresses— that shiny slippery stuff in the wintertime that got to make a noise every time you move your ass a inch on them hard old benches. And that scratchy starchy stuff in the summertime with all them scratchy crinolines. Had to carry a pocketbook and wear them shiny shoes. And the church we went to was all the way over on Summit Avenue, so the whole damn neighborhood could get a good look. At least all the other kids'd be dressed the same way.

The boys think they slick 'cause they get to wear pants, but they still got to wear a white shirt and a tie; and them dumb hats they wear can't hide them baldheaded haircuts, 'cause they got to take the hats off in church.

There was one Sunday when I musta been around eight. I remember it was before my sister Corletta was born, 'cause right around then was when I put my foot down about that whole sanctimonious routine. Anyway, I was dragging my feet along Twenty-fifth Street in back of Mama and Vincent and them, when I spied this lady. I only seen her that one time, but I still remember just how she look. She don't look like nobody I ever seen before. I *know* she don't live around here. She real skinny. But she ain't no real young woman, neither. She could be old as my mama. She ain't nobody's mama—I'm sure. And she ain't wearing Sunday clothes. She got on blue jeans and a man's blue working shirt, with the tail hanging out. She got patches on her blue jeans, and she still got her chin stuck out like she some kinda African royalty. She ain't carrying no shiny pocketbook. It don't look like she care if she got any money or not, or who know it, if she don't. She ain't wearing no house shoes, or stockings or high heels neither.

Mama always speak to everybody, but when she pass by this lady she make like she ain't even seen her. But I get me a real good look, and the lady stare right back at me. She got a funny look on her face, almost like she think she know me from someplace. After she pass on by, I had to turn around to get another look, even though Mama say that ain't polite. And you know what? She was turning around, too, looking back at me. And she give me a great big smile.

I didn't know too much in them days, but that's when I first got to thinking about how it's got to be different ways to be, from the way people be around my way. It's got to be places where it don't matter to nobody if you all dressed up on Sunday morning or you ain't. That's how come I started saving money. So, when I got enough, I could go away to someplace like that.

Afterwhile I begun to see there wasn't no point in waiting around for handouts, and I started thinking of ways to earn my own money. I used to be running errands all the time—mailing letters for old Grandma Whittaker and picking up cigarettes and newspapers up the corner for everybody. After I got bigger, I started washing cars in the summer, and shoveling people sidewalk in the wintertime. Now I got me a newspaper route. Ain't never been no girl around here with no paper route, but I guess everybody got it figured out by now that I ain't gonna be like nobody else.

The reason I got me my Peugeot was so I could start to explore. I figured I better start looking around right now, so when I'm grown, I'll know exactly where I wanna go. So I ride around every chance I get.

Last summer I used to ride with the boys a lot. Sometimes eight or ten of us'd just go cruising around the streets together. All of a sudden my mama decide she don't want me to do that no more. She say I'm too old to be spending so much time with boys. (That's what they tell you half the time, and the other half the time they worried 'cause you ain't interested in spending more time with boys. Don't make much sense.) She want me to have some girl friends, but I never seem to fit in with none of the things the girls doing. I used to think I fit in more with the boys.

But I seen how Mama might be right, for once. I didn't like the way the boys was starting to talk about girls sometimes. Talking about what some girl be like from the neck on down, and talking all up underneath somebody clothes and all. Even though I wasn't really friends with none of the girls, I still didn't like it. So now I mostly just ride around by myself. And Mama don't like that neither—you just can't please her.

This boy that live around the corner on North Street, Kenny Henderson, started asking me one time if I don't ever be lonely, 'cause he always see me by myself. He say don't I ever think I'd like to have me somebody special to go places with and stuff. Like I'd pick him if I did! Made me wanna laugh in his face. I do be lonely, a lotta times, but I don't tell nobody. And I ain't met nobody yet that I'd really rather be with than be by myself. But I will someday. When I find that special place where everybody different, I'm gonna find somebody there I can be friends with. And it ain't gonna be no dumb boy.

I found me one place already that I like to go to a whole lot. It ain't even really that far away—by bike—but it's on the other side of the Avenue. So I don't tell Mama and them I go there, 'cause they like to think I'm right around the neighborhood someplace. But this neighborhood too dull for me. All the houses look just the same—no porches, no yards, no trees—not even no parks around here. Every block look so much like every other block it hurt your eyes to look at afterwhile. So I ride across Summit Avenue and go down that big steep hill there, and then make a sharp right at the bottom and cross the bridge over the train tracks. Then I head on out the boulevard— that's the nicest part, with all them big trees making a tunnel over the top, and lightning bugs shining in the bushes. At the end of the boulevard you get to this place call the Plaza.

It's something like a little park—the sidewalks is all bricks and they got flowers planted all over the place. The same kind my mama grow in that painted-up tire she got out front masquerading like a garden decoration— only seem like they smell sweeter here. It's a big high fountain right in the middle, and all the streetlights is the real old-fashion kind. That Plaza is about the prettiest place I ever been.

Sometimes something going on there. Like a orchestra playing music or

some man or lady singing. One time they had a show with some girls doing
some kinda foreign dances. They look like they were around my age. They
all had on these fancy costumes, with different color ribbons all down they
back. I wouldn't wear nothing like that, but it looked real pretty when
they was dancing.

I got me a special bench in one corner where I like to sit, 'cause I can
see just about everything, but wouldn't nobody know I was there. I like to
sit still and think, and I like to watch people. A lotta people be coming there
at night—to look at the shows and stuff, or just to hang out and cool off.
All different kinda people.

This one night when I was sitting over in that corner where I always be
at, there was this lady standing right near my bench. She mostly had her
back turned to me and she didn't know I was there, but I could see her real
good. She had on this shiny purple shirt and about a million silver bracelets.
I kinda liked the way she look. Sorta exotic, like she maybe come from
California or one of the islands. I mean she had class—standing there posing
with her arms folded. She walk away a little bit. Then turn around and walk
back again. Like she waiting for somebody.

Then I spotted this dude coming over. I spied him all the way 'cross the
Plaza. Looking real fine. Got on a three-piece suit. One of them little caps
sitting on a angle. Look like leather. He coming straight over to this lady
I'm watching and then she seen him, too, and she start to smile, but she
don't move till he get right up next to her. And then I'm gonna look away,
'cause I can't stand to watch nobody hugging and kissing on each other, but
all of a sudden I see it ain't no dude at all. It's another lady.

Now I can't stop looking. They smiling at each other like they ain't seen
one another in ten years. Then the one in the purple shirt look around real
quick—but she don't look just behind her—and sorta pull the other one right
back into the corner where I'm sitting at, and then they put they arms around
each other and kiss—for a whole long time. Now I really know I oughtta
turn away, but I can't. And I know they gonna see me when they finally
open they eyes. And they do.

They both kinda gasp and back up, like I'm the monster that just rose
up outta the deep. And then I guess they can see I'm only a girl, and they
look at one another—and start to laugh! Then they just turn around and
start to walk away like it wasn't nothing at all. But right before they gone,
they both look around again, and see I still ain't got my eye muscles and
my jaw muscles working right again yet. And the one lady wink at me. And
the other one say, "Catch you later."

I can't stop staring at they backs, all the way across the Plaza. And then,
all of a sudden, I feel like I got to be doing something, got to be moving.

I wheel on outta the Plaza and I'm just concentrating on getting up my speed. 'Cause I can't figure out what to think. Them two women kissing and then, when they get caught, just laughing about it. And here I'm laughing, too, for no reason at all. I'm sailing down the boulevard laughing like a lunatic, and then I'm singing at the top of my lungs. And climbing that big old hill up to Summit Avenue is just as easy as being on a escalator.

THE CHANEYSVILLE INCIDENT

David Bradley

Sometimes you can hear the wire, hear it reaching out across the miles, whining with its own weight, crying from the cold, panting at the distance, humming with the phantom sounds of someone else's conversation. You cannot always hear it—only sometimes; when the night is deep and the room is dark and the sound of the phone's ringing has come slicing through uneasy sleep; when you are lying there, shivering, with the cold plastic of the receiver pressed tight against your ear. Then, as the rasping of your breathing fades and the hammering of your heartbeat slows, you can hear the wire: whining, crying, panting, humming, moaning like a live thing.

"John?" she said. She had said it before, just after she had finished giving me the message, but then I had said nothing, had not even grunted in response, so now her voice had a little bite in it. "John, did you hear me?"

"I heard you," I said. I let it go at that, and lay there, listening to the wire.

"Well," she said finally. She wouldn't say any more than that; I knew that.

"If he's all that sick, he ought to be in the hospital."

"Then you come take him. The man is asking for *you*, John; are you coming or not?"

I listened to the wire.

"*John*." A real bite in it this time.

"Tell him I'll be there in the morning," I said.

"You can tell him yourself," she said. "I'm not going over there."

"Who's seen him, then?" I said, but she had already hung up.

But I did not hang up. Not right away. Instead I lay there, shivering, and listened to the wire.

Judith woke while I was making coffee. She had slept through the noise I had made showering and shaving and packing—she would sleep through Doomsday unless Gabriel's trumpet was accompanied by the smell of brewing coffee. She came into the kitchen rubbing sleep out of her eyes with both fists. Her robe hung open, exposing a flannel nightgown worn and ragged enough to reveal a flash of breast. She pushed a chair away from the table with a petulant thrust of hip, sat down in it, and dropped her hands, pulling her robe closed with one, reaching for the mug of coffee I had poured for her with the other. She gulped the coffee, straight and hot. I sat down across from her, creamed my own coffee, sipped it. I had made it strong, to keep me awake. I hated the taste of it.

"Phone," Judith said. That's how she talks when she is not quite awake: one-word sentences, and God help you if you can't figure out what she means.

"The telephone is popularly believed to have been invented by Alexander Graham Bell, a Scotsman who had emigrated to Canada. Actually there is some doubt about the priority of invention—several people were experimenting with similar devices. Bell first managed to transmit an identifiable sound, the twanging of a clock spring, sometime during 1876, and first transmitted a complete sentence on March 10, 1876. He registered patents in 1876 and 1877."

Judith took another gulp of her coffee and looked at me, squinting slightly.

"The development of the telephone system in both the United States and Great Britain was delayed because of the number of competing companies which set up systems that were both limited and incompatible. This situation was resolved in England by the gradual nationalization of the system, and in America by the licensing of a monopoly, which operates under close government scrutiny. This indicates a difference in patterns of economic thought in the two countries, which still obtains."

She just looked at me.

"The development of the telephone system was greatly speeded by the invention of the electromechanical selector switch, by Almon B. Strowger, a Kansas City undertaker, in 1899."

"John," she said.

"I didn't mean to wake you up."

"If you didn't want to wake me up you would have made instant."

I sighed. "Jack's sick. Should be in the hospital, won't go. Wants me." I realized suddenly I was talking like Judith when she is not quite awake.

"Jack?" she said. "The old man with the stories?"

"The old man with the stories."

"So he's really there."

I looked at her. "Of course he's there. Where did you think he was—in Florida for the winter?"

"I thought he was somebody you made up."

"I don't make things up," I said.

"Relax, John," she said. "It's just that the way you talked about him, he was sort of a legend. I would have thought he was indestructible. Or a lie."

"Yeah," I said, "that's him: an old, indestructible lie. Who won't go to the hospital." I started to take another sip of my coffee, but I remembered the rest room on the bus and thought better of it.

"John?" she said.

"What?"

"Do you have to go?"

"He asked for me," I said.

She looked at me steadily and didn't say a word.

"Yes," I said. "I have to go."

I got up then and went into the living room and opened up the cabinet where we keep the liquor. There wasn't much in there: a bottle of Dry Sack and a bottle of brandy that Judith insisted we keep for company even though Judith didn't drink and we never entertained. Once there would have been a solid supply of bourbon, 101-proof Wild Turkey, but the stockpile was down to a single bottle that had been there so long it was dusty. I took the bottle out and wiped the dust away.

I heard her moving, leaving the kitchen and coming up behind me. She didn't say anything.

I reached into the back of the cabinet and felt around until I found the flask, a lovely thing of antique pewter, a gift to me from myself. It was dusty, too.

"Do you want to talk about it?" she said.

"What's there to talk about?" I said. I filled the flask.

"Well," she said, "I just thought there might be something on your mind."

"What would make you think that?" I said.

"You want me to be a bitch," she said. "You want me to say something about starting to drink again. . . ."

"I never stopped," I said.

"Not officially. But you haven't been doing as much of it. And you want me to say something nasty about you starting again. But I won't."

"I thought you just did," I said.

She didn't say anything.

"It gets cold out there in those mountains," I said. I turned around and looked at her. "You don't understand how cold it gets."

She opened her mouth to say something, then thought better of it. I put the flask in my hip pocket.

"We could talk about it," she said. "About whatever it is that's bothering you."

"There's nothing bothering me," I said, "except being up at midnight with no bed in sight." I looked at my watch. "And it's time to go, anyway." I turned away from her and went to the closet to get my coat. She followed me.

"Someday," she said, "you're going to talk to me. And when you do I'm going to listen to you. I'm going to listen to you so goddamn hard it's going to hurt."

I didn't say anything; I just got out my heavy coat and made sure I had my fleece-lined gloves and a woolen scarf and a knitted wool watch cap stuffed into the pockets.

"John?" she said.

"Yeah?"

"Would you like me to come with you?"

"What about the hospital?" I said.

"I'll get somebody to cover for me. God knows there are enough people who owe me. I'll come tomorrow after—"

"No," I said.

She didn't say anything.

I turned around and looked at her. "You don't understand," I said. "It's not just like visiting friends. . . . I can't explain."

"Forget it," she said.

"Look," I said. "If you want to help, just call the department for me. Tell them . . . tell them it's a family illness. They can get anybody to do the Colonial History lecture—it's not until Wednesday. The Civil War seminar can take care of itself."

"All right," she said. "How long . . . I guess you don't know." Suddenly there was a lot of concern in her voice, which told me I must be looking and acting pretty bad. Judith is a psychiatrist; she's seen a lot of troubled people, and she never wastes undue concern on cases that aren't critical.

I smiled at her. It was a good smile, full of teeth; it would have fooled most people. "Now, dear," I said, "I'm just takin' a little run up the country, seein' a sick friend. Now, as every student of marital infidelity knows, a sick friend is just a tired euphemism for a willing wench. Seeing as we're not what you call legally espoused, it isn't precisely adultery, but—"

Judith said something highly unprintable and spun me around and wrapped her arms around me. I felt the shape of her body fitting the shape of mine like a template. Her hand moved over my clothes, finding the space between my shirt buttons and sliding through until it found the place at the base of my belly that somehow never seemed to get enough warmth. I let her hand rest there for a moment, and then I stepped away from her and turned and held her as tightly as I could, my nose buried in her hair, my hands feeling out the shape of her back. Then my hands stopped moving and we just stood there, very still, so still that I could feel her heart beating, slowly, rhythmically, steadily. And then I felt my own heartbeat steady. I pulled my face from her hair and kissed her. She stepped back and, with her head down, fastened the zipper of my coat.

"Stay warm," she said.

The key to the understanding of any society lies in the observation and analysis of the insignificant and the mundane. For one of the primary functions of societal institutions is to conceal the basic nature of the society, so that the individuals that make up the power structure can pursue the business of consolidating and increasing their power untroubled by the minor carpings of a dissatisfied peasantry. Societal institutions act as fig leaves for each other's nakedness—the Church justifies the actions of the State, the State the teachings of the School, the School the principles of the Economy, the Economy the pronouncements of the Church. Truly efficient societies conceal the true nature of the operations, motivations, and goals of all but the most minor institutions, some even managing to control the appearances of the local parish, courthouse, board of education, and chamber of commerce. But even the most efficient society loses control at some point; no society, for example, is so efficient that it can disguise the nature of its sanitary facilities. And so, when seeking to understand the culture or the history of a people, do not look at the precepts of the religion, the form of the government, the curricula of the schools, or the operations of businesses; flush the johns.

America is a classed society, regardless of the naïve beliefs of deluded egalitarians, the frenzied efforts of misguided liberals, the grand pronouncements of brain-damaged politicians. If you doubt it, consider the sanitary

facilities employed in America's three modes of public long-distance transportation: airplanes, trains, and buses.

America's airports are built of plastic and aluminum. They gleam in the
sun at noon, glow at night with fluorescent illumination. They are reached
most conveniently by private autos, taxicabs, and "limousines." In the airport
there are many facilities for the convenience of the traveler; for example,
there are usually several bars which serve good bourbon. The planes themselves are well maintained and are staffed by highly paid professional people—
pilots ("captains") chosen for their experience and reliability, hostesses chosen
for their pleasantness and attractiveness. There are usually two classes of
accommodation; in one both food and liquor are free, in the other the food
is complimentary and alcohol can be obtained at a reasonable cost. The
companies that operate airplanes are known by names that reek of cosmo-
politan concerns: American, National, United, Trans World, Pan American.
The average domestic fare is on the close order of two hundred dollars, and
the preferred mode of payment is via "prestige" credit card—American Express, Diners Club, in a pinch Carte Blanche. The sanitary accommodations,
both in the airport and on board the plane, are almost invariably clean.
Soap, towels, and toilet paper are freely available; on board the plane, the
complimentary offerings often extend to aftershave lotion and feminine protection. Most significantly, the faucets turn. The sinks drain. The johns
flush. And if they do not, they are speedily repaired.

America's train stations are built of granite and brick, smoked and cor-
roded from the pollution in city air. Their dim, cavernous hallways sigh of
bygone splendor. They straddle that ancient boundary of social class—the
legendary "tracks." They are reached with equal convenience by private auto
and public transport. There is rarely more than the minimum number of
facilities for the traveler; rarely, for example, more than one bar, and that
one oriented toward the commuter trade—the bar bourbon is of the cheaper
sort. The trains are frequently ill-maintained. The operator ("engineer")
wears a flannel or work shirt, in contrast to the airline pilot's quasi-military
uniform, and the attendants, who take tickets rather than provide service,
are most often elderly gentlemen; the overall aesthetic effect is somewhat
less pleasing than that presented by an airline hostess. There is class-
differentiated accommodation, but the actual difference is somewhat ques-
tionable; meals and liquor, when available at all, must be purchased in both
classes. There is now only one passenger train company, really a gray government agency with a name dreamed up by some bureaucrat's child, too
young or too stupid to know the proper spelling of the word "track." Before
the government took over the passenger trains, the names of the companies
sang of regionalism; instead of a United or a National there was a New York

Central and a Pennsylvania, and in lieu of a Trans World or a Pan American there was a Southern and a Baltimore & Ohio. The average railroad fare is on the close order of sixty dollars, and payment is often made in cash. When credit cards are used they are often bank cards (which allow time payments) as opposed to prestige cards (which do not). The sanitary accommodations associated with rail travel are somewhat less civilized than those associated with travel by air. In the station there is usually only one central rest room for each sex, that one poorly attended. The items freely provided for use are the bare essentials in theory and often less than that in fact—the wise traveler checks for towels before he wets his hands. Perhaps 50 percent of the johns are operable at any one time; the others are clogged with excrement and cigarette butts. Repairs are delayed more often than expedited. Recent environmental concerns have favorably altered the conditions in the on-board sanitary accommodations; the newer trains have flush toilets modeled after those on planes. Still, until quite recently—within the last decade, in fact—the accepted mode of getting rid of human waste was to eject it through a pipe at the bottom of the car, where it fell to the ground and lay exposed until natural decomposition could eliminate it.

America's bus stations tend to lurk in the section of town in which pornographic materials are most easily obtained. Like airports, they are built of plastic, but it is plastic of a decidedly flimsier sort. They are reached most easily by public transportation or "gypsy" cab; except in largest cities and smallest towns, ordinary taxis shun them. The facilities for traveler convenience are virtually nonexistent; in lieu of a bar there is a lunch counter, which (if one can attract the wandering attention of the attendant, who is usually of the gender of an airline hostess and the appearance of a train conductor) will offer up a buffet of *hot dog au grease* and sugar-water on the rocks. The buses are at times in good repair, at times not, but always uncomfortable. The drivers look like retired sparring partners of heavyweights who never have been and never will be ranked contenders. There is a single class of accommodation—fourth. *Nothing* is served on board; a sign in the on-board rest room cautions against drinking the water. The names of the bus companies sing of locality (White River, Hudson Valley), private ownership (Martz, Bollman), and dogs. The average fare is on the close order of twenty-five dollars; the maximum one-way fare to the most distant portion of the United States is only eighty dollars. The preferred mode of payment is cash; if, as with the larger bus lines, credit cards are acceptable, they are bank cards, never prestige cards. The sanitary accommodations are much in keeping with the rest of the scene. Inside the station, the rest rooms are of a most doubtful nature; usually they are wholly or partially closed for repairs that are so long delayed and so temporary in effect that they seem mythical.

The on-board accommodation is hardly better. The john, which is not even supposed to flush, is merely a seat atop a square metal holding tank; below it the curious—or perhaps "sick" is a better adjective—traveler may observe the wastes of previous users swimming blissfully about like so many tropical fish.

The various degrees of civilization represented by the sanitary accommodations inevitably reflect class status that the society at large assigns to the passengers. It is no accident, then, that airline patrons are usually employed, well-dressed, and white, while train passengers (except the commuter) are more likely to have lower incomes, cheaper clothing, and darker skin. A randomly selected bus passenger, at least in common belief and easily observable fact, is, far more than the patrons of planes or trains, likely to be: un-, partially, or marginally employed; un-, partially, or cheaply dressed; in- or partially solvent; in- or partially sane; non- or partially white.

The Greyhound bus station that serves Philadelphia sits in the center of town, a prematurely deteriorating, fortunately subterranean structure that cannot escape its surroundings—the skin flicks down the street, the bowling alley on one side, the Burger King on the other. I emerged from the subway a block and a half from the station, ran the gauntlet of improbable offers from gypsy cab drivers, winos, and whores, entered the station, and stood in line to buy a ticket to a town that existed as only a dot—if that—on most maps, a town noted for its wealth of motel rooms.

Now the county seat and watermark of westward expansion is a town served by only two local buses a day. If you're in too much of a hurry to wait for one, you can buy a ticket and take your chances on begging or bribing the driver of an express bus to make a brief unscheduled stop on the 'pike, and walk four miles from there. I was in a hurry. I took my chances. The ticket cost eighteen bucks and change.

Three and a half hours later my bus was boring up a moonlit slab of highway, the snarl of the exhaust bouncing off the walls of rock that towered on either side of the road. Except for the bus, the Turnpike was empty; four barren lanes, the concrete white like adhesive tape applied to the wounds the machines had slashed into the mountains. The bus moved swiftly, slamming on the downgrades, swaying on the turns. The driver was good and he knew the road; we were ahead of schedule, and long ago we had reached the point where the hills were familiar to me, even with just the moonlight to see by. Not that I needed to see them; I, too, knew the road, could pinpoint my location by the sways and the bumps. I knew that in a minute the driver would downshift and we would crawl up a long hill, and the road would be straight as an arrow from bottom to top, then twist away suddenly to the right. I knew that at the crest, just before the twist, there would be a massive gray boulder with names and dates scrawled on it, a cheap monument to the local consciousness: DAVID LOVES ANNIE; CLASS OF '61; MARGO AND DANNY; BEAT THE BISONS; DEEP IN YOUR HEART YOU KNOW HE'S RIGHT; SCALP THE WARRIORS; NIXON THIS TIME. After that the road would twist and turn and rise and fall like a wounded snake for eighteen miles, and then I would be there, or as close as this bus would take me.

And so I settled myself in my seat and took another pull on my flask and looked out the window at the mountainsides black with pine, and thought about how strange home is: a place to which you belong and which belongs to you even if you do not particularly like it or want it, a place you cannot escape, no matter how far you go or how furiously you run; about how strange it feels to be going back to that place and, even if you do not like it, even if you hate it, to get a tiny flush of excitement when you reach the point where you can look out the window and know, without thinking, where you are; when the bends in the road have meaning, and every hill a name.

A truck swung around the turn ahead of us, its running lights dancing briefly in the darkness, the sound of its diesel penetrating the bus, audible over the rumble of the bus engine, and I thought of the nights when I would lie in bed, listening to the trucks on the 'pike grinding on the grades, bellowing like disgruntled beasts, and promise myself that someday I would go where they were going: away. Bill had done that, too, had lain and listened to the trucks. He had told me—but not until years later—how he had lain there, night after night, chanting softly the names of far-off cities to the eerie accompaniment of the whine of truck tires. I had done the same, in my own way: I would start with the next town to the east or the west along the 'pike and move on, saying the names of the exits one by one, as if I were moving by them. Once I even reached New Jersey before I fell asleep. And I remembered thinking, when Bill told me of his game and I told him of mine, that his was so much better; that he had visited and revisited Paris, Hong Kong, Tokyo, Peking, while I was struggling to get out of the state. Later, I had wondered if it would be that way all our lives, he flying from place to place while I crawled, making local stops. I had watched with some curiosity to see if it would work out that way, and to some extent it had; he flew to Vietnam and never came back, and while I had taken a few leaps, I had ended up in Philadelphia. And now I was coming back, passing little towns, knowing their improbable names—Bloserville, Heberlig, Dry Run, Burnt Cabins, Wells Tannery, Defiance, Claylick, Plum Run, Buffalo Mills, Dott. The bus was an express, nonstop between Philly and Pittsburgh, but I was making local stops.

The truck vanished behind us, leaving an afterimage on my eyes, and the bus rolled down into a valley and across a bridge. The stream below it was called Brush Creek, and this time of year it would be low. The logs would stick out from the banks and gouge gurgling hollows in the sluggish water. Half a mile upstream, near the hulk of a dead hickory, was the place where, surprising no one so much as myself, I had caught my first catfish. Old Jack had helped me bait the hook, had shown me how to get the fish off it. And then he had taken his knife and shown me how to scale the fish and gut it, and we had built a fire and fried the fish in bacon grease in a black iron skillet he had packed along. It was a lot of trouble to go to and it could not have been much of a meal for him—it wasn't much of a fish— but he said there was something special about a boy's first catfish, no matter how small it was.

Then the bus was moving along the southern slope of a mountain—raw on one side, empty space on the other. I was almost there. I emptied the flask, capped it, put it in my pocket. I pulled my pack toward me, tightened the laces, checked the knots. Then I stood up and made my way toward the front. Five minutes later I stood by the side of the road, shivering in the sharp, clear mountain cold, and watched as the bus roared away into the darkness. And then I began to walk.

I WAS HERE BUT I
DISAPPEARED

Wesley Brown

1 Sometimes you can know too much about a person. Sometimes you don't know nearly enough. And sometimes it doesn't matter what you know. Faye always made sure I knew more than enough about her! We met at the apartment of a mutual friend who lived in Esplanade Gardens, overlooking the Harlem River. When I walked her home to another part of the same complex, I asked for her phone number. She leaned back against the glass door of her building, studying me in the light of my request. A muscle in her face pulled at the corner of her mouth, showing a playful mixture of irritation and delight.

"Tyrone, if you ask for *my* number, I assume you intend to dial it, not just juggle it around with a lot of others. So, if you want to see me again, don't wait too long to call. I also have a nine-year-old son named Cecil." The disturbance around her mouth gave way to a smile.

Faye was no less blunt the first time we made love. Crossing that chasm

of intimacy with a woman for the first time has always made me queasy. It's
not so much that I fear rejection but that I want to know what will be the
outcome of a strong physical attraction. Not wanting to be caught gagging
on my own chauvinist pork, I overreact. It's as if being aroused by a woman's
physical presence were something shameful. But as a blues singer once said,
"It may be a scandal, but it ain't no shame!" During those first times with
a woman when desire is consummated, I always hear both need and the fear
of needing speaking through my pleasure.

Faye and I were in a wild fit of earnest and awkward attempts at pleasing
one another with our mouths and hands when she pulled away, took my
hand, and led me from the sofa to her bedroom. She asked if I had any
condoms while we shed what was left of our clothes. I said no. She stopped
undressing and left the room. When she returned we hissed and cursed our
way free of restraint. As I gave in to her guidance, I reminded her that I had
no protection. She said she'd heard me the first time, which was why she
had left the room to put in her diaphragm.

"Don't fall asleep, Tyrone," she said later. "You have to leave before
Cecil wakes up. He wouldn't understand finding you in bed with me." Faye
also informed me that I'd have to share responsibility for the possible consequences of our pleasure. She said she was aware that prophylactics had
historically been bad-rapped, but felt we should see about that for ourselves.
She was right, of course. I hadn't acted responsibly. But there was something
about her righteousness in pointing it out that bothered me.

We began to see more of each other and got along quite well. I'm not
exactly sure why that was. The night I met Faye I was immediately attracted
by her disposition. When she moved, I marveled at the lack of pretension
in her body. The other thing that might have made us compatible was the
intimacy of our silences. Often on nights when Cecil had finally collapsed,
exhausted after using every ploy to hold Faye's attention, she would put him
to bed and for the rest of the evening we would not exchange one word. I
could understand Faye's wanting to savor the only hours during the day that
belonged to her. She would usually read and I would work on my fifth-grade
lesson plans. She never assured me that her silence was not a reflection on
me, and I never needed to be reassured.

One Saturday night Faye and I were supposed to go to a party. I went
by to pick her up and Cecil answered the door. He and I had felt each other
out during those first months. It was clear that at first he saw me as an
interloper, then later as a tolerable presence. His suspicions had unnerved
me. I didn't force myself on him except once when I showed too enthusiastic
an interest in how he was doing in school. He answered with more than a
little hostility: "I thought you were here to see my mother!" He had every

right to be angry at my familiarity, since I saw him then as an obstruction and was trying to bribe him with attention. So I was surprised that evening when he began talking to me.

"What you and my mother gonna do tonight?"

"We're going to a party."

"What you gonna do there?"

"Eat, dance, and talk."

"Is that how you play when you a grown-up?"

"In a way."

"Are you playin' when you and my mother in the bedroom with the door closed?"

"I guess you could say that sometimes we're playing."

"What do you do?"

"Well, we show each other how much we care about each other."

"What do you mean by 'show'?"

"Hugging. Kissing. Like that."

"How come you just can't tell how you care insteada showin'?"

"Because people believe you care more when you show them than if you just tell them."

"You never tell or show me how much you care about me."

"I didn't know you cared how I felt about you."

"I was just wonderin', that's all."

"I like you a lot, Cecil."

"When you gonna show me?"

"What do you like to do?"

"Go to the zoo and baseball games. Stuff like that."

"You sure you're not just saying that because you don't like me going out with your mother so much?"

"No, I just wanna have some fun, too."

"Don't you have fun with your friends?"

"Yeah, but I ain't had none with you yet."

Faye came into the front room. From her expression, she had obviously overheard our conversation. She told him she wanted to talk to me alone and that he could go and watch television until the sitter came.

"What are you grinning about?" I asked.

"You two do all right together."

"So I noticed."

"Well, let me be the first to tell you, in case you hadn't noticed, that you and I aren't doing as well."

"What's wrong?"

"The fact that you never seem to know is part of the problem."

"Faye, are you going to make a suspense thriller out of this or are you going to tell me what it's about?"

"I like the way you turn things around like I'm the one who's been inconsiderate."

"I'd be glad to show more consideration if you'd first consider *telling* me!"

"Tyrone, our seeing each other doesn't mean you have to do anything for Cecil and me. I've never put that on you. But if you're involved in my life, you should be sensitive to my situation. Whenever we go out I have to pay a sitter to stay with Cecil, and we go out a lot. It doesn't seem to have occurred to you to *offer* to pay the sitter."

She was right, as she so often was about me. But what bothered me about Faye's keen ability to flush out my oversights was her equal interest in making me feel guilty. As the body needs impurities to build up a tolerance for what is harmful, Faye needed my flaws to protect her from my more endearing qualities.

I didn't mind being needed in spite of my faults, but not because of them! I resented the accuracy of Faye's criticisms and their frequency. Instead of sticking up for myself, I began to cooperate with her search-and-seizure missions into my baser impulses. I started acting unnatural—deliberately not doing things I'd promised. Faye was shocked by my strange behavior and told me it was unworthy of me. As a result, her incisive critiques of me turned into pettiness, which annoyed me even more.

With the school year ending, I was planning to visit a friend who was living in San Francisco. I mentioned it casually to Faye during a telephone conversation, and I immediately detected a pronounced change in her voice.

"I see," she said. I knew from her tone that she was upset because I hadn't suggested that she go with me. I was somewhat relieved that I'd finally hurt her in a way that wasn't forced. However, there was something gone in her voice that was always there when she took me to task. Her tone spread over both words equally, and for the first time she sounded resigned to what she disapproved of in me.

"You think you might want to come?"

"My situation's not the same as yours. In case you hadn't noticed, there are things I have to consider before I go somewhere, other than whether I want to go or not!"

"Well, maybe we could—" But my sentence was severed by Faye's slamming down the receiver. I called her right back, but she didn't answer the phone. I tried calling her at work the next day, but again she wouldn't talk to me. That night I went by her apartment, but she refused to buzz me in. In the past Faye had been willing to call me on my ways, probably because she understood my intentions sometimes better than I did. But now her pettiness, which I had helped along by deliberately untidying myself, had exhausted her to the point where she could not or would not see me beyond one callous act.

Seeing so clearly what had happened to us and being helpless to do anything about it became unbearable. One day after school I went to midtown Manhattan and stationed myself outside the building where Faye worked. A little after five she came through a set of revolving doors and walked in the opposite direction from where I stood. I caught up with her and spoke as if I were trying to wake her from sleep.

"Faye, I want to talk with you."

"You ought to try listening. If you did, you'd know I don't want to see you!"

"But that's what I don't understand, Faye. Why don't you want to *see me*? I mean *really see me* the way you used to?"

"Because I'm tired of being your eyes. There are some things you should've never let me make you aware of."

"I know," I said in a voice free of everything except my acceptance of what she'd said. My unadorned admission brought sympathy to Faye's face, but only for an instant.

"I have to go," she said, turning away from me and moving into the crowd. I didn't bother going after her.

 I felt I owed myself the trip to California, since it was indirectly responsible for my breakup with Faye. What better way to remind me of my sins of omission than to take the trip by myself?

I hadn't seen Rudy in almost five years. He had left New York for the same reason many people I knew had: overstimulation. We'd been involved in a community action project after graduation from college in 1967. Rudy had been hurt into leaving New York by truly believing change was possible, beginning with himself. He was much more sensitive than I to the righteousness of many people we worked with, people who needed to be right more than they needed the world to be different. Rudy, who admitted to not always being sure, paid dearly for not closing his mind down to change.

I had never been to California before but had heard enough to give me something to think about on the flight. People had told me it wasn't just the three-hour time lag that distinguished New York from California; it was the different way time was perceived. In New York time was something outside of you. You kept up with it so you wouldn't lose track of yourself like someone without a *TV Guide*. In California time was just there, a permanent fixture in the landscape like the San Andreas Fault, the Golden Gate Bridge, and Johnny Carson.

After the landing I walked through the gigantic nozzle connecting the plane to the terminal, anticipation making me feel that my nerves would burst through me like the springs of a broken-down mattress. None of Rudy's letters had mentioned that Alex, the woman he lived with, was white, which surprised me when I heard it through a mutual friend. It was so uncharacteristic of Rudy—he was never one to avoid the confrontation between his choices and the social cost.

I saw them before they saw me. Rudy looked thinner than I remembered; his forehead reached farther back into his scalp to hair grayed, no doubt, by the concerns that had driven him to California in the first place. Typically his reaction to the commotion around him made it impossible for him to see me. The woman with Rudy, who I assumed was Alex, must have seen me smiling at them. She motioned for him to look in my direction.

"AwwRrriiight! Rriight! Shit! Damn, Tyrone! This is somethin'!"

"I see you're just as articulate as always."

"Shit, yeah! You got that right!"

We embraced but it was awkward as most reunions initially are. "Hey, man, this is Alex."

"Hi. It's good to finally meet you," she said, enclosing my hand in both of hers. She was very long in the body—not so much tall as stretched out, fully extended, like a dancer.

Rudy and Alex rented the bottom floor of a two-family house. I walked into a world made up of references from any number of experiences: posters, wine bottles, driftwood, books and records, a huge cable spool that served as a table. However, no room in the house showed a clear prejudice toward any particular experience of Rudy's that I was familiar with. Sure, living with someone can blur some of the manifestations of who they are as individuals. But I couldn't point to any area of the house that had Rudy's singular character. I wondered if anything remained of the person I had known.

"Well, tell me what you've been doing," I said, when we settled in the front room for coffee.

"Jobwise, I've been working at this health food restaurant in Berkeley. Other than that, Alex and I have been looking for a community that we can be a part of and not be hassled."

"Is there any such place?"

"It's right up here," he said, tapping a finger against his temple. "It's taken me almost three years to get to the point where I am now, mentally."

"Where's that?"

"Being able to make something the way I want it, just by thinking it."

"I'm not sure I understand what you mean."

"It's like when I stopped eating meat. After a while my body didn't crave it anymore. The same thing happened with all the inner turmoil I brought with me from New York. When I stopped putting all that energy into thinking about racial conflict or the sorry state of the world in general, none of it bothered me anymore."

"Just because you've developed a healthy tolerance for things you can't change right now doesn't mean the world is any different. It's just your attitude that has changed."

"But if my attitude toward things has changed beginning with what I put in my body, then it follows that diet is a way toward political change."

"But I don't see how diet can change attitudes that are so ingrained most people aren't even aware of them. Isn't that what you always used to say— consciousness has to change before real change can take place?"

"You're right. I used to believe that. But I've come to the conclusion that instead of consciousness changing, much of it needs to be eliminated!"

"I'm not sure I follow you."

"I mean it's impossible to change most of the things that go into shaping us. There's too much reinforcing it. So Alex and I, and a lot of other people we know, have found a way of short-circuiting the flawed parts of ourselves that we have no hope of changing."

"How?"

"By breaking with the parts of our past that produced our defects."

"Am I part of that past?"

"That depends on whether you brought any of it with you." His tone, though not accusatory, was blunt. It implied that I was the best judge of where our shared past put me in relation to his present. His expression reminded me of Faye's just a few days before, when I told her how much it had cost us to get where we were. While I was willing to pay the cost for knowing them in a particular way, Rudy's look, like Faye's, told me he wanted no part of it.

I turned toward Alex in time to see her react like someone witnessing a minor accident that suddenly turned into something disastrous.

"Are you getting hungry?" Rudy asked.

"That's why I came out here."

"Well, if we're going to make sure you're well fed, we'd better start with the body."

We went out to eat over in Berkeley at the health food restaurant where

Rudy worked. Once we were in public, I noticed how Rudy began speaking in the exclamatory, monosyllabic way he had at the airport.

The next morning Rudy and I got up around six to run. We ran through Golden Gate Park to the ocean. When we reached the Pacific, it inspired more awe in me than I have ever felt in the presence of the Atlantic. It reminded me that most people who came or were brought to America moved from east to west. By the time they got to the West Coast they had probably taken in much of the psychology of the nation. Perhaps the West Coast represents not only the farthest migration but also all the extremes of the American psyche that have been dragged across the country. Maybe that's why the Pacific rears up so menacingly as its tides taste land. It has had well over a century to witness what the expansion to its shores has wrought.

We ran for about another mile before stopping and then began walking back. "See that?" Rudy asked, pointing at something written on the concrete wall that protected the shore from high tides. Lettering three or four feet high said I WAS HERE BUT I DISAPPEARED.

"I wrote that," he said.

"When?" I asked.

"About a year after I came out here. There was this dude I'd gotten friendly with who was a painter. He'd gotten this commission to do a painting of Christ's crucifixion and asked if I'd pose for it. I was glad to do it. The money came in handy, since I wasn't working. When I looked at the painting I was shocked because it wasn't me. I mean, it was my body, minus the color. And the face looked more like Max Von Sydow's.

"When I pointed this out to him, he told me he hadn't wanted to inject race into the painting. He had done precisely that by using me as a model and then leaving out a physical trait that was intrinsic to being me! I was outraged. He told me I was overreacting. I said I didn't want to impose on him my notion of what Christ looked like, but if he knew what he wanted he should have gotten someone who resembled it more. He said that was too limiting. As an artist it was his task to take what was and make it into something else. That was fine with me, but as a human being I resented him taking what I was and making me disappear."

We kept walking and Rudy continued speaking, not seeming to need or expect any comment from me. "This painter said distinctions between people on the basis of race were a medieval notion and that people's consciousness was moving toward a more amoebalike phase where everything would be everything. I said, you mean white. He said no, what he was getting at was that the things plaguing humanity had to be combatted by reducing their importance. He felt that Lenny Bruce had been right about taking the power out of words like *nigger* by using them as if they meant nothing.

"I asked him how you take the power out of someone's behavior. He said, 'By acting as if the things that can most readily be used against people no longer exist.' I wasn't convinced. Since he had seen fit to eliminate my blackness, what was he doing about his whiteness? How was he making sure the advantages it gave him would also disappear? He said that for the past few years he'd stayed out of situations that traded on privileges that harmed others. But we're not in the world by ourselves, I said. What about all those people who don't have your understanding and don't want to see anything disappear? 'There's not much we can do about that,' he said. 'But by not reacting to how others see us, we take away their power over us.' "

Without even a glance at me, Rudy went on. "He left me with a lot to think about. I had spent most of my life being affected by almost every twitch coming from another person, and what had it gotten me except colitis and an intuitive grasp of injustice?

"And then one day, while I was walking through the Fillmore district, I saw YOU ARE WHAT YOU EAT scrawled on the wall of a handball court. On impulse I went to the library and took out a number of books on men who were megalomaniacs. The biographies ran the gamut from Taras Bulba to Richard Nixon. Without exception there was a correlation between being power hungry and eating meat.

"So I decided to carry out an experiment, keeping meat and all unnaturally grown food out of my body, and found I stopped desiring what I used to crave. When that happened I was convinced that I could keep out of my system everything I didn't need. It didn't matter that these things were present in others. The important thing was: I could eliminate them from me!"

I didn't once interrupt Rudy or take issue with any of what he said. He seemed unaware of my presence anyway, in a near-rapturous state.

Rudy left for work soon after we returned to the house. Alex didn't have to be at work until later in the afternoon. As we sat alone in the front room drinking Mexican coffee, I held up the mug and felt the heat seep under my eyelids. Alex put on a Crosby, Stills and Nash album; the spiraling harmony of their voices mixed with the strong aroma of the coffee and gave me a nice buzz.

An uneasiness between us made me wonder if we were feeling the usual tensions between a man and a woman alone together. Add to that my being black, and her being white and the lover of a close friend who was black, and you had a situation tasty with psychosexual import.

I tried dislodging some of my own tension by looking at her very carefully and realized I wasn't particularly attracted to her.

"Does Rudy have many black male friends?" I asked.

"Why do you ask?"

"I get the feeling you aren't all that comfortable around me."

"We just met and I don't know you. It's got nothing to do with your being black."

"You ever wonder how it can be that in a country so preoccupied with race, people can say race has nothing to do with anything?"

"All right. I am kind of nervous around you. There've been times when black guys who know Rudy have tried to hit on me when he's not around. I was hoping I wouldn't have to go through that with you."

"You ever make it with any of them?" I asked with intentional cruelty.

"It never fails! Most of the black men I've met through Rudy have tried to get over with me or wanted to know if I'd ever made it with any of his other friends. I had hoped you would disappoint me on both counts."

"I'm sorry. I didn't mean to say that."

"Oh, yes, you did! You strike me as the kind of person who *means exactly* what you say! So, yes, I did make it with one of Rudy's friends once. He knows all about it. I've also straightened out my own head. Living with a black man and being attracted to other black men doesn't make me some crazy nymph after black flesh! If you're one of those black men who need a white woman's desire or fear to boost your ego, I'm not the one to flatter you that way!"

As Alex's anger and the last few bars of the music played out, I concluded that she was much more attractive than I originally thought. "How did you meet Rudy?" I asked. Her face knitted a fabric of recollection, then she burst into raucous laughter. "What's so funny?"

"Have you ever heard of Lombard Street?"

"No."

"Well, it's a street that's like the first drop on the Cyclone at Coney Island. Only twice as long. It's an absolute, geometric horror to see these houses built on a surface that steep. It's like being in a landslide that's on hold. That's where I met Rudy. He was sitting on the curb and I was walking by. He made a remark about Lombard Street resembling the condition of his life and wondered how the people living there managed to keep their equilibrium. There was something about the way he talked, not that it was peculiar or anything. Just different in a way that impressed me, though he wasn't trying to."

"Are you from California?"

"No. I'm from a place called Mexico, New York."

"How long have you been out here?"

"About five years."

"Has your life led you to the same conclusions as Rudy?"

"Pretty much."

"How much is that?"

"As much as it takes to know when someone really wants to know something about me and when they're trying to put me down!"

"You sound battle tested."

"I am, and by people a lot better at it than you. I'm sorry, Tyrone, if
Rudy and I are a disappointment to you, but we had no way of knowing
what you'd want of us when you got here."

"You're right. I just broke up with a woman. What I've needed most
since it happened was to feel that my ties with people I care about are still
there. So I come out here and Rudy's talking about dispensing with his
awareness of things we've both experienced."

"You can understand why, can't you?"

"Of course I understand, but that doesn't help."

"Coming from New York City, you probably don't know what it's like
to grow up in a place without any anonymity—where everything is known
about everybody, or at least people talk as though it were. Your most private
thoughts become the topic of public discussion. After that, I wanted to be
someplace where I wouldn't know almost everyone."

"So you think what you don't know can't hurt you?"

"Something like that."

"I find that strange, given whom you're living with."

"You mean about Rudy being black?"

"Oh, so you've noticed!"

"Rudy has never dealt very well with the hostility we get in public. You
probably noticed the difference in the way he talks when we go out."

"That's right! Like at the airport! He was barely coherent. I thought it
was because we hadn't seen each other in so long."

"It's real, what Rudy said about needing to eliminate certain things from
his consciousness. Unlike you or me, he's never developed a thick enough
skin. The verbal attacks we get from blacks, especially black women, are
why he doesn't talk very well in public."

"How do you take the abuse?"

"That's just it. I take it *all* because he can't. I try to ignore it. I've never
baited black women, but it usually doesn't matter. Once when we were
walking home from the movies, a group of black women passed us. One of
them went into a tirade against Rudy, saying that his sin of commission was
me, which made him guilty of the ultimate sin of omission—*them*. She was
quite vicious, but in a perverse way I was impressed by how articulate and
controlled her venom was. When she finished, she waited, like she was
expecting us to say something. I had no intention of saying anything, but
Rudy tried. Well, you know what happened? He started stammering and
couldn't put more than three words together at a time. If you could have
seen the expression on that woman's face. After the shock wore off, they

began laughing. The one who started it all was yelling after us that she could see why Rudy and I were together—since he wasn't well-spoken, it was clear that he must be well hung."

"How do you remove an experience like that from your consciousness?" I asked.

"Well, we've become part of a group that's been able to minimize it to a great extent."

I discovered that "minimize" was indeed the crucial word. One evening soon after my talk with Alex, she and Rudy took me to a place called The Center for Minimalist Living. The building was furnished sparsely with folding tables and chairs. The walls were bare except for framed signs, which read CARES AND WORRIES ARE EXPENDABLE and MINIMALISM IS THE ABSENCE OF WHAT YOU NEVER THOUGHT YOU COULD LIVE WITHOUT.

We sat down to what was called a "minimalist meal." Whatever it was tasted like a kind of ghost food, giving me the aura of a meal but not the experience. After we'd eaten, a man got up at the other end of the table and said it was time for each of us to make a testimonial about how we had practiced minimalism during the previous week. Rudy leaned over and informed me that the man was the painter who had used him as a model. He was truly minimal, reminding me of nondescript television game-show hosts whose on-air identities are tailored to the tight design of their stylish clothes.

One after another people spoke of how they had eliminated some more strife from their lives and how every day the crooked stick of experience was being pulled into a straight lick. It was like a session with Oral Roberts without the laying on of hands, which meant that healing had been disavowed. To speak of scars would have been an admission that there were gashes whose closing had left a record of the pain. I was so dumbfounded by these emotional amputees that I didn't hear Rudy's voice.

"Tyrone! Tyrone! It's your turn!" I opened my mouth, but not only did words fail me, so did the thoughts I needed to measure my words against.

"It's all right. Take your time," said the painter. How fitting it was for someone who had transcended color to sympathize with my inability to find words. Finally I shook my head, deciding to let that gesture stand as my testimony. The reaction was a collective nodding in agreement, as if I had just scaled some new height in minimalist expression. After the testimonials ended, people came over to thank me for showing them that the most appropriate epitaph for the death of conflict was not even to talk about it.

My rapport with Rudy and Alex deteriorated rapidly after that. I never could engage either of them in any conversation other than the fingertip of here and now or some minimalist speculation about the future.

The night before I returned to New York, I persuaded Rudy and Alex
to take me to see Lombard Street. We parked on a nearby street and walked
the rest of the way, stopping when we reached the top of the block. It was
truly remarkable! All those houses leaning as if on the verge of some terrible
spill into the avenue at the bottom of the hill.

"I would've thought coming here would remind you of too much you
don't want to think about," I said to them.

"That's why we come," Alex said. "It reminds us of the dangers we can't
foresee, so when terrible things happen that are unexpected, we're really not
affected that much."

There was much I wanted to say, but I kept my own counsel and looked
down into the doom and descent of Lombard Street.

"Why so glum, Tyrone?" Rudy asked. "Sorry you came?"

"No."

"We've chosen the way we want to live at a cost we can bear."

"Well, if you can bear the cost of living an undisturbed life, then I guess
that's all that matters. But I don't think I could live that way."

"How *do* you live, Tyrone?"

"With difficulty."

"You mean like this," he said, grabbing Alex's hand, and she grabbed
mine. Before I knew what was happening, we were running wildly down
Lombard Street. It was all I could do just to keep up with them. When we
reached the bottom, we were all quite winded.

"Like that," Rudy said, heaving to catch his breath.

"Something like that," I said.

"Your life's a bit too strenuous for me."

"I feel the same way about it myself sometimes."

"What do you do about it?" Alex asked.

"I try not to think about it."

"Sounds like creeping minimalism to me," she said, and to my surprise
I heard myself going along with her.

"Shit, yeah! You got that right!"

 My plane arrived at Kennedy
Airport around ten in the evening. I called Faye but a recorded message
informed me that her number had been changed and was unlisted. The next
day I tried to reach her several times at work, but it was obvious by the way

the woman who answered the phone put me off that Faye didn't want to talk to me.

One evening soon after my return, I went out with friends to a mid-Manhattan disco. The crowded dance floor was made to seem even more dense by a mirror covering an entire wall. While dancing with one of the women I came with, I was very much aware of how easily the music enlisted me into the hup-two cadences of the bass line. It was as if I were in the grip of some benign undertow. I also noticed that many of the dancers seemed much more involved with their reflection in the mirror than with their partners. I watched a man and a woman shiver and suck in air from the attention they were giving their bodies with their hands. I must have been as dissociated from myself as others were attentive to themselves, since I had only the vaguest memory of stopping dancing and buying the glass of brandy in my hand.

Where was I in all this? At least Faye, Rudy and Alex, and those on the dance floor cloning their own orgasms, had made their choices. Maybe my stance was to be luminous about what I needed only after I made sure I couldn't get it, even by accident.

"Would you like to dance?" I turned toward the voice and felt at a disadvantage. A woman had walked boldly over to a group of people she didn't know and asked one of the men, me, to dance, not bothered by the fact that we were a group and were probably coupled off, or that she was white and I was black.

After the initial jolt, I said yes, attracted not only by her nerve but also by something in her face. It told me that even if she saw me as a piece of exotica, she was game enough to see where we would take it.

For some reason we didn't go into the face-off posing that so much of dancing has become. Instead, our hands and arms curved to holding as we began the hustle. As unfamiliar and unrehearsed as we were with one another, I began to feel through our shift and swivel a connection directing what we would do. We never once looked in the mirror but relied on our facial expressions to tell us how we felt. She showed a self-possession that was not self-absorbed, and a stylishness that was not stylized. I watched her chestnut ponytail whip back and forth as she swung out from me at arm's length, then felt the strong pull of her leg as she kicked out from the hip and spread her violet dress to full sail. By the time she spoke again, I was pretty far gone.

"I'm Madeline," she said.

"I'm Tyrone."

"The people I came with are ready to go," she said, "so I have to leave now. I really enjoyed dancing with you."

I walked back over to the people I had come with. Their looks seemed severe with tribal inquiry into why I had obviously enjoyed dancing with a white woman. I felt they had a right to the question, since it came from something common to all attraction: whether we are more thrilled by the idea of someone than by the person themselves. Short of asking them, I had no way of knowing if they believed I was attracted to her whiteness instead of her nerve. But I was willing to accept whatever they thought if my enjoyment reflected unfavorably on tribal loyalty.

Perhaps Rudy and Alex had been right. Why expose yourself to life at all if you didn't want the responsibility for what you felt? All my opposition to how they minimized disruption in their lives was obviously self-serving. I wanted to live in a way they had spurned. Yet I couldn't even enjoy dancing with a woman without casting myself as some perverse dealer in the dreaded sexual traffic moving back and forth across the border of race.

I went over to the bar, ordered another brandy, and nursed it while looking at the people in the mirror. Gradually I settled on my own reflection and considered how people get to the planned obsolescence of the high cost of living. As I acknowledged the impressive evidence that justifies cordoning off life to avoid discomfort, my mirror image began to fragment and disappear. All that was left of me was a curved slice of moon about to go into total eclipse. But just before I vanished, some nagging streak in me that had been weaned on risk reasserted itself. I realized I was not about to exempt myself from the terrors of being alive.

I squeezed between two fingers the skin joining the bridge of my nose with my forehead and looked back in the mirror. I was intact again, distorted but recognizable. That brandy must have been a lot stronger than I thought. But when I looked into the brandy snifter, it had barely been touched.

"Something wrong with the drink?" the bartender asked.

"I wish there was," I said. "It would make things a lot simpler."

WILD SEED

Octavia Butler

Doro discovered the woman by accident when he went to see what was left of one of his seed villages. The village was a comfortable mud-walled place surrounded by grasslands and scattered trees. But Doro realized even before he reached it that its people were gone. Slavers had been to it before him. With their guns and their greed, they had undone in a few hours the work of a thousand years. Those villagers they had not herded away, they had slaughtered. Doro found human bones, hair, bits of desiccated flesh missed by scavengers. He stood over a very small skeleton—the bones of a child— and wondered where the survivors had been taken. Which country or New World colony? How far would he have to travel to find the remnants of what had been a healthy, vigorous people?

Finally he stumbled away from the ruins bitterly angry, not knowing or caring where he went. It was a matter of pride with him that he protected his own. Not the individuals, perhaps, but the groups. They gave him their loyalty, their obedience, and he protected them.

He had failed.

He wandered southwest toward the forest, leaving as he had arrived— alone, unarmed, without supplies, accepting the savanna and later the forest as easily as he accepted any terrain. He was killed several times—by disease, by animals, by hostile people. This was a harsh land. Yet he continued to move southwest, unthinkingly veering away from the section of the coast where his ship awaited him. After a while he realized it was no longer his anger at the loss of his seed village that drove him. It was something new—an impulse, a feeling, a kind of mental undertow pulling at him. He could have resisted it easily, but he did not. He felt there was something for him farther on, a little farther, just ahead. He trusted such feelings.

He had not been this far west for several hundred years; thus he could be certain that whatever, whomever he found would be new to him—new and potentially valuable. He moved on eagerly.

The feeling became sharper and finer, resolving itself into a kind of signal he would normally have expected to receive only from people he knew—people like his lost villagers whom he should be tracking now before they were forced to mix their seed with foreigners and breed away all the special qualities he valued in them. But he continued on southwest, closing slowly on his quarry.

Anyanwu's ears and eyes were far sharper than those of other people. She had increased their sensitivity deliberately after the first time men came stalking her, their machetes ready, their intentions clear. She had had to kill seven times on that terrible day—seven frightened men who could have been spared—and she had nearly died herself, all because she let people come upon her unnoticed. Never again.

Now, for instance, she was very much aware of the lone intruder who prowled the bush near her. He kept himself hidden, moved toward her like smoke, but she heard him, followed him with her ears.

Giving no outward sign, she went on tending her garden. As long as she knew where the intruder was, she had no fear of him. Perhaps he would lose his courage and go away. Meanwhile, there were weeds among her coco yams and her herbs. The herbs were not the traditional ones grown or gathered by her people. Only she grew them as medicines for healing, used them when people brought their sick to her. Often she needed no medicines, but she kept that to herself. She served her people by giving them relief from pain and sickness. Also, she enriched them by allowing them to spread word of her abilities to neighboring people. She was an oracle. A woman through whom a god spoke. Strangers paid heavily for her services. They paid her people, then they paid her. That was as it should have been. Her people could see that they benefited from her presence and that they had reason to fear her abilities. Thus was she protected from them—and they from her—most of the time. But now and then one of them overcame his fear and found reason to try to end her long life.

The intruder was moving close, still not allowing her to see him. No person of honest intentions would approach so stealthily. Who was he, then? A thief? A murderer? Someone who blamed her for the death of a kinsman or some other misfortune? During her various youths she had been blamed several times for causing misfortune. She had been fed poison in the test for witchcraft. Each time, she had taken the test willingly, knowing that she had bewitched no one—and knowing that no ordinary man with his scanty knowledge of poisons could harm her. She knew more about poisons, had ingested more poisons in her long life than any of her people could imagine. Each time she passed the test, her accusers had been ridiculed and fined for their false charges. In each of her lives as she grew older, people ceased to accuse her—though not all ceased to believe she was a witch. Some sought to take matters into their own hands and kill her regardless of the tests.

The intruder finally moved onto the narrow path to approach her openly—now that he had had enough of spying on her. She looked up as though becoming aware of him for the first time.

He was a stranger, a fine man, taller than most and broader at the shoulders. His skin was as dark as her own, and his face was broad and handsome, the mouth slightly smiling. He was young—not yet thirty, she thought. Surely too young to be any threat to her. Yet something about him worried her. His sudden openness after so much stealth, perhaps. Who was he? What did he want?

When he was near enough, he spoke to her, and his words made her frown in confusion. They were foreign words, completely incomprehensible to her, but there was a strange familiarity to them—as though she should have understood. She stood up, concealing uncharacteristic nervousness. "Who are you?" she asked.

He lifted his head slightly as she spoke, seemed to listen.

"How can we speak?" she asked. "You must be from very far away if your speech is so different."

"Very far," he said in her own language. His words were clear to her now, though he had an accent that reminded her of the way people spoke long ago when she was truly young. She did not like it. Everything about him made her uneasy.

"So you can speak," she said.

"I am remembering. It has been a long time since I spoke your language." He came closer, peering at her. Finally he smiled and shook his head. "You are something more than an old woman," he said. "Perhaps you are not an old woman at all."

She drew back in confusion. How could he know anything of what she was? How could he even guess with nothing more than her appearance and a few words as evidence? "I am old," she said, masking her fear with anger. "I could be your mother's mother!" She could have been an ancestor of his mother's mother. But she kept that to herself. "Who are you?" she demanded.

"I could be your mother's father," he said.

She took another step backward, somehow controlling her growing fear. This man was not what he seemed to be. His words should have come to her as mocking nonsense, but instead they seemed to reveal as much and as little as her own.

"Be still," he told her. "I mean you no harm."

"Who are you?" she repeated.

"Doro."

"Doro?" She said the strange word twice more. "Is that a name?"

"It is my name. Among my people, it means the east—the direction from which the sun comes."

She put one hand to her face. "This is a trick," she said. "Someone is laughing."

"You know better. When were you last frightened by a trick?"

Not for more years than she could remember; he was right. But the names . . . the coincidence was like a sign. "Do you know who I am?" she asked. "Did you come here knowing, or . . ."

"I came here because of you. I knew nothing about you except that you were unusual and you were here. Awareness of you has pulled me a great distance out of my way."

"Awareness?"

"I had a feeling. . . . People as different as you attract me somehow, call me, even over great distances."

"I did not call you."

"You exist and you are different. That was enough to attract me. Now tell me who you are."

"You must be the only man in this country who has not heard of me. I am Anyanwu."

He repeated her name and glanced upward, understanding. Sun, her name meant. Anyanwu: the sun. He nodded. "Our peoples missed each other by many years and a great distance, Anyanwu, and yet somehow they named us well."

"As though we were intended to meet. Doro, who are your people?"

"They were called Kush in my time. Their land is far to the east of here. I was born to them, but they have not been my people for many years. I have not seen them for perhaps twelve times as long as you have been alive. When I was thirteen years old, I was separated from them. Now my people are those who give me their loyalty."

"And now you think you know my age," she said. "That is something my own people do not know."

"No doubt you have moved from town to town to help them forget."

He looked around, saw a fallen tree nearby. He went to sit on it. Anyanwu followed almost against her will. As much as this man confused and frightened her, he also intrigued her. It had been so long since something had happened to her that had not happened before—many times before. He spoke again.

"I do nothing to conceal my age," he said, "yet some of my people have found it more comfortable to forget—since they can neither kill me nor become what I am."

She went closer to him and peered down at him. He was clearly proclaiming himself like her—long-lived and powerful. In all her years she had not known even one other person like herself. She had long ago given up, accepted her solitude. But now . . .

"Go on talking," she said. "You have much to tell me."

He had been watching her, looking at her eyes with a curiosity that most people tried to hide from her. People said her eyes were like babies' eyes—the whites too white, the browns too deep and clear. No adult and certainly no old woman should have such eyes, they said. And they avoided her gaze. Doro's eyes were very ordinary, but he could stare at her as children stared. He had no fear, and probably no shame.

He startled her by taking her hand and pulling her down beside him on the tree trunk. She could have broken his grip easily, but she did not. "I've come a long way today," he told her. "This body needs rest if it is to continue to serve me."

She thought about that. *This body needs rest.* What a strange way he had of speaking.

"I came to this territory last about three hundred years ago," he said. "I was looking for a group of my people who had strayed, but they were killed before I found them. Your people were not here then, and you had not been born. I know that because your difference did not call me. I think you are the fruit of my people's passing by yours, though."

"Do you mean that your people may be my kinsmen?"

"Yes." He was examining her face very carefully, perhaps seeking some resemblance. He would not find it. The face she was wearing was not her true face.

"Your people have crossed the Niger"—he hesitated, frowning, then gave the river its proper name—"the Orumili. When I saw them last, they lived on the other side in Benin."

"We crossed long ago," she said. "Children born in that time have grown old and died. We were Ado and Idu, subject to Benin before the crossing. Then we fought with Benin and crossed the river to Onitsha to become free people, our own masters."

"What happened to the Oze people who were here before you?"

"Some ran away. Others became our slaves."

"So you were driven from Benin, then you drove others from here—or enslaved them."

Anyanwu looked away, spoke woodenly. "It is better to be a master than to be a slave." Her husband at the time of the migration had said that. He had seen himself becoming a great man—master of a large household with many wives, children, and slaves. Anyanwu, on the other hand, had been a slave twice in her life and had escaped only by changing her identity completely and finding a husband in a different town. She knew some people were masters and some were slaves. That was the way it had always been. But her own experience had taught her to hate slavery. She had even found it difficult to be a good wife in her most recent years because of the way a woman must bow her head and be subject to her husband. It was better to be as she was—a priestess who spoke with the voice of a god and was feared and obeyed. But what was that? She had become a kind of master herself. "Sometimes one must become a master to avoid becoming a slave," she said softly.

"Yes," he agreed.

She deliberately turned her attention to the new things he had given her to think about. Her age, for instance. He was right. She was about three hundred years old—something none of her people would have believed. And he had said something else—something that brought alive one of her oldest memories. There had been whispers when she was a girl that her father could not beget children, that she was the daughter not only of another man, but of a visiting stranger. She had asked her mother about this, and for the first and only time in her life her mother had struck her. From then on, she had accepted the story as true. But she had never been able to learn anything about the stranger. She would not have cared—her mother's husband claimed her as his daughter and he was a good man—but she had always wondered whether the stranger's people were more like her.

"Are they all dead?" she asked Doro. "These . . . kinsmen of mine?"

"Yes."

"Then they were not like me."

"They might have been after many more generations. You are not only their child. Your Onitsha kinsmen must have been unusual in their own right."

Anyanwu nodded slowly. She could think of several unusual things about her mother. The woman had stature and influence in spite of the gossip about her. Her husband was a member of a highly respected clan, well known for its magical abilities, but in his household it was Anyanwu's mother who made magic. She had highly accurate prophetic dreams. She made medicine to cure disease and to protect the people from evil. At market no woman was a better trader. She seemed to know just how to bargain—as though she could read the thoughts in the other women's minds. She became very wealthy.

It was said that Anyanwu's clan, the clan of her mother's husband, had members who could change their shapes, take animal forms at will, but Anyanwu had seen no such strangeness in them. It was her mother in whom she found strangeness, closeness, empathy that went beyond what could be expected between mother and daughter. She and her mother had shared a unity of spirit that actually did involve some exchange of thoughts and feelings, though they were careful not to flaunt this before others. If Anyanwu felt pain, her mother, busy trading at some distant market, knew of the pain and came home. Anyanwu had no more than ghosts of that early closeness with her own children and with three of her husbands. And she had sought for years through her clan, her mother's clan, and others for even a ghost of her greatest difference, the shape changing. She had collected many frightening stories, but had met no other person who, like herself, could demonstrate this ability. Not until now, perhaps. She looked at Doro. What was it she felt about him—what strangeness? She had shared no thoughts with him, but something about him reminded her of her mother. Another ghost.

"Are you my kinsman?" she asked.

"No," he said. "But your kinsmen had given me their loyalty. That is no small thing."

"Is that why you came when . . . when my difference attracted you?"

He shook his head. "I came to see what you were."

She frowned, suddenly cautious. "I am myself. You see me."

"As you see me. Do you imagine you see everything?"

She did not answer.

"A lie offends me, Anyanwu, and what I see of you is a lie. Show me what you really are."

"You see what you will see!"

"Are you afraid to show me?"

". . . No." It was not fear. What was it? A lifetime of concealment, of commanding herself never to play with her abilities before others, never to show them off as mere tricks, never to let her people or any people know the full extent of her power unless she was fighting for her life. Should she break her tradition now simply because this stranger asked her to? He had done much talking, but what had he actually shown her about himself? Nothing.

"Can my concealment be a lie if yours is not?" she asked.

"Mine is," he admitted.

"Then show me what you are. Give me the trust you ask me to give you."

"You have my trust, Anyanwu, but knowing what I am would only frighten you."

"Am I a child then?" she asked angrily. "Are you my mother, who must shield me from adult truths?"

He refused to be insulted. "Most of my people are grateful to me for shielding them from my particular truth," he said.

"So you say. I have seen nothing."

He stood up, and she stood to face him, her small, withered body fully in the shadow of his. She was little more than half his size, but it was no new thing for her to face larger people and either bend them to her will with words or beat them into submission physically. In fact, she could have made herself as large as any man, but she chose to let her smallness go on deceiving people. Most often it put strangers at their ease because she seemed harmless. Also, it caused would-be attackers to underestimate her.

Doro stared down at her. "Sometimes only a burn will teach a child to respect fire," he said. "Come with me to one of the villages of your town, Anyanwu. There I will show you what you think you want to see."

"What will you do?" she asked warily.

"I will let you choose someone—an enemy or only some useless person that your people would be better without. Then I will kill him."

"Kill!"

"I kill, Anyanwu. That is how I keep my youth, my strength. I can do only one thing to show you what I am, and that is kill a man and wear his body like a cloth." He breathed deeply. "This is not the body I was born into. It's not the tenth I've worn, nor the hundredth, nor the thousandth. Your gift seems to be a gentle one. Mine is not."

"You are a spirit," she cried in alarm.

"I told you you were a child," he said. "See how you frighten yourself?"

He was like an ogbanje, an evil child spirit born to one woman again and again, only to die and give the mother pain. A woman tormented by an ogbanje could give birth many times and still have no living child. But Doro was an adult. He did not enter and reenter his mother's womb. He did not want the bodies of children. He preferred to steal the bodies of men.

"You are a spirit!" she insisted, her voice shrill with fear. All the while part of her mind wondered why she was believing him so easily. She knew many tricks herself, many frightening lies. Why should she react now like the most ignorant stranger brought before her, believing that a god spoke through her? Yet she did believe, and she was afraid. This man was far more unusual than she was. This man was not a man.

When he touched her arm lightly, unexpectedly, she screamed.

He made a sound of disgust. "Woman, if you bring your people here with your noise, I will have no choice but to kill some of them."

She stood still, believing this also. "Did you kill anyone as you came here?" she whispered.

"No. I went to great trouble to avoid killing for your sake. I thought you might have kinsmen here."

"Generations of kinsmen. Sons and their sons and even their sons."

"I would not want to kill one of your sons."

"Why?" She was relieved but curious. "What are they to you?"

"How would you receive me if I came to you clothed in the flesh of one of your sons?"

She drew back, not knowing how to imagine such a thing.

"You see? Your children should not be wasted anyway. They may be good—" He spoke a word in another language. She heard it clearly, but it meant nothing to her. The word was *seed.*

"What is seed?" she asked.

"People too valuable to be casually killed," he said. Then more softly, "You must show me what you are."

"How can my sons be of value to you?"

He gave her a long, silent look, then spoke with that same softness. "I may have to go to them, Anyanwu. They may be more tractable than their mother."

She could not recall ever having been threatened so gently—or so effectively. Her sons . . . "Come," she whispered. "It is too open for me to show you here."

With concealed excitement, Doro followed the small, wizened woman to her tiny compound. The compound wall—made of red clay and over six feet high—would give them the privacy Anyanwu wanted.

"My sons would do you no good," she told him as they walked. "They are good men, but they know very little."

"They are not like you—any of them?"

"None."

"And your daughters?"

"Nor them. I watched them carefully until they went away to their husbands' towns. They are like my mother. They exert great influence on their husbands and on other women, but nothing beyond that. They live their lives and they die."

"They die . . . ?"

She opened the wooden door and led him through the wall, then barred the door after him.

"They die," she said sadly. "Like their fathers."

"Perhaps if your sons and daughters married each other . . ."

"Abomination!" she said with alarm. "We are not animals here, Doro!"

He shrugged. He had spent most of his life ignoring such protests and causing the protesters to change their minds. People's morals rarely survived confrontations with him. For now, though, gentleness. This woman was valuable. If she was only half as old as he thought, she would be the oldest person he had ever met—and she was still spry. She was descended from people whose abnormally long lives, resistance to disease, and budding special abilities made them very important to him. People who, like so many others, had fallen victim to slavers or tribal enemies. There had been so few of them. Nothing must happen to this one survivor, this fortunate little hybrid. Above all, she must be protected from Doro himself. He must not kill her out of anger or by accident—and accidents could happen so easily in this country. He must take her away with him to one of his more secure seed towns. Perhaps in her strangeness, she could still bear young, and perhaps with the powerful mates he could get her, this time her children would be worthy of her. If not, there were always her existing children.

"Will you watch, Doro?" she asked. "This is what you demanded to see."

He focused his attention on her, and she began to rub her hands. The hands were bird claws, long-fingered, withered, and bony. As he watched, they began to fill out, to grow smooth and young-looking. Her arms and shoulders began to fill out and her sagging breasts drew themselves up round and high. Her hips grew round beneath her cloth, causing him to want to strip the cloth from her. Lastly, she touched her face and molded away her wrinkles. An old scar beneath one eye vanished. The flesh became smooth and firm, and the woman startlingly beautiful.

Finally she stood before him looking not yet twenty. She cleared her throat and spoke to him in a soft, young-woman's voice. "Is this enough?"

For a moment he could only stare at her. "Is this truly you, Anyanwu?"

"As I am. As I would always be if I did not age or change myself for others. This shape flows back to me very easily. Others are harder to take."

"Others!"

"Did you think I could take only one?" She began molding her malleable body into another shape. "I took animal shapes to frighten my people when they wanted to kill me," she said. "I became a leopard and spat at them. They believe in such things, but they do not like to see them proved. Then I became a sacred python, and no one dared to harm me. The python shape brought me luck. We were needing rain then to save the yam crop, and while I was a python, the rains came. The people decided my magic was good and it took them a long time to want to kill me again." She was becoming a small, well-muscled man as she spoke.

Now Doro did try to strip away her cloth, moving slowly so that she would understand. He felt her strength for a moment when she caught his hand and, with no special effort, almost broke it. Then, as he controlled his surprise, prevented himself from reacting to the pain, she untied her cloth herself and took it off. For several seconds, he was more impressed with that casual grip than with her body, but he could not help noticing that she had become thoroughly male.

"Could you father a child?" he asked.

"In time. Not now."

"Have you?"

"Yes. But only girl children."

He shook his head, laughing. The woman was far beyond anything he had imagined. "I'm surprised your people have let you live," he said.

"Do you think I would let them kill me?" she asked.

He laughed again. "What will you do then, Anyanwu? Stay here with them, convincing each new generation that you are best let alone—or will you come with me?"

She tied her cloth around her again, then stared at him, her large too-clear eyes looking deceptively gentle in her young man's face. "Is that what you want?" she asked. "For me to go with you?"

"Yes."

"That is your true reason for coming here then."

He thought he heard fear in her voice, and his throbbing hand convinced him that she must not be unduly frightened. She was too powerful. She might force him to kill her. He spoke honestly.

"I let myself be drawn here because people who had pledged loyalty to me had been taken away in slavery," he said. "I went to their village to get them, take them to a safer home, and I found . . . only what the slavers had left. I went away, not caring where my feet took me. When they brought me here, I was surprised, and for the first time in many days, I was pleased."

"It seems your people are often taken from you."

"It does not seem so, it is so. That is why I am gathering them all closer together in a new place. It will be easier for me to protect them there."

"I have always protected myself."

"I can see that. You will be very valuable to me. I think you could protect others as well as yourself."

"Shall I leave my people to help you protect yours?"

"You should leave so that finally you can be with your own kind."

"With one who kills men and shrouds himself in their skins? We are not alike, Doro."

Doro sighed, looked over at her house—a small, rectangular building whose steeply sloping thatched roof dipped to within a few feet of the ground. Its walls were made of the same red earth as the compound wall. He wondered obscurely whether the red earth was the same clay he had seen in Indian dwellings in southwestern parts of the North American continent. But more immediately, he wondered whether there were couches in Anyanwu's house, and food and water. He was almost too tired and hungry to go on arguing with the woman.

"Give me food, Anyanwu," he said. "Then I will have the strength to entice you away from this place."

She looked startled, then laughed almost reluctantly. It occurred to him that she did not want him to stay and eat, did not want him to stay at all. She believed the things he had told her, and she feared that he could entice her away. She wanted him to leave—or part of her did. Surely there was another part that was intrigued, that wondered what would happen if she left her home, walked away with this stranger. She was too alert, too alive not to have the kind of mind that probed and reached and got her into trouble now and then.

"A bit of yam, at least, Anyanwu," he said, smiling. "I have eaten nothing today." He knew she would feed him.

Without a word, she walked away to another smaller building and returned with two large yams. Then she led him into her kitchen and gave him a deerskin to sit on since he carried nothing other than the cloth around his loins. Still in her male guise, she courteously shared a kola nut and a little palm wine with him. Then she began to prepare food. Besides the yams, she had vegetables, smoked fish, and palm oil. She built up a fire from the live coals in the tripod of stones that formed her hearth, then put a clay pot of water on to boil. She began to peel the yams. She would cut them up and boil the pieces until they were tender enough to be pounded as her people liked them. Perhaps she would make soup of the vegetables, oil, and fish, but that would take time.

"What do you do?" she asked him as she worked. "Steal food when you are hungry?"

"Yes," he said. He stole more than food. If there were no people he knew near him, or if he went to people he knew and they did not welcome him, he simply took a new strong, young body. No person, no group could stop him from doing this. No one could stop him from doing anything at all.

"A thief," said Anyanwu with disgust that he did not think was quite real. "You steal, you kill. What else do you do?"

"I build," he said quietly. "I search the land for people who are a little different—or very different. I search them out, I bring them together in groups, I begin to build them into a strong new people."

She stared at him in surprise. "They let you do this—let you take them from their people, their families?"

"Some bring their families with them. Many do not have families. Their differences have made them outcasts. They are glad to follow me."

"Always?"

"Often enough," he said.

"What happens when people will not follow you? What happens if they say, 'It seems too many of your people are dying, Doro. We will stay where we are and live.' "

He got up and went to the doorway of the next room where two hard but inviting clay couches had been built out from the walls. He had to sleep. In spite of the youth and strength of the body he was wearing, it was only an ordinary body. If he was careful with it—gave it proper rest and food, did not allow it to be injured—it would last him a few more weeks. If he drove it, though, as he had been driving it to reach Anyanwu, he would use it up much sooner. He held his hands before him, palms down, and was not surprised to see that they were shaking.

"Anyanwu, I must sleep. Wake me when the food is ready."

"Wait!"

The sharpness of her voice stopped him, made him look back.

"Answer," she said. "What happens when people will not follow you?"

Was that all? He ignored her, climbed onto one of the couches, lay down on the mat that covered it, and closed his eyes. He thought he heard her come into the room and go out again before he drifted off to sleep, but he paid no attention. He had long ago discovered that people were much more cooperative if he made them answer questions like hers for themselves. Only the stupid actually needed to hear his answer, and this woman was not stupid.

When she woke him, the house was full of the odor of food and he got up, alert and ravenous. He sat with her, washed his hands absently in the bowl of water she gave him, then used his fingers to scoop up a bit of pounded yam from his platter and dip it into the common pot of peppery soup. The food was good and filling, and for some time he concentrated on it, ignoring Anyanwu except to notice that she was also eating and did not seem inclined to talk. He recalled distantly that there had been some small religious ceremony between the washing of hands and the eating when he had last been with her people. An offering of food and palm wine to the gods. He asked about it once he had taken the edge off his hunger.

She glanced at him. "What gods do you respect?"

"None."

"And why not?"

"I help myself," he said.

She nodded. "In at least two ways, you do. I help myself, too."

He smiled a little, but could not help wondering how hard it might be to tame even partially a wild seed woman who had been helping herself for three hundred years. It would not be hard to make her follow him. She had sons and she cared for them, thus she was vulnerable. But she might very well make him regret taking her—especially since she was too valuable to kill if he could possibly spare her.

"For my people," she said, "I respect the gods. I speak as the voice of a god. For myself . . . in my years, I have seen that people must be their own gods and make their own good fortune. The bad will come or not come anyway."

"You are very much out of place here."

She sighed. "Everything comes back to that. I am content here, Doro. I have already had ten husbands to tell me what to do. Why should I make you the eleventh? Because you will kill me if I refuse? Is that how men get wives in your homeland—by threatening murder? Well, perhaps you cannot kill me. Perhaps we should find out!"

He ignored her outburst, noticed instead that she had automatically assumed that he wanted her as his wife. That was a natural assumption for her to make, perhaps a correct assumption. He had been asking himself which of his people she should be mated with first, but now he knew he would take her himself—for a while, at least. He often kept the most powerful of his people with him for a few months, perhaps a year. If they were children, they learned to accept him as father. If they were men, they learned to obey him as master. If they were women, they accepted him best as lover or husband. Anyanwu was one of the handsomest women he had ever seen. He had intended to take her to bed this night, and many more nights until he got her to the seed village he was assembling in the British-ruled Colony of New York. But why should that be enough? The woman was a rare find. He spoke softly.

"Shall I try to kill you then, Anyanwu? Why? Would you kill me if you could?"

"Perhaps I can!"

"Here I am." He looked at her with eyes that ignored the male form she still wore. Eyes that spoke to the woman inside—or he hoped they did. It would be much more pleasant to have her come to him because she wanted to rather than because she was afraid.

She said nothing—as though his mildness confused her. He had intended it to.

"We would be right together, Anyanwu. Have you never wanted a husband who was worthy of you?"

"You think very much of yourself."

"And of you—or why would I be here?"

"I have had husbands who were great men," she said. "Titled men of proven courage even though they had no special ability such as yours. I have sons who are priests, wealthy sons, men of standing. Why should I want a husband who must prey on other men like a wild beast?"

He touched his chest. "This man came to prey on me. He attacked me with a machete."

That stopped her for a moment. She shuddered. "I have been cut that way—cut almost in half."

"What did you do?"

"I . . . I healed myself. I would not have thought I could heal so quickly."

"I mean what did you do to the man who cut you?"

"Men. Seven of them came to kill me."

"What did you do, Anyanwu?"

She seemed to shrink into herself at the memory. "I killed them," she whispered. "To warn others and because . . . because I was angry."

Doro sat watching her, seeing remembered pain in her eyes. He could not recall the last time he had felt pain at killing a man. Anger, perhaps, when a man of power and potential became arrogant and had to be destroyed—anger at the waste. But not pain.

"You see?" he said softly. "How did you kill them?"

"With my hands." She spread them before her, ordinary hands now, not even remarkably ugly as they had been when she was an old woman. "I was angry," she repeated. "I have been careful not to get too angry since then."

"But what did you do?"

"Why do you want to know all the shameful details!" she demanded. "I killed them. They are dead. They were my people and I killed them!"

"How can it be shameful to kill those who would have killed you?"

She said nothing.

"Surely those seven are not the only ones you've killed."

She sighed, stared into the fire. "I frighten them when I can, kill only when they make me. Most often they are already afraid and easy to drive away. I am making the ones here rich so that none of them have wanted me dead for years."

"Tell me how you killed the seven."

She got up and went outside. It was dark out now—deep, moonless darkness, but Doro did not doubt that Anyanwu could see with those eyes of hers. Where had she gone, though, and why?

She came back, sat down again, and handed him a rock. "Break it," she said tonelessly.

It was a rock, not hardened mud, and though he might have broken it with another rock or metal tool, he could make no impression on it with his hands. He returned it to her whole.

And she crushed it in one hand.

He had to have the woman. She was wild seed of the best kind. She would strengthen any line he bred her into, strengthen it immeasurably.

"Come with me, Anyanwu. You belong with me, with the people I'm gathering. We are people you can be part of—people you need not frighten or bribe into letting you live."

"I was born among these people," she said. "I belong with them." And she insisted, "You and I are not alike."

"We are more like each other than like other people. We need not hide from each other." He looked at her muscular young man's body. "Become a woman again, Anyanwu, and I will show you that we should be together."

She managed a wan smile. "I have borne forty-seven children to ten husbands," she said. "What do you think you can show me?"

"If you come with me, I think someday I can show you children you will never have to bury." He paused, saw that he now had her full attention. "A mother should not have to watch her children grow old and die," he continued. "If you live, they should live. It is the fault of their fathers that they die. Let me give you children who will live!"

She put her hands to her face, and for a moment he thought she was crying. But her eyes were dry when she looked at him. "Children from your stolen loins?" she whispered.

"Not these loins." He gestured toward his body. "This man was only a man. But I promise you, if you come with me, I will give you children of your own kind."

There was a long silence. She sat staring into the fire again, perhaps making up her mind. Finally, she looked at him, studied him with such intensity he began to feel uncomfortable. His discomfort amazed him. He was more accustomed to making other people uncomfortable. And he did not like her appraising stare—as though she were deciding whether or not to buy him. If he could win her alive, he would teach her manners someday!

It was not until she began to grow breasts that he knew for certain he had won. He got up then, and when the change was complete, he took her to the couch.

MUZ AND THE
SPHERE OF MEMORY

Xam Wilson Cartiér

Why is it that radical reviews always start at the core of your current and clack back through your mucked-up life? It's standard operating procedure; no one escapes the railroad express with its scenic view of the past.

In this way, in the liquor store of today, I find myself suddenly subjected to passing-flash memory of still-married me, sorrowful and contrite for being boozed again, and in front of husband Charlie, motherly Muz, and young chick Mia, who's four years old at the time. This all goes down when it's 98-degree serious summer in Saint Brew and I've been tucked away all day with my usual beers on the back porch so that Mia can play outside where there's hope of a breeze. All day long I've been home, and I'm not the only one—we're all here, inside neighborly fences with our food-stamp beer and watermelons—students, artists, retirees, unemployees, and captive mothers like me, spontaneously combustible fire-tempered folks as far as the eye can see.

Before the day can broil away, I've wound up screaming fed-uply at Muz, which releases the regular rash of guilt and reproach from within, then I yank Baby Mia and scream at her till she cries, due to fury at Muz and at Charlie, who's squalled into his Me-Tarzan-You-Shit act; and hell, I'd rather be Cheetah than Jane—Cheetah's *supposed* to be slow so can excuse his shortcomings in matters of scuffling to please and then shuffling aside with a monkeyish grin. Charlie's been waving his paycheck in my face and enlightening me with wisdom like "I'm sick of your constant comments. Don't let your mouth take you where your ass can't follow!", which brings on my tailormaid trip of repentance for harmony's sake, so I smile and refuel with my beer after beer. . . . That's me, for example, cooking subthermal Charlie a midnight supper when he gets in from the later day's work. And yep, that's the Kid again hovering over the stove, hand-slaving a pound cake solely for Muz. Hostility grates me like a gristmill, and I know what I'm doing, yet do it anyway, nevertheless, asinine-regardless . . . stupid, stupid, Jane, after all.

My atonement includes mopping and scrubbing the kitchen and bathroom floors, all after a clandestine slap from Charlie back in the kitchen, but I deserve it, I think at the time, and Charlie only hit me once—he held his temper despite the lure of my guilt.

Why is it that I wash my sins away with repentant floor cleaner suds and a beer or two, feel confessional fresh, then am At It again in no time at all? I despise myself when I can't help but drink—I hate what I feel and hate what I do when my shadow splits off and takes over the show while I watch it from shut-away closeted wings, and I see it upstage the bright best of myself. . . . Damn you, dense shade of relentless intent, bent on venting self-consummate force at any event, whenever my pressure cooks up to max—hooch never helps, and I know it!

Like this I go on thinking, chew-thought ruminating about past repeated error of the same foolish type, till deliberately, as part of my cure from the lure of further gloomination, I conjure up the virulent vision of my healing throes after that booze bout of yore. Instantly I see Charlie, who lopes into view right on cue with his knack for kicking a sucker. I can still see him now, can't forget how, how he—See? He's dragging Baby Mia into the bathroom to watch me throw up bile and drops of blood, my bitter dues on the installment plan once an hour, despite my dose of Pepto Dismal. . . .

Look! Look! See Mommy squirm!

So it is that noxious recall spews me into a course of the current and heaves me up to right now, where I am in this liquor store buying visiting house guest Muz her fifth of Cutty Shark—this being my goal and sole mission. *Just show Muz how cope-able I am, now that I've moved on my own to San Fran.* . . . From here at the counter I can see the beer glistening in the back-of-store refrigerator, which I soon find myself headed toward in a natural way like the rest of recidivist nature. So what? So I'll pick up some cans of malt liquor. This stuff serves its purpose—it cures tough congestion, shrinks swollen membranes. . . . Ask the two women in line to the counter. Just to hear these she-roes talk, you know that they know what they're here for.

Woman One: ". . . *too* cold!"

Woman Two: "Was I cold? I said to George, 'Listen. Our relationship, if you want to call it that—well, it didn't exactly start out to be one of those everlastin' hookups. I mean it had to end sometime, right? And now time's just up, that's all, no blame. . . .' Had to bust myself right there; I almost said 'the jig'—'the jig is up.' Yeah, fool, the jig, the stroll, the hustle, and so's your slow drag through my life—"

"I hear you!"

"By the time we broke up, George was sayin', 'Well, wait. Let's talk, baby. Don't be rash.' "

"Say what?"

"Now you know I been tryin' to talk to this nut for four years—"

"That all?"

"And by the time he hauls his wide-ego self over to tryin' to get me back—when he finely drags his bag all the way over to the 'let's talk' stage—well, it turns out we've developed these two different accents—not whole separate lingos, but damn close, worse even when you think about it. You're talkin' the same, *sounds* almost the same, and that's what leads you off and runnin', see—but everything you say you get 'Hello? Hello?' See what I'm sayin'?"

"For sure."

"So all I want to know is, how come, when a man and a woman hook up in all seriousness and respect—this ain't no drop-in love affair now, no kid on the way or any other time bomb in the scene, just a matter of choice, adult agreement between two consenting fools—why is it that from the moment you get married, the countdown to hell begins? Five, four, three, two . . . *and now, my friends, at the sound of the bang, your bag will turn into a box.* Hell, what's missing in this picture?"

A piece of familial puzzle—Muz has her own, which she brandishes the minute I'm back in the car. "For your sake," she says, "I hope Mia has a smooth adolescence! I know she's only nine now," she answers my quizzical eyebrows and forges ahead, "and I know you think there's a huge gap between mothering a child of nine and mothering a teenager-to-be. But believe me, adolescence is right around the corner. It'll be up on you before you know it!"

When I see her shoulders sag for a moment, I can't help but remember how she turned to me with tears in her eyes at daybreak on the day after

Double died at the axis of my adolescence, right when a Girl Needs a Father Most. "You're all I've got," Muz said at the time. And yet so far as a teenager, she said, I'd been spending damn near all my better energy, working overtime at it, just grieving her to the hilt ("Words aren't made for this," she grieved), with my persistent Courting of Disaster. Then came the nostalgic tidbits from my mottled past, proof of my rotten response to the challenge of growing up, episodes handpicked and promptly produced, fresh from her time-tight bag of miserable memories.

Now, as she turns to glance across the car seat at me, for a moment I look straight into the opaque wool brown of Muz's eyes and I'm struck by their lack of a spark of zest (as Double's had), and the old Eyeball Theory, as Double called it, comes ogling up from my childhood straight through my grown-up cool.

According to Double's hypothesis, which dealt with eyes as windows of the soul, sole windows that the inner self looks through and can be seen in, one of the key signs when reading eyes is the presence of absence of telltale spark in the optical lens, that little flame flaring from time to time. Since Double's research had unearthed bright-eyed folks who were *bon vivants* and who yet were sparkless, his conclusion was the eye spark is produced by zest for life, but not vice versa, in those who're on the up and up. So seeing lusterless Muz of today, I'm pierced from inside by a pang of connection with her ongoing grief and with her loss of hope in deadening widowhood. After all, I'm a widow, too; look at my funereal marriage here on the bier.

"You know what, though?" Muz said to me a scant year ago, "I keep thinking if I'd just gotten up there"—to K.C. MO, where Double'd moved in search of work—"if I'd've managed to go see him before he died, he never would've died. I know he wasn't *doing* for himself like he should've, you know, and if I'd only made myself go on up there! But that was around the time the windows needed sealing—remember?—and everything all over the house would've got ruined—it was raining and storming all that winter, remember? But somehow I could have managed it; I should've done what my better judgment told me, should've followed my first mind, something *told* me—"

"Wait," I cut in, "hear me out. And I want you to know, if I seem like I'm not responding when you tell me something like this, it's not 'cause I don't feel a thing or nothing, it's just that I try not to flap right off the top, see. My way is to shut down and gather my steam for as long as I can; I just shut down all operations till I can hear myself think—"

"*Lord*, you're my daughter!"

"—so I can stop and mesh things through—"

"—just *like* me!"

"Now here's what I want to say—"

"You do exactly like me, that's me all over again!"

"All right now let me express myself—"

"Okay."

"The thing to keep in mind is *we* don't say when it's time to die—"

"God says that; it's up to Him!"

"We're not the ones who say when it's time to go; we can't postpone anybody's death when it's time for them to go. When it's time for them to go, then it's *time*—and they go."

"I'll buy that! Go on, you're *helping* me."

"Then, too, his life had been painful for a long time now. We can't exactly peep the Spirit's hand, you know, but sometimes I think *I* can tell what's on Her mind—"

"Now you're talking."

"So it was time for him to go. Besides, Double's still here, you know. People don't evaporate when they pass, they literally pass into another phase just like everything else on this earth. The waves are the same waves, this is the same dirt we're walking—we keep digging up old shit from millenniums ago, don't we? And *we're* the same, same bodies even. God don't throw nothin' away—"

"Go on; I'm with you—"

"Everything on this earth is recycled. And the world runs on a master plan down to the protoplasm. So are human beings the only exception? Aw, come on."

"Damn! You're helping me; you're good!"

"Coulda told you that."

"Oh, you wouldn't be telling *me* anything. One thing about me, I'm wide-awake in this world. Not too much slick stuff slides past me!"

Muz is silent now; she's facing the scene at the car window on her right, the outside world with its current view of the Spansamerica Pyramid glimmering in the heart of San Fran's Financial District for a concrete case in point, with its bustling office workers visible in fluorescent windows on their way to the downward escalator and out the front door. At the downstairs door they'll meet—I can see this upcoming incident and so feel like God for a moment—at the outer building door they'll meet a waiting bevy of slow-moving downhearted derelickeds gathered at the end of their own long, hard hustle. These bums have dealt with flat-pocketbook office workers all day long, and hope hangs heavy in an empty hat outstretched by necessity. Two ragged men limp among the fleeing nine-to-fivers, begging-handout denizens maintaining their own practical plodding pace in a whirlwind of commuters all around, but no one sees them, of course not—who'll look at those barely mobile mirrors of our desperation, inner wound in outer form?

Here on the edge of rush hour we're barely making any time at all up this hill of Sacramento Street, inching uphill toward gilded bliss of Nob Hill up ahead where the Mark Hopkins Hotel leans discreetly into view on the left and St. Mary's Cathedral is a squinted vision of faithful landmark up ahead on the right. Looking beside me at Muz's back, I can see her straightening erect in the airport last night, saying, "Let me know when you see that dowager's hump again. . . ."

Dowager's hump? I'd told her only that lately her back seemed curved when she was standing relaxed, but oh, I remember heartlessly adding, "and it looks like you don't have a neck. . . ." Why did I have to say that anyway— I always lash out instead of just covering my head; I never lean back and let myself grow defensive in a natural way. What is it that makes me so wary of Muz and her comments and even of her life advice that proves so on time and works like a charm to banish the barbs on each fence to my future?

This query makes my spirit sag, and I can't resist anymore, it seems for a moment; I scramble for a toehold on renitent optimism, scramble up to the edge of it and dangle for a moment, but I'm sliding, I'm sliding backward and downward inside my outer eye, where I'm eight-year-old me sidling up to Muz, bearing puny kidhood tributes, scuffling to buy out her freeze play, her motherly noncommitment with attempted bribes of peppermint sticks, one each week at faithful allowance time, which Frozen Muz promptly sets aside to throw away. But hell, she did her best, I guess, with her functional focus flat on the ground. Besides, Muz has given me a lot to be grateful for: her share of the family sass factor, and do-or-die grit. And what the heck, I'm a big girl now, all begrowned and done up in my own chunked-off life. So why's it that I can't climb for good out from under this mother-mother lugluebrication that hits the fan when my mind is turned?

After I'd left Charlie, I remember how in the middle of the night or anywhere else, for solace and rapport I'd want to jump up and call Muz, or even Charlie himself, for that matter. Two potentially crippling calls, but it was a time when I needed a witness and I couldn't be choosy, 'cause right then I couldn't bear to grin-talk with anyone who wasn't at the scene of my marital accident. When I met people those days, I was full of bleeding gut material from once-upon-a-time, when all my madnews was just surface scum floating topside on the real-life layer. When I was some(hapless)body's wife, in a former life. (Amazing!) Once upon a time of marriage, carriage, his-and-hernias . . . with sounds of the same nightmare chase coming from both sides of the bed.

But all I have to do now is to bring myself to speak up to Muz about my ongoing woe of having left Charlie last year; she'll understand, although in considering my problems she never discloses any comparative agony from her own experience as most people match misery with you in a polite gesture of attempted shared humanity.

Yet closemouthed as Muz is—"In case you don't know it, I'm a *private* person," she once said in irritation at my demand for personal data that she was keeping clutched to her chest—Muz is willing to share her own rooted resources with me, her only child, when the time seems ripe according to her practiced perspective. Besides, it's not her fault, that reticence; she was brought up to be closemouthed in the deadening days of the Great Depression, with its flamboyant poverty only a meal or a job away if you called attention to your dark situation. When there was no space to study at home, so it was your turn finally to take your books and tag along with your father to his stint at the country club, you knew better than to mention his working two jobs to send you and five younger brothers and sisters to teachers college in 1936 while the rest of the world was on welfare and even whites were panicking in open desperation, though not enough to stop them from calling, "Waiter!" Then, when waiterly Grandad appeared at their beck, they'd nudge each other (Is this the one with the college pretensions?) and smile, "Here!" so when Grandad held out his hand, they'd slip him an open napkin of spit and chewed food to discard, and they'd watch his silent retreat from the table, then next from his job, due to mysterious layoff by the powers that were. . . .

Yet last time I really talked to Muz, I mean laid my soul bare, Muz gave her testimony right on time when I needed it in the wake of my miscarried marriage, just as I was reconsidering my move from Charlie as I continue to do in spare moments of free-floating loss. That time, when my wound was still fresh, I was convincing myself that I needed to leave Charlie for survival's sake by comparing my getaway to the way the old pioneers used to throw goods off their covered wagons when times got tough and they had to pick up speed under attack. *Blip!* There goes the family stove. *Blam! Fuck* this trunk of household tools!

And it's still your heavy wagon time, I said to myself as I unpacked personal things at my new apartment in San Fran, delving into a box of remnants of my old life with Charlie, including agonizing memorabilia such as harmless-seeming shapshot chronicles of our transient joy. Look, I thought *re* one photo, here we are smiling in that ridiculous lowlife niteclub in East St. Lou, where Charlie got so wasted he confessed that he loved me more than anything. And check it out, here's Charlie's Record (as I persisted in calling it, though he gave it to me one birthday when he'd brought me no gift and I put up such a fuss)—here's Charlie's record of John Coltrane's

"My Favorite Things," that painful trickling joy of jazz in fluid process, riding on a riff of "Be Here Now. . . ."

Oh, no, and here's Charlie's half of our honeymoon toasting goblets, our gift from Muz and Double—look at this engraving: "Love Is the Only Elixir." (My God, but where's the antidote?) And here's our favorite T-shirt that we shared. I can't help but sniff it for illusion of comfort from Charlie's friendly body smell, then I can't help but pretend he's right here in this room, helping me unpack—he's my best friend, Charlie is, so maybe he'll help me over the hump of my lump, help me, help me manage to get over Charlie. . . .

Stop! So I use the shirt as a towel for my tears while I gather all the keepsakes and hurl them down the garbage chute, one by clattering one. Simultaneously I'm discarding each companion memory in ritual, or so I tell myself at the scene; yet I hold on to one—I can't bear to throw away Charlie's Trane, which leaves "My Favorite Things" as all that remains of my favorite things.

I recall my attempted takeover the time Charlie said, "I'll fill out my own school scholarship forms," meaning "no thanks to you," and I can't manage to blame him; in my quest to see our two egos comfy, side by peery side (we'll get along so much better when Charlie has his bachelor's degree, I'm thinking; it'll help him withstand the grit of my wit)—in my zeal I've boiled up to the bitch point where I'm pointing out to Charlie how he never reads instructions the right way, which is from top to bott: instead he swoops onto the middle of the page and scans to the bottom, then back to the top. So I tell him how he misses and mucks up major information with his offbeat reading that's completely out of step with the data digestion process (Hup Two . . .).

"You either swoop from the top, or you'll crip your way through on one wing," I throw out, steaming and swigging beer. "Right?" And on I roar with righteous fume, knowing full well that halo glare's malignant. It's one of those times when I can feel the Muz raging in me, can hear Double say to Muz with quiet force, "Okay, so I'm wrong! Well, lead me to the guil-lotine!" A time when I'm caught up in the sort of needling that drives a man into the street searching for a pliant partner to override, consideration of which incenses me further, past logic and back around the spiral to bitch again.

"Well, I'll do the goddamn forms myself," Charlie said then. "No, look—" he says with warning stop-still-or-I'll-stop-you look at me reaching for them anyway. So I stop, aborted and drinking a bracer of beer, noting through my fog how I'm spun back in time with Charlie to repeat-perform

Muz and Double's scenes of tryst over the same basic issue. Muz and I could be a duet, singing to Charlie and to Double before he died: "I'll help you, but I'll take my just due for it!" A bitch serenade rasped from our martyring flame, as if we can't help but add char to their hard row to hoe.

Charred row to hoe, stiff way to go with no time to gather moss of rest away from strife—what a life of dry-spell disunity! Our men always versus our women. . . . Here's what I'll say to Muz about that and my role in such ingrown-type underground war: "These days . . . these days most men think I'm cold, based on my tendency to jump away from their first reach to embrace even physically," including once (and I'll keep this to myself) when I'm wearing nothing but thin see-through T-shirt and tight jeans of seeming provocation, tucked-in tease. I'm greeting a would-be beau who reaches to hug me hello, and what I'm jumping away from really is the palpable prospect of ah, the sweet feel of his force pulsing hard deep inside me, the tart taste of my sauce on his lips, with no follow-up food for my heart that still throbs like my hot spot, with rhythms now different, no longer in sync.

But Muz (here's what I'll say about the snag that still vexes my life)— Muz, do you see how the past has flowed forward to taint my today? Since my break made from Charlie, it seems I can never elate with full glee or be buoyed up for long by lighthearted levity. There's something holding my happiness back; something's hanging onto the hem of my bliss. Wait, let me rephrase this. What is it that makes me farm through my mind in moments of soon-to-be happiness away from past woe? It seems I can't stand joy straight but have to dredge up past sadness to water it down. Most of my growth's in the past, underground; and the green clump of vigor that strangers can see ("Hey, look at me! I'm finally free!") is merely surface-type growth yet to be. Am I right? Muz, you tell me!

EMMA

Carolyn Cole

My last fifty cents. She'll never hit me. She wants to tonk out. That's why I'd rather play with Maria. Grown-ups get tired too fast. And when they get tired they can think of zillions of ways to end a good game. Maria would have hit me. And if she'd won my last quarter, she would loan me some more. The game would never end. Never, not until a grown-up would say, "You've got to go to bed now." Maria told me that is Emma's favorite.

Maria knows a lot of things, especially about Emma. I do, too. We've decided to be just like Emma when we grow up. We'll play games with the children, read stories to them, take them shopping and to New Orleans. Even when their daddy doesn't want them to go. We'll let them dress up in our pretty red dresses and long white beads. Not the long ones that hang all the way down to your waist. Not those kinds. Not like the lady at the train station.

When we're grown up, we'll go to dinner and to parties. We'll wear long black dresses with real wide skirts. Skirts that spread way out like umbrellas when you spin around. And we'll wear lots of sparkling jewelry. We won't leave home until ten at night. And when we come home, it'll be real late—almost the next day. The house will be quiet and real, real dark. The children will be in bed. But we won't forget about them. We'll tiptoe into their rooms and kiss them on their heads. We'll make sure they're still asleep first. That's the way Emma does.

I like the long black dress. It's shiny and it smells good. When Emma walks, it sounds like paper rattling. That makes me think about presents. She always brings presents back for me and Maria, wrapped in real pretty paper. But not Christmas paper. Maria and I will always remember to bring presents for the children. Maria likes the long black dress, too. She says you should only wear it at night like Emma does. I guess the lady at the train station doesn't know that.

The next morning Maria and I will call each other on the phone and talk for hours about the latest dances and our aching feet. I'll say, "Such fantastic food and wine." Maria will say, "We really should do this more often." I'll throw my head back and laugh. I'll twist my hair around my fingers, get real serious, and ask Maria, "Was 'she' there?"—like Emma does. I asked Maria if "she" meant the lady at the train station. Suddenly, for no reason, Maria would get this real mean look on her face. She'd press her lips together real tight. "You've gotta promise to never tell Emma, Dory, or I'll get in trouble." I asked her what kind of trouble. When she wouldn't tell me, I told her I'd tell Emma. But she grabbed my arm and twisted it real hard. "I'll break it!" she yelled.

Sometimes she'd squeeze my arm so tight that I thought she was really going to break it. I'd scream real loud and she'd let go. I knew she wouldn't break it. She's my best friend in the whole world. But sometimes I'd keep right on screaming just to see how loud I could scream.

I heard Emma scream one time. Daddy was fussing at her. She picked up the phone. Then she dropped it and just stood there screaming. Daddy tried to cover her mouth like Maria does me. But she bit him. He snatched his hand back real fast. They stood at the end of the bed, staring at each other. I held my breath 'cause I knew that was going to be it. But they just started laughing real crazylike. Just laughing and rolling all over the bed. One day I'm gonna bite Maria. Maybe she'll think it's funny, too. Yeah, she'll think it's funny. She knows it's just a game. She told me about it.

Maria said grown-ups have a special grown-up game to play. That's the game they play with the lady at the train station. I'm not sure how to play this game. All I know is that I want to play on Emma's side. I don't want her to lose this game. She's my mommy. I think it's fair for me to be on her team. So I asked Maria a lot of questions about it. She said what she always does, "Dory, you ask too many questions. All you need to do is play fair. Like when we play spades. You wouldn't look in someone else's hand and tell that they have the little joker when the big joker is the card that

beats everything. Now would you?" I told her no. But when I know who
has the little joker I can play my other cards smarter. I told her that, too.
All she said was, "Fine, Dory, fine. You're gonna do what you want to do
anyway. You're a spoiled brat and you just want to have everything your
way." She never sounded like herself when she said stuff like that. She
sounded like a grown-up. Emma says Maria is growing up. She's nine years
old. She said I'll probably sound just like that next year.

Yesterday Maria was trying to work a puzzle. She hates for people to talk
to her when she's trying to work those puzzles. But I kept talking anyway,
begging Maria to tell Emma just a little bit about the lady at the train station.
She said we could give Emma a hint right after lunch. But when she came
back, she didn't want to tell Emma anything. I knew it was because of her
mama. But she was mad enough already. I don't like it when she gets too
mad at me. She always gets mad at me when she's really mad at somebody
else. Mrs. Robinson must have done something to her when she went home
for lunch. She's always doing something to make Maria mad. On Saturday
she fixed Maria's hair in corn rows. Maria hates corn rows. Last time Maria
asked for sneakers, her mama bought bobos. Mrs. Robinson's kind of weird.
One time I heard Emma tell Miss Watson that she has a green-eyed monster.
I don't know where she keeps him, but I don't go in that house. I don't
think Maria knows about him. I don't think she'd go back home if she did.

I felt Emma kick my leg under the table, but not real hard. "Are you
going to play in this life or the next?" she asked me. "Huh?" I asked. She
held up the cards, almost showing me what she had in her hand. "Do that
one more time," I said. She made a funny face and pressed the cards to her
chest, acting like a little girl. She pushed her hair back and looked up at the
clock. I knew what she was going to say next. "We've been playing for an
hour, Dory. It's getting late. I think you're tired. You really should go to
bed now." I begged, "Please, just a little longer, Emma?" Oops, it slipped.
I covered my mouth. "What did you call me, Dorian?" she asked. I told
her that I was sorry. That's what Maria and I call her when we're playing
grown-up. She kind of smiled and didn't say anything. So it must have been
okay. She looked at the clock again. Then she looked at her watch. I knew
she was waiting for him. I wondered if he was still with the lady at the train
station. I hate it when he makes us wait like this. "Do you want to do
something else, Mommy?" I asked. Before she answered, I said, "I know
what we can do. We can play hang the man." She shook her head. "Monopoly?" She shook her head again. "I know," I said, "let's dance." I stood
on my chair to turn on the radio. I knocked over the sugar can. She caught
it as it rolled off the counter. She pulled me back down into my chair. "No,
we will not dance," she said. "Well, then, here," I said, pushing the book

across the table. "Let's finish *Little Women*." She smiled a little bit. I think she was going to do it, but we heard Daddy's car pull into the garage. Emma threw her cards on the table and ran to the back door. She was so happy to see him. She acted like a puppy licking and kissing his face. He was sort of happy to see her. But not happy like when he sees the lady at the train station.

Every night I would sit at the top of the stairs next to their door. Sometimes I could hear him telling Mommy that he loved her. She would ask, "Only me?" Daddy said, "You're the only woman in my life, Emma." They would talk some more and the bed would squeak a lot. I couldn't hear them talking anymore so I would go to my room. I told Maria about it. She said, "See, I told you, Dory. It's all just a part of the game." I told her, "Humph, it's not much of a game to me. I don't like this game at all." It just seems to me that Emma should know who has the little joker.

The next morning when I woke up Emma was bouncing up and down on my bed singing, "Wake up, sleepyhead." I sat up on my elbows so I could see if the sun was in Mr. Teddy's cup. When Grandaddy was here last summer, he teased me a lot about staying in bed too long. He said Emma did the same thing when she was a little girl. Grandaddy has lots of funny ideas. He propped Mr. Teddy on the rocker and tied my yellow cup on his arm. "Now, Dory," he said, "when the sun is in this cup, it's twelve noon. All little girls should be up by then." "Why?" I asked. "So you won't miss anything," he told me. When I asked him how he knew it was noon, he said it was because he lived on a farm and farmers just know about these things. Grandaddy told me a long story about farmers. There was a lot of stuff about chickens and getting up early.

I told Maria. She thought I was real smart. Grandaddy said even Emma could tell time by the sun. Maria liked that part a whole lot. That's why she let me teach her how to tell time in Mr. Teddy's cup. Grandaddy said this was our little game. We shook hands and all that stuff. I liked Grandaddy. He always came to my room to talk to me. Daddy never came in my room unless it was to get Mommy. I hugged Grandaddy every day that he stayed with us. His gray whiskers stuck in my face, but I hugged him harder anyway. He'd pick me up so I could almost touch the light. Then he'd bounce me on my bed a while and just stand there staring out the window. Sometimes he took his pipe out of his pocket and beat it in his hand. He told me that holding the cup would keep Mr. Teddy busy. "That's funny," I said, "'cause Mr. Teddy needs something to keep him busy, and Daddy said you need something to keep you busy." That made him laugh. Then he said the strangest thing. He said Daddy was busy enough for both of them. Then he called me Emma. Grandaddy had a strange look on his face when he said that. "I'm not Emma," I told him. "I'm Dory." He pulled my braid and said, "You seem to be one and the same to me, Dory." I wasn't sure what he meant, but I like him thinking I was the same as Emma.

We had a real good time that summer. Daddy came home early every night. He even stayed home from work one day. He wore blue overalls like Grandaddy. Emma and I wore some, too. We dug up the backyard and planted a garden. We worked in it all summer, getting dirty and laughing a lot. Maria worked in the garden with us. Mrs. Robinson never came over, but Emma sent vegetables to her. Sometimes she sent them back cooked into vegetable pies. I didn't really like them, but Emma and Grandaddy liked them a lot. So I pretended to like them, too. When summer was almost over, Grandaddy went back to his farm. Daddy drove him to the airport early one morning before the sun was in Mr. Teddy's cup. Emma sat on the steps with me and Maria and watched them drive away. She started to cry. Maria and I cried, too. I missed him. He made everybody happy at our house. I forgot about the lady at the train station. I think Daddy forgot about her, too.

One day Maria told me that she wanted to live on a farm when she grew up. "I thought you wanted to be like Emma," I told her. "I do," she said. "Emma lives here. You can't live on a farm and be like Emma," I said. But she told me that she could be Emma when she used to live on a farm. Maria didn't even know Emma then. I asked her how she could do that, but she told me not to worry about it. I didn't have time to worry about it because Emma came to the door talking real fast about new school clothes, a busy day, and hurry.

Mrs. Robinson was already in the car when we got to the garage. It didn't take long to get downtown. We went to a lot of shops. Emma had me trying on all kinds of stuff. I lost Maria for a while. I guess Mrs. Robinson had her someplace trying on a bunch of stuff, too. We found them and drove to the mall. Maria and I talked about our new clothes. Emma and Mrs. Robinson were talking, too. I wanted to listen, but they were so quiet. Besides, Maria kept talking. When we got to the mall, Maria and I went to the arcade. We played Ms. Pac Man until we ran out of tokens. "What do we do now?" I asked Maria. I knew what Maria wanted to do. We said it at the same time. "Let's go to Gino's and eat with Emma." I added, "And your mama, too."

Emma and Mrs. Robinson were sitting out front at Gino's watching the ice skaters. Maria wanted to ice-skate, but I wanted to roller-skate. After she found out that I put her roller skates in the car instead of her ice skates, she was a little bit mad. She kept calling me a brat. It didn't matter as long as I knew she was going to the train station to skate with me. Mrs. Robinson and Emma were talking with their heads close together. Emma's black hair and Mrs. Robinson's red hair looked pretty. It looked like they had one head with two colors. Like Jabo, the downtown clown.

Then Maria said, "Let's play Emma and Ruby. You can be Ruby and I'll be Emma," she told me. I like to play grown-up, but I don't like it when I have to be Maria's mama. Maria and I got into another fight. She wanted me to be her mama 'cause I'm short like her mama. I might be short like her mama, but I dress like my mommy. When I told Maria that, she just said, "Well, then, your stupid Teddy Bear could be Emma 'cause it dresses just like her, too." That made me mad because Mr. Teddy is a boy. I yelled at Maria. She got angry and grabbed my arm. She squeezed it real tight. I screamed, but she wouldn't let go. I screamed again. She tried to cover my mouth with her hand. I was going to bite it when her mama yanked her away from me. Mrs. Robinson pushed Maria into a chair. "I'm surprised at you two," she said, "making all these loud noises in public." She didn't sound surprised to me—just long and boring. No wonder Maria wants to be Emma, I thought. Mrs. Robinson kept talking on and on. I kept waiting for her to stop, but it was taking a long time and Maria was making some awful faces. Mrs. Robinson waved to a lady passing by. I whispered to Maria, "Okay, you can be Emma." Maria smiled. Emma touched both of us on the hand and said, "Now, isn't this much better than fighting?" Mrs. Robinson said, "They're both impossible. You should have both of them, Emma." Emma smiled and winked at us. "Maria would pack up and leave with you at a moment's notice," she said. Emma said, "That would be nice. Dory needs a sister to share her things. It will keep her from being spoiled." I said, "I'm not spoiled, Mommy." She pulled my braid. "You're not spoiled too bad," she said. I pushed her away. I always pretended not to like it when she did that. It always made her do it again.

The waitress came over to our table. I was already waving my hand, telling everybody that I knew what I wanted. Maria squeezed my hand under the table. I pulled it away, trying to pretend I didn't know what she wanted. Then she kicked my knee. I knew what she wanted then. I licked my tongue at her. She grinned at Emma. "You order first. I'm having whatever you have." So Emma ordered a hot fudge sundae and a glass of water. Mrs. Robinson said, "Does that mean you and I are on a diet, Dory?" I mumbled, "I guess so." She ordered frozen strawberry yogurt and coffee. Mrs. Robinson went to the bathroom. When Maria wasn't looking, Emma fed me her sundae, drank my coffee, and ate that awful yogurt. When Mrs. Robinson sat down again, she smiled at me. "I see you like yogurt, Dory." I smiled back and made a face when she wasn't looking. She leaned over and asked Emma, "Why don't you have another child?" Emma made a face and said,

"Heavens, no! Jack wasn't ready for Dory. We're not going to talk about another baby until he gets the business of Dory straight in his head." Mrs. Robinson said, "I guess it was a big change for him, from the great player to the great father and husband. That is quite a change." Emma said, "I was thinking more of the things that we gave up as a couple." Mrs. Robinson said, "I can't tell that he's given up anything. It seems to me you've given up everything." Emma sat back in her chair and looked at Mrs. Robinson like she looked at me when she didn't understand something that I had done. I was staring at Mommy. I guess she didn't like that either. She reached into her pocketbook and handed me a deck of cards. "Play with these and stop listening to my conversation," she said. I pushed the cards over to Maria. She pulled her face out of her bowl and opened the cards. Mrs. Robinson said, "I could keep Dory for you, sometimes." Emma said, "Thank you, but we need to spend time with Dory. Besides, Miss Watson comes whenever I need her."

Mommy bent down to put her pocketbook on the floor. Mrs. Robinson smiled that awful smile. When Mommy sat up she said, "You know, he's a very handsome man, Emma." She smiled and drank some coffee. "He makes good money," she added. She smiled again and drank some more coffee. Mommy shook her head. "Yes, he's handsome and he does earn good money." Mrs. Robinson said, "There's a lot to be said for men and their money." She smiled a third time and picked up her cup. She touched it to Mommy's glass. "Here's to a man with money," she said. "Wish we all had one." Mommy snatched her glass back so fast she spilled the water in her lap. Mrs. Robinson smiled as Mommy tried to wipe the water off her dress. She kept right on talking like nothing happened. "And to their ladies of leisure," she said. Mommy bit down on her lip like Maria does when she's getting ready to twist my arm. She just looked at Mrs. Robinson for a long time. Then she said, "I think we should drink to minority business loans and women who work hard to make men's dreams come true. Or better yet," she said, "let's drink to ambitious women who bleed men dry." She slammed her glass down hard on the table. Mrs. Robinson stopped smiling. Mommy looked at me. I was staring at them with my mouth open. I guess she didn't like that either. "Play with those cards," she said. She looked up like she was talking to God and said, "That child will repeat every word of this tomorrow." I pushed the cards over to Maria. She pulled her face out of her bowl and opened the cards. Mrs. Robinson said again, "I could keep Dory for you sometimes if you'd like to go with your husband more." Emma said, "Thank you, but it's like I told you, we need to spend time with Dory." Maria squeezed my arm. "Would you please stop staring at them and play cards with me?" I didn't want to play. Something was going

on. Emma was getting mad, and Mrs. Robinson acted like she wanted
her to.

Mrs. Robinson said, "Emma, why don't you put Dory in boarding school
or get a live-in housekeeper?" Mommy was looking at the ice skaters. I guess
she didn't hear Mrs. Robinson. So Mrs. Robinson kept on talking. "I would
if it were me," she said. "I'd put Maria in a boarding school in a minute."
Maria looked at Mrs. Robinson kind of madlike for a long time. You heard
that, I thought. Mrs. Robinson didn't seem to mind, though. She kept right
on talking. "You better go with him, protect your interest," she said. "I'm
afraid that's not all there is to it," Mommy said slowly. "That's all there was
to it when Frank left me," said Mrs. Robinson angrily. "Jack is a player,
just like Frank," she went on. "Men like that don't want women and kids.
Why don't you admit it? And don't give me that responsibility shit either."
Me and Maria's eyes got real big. We covered our mouths. Ooh! Mrs.
Robinson said a curse word. Mommy said, "That's enough, Ruby," real
loud. Mrs. Robinson looked real scared then. Maria and I sat real quiet,
pretending to put the cards back into the box. Finally Mommy said, "Come
here, Dory." She held up the prettiest ribbons I had ever seen. They were
supposed to be for school, but I talked her into letting me wear mine now.
Maria got a present, too. She gave Maria a box of headbands with a lot of
different colors, just like my ribbons. It was so funny when Maria told
Mommy thank you, 'cause she slipped and called her Emma. I thought it
was funny, but Mrs. Robinson started fussing at her. She would have fussed
a whole lot, but Mommy said, "Ruby, please, let's not make a big deal of
it." Mommy pushed her chair back and stood up. She had a big wet spot
on her pink dress where the water spilled on her. "I've got a few more things
to pick up and I can go home and . . . and get out of this wet dress." Me
and Maria finished the sentence for her. All of us started laughing, even
Mrs. Robinson. I still didn't feel like being around her anymore, so I asked
if Maria and I could take the bus to the old train station and skate. Mommy
said, "No," but Mrs. Robinson said she thought it was a good idea. Mommy
said, "Ruby, all kinds of people go there. The worst kinds." I turned around
for her to tie my ribbons. "Why do you like that place anyway, Dory?" she
asked. "Why don't you let me take you to a nice clean skating rink?" I said,
"'Cause I like to skate outdoors." Maria said, "Me, too. And I like the smooth
pavement. All the kids go there, Mrs. York." Mrs. Robinson said, "See, you
have nothing to worry about." "Okay, okay," Mommy said, "if you like old
run-down buildings, rusty pipes, broken windows, and peeling paint, go right
ahead."

Mrs. Robinson wanted to come by the train station and pick us up. I
told her we could walk home. "Fine, Dory, just do whatever you want to

do." She sounded just like Maria. After we got our skates from the car they waited with us until the bus came. Me and Maria hugged Emma before we left, but I still didn't feel good about leaving her. I just kept thinking that me and Maria had taken Mrs. Robinson's side against her. I would never do that.

I was looking out the window, thinking about my mommy and daddy. I wanted to grow up as quickly as possible, so I could understand things like Maria. I tugged on Maria's arm. She stopped gooing and cooing with the baby across the aisle. "What's a player, Maria?" I asked. "Just someone who plays like a card player or a baseball player or a piano player," she said. I asked, "Are you sure, Maria?" She just gave me that look. I was just looking to make sure she was telling me right. She'll be a grown-up soon. And I know they don't tell you everything. Anyway, I wanted to know what a boarding school was and all that other stuff I heard Mommy and Mrs. Robinson talking about at Gino's. I turned back to the window. Maria went back to her cooing and gooing with the baby across the aisle. I thought about Mrs. Robinson trying to get my Mommy to have another baby. I almost fell out of my seat trying to see the baby across the aisle. It was wrapped in a yellow blanket with only its head showing. It looked like a turtle. I sat back in my seat. I hate turtles.

When we got to the train station, Maria and I strapped on our skates and moved in with other kids. We skated fast and held hands. We were skating around and around the big poles when we saw the lady sitting on the steps wearing her black dress and long white beads. Maria pulled me over behind an old boxcar. "It's her, Dory," she whispered. "I know," I whispered. "But I think this game is over, Maria. Grandaddy told my daddy something when he was here that made him forget all about that lady. Remember how he came home early every night. I told you, Maria, he said Mommy was the only woman in his life." Maria smiled. "I don't think he's coming either." We watched her as she walked up one side and down the other, looking all around. She almost caught us looking at her one time. She sat down on the steps again. We watched her cross her legs and sway back and forth like she was listening to the music. We heard footsteps. She heard them, too. I saw my daddy's shiny black shoes and gray pants. She jumped up and ran toward the old passenger waiting shed. She threw her arms around my daddy's neck. He kissed her just like she was Mommy. He was turning her around and around like he does Mommy. I smelled his perfume all over the train station. The train station was just like Mommy's room when Maria and I sprayed too much perfume. Mommy always said, "Don't spray too much; it'll make you sick." It was too much perfume. It was just too much. It made me sick.

I looked at Maria. She stood there with her hand over her mouth. Then she said, "She's not tall like Emma." I said, "She doesn't have pretty black hair like Emma." Maria said, "She doesn't have pretty white teeth like Emma. Not even a pretty smile like Emma." I said, "To tell the truth, she's kind of fat. She can't even walk pretty like Emma." A freight train passed by, blowing its horn long and loud. When the last car rolled by, Emma and Mrs. Robinson were standing there like they had just gotten off the train. Mommy rushed over to me, brushing my hair and dusting off my dress. "Look at you, Dory," she said. "You're a mess." Mrs. Robinson saw Daddy and the lady on the other side. "Well, well," she said with that same smile on her face, the smile she had at Gino's. "I think you've got a bigger mess than that on your hands." She pointed right at Daddy and the lady. Mommy looked at them. She walked closer to them, looking like she wasn't sure they were there. I looked at Mrs. Robinson. She still had that weird smile on her face.

Mommy screamed real loud and ran away. Daddy called out for her to come back, but she kept walking and running real fast. When she ran past me she almost knocked me down. She was crying, crying real hard. I tried to catch up with her. It was hard to run in skates. But I caught up with Mommy at the bottom of the hill, waiting to cross Georgia Avenue. Daddy ran up behind her and caught her by the arm. She snatched away from him and ran into the street. I don't know exactly what happened. After that, I was lying in the street. People were standing over me talking loud. Red lights were flashing. Some lady was yelling, "Oh, my God!" and a crazy man was yelling, "I didn't see them." I sat up on my knees. My head hurt and blood was dripping from my nose. A man in a white coat said, "Don't move, little girl. Help is coming for you." I didn't need help. I just needed my mommy. My arms were bleeding, but they didn't hurt. I stood up, looking around for her. Mommy was there, lying on the ground. Her face was real bloody. It didn't look like Mommy. The men from the hospital were doing something to her. They said they were going to make her all right. But they didn't. Daddy was crying and saying her name over and over. Mrs. Robinson had her arms around him, patting his back and saying a bunch of stuff. But where was Maria? I was going to get Maria to help me. That's when the man hit my mommy real hard with his fist. There was a real loud scream. Loud and long like when I heard Mommy scream before. But not just like it. The scream was getting closer and closer, louder and louder. It was Maria. She put her arm around me. She was screaming and saying, "We've got to do something, Dory!" Me and Maria tried to push the policeman, so we could help Mommy. But the man in the white coat shoved us away, real hard. "Somebody get these kids!" he yelled. The policeman picked me up.

I saw a lot of people looking at me—a lot of people I had never seen before. I saw Mommy's pocketbook open on the ground. Everything was scattered on the street. My cards were everywhere. I started counting, looking for all of them. The last one was lying beside Mommy's hand, the little joker, bloody. She was lying there like a broken doll. I knew we couldn't play with those cards ever again.

Emma never came home after that day. I wish she had. I missed her. Everything was different in our house. No one ever talked to me about anything, except Maria. She did all the things with me that Emma used to do. She even played Monopoly with me. She used to hate Monopoly. Sometimes we would stare at the picture of Emma in the hall for a long time without talking. It was real lonesome for me and Maria, just like when Grandaddy left. We tried to be good. That's the way Miss Watson said Emma would have wanted us to be, real good, not causing any trouble for anybody. We were good, but we could never be good enough for Mrs. Robinson. She always fussed at us. Something was always wrong. One day she told me and Maria that she was going to get rid of us soon as she could. She pulled my hair real hard—not the way Emma used to, but real hard. "The very next thing you do, I'm sending you away from here," she said over and over again. I wondered how she could send me away. I didn't live at her house, and she wasn't my Mommy.

She's playing that game that grown-ups play. I told Miss Watson about it. She fussed with Mrs. Robinson. But it doesn't matter now 'cause she's sending us all away now, even Miss Watson. Daddy and Mrs. Robinson put me and Maria on the train early one morning. Mrs. Robinson was smiling that awful smile. Daddy never looked up at me and Maria, not even when he said good-bye. Maria told me that we were going to Saint Agnes House, a boarding school in the country. Maria stopped talking. She was staring out the window. I looked where she was looking. Mrs. Robinson and Daddy were kissing. I told Maria about her mama in Emma's bed that night when I heard it squeaking. It's because of me that we had to leave. I told Maria about telling Miss Watson, and how she fussed at her mama. "I'm sorry, Maria," I told her. "I wouldn't have gone in the room, but I thought Emma had come home again." Maria didn't say anything for a long time. She was pointing at trees and houses passing by like she was counting them. I didn't know what to say, so I just didn't say anything. Maria stopped counting or pointing or whatever. "It's not your fault," she said. "It's just grown-ups and all those games." "I don't know if I want to grow up," I said. Maria was crying. I didn't know what to do, so I held her hand the way Emma used to hold my hand when I cried. Maria told me that she was afraid that we would die just like Emma. But I told Maria that we wouldn't because I learned a lot about this game. When it's our turn to play, we'll play smarter. Maria smiled. It was a nice smile like Emma's smile. It was good to see Maria smile again. She said she was going to take care of me and Mr. Teddy, so I told her that when we get to Saint Agnes House she can be Emma when she used to live on a farm.

LONNIE'S COUSIN

Wanda Coleman

I'm so glad you're home. I was so alone. No one here but me and the baby.

It's okay. I'm back now.

I tried so hard to keep it together. But the neighbors—that Lonnie and his people. They smile and they act nice to you, but they ain't your friends, and they ain't mine.

What do you mean?

While you were gone, they tried to fix me up with their cousin.

What?

I was so stupid. I thought they wanted to be friends—thought they were looking out for me because you were gone.

Uh-huh.

They tried to get me into trouble—to do something I didn't want to do.

What happened?

You know what they think of us, don't you?

What do you mean by that?

They see you got a black wife. And you livin' down here in the ghetto. You got to be pretty stupid for a white man. That's what they think of you. The only reason they pay any attention to me is because I'm with you.

We're friends—Lonnie and me.

You're the manager and they're the tenants. They've been in this building longer than we have. The owner—the only reason he made you manager is because you're the only white face in here. You're cheaper than hiring outside help. And he don't trust nobody black.

What you're saying is really ugly. I don't believe it.

Listen to me. Listen good. They wanted their cousin in my panties. To bring us down. You hear that?

I'm not sure what I'm hearing.

Fool.

Don't cry. Look, honey. I'm willing to listen. Tell me what they did to you.

Okay.

Sunday I was planning to make you some fudge for when you got back. I was getting the cocoa and stuff ready in the kitchen—about eleven o'clock. And the baby woke up and started crying. I had his crib in there in the living room near the stereo, and I'm in the middle of finding out he's wet when the doorbell rings.

So I run to the door. And Lonnie is there, grinning all in my face—acting friendly. He sure fools me, talking about why don't I bring the baby and come downstairs and visit with him and his wife. I figure it's safe because he's married. Even though I don't know them, I've seen his wife and she looks like someone I'd like to befriend. But I hesitates because I'm making fudge. But he says to come just a little while because he knows I must be lonely, you being away. Well, I was. So I changed the baby, bundled him up, put a bottle and a couple of diapers in the bag, and went downstairs.

See. He was just being neighborly. I knew it.

Hush up and let me tell it.

So when I get down there there's this other couple and they's dancing, smoking, and drinking beer and all—having a good time. And then they introduce me to this ugly old man—he's their cousin.

What's his name?

I don't know. I forgets it. But I'll remember him as long as I live.

What did he do to you—if anything?

He put a spell on me. He hexed me.

Come on. Bullshit.

Listen.

He put a spell on you?

Those things happen. Whether you believes or not.

This is the twentieth century.

You gonna hear me out?

Go ahead.

Lonnie's wife, she come up to me cooing about the baby, asking me the usual stuff like she's really interested. She takes the baby and lays him on the loveseat near the door where I can watch him. So that means I got to sit opposite him on the couch next to Lonnie's cousin. I don't think about that. I'm just sitting there. They offer me a beer. I tell 'em I don't drink, 'specially beer because I think it tastes like cow piss. And they laugh. So Lonnie's wife she gets some cherries and she fixes me a drink with lots of cherry juice in it real cold over ice. And it don't taste too bad—like punch with a twang. Lonnie's friend—the other guy—he come over and ask me to dance.

What about the cousin?

I'm getting to that. The friend he asks me to dance. We all up dancing and the friend's lady, she's dancing, too, by herself off on the side so she can change the 45s on the stereo.

Then what?

Then I notice his cousin is looking at me. He don't seem to be, but I can feel his eyes got feet and they walking all over me. And they strange, heavy eyes—got them thick lids. Look like he damn near half asleep or something.

How old a man is he?

I don't know. Forty, maybe fifty. Way older than us. One of these country-looking men, but he's not. He had on this stingy brim panama and belted slacks *and* suspenders both, like he about to lose his pants. And they was khaki. And he had on a pink shirt.

Did he have an accent?

No. He talked regular like us. And he was *real* dark. Twice—three times my color. Dark as that there fudge I made.

And all he did was look at you?

At first. But after a couple of records Lonnie pushed him up from the couch to dance and I was his partner. But he didn't touch me. We just fast-danced. He just made like he was dancing enough to make us laugh, then he sat down again. By that time I was having a good time. And I just naturally was relaxed and started talking to him.

Talking about what?

About stuff. Whatever he asked me or came up. You and me. The weather. Television and movies. Like that. But I felt his eyes pulling at me, drawing me into them. My heart started beating real fast. I felt hot and all sticky under my arms. And I started falling into his eyes. And then I pulled my eyes away, but they got stuck on his lips. He had real thick lips. Big, dark, and smooth. And he moved closer to me. I scooted back. And he eased still closer to me. And I'm on the couch with no place to go, backed against the arm of it, even leaning backwards. But I'm deeply drawn to him at the same time. I'm not talking anymore. I'm listening. He's telling me I'm beautiful. I don't know how beautiful I am, he says. And he reaches his hand up and brushes my hair back. And a feeling goes through me I've never felt before. He put his spell on me right then.

What kind of feeling was it?

I don't know. Like, if I'd've been standing, my feet woulda gone out from under me. He took his other hand and stroked my thigh and I almost passed out.

Describe it.

Like electricity near about. I don't know what. But I knew that if he kept touching me like that he was gonna have his way with me. And I wouldn't be able to say no to nothing.

Then what?

He put his arm around my head and kissed me, pulling me in against his chest.

Then what? Come on, tell me what it felt like. Quit crying, woman. I'm not angry at you—honey, tell me.

I'm so ashamed.

Don't be. Not at all. I'm here and I'm listening.

He kissed me to my soul. I couldn't break free. I kissed him back. I couldn't help it. I was under his spell. When he let go, everybody was looking at me. Lonnie and his wife and the other couple—dead in their tracks— like they were all kissing me. Like voodoo or something. It felt real strange. The strangest feeling I ever felt. I could hear what they was thinking. I came halfway to myself. I said how it was getting late and I had to go finish making that fudge I'd promised you. So I scooped up the baby and hurried out of there so fast I forgot his little diapers and stuff. I ran back upstairs here.

And that's all?

He followed me up here after a few minutes. He was carrying the baby's bag.

And you let him in.

I tried not to. But he put that spell on me again—I was still under it. He just reached through the screen door when I grabbed for the bag and caught my hand. And it was his touch—he got a touch like satin and a voice like satin. Black satin. Standing right there in the doorway. Then he pulled me to him and started feeling me all over. Hands and eyes. He lifted me right into him, and I could feel him hard through his trousers. I was lost to him.

You did that?

I didn't know I was so weak. I swear I could not help myself. He had greater powers than I had. Will power don't work against no spell.

Then what?

The baby woke up and started crying. I ran over and got him and put him between us. Then I made him hold the baby while I started making the fudge. He got uneasy and said he was going downstairs and get something to drink so would I please take the baby back. Soon as he left I pulled all the curtains and locked the door. I took the baby into the bedroom here and turned up the television so loud I couldn't hear the doorbell ring when he got back. Later I fixed us dinner. Me and the baby fell asleep in here on the bed. Then you woke us up coming in this morning.

And that's all? That's it?

Ain't that enough?

You're positive you didn't let him fuck you.

I couldn't. I love you, honey. I couldn't do that and live with myself. I know that now. Spell or no spell.

You didn't let him fuck you.

Because of you. You and the baby. Plus I couldn't give Lonnie and his bunch the satisfaction of knowing their cousin got me. The thought of them laughing at us behind our backs really makes me mad. They'd love the chance to run us out of here. That's the kind of lowlife they are.

Why should I believe you didn't let him fuck you? You wanted it.

I didn't want that ugly old man. He made me want him. That's how a spell works. He was so ugly he was beautiful. He the kinda man Mama Creole used to warn me about. The kind that know women better than women know themselves.

And he touched you—your breasts.

He reached up under the blouse I had on—my little white top with the angel sleeves.

Did he kiss you at the same time?

Yes.

What else did he do?

I don't want to talk about it no more.

But I want to talk about it. I want to hear it again. All of it.

That was all of it.

I have a right to know what he did to you. I'm not sure you're telling everything.

But I said.

That was too general. I want specifics. You said he was darker than you are.

Yes. Almost purple-black. Much darker than Lonnie and his wife. It's hard to believe they're blood kin.

His hands. How big were his hands? Bigger than mine?

Why? You seen him around before?

No. I just want to know.

In case you see him again?

Quit stalling and tell me.

I'm not stalling. I'm just concerned. Yeah—his hands was twice—three times bigger than yours.

And his lips.

Thick. Very.

Did he smell?

Yeah, come to think of it.

Like what?

I hadn't thought till you asked—but he had a real strong funk to him. Like a wino. Only not so bad. Kind of pleasant. But strong and musty.

And his eyes. What were they like? What color?

Black-brown. Like big old olives swimmin' 'round in a yellow dish. You could see the veins in them. They was eyes that's done lots of living.

What was he built like? Was he as tall as me?

By about half a head. And he was lanky. But real strong. Like a man that works the earth.

And he kissed you.

Yes. It made me weak all over when he kissed me. Don't make me keep telling it.

Don't I ever make you feel the way he did?

It's not the same thing. You're my husband. He had me under a spell. I love you and you love me naturally. What he was about was no good.

Tell it to me again. From the beginning. Word-for-word.

No.

Come on. Tell it.

Please don't make me.

Look, honey—relax. I've forgiven you. I believe you. Really, I do understand. Things like that happen.

Do you? Oh, thank you—*thank you.*

Now you said you felt a weakness all over when he touched you.

I was so scared. I was afraid you'd be angry and want to leave me. I was so afraid to tell you. But I had to. You needed to be warned about Lonnie and them in case they try another trick.

No, honey, I'm not going to leave you. Not because of something like that. So don't worry. And don't worry about Lonnie. I'll deal with him. Now tell me again, and start at that part about how he made you feel when he first touched you.

I don't want to talk about it no more. I want to forget it ever happened.

That's all right. I want to hear it. From the start. When you first saw him—Lonnie's cousin.

You mean, when he was telling me how beautiful I was and stroking my hair.

Yeah. Start with that part.

Are you serious?

And then he touched your thigh. Like this?

Near about. But it felt different because I was under the spell, remember.

But what exactly did he do that caused the spell. What did he say?

It wasn't what he said as much as what he didn't say. Why you looking at me so funny like?

It's all right, honey. It's really all right. Tell it to me slowly, like it's in slow motion. Close your eyes and tell it to me again. From the start. From feeling so alone—me gone—just you here and the baby—and then Lonnie comes up to the door. And when you get to the part where he touches you, tell it extremely slow. Moment to moment so I can imagine what it felt like.

What?

Come on, honey. Do it for me.

Am I hearing what you're saying?

Don't be hurt. Believe me, baby—believe in me. You believe in spells. Give me your hand. There, now. Feel that. See how hard and good that feels. And it's all yours. And after you finish telling me that story again, I'm gonna give it all to you. But before I do, I want to hear it all one more time. And don't cry when you tell it. Tell it like you enjoyed it.

Tell it just like it happened.

THE LIFE YOU LIVE

(MAY NOT BE YOUR OWN)

J. California Cooper

Love, marriage, and friendship are some of the most important things in your life . . . if you ain't sick or dyin'! And, Lord knows, you gotta be careful, careful 'cause you sometimes don't know you been wrong 'bout one of them till after the mistake shows up! Sometimes it takes years to find out, and all them years are out of your own life! It's like you got to be careful what life you live, 'cause it may not be your own! Some love, marriage, or friend done led you to the wrong road, 'cause you trusted 'em!

Of course, I'm talkin' 'bout myself, but I'm talkin' 'bout my friend and neighbor, Isobel, too. Maybe you, too! Anyway, if the shoe don't fit, don't put it on!

I might as well start at the beginning. See, Isobel and I went to school together, only I lived in town and she came in from the country. Whenever she came. Her daddy was always keepin' her home from school to do work on that ol' broke-down farm of his. He was a real rude, stocky, solid, bearlike, gray-haired man with red-rimmed eyes. Can't lie about him, he worked all the time hisself. But that's what he wanted to do with his life. His kids, they didn't mind workin', but not ALL the time! He never gave them any money to spend on pleasure things like everybody need if they gonna keep workin' all the time.

He was even stingy at the dinner table. Grow it or don't get it! Even his horses and cows was thin. Everything on his farm didn't like him. All his kids he hadn't put out for not workin' left soon as they could, whether they was out of school yet or not! That finally left only Isobel. She did farm work and all the housework, small as she was. Her mother was sickly. I 'magine I'd get sick, too, if I knew that man was comin' home to me every day!

He ran all the boys off who came out to see Isobel. He either put them to work on some odd job or told 'em not to come back. I know, 'cause when we was 'bout sixteen and still in high school I rode out there with one boy who was scared to go by hisself. I wasn't scared of nothin' . . . then!

I saw that ol' man watchin' and waitin' for us to reach the house. Isobel was standing in the doorway, a pot in her hands and a apron on, getting ready to go slop some pigs. She looked . . . her face was all cracked, it seemed. Not 'cause she liked that boy so much, but because she wanted to be young, 'stead of old like her father. We left.

Now me, I grew up any which way in my parents' house, full of kids and everybody building their own world right there inside that house. We had the kind of family that when Mama and Daddy was gone off on some business or other and we s'posed to clean the house? we would slop soapy water all over the kitchen floor, put our skates on and have a skating rink party. Oh! That was fun, fun! Then as soon as Mama and Daddy drive up, them skates be off! We could mop, dust, wash dishes, make beds, whatever, before they got in the house! There! Poor, for sure, but happy!

Well, you know you grow up and forget everybody and everything 'cept your own special business. That's what I did. I was grown and married twelve years when Isobel came back into my life. She had been married 'bout seven years then herself.

Tolly was her husband's name, and he had done got to be a good friend of my husband. Tolly was a travelin' salesman, for true. He had traveled right on Isobel's daddy's farm and stole that girl right out from under her daddy's time clock she was still punching at. She was twenty-four years old then, still not ever married. We was both thirty-one or so when they moved next door to me and Gravy.

I was very glad to have a old school chum for a neighbor. I had just at that time left one of them ladies' clubs that ain't nothing but fussing, gossip, and keepin' up with the Joneses type of thing. Not doin' nothin' important! Just getting together to go to each other's houses to see how everybody else was livin'! Stuff like that. My usual best friend had moved away from this town, and I didn't have a new one I trusted. My mama had told me that I would look up one day and could count my friends on one hand and sometimes one finger! She was right . . . again.

One day, just before Tolly and Isobel moved in their new house, he was over to see Gravy, and I told him, "You all have dinner over here with us on your movin' day. Tell Isobel don't bother with no cookin'!"

He looked at me like I was in space. "Better not do that, Molly. I been puttin' off telling you that for some reason Isobel won't tell me, she does not like you . . . at all!"

I was honestly shocked. "Not like me? Why?"

He frowned and shook his head. "Won't tell me why. Just got awful upset when I told her you was going to be our neighbor."

I never heard of such a thing! "Upset?"

He nodded his head. "I mean she was! Almost didn't want to move here! There just ain't nowhere else I like right now, and the price is right."

I thought a minute. "Well, when you all move in, I'll find out what's wrong! I can't remember nothing I ever did to her. I was lookin' forward to havin' you two close—"

He cut me off. "Don't count on it! Isobel is kinda sickly, and it makes her awful mean to get along with! Sometimes I want to give up, but we married and I'm gonna make it work, single-handed if I have to!"

I sat down, wondering. In all the time we knew him I never had guessed they had a problem marriage.

He turned to my husband. "Man, you lucky havin' a wife like Molly. Molly got sense. My woman think everybody always lyin' to her!" He turned to me. "If you ever run into her accident'ly don't mention nothin' 'bout my name! She b'lives every woman is after me! Anyway, she say you already done told all kinda lies on her when you all was in school."

I gasped, 'cause it wasn't true!

He kept talkin'. "She told me some terrible things about you! But I know how she lies, so I didn't pay them no mind."

Gravy was looking at him with a funny-lookin' frown on his face. I looked like I was being pushed out of a airplane.

Tolly ended up telling us, as he shook his head sadly, "She goes to bed . . . and every mornin' when she gets up, the pillowcase be just full of blood. Her mouth bleeds from rotten teeth. Her breath stinks! Bad! She don't never bathe. I have to make her! We don't have kids like you-all 'cause she hates 'em! Hates sex!" He looked at Gravy. "I have to *fight* her to get a little lovin'!"

Oh, he told us so many bad things about his own wife!

When they moved in, I pulled the shades down on that side of the house. And—don't this sound dumb?—we never hardly spoke for twelve years! Twelve years!

If I happen to come out to empty garbage or do something and see her over the hedge, we just did nod and sometimes we pretended we didn't see each other. At the market either, or . . . or anywhere!

Sometimes at some holiday gatherings when we all happen to be there I'd see Isobel. She'd be in a corner somewhere. Sad eyes, mouth always closed, and when she did talk, she put her hand over it. Which made what Tolly said seem true.

Sometimes when I had problems, I'd look over there and wish we were friends. Tolly was gone 'bout four days out of every week. Even when he was home they never went anywhere or had any company. So I knew she had to get lonely sometime. But when Tolly would come over, he always reminded me by some word or other that Isobel did not like me . . . at all.

The twelve years passed without us ever getting together. Ain't that dumb?

You remember I mentioned my problems? They didn't seem to be big ones. All the ladies said I was lucky to have a husband like Gravy. The fact is I got so many things to tell you that happened all at the same time, I don't know how to start.

Now, Gravy was a good husband, good provider. We raised our kids right. One went to college, one got married. Now we were home alone together.

All down through our married years, he always liked me lookin' kinda messy. Said it made me look homey and woman-warm. He urged me to eat to get meat on my bones till you couldn't tell I had any bones! He liked gray hair, so when mine started turning, he wouldn't let me dye it. He didn't like makeup, so I didn't hardly wear none. Just liked my cooking, so we never went out to dinner, I always cooked! He liked me in comfortable clothes, so I had a lot of baggy dresses. Didn't want me to worry my "pretty head," so he took care of all the money.

I looked, by accident, in the mirror one day . . . and I cried! I was a fat, sloppy-dressed, house-shoe wearin', gray-haired, old-lookin' woman! I was forty-three and looked fifty-five! Now, ain't nothin' wrong with bein' fifty-five years old if that's where you are. But I wasn't there yet! I had been lookin' in mirrors through the years, and I could see myself then. I felt bad, but I could take it if it made my husband happy. That last day though, I couldn't take it!

That was the day I saw Gravy in the park. A Sunday. He had gone out to do somethin'. Hadn't said what. I was sitting in the park, on a cold bench, by myself. THEY was walkin', laughin' and holding hands. He even peck-kissed her every once in a while, throwing his arm around her shoulders and pulling her to his old slim body. Not a gray hair on his head 'cause he said his job might think he was gettin' old. He dyed his hair. He just liked mine gray.

Let me tell you, PLEASE! She was slim. Wasn't no potatoes, biscuits, and pork chops sittin' on her hips! She had plenty makeup on. I'd say a whole servin'! Black hair without a spot of gray in it! High-heeled shoes and a dress that kept bouncing up so you could see that pretty underwear she had on. She was half his age! Why, she wasn't his type at all! And I could tell by lookin' at her she didn't know how to cook . . . he took her out!

Big as I was, I jumped behind the bushes and watched 'em slowly pass by, all my weight on my poor little bended knees. Cramped. By the time he got in front of me, I could have yelled a Tarzan holler and leaped on him and beat him into a ass pate.

But . . . I let them pass. I didn't want HER to see how bad I looked! I know I looked crazy, too, as well as ugly.

When they was well past me, I walked like a ape out of them bushes 'cause I couldn't stand up straight too fast! Some kids saw me come out them bushes and musta thought I had gone to the bathroom in there, 'cause they said something about a "swamp" and ran off laughin' . . . at me! I cried all the way home.

I'm telling you, I was hurt. Now, you hurt when somebody meets you and loves you up and in a few days you don't hear from them no more. But . . . this man been lovin' me up twenty-four years! Settin' my life, my looks, and my thoughts! I let him! Well, that hurt filled my whole body and drug my heart down past my toes, and I had to drag it home, forcin' one foot at a time. Going home? Wasn't no home no more. Chile, I hurt! You hear me?!

Now, I'm going to tell you somethin'. If you ain't ready to leave or lose your husband . . . don't get in his face and tell him nothin'! You wait till you got yourself together in your mind! You wait till you have made your heart understand . . . you can and will do without him! Otherwise, you may tell him you know what he's doin', thinking YOU smart and he's caught! And HE may say, "Well, since you know, now you know! I ain't giving her up!" Then what you gonna do?

Tell you what I did. But wait, let me tell you first things first. Gravy came home, sat in his favorite chair lookin' at TV, smokin' his pipe. I stared at him, waiting for him to see that I knew. He didn't see me so I got up, put my hands on my fat hips, nose flaring wide open, and I told him I KNEW!

Gravy put his pipe down, just as calm as I ever seen him in my life, turned off the TV, sat back down, put his hands on his knees, and told me . . . he wanted a divorce.

A DIVORCE?!

I felt like someone had dipped me in cement. I couldn't move. I couldn't speak. I couldn't do nothin' but stare at Gravy. My mind was rushin' back over our years together. Over the last months . . . looking for signs.

We had been so . . . comfortable.

He said to me, "You have let yourself go. You make me feel old. You ARE old."

I thought of answers, but my mouth wouldn't act right. He went on and on.

"I ain't got but one life, it ain't over! I got some good years left!" He patted his chest. "I need someone can move on with me. You don't and can't compete with nobody. You don't know how to do nothin' but cook and eat! You ain't healthy! All that fat! Look at your clothes! Look at your head! A lazy woman can't 'spect to keep a man! You been all right . . . but . . . I GOT to GO! You tell the kids."

My heart was twistin' around in my breast. I was struck!

He went on and on. "We'll sell this house and each get a new fresh start."

At last my lips moved. "Sell this house? My house? My home?"

His lips moved. "Ain't no home no more. Just a house." He got up talking, putting his foot down. "We gonna sell it and split the money and go each our own way."

I said to myself, This m———— f————!

Then I said to him, "You m———— f————!

He walked away. "Ain't no sense in all that. It's too late for sweet names now!"

Now, at first I had been feelin' smart, but that flew out the window. Chile, I lost all my pride, my good sense. Tell you what I did.

I fell out on the couch, cryin', beggin' him to think of our years together, our children, our home, our future, his promises, our dreams. I cried and I begged. Got on my knees, chile! Tears running down, nose running, mouth running, heart stopping. I fought in every way, using everything I could think of to say to hold that man! That man who did not want me! If I had waited till my sense was about me, I'd maybe begin to think of the fact of why was he so much I had to want him? After all, he wasn't no better, no younger than me! I had already had him twenty-four years . . . maybe that was enough! For him AND for me! But I didn't stop to think that. I just cried and begged.

I had heard some old woman say, "If your man 'bout to fight you or leave you, go somewhere, take your drawers off, go back where he is and fall out on the floor and kick your legs open when you fall back! That'll stop him!" Welllll, it don't always work! It don't always stop him as long as you want it to! Gravy stopped for 'bout thirty minutes, then that was over. I was back where I started.

He left, GOING SOMEWHERE. While I sat in my house that would soon be not mine.

Then I fought for that house like I had fought for him. Why, it stood for my whole life! It's all I had, 'sides my grown children, and they was gone on to live their own lives, have their own children, their own husband and wife.

I was alone.

Just yesterday I had a family. A home. I thought it was the worse moment in my life! But, you see, you never know everything till everything happens!

Then all this stuff started happenin' at the same time! Before my house was sold, when Isobel and Tolly had lived next door twelve years, Tolly died. Had a heart attack. A young man, too! Prove that by the fact that he had that attack in bed with a seventeen-year-old girl! Isobel was forty-three, like me. Now she was alone, I was half dead.

I decided to just go on over there, whether she liked me or not! I baked a cake and went to the wake. She was lookin' like a nervous wreck before Tolly died. Now she still looked a wreck but not so nervous. She looked like she was holdin' up quite well. So well I wished Gravy had died 'stead of getting a divorce. Anyway! She looked at me, her lip dropped, her eyes popped. I slammed the cake down as easy as I could, not to hurt that cake, you know, and said, "Yes, it's me! I'm doin' the neighborly thing whether you like me or not, and whether you eat it or not!" Then I turned to go and she grabbed my arm.

"Whether I like YOU?" she asked.

I turned to her. "Yeah! I don't care if you don't like me. I think all this mess is foolishness! I ain't never done nothin' to you!"

She looked kinda shocked. "Why . . . you're the one who does not like me! You didn't want to be friends with me! Tolly told me all those bad things you said about me!"

It was my turn to look shocked . . . again! You might say I was at the time of life where ever' which way I turned, I got shocked.

I gasped. "I never said anything bad about you! I wanted to be your friend."

Her eyes opened wide. "I wanted to be your friend. I needed a friend! I didn't never have nobody but Tolly."

We looked in each other's eyes till we understood that Tolly had planned all this no friendship stuff.

Well, we became friends again. She told me her new name was Belle, said, "Who wants to be named Is-so-bel!" Said, "Now that I am free, I can change my name if I want to! Change my whole life if I want to!" Now!

I learned a lot I did not know, just on account of my not stopping to think for myself. Listenin' to others, taking their words. Trusting them to THINK for me!

Tolly had told Belle the same thing he had told me. PLUS, he ruined that girl's mind! Just shit in it! Told her things like when she talked and opened her mouth, spit stretched from some teeth to some other teeth and just hung there. So she tried never to talk to people.

Told her all kinds of mean, violent things. Every time he went to the store alone, he would tell her stories, like someone was beatin' his wife 'bout tellin' lies. Or someone had killed his wife for lying! Sneaking out on the side! Every day he had things like these to tell her. He would slide out of bed and tell her she was the one left streaks of shit on it, 'cause she didn't wipe herself right! She got where she almost bathed when she went to the bathroom.

He had her believing nobody liked her! Everybody told lies on her! She was weak-minded. A fool about life. Was even ugly. Had a odor. Was very dumb and helpless. That she lost things.

He had taken her wedding rings once, for two years. Hid them. She found them in the bottom of a jar of cold cream. He told her she put them there. She knew she hadn't.

He told her she needed therapy and made her take—GAVE her—hot, hot baths, let the water run out and then he ran cold, cold water on her, holdin' her down in the tub. He threw her food out, said she was tryin' to poison him. Him! Complained he was sick after he would eat somethin' of hers. Whenever they was gettin' along all right and she wanted to go somewhere, he would dress, get to the door, then get very ill. If it was the show, he'd wait till he was in the line almost at the ticket window, then he'd get sick. If they went to the market together, he'd accuse her of talkin' and huggin' a man who had never even been there. He didn't allow her to spend any money except for the house note, food, and insurance. She bought plenty food, paid the house notes, and bought lots of insurance, 'cause that's all she could do!

Wouldn't let her join any clubs. Well, that mighta been good. I was in one at the time I needed to get out of. Tell you about that later!

He kept her up hundreds, thousands of nights, wouldn't let her sleep! Makin' her tell him about her past, and she really didn't have any. From her daddy to him. He had to know that. He did know that! He was sick, crazy. The kind of crazy that can walk around lookin' like everybody else and get away with it! I bet he told Gravy about all them ugly bleeding teeth, bad breath, oh, all them things to keep Gravy away from her when he was out of town!

I never did see her cry.

The slick bastard!

Well, you know. You know all about things like that.

We became friends again. I helped her settle her affairs and all. She said, "I'm gonna sell this prison."

I said, "Sell your only home?" Aghast.

She said, "Money buys another home."

I thought about that!

She said, "Some of the worst times of my life was spent here! First I was glad to leave my daddy's house. Now I'm glad to leave Tolly's! The next house I get is gonna be mine. MINE! I'll live in that one in peace."

I thought about that.

I went to the bank with her to get all the matters set straight. The lady at the desk heard the word *deceased* and looked up in sympathy. But Belle was smiling, a bright, happy smile. She was the happiest woman in the bank!

She sat there in front of that lady, a little ragged, hair undone but neat. Nervous breakdown just leavin', but still showing around the edges. Nails bit off. Lips bit up. Graying hair saying she was older, but bright future-lookin' eyes saying she was ready! MY friend!

That woman really had bought a lot of insurance! Over a hundred thousand dollars' worth! And insurance to pay the house off, the car she couldn't drive yet, off, and any furniture they owed for, off. That's one thing he did for her, he let her buy insurance. And she sure did!

Belle was gaining weight, lookin' way better as time went by. And she was going to the hairdresser, buying clothes, going to shows, nightclubs and restaurants. I went with her most times. I was still in my clubs, a reading club and a social club. I left the reading club 'cause they wanted us to make reports on what we read. I didn't want to make no report! I just wanted to read in peace . . . exchange books, eat, things like that. I dropped out that club and just started buying my own books.

Both Belle and me was lookin' better, healthier, and was more peaceful every day. She was taking painting lessons now and music appreciation. Tolly hadn't liked her to go to school; she might meet somebody. He always told her as he laughed at her, "What kinda thing you goin' over there to waste time doin'? Showing them people how clumsy and dumb you are! Girl, throw that mess out of your mind!" He put little holes in her plans, and her confidence just leaked out. The desire to go had stayed, though. She was the busiest widow I ever did see! Some people might turn over in their graves, but I knew if Tolly could see her he was spinning in his!

I looked at her livin' her life, and I began to really like what I saw. 'Stead of staying home in case Gravy called, I started goin' to a class to lose weight

'cause Belle said it was healthier and I would look better, too! I started goin'
to the hairdresser. Not to dye my hair—that's too much work to keep up—
but a natural ain't nothin' but a nappy if you don't take care of it! It's shaped
and highlighted now. Belle was learning and showed me how to use a little
makeup right. Don't try to hide nothin', just bring out what you got!

She gardened a lot, and I began to help her. We ate fresh vegetables and
bought fresh fruit. Dropped them ham hocks and short ribs, chile, less we
had a special taste for 'em sometime. I didn't miss 'em! Found out all that
rice and gravy and meat was really for Gravy. Wondered how he was eatin'
lately, but threw that out my mind 'cause I had to get to my financial-
planning class or my jewelry-making class or my self-awareness class. The
only one I dropped out of was self-awareness. I knew myself. I was learnin'
my strength every day. I already was over my weakness.

I missed a man beside me at night, but I was so busy when I looked up
six months had passed and I hadn't cried once.

I didn't fight for the house no more. I wanted it to be sold. I didn't fight
for Gravy no more. I was glad he was gone. Mostly. He had done me a big
favor by giving me MY life back. You hear me? He handed my life to me
and I had fought him! Fought him to take it back! Keep it! Use me some
more! Chile, chile, chile.

Gravy noticed when he dropped by to check on the house. He noticed
a lot 'bout the new me. He slapped me on my behind. I didn't say nothin';
after all, he had been my husband. I sashayed it in front of him as I walked
him to the door. I put him out 'cause I had to get to school or somethin'.
Or maybe just lay down in peace and think of my new future. Or take a
bath and oil and cream my skin for the next man in my life who I might
love . . . anything! Whatever I want to do! Now!

I prayed for the house to sell. I wanted MY money! 'Cause I had plans.

Belle's house was sold. She moved in my spare rooms while she looked
for somethin' she wanted to buy.

I asked her, "You gonna buy a smaller house this time? You don't need
much room."

She looked at me thoughtfully. "You know, I been thinking. A house
just sits you in one spot and you have to hold your life into that space and
around the town it's in. I don't need much room in a house, but I need a
lotta space around me."

I thought about that.

Soon after that, she told me she had bought five acres on the edge of a
lake. She was goin' to buy a mobile home, nice, roomy, and comfortable.
Live there with the lake on one side, the trees on the other, and the town
where she could reach it if she wanted to.

I thought about that, liked it, but I couldn't afford that. I told her, "I like that. That's really gonna be nice."

She answered, "Well, come on with me then!"

I know I looked sad. "Girl, my money ain't that heavy. Not for land AND a mobile home. You got over a hundred thousand dollars; I MAY get twenty thousand."

She say, "I can't live all over my five acres. Get you a mobile home and live on my land!" I know I smiled big as she went on talkin'. "Better still, I'll buy your mobile home 'cause you gonna need your money to live on. You buy the landfill I want for the garden 'cause I want to grow my own food."

I thought only a minute; I wanted this to be MY life. So I told her, "The land is yours. If I buy landfill, if I ever leave, I ain't gonna take it with me so it will still be yours, too. Tell you what, I'll buy my mobile home and pay you rent for use of the land. Then if I ever move, you can buy my home, cheap."

She laughed. "Girl, the land is paid for. I don't need no rent for land that's gonna sit there anyway! You my friend! The only one I got now."

I was happy, said, "You my only friend, too!" I was happy 'cause friends are so hard to find. People count their money 'fore they count friends.

Then she was serious. "I want to be alone. Don't want no man, woman, chick or child tellin' me what to do no more!"

I shook my head. "Me neither! Lord, no!"

She went on. "But everybody need some company sometime. You keep me from gettin' lonely enough to run out there in them silly streets and bring somethin' home I don't want!"

I spoke. "You got me started on my new life . . . school and everything!"

She was still serious. "I trust you."

I got more serious. "I trust you."

She kept talkin'. "I'm goin' to try to pay for everything in cash. Pay it off! Don't want to owe nobody nothin'!"

I added, "And grow our own food."

She nodded. "Come into town for whatever we need or want."

I was eager. "Don't need no fancy clothes."

She smiled. "We can live on a little of nothin' . . . and be fine! Don't have to go to work or kiss nobody's behind for nothing!"

I laughed out loud. "NOTHIN'!"

You know what we did? We went downtown and bought cowboy jeans, hats, boots, and shirts! We was dressin' for our country life. We was sharp!

It was finally time for her to go, everything ready for her. She drove off with a car full of paints and canvases. I forgot to tell you, she had learned how to drive and had a little red sports car! She wore dark goggles and a long scarf around her neck, just a-flyin' in the wind.

One day, for a minute, just for a minute, she looked sad to me. I looked sad to me. Two older ladies lookin' for a future. Goin' around acting like we was happy. I felt like crying. Belle saw me and asked why, and I told her. Then I did cry.

She put her hands on my shoulders. "Molly? You 'bout forty-five years old."

I corrected her—"Forty-four"—as I sobbed.

She didn't laugh at me. "Well, s'pose you live to be eighty?"

Somethin' in my breast lifted.

She went on. "What you gonna do with them other thirty-five years? What you gonna call 'em if not your future?"

The tears stopped.

But she didn't. "Now, Molly, you my friend. But don't you move out there, away from all your clubs and people, if you gonna be sad. I don't want no sad, depressed killjoy for a neighbor, messin' up my beautiful days! Don't move!"

I could see she meant it. I thought of my clubs where I couldn't stand nobody hardly. I thought of my empty days of food with Gravy. I even thought of my kids who had their own families now. I shook my head so hard. Clearin' it! Shit!

She looked at me steady. "If you even THINK you might want to stay here, PLEASE stay! Till you get all of what you need. 'Cause if you get out there and you got a complaint, I don't want to hear it! 'Less it's 'cause you sick or somethin'!"

She left.

At last my house sold. I went and told the mobile-home man I was ready, gave him a check with no signature on it but mine!

Then I gave my last club meeting, 'cause I knew I was never gonna have to be bothered with them again!

One woman specially, Viola Prunebrough, always was talking 'bout me and laughin' at me. This meeting was specially for her, but the others deserved it, too.

In my reading class we had read Omar Khayyám, and I learned about wrapping food in grape leaves. At the last meeting before this one, I had served them, thinkin' it was some high-class stuff. I didn't know what to put in them, so I stuffed them with chitterlings. It was good to me! Viola had talked about me and laughed all over town. Made me look like a fool in front of everybody. Now you know why I wanted to pay her back. It's ugly, but it's true.

I let everybody in the club know the date for comin'. Then I went to try to find me some marijuana. It was hard to get! Didn't nobody know me that sells the stuff! But I finally got some. A quarter pound! When I prepared the food for that meetin', I mixed that stuff in everything I cooked. I put on a big pot of red beans. No meat, no salt, no onions, no nothin'! Just cooked. I had a plan, see?

When them ladies, all dressed up so nice to show off, got to eatin' all my good food, they went to talkin' loud, laughin', and jumpin' all over the place, saying stupid things. Eatin' and drinkin' everything in sight! I had to snatch some things right off the trays and hurry up and replace 'em 'cause them ladies was gonna eat my dishes and furniture if I didn't! Dainty painted lips just guzzled the wine.

Then I just happen to put on some records by Bobby Blubland. Chile! Them ladies was snapping their fingers, movin' around, shaking their behinds and everythin' else. Dancin' like they hadn't moved in years! Some was singing so loud they drowned Bobby Blubland out. They'd have got me put out if it wasn't my own house. We hadn't had no meeting yet, either!

Then all the food was gone 'cept the beans. Them women musta been still starved, 'cause B. B. King was singing when I looked up and ALL them ladies was bearing down, coming on me in the kitchen, lookin' for anything they could get their hands on to eat. That marijuana must be something!

They got hold of them beans and ate them all. Gobbled them, smacking their lips and ohhhhhing and ahhhhhing till every bean was gone. I laughed till I cried. Why, these were ladies! Beans were in their clothes, in their shoes, even in one lady's hair. I shoulda felt 'shamed, but I didn't. I didn't eat anything myself! Some of them was getting sleepy. Well, they sure were full! Lou Rawls couldn't keep them up anymore. I told them they better go, and then I fixed something for Viola's stomach: a cup of hot tea with a little Black Draught in it. I rushed her out then. I know when she got home she didn't get no rest! I played music for her exit; she wanted to stay and talk and hug and cry between belches. She danced out the door with her fat self, cramps only beginnin' to hit them beans in her belly. Then they were all gone. When they came to theirselves, to ask me what I had cooked, I was gone, too!

I picked up all the supplies I would need for my jewelry makin'. I had found out I was very good at it. People always wanted to buy whatever I made. I was goin' to make a little livin' on the side!

I moved into my new two-bedroom mobile home with the little fireplace. I always wanted one. As I drove over there for the first time, the smile on my face liked to stretched from here to yonder! I laughed out loud, several times . . . and wasn't nobody in the car but me!

We each had a little sun porch built facing the lake. Just listen! 'Most every morning we wave to each other as we sit on that porch and watch the sun finish coming up, while we have coffee or tea or whatever! If it's warm, after the sun is up good, I always go for a swim. Belle usually comes out and sets up her painting stuff. Then maybe I fish and catch my lunch. I take her some, or if her sign is out that says "DON'T," then I don't!

Next, maybe I either put on some music I have learned to appreciate or go in my extra bedroom that is my workroom, 'less my kids are here visiting, and make jewelry to sell when I want to. Or I work in the garden, which is full and beautiful. Or I read. The main thing is I do whatever I want to, whenever I want to.

Sometimes I don't see Belle for days. I see her in the distance. We wave, but we don't talk. We ain't had a argument yet, except on where to plant the onions, tomatoes, or potatoes. Something like that.

I'm telling you, life can be beautiful! Peace don't cost as much as people think it does! It depends on what you want. Not money. People with plenty money don't get peace just 'cause they have money. I get lonely, but I never get sad or depressed.

We both got lonely for a man sometime. But we didn't know any that wouldn't come out here and mess things up . . . in some way.

Then the generator broke down and we had to call in a repairman. He came. A little, thin, bowlegged, slow-walkin', half-ugly man. He was the sweet kind. Anything you need, he wants to fix it for you. Well, there is always something that needs a little fixin'.

He would work, but he wouldn't talk 'bout nothin' but sex while he worked. He talked 'bout how many women loved him. Loved him makin' love to them. What a lover he was. That kinda stuff. He would stop and look for a wrench or screwdriver or hammer, look off in space and tell you 'bout that last beautiful woman who wanted to leave her husband for him, but he don't take nobody's wife! Or the sister who said, as she took off her clothes, "My sister told me how you make her feel. Now you ain't leavin' here till you make me feel thataway, too!"

I don't know was he lyin' all the time, but he did put stuff on your mind.

One day he came back by when everything had been done (and nobody had taken their clothes off once). He went to Belle's. She showed him her shotgun and told him, "If I don't send for you, don't come! I bought this to use and I know how! Don't bring no clouds 'round here, 'cause I will make it rain!" He left, wavin' his hand, telling her he didn't mean nothin' wrong. She thanked him and shut her door.

Now, it had been raining all night and the leaves was dripping over my roof. I could hear the steam sizzle as some of 'em hit my fireplace stack. I had awakened, and instead of putting on Percy Faith or somebody, I had put on B. B. King. When Mr. Repairman passed my house I told him, through the window, I had somethin' needed fixin'! He came on in.

The big LIAR! He couldn't do nothin' he bragged about!

He wanted to lay around in my bed and smoke a cigarette, drink a little wine, and talk. I told him, "You got to go!"

He left, saying, "All you women are crazy! That's why you ain't got no man!" I just laughed.

He still comes to fix the generator when we need him. But that's all!

At that time, Belle's loneliness came out in another way. See, when you have all this space and beauty, it seems to bring you closer to God. Belle decided she ought to know Him better.

This is what she said: "I know the human race ain't no accident. Be 'bout three billion accidents now! And ain't no new kinda accident happenin' all by itself! Nowhere!"

I started to give my opinion, but she wasn't through.

"And another thing," she went on. "There has got to be some truth somewhere! Some of this stuff got to be lies! If we die and rush up to Heaven right away, what is the resurrection for? What is Judgment Day gonna be if everybody is already gone on to Heaven? And if everybody returns to God, then who is on that big, wide road Jesus said would be so packed full of people?"

She made good sense, and it felt warm talking 'bout it. She got some books, and pretty soon she had a Bible study man coming out here. They'd sit on that porch of hers and study, argue, and talk for two or three hours every week. Then she would teach me what she learned. Show it to me in the Bible even! I enjoyed it and was reading the books myself.

On one of Belle's trips to town in her little red sports car she ran into Gravy. He said he needed to see me. She called me and let him talk, 'cause it was my business to give out my own number. I told him he could come out and talk.

He came. He drove up early one morning in a very big, nice blue car. I know he came that early 'cause he wanted to see was anybody there with me. There was only me . . . and peace. I thought I'd be nervous, but I wasn't.

He stepped in the door, head way out in front of him, looking in and around. His shiny pointy-toe shoe slipped on one of my small steps and he went down on one knee. I know it hurt and he wanted to holler, but he held hisself together and limped on in.

Said, "Hot damn, Molly, you got to do somethin' 'bout that step! Shit!"

I told him, "I ain't never slipped on it. Come on in, sit down. Want some coffee?"

He set. "Yeah, bring me some of that good coffee of yours. You make the best coffee in the world!"

While I got everything together I was lookin' at him lookin' at my place, my home. I really looked at him tryin' to see my twenty-four years. I ain't gonna talk about him. He didn't make me do nothin'. I let everything that happened happen. Other than Mala, his girl. Maybe that, too. Remember, I begged to stay with him even when I knew he had her!

He had changed, naturally, a couple of years had gone by. I looked at his hair. He was letting it go, and it was pretty damn near all gray now. He saw me lookin' and patted his head, sayin', "Mala like this ol' gray hair, say it makes me look mature." He laughed a low, empty, scratchy laugh.

My eyes happen to look down at his stomach when I handed him the napkin. He saw that, too, and said, "Mala say she like a round, cozy stomach. Say it's a sign of satisfaction!"

I thought to myself, Or constipation.

He stirred his coffee. "She like all them hamburgers and hot dogs, boxes of candy, jelly rolls from the bakery. Say all that meat and gravy is too heavy to be healthy." His voice was tryin' to sound happy and young, but it still came out disgusted. He looked at me. I was a slim-plump. Meat all where it ought to be, and healthy!

I sat and crossed my legs, the ones he hadn't seen in twenty-four years. He looked, and took a swallow of hot coffee. It was too hot, but he couldn't spit it out. He finally got it down.

I asked, "How is Mala?"

He put the cup down. Said with a surprised look, "You know, I came down a little sick and she got mad at me for it! Like I could help it! One little ol' operation!"

I said, "For Heaven's sake!"

He said, "Yeah!" He started to take another swallow of the coffee, but put the cup back down.

I asked, "Well, things are better now since you up and all?"

He pursed his lips and rubbed that sore knee. Said, "I don't rightly know. She left me 'bout two months ago." He looked outraged. "Do you know, the judge ain't gonna make her sell that house I bought? 'Cause she got two kids! Them kids ain't mine! Mine is grown and got they own homes! Them some other man's children livin' in my house that she won't let me live in!"

I sat up. "Well, what happened, for God's sake?"

He looked like he could cry. "She told me she like this gray hair . . . this . . . this belly and my . . . my . . . 'scuse me, Molly—my lovin'! Then she got tired of my gray hair, my cozy belly, and my gas, and the way I cough in the bathroom in the mornings! Have you ever heard of such a thing?! You got to cough in the mornings to clear your throat! She crazy! That's what! Crazy!"

I sat back. "Well, I'll be damned!"

He was ready to really talk. "Ain't it a damn shame! And I have seen that man—that boy! She got him coming to MY house after dark! Nothin' but a kid! I could tell him somethin' 'bout what he is gettin' into! She ain't shit! She is a lyin' cracked-butt bitch!"

I sat up. "Don't talk like that in my house, Gravy. I got a special kind of vibration and atmosphere in my house. PEACE. I won't allow it to be disturbed."

He looked at me like I had just said, "Let's get in my flyin' saucer and go to Jupiter today!"

Well, I'm not goin' to bore you with what-all he said. He added up to him and me goin' back together, "like we always shoulda been in the first place." After all, I was the mother of his children. He missed me. When he got to the part where he had always thought of me, even in her arms, I gave him a look that he understood to mean "You are really killin' it!"

I didn't tell him, but I thought clearly, He don't have nothin' to show for twenty-six years of livin' now, 'cept gray hair, potbelly, and a blue car. I had a home . . . with atmosphere. I had a place where my children and grandchildren come spend the summer. I looked good. Because I was healthy. I ate right. Wasn't gonna go back to cookin' all that shit again!

I didn't need to say all those things. I didn't WANT him. No more, ever again, in this life, or no other life. I didn't love him.

I loved me.

Trying to hug me, he left, saying he'd be back bringing me something pretty. I told him, "Call first. I may be busy." As he drove away, he was the most sad, confused-lookin' man I had seen in a long, long time.

I never let him come back. He had done been free to pick and he had picked.

Belle got married to the Bible study man. She said to me, "Ain't it funny? People go to bars, be around purple-headed, shaved-headed, or even normal-lookin' people, lookin' for a mate. Why do they cry when things go wrong? What did they expect to find in a place like that? Moses?" That's the way she talks. Then she say, "How you doin', girl? Need anything?" That's what she says to me. My friend!

As a matter of fact, I'm doin' all right! I got a couple of fellows I go out with sometime. My jewelry makin' is so good I sell it fast as I can make it.

To think I fought this! Well, I don't know.

I don't have anyone I want to marry. Well, hell, I'm only goin' on fifty. I got a future if I live right. I got dreams. Now I swim in the lake. Maybe someday I'll try a ocean!

I get lonely sometime. But not looooooonely.

I might even get married again someday. That'd be nice, too. Only this time I know what kind of man I'd be lookin' for! 'Cause I have done found ME!

I love myself now . . . and everything around me . . . so much.

I know if I got a man there would be just that much more to love. But believe me, I'm doing all right!

You hear me?

UPWARD BOUND

Steven Corbin

The summer between sophomore and junior years in high school, I had the opportunity to attend college. Upward Bound was a year-round, government-funded program designed for academically gifted inner-city students to whet their taste for college life. The locale was Upper Montclair, New Jersey. The school Montclair State College.

Out of my element, I wasn't certain how I felt about being away from home for six weeks. Accustomed to a raucous, crime-ridden, poverty-ravaged neighborhood, I wasn't used to the open space of green campus, the rolling hills, the serenity. Arriving at the campus, I wanted to turn around and go home.

Stone Hall, the boys' dormitory, was located—or isolated, as it were—at the northern end of campus. One was forced to tour the entire campus en route to breakfast at Freeman Hall. My room—luckily I didn't have a roommate—was all of one hundred square feet. There was hardly space to bend over. But it was mine. All mine. Compared to the cramped bedroom I shared with two brothers at home, this was the Taj Mahal.

Though only the first day, it seemed, by the chatter and laughter ringing through the halls, that everyone knew one another. A familiar alienation; I never fit in. As a child, some of my playmates wondered why I'd abruptly desert them in a game of stickball and run home to draw pictures and write poetry. Male members of my family considered me weird for not sharing their enthusiasm for professional contact sports. They didn't understand why crashing helmets on the thirty-two-yard line and pulverizing left hooks to the jaw in a boxing ring were, to me, insufferable. And, as I was fifteen-and-a-half years old—going on sixteen in four months—my peers were beginning to speculate about why I was seemingly not into pussy. Why I never talked about it. Hell, I'd never even had any.

Walking down the dormitory's corridor, which seemed to go on forever, I surreptitiously glanced into several rooms where students were getting acquainted through loud, animated discussions, laughter, swearing, water balloon and pillow fights. I felt fortunate about rooming alone. Unless I could choose my roommate, I was in no mood for surprises. Be just my luck to be paired with a star quarterback who plastered *Playboy* centerfolds along his wall and who, in the middle of the night, might ask me to make myself scarce so that he could ravish the coed he'd managed to slip into the dormitory against the counselors' knowledge.

Put simply, I didn't know if I could endure the next six weeks.

Evening. A cool breeze calmed the campus, the towering pine trees whispering to each other, bowing, curtsying, swaying as if in a mating dance, sunlight peeking through the leaves in quick snatches. The sun slowly set, tinges of burnt orange dramatically reflecting off the skyscrapers of New York's skyline on the far eastern horizon.

Dr. Greene, the program director, was winding up a tedious welcoming speech in the dining hall, and made special mention of the students attending for the first time. As my eyes panned the room, studying the brown, black, yellow faces I knew would never become my friends, I wondered just what the hell I was doing there. So far, what I liked best about being tucked miles away from home was the cafeteria. All you could eat. The perpetually ravenous, skinny teenager that I was, my insatiable appetite was often unfulfilled at home. My mother, a factory worker, struggled to feed and clothe three growing sons, and though we'd eat three meals a day, I never got as much as my appetite demanded. Dr. Greene told us why we, the academically promising black and Puerto Rican and some Asian students, had been chosen, driving his point home by paternally placing his hands upon the shoulders of Angel Rodriguez, who'd be attending Harvard in the fall.

Bored, my mind wandered to my home in Jersey City. I could see my brothers, both poor eaters, sweating it out in the hot and sticky, roach-infested kitchen, languidly devouring their food, distractedly twisting their hair, cheeks puffed out like hamsters storing seed. In my family I was the best eater—which meant I'd eat anything. Garbage mouth, they called me. My younger brothers were finicky, which drove my mother crazy. She professed two basic philosophies about food. A child of the Depression, she abhorred the waste of food. Secondly, she never refused a hungry person a meal. In our home we were never sent to bed without dinner as a punishment, regardless of what we'd done. "Because," she was known to say, as her mother had before her, "people gotta eat, and food ends up as shit, anyhow."

Before classes began that week, students were cramming in as much partying as possible. The dance season kicked off in Chapin Hall, the girls' dormitory, where they played mostly 45s and Shing-a-linged and grinded the night away. I felt suspended inside a bubble of isolation, so distanced from it all, balancing myself on the periphery, though I could reach out and touch any one of them. From outside on the veranda, I could smell marijuana seeping through the open windows, carried by the pine-sweetened breeze, and I hoped for an invitation to take a hit.

Surprisingly, the blacks and Latins seemed to mingle, which was uncharacteristic of the territorial neighborhoods we hailed from. The music even fluctuated from the smooth, sweet soul of The Temptations and the raw, sweaty funk of James Brown, to the brassy, timbal-punctuated salsa rhythms of Ray Barretto and Willi Colon. The Puerto Ricans—the PRs, we called them—were jazzed about teaching blacks their style of dancing: mambo, cha-cha, and merengue; they were no more enthusiastic than the blacks who were eager to learn.

I couldn't get into it.

I could dance all right. I could even do the mambo and cha-cha. But I'd been spoiled by having spent my weekends in Greenwich Village with members of my track team. We frequented gay bars where we were never carded. So, sitting there in Chapin Hall on the campus of Montclair State, listening to the slow, uptempo, and salsa music, it wasn't as if I didn't want to dance. I refused to dance with girls. In all of my two years in high school, I'd never been forced to before. I wasn't about to start now. I knew myself. Knew what I wanted. And it didn't come in a skirt and panty hose. Nearly all the good-looking guys on the dance floor grabbed at anything with breasts while I, sitting forlorn and unapproachable, squeezed into a dark corner, fantasized that they'd grab for me instead.

This simply isn't working out, I kept thinking.

And just as the party was over, and we headed back to our separate dormitories in compliance with the eleven o'clock curfew, and I was feeling sorry for myself for being cast into yet another social circumstance where I didn't fit, walking back alone to Stone Hall while, seemingly, everyone had someone, a friend, a roommate, a lover to talk to, the warm night air ignited with mosquitoes, lightning bugs, crickets whirring, the breezy fragrance of pine, it happened suddenly, as if a cone of celestial light had been thrown upon the darkness.

I saw *him*.

The boys' showers were crowded.

With my towel, I had to wait in line for an available stall. I was uncomfortable standing in the buff before a group of males. Changing clothes in my high school locker room for Phys. Ed., I'd protect and guard myself as if something immeasurably valuable existed beneath the towel. Conversely, watching other boys soap their lean bodies became a pastime, a ritual I would come to live for every morning for the next six weeks. Sight-seeing, I called it.

I stepped into the shower. Adjusting the hot water, I took the bar of soap, turned, glanced over my shoulder, and nearly gasped out loud. There *he* was. In the opposite stall, *he*—I thought I heard someone call him Lorenzo—caught sight of me dropping the soap, nearly tripping over myself to retrieve it. I tried to calm my shaky hands, to slide the soap across my body and work up a lather as I'd done a thousand times before. Whenever I could, I tried to steal glimpses of him without appearing obvious. That's all I needed. For my secret to be unleashed among a bunch of hormone-exploding, homophobic, perhaps fag-bashing teenage boys I didn't know. I thought that he caught me staring several times. My eyes met his, then dropped when I thought he wasn't looking. He must've noticed me checking him out. Suddenly he turned away. My view had been reduced to his backside and the hefty calves of his hairy legs. He, too, had dropped his soap. I used the opportunity to exchange a smile with him. He didn't return it. And if I wasn't mistaken, he flashed me a dirty look. The "What the hell're you staring at? You faggot!" look. For the remainder of the shower, I kept to myself. But I had to look at him once more. When I turned, he was gone. In his place stood an obese guy who sang out loud while he bathed. Unflinchingly, he stared at my nakedness. He swung around to adjust the water. When he turned back, I, too, was gone.

During my classes I daydreamed about my family back home. How my brothers were faring in my absence. The brother closest to me in age had begun an experimentation of sorts in our drug-infested community. He'd made the quantum leap from diet pills to heroin. By age fifteen he was shooting up, or mainlining, as the phrase went. It concerned me gravely.

Though we'd always been close and acted as utmost confidants for each other—I was closer to no one than my brother—I had felt compelled to tell my mother of his doings, but my loyalties to him wouldn't allow me to part my lips. He'd assured me that he had it under control. But then so did many others who were no longer around to tell about it. The crowd I ran with was nothing to write home to my mother about, either—especially the boys from my high school track team who accompanied me to Greenwich Village gay bars on weekends—but the crowd my brother hung with was another story. I even thought myself "better" than my brother because I "snorted" heroin occasionally, while he was doing heroin as junkies did it. Telling my mother—or my father, who didn't live with us—might break the sinewy chain of our male bond. And consequently he could turn around and tell my parents that I slept with guys.

As a child, I was in touch with my sexuality at an age when most boys don't know how to write their name. Though I couldn't divulge or exercise it, except through bonding games of Truth and Dare with the neighborhood boys, I never experienced shame or remorse over it. Later, as a teenager, I even thought myself superior to straight boys. They were not as bright or creatively talented as I was. They didn't know themselves as I knew myself. They were not as discerning as I. I was privy to two worlds; they, one. They knew virtually nothing about sensitivity—maybe individually, but not as a group. They couldn't open up and reveal themselves as I could. They couldn't make love. Oh, they could fuck. But they couldn't really love their women. I knew. My female friends and my mother and her sisters chronically complained about it.

That wasn't true of gay boys. We could go for hours without climaxing, caressing and cuddling with endless foreplay. Masters & Johnson even wrote a *Newsweek* cover story about it, detailing their sex study findings, substantiating it with statistics and laboratory observations.

My baby brother was still young enough that I didn't feel cause to worry. Not yet. In a few years that would sweep by as swiftly as this six-week college stint, there was no telling what he'd be subjected to. Coming of age in our community, there was little chance that he wouldn't dip and dab in hardcore drugs. In our neighborhood it was recreation. While suburban middleclass kids went away to summer camps and vacations along the Jersey shore, we turned to deserted parking lots, rooftops, and abandoned buildings to experiment furtively with chemicals capable of wiping us out in a single afternoon.

"Your dime," my smart-aleck brother said, answering the phone.

"It's me, bucket head."

"Yo!" my brother said. His voice was hoarse, scratchy. Heroin coated.
"What's happening?"

I pictured him with a needle in his arm, slumped in a corner on the
bathroom floor, his dilated pupils flickering to the back of his head, while
Ma cooked dinner in the kitchen next door, assuming he was taking a leak.

"You're what's happening, man," my brother said. "How's college?"

"It's okay. Where's Ma?"

"She ain't here. She'll be back later."

"How's everything at home?"

"Same ol' shit, man."

"Why's your voice so raspy?"

"It ain't—"

"Are you? . . . You know."

"What?"

"You know."

"Yeah, I'm high, if that's what you mean. I only do it once in a while."

I sighed heavily into the mouthpiece. "I don't know," I said, defeated.

"Know what?" His joviality turned defensive.

"Well, I was just thinking that . . . well, what if Mommy or Daddy
found out—"

"You mean, what if you *told* them, right?"

"Well, sometimes Ma asks me about the crowd you run around with—"

"Yeah, and she asks me how come you never go out with girls, but do
I tell on you?"

"But what I do won't kill me."

"Oh, yes, it will. If I tell Ma or Daddy, it will."

Watching a grainy, black-and-white Malcolm X documentary in class, my
mouth gaped at the rare opportunity this afforded. Everything I'd ever seen
or heard about Malcolm X had been through the bigoted American press,
which continually berated and lambasted him. But Professor Maddox—a
black man who jokingly made it clear that he was no relation whatsoever to
Lester of Alabama—heralded the slain leader's immense contributions to the
black community, especially in the way of fostering black pride. Because of
Malcolm, he said, we'd ceased being "colored" *and* "Negro" and for once
took unadulterated pride in being exactly what we were: black. I found this
fascinating. It might've been the moment I realized that I would be getting
a special, even alternative education in this Upward Bound program.

At any given moment in the dormitory all I ever heard about was pussy.
Pussy this. Pussy that. And yet, when the opportunities availed themselves,
these pussy-crazed juveniles engaged in antics beyond my comprehension.

One day there had even been a fistfight between two roommates. Apparently, one fellow admitted a bunch of the guys into the room in the middle of the night while his roommate slept. Several of the boys took turns prodding his open lips with their erections or sticking them against his teeth. When he woke up, I could hear the noise from my second-floor room, though the incident happened upstairs and down the hall.

My optimism shattered when it became common knowledge on campus that *he*—Lorenzo Gonzales, a Cuban—relentlessly chased a cute black girl from his high school who made no bones about the fact that she had another "real" boyfriend back home. While she went steady with Shorty, her beau in Jersey City, Lorenzo was a hobby she could indulge during her spare time. I thought her stupid, even cruel. How, I wondered, could she pass up this sexy Latin hunk of toned flesh with the mink-brown eyes and thick eyebrows? He adored her and didn't care who knew it. I admired his tenacity. It was rumored that reports of his liaison with Maxie had gotten back to Shorty and inevitably there'd be a showdown. I hoped as much. That's what he'd get for messing around with someone who didn't want him half as badly as I.

As much as we attended classes, studied, and composed term papers, there were just as many recreational outlets. It took little or no excuse to throw a party, even if it was only playing records in the Rec Room. Not unlike in the streets and schools we'd left behind for six weeks, drugs flowed and passed hands with similar frequency and visibility. Despite our status as so-called academically gifted students, many of us couldn't shake inner-city habits like marijuana, amphetamines, barbiturates, cocaine, and heroin. Removed from the world, we weren't allowed to leave the campus unless chaperoned by one of the counselors. Similarly, we were prohibited from harboring anyone else on campus or in our dormitories, aside from Visitation Day. Neither of which stopped us from periodically sneaking off campus to buy drugs in nearby New York City. Curfew was taken seriously. Campus legend boasted that someone had been fifteen minutes late getting back to his dormitory. The counselors called his parents and announced that they'd be delivering him back to Jersey City within the hour. Like clockwork, one-two-three, he was gone.

As my warped sense of humor disseminated among my peers, I began to relish a popularity I hadn't anticipated. People were a lot friendlier than I'd given them credit for. Usually it was effortless to befriend girls. Easier to get along with, there was less to prove with them, which allowed me to be myself. With the guys, I'd feel pressured to discuss the Yankees, the Knicks, the Mets, the Jets. And of course, pussy.

There were two other guys like me. They liked boys, too, I could tell. Over the weeks we became friends. But we never let on about ourselves among each other. Like a secret code, we always talked around it. They, like me, never pursued the girls or even discussed them. We talked about everything *but* sports and pussy. I wanted to invite them to hang out with my friends and me at Stonewall or the Bon Soir in the Village when the six weeks were through. Yet I felt as if I'd be violating the tacit code we perpetuated. So I said nothing.

There were times, especially on Friday and Saturday nights, when I'd sit atop a hill near Stone Hall overlooking the rolling hills, the green pastures, and the New Jersey Turnpike. Beyond that, New York shone like the Emerald City in *The Wizard of Oz*. No matter what fun I was having with the Upward Bound students, it never equaled the antics I was missing with my friends in the Village. Given the hour, I knew precisely where they were and what they were doing. At eight o'clock or so, they were arriving at the PATH Ninth Street train station, crossing the street, passing by Trude Heller's. They'd walk to Nathan's on the corner of Eighth Street and Sixth Avenue, then continue up the street to the Bon Soir. Friday and Saturday nights my crowd openly cruised, even harassed good-looking guys and gave "street shows" for the busloads of tourists who flashed their cameras like paparazzi. By two o'clock in the morning they'd be hitting Nathan's for a bite. Then they'd end up at the Pitts Street pool for a swim and whatever, or Stonewall in the Village, or Bosco's in Harlem, or another after-hours spot somewhere between Brooklyn and the Bronx.

I joined the newspaper staff as a reporter. Our campus rag was called *Up*. The stories were average, the graphics mediocre. The outstanding newspaper feature was the art work. Sketched by some incredibly talented artist, it put everything else to shame. When I looked closer to examine the signature, I read the initials L.G. Could it be? I thought. Upon further inquiry, I was told that Lorenzo Gonzales had long ago established quite a reputation as an artist. He did much of the impressive work in his high school yearbook. There was nothing or no one he couldn't draw. I believed that and appreciated his talent, since sketching was one of the first artistic outlets I had exhibited as a child.

I never again saw him during my favorite part of the morning, watching wet flesh. He was either leaving when I arrived, vice versa, or I saw him nowhere near the showers at all.

Dr. Greene, his assistants, and counselors took us on field trips. We were exposed to cultural and artistic events relevant to us as blacks, Latins, and Asians. During the six weeks, we visited New York several times to see Broadway plays, such as *Purlie Victorious* and *Two Gentlemen of Verona*. We toured the Metropolitan and Guggenheim museums. Saw R&B and salsa concerts at Madison Square Garden, recitals and operas at the Met. They took us to Boston to see James Earl Jones play *Othello*. In Philadelphia, my one and only time there, we saw the cracked Liberty Bell on the Fourth of July. We frequented the movies and shopping malls, where we spent our weekly stipend. And once, they took us, by bus, to Washington, D.C., for the weekend where we did all the usual tours of the virgin white buildings that housed our government. Except it wasn't that new to me. When I was a child, my parents visited Virginia annually to see my father's family. We passed through D.C., to and from, and took rolls of slides on the steps of the Capitol or the Lincoln Memorial.

"Who do you think is the most athletic?" I asked my closeted friends one night, sitting in the dormitory, passing around a joint, whistling through clenched teeth.

"What?"

"You heard me."

"Franklin," one said.

"Elijah," the other said.

"What about Lorenzo?" I said.

"Oh, yeah!"

"I forgot about Lorenzo!"

Their emphatic responses to Lorenzo struck a chord. I decided to explore it.

"And . . ." I said, slowly and deliberately, sucking in a lungful of marijuana, "don't you think he's the cutest, too?"

Eyes dropped to the floor. The room turned suddenly quiet. I had gone too far.

"Well?" I went further.

"What do you mean, cute?" one said.

"C'mon. Cute is cute," I said. "Okay . . . I'll say it first. I think . . . he's the cutest boy on campus."

Eyes lifted slowly from the floor.

"Well . . . " one said, his eyes moving around the room, eyes moist, cloudy, and glossed by Panamanian Red, "if you think he's cute . . . then . . . I think so, too."

"Me . . . too," the other said. We burst into a round of forced laughter.

"And how about Maxie Bryant?" I said. "See how she treats him? Don't they make a terrible couple?"

"He's a fool for her. I don't understand it," one said.

"Bitch," the other said.

"This conversation will stay in this room, won't it?" one said.

I liked thinking of Lorenzo as my proverbial "first love," though he'd never said one word to me. Except I'd been involved in an affair earlier that year. Ramon Diaz—my track teammates teased me about my proclivities for Latin men—was actually my first love. He was twenty-one, I fifteen, though I lied and said I was sixteen. A Brooklyn Puerto Rican, he lived near Jay Street Boro Hall with his lover. I didn't find out about the lover until emotionally it was too late. Anyway, he was a dog. I was willing to do "anything" for him. He knew it, and used me accordingly.

I was awakened one night by loud whispering outside my door. Whoever it was—I didn't recognize the voice—stood outside the corridor telling someone that a faggot lived in this particular room. I was convinced that it was meant for me to hear. As the voices subsided and I turned over to get back to sleep, I heard something roll under my door. Quickly I jumped up, turned on the light, and noticed a blue-and-white firecracker, its fuse fizzling. A dud, it never went off.

A couple of hours later that same night, I heard rooms being broken into by the dorm director and counselors. They were ransacking the rooms in search of illicit drugs. Some students were quick enough to flush whatever they had down the toilet. Those not so lucky were apprehended, and told to start packing. I had a few joints and a two-dollar glassine bag or two of heroin—a deuce, we called it. Why they never bothered to raid me, I don't know. Nor did I bother to flush any of my drugs.

As the six weeks inched to a close, I discovered a thing or two. Without a doubt, I would attend college after graduation. Additionally, I'd developed the desire to go away to school which, before the Montclair experience, had never occurred to me.

The annual banquet was approaching—Upward Bound's version of a prom. The students got dressed up, had corsages, made dates, and attended the dinner where we would receive awards, say good-bye to each other, and party the last night away.

I anguished over whom to ask. This brand of protocol worked against my grain. Finally, after much contemplation and process of elimination, I asked a girl who'd be an easy, sure bet.

When I asked, Patrice replied affirmatively before I could finish the question.

I speculated about my father's pride in my accomplishments. After the first four weeks at Montclair State, I'd been chosen as one of the exemplary students to be written about in a newspaper article in our home town. Everyone read the *Jersey Journal*, and I felt that Daddy had seen the article and my photograph. It might've been the first time in years that he had seen me, in a photograph or otherwise. He lived all of seven blocks away from my mother, brothers, and me. But the divorce between him and my mother had been so bitter that for some twisted reason he took it out on his children as well. None of us ever understood his despicable behavior. Before the breakup he'd been a caring father, as good as any.

Despite his comparatively well-to-do economic status, his frequent fishing trips to Costa Rica, or the fact that he hit the numbers for several thousand dollars several times a year, he never gave us a penny. Adding insult to injury, he was characteristically delinquent with his child support payments. Frequently my mother was forced to confront him in a court of law for a measly forty dollars a week. "Ain't that a damn shame," my mother and her sisters would say, my aunts shaking their heads and sucking their tongues in unison. While he traipsed about town in silks, mohair, monogrammed jackets, and designer shirts, his three boys wore the same pants to school every day, their shoes had holes in the soles—especially mine—and we hardly got anything new unless it was Christmas or Easter. Even then, nothing was guaranteed.

My father had groomed me academically. Throughout grade school he encouraged my straight-A report cards and convinced me that I would be attending college. *College.* That word frightened me. I thought yeah, I'm smart all right—the word they used in those days in lieu of bright or gifted—but I didn't think I had what it took to survive a college education. This was highly unusual. My father entertained middle-class values amid a low-economic neighborhood. I know of no other fathers on the block, or mothers, who insisted that their children were to attend college.

Now that I was performing the deeds my father expected of me, it seemed to hardly matter to him. Not once did he ever call to congratulate me or tell me to keep up the good work. Although he never pressured me to be a lawyer or a doctor or any other kind of professional, he had always let me know that he expected something important from me. Now he didn't seem to give a rat's hair what I did academically.

I was awakened by light taps on my window. Frightened, I glanced up at the window above my bed. I rubbed my eyes, blinked them repeatedly, but I couldn't believe them.

Lorenzo, a look of desperation distorting his face, was asking me to let him in. I had no idea what he wanted. Or what he was doing on the ledge outside my window in the middle of the night. I might've fantasized the situation along the lines of some Romeo and Romeo romance. But his facial expression said something entirely different. I hurried and opened my window so that he could crawl in.

At first he said nothing, panting, out of breath. He motioned me to "Shh!" with his forefinger pressed against his lips. When he caught his breath, he told me that he'd been out past curfew. He'd gone to New York to buy drugs, and he promised to slip me a free bag for my troubles. Groggily, I accepted the reward for my deed.

"Thanks a lot, man," he said. "What's your name again?"

I knew that he knew my name. He also knew I had the hots for him. He was playing it safe.

"You know my name," I replied.

"Well, thanks a lot."

"Anytime."

"Well," he said, clearing his throat, his discomfort apparent as he searched for the next thing to say. "So, man, who you taking to the banquet tomorrow night?"

"Patrice Jackson. . . . You?" It was weird, knowing the answer before asking the question.

"Maxie," he said, anxiously jiggling the change in his pocket.

"Of course."

"Hey, man, I didn't know you and Patrice had a thing."

"Maybe that's because we don't."

"Oh. . . . Well, anyway, she's cute."

"Yeah, I guess."

"It's late," he said, looking at his watch, as if he hadn't known that before waking me up. He slapped his forehead with the palm of his hand. "I really should be going—"

"Are you and Maxie going steady?"

"Why?"

"Just asking," I said, now embarrassed by my prying—embarrassment stemming from the suspicion in his inflection. "I think you two make a nice couple."

"Well, man," he said, removing his shoes, tiptoeing across the floor, opening the door, turning to shake my hand. He looked both ways before stepping into the corridor, and whispered, "Thanks a lot for helping me out tonight. If there's anything I can do for you, man, let me know."

After he left, I clicked off the light and climbed back into bed.

In the darkness, against the whirring of crickets, the buzzing of mosquitoes, my back sticking to the humid, muggy, sweat-soaked sheets, I masturbated. Fourth time that day. All of them over him.

At the banquet I watched Lorenzo more than my own date. Admittedly, he and Maxie made an attractive couple. As speeches were read and awards handed out to the high achievers, I worried about having to kiss Patrice at the end of the night. Contemplating it there at our table, I realized that I'd never kissed a girl. Would she expect me to kiss her? Would she kiss me back?

My contributions to the campus newspaper were cited by Dr. Greene and Professor Maddox. I was asked to stand, which I did. The entire room broke into a thunderous applause, which startled me. I hadn't known I was so well-liked. In the distance I could see Lorenzo clapping loudest and whistling with his pinkies stuck in the corners of his mouth. As soon as he had finished clapping and whistling, he placed his arm around Maxie's bare shoulder, and I sensed a quickly passing wave of jealousy.

Toward the end of the night Lorenzo approached me, slapped me five, and reiterated how grateful he was to me for letting him in my window. Apparently, two other people had refused, afraid they'd be expelled along with him if caught. "Too bad we didn't have the chance to know each other better," he said.

Too bad, indeed, I thought.

All I could think of was having to kiss Patrice. Should it be a peck? On the cheek or the lips? Is she expecting tongue? Or more? I knew she expected something by the way she kept looking at me, and the manner and tone she employed when she spoke. I'd never heard it before. She was acting as if we were going together. She hadn't had a boyfriend all summer. Perhaps she needed an escort to make a statement. All week long, her roommate and girlfriends had teased me about her wherever I saw them—in class, the cafeteria, the bookstore. Sounded as if she'd told them we'd been engaged.

I'd known Patrice over the past six weeks as a fellow student and acquaintance. Like other students, she was as significant to me as the mosquito buzzing in my ear the night before.

Yet just this side of a week, her innocuous expectations had vexed me. I resented her for it. But I soothed myself with my only option. Control. Take charge, I told myself. She's the girl, and she expects you to be in control. She'd accept whatever I gave her. Even if it was a handshake.

When I walked her back to Chapin Hall, we stood on the wide veranda gazing nervously into each other's eyes. She obviously wanted me to kiss her. I was fumbling, and flirted with the idea of pecking her on the cheek before fleeing into the pitch darkness. After tonight I never have to see her again, I reminded myself.

I wrapped my arms around her, pulled her to me, and planted the kiss upon her lips for which I assumed she'd been waiting all night.

It was easier than I'd thought.

I just imagined it was Lorenzo.

STARS IN MY POCKET
LIKE GRAINS OF SAND

Samuel R. Delany

"Of course," they told him in all honesty, "you will be a slave."

His big-pored forehead wrinkled, his heavy lips opened (the flesh around his green, green eyes stayed exactly the same), the ideogram of incomprehension among whose radicals you could read ignorance's determinant past, information's present impossibility, speculation's denied future.

"But you will be happy," the man in the wire-filament mask went on from the well in the circle desk. "Certainly you will be happier than you are." The features moved behind pink and green plastic lozenges a-shake on shaking wires. "I mean, look at you, boy. You're ugly as mud and tall enough to scare children in the street. The prenatal brain damage, small as it is, we still can't correct. You've been in trouble of one sort or another for as long as there are records on you: orphanages, foster homes, youth rehabilitation camps, adult detention units—and *you* haven't gotten along in any of them. Sexually . . . ?" Lozenge tinkled against lozenge: the man's head shook. "In this part of the world your preferences in that area can't have done you any good. You're a burden to yourself, to your city, to your geosector." Lozenges lowered, just a bit: the man moved forward in his seat. "But we can change all that."

He pushed back in the sling that was uncomfortable and costly. A blank and intricate absence on his face, he raised one big-knuckled hand to point with a finger thick as a broom handle—for the technology of that world still made lathes, lasers, bombs, and brooms: the nail was gnawed almost off it, as were the nails on his other fingers and thumbs. Crowding his wide palms' edge, whether flailing before him or loose in his lap, those fingers seemed not only too rough and too heavy for any gentle gesture, but also—though, if you counted, there were only ten—too many. The finger (not the fore but the middle) jabbed brutally, futilely. "You can change me?" The voice in his nineteen-year-old throat was harsh as some fifty-year-old derelict's. "You can make me like you? Go on! Make me so I can understand things and numbers and reading and stuff!" As brutally, the finger came back against the horse-boned jaw: a mutated herpes virus, along with some sex-linked genetic anomaly, had, until three years ago when the proper phage was developed, rendered the ordinary adolescent acne of the urban males in that world's lower latitudes a red, pitted disaster. "All right, change me! Make me like you!"

Either side of a plastic diamond, the mouth's corners rose. "We could." The plastic swung with breath. "But if we did, then you wouldn't really *be* you anymore, now, would you?" From the black ceiling, through the orrery of masking bits, a hanging lamp dappled the man's naked arms. "We're going to make a change in your mind—a change in your brain—a very small change, a change much smaller than the one you just asked for. We're going to take that little knot of anger you just waved at me on the end of your finger, that anger you just threw back at your own face—we're going to take that knot and we're going to untie it. Maybe thirty brain cells will die by the time we're finished. Maybe six thousand synapses will be shorted open and left that way. Maybe another thousand will be permanently closed. The illegal drugs we know you've put in your belly and your lungs and your veins over the past twelve months, not to mention the past twelve years, have already wreaked more biological havoc among your basic ten billion than we will, by a factor of several hundred thousand. Indeed, a side effect of what we intend to do is that you simply won't *want* any more drugs. You'll be happy with who you are and with the tasks the world sets you. And you must admit that, as worlds go, this is a pretty beneficent one."

He didn't know what "beneficent" meant. And though he'd heard that there were other worlds, other cities (other than the three in whose slums and institutions he'd grown up), other counties, other geosectors, even other worlds with beings who were just not human, it all struck him as only dubiously credible.

Behind the mask with its plastic shapes a-bob, the man was saying: "It's a decision many men, not to say women, make. . . . Indeed, I read a report last week that said almost three times as many women as men on our world make this decision, though it doesn't seem my experience. The men—and women—who've made the decision we're asking of you include some fine folks, too: artists, scientists, politicians, well-respected philosophical thinkers. Some very rich and powerful people have decided to abandon their worldly acquisitions and come to the Institute here. They feel, I suppose, we have something to teach them. And though we certainly would never claim such a thing—our method is much too simple—perhaps we do."

"I can learn things," he suggested hoarsely, pulling back in the sling and looking down, for the tests he'd been given over the years suggested strongly that he couldn't. And the few times he'd hung around the places that were a confusion of books and tapes and films, they'd asked him to leave, or put him out, saying much what this masked man was saying now and saying it much more angrily. "I could learn if you taught me. . . ."

"You've learned to beg. You've learned to steal. And I gather in the last year or two you've learned that, for you, begging is better than stealing because you haven't learned to steal well enough to keep from getting caught. That stands you in good stead here." The mouth's corners rose again.

Deciding it must be a smile, he tried a small smile back—an expression he seldom let hold his long, rough face for any time.

"As I said, we're not out to change the fact of who you are. We only want to change that small bit of you grossly unhappy *with* that fact. All right. Do you choose happiness? You have only to say 'yes.' "

He said: "Will it—"

"Destroy your will? Oh, we don't do anything so simple or unsubtle. If you can make fine, fast, and fertile decisions now, you'll be able to make them afterward. You simply won't be inclined to make new *kinds* of decisions, at least without instructions."

He said: "Will it *hurt* . . . ?"

"Say 'yes.' There's no pain, I assure you—either physical or emotional. After all, what did you come here for?"

He said: "Well, yeah. Sure. That's why I—"

"Say 'yes.' We need a voiceprint of the actual word; this is being recorded. Otherwise it isn't legal."

Which confused him. " 'Yes . . .'? Yeah, but that's what I—" and felt something terrible in him pull away or something gigantic in him vanquished; and its departure or defeat was a relief or a release, which, because he had never felt *any*thing before to such an extent, seemed more something that hadn't, rather than something that had, happened: not an overwhelming occurrence to him so much as a total surround revealed—or removed. He asked, because the question had been struggling with the back of his tongue and came out through momentum rather than desire: "When you gonna do it?"

"We just did." (He really didn't want to know . . .) "You, of course"— the man laughed—"expected lightning to whip down from electrodes in the ceiling and crackle about your beleaguered skull—really, we *must* do something with that ringworm! I mean, on a young man *your* age? Actually, we use midrange gamma-ray lasers . . . but you wouldn't understand. Put your thumbprint here." From beneath the desk the man took out a yellow cube, extended it.

He reached forward to press the great sausage of his thumb on the transparent face.

"There. That gives the RAT Institute license to sell you to a labor project that, in our estimation, will be both profitable and humane. Let's see . . ." The man's other hand came up to scatter more cubes, clicking, across the desk. Lozenges dipped to study the inscribed marks: turquoise, orange, lavender. "You had a vasectomy in the orphanage back when you were"—he turned one to another face—"thirteen . . . apparently a reversible one, should you or anyone else want to bother. Well, though you're not likely to initiate anything in that department now, it's astonishing how many people still try to use slaves for sex. And we haven't done anything that'll stop you from responding—if your accustomed stimuli are applied. But that's no longer our concern." Lozenges lifted. Those over the eyes (purple left and green right) were transparent enough to see through to blinking lids. "You're as happy now as you can be, aren't you?" (The silence welling in him obliterated any need to deny, and, anyway, he had never been much for denying what was told him with sufficient authority.) "But I don't have to say that to you. You know it. If you'll just go through there . . . ?"

He stood.

On the arched door were the three hieroglyphs: *Radical Anxiety Termination.* In his search for the Institute, he had finally come to recognize them, though he still could not really read them, if only because—as a number of people had explained, patiently or impatiently, while he'd been searching—he could pronounce none of the three correctly, even after they'd been repeated to him many, many times.

He did not think this as he pushed through the flap, where, after waiting nine hours, he was given a shower with some fifteen or twenty others in a hall set up to wash hundreds.

Three hours later he was given a shirt too loose over his shoulders and pants too tight under his crotch, both of them as usual ridiculously short for his long, long legs and arms—he was just shy of seven-foot-four; and though on that world six-foot-eight or six-foot-ten was not unusual for a man or a woman, still all of that world's beautiful people (and the vast majority of its famous ones) were under five-foot-five.

An hour after that, in a narrow room, he ate a meal standing elbow to elbow with a number of others it did not occur to him to count at a chest-high trough—on him, to his ribs' bottom. They ladled up metal cups of lukewarm broth, drank, then ladled up more, drank those, ladled up still more. Some wiped where the broth ran down their chins with the backs of their sleeves. He didn't—because they hadn't changed who he was, and he certainly wouldn't have otherwise.

For five hours he slept in a blue dormitory with green plastic sleeping pads fixed permanently to the floor: in better condition than those at the detention house he'd been in three months ago, which was the last time he'd slept indoors. There the edges had been split, the stuffing soiled and lumpy. He looked at these, remembered the others, and was aware of no contrast.

For three days he was transported in a freight car through underground tunnels, during which time he was not fed at all—an oversight, apparently, from the resigned humor of the supervisor at the other end who discovered it: "Look, if you don't feed the rats, they ain't gonna scurry."

"It was an accident, man! Besides, I hear you can let 'em go thirty, forty days without food and they'll still—"

"Just do your job and feed 'em?"

For six years he labored among the dozen porters at a polar desert research station where, at the printed orders of the computer console in the research station vestibule, he carried small machines strapped on his side to an information relay outpost fourteen kilometers away; and carried papers and tapes back to the research station in a dark yellow canvas bag with a dim picture of a lizard in brown and gold above the self-sealing flap.

At the orders of the men and women who worked there, he dollied medium-sized machines up and down from the station's underground refrigeration crypts, where his bare feet left wet prints on the frosted metal walks, where the thrum of some machine down one of the storage corridors made a purple tubelight near the double doors flicker every time the mechanical hum suddenly speeded or slowed, and where the hanks of cable looping under the studded ceiling plates were nobbed along their length with glimmering transparent lumps called "ice"—which had something to do with water, though he didn't know what.

Once he was told to make a special trip at four-thirty in the morning out to the relay station to pick up some readings, only the man who told him was new and pointed in the wrong direction. He knew it wasn't right, but he thought that's where they wanted him to go anyway. So he walked for six hours while the sky went from starless black to cloudy red in flaming streaks above the sand, brightening to orange and becoming hotter.

And hotter.

And hotter . . . .

They found him, sitting, his feet moving a little, one, then the other, as if still trying to walk, his eyelids swollen closed, his lips dusted gray, cracked here and there, the blood in the cracks dried to black, and the black dusted gray again, his huge hand over the embossed lizard, protecting it from the sun.

They had come after the bag, of course. It had a signal-locator built in that let them find it anywhere, and it might have had some things in it they needed. No one had known for sure what it contained when they'd discovered it was gone that morning.

They took him back, too.

He lay on an old piece of canvas in the sunscreened rear of the transport with a wet rag in his mouth. One or the other of them took it out every few minutes and re-wet it so that he could suck it.

No one ever asked him why he'd gone the wrong way—though he could have told them. After that they just said he was very stupid.

Even for a rat.

One night during his third year there, three of the porters sleeping on the sand beside him began to shiver, vomit, and make strangling noises. After four hours, while he lay awake watching, first two, a few minutes apart, then half an hour later the third, died.

The next morning the woman first in charge of the station beat him with a steel pipe:

"You *brainless*, moronic, *worthless* . . . ! *Why* didn't you come *in* and *wake* somebody *up*! You idiotic—!"

The man second in charge pulled her away by her loose, sleeveless shirt. "Come on, now! Cut it out!" (Whatever had been done to him six years ago, though it had stopped any necessity to respond to pain with expressions either of fear or defiance, did not make pain hurt any the less.) "They only do what you tell them. Nobody's ever told this one anything about q-plague."

"Then what does he think the rest of us are all up here *studying* it for! . . . I know: he *doesn't* think!" Before her, plastic careened and swerved and rattled. "But seventy-six SI-units apiece those three cost me! And they actually had some skills." (By now he knew he'd only cost twenty-eight.) "Why couldn't *he* have gotten infected! He's been here longer than the rest. You'd think—" Then, not thinking, she struck him again, on the knee, so that he finally fell to the mottled thermoplast flooring, one hand over his bleeding ear, the other feeling around his agonized patella.

"Come *on*, now! Just leave him a—"

"What I want to know is how the virus got out into the rat cage anyway. I mean nobody was supposed to—" Then she turned, flung the pipe away— it rolled to clank the baseboard—and stalked off. The man second in charge put him back to work an hour later, where he heard three of the other men talking outside behind the station:

"Did you see the way she went after that damned rat? I mean I was just up the hallway when she lit into him, man!" (*Rat* was what you called someone who'd been to the Institute: *man* was what you called someone who hadn't.) "With a steel pipe! I thought she was gonna kill him!"

"It's working for a woman, man. That's all. I just never was that comfortable working for a damned bitch." (*Bitch*, on that world, was what men called women they were extremely fond of or extremely displeased with when the woman was not there.) "It just isn't right."

"Well, you know the boss. She's been under a lot of pressure, right through here. And I've worked for worse."

"I know, I know. Still, it gets me, to see her go after somebody—even a rat—that way." Shaking their heads, they went on talking.

Their lozenges tinkled.

He took down the work gloves from the rack of gloves along the hangar door's back and pulled them on. One fraying pressure bandage deviled the bottom of his vision along his right cheek. The other was bound just a little too tight on his left leg. He rolled orange-rimmed drum after orange-rimmed drum to stand beside the lift rail of the thirty-meter sled.

". . . as soon as a bitch gets any power, man. And with a damned rat . . ."

He walked back for another drum and did not think: They talk of me as though I were invisible. But as he tipped the container to its rim, he saw the woman (besides the woman who was first in charge, she was one of two others—excluding rats—on the station staff) who directed the loading. She stood about two meters from the men, a hank of strings hanging from her fist. Threaded on each were the dozens of tiny cubes about which were glyphed the loading, packing, and shipping orders for the station. She had turned her wire mask around on her head so that the intricate plastic shapes, translucent and opaque, hung by her ears.

Her naked eyes were green.

In the lined flesh about them (she was not a young woman, but she must have been handsome once, for she was not above five feet tall), he read an expression he recognized as one that had, from time to time, before all this, fixed his own face. (Since the vestibule console had been dropping its oversized message-cubes into his hands every morning, hieroglyph on one side, a simple picture explaining it on another, and on still others the totally mysterious alphabetics, he had been learning—for they had *not* changed who he was, and he had *said* he could learn things—to read.) He could not have spoken what was written in her face now.

"Hey, man," someone called to her from the corner of the sled, "you better check out your stacking schedule . . ."

What he did think was: a damned bitch . . . a damned rat. . . . He watched her watch him. Slowly she reached up. Strings swung, cubes *clisked,* plastic clattered as she twisted her mask to place. She breathed out, making no sound and taking a long time doing it. Then, wrapping the hanks of string efficiently around her forearm, she turned to go after three other rats struggling with a distillation unit just inside the hangar door.

He began to roll his drum.

In his sixth year there, an important personage came to inspect the station. He noticed, and did not think about, the titters and whispers passed on station rampways and at turns in the halls. ("I don't care *how* tall they look! You better stop talking like that, or somebody just might start wondering about *you* . . . !") The day before, the woman first in charge had suddenly resigned, and he had heard men talking in the corridors, behind purples and greens and blacks and yellows: "She told him she was going back south and commit herself to the rat-makers! I mean, can you imagine someone who's reached *her* position doing *that* to themselves? She's got to be crazy, man. I always told you she was crazy—although you have to respect the bitch." And the other woman had left the station a long time ago anyway.

That night he turned over on the ground, waking, to see the station's back door open on a silhouette in yellow light. (Inside the station the halls were always illuminated with yellow tubelights during the hot polar winter.) A body sheath of gold—possibly a silver that just looked gold in that mustard glow—a tall cylindrical mask, black and set with dozens of reception and projection lenses, black boots with decameter-thick soles . . .

He did not know, nor did he wonder, which lenses worked.

"Well . . ." The short laugh was mechanically distorted. "I just thought I would come out and see for myself."

Around him on the ground lay an oval of blue, which came from one of the lenses. At one edge was the foot of the rat sleeping to his left; on his other side was the blued elbow of the rat to his right.

"I always check with the Institute before I embark on one of these expeditions to the outer reaches. Shutting down a station like this, this far away from civilization, is never pleasant. Still, you'd be surprised what you can find in the rat cage if you look. For example, the Institute told me before I came that you—yes, you—and I share complementary predilections that might have resulted in an hour or so of pleasure for us both." The mechanical laugh again. "I'm afraid, however, I hadn't counted on—" The glow around him changed to red; nothing else happened—"your looking quite like that. Your face . . . ! Well, I shall simply retire to my rooms. And perhaps cut my stay here short by a day or two. Sorry to have disturbed you. Go back to sleep." The figure in the high-soled boots retreated, tottering, behind the door and closed it.

He lay on his back, curious at the warmth flickering low in his belly, in his thighs, a flickering which, as he recognized in it an almost forgotten arousal, ceased.

He slept. And woke with a gentle shaking of his shoulder. He blinked in the orange dawn-light. A thick sole rocked him back and forth. Above, the speaker-distorted voice said: "All right, up you go. Time to get up." The masked figure moved on to kick another rat awake, but gently—which was not the way they kicked him awake other mornings. "All right. Everybody up. Well, rats, what do you think of the new job you're going to, hey?" The figure stopped to brush sand off the shoulder of one woman porter.

"Think . . . ?"

The figure laughed. "You *can* think, you know—though they don't encourage it in places like this." In the tight, metallic suit the man moved among shambling rats. The cylindrical mask revolved. Lenses retracted; lenses appeared. Then the figure paused. "Didn't they tell you yesterday that all of you had been sold?"

One rat said, "No. They didn't tell us."

The cylindrical mask revolved again. "I hate it when they treat rats that way. It isn't necessary. They could have told you. I hate it." A light behind one lens changed from deep red to green, but under the streaked sky it wasn't that noticeable. "Well, you *have* been sold, the lot of you. Most of you are going north again."

It was another underground station with sandstone walls up to the wire mesh below the ceiling. The masked figure was with them.

He stared at the lensed headmask, unblinking—not feeling any of last night's lust but remembering it, wondering if it would come again. The creature behind the lenses didn't seem to notice at all—until the car roared up.

"Okay, inside you go. Inside!" and the little hand reached way up to give him a friendly push on the shoulder. "Sorry, rat. . . ." Then the door of the transport shut behind him and he was in the dark with the others. (There should have been some lights. But they probably weren't working.) He nearly fell when the car moved.

Many hours later, they shot from darkness into pale, blinding blue. With his eyes squinched against the glare, forcing them open, closing them, then forcing them open again, he realized that the curved roof and the upper half of the walls as well as large parts of the floor were transparent.

Between the rings that, every few seconds, flashed back around the hurtling car, he saw cloud and, way below, rock. Here and there something flickered as though the stones were afire. Hundreds of meters or hundreds of kilometers ahead a mountain wall drew closer, darkening.

Red and brown rocks towered about.

Moments before the car smashed into the stone-face, he saw the hole with still another ring around it.

Another rat in the car mumbled: "Another world . . . ."

They plunged into it: darkness.

He'd known his world contained cities and sand. But the canyon, with its rocks and rampant clouds, made him, though he could not have said how, change his vision of what a world was.

After the ride there was another station, another shower. The man who ushered the hundreds of rats who'd been collected here into the hangar, under water nozzles along the ceilings and walls, stopped him long enough to say, "Jeeze! *You* look like you ain't been washed since you *got* to the Institute!" (The rat cage in back of the polar station, though it had been disinfected and deodorized once a month, had not had any water for washing rats.) After the shower they were issued more clothes. (The ones he'd been given back at the Institute had, down at the polar station, come apart, bit by bit, first at the places they'd been too tight, then all over, now a sleeve falling off, now a pants leg torn away; for the last year he and the other porters had done their work naked.) He was fed from another trough.

Under girders and wires and behind round windows that distorted things at their edges, he worked for three weeks at the industrial yard before he associated the frequently repeated name *Muct* with the unknown hieroglyph above the doors and on the first cubes of all instruction strings and stenciled in yellow over the brown and green enameled machines. There were seven machines from which he had to clean the soot and soiled lubricant that blackened his hands and stiffened his clothes. Unlike the polar station, here he was fed twice a day, washed every three days, and his work togs changed biweekly. Around him, thousands of rats serviced the great city full of machines, called Muct.

The man in charge, of him and some thirty-two others, told him many things, now about one machine, now about another, told him the things softly, simply, clearly—told him to remember them; and what he was told to do, he did. In six months he had learned how to drive two of the machines and how to repair four others so well that frequently he did not see the man who was in charge for three or four days at a time.

Sometimes the man came in to where he was working, with another man who himself was being trained to be a rat trainer. "Now who says they can't learn? Look at this one here, for instance. You just got to know how to teach 'em, is all. They learn better than an ordinary man. I mean, you tell them to do something, they do it. And they remember it—*if* you tell 'em to remember. You just got to know what to tell. I always say to you new guys, you tell a rat to take a shit, you gotta remember to tell 'er to pull her pants down first and then pull 'em up afterwards. Or you gonna have a rat with shitty pants." (Most of the rats back at the polar station and most of the rats at Muct were women.) "But some guys don't have the patience. You gotta be patient with a rat. Man, I can get these damned rats to do anything a damned man can do. I can even get them to do things you wouldn't think a damned bitch could do. Once I taught a rat to cook food for me, just as good as a man."

"Oh, I know women who can cook!"

"Well, yeah. But those were exceptions," the trainer said. "And I mean, a damned rat . . . ?"

"What else did you teach her?" The interlocutor's lozenges tinkled.

The man in charge, who didn't wear a mask (like a rat himself), just grinned as they went out.

Sometimes between work shifts the man would sneak several rats into his own quarters and tell them to do odd things. Several times other trainers came and kidded him about it or, occasionally, yelled at him about it. Sometimes he kidded or yelled back. But he didn't stop. "I mean," he said, "they all do it, too. Even some of the bitches. It ain't nothing. It goes along with keeping you rats in line. I mean, what's a damned rat for, anyway? I ain't never heard one of you complain about it—hey, rat?" And *he* wasn't one of the rats the man took off with him, anyway.

He had a sleeping pad again. During those hours of the afternoon or night when his shift was not working, he sat on a long bench, watching a high screen, on which were projected stories about men and women who wore the dangling masks. Somewhere before the end of each story one man or another would rip a woman's mask off and the woman would turn her face away and cry. If the wrong man did it, the right man would kill him— or sometimes kill the woman.

A month after he got there, they fixed the sound on the projector; after that the stories made more sense.

He worked and watched stories for three years; then one morning the man in charge came to kick him awake.

He pushed himself up to his elbow.

"They sold you!" The man kicked him again, about as hard as he'd ever *been* kicked, so that he fell back down and had to push up again. "How you like that! They sold you out from under me! I've really *worked* on you, too, you mindless rat! You don't treat a damned man like that. You don't treat a rat like that, either!"

He thought the man was going to kick him again. But he didn't.

"They said they needed some rats with some kind of experience down in the south. You didn't *have* no damned experience when you came here. You didn't know a thing. Now you got some you can use to do something useful, and they're gonna take you off, who knows where, and use you for who knows what! It ain't fair, not after all the words I shoved into your dirty ears! It ain't fair!"

The man went away. But that evening, after work, he came back. "Come with me, now."

So he got up off his pad and went.

The man's quarters were not large. The other male rat and the five females they had picked up on the way almost filled the cluttered cubicle.

"Okay, okay, get your clothes off. Get 'em off, now." The man was tall (almost as tall as he was), and he put an arm around his shoulder. "This is going to be a going-away party for our friend here. He's been sold south, you see. He's going away tomorrow—and it's a damned shame, too. It ain't fair. So come on! Get your clothes off now. Put 'em over there. There're some masks. Put 'em on—no, on your *head*, shit-for-brains! Come on, you been here before. You remember now, for next time. Put on the masks; then you can feel like real people for a while." He scratched his ear. "I don't think it does a damned rat no harm to feel like a real bitch—excuse me"— to a rat who'd dropped her splotched tunic to adjust a wire headframe from which more than half the plastic pieces were missing—"or a man. Myself, I think it makes 'em work better. And it don't hurt 'em much, don't care what they say. . . ."

That night he was told to do some odd things. ("I want you to do just like you'da done at this kind of party before you come to the Institute. Exactly like it, you understand? You can use that one, or that one, or that. Only not her—she's my favorite, right through here, you see? Unless of course she's got something you really like a lot.") The man in charge never did put on a mask himself. For much of the evening he made love to one of the masked women while the other masked male struck him on the shoulders and buttocks with a piece of frayed copper wire and called him "a tiny rat" and other things.

There *wasn't* much he'd have done at this kind of party except sit, watch, and bite at his cuticles and nails. (As a boy he'd been to a couple like it.) So that's what he did. After half an hour the man in charge, who had spatters of blood all over his shoulder blades by now, looked up and noticed. "Okay, then," he said. "I want you to play with yourself until you come. You, too—" which was to a female rat.

So he did.

It felt astonishing and surprising and pleasant—the most powerful thing that had happened to him since the moment he'd said "Yes," at Radical Anxiety Termination. When the man in charge sent him outside to go back to his sleeping pad, the female rat had not finished.

The next day some women in plain beige face covers got him and took him to another station where he was put on another car. Days later he got out at a station with sandstone walls, wire mesh on the ceiling.

Among the men who came to pick up the six rats who'd been delivered, he recognized one, and after a few minutes, while he was checking them for hernias and bad teeth, the man recognized him. "Hey, this one was here six years ago!" he said to his companion. "A real idiot! *He* couldn't do nothing right! I think they sent us the wrong rat! The order was for rats with some experience of what we were doing up here. But I didn't mean just any rat who'd *been* here before and couldn't *do* anything!"

"What're you gonna do? Send him back?"

"Naw. We can use him for porter work. That's what they used him for before."

He worked at the polar station, which had been reopened, doing pretty much what he'd done—carrying the bag back and forth to the data station— for seven years more. Lots of things were different, at least at first. There was another man in charge. Though he didn't know exactly what, the station was now studying something other than q-plague. Now there were several large, spidery instruments that sat out in the sand with great arms yearning toward the orange sky. And the wall behind the rat cage had been painted blue.

For a while the rats at the station were given clean clothes each month or so. But they missed the laundry more and more frequently. One morning, when their clothes hadn't been changed for three months, a man came out to the cage. "Okay, come on. Take 'em off. We're going to go back to the old way. Naked's better than walking around in that stuff." Feeding went back to once a day after that, too.

Coming back across the sand, by the power pylons, he saw the green transport sled and walked by its high, sand-scarred flanks into the station vestibule to lift up the lizard-embossed flap of his canvas bag and empty the elliptical spools of data tape into the receiving slot. About an hour later someone called him and three female rats into the office of the man in charge.

Years ago, it seemed, he'd been in the room to take out tubs of old message strings and bits of discarded packing foam. Today the walls were blue, like the back wall of the rat cage.

A very tall woman sat on a cushion on the black tiled floor, one sandaled foot on the desk's lowest shelf. Her heel had overturned a stack of multicolored cubes. Some had fallen to the ground.

"You know that what you're asking is illegal."

The woman made a barking sound, becoming a laugh that would have set her lozenges shaking only for some reason she'd taken off her mask and tossed it on the tile so that the colored bits lay in a tangle. "You think a bitch like me doesn't know that? Do you think a bitch like me would come in here and ask what I'm asking of you if this station were three thousand kilometers closer to the population belt?" She pulled her foot off the shelf. It dropped to the black, along with three bright cubes. She smiled, as if she knew that behind his plastic bits the man currently in charge smiled back. "What kind of bitch do you think I am?"

"I think—" The man coughed. "Well, really, I don't know why I'm doing this. It's irregular—"

"I only said you should bring them in and let me look them over." She drew her heel back to the cushion and put her arms across her knees.

"And I have." The man coughed again. "I have. There they are . . . but I don't know why I'm doing it. It's irregular, and it's illegal, and—"

"I'll tell you why you're doing it." The smile softened on her dark face. "The economy in over a third of the equatorial geosectors is failing. Neither the political swing toward the extreme Yellow, the insurgent Crazy-Grays, nor the Free-Informationist backlash is going to mean a return to the soft-money economy that will benefit any of the polar projects, north or south. I took a look at the shape your rat cage was in before I came inside. Hot stars and cold magma! You men haven't been properly staffed in three years, and getting rid of another mouth to feed—even a rat's—is going to be more help than hindrance. You know it. I know it. And that's why you'll do it—"

He didn't know why she paused, but he expected her to pick up her discarded mask and put it back on now; that's what the women on the projection screen at Muct had always done after they paused meaningfully. But that had been years ago, somewhere else in the world.

This woman still smiled, face still bare.

The masked man behind the desk took a silent breath. White hair moved on his chest under his shirt's soiled net. "You're quite a woman."

"I'm quite a bitch." She threw back her head, and her hair, which was dark and wiry, did not swing. "That's how you'll say it when I'm gone. Say it to me that way now."

Behind the swinging fragments, the man coughed again. "Well, I guess you are." He rose, stepping from behind the desk. "A bitch. At any rate. These are the ones I can let you choose from."

She turned on the cushion, rising to her knees. She had an expression of great concentration now, an expression the women in the projected stories never wore. After seconds she stood. "I told you I was interested in males."

She touched her chin with her fingertips, moving them a little as if scratching some half-felt itch. She was a good head-and-a-half taller than the man in charge.

"Well, we have more females here." The man shrugged. "These are the ones we can spare."

"Mmmm," she said, as though she knew that already. Then she said: "Which more or less limits me to this one. Tell me"—she turned to face him—"are you ready to come away with me to strange climes and stranger lands and be my slave forever, to obey my every command, to fulfill any and every whim and caprice I should articulate, no matter how debased or lascivious?"

He did not know what "articulate" or "lascivious" or some of the other words meant. "Yeah . . . ?"

The man in charge coughed once more.

The woman chuckled over her shoulder. "That was mostly for your benefit. He isn't exactly what I pictured, I admit." She turned back, reached forward, touched his naked cheek, grimacing as if she questioned some terribly important point to which he was oblivious. "But you'll do. You'll have to, won't you? It's cut into your brain now, that you'll do . . . do what I say." Her hand fell from his face, a finger brushing his collarbone in the fall. "How much do you want for him?" She turned to the man in charge and, stepping over fallen cubes in her scuffed sandals, took out a coil of silver string from her leggings pocket and began to unroll it, silent lips counting the evenly spaced black beads along it to which cubes could be clipped.

The man mentioned a price so far above twenty-eight SI units he simply decided that they weren't discussing him after all.

The woman kept wrapping silver around her fist, kept counting. Finally she popped the credit cord, rolled it from her palm with her thumb, and put the SI payment on the desk. "You know you're overcharging me by even more than some black-market slaver might in some mildewed equatorial bazaar." She still smiled.

"You know," the man said, "the only reason I'm doing this at all is because—"

"—is because you think you can get away with it." She put the remaining credit roll back in her pocket and bent to pick up her mask with a swipe of her arm. "That's why I'm doing it, too." Lozenges clicked and tinkled on tangled wire. "Would you like me to take him out the back? We'll attract less notice that way."

"Yes," the man in charge said. Then he said, "Just a moment." He reached behind the desk, opened a lower file, and pulled out one of the

yellow canvas bags with the embossed lizard. "He can put his things in this."
He handed it across the desk.

"Thanks." She took it and slipped the strap over her arm. "This way?"

"Yes," the man repeated. He came around to the front of the desk to pick up the cubes she'd knocked from the desk shelf. He knelt. "The back way. Yes, that would be best."

LOVE STORY

BLACK

William Demby

"Miss Pariss? Miss *Mona* Pariss?"

"Who are you? You my new welfare worker?"

"No, ma'am—I'm—well, I'm a writer . . ."

Hastily I backed away from the triple-chained crack in the door through which her darting suspicious eyes were studying me, and I assumed the smiling expression of a kindly undertaker to convince her, and myself as well, that I was neither a criminal nor a policeman—though my nose was vibrating convulsively from the exotic stench of collard greens, pork fat cooking, and powerful incense leaking out onto the darkly sinister landing of the fourth floor walk-up apartment where the great lady lived.

"How come those people down at welfare always changing my worker?" she whined, she too shuffling back cautiously from her side of the door, so that I caught a fluttering glimpse of what looked like a tattered Oriental robe of embroidered dragons and poisonous flowers draped over a slender body like an oversized flag around a corpse.

"I'm not a welfare worker, Miss Pariss," I repeated loudly, thinking perhaps she was deaf. "I'm a writer—"

"Oh, you one of them welfare *auditors*. Well, I ain't got nothing to hide from the government. But where's my Miss Hollygreen—that nice red-headed white girl got me my telephone put in. I ain't seen hide nor hair of her since way before Christmas, and my arthritis been accumulating something terrible . . ."

"Miss Pariss," I said wearily, "I've been sent by *New Black Woman* magazine to interview you, or at least seek your permission for such an interview—"

Nervously I fumbled in my jacket pocket for the letter Gracie had had her secretary prepare for me, neatly typed and very official looking on heavy bond paper, and bearing the self-consciously elegant *New Black Woman* letterhead. I pushed the crisp letter through the crack of the door, but Miss Pariss only took another step backward.

"I already been interviewed by the welfare people," she said, sidestepping the letter, "three times—twice at the Center, and they didn't even pay my busfare, and once by some pimply-assed dude who came snooping around the apartment looking for rats and cockroaches, pretending he was an exterminator, when I could tell right away he was an inspector from the Department of Social Services by that skinny black tie he was wearing and those cheap two-toned Thom McAn shoes, and he had on one of those skinny-brimmed Jewish black hats—"

"Please, Miss Pariss—!"

"Now come to think of it—how come you know my real name before I was married? How come you know my stage name? You a detective from the Bureau of Investigation? If you are, I don't know nothing about the nigger they found cut up into stewing beef in the apartment across the hall. My motto is 'See no evil, hear no evil, and talk no evil. . . .' I'm a religious woman, and I stay out of trouble like trouble stinks, and trouble stays away from me like I stink—if you'll pardon the metaphor, that's show business talk you know—"

"If you'll just read this letter, Miss Pariss, it will explain everything."

Bony fingers heavily burdened with many gaudy rings and with long purple-painted nails snatched the letter from my hand.

"I got to get my reading glasses," she said, "so you stand right there and cool your heels while I go and verify your credentials."

Abruptly and definitively the door slammed shut, and there was the grating sound of locks being turned, and I was left standing there on the dark landing, feeling humiliated and impotent, my initial elation over the assignment having abandoned me already, as though the stench of collard greens, pork fat, and incense had the effect on my already shaken psyche of a depressant gas.

I lit a cigarette and glanced at my watch, thinking that if I could get this over within half an hour or so I would still be in time for my first class of the fall semester. But when almost fifteen minutes passed and there was still no sound from within Miss Pariss's apartment, I knocked urgently on the door—the way detectives knock on doors in the movies.

Still no sound from within. But now in the abrupt silence I heard faltering footsteps climbing the creaky wooden steps that had evidently replaced the concrete steps long since disintegrated, for Miss Pariss lived in an ancient town house that had undergone countless transformations in its century-old existence.

In a few minutes a light-skinned black man with the puffy jowls and slow shuffling one-sided walk of a waiter still carrying an invisible tray appeared on the landing. He was wearing a jaunty red, black, and green wool ski cap and a frayed black minister's coat which was several sizes too small for his flabby cucumber-shaped frame. Under his arm he carried a hand-carved cane with a crudely wrought Coptic cross on the head, and with his free hand he was hugging a gallon jug of red Gallo wine, which he delicately placed on the sagging floor in front of the apartment adjoining Miss Pariss's and began to fumble clumsily in his bulging coat pocket for his keys. Apparently he was in a drunken stupor, but after several unsuccessful attempts at fitting the key into the lock, his eyes narrowly focused on me and he turned, his blood-streaked eyes narrowed with suspicion.

"You the new welfare worker?" he asked in a squeaky belligerent tone of voice.

"No, I'm not—I'm waiting for Miss Pariss. . . ."

"Miss Pariss? Maybe you mean Madam Sheba Smith—anyway, she ain't home. She gone for the week. Her sister down home in Cedric, North Carolina, died—besides she already been inspected by the exterminator—"

"But I just spoke with her—I'm waiting for her to open the door—"

"You musta been speaking to a ghost then, 'cause she ain't back from the funeral. I thought you was the new welfare worker, 'cause that hinckety white girl ain't been back since the week before Christmas, and she promised me an emergency clothing allowance on account of the fire last Thanksgiving when they turned off my electricity and I had to use candles. . . ."

Wheezing as though he had a console of tiny whistles embedded in his chest, he promptly forgot me and, having finally found his keys, he began unlocking each of three locks with the solemn concentration and dignity of the night watchman of a bank.

When the door closed behind him, I lit another cigarette and resolved that if Miss Pariss didn't open the door within a few minutes I was going to leave and renounce the whole project of interviewing her, no matter what Gracie would say about novelists lacking "journalistic initiative," the exact phrase she had used when I first approached her about doing a "literary" piece for her new magazine.

"We're not printing any of that washed-out white literary chichi bullshit," was her scathing retort. "We're trying to get to the nitty-gritty shit about the black experience!"

Gracie didn't like my novels and said I'd lived in Europe too long.

"You've got to take that brain of yours out of that white plastic bag!" she said.

And maybe she was right. At any rate, here I was standing like a fool in a toxic cloud of collard greens, cooking fat, and incense waiting for Miss Pariss to open the door. And just as I was about to knock one last time, the door opened wide and Miss Pariss appeared, a sly smile on her nut-brown face.

She looked much younger than I expected. Gracie said their research indicated she must have been at least eighty-four years old. But in that dismal light she appeared to be a well-preserved sixty, her true age, whatever it was, betrayed mostly by the shrunken and wrinkled skin on her long clawlike hands, in both of which she still clutched the letter of introduction as though it were an official proclamation to be read before an audience.

"What kind of magazine this *New Black Woman?*" she demanded. "I ain't never heard of no magazine like this—"

"Well—it's kind of like a fashion magazine—" I lied, imagining all too well Gracie's obscene reaction had she heard me.

"Kind of like a black version of *Vogue* magazine—"

Miss Pariss looked down at the letter again, her lips moving as she read, and then began to study me for such a long time that I coughed and involuntarily scratched my head.

"It's a rather new magazine of its kind," I said in a sinking voice. "As its title suggests, it attempts to reflect the new awakening of the black woman. I might add that it is doing quite well financially. Actually, I should have brought along a copy to show you—"

"You one good-looking dude, even with that Jew-boy nose—you ain't one of them dancing queens downstairs keep everybody awake playing that symphonette music on their hi-fi, is you?"

"I'm a writer, a novelist—and I teach college—"

"Well, you talk educated white. Those dancers, they's homosexuals, if you get what I mean—funny fairies, I call them, not that I hold that against them, but I like my black dudes doing their stud business through the front door like the good Lord ordained—"

"About the interview, Miss Pariss? I'm afraid I'm running short of time;

I've got a class to teach and this is the first day of the semester. I hope you don't misunderstand my rushing you like this. But what about the interview?"

"You sure you ain't no welfare inspector?"

"No, ma'am—nor a detective either—perhaps it would be more convenient if I phone you for the interview—"

"My phone been turned off for two months—"

"But you *do* agree to the interview?"

"I ain't agreed to nothing—"

She was studying me now with such intensity, her mouth slack in a sly, mocking smile, that I could feel my hands perspiring, and I began to rub them nervously along the sides of my trousers.

"You sure one good-looking dude," she said suddenly, "and you say you ain't one of them funny fairies from downstairs—"

She took one more look at the letter, read it through word for word, then meticulously folded it and placed both the letter and the envelope in her sunken bosom.

"Well, I'll tell you what I'll do—" she said, lowering her voice to a conspiratory whisper. "You come back this evening, just before "The Bill Cosby Show" go on the air. There ain't no lock on the door downstairs, but when you come up here to *my* door, you knock three times just like this—"

And she rapped on the door three times in a rapid signallike manner.

"That way I'll know it's you and not that wino bum Reverend Grooms lives next door—because he's not supposed to know I'm back yet—"

 Promptly at five minutes before eight, the hour "The Bill Cosby Show" went on the air, I was back on the dark landing in front of the door to Miss Pariss's apartment. But now the jubilant hubbub of TV sets and the thumping basso profundo beat of hi-fis reverberating all up and down the dismal stairwell of the prisonlike interior of the derelict West Side building created a less sinister impression and, indeed, I felt the almost childish euphoria of embarking on some mystery magic tour. Also contributing to my high spirits was the fact that the first day of the semester had gone rather well—and my usual air of self-conscious timidity was replaced by a deep-voiced stance of authority, enhanced no doubt by a snappy teaching outfit I had purchased two days before with Gracie's assistance (she had always complained that my pseudo-Ivy League clothes made me look like an equal opportunity insurance company trainee), consisting of a brown velvet combat jacket, bell-bottom velvet trousers, and a very expensive stamped nylon body shirt with a bright red-and-green tribal motif. After holding forth somewhat pompously on the importance of honesty in writing, I had had the class write a short paper about themselves in the third person—as though they were describing someone else, with the emphasis on honesty rather than style. Most of my students are working-class Irish and Italians from Staten Island and the Bay Ridge section of Brooklyn, and for most of them, having a more or less young and hip black professor is something of a novelty, which of course enhances my authority and permits me to get away with certain theatrics and pomposities I would be ashamed to indulge in had I been teaching in an Ivy League college. But as a novelist and an exotic black professor who has lived many years abroad, hamming it up is as much a professional stock-in-trade as it is for a ward politician, and my students love it. Especially my black students, of which there are only a sprinkling in my classes, with the exception of my black lit class, which is made up almost entirely of black students. At the end of the hour I hadn't had a chance to glance at all the papers as they were sheepishly turned in, but one paper, turned in after less than fifteen minutes of frantically confident pen-scratching by a fat black girl, was so cryptic and strange that I read it to myself three times, long after the classroom was deserted.

(This girl she 5'6" tall and has weight of average person, has large Afro on her head, wear a skirt about 3 inches from her knee. Complexion medium brown. Like dark colors. Walk fast always. Wear a black coat with gold button down the front. Appears a very likeable person. Was at one time very active in football, basketball, handball. Like children. Once start something always hope to finish the project. But she only visit your English class. Is always dieting never losing more than a few pounds at a time. Rainy days are her best day. She hate math. But would like to drive a car or airplane or truck. Has hope of completing her education and traveling around some. Wish to have at least six or seven kids, they are all tax deductible. Not like to get up early in the morning and refuse to go to bed at night. I like this class, but I am not in it officially. Thank you for letting me sit in.)

What did she mean by that: *Not in my class officially?* Was she some kind of spy sent by the dean—or, even worse, sent to spy on me by the ultra-militant Afro-American Student Union, some of whom have already accused me of being a Negro Bourgeois Lackey for having lived in Europe?

But now I rapped on the door three times as Miss Pariss instructed me to do. And this time the door opened widely, almost before I had finished knocking, and Miss Pariss invited me inside with the nonchalant flourishing gesture of a duchess welcoming a visiting ambassador.

"Come right in, sir," she said, her accent now stilted and cultivated, almost European. "You are right on time—'The Bill Cosby Show' is due to go on the air in just five minutes."

The entrance hall was completely dark, and by now there was only a lingering scent of pork fat and greens. But the overwhelming sweet density of incense that permeated the musty air after she carefully secured the locks gave me the odd impression of entering an opium parlor like one I once visited in Macao—an impression enhanced by the tiny pink-shaded boudoir lamps scattered strategically about the living room to create a romantic or funereal atmosphere, and the eerie moving shadows on the TV screen, the colors of which, due to some long neglected technical breakdown, were predominantly yellows and greens.

"Have a seat, young man," Miss Pariss said graciously, assuming the tone and mannerisms of a TV commercial hostess, "over there on the sofa in front of the TV—Reverend Grooms, get off your fat lazy ass and get our writer guest a drink!"

Only now did I recognize the shadowy form seated on the far corner of the sagging sofa as the strangely garbed man I had met on the landing while waiting for Miss Pariss to open the door. The console of whistles again wheezed jarringly in his chest, and he cast an evil glance of resentment in my direction as laboriously he hoisted his flabby frame up from the sofa and limped over to a round table, in the very center of the room, covered with a yellow velvet tasseled cloth upon which were lit two candles in altarlike candlesticks and between which were two glasses with likenesses of Martin Luther King and Bobby Kennedy stamped on them, a plastic bowl of ice cubes, a pitcher of water, a huge can of mixed nuts, a freshly opened bottle of medium-priced scotch whiskey and a nearly half-empty jug of red Gallo wine, no doubt the same jug Reverend Grooms was nursing under his arm when I first encountered him. Now Reverend Grooms was wearing a spotted black suit and a clerical collar at least two sizes too large for his neck, which in spite of his flabby overweight body was strangely skinny, like the neck of a hormone-fattened turkey.

Sulkily Reverend Grooms prepared two drinks of scotch and clumsily handed me my drink first, almost spilling it.

"You should have asked our guest if he wanted his straight," Miss Pariss said as she settled down in an armchair draped with a needlepoint effigy of an African warrior, in the heroically contracted pose of a black Mr. America, on the back as a headrest.

"Oh, this will be fine," I said, moving toward the side of the sofa as far from Reverend Grooms as possible, and away from the glare of the TV set, whose wavering yellow and green images were already making me dizzy.

"Well, I want more scotch in mine, Reverend Grooms," Miss Pariss said curtly. "You don't have to be skintchy with *my* scotch. . . ."

Stifling a grumbling remark, Reverend Grooms dutifully splashed more scotch in Miss Pariss's glass and handed it to her with exaggerated deference— so much so that I could not help but come to the conclusion that he must function as Miss Pariss's butler. He had just returned to the table and was filling a chipped water glass with red Gallo wine, pausing to gulp down over half the contents of the glass before refilling it, when Miss Pariss shouted:

"The nuts, Reverend Grooms! The nuts! Offer our guest the mixed cocktail nuts—"

"Oh, I've just had dinner," I said hastily. "The drink will be just fine—"

"Well, *I* want some of them mixed cocktail nuts. Reverend Grooms is just being his usual evil self—he knows perfectly well I always have mixed cocktail nuts with my *good* scotch—it enhances the aroma of the malt—I learned that in Edinburgh from a scotch whiskey broker who was a great admirer of my talent when I was on one of my European tours—"

"Yeah, I can just imagine what kind of talent of yours he was admiring—"

"Reverend Grooms, you've got a mind that goes swimming every night in the sewers—and you still have the liver gall to call yourself a man of God!"

Reverend Grooms settled back against the sofa and smiled dreamily and took another long drink of wine.

"Girl, we going to miss the beginning of the show with Lola Falana and all them dancing girls prancing around and doing their thing—and I don't want to miss all those cartoons at the beginning either—"

"I don't want to hear you calling me 'girl'—you ain't got no business getting familiar with me around our writer guest!"

"You keep eating all those mixed nuts you're going to end up with your intestines turning into a peanut butter sausage! You know you got regularity trouble as it is—"

"You better get me my mixed nuts, you jackleg wino hypocrite!"

By now "The Bill Cosby Show" was flashing on the screen with all its synthetic jive and super-hip poor-mouth humble ghetto jokes and the fantastic bedtime sexuality of the dancing girls. "The Bill Cosby Show" is my favorite show-business special: I do my best thinking while watching it and find it especially conducive to marking boring student themes while it is on. But that night, in the strangely obsessive presences of Reverend Grooms and Miss Mona Pariss, I couldn't keep my eye on the screen. My mind was jumbled with confused misgivings about the interview. How should I approach Miss Mona Pariss's life? Humorously, nostalgically, reverentially— the combined saintliness of Josephine Baker and Bessie Smith? But suddenly now there was dead silence in the room, the abrupt silence of a church when the passing of the collection plate is announced. The show was over and the TV set turned off.

Reverend Grooms broke the silence, shaking his head and cackling with appreciation.

"That Bill Cosby sure puts on a show! Even if he is only a colored boy from South Philly, I say he puts on a better show than Johnny Carson! And that's the gospel truth!"

He had shuffled over to the center table and was pouring himself another glass of wine, his puffy, misshapen face relaxed in a smile of complete digestive and libidinous satisfaction.

"You may go now, Reverend Grooms!" Miss Pariss announced imperiously. "And take that jug of wine with you—I simply can't endure the stink of that cheap dago red!"

Chastised, Reverend Grooms's face melted into a sullen, formless pulp. Casting an evil, resentful glance in my direction, he defiantly wiped his lips on his sleeve, tucked the jug of wine under his arm, and struggled to walk with dignity toward the door, his thick lips pursed tightly in offended silence. When the door closed behind him, Miss Pariss rose for the first time since my arrival and again performed the meticulous ritual of securing all the locks. Then, smiling coyly, she turned to me and said in a formal yet cute tone of voice:

"And now, sir, shall we begin the interview?"

Suddenly it occurred to me that I had neglected to bring a tape recorder. From her initial reaction to the proposed interview I had naturally assumed that my purpose in being invited that evening had been to begin a long period of negotiations as to whether or not she would even consent to be interviewed. But apparently her decision had been made.

"Shall we begin the interview, sir?" she repeated, rising slowly and approaching me with her hands on her hips, with the slow, studied, undulating walk of a nightclub singer coyly approaching the microphone after the spotlight centers on her figure.

"Why, yes—of course," I stammered, taking a step backwards and almost knocking over one of the pink-shaded boudoir lamps set on a fragile corner table.

"But I'm afraid I didn't bring my tape recorder with me. You see, I assumed you would want to discuss the kind of interview the magazine has in mind first—"

"Never mind," she said, her voice lowered to a husky challenge. "I'm sure the interview will go along just perfect. So if you don't mind let's go into the other room where we'll be more comfortable—"

And she picked up the bottle of scotch and our two glasses and led the way through a heavily curtained door opening into a short, cluttered hallway, on one side of which was a tiny kitchen, the door blocked with an overflowing trash can, to still another door, this one also heavily draped with red velvet hangings.

"This is where I do my meditating and futurizing," she said nonchalantly as I followed her through the drapes, finding myself in a huge high-ceilinged room with hand-painted beams, a spacious, thick-walled room with a fireplace and glassed-in balcony thick with a jungle growth of plants with huge, waxy, luxuriant leaves.

The room was at least twice as large as the sitting room we had just left, and even with the canopied bed that dominated the center of the room it gave the impression more of a temple or the chapel of a funeral parlor than of a bedroom.

"This is where I do my meditating and futurizing and my praying exercises," she repeated, as if to emphasize not only the difference of function of the two rooms but the transformation of personality each room apparently enhanced.

There was no overhead lighting, just tiny imitation candle-shaped electric lights set under the figures of plastic saints, such as one sees in the Puerto Rican magic medicine shops in my West Side neighborhood, though all the saints' faces had been painted jet black (the blond hair of one saint, however, had been incongruously left painted in bright yellow). The huge canopied bed that dominated the center of the room was covered neatly with a damask bedspread. And on either side of the bed were petite boudoir chairs, they, too, covered with cheap red velvet. In one corner of the room (there was no other furniture, which further contributed to the funeral parlor-temple atmosphere and spaciousness of the room) there was an old-fashioned rolltop desk, upon which she placed the bottle of whiskey and the two glasses.

"Too late in the night for ice," Miss Pariss said brightly as she began pouring two drinks of straight whiskey, filling each of the Martin Luther King–Robert Kennedy memorial chalices nearly half full.

My attention had been drawn to the water-stained wall opposite the draped window upon which were hanging, in random gallery fashion, an incredible number of framed posters and faded glossy photographs of Miss Pariss during many stages of her career. On one very large gilt-framed photograph prominently placed in the center of the display, she was mounted on a huge white horse; she was wearing a floppy garden party hat, a tight-waisted long-skirted lace dress, and carrying a parasol. Apparently she wasn't ready yet to discuss the photographs and posters, for she hurried over to where I was standing and prodded me on the arm with the glass of whiskey.

"Let us relax first and gain inner harmony," she said in yet another change of voice, this one the deep-throated voice of an oracle.

Then, holding her own glass in her free hand, she took me strongly

by the hand and led me to one of the chairs beside the enormous canopied bed.

"You sit yourself down and make yourself comfortable," she said, "while
I stretch out so I can get my thoughts together—I never could do no meditating or futurizing sitting down or standing up—"

She was staring at me, not exactly directly, but with her eyes half-closed,
as if staring at the inside of my mind. But at the same time she was looking
at me as a sexually aroused woman looks at a man. And this was very
unnerving, especially in those mumbo jumbo surroundings. Nervously I
took a deep drink from my glass and was about to comment on the photographs to distract her powerful gaze when suddenly she began to giggle.

"This like one of them welfare psychiatrist sessions, ain't it the truth!
You sitting there with your notebook and pencil ready to write down what
I say and me stretched out here all comfortable and relaxed getting myself
together to start memorizing—"

The incense burning somewhere in the room and the whiskey were
beginning to give me a high, as though I were floating beneath water or in
a dream. To regain control of my critical faculties I forced myself to concentrate on the details of her appearance, but I was only able to observe the
dress she was wearing, so mockingly intimidating was her powerful gaze. It
was a kind of evening gown of faded black satin with fringes around the
bosom and halfway down the skirt—a theatrical costume of some long-past
era, I decided, making a mental note of the fact.

"You like this dress?" she said, primly pulling down the skirt, which had
bundled up above her knees when she stretched out on the bed.

"I find it extremely attractive," I said, "a most original creation. Did you
make it yourself?"

She laughed so hard she began to choke.

"Of course I didn't make this dress—Reverend Grooms he designed it
and made it himself. That wino fool could of made hisself a fortune designing
clothes if he hadn'ta been born black and decided to go into the gospel
preaching business. That nigger's been designing my clothes for over fifty
years! And he ain't no funny-fairy folk either!"

She said this with such earnest conviction and affection that I again had
to make a mental note to investigate and reevaluate the relationship between
Miss Pariss and Reverend Grooms. But I realized with an ever-deepening
sense of dread that my scrupulous schematic approach to this interview would
have to be completely cast aside.

For even then I knew that this was no simple human interest story of a
long-neglected black entertainer. Whatever this woman was about, it was
drenched with the balsam of mystery from which ancient myths derive. And

perhaps she sensed the chill of uneasiness that had come over me, for she said, again in her normal (if she indeed had a normal voice) bantering tone:

"I call it my memorizing and meditating dress— I always put it on when I do my meditating and futurizing—"

"Then you agree to the interview?" I said, a bit too eagerly, involuntarily leaning forward as if to settle down to hear a story.

For what seemed an eternity Miss Pariss said nothing, and I began to fidget on the edge of the chair.

"Well, I must say I'm very pleased," I said in a cheerfully altered voice. "I think it's safe to tell you that the editor of the magazine even thinks your life is so important to black history that the interview series may well be expanded into a book."

Still, Miss Pariss said nothing, and continued her relentless staring, making me so nervous that I took a long drink from my glass, knowing well that it was completely empty. At the same time I was beginning to feel slightly drunk, and my eyelids had become so heavy that for a moment of panic I entertained the ridiculous notion that perhaps she was hypnotizing me.

But then, in a tiny secretarial voice that seemed to penetrate my consciousness from some faulty long-distance telephone connection, I heard her saying:

"Yes, indeed, child—my life's a book all right. Course everybody's life is a book, but ain't nobody's life a book like my life's a book! Yes, child, my life's a book, all right—a holy book, and I don't mean to be sacrilegious!"

Another long pause with the incense-laden silence vibrating with the obsessive bass beat of the hi-fis on the floor below.

"Pour me some more whiskey, youngblood!" she ordered almost angrily.

I jumped to my feet as though a whip had been cracked around my neck and rushed to fill her glass, which I ceremoniously handed her as an acolyte serves a priest.

"You pour yourself a drink, too," she said, her tone now maternal and protective. "If you want to hear the story of my life you've got a lot of listening to do, so you better come right over here on the bed and stretch out comfortable here beside me—"

Then while I was pouring myself yet another drink, my hands shaking, she rose up on her elbow and moved over to the far side of the enormous damask-covered bed.

"Now then—" she said, as I gingerly stretched out alongside her, biting my lips to fight the sinking feeling of dizziness that was overcoming me from too much to drink. "You just lay there and relax your body and soul. You sure one cute dude for not being one of those funny fairies from downstairs—

"They nice polite fellows, mind you," she continued after a thoughtful pause. "Sometimes I invite them up here and tell their fortunes, and tell them the ins and outs of show business when they're out of work—which is most of the time, now that they stopped using colored on the stage in favor of all those long-haired whites twanging their guitars. Cornfield music, we used to call it. But they so mammy hungry they get on my nerves always asking me 'should I do this' or 'should I do that' or would I mind sewing a button on their crotches. Makes me feel old, and while my flesh may not be as young as it used to be, my blood runs as hot as peppermint tea soon as I get a little scotch in me. Yes, Lord! Don't talk to me about no geriatrics! When geriatrics starts heading my way, they won't have to put me in the grave, I'll dive in headfirst!"

And she laughed so hard I thought she was having a fit. Finally, though, she caught her breath and regained her poise.

"Now if you'll just take off your jacket and make yourself at home so to speak, we might as well get down to work on this interview of yours—"

I quickly jumped off the bed, overjoyed to be doing something that was at once real and familiar and not something out of a waking nightmare, and fumbled for the notepad and pencil in the inside pocket of my jacket.

"While you up," she said, "you might as well take off your clothes—"

"Take off my clothes?" I gasped, turning.

"What's the matter with you, youngblood? Are you sure you ain't one of them funny fairies from downstairs? Don't you understand plain English?"

"You want me to take off my clothes and get in bed with you?"

"You heard what I said. Don't you know what I'm talking about?"

"Do you mean you want me to—er—to—to go to bed with you before you'll give me an interview?"

Again she broke out into that high-pitched, screaming laugh of hers.

"You been reading my mind, youngblood."

My own forced laughter was at once cautious, involuntary, and forced—gallows laughter. And a spasm of shock and terrified reverence completely paralyzed my thinking.

"But, Miss Pariss," I stuttered, averting my eyes, but choosing my words as delicately as I was able.

"But, Miss Pariss—" I repeated clumsily. "This is—well, ridiculous, I mean this isn't exactly what I had in mind—"

"You mean you don't want to share my bed with me?"

"I by no means wish to give you the impression that I don't want to share your bed with you. It's only that—"

"Just because you a pretty youngblood dude, you think you too good to share my bed just because you think I'm a senior citizen or one of them geriatric cases—"

"Believe me, Miss Pariss. We've known each other only a short time, hardly a day—and yet I am convinced you are the most remarkable woman I have ever met—"

But even as the words came out of my mouth I knew that I was only rehearsing the very words I would be repeating to Gracie the next day when inevitably she would ask me how I thought the interview would go. After all, Gracie had her problems with the editorial staff at the fledgling magazine, and she had already told me she was having a very hard time thinking up new ideas for articles that were both "interesting to a large black mass audience and provocative."

If for no other reason than Gracie's courage and trust in me I had no choice but to go through with the interview no matter what the cost to my personal sensibilities. And besides, I desperately needed the money.

So with the slow stagy motions of a striptease artist I began to undress. And when I was down to my leopard-skin briefs (the room now completely dark except for a single pink electric candle under a plastic black-faced St. George slaying a dragon), her now deep oracle voice boomed through the fumes of incense and she said in a priestly command:

"Take it off! Take it all off! Ashes to ashes, dust to dust—"

Then as I sat gingerly on the edge of the bed, she took my hand and placed it against the rouged smoothness of her sunken cheek.

"Now don't that feel as soft as a baby's behind?" she said gently.

I felt heat and throbbing blood. And, after what seemed to be an endless moment of mystical anticipation, not unlike the elevation of the mass, she placed her withered hand between my naked legs and let out a glory shout.

"It's up, youngblood, it's up! May the good Lord be praised! I could tell by that funny slant in your left eye you was some special kind of dude, so now get ready to hear the truth—the true truth, the whole truth, and nothing but the truth, straight out of the holy book of the life of Madam Mona Pariss Babu!"

THE BOY WITH BEER

Melvin Dixon

It was Friday night and crowded. He stood alone outside the club, trying to see into the front window, where his breath clung to the tinted glass and people were blurred shapes of rising and falling colors. He left the window and returned to it. The doubt in him was as real as the cold outside. He approached the window again, then the front door, shoving a course notebook into his coat pocket as he went. He held it there. Maybe next weekend, he thought. He felt the night air on his neck and knew it would be warm inside. For the third time he told himself, "I have to," but the voice questioning inside him was cautious.

—*What if Mama finds out?*
—She won't know anything about it, I'm sure.
—*And Larry?*
—Larry. He's gone.
—*And she won't know?*
—I won't tell them who I am.
—*They already know.*
—I'm going in anyway.
—*No, you're not.*

—I have to.
—*Do you remember the words?*
—I'm going in anyway.

People laughing somewhere behind him brought his attention back to the street. Suddenly his neck felt wet. The air on his sweat made him aware of a cool emptiness growing inside him. Real voices came from the laughter behind.

"Ha, ha, chile, I'm a little too tired tonight. And you all sure are some crazy folks, I swear! Dragging me out of my house in this cold. Humph! Just being with you crazy children is too much. Ha, ha, I swear."

"Well, honey," another one said, "we'll just leave you behind then. I been sitting home all week, let me tell you, waiting for that man to call. That's right. *All week.* And that bum ain't called yet. Bet you I ain't sitting home for nobody no more. I ain't about to rot for nobody."

A third one joined the group. "Yeah, but you said he was worth waiting ten years for."

"That was last week, darling. I'm in the market for something better-looking tonight," the second one answered.

"Whooooo, for days, chile," the third one said.

"Quit running your mouths," said the first, "so we can get one good drink before the night's through."

The voices came toward him. He moved quickly away from the entrance, relieved that the three hadn't noticed him. He watched the red front door open for the new guests, and he listened as the sounds of black night life flew out into the street. Then quietly he followed the trio inside.

—*It ain't easy, girls, it ain't easy*
  It ain't easy, girls, it ain't easy . . .

He recognized the song from the jukebox. Its rhythm made him feel more of a willing captive to the smoke, the wine, the music, and the solitary bodies. Several heads turned in his direction, and he felt a dull pain in his chest. One by one, the heads turned back to their drinks as if he was not the one they expected.

As he walked farther inside the bar, he thought again of what she would say if she saw him. But she's far away from me now, he thought. Far away. But her voice returned to him, and his legs went stiff.

—*You're Mama's little man. That's who you are.*
—*Yes, Mama.*

—*Now don't you look nice?*
—*I guess so.*
—*Sure you do.*
—*Mama?*
—*I know you're going to like church today. Youth Choir singing?*
—*Yes.*
—*Should I sit near the front to hear your solo?*
—*I don't have a solo.*
—*No?*
—*Mama?*
—*Yes, son. Oh, is my hat on straight? Here, zip me up quick. We can't be late.*
—*Mama?*
—*What is it, son?*
—*I don't feel well.*
—*You'll be all right. Reverend Jones preaches a fine sermon. He'll make you feel real good.*
—*Mama?*
—*Come on now. We're going to be late. Watch your step.*
—*Mama?*

All the way inside the bar colors danced around him in pink knits, tailored orange sharkskins, and burgundy velvets. The burgundy velvet blew its cheap wine breath across the glossy dance floor to meet him. A forest-green jacket and a pair of chartreuse shoes slid into action in front. But instead of joining them he moved beyond the dancers, the empty beer bottles, the cigarette fog, and settled in a booth near the door to the back kitchen.

Order a beer. "That's not too expensive," he told himself. "What with the little change I brought." Drink it slowly. Nurse each swallow. Make it last.

But he was afraid.

"Ballantine, please."

No response.

Then louder, deeper. "Ballantine, please!"

"Comin'." The response was electric.

He returned to his seat with a glass, hugging the neck of the brown bottle and jiggling with his walk. He thought for a moment that he would not be able to stay the whole night. Fear danced inside him and voices kept coming to his mind. They warned him to leave. "No, not yet," he said to himself. He tried to focus on the bar, the Ballantine, the thirst, but the voice of his father reached into him and chilled.

—*Willis! What the hell you doing in here making a damn cake? And with your mother's apron, on too! Come on out here and help me clean up the yard.*

—He's helping me.
—Helping you nothing, Sarah. He should be out doing some man's work like
    the other boys his age. Not laid up in some damn kitchen!
— If he wants to bake a cake, let him.

The first gulp of beer was so icy it numbed his insides. Willis looked around
him at the rows of laughing faces and bodies, the people in couples, some
standing alone, watching. He wondered what he should say to them. What
he should do. Maybe Larry would know. He remembered asking:

—Larry, will you be my friend?

and asking him again, but Larry had gone.

—Willis?

Someone else was calling.

—Wwwwwwiiiiilllliiissssss. Come home!

Her voice calling was not like his father's voice, which was tender only after
collard greens and three cups of pot liquor. He often forgot birthdays and,
once, even Christmas. Willis remembered his own birthdays, twelve of them,
passing unnoticed. He was six when he received his last gift from his father,
a battery racing car that fell apart after three days.
    His father used to scare away friends. Like Larry when they listened to
records, read comic books, and sometimes played catch outside. His father
said they made too much noise, so Larry could never stay long. Yes, he and
Larry were friends. Good friends. Until.

—Larry?
—Yeah.
—We're still friends, aren't we?
—Sure. Good friends. Yeah.

Larry. The green house across the street. Larry. A year older. They went to
the same school, and every day they would shine shoes for a quarter downtown until Willis was fourteen and Larry spent the night. Willis felt awkward.
Larry's hands were cold and hard. Willis had warm fingers, and that night
they touched, fumbled nervously, and shook. He remembered what they
said about his hands.

—Sarah, what firm, wide hands your son has.
—He used to play the piano.
—That's so nice.
—He practiced every day.
—That's so nice.

And Larry, who was his friend.

—But listen, Willis.
—You do understand, don't you?
—Naw, I don't think so.
—Larry?
—Look, Willis, man, I don't think we can be friends anymore. Not that way. Understand? You understand?
—I guess so.
—Look, man, don't act like you're gonna cry.

Larry. The face and the voice came too sudden. Harsh. Willis tried to blur the memory. He swallowed hard and concentrated on the drops of water forming on the beer bottle. He took another swallow and rinsed his gums before dropping it deep into his throat. He looked at the men and the few women around him.

He remembered Sandy, who was the color of cinnamon with short bristly hair and agile enough for the girl's track team at Eastern High. All the girls moved like athletes then, he thought. Willis took her to the Sophomore-Junior Prom, where they drank from the quart of Calvert L.B. had hidden under his dinner jacket. Nothing mattered then; he was with Sandy. He remembered her body growing warm against his as they danced. In the morning they drank the last of the whiskey.

—Willis?
—Yes.
—Why do you drink so much? You know it's wrong.
—I don't know.
—I don't like you to drink like this. It's not good.
—All right.
—You know, Willis, I feel so lucky.
—Why?
—All the girls in my homeroom are jealous because we're going together.
—Oh? But I just took you to the prom.
—And I like you because you're not like the other boys. You're different, and for me that's special.

Her voice vanished quickly from his mind when Willis saw a figure come near his booth. He held the beer bottle tighter and shifted in his seat. He saw a black satin gown, streams of costume pearls flowing about a thick brown neck, a blond bouffant wig covering the head. When he saw that it was a man Willis shivered, but his eyes remained glued. The man glided past like a ghost, catching him in the perfume lagging behind. Out of the mist an angry face loomed near. Imaginary, but its voice was menacing.

—*What took you so long in there?*
—*I was brushing my teeth.*
—*You know I got to shave.*
—*Sorry.*
—*And take a shower.*
—*I'm sorry, Daddy.*
—*Hey, come here, Willis.*
—*Yes?*
—*Closer. What's that black mess around your eyes? And that red on your cheeks?*
—*Nothing.*
—*Nothing, huh? Boy, you better get away from me looking like that.*

The summer after high school, Willis remembered, had been lonely. He'd sit in the park. Watch people. He wondered why they didn't respond to his looking. Why they didn't sense the doubt inside him. He wanted to ask someone, anyone, if he was always to be lonely. Or could he face the steady torture in his father's eyes? Should he leave home? Where could he go? He had measured his misery by the blankness of the faces passing him and wondered why he was even there. If he could have remembered the words, maybe the emptiness would have gone away:

The Lord is my shepherd; I shall not want.

And Sandy?

I shall not want. He maketh me to lie down in green pastures. He lead-eth me.

Sandy, I love you.

He leadeth me beside the still waters. I shall not want. He restoreth my soul.

Sandy, we can't anymore.

He leadeth me in the paths of righteousness for his name's sake, for his name.

How would he welcome the funeral of his body and the touching, the steady touching of him? To lie alone like a corpse in an abandoned field without flowers, where on top of his body the grass grows yellow and the sky above is empty? Is empty.

Willis thought of last summer when the neighbors talked of nothing but the two boys caught fondling each other in the bushes near the park's pond.

Yea, though I walk through the valley . . .

The bar was too crowded now, and the night was continuing. Willis participated in the funeral not yet welcomed. He repeated to himself

of the shadow of death, I will fear no evil. No evil. For Thou art with me; I shall not want . . . he leadeth me . . . I shall not want.

His back felt the stiffness of the pewlike booth, but there were no altars here. He could not pray; but he could remember. And he remembered the Church School Children's Day Program, the deacons who shook his hand, the church mothers who kissed him when he recited the verses in his clearest voice.

Suddenly a hand brushed against his thigh. He turned sharply and searched the crowd. Did he just imagine the touch? Was it his own hand and fingers that crept so often to his groin and pulled and pulled until he had released himself to sleep? His body sank into the pew-booth again and the recitation grew louder, louder inside him.

Thou preparest a table before me in the presence of mine enemies thou anointest my head with oil my cup runneth over and over and over and over and surely goodness and mercy shall follow me all the days all the nights in the night of my life and I will dwell in the house in the bar of the house of the Lord forever and ever and ever

The journey into him was taking too long. "Don't touch me!" The words choked him inside.

—Reverend Jones preaches a fine sermon in his way. You listen to Mama. Join the church, son. Mama knows. Baptism will help you.

The coldness of the water then made his chest feel empty. He felt the bottom of the pool until his toes couldn't touch anymore. Willis folded his arms across the chest as if he were dead and went down. When the preacher lifted him up, he broke the water with his cheeks puffed out. His mother saw him and she believed. Still he couldn't answer when she asked,

—Willis, why are you looking at those boys like that?
—I'm not, Mama.
—You are, son. You are.
—No, Mama.

—*They're wearing the same white robes you are. They have the same thing
  you have.*
—*I know, Mama.*
—*They're just as wet as you are.*
—*But I'm not. I'm not looking at their legs or their thighs.*
—*Here, take this towel and dry yourself good.*
—*I'm not looking at them.*
—*Hurry up now before you catch cold.*

What had the preacher said? Willis tried to remember when a girl in a short
blue dress staggered to his booth and was sick and falling near him. Willis
wanted to leave the booth, and he couldn't leave the booth, and he was
afraid to stay. The door to the back kitchen flapped open and a man came
out to take the girl away. The preacher said he would be safe.

The waters of grace shall set you free. Repent, brethren, repent!

His glass of beer dropped to the floor. Cold liquid oozed down his leg
and dripped into his shoe. The chill filled him inside. Willis was too embarrassed to ask for a napkin. He let the wetness stay.

Black shapes and colors dancing and melting into fuzzy silhouettes made
him want to laugh, and he did. He touched his wet leg and laughed again.
People around him were laughing and singing with the music and sharing
each other's secrets. No one knew Willis's secret, but still the people laughed.

Then a hand on his shoulder. A man's voice. Willis stopped laughing,
stopped breathing, stopped thinking, stopped living. Could not die. Was it
his father's voice?

—*Willis?*
—*Yes, Daddy.*
—*Be strong, hear. You hear me?*

No, don't move, Willis thought. Hold on to the hand. But he did nothing.
He said nothing; he listened.

"Hi."

It didn't sound like his father.

"I said *hello* there."

The voice was not his father's voice. Still he was afraid to answer. After
a moment Willis spoke.

"Oh, I didn't quite hear you."

"May I join you?"

"No, no, I don't mind at all."

"You sound nervous."

"I was hoping it wouldn't show. Well, not that much anyway."

"Can I get you a drink?"

"No, thanks."

"No?"

"I'm still on this one."

"Been here before?"

"No."

"No?"

"Actually, I was on my way home from—"

"Yes?"

"Well, from class. We had this evening lecture that—"

"Still in school, huh? That's good."

School. His mother's voice found him again.

He was always such a good student, my son. You know my son, don't you?
Willis? They call him Willie sometimes, but his name is Willis.

The man, sitting opposite, looked straight into him. "You like school?" And
Willis shuddered to forget what had happened there.

> —*I'm gonna kick your skinny ass all the way home, chump. You hear?*
> —*But why, Jake?*
> —*I can get an A, too, chump. An A right upside your head. You cheated*
> *on the test anyway.*
> —*I didn't, Jake. And I haven't done anything to you.*
> —*Just be by the playground gate, I'll show you who's smartest.*
> —*I won't be there.*
> —*Yes, you will.*

Willis watched the man and listened again. He noticed the smooth skin,
the moustache neatly trimmed and moving up and down with his words,
calm, like his eyes; the eyes shining like coal from the clear brown face, the
face moving gracefully toward his.

"I bet you're a science major. Probably going to be a doctor, huh? We
need doctors."

"No."

"Maybe a lawyer, then? You look like a lawyer."

"I like music."

"Music?"

"And I might teach." As Willis spoke and tried to smile, the voices inside
him rang together like a bell, stiffening him and hollowing him and emptying
him of his troubled song.

—*He's my son. I was the proudest mother on Parent's Night.*
—Larry, will you be my friend?
—*Shadow of death and valley, comfort me. I am wanting, I am wanting*

Then silence. Silence inside him and out. The jukebox finished. Feet shuffled off the dance floor. The cigarette fog rose up again and blurred the crowd. With his eyes Willis reached deep into the face before him for the music he could share. He was sure now, if only for a few hours until the voices reached for him again.

"Your glass is empty," the man said. "Here, let me get you another beer."

"Thanks."

"What are you drinking—Schlitz?"

"No, Ballantine."

"By the way, I'm Jerome."

"My name is Willis."

THE VIBRAPHONE

Rita Dove

Christie Phillips was a student in musicology—concentration baroque. Her parents never knew what to make of this—to them, gospel was the only serious music, and whenever she went home to Toledo, they would try to drag her to their AME church to play the organ.

The requirement in college to master at least three instruments had led Christie to the harpsichord—and suddenly she was plunged into the narrow yet measureless world of early music, where embellishment rippled into formata, where time changed to suit one's mood.

When Jerry Murdon had his debut at Carnegie Hall, Christie managed to get a ticket, even though the concert was sold out. Murdon had all the promise of young genius—piano study with the best teachers at Berkeley and then Juilliard, first prize at the National Bach Competition for young performers, several years' experience as a soloist at Spoleto. Half of the female music students at the prominent music schools in the country were in love with him. "There is nothing," the critics were fond of saying, "to keep Murdon from becoming one of the greatest pianists of our time."

At Carnegie Hall he burst onstage, correct and handsome in tails, his reddish Afro like an explosion under the spotlight, a tensed authority in the jagged face. He seated himself, long curved fingers poised for the Bach Sonata in D Major . . . there was silence. Silence that deepened and chilled the longer he played, for there was something different in this familiar music when he played it—something pepped up, askew. Stunned silence, then, and finally, hissing. Husbands walked out; their wives, some actually in tears, followed more slowly. Jerry Murdon kept on playing; the concert was being recorded, and the sound engineers let the tapes run, more from a morbid curiosity than any sense of duty.

Columbia refused to release the tapes; they bought themselves out of the contract, and Murdon used the money to produce his own record. He called his label Lunar Discs—a reference to the fact that Bach had milked his eyes blind copying music by moonlight. The album jacket showed Jerry Murdon at the piano, tails flying and Afro exploding, in the far-right corner of a star-thick sky a hovering full moon, and the man in the moon was Johann Sebastian Bach. The title spilled across the sky in cobalt script: "Recreation of the Soul. Murdon Plays Bach."

Of course Christie bought the album. The record became a hit. It was Bach of the twentieth century—industrialized, anonymous, defiant, the playing technically exquisite. She tried to duplicate certain passages on the conservatory pianos but always came away discouraged. When, on his next LP, Jerry Murdon switched to electric piano, she switched with him.

Five years Jerry Murdon dominated the jazz scene, his Bach interpretations growing more estranged. Then, quite suddenly, there were no more concerts, no more recordings. His rivals claimed he had run out of ideas; gossip columnists predicted yet another victim to drugs. *Billboard* reported seeing him on a beach somewhere in Italy. No confirmations or contradictions were made in this chaos of wild speculations; Murdon, wherever he was, kept silent, and the public, disappointed and just a bit insulted, dropped him. Jerry Murdon, King of Bach, was soon one of the forgotten.

In the meantime Christie had started on the theoretical section of her dissertation, an analysis of her own transfiguration of an obscure seventeenth-century Italian instrumental "opera" for harpsichord, viola da gamba, and baroque flute. The composer was very obscure indeed; most of the documents weren't available. She grew tired, discouraged, and humiliated; more from despair than the hope of finding any material, she finally applied for a summer scholarship to conduct research at the musical institute in Florence . . . and was accepted.

Florence was like walking through an oil painting, one of those thronging street scenes radiating with color and the newly discovered landscape of perspectives. She had more than enough time to decipher those manuscripts waiting for her; September was two weeks gone and the days still warm . . . what better time to take off for a weekend?

That Friday she took a train to Pisa, made the obligatory snapshots of the tower, then caught a local bus to Viareggio. Viareggio was like any Italian resort town—a beach littered with beer cans, tar, and seaweed, and—parallel to the beach—the promenade, a broad avenue lined on either side with expensive jewelry stores and bright boutiques.

It was too windy for swimming; the beach was deserted. She turned back toward town. Immediately behind the promenade, the city sprouted into a thicket of smaller, grimier streets where the Italians lived and shopped. She wandered around, looking for an intimate café, something—when, about two blocks away, a black man with a dog stepped out into the street—his long head, the reddish Afro, the silhouette so familiar from a distance. . . .

He was gone. She quickened her pace; but the street she thought he must have turned into was empty. Perplexed, she returned to the corner and walked slowly to the spot where he had appeared. She was standing in front of a music store.

The small round man behind the counter looked at her with a patient, dubious smile. *"L'americano?"* he repeated, scratching his head.

"Si," she said. "He's a pianist, isn't he?"

"Paese," he replied. He took her to the door and pointed up the street energetically.

Several times she stopped to ask an old woman or a passing schoolchild the way to Paese, for the street had a maddening habit of dissolving into spidery alleys. Finally the last stucco house was behind her and the streets curved upward sharply, into the vineyards. There she stopped and put out her thumb.

A cherry-red Alfa Romeo pulled over, and a middle-aged man in a slinky shirt rolled down the window. "I'll take you wherever you want, signorina!" No other car stopped for a good fifteen minutes. Then she got lucky.

A battered, three-wheel pickup halted, and a young man in baggy white overalls and paint-splattered boots opened the door. He was employed at the new villa going up outside the village of Paese, where he hauled plaster every day, and once—about this time of day, three or four—the black American with the dog. . . .

The pavement was broken in places, and for a while they rode in silence, the pickup slamming hard into the rutted path. Directly outside the village, they stopped.

"This is as far as I go, signorina."

"But—the American?" she stammered.

"This is as far as I took him, signorina. As far as Paese." He hesitated. "The signorina has been looking for the American for a long time?" His voice grew dark, solicitous.

"Not really. That is—"

The disappointment in his face surprised her—what had he been expecting? Then it hit her: in his head an elaborate melodrama, a scenario in the operatic mode, was brewing. She gasped and swallowed at the same time, bringing tears to her eyes.

"Signorina!"

He held out a hand, checked himself. She buried her face in her hands.

"Signorina, don't cry! Please."

A hand on her arm, patting it as a child pats a doll.

"Don't cry," he repeated, his voice hardening. He put the pickup in gear. "Don't worry, signorina. We will find him."

Pulling up in front of a crumbling pink church at the village square, he got out and walked over to the neighboring café, where a group of old men were playing dominoes. The consultation was brief; he returned smiling. The path led through Paese and out the other side, where the road became a dirt trail twisting still higher into the mountains. After another ten minutes of hairpin curves and teeth-jarring potholes, they pulled up behind a rusty Fiat parked at a dilapidated gate that seemed to hang in midair, suspended by a wilderness of overgrown vegetation.

There was no bell, no mailbox. The gate stood ajar, and beyond it she could just make out the flagstones of a walkway curving through the trees. Christie stepped through the gate. The air was heady with the mixed scents of rosemary and rotting olives. The path swerved to the left.

A bright, clipped lawn, as neat as a starched tablecloth. Rows of flowers, perfectly ordinary daisies and petunias. Dainty white picket fences encasing the plump beds and even a rose arbor.

The house was less spinsterish, two stories high, stone whitewashed to blinding perfection. It was abnormally long, and its length was punctuated, from roof to foundation and from pole to pole, with windows.

Then it came, out of nowhere. Music. Sounds wrung from joy and light and squeezed through voltage meters, a whine that twitched like electrocution and sobbed like a maniac; music that robbed the air it rode upon, vibrations that rattled her breath and shoved it back down her throat. It was a sound that made the garden, in its innocent stupidity, glow like a reprimand—a warning from a lost childhood or a lost love, or anything as long as it was lost, lost. . . .

"If it bothers you, I can turn it off."

He looked older than forty—he had grown a beard, which was black, and the reddish Afro, his trademark, straggled dully around the mistreated cowl of a speckled gray sweater. The beginnings of a paunch. Hips sunken in, lips full and somehow vulgar in the haggard brown face, dimples cutting along the sides of his cheeks like scars.

He went back inside. A moment later the terror had stopped.

He reappeared. Wordless, he led her into the house.

The music, and the sight of him so suddenly near, so changed, had acted as an anesthetic. She didn't know what to think of the situation, though curiosity and the thrill of adventure helped placate the small anxieties trying to surface.

They entered a large room, airy and bright, an ideal studio. But it was full of reel to reel tape recorders and electronic devices—dubbing machines, splicing decks, amplifiers. Wa-wa pedals littered the floor like poisoned field mice, electrical cords squirming in a maze toward every corner.

Jerry Murdon moved through the room, flicking switches, plugging in cords, adjusting tone levels, checking balances. He came to rest at a vibraphone in the center of the room.

"The motif," he said, picking up the mallets. She recognized it as the organ prelude to the fifty-second Cantata: *Falsche Welt, dir trau' ich nicht.*

"—And here it is again."

He flipped a switch and the melodic line, amplified, wailed from massive quadraphonic speakers. He flipped another switch, and the same melody, shaken and broken down nearly beyond recognition, rose from the floor. Another switch, another—and a roar of sound, grace notes proliferating like bacteria, chords like a dying train, poured over her . . . and beneath it all the characteristic undulation of the vibraphone, its relentless throb taking over her pulse.

"There they are, twenty-four from one. A single source. Can you find the core again?"

"I've—I've lost it."

"But it's there. It's there, you can tell, can't you? Don't try to listen; feel for it."

She nodded weakly. He went over to the back wall and pulled a lever. The music stopped.

"See that hatch?" He pointed to a small square in the ceiling directly above her. "That's where it all goes. Come on."

He led her upstairs. At first she couldn't make out anything; the shutters were drawn. Then she saw a bed, unmade, and an aluminum ladder hanging from hooks on the wall. She jumped—something growled. Red eyes glittered from the pillow.

"Quiet, Sebastian!"

The dog grew still. He walked over to the bed, knelt beside it, and threw open the trapdoor. The light from the studio streamed up.

"At night," he said softly, "I open the hatch and let my latest composition come up. Then I fall asleep and dream the variations." He smiled, his face suddenly very young.

Christie looked at the blazing hole; it seemed to spread toward her. "Don't you ever"—she searched for the right word—"get seasick?"

He laughed. "The throbbing, you mean? That's the beauty of it. To float on the lap of the sea, to move with the pitch and reel. To stand up in the center of things with no point of gravity but your own." He slammed the hatch shut.

"Would you like some tea?"

This room was much smaller. There was just enough space for a table— a hexagonal, carved mahogany piece of Oriental design—and two tall leather chairs whose curved backs and armrests were covered with intricate tooling.

"Have a seat—be back in a sec."

She sat down; in the center of the table stood a shallow dish filled with black candy drops. Licorice. She counted the pieces.

There were exactly twenty-four.

Christie looked around, suddenly uneasy. The windows were covered. Panels of heavy dark red cloth were draped from floor to ceiling to create an illusion of a six-sided space, like the table. Brocade dragons scaled the cloth panels.

Jerry Murdon returned, tea things aloft.

"It's not so often I get visitors; I must take advantage of you."

"In what way?" she asked lightly. She looked over the tray he had placed between them—smoked oysters skewered with toothpicks, black olives, sesame rounds, cheese cubes. A bottle of something clear and alcoholic. Cigarettes.

The teapot exhaled an acrid perfume, jasmine.

"You see," he said, pouring the tea, "I realize you didn't come all the way up here for nothing. Perhaps you came because you're a bored, spoiled little American who thought it would be a blast to see how old Murdon has degenerated. . . ."

"I'm a music student," she said lamely.

"So," he replied, leaning back, "a music student. Piano, I suppose."

"Harpsichord. I play in a baroque consort."

"More than one way to get at the core," he said, nodding. "Bach, of course, was the purest of them all—but baroque was better than what came afterward. That maniac Beethoven obscured vision for over a century. Would you like some vodka?"

"No, thank you."

He poured himself a drink. "So why don't you tell me what brings you here."

"I'm studying in Florence." Christie hesitated. "It wasn't easy to find you."

"I can imagine," he countered. "Therefore I won't let you get away unrewarded."

She reached for an oyster, not daring to look him in the eye. He waited, enjoying her discomfort. She thought of her dissertation, in a box in her room in Florence. She thought of the pale sandwiches at the Trattoria. She thought of her first violin, she thought of the first Murdon album with Bach as the man in the moon . . . but none of these thoughts stayed in her mind long enough to count as a full idea. He lifted his shot glass and tossed it off.

"Don't worry," he said, relenting. "You came for my story, didn't you— why I left, how I got here, the whole deal, right?"

She nodded.

"Now then—you might remember, being a fan of mine"—he threw a glance at her, testing—"my keyboard style changed three times during my career. First, of course, there was the classical perfection of Jerry Murdon, the best young pianist of a generation. Then the furor at Carnegie Hall, my real debut in more ways than one. You see, I knew what I wanted; I was just looking for the right break. Colleagues called me an opportunist, critics called me a confidence man. Remember this article?"

He opened one of the table's drawers and extracted a newspaper clipping. "First he encourages our outrage by his circus antics at Carnegie Hall; now, assured of our attention, he has set out systematically to destroy all that Bach has created. Where, I ask you, in this cacophony, this parodic bebop, is the spirit of that great man who said he composed "for the glory of God and the recreation of the soul"? What Jerry Murdon is doing amounts to blas- phemy.' " He put the clipping away. "Fools," he muttered.

"My second change was in many ways more dramatic than the first. It came a year later, a scant three months after my smashing success at Newport." His dark eyes fixed her like a specimen moth. "My playing be- came—how shall I describe it?—less agitated, more melodic. One *Downbeat* critic dubbed it 'The Golden Age of Murdon.' The real story begins here. It begins with a woman, naturally.

"She had heard me at Carnegie Hall and was convinced I was a genius. She was tall, attractive, Italian-Jewish descent. She did textile prints for the big ones—Cardin and Blass. Her faith in me was exciting; indeed, her complete trust spurred me on in more than the musical sphere. I began to see other women, although Elizabeth satisfied me completely. It was an irresistible chain of events; her very submissiveness lured me into more affairs. I was unscrupulous; I wanted her to find out. But she never noticed any- thing—an intelligent woman, mind you—she chose never to notice any- thing. I would come home at seven in the morning, stinking of martinis and perfume, with some tale about a new piece I had been working up with the band, and she accepted my story—even if the drummer had phoned the night before to ask where I was.

"I shocked no one except, perhaps, myself. No reproaches, and the thrill fades. Betrayal became time-consuming and, eventually, boring . . . so I stopped. Enter the Golden Age."

He lit a cigarette. "Contrary to the rumors circulated by the press," he added wryly, "I have never been very highly sexed."

He pulled the smoke deep into his lungs, leaning back to let it drift down his throat before pushing it out again in a thin gray stream. "When I am making music, I have no time, no room, for anything else. My body disappears. You could call it a byproduct of creation. I'm sure, in fact, that if someone investigated the matter, they would find out that God, the supreme artist, has no penis." He smiled. "What is creation, after all, but a godly act? And what do I need with the pitiful palpitations of human tissues and fluids when my music"—he sprang forward in his seat—"when my music will last forever?"

He leaned back, that youthful look on his face again. Innocent. A fawn.

"Cases of sexual disinterest are not so uncommon among artists. Dylan Thomas, for example, neglected his wife—and every other female of the two-legged species—whenever he was engrossed in a poem. And when he had finally written the last line, drunk and freezing in his drafty shack in the Welsh countryside, the rush of creation still glowing, that incredible deranged energy tingling in his groin—do you think he remembered Caitlin, fair and lonely in their farmhouse up the hill? Do you think he thought of a warm bed and the soft words of love?" He paused for effect. "No—he masturbated."

Determined not to give him the satisfaction of showing her shock, Christie held her face impassive. He turned aside abruptly and grimaced. She sipped her tea carefully.

"I finally had what every man or woman of genius needs—a wife."

"So you married her?" she asked naïvely. The triumphant look he shot her made her wish she had kept her mouth shut.

"I don't mean marriage contracts and golden rings. I mean wife in all its philosophical implications—that circumstance in which another soul serves as a standard, a foil by which to measure one's progress—or, if you will, one's aberration. I mean the home one turns one's back on, the slippers one kicks aside. The person who believes in you unconditionally. In colloquial terms, a wife."

He paused. "Those were the *cantabile* years. Four years—a perfect quartet. The highest praise"—and he reached in the drawer again, spreading the clippings on the table, articles from *Jazz Monthly*, *Billboard*, *Village Voice*, *Downbeat*—"was written then. When things were almost over. Oh, there were signs. I was dissatisfied. My last record was listless, secondhand, and I knew it. The third stage flared up—a return to the *prestissimo* of my post-

Carnegie days—but my technique had more style than . . . well, brilliance or profundity. I was afraid.

"Then without warning, a woman dies. Elizabeth finds a letter in her mailbox from the attorney in charge of the woman's estate. I didn't think she knew anyone west of the Alleghenies, but there it was, black on white—a sixty-five-year-old woman dead of asthma complications in Phoenix, Arizona. Elizabeth was an heiress—no considerable fortune but an interesting one nevertheless—namely to all the household and personal possessions of one Mrs. Aaron R. Rosenblatt."

"Her mother?"

He snorted. "Elizabeth was alone in the world. Her parents had died long ago. More tea?"

She shook her head. "I'm ready to try the vodka, please."

"Wise decision."

The room was very still. Was it soundproof?

"When I asked her, Elizabeth claimed she had been just an acquaintance, an old neighbor from Brooklyn for whom she bought groceries when she could no longer get around. Okay, I thought, I'll go along with that. It was my turn to believe unconditionally.

"We flew to Arizona. Elizabeth wanted to go alone, but I argued that there were certain business details—liquidating the condominium, for example, or deciding the fate of a six-month-old diesel Mercedes—where two heads would be better than one. Besides, I had just finished my fifth record, 'Murdon's Requiem,' and I needed a break. 'A little cactus juice will do me good,' I joked. Reluctantly she agreed.

"I had never been to the Southwest before. It made a very powerful impression on me—a barbarous landscape, raw and beautiful as a baboon's ass."

He looked up, his eyes fierce, bloodshot. "Our great civilization, with its skyscrapers and automobiles"—he was smiling now—"seemed no more than a huge, complicated toy. Mrs. Rosenblatt's condominium complex looked like a battery of cereal boxes hastily set up to ward off a hurricane. We located the correct building, obtained the keys from the manager, and let ourselves in. It was an apartment like any other—prefab walls, balcony, built-in shelves, dishwasher and freezer. Color TV, glass coffee table. At first glance there was little we saw we could use ourselves—maybe the music box from Austria, shaped like a breadbox, with interchangeable melody rolls. Elizabeth discovered a camera with the film still in it. . . .

"We moved on to the kitchen. Spotless Formica, stainless steel sinks gleaming like sunken mirrors. A woman who kept things up, who would never be caught off guard by unexpected visitors. The kitchen yielded a few odds and ends—a very good old-fashioned meat grinder, like the one my grandmother used, a waffle iron that baked scalloped cakes imprinted with interlocking hearts.

"On to the bedroom, then. A dressing table with the usual assortment of talcs and perfumes, a jewelry box with a ring in it, a diamond in an overladen setting. In the closet, tucked behind polyester pantsuits and cotton sundresses, a very nice mink coat. Elizabeth didn't even want to try it on. 'What's wrong?' I asked, teasing. 'Don't tell me you're superstitious.' 'I don't like mink,' she snapped, walking out of the room. I had never known her to lose her temper before.

"But I was patient. You see"—he fixed Christie with his bloodshot eyes again—"it was my turn to play wife.

"I decided to explore the rest of the apartment. The bathroom was typical, pink tiles and the smell of bath salts and disinfectant. At the end of the hall a broom closet—nothing to see there—and next to it, opposite the bathroom, another room. The door was shut, but the key stood in the lock, so I turned it and pushed the door open.

"The shades were drawn. A single bed, made up like an army cot, stood to the left, the blue blanket folded in a precision envelope and laid at the foot of the mattress. Next to the bed stood a night table, but no lamp. Likewise a bureau against the far wall, devoid of ornaments—no lamp, no knickknacks, no doilies. The very barrenness of the room, couched in the half light of a day turned dingy by window shades, made me realize how full of life this 'apartment like any other' had been so far. Strange, I thought, a guest would hardly feel comfortable here—and that's when I saw it, in a niche in the far right wall. . . ."

His voice trailed off, and his gaze, directed toward her but not seeing, was the gaze of the poodle on the bed, a reflected and opaque brilliance.

"The niche," he continued, softly, reverently, "was hidden by a heavy black cloth, with a fluorescent light fastened to the wall above it." His gaze focused briefly, slid away again.

"I went over and lifted the cloth. As with everything Mrs. Rosenblatt owned, this, too, was in perfect condition, but there was a difference—for, although the keys' high sheen testified that they had been wiped every day, though the felt damper bar was free of dust, the mallets had not been placed in their holder but lay ready, both pairs, across the keys. As if someone had just left off playing. All this I saw and registered automatically; only much later, in my New York studio, did I put together the entire constellation.

"I found the cord and plugged it in. The discs in the pipes slowly began to turn. I released the damper pedal so that the keys could resonate, picked up the mallets, arranged them to strike perfect fourths. First a C scale—the fourths were nice, and I liked the curious lurching tone of the vibraphone. I was just about to try a few chords when I heard Elizabeth scream in the living room. . . .

"There was a freezing stillness, then the sound of running steps in the hall. She stopped at the door and hung there, holding on to the sides of the doorjamb with both hands. Haunted, face drained of color, she stared at me. Then she fainted.

"By the time she came to, I had carried her into the living room and begun to administer all the first aid one learns from the movies—a cold towel on the forehead, cognac at the lips. She came to and smiled. When she remembered, she jumped up, hysterical, and demanded to leave the house. I complied. What else was there to do? We got into the car and drove out of the condominium village, into the desert. The endless vistas of scrub grass, the wild, magic mountains, seemed to soothe her. I, too, was calm, but it was a calmness of despair. I had lost something—I was certain of it— but I couldn't put my finger on what. We drove for nearly an hour. I think we drove in circles; the same adobe ruin loomed up at rhythmic intervals, a caved-in hut with a spot of bright green—a scrap of cloth or a candy wrapper—wedged between two bricks. I said nothing; there was nothing for me to say.

"They had met at a jazz club—one of the countless smoky cellars in Manhattan where young musicians go to try out their wings. He played with a group that did commercial jazz; he was much better than the others. She went up to him afterward and told him so. They talked. His name was Daniel Rosenblatt."

Christie shifted her position; the chair was very hard. Misreading her restlessness, Jerry Murdon sniffed and laughed shortly.

"I know. It sounds like the typical love affair. In a way, it was. They moved in together after a few months. He took her to meet his mother, who was upset until she learned that Elizabeth was technically Jewish. Then the mother began to hint marriage. She hinted for seven years. Seven years! Finally, they decided to get the license—but first, they said, we'll take the honeymoon. When we come back, we'll tell her. . . .

"Where can a young couple go after seven years of blissful shacking up? Somewhere sunny, somewhere south—but not the Bahamas, not Capri, no—a place with a difference. That's when Elizabeth remembered the other half of her blood—peasant blood, her father's, and her grandmother's tales of a life in the mountains, surviving from olives and wine. That's how they decided on Italy."

Tuscany, Christie thought. Paese. *Here.*

"Well, they left Mama in her mink on the airport observation deck, wringing her hands, and to Italy they went—on the beach in the morning, on the mountain paths in the afternoon, and at night in restaurants, wining and dining themselves silly—saltimbocca and fritto misto and cannelloni, cappuccino in the morning and espresso at night.

"One evening Daniel decided to have a pear for dessert. There was no reason for either of them to suspect anything; the restaurant, listed with the tourist office, even boasted two stars. The service was swift and polite, the meal impeccable. Who would have suspected that the fruit had been washed too hastily that evening? Who would have thought a simple unwashed pear could breed on its blushing surface such a rare bacillus? Back in their room, Daniel complained of pains in his stomach. An hour later he couldn't move his legs. . . ."

Murdon lit another cigarette, flung the snuffed match on the floor. "She telephoned an ambulance and rushed him to the hospital. His stomach had stopped hurting, but he was numb up to his nipples. The doctors were helpless. 'A virus,' they said, throwing up their hands. 'Where can we start, there are a million of them in the air. . . .' By morning Daniel Rosenblatt was dead."

Christie watched the cigarette disintegrate, unnoticed, between Murdon's fingers. Was he lying—was the entire story merely invented, a noble allegory of his jumbled ambitions and private doubts? For all the pathos of the story there was also a coldness to it, something structured—as if he had gone over it many times, revising and ornamenting, lying on his bed in the dark with the amplified swell of twenty-four vibraphones frothing below him.

"Now that she had told me," Murdon resumed, the words issuing from his lips almost mechanically, "she felt better, almost cheerful. The energy with which she took charge was baffling. She contacted the lawyer and turned over the management of the remaining personal effects. She decided to keep the Mercedes. As for the vibraphone—Elizabeth's suggestion was to take it to New York with us, where it would bring a better price. I was put in charge of selling it.

"Back in Manhattan, it was as if nothing had happened. She never mentioned Daniel Rosenblatt again, and I never asked. I put an ad in the Times, set up the vibraphone in my studio, and waited. But every time I opened the door and saw a prospective buyer's anxious, hopeful face, it was Elizabeth's face I saw, terrified and inscrutable—and I wouldn't sell. When I remembered that face I couldn't practice, either. Instead I sat and looked at the vibraphone, its thirty-six steel plates, those churning columns of sound. What I couldn't understand was why she had never talked about him before. We were an enlightened couple. There was no reason, no reason at all.

"After two weeks had passed, Elizabeth asked me if I had had any luck.

I said I had someone coming in in the morning who seemed interested. The next morning I withdrew three thousand bucks from the bank, gave her the money, and told her the customer was satisfied. Then I went to a bar in Soho and got drunk. That night I slept in the studio."

Christie's head was pounding, a dull, wrenching pain to match the thump of her heart, a muffled yelp—but it wasn't her heart at all. It was the poodle, barking at the other end of the hall.

"Quiet, Sebastian!" Murdon yelled.

His hand trembled as he reached for the vodka bottle, and his voice had an edge to it. "I taught myself to play vibraphone," he said. "I had to play; it was the only way out. I stayed in the studio. When I felt hungry, I heated up a can of soup; when exhaustion overwhelmed me, I fell asleep as I was, the mallets in my hands.

"I was asleep when she knocked. I remember it was late afternoon, because the sun slanting through the windows struck the instrument and threw bars of light and shadow on the floor. She demanded an explanation. She began to cry. She said I had to sell it. She begged me to stop playing. 'I can't stop,' I said. I was telling the truth, but she didn't believe me."

Murdon reached for a drawer. A vicious tug sent packets of letters, bound with red string, spilling onto the rug.

"They're all the same," he said, pushing the letters together. "Variations on a theme. She can't leave me alone, but she can't come to me, either. So she writes to me. My fan mail," he whispered, gazing at the heap of envelopes.

He stood up abruptly. "If you'll excuse me, I have work to do."

He was kicking her out; shocked, disappointed, Christie picked up her purse and followed him downstairs. He opened the door and stood back to let her by, his face a contemptuous mask.

"They all go in the end, with their tails tucked under," he said. "Don't flatter yourself. You're not the first one to seek Murdon out in the wilds of Tuscany. Every summer someone shows up, sits still, and listens."

Christie held out her hand to say good-bye, but he stood transfixed, leaning against the door and staring at some point beyond the arbor. "It's the strangest thing," he whispered. "I talk and talk, and you listen. But you never tell anyone else, not a peep"—his face twisted suddenly—"his spell is that strong."

The door closed. Christie turned and began walking slowly down the path. Behind her, the music started up again, that surging, choking wail, a clamor against wasted innocence—she shivered looking over the garden—a search for the contentment lost long ago, without anyone knowing it.

IN THE SHADOW OF THE PEACOCK

Grace Edwards-Yearwood

Frieda heard the sound and ignored it. When she heard it again, she opened the window and leaned out. The noise had come from the direction of the avenue and was faint, barely distinguishable from the other, ordinary night summer sounds. She strained for a better view but, as usual, was blocked by the fire escape.

She listened intently for the sound of a motorcade. Perhaps it was another Negro Freedom rally organized by Paul Robeson, or it might be Mayor La Guardia again, touring Harlem as he had done a few weeks ago with the Liberian president. But those motorcades always came up Seventh Avenue, and this sound, this noise, was different.

Directly below, she noticed that the loungers had given up top positions on the stoop, and strollers, in frozen attitudes, appeared to be listening for some extraordinary signal. Across the street, flowered, striped, and gauzy curtains were torn aside and windows were suddenly filled with wide-eyed, frightened faces.

She thought of climbing outside, but wondered what Noel would say if he came in and found her on the fire escape in her condition. The thought

was broken again by the sound, no longer an undercurrent but elevated high on the hot night wind.

It was heavy and pulsating, a roar rolling before the measured tread of an army on the march. It poured up the avenue, preceding the mob by several minutes. It engulfed the strollers and loungers, sucked them in and swelled the dimensions of the sound and the mob.

Fragments:

"Whut?? Whut happened, man?"

"Cop kill a Gee-Eye . . . outside the Braddock!"

"Naw!"

"If I'm lyin', I'm flyin'."

It happened in Chicago, Texas, and Alabama, where a colored man in uniform, momentarily confused by the heady breath of patriotism, might forget himself and then pay for the lapse. But this was New York. Harlem. Where there was safety in collective anger.

"Mmm . . . uhm! Cats gon' raise some hell tonight, betcha that!!"

At first the bricks connected only with the streetlights and glass rained down in darkness. All but invisible, the mob, a solid sea of blackness, surged up the wide avenue. Their familiar badges of mops and brooms now transformed into torches that winked dangerously in the blackness. Then came the sound of heavy glass. Storefront glass. Pawnshop glass.

Frieda listened, thought of Noel, and left the window where she had crouched.

"Don't let nuthin' happen to him . . . don't let him be in the middle of this, whatever it is. . . ."

She had abandoned prayer as comfort years ago, but her mouth moved anyway as she made her way down the stairs. At the bottom of the landing, she paused, breathing heavily, and realized that she had not run this fast in a long time. She sat on the third step from the bottom, feeling her breath leave and enter, leave and enter in fitful bursts, burning her nostrils and drying her mouth.

. . . calm . . . calm . . . quiet . . . don't . . . don't get too excited . . . not now, not now. . . .

The lobby door swung open and she recognized Sam and Dan as they slipped out of the darkness of the street into the dim hallway. They moved toward the steps, huge, handsome young men burdened with the weight of several large cartons. Despite their size, they had the quick, quiet grace of street cats. They stopped when they saw her.

"Frieda! Outside ain't no place for you. Not tonight anyway!"

Sam turned to his twin. "Where this girl think she goin'?"

"He's right, Frieda. Things is jumpin' off out there," said Dan as he surveyed the dim hallway for a place to stash his take. It was going to be a

long night, and he didn't plan to make more than one trip up four flights, no matter how much he stole.

The only available space was the shallow alcove behind the stairs. Anything placed there would be visible from the lobby, easy pickings for any common thief who had no respect for another person's hard labor.

"Hell with it," he sighed, turning again to Frieda. "Looka here now, you can't go outside. Not in your condition. . . ." Frieda instinctively put her hand to her swollen stomach.

"Dan . . . I didn't mean . . . what's goin' on . . . you seen Noel?"

"Ain't seen nobody 'cept wall-to-wall busted heads. The bulls is swingin' and we swingin' right back."

"But why? What happened . . . ?"

"Gee-Eye took a bullet," said Dan as he started up the stairs, "right here on his own turf. Didn't even git overseas and he a casualty. And they don't be dealin' no purple hearts for the Braddock."

Frieda was surprised. The Braddock restaurant had always been a lively, crowded place where people waited hours to taste Miss Beryl's West Indian cooking, but there had never been any trouble.

"Listen," said Dan, pausing as he passed her, "don't go out there. Them people'll run right over you, pregnant or not. You won't stand a chance."

"Besides," said Sam, "we goin' back out. Give us a list. We'll git anything you want. . . ."

Frieda, silent, stared toward the door with wide eyes, trying, all at once, to absorb what she had just heard, and listening for some new sound.

"Girl, stop worryin'. Noel, he all right. Now look, you place your order while the gittin's good. We deliver. No money down and no monthly payments. Not even a slight installation charge. You name it, you got it—basins, bowls, bassinets, bottles, brooms, everything and anything for the pretty little mama . . ."

His sales pitch was interrupted by a howling scream outside that caused the three of them to recoil.

A woman was running, crying. "Help me git 'im to the hospital. His hand is nearly off!! Help me . . . !"

"Who tol' 'im to put his fist through the goddamn window in the first place," someone yelled back. "Everybody else usin' garbage cans, and this nigger wanna play King Kong. Oughtta bleed to death on gee-pee. Come on . . . but dammit, don't bleed all over my car!"

The screaming continued down the block in a long, unbroken wail. Sam shook his head and started up the stairs after his brother. At the top he leaned over the railing. "Don't you worry 'bout Noel. He all right. You just sit tight. Things is too hot out there. Just sit tight."

As soon as their footsteps faded, Frieda opened the door. The streets had gone from wartime brownout to total darkness. Only the lights from the hallways sliced the night at measured intervals. Broken glass covered every inch of sidewalk, and runners, heading for the avenue, performed strange arabesques as they slid and skated in and out of the dim yellow pools.

She left the stoop. Where was she going? Suppose Noel came from another direction . . . no . . . he always came this way . . . from the avenue . . . I know . . . I know . . .

She stayed near the buildings, clinging to the handrails as she crept along. The roar by now had become so sustained that she felt it had always been there, as part of the background. Except for the futile howl of a burglar alarm and an occasional scream louder than the rest, the noise reminded her of the waterfall back home in the South.

She remembered a night like this. A different kind of mob running wild. Heavy, sweating faces staring down the barrel of a shotgun. Retreating, retreating . . .

She shook her head. . . . Calm . . . calm . . . once I see Noel . . . calm . . . calm . . .

At the corner, two men carrying a huge orange sofa blocked her way. "You be careful out here, little girl. . . ." They maneuvered their cargo around her with a series of grunts and groans and were gone. A woman followed in their wake with a portable sewing machine balanced delicately on her head. Graceful as a ballerina, she stepped lightly over the shards of glass and disappeared in the dark.

Eighth Avenue was devastated. Windows were smashed, and locks and gates were bent into intricate curlicues. Broken furniture spilled from discarded cartons, and headless mannequins, stripped of clothing, lay amid the debris, their stark plaster limbs spread at impossibly obscene angles.

Frieda crept past Johnson's meat market and Clark's grocery store, two places where she shopped every chance she got because the mysteriously abundant displays of food reassured her and she didn't have to think about the war and shortages and red and blue ration stamps. Now, both places, side by side, appeared to have been sucked out by a giant vacuum. Even the refrigeration systems had been destroyed.

. . . how could this happen . . . they say somebody shot a soldier . . . what did he do . . . is he dead . . . what could've happened to cause all this . . .

She concentrated on the devastation to keep from thinking about Noel, but that was impossible. Somehow the two were intermixed. She felt cold standing there, trying to think and not think.

The siren clanging above the roar distracted her, and she saw, four blocks away, the faint glow as it spread in the dark, small at first, then, seconds later, leaping in long orange tongues up the side of the building from the store below, bursting windows and buckling frames.

Frieda could hear the screams from where she stood. The tide, which had been flowing away from the wreckage, stopped in wonder. "Who the hell set that fire?? Don't they know there's people upstairs over that store? Who set the fire??"

The question shot out of the darkness, and the tide reversed itself. People began to run toward the building, careless of the glassy pavement, as the screams of the trapped rose above the roar.

Frieda was overcome with confusion, and the terror that had crept up her back by inches now immobilized her.

"What's goin' on? What's goin' on?"

There was no answer as the mob pressed in. That is, she heard no distinct answer. Only the hollow scream that rolled out of the darkness as she was swept like flotsam into the tide that enveloped her.

A few blocks away, the "A" train pulled into the 145th Street station, and Noel was asleep as usual. He slept with his head thrown back, but the rest of his six-foot frame was curled into itself protectively.

Al glanced at him. He did not understand how Noel could have accustomed himself so quickly to the fast pace of the city and, worst of all, the grinding noise of the subway.

Damn, he thought, dude in the city less than a year and he cattin' like he born here. Probably sleep right on through a Jap attack. . . .

He poked Noel lightly with his elbow. "Rise and shine, man. This is it."

Noel was awake, instantly alert although his eyes retained a sleepy, languid look. He rose from his seat and suppressed an urge to stretch. Several women in the crowded car looked up from knitting and newspapers and put a smile on the edge of their lips just in case he glanced their way. But Noel was too tired to notice. He yawned and waited impatiently for the train to stop.

"Tell me somethin'," Al said, "what you gonna do when I catch my digit and quit this job? You liable to ride all the way up to the yards some nights. . . ."

"You can hit the number all you want to," Noel replied, "but you ain't quittin' this job. This the most and steadiest money you seen in your life."

"That's only 'cause of the war," Al said as they made their way to the door with the crowd, "only 'cause of the war. And how long can it last? Six months? A year at most? Sam got a B-24 rollin' off the assembly line every hour. What them Japs got? They just a dot in some ocean nobody never heard of. How long can they last? This war could be over tomorrow, then what? Where we gonna be? Worse off than ever, that's where. . . . They singin' that stuff 'bout 'praise the Lord, pass the ammunition and we'll stay free' don't mean us, you know."

They headed for the exit, both feeling the weight of the twelve-hour, six-day work shift. Noel only half listened as Al spoke. He was too tired to argue.

He thought: That's what happens when a man been catchin' hell too long. He never forget it. Then again, he ain't supposed to . . . keep 'im prepared for whatever comes up . . . but hell, he ain't the only one seen a bad time. . . .

He knew what was coming and with effort tried to rechannel his thoughts. He had promised himself, once he and Frieda had gotten safely away, that he would live only in the now and think only of the future. But sometimes, in that hour of the night when the mind exercises the least control over the body, Noel would waken out of a deep sleep, bolt upright in the bed, arms and legs twitching frightfully as he saw the flames, smelled the terrible odor, and tried to close his ears to the screaming that never stopped.

Sometimes Frieda would wake him. And they would wrap themselves into each other, silently, and remain like that until dawn.

. . . I'm tired, he thought, I'm just tired, that's all. Got enough grit on me to weigh a ton. Nobody'd believe that Navy Yard could be so dirty. They don't show that on them posters. A slip of the lip might sink a ship. Pitch in for democracy. Shit. They hired the women, old men, even the crippled folks, then they hire us. Give us the dirtiest jobs left over and swear to God they doin' us a favor. Ah, hell with 'em. Right now the first thing I'm gonna do when I git home is hit the tub. Nice . . . warm . . . let Frieda rub my back a little.

But it wasn't his back that was bothering him. He relaxed, slackening his pace as he imagined the touch of her hands, soft and gentle, on his back, neck, and shoulders and, finally, sliding between his thighs in the warm, soapy water.

. . . sure be glad when the baby finally git here, awh, Jesus . . .

"Hey, Noel! Man, you sailin' 'long like you in a trance," said Al, "bet you didn't hear a word I said. If I'd a known the dream was that good, I'd a left you on the train. Didn't mean to disturb you."

"Naw, man, naw. It ain't like that. Just thinking," said Noel. He did not remember coming through the turnstile or passing the change booth. They had come to the stairs, and he was surprised to find the exit blocked, jammed with people.

"What's goin' on?" yelled Al. "Come on, let's move. I'm tired and wanna git home."

Al was short and powerfully built and had a scar near his ear which he had never spoken of to Noel. They had both arrived in the city on the same bus a little less than a year ago and wound up working on the same job and living in the same building.

Noel seemed quiet and easygoing, and it puzzled Al when he noticed that Noel never smiled and never talked about home, wherever that was. But, on reflection, he realized that he himself said very little.

"Come on," Al yelled again, "what's goin' on up there?"

"We trottin' fast as we can," someone shot back, "keep your drawers on, for Chrissakes."

Outside, on the avenue, they stared in openmouthed surprise.

"What the hell happened?"

"Look like the Japs got us. . . ."

"Man, where in hell alla these people come from . . . ?"

". . . and lookit all that smoke. . . ."

They heard the story on the run—in distorted, disjointed chapters.

". . . they say she wasn't nuthin' but a trick. . . ."

"So what? That don't give no wop cop no right to be beatin' on her. . . ."

"Braddock'll never be the same."

"Sho' won't. They done crisped the joint. . . ."

". . . poor Miss Beryl . . . work so hard. . . ."

"Heard the Gee-Eye come from uptown. Ex-Jolly Stomper . . ."

"Good God a'mighty. No wonder he so bad."

"Took that cop's billy an' made 'im eat it. Them uptown cats 'bout the baddes' things on two feet. . . ."

"He still alive? Heard he took three bullets. . . ."

"In Sydenham, they say."

"Naw, took the cop to Sydenham. The Gee-Eye up at Harlem."

"Hell . . . make it to Harlem breathin', he make it all the way. They say 'what come in, if it's still squawkin', guaranteed it'll go out walkin'.'"

The crowd flowed in all directions, its members imagining in the dark confusion that anyone or anything flowing against them was a mortal enemy. The thick, wet smell and taste of blood was in the air and on the tongue.

"Hell gon' pay tonight. . . ."

Al and Noel were out of breath when they approached the burning building. The heat radiated out and over the scene. Fire engines and yards of tangled hose cluttered the area. The crowd, uncontrolled by the few police still present, milled around the blaze. The flames had reached the third floor, and one by one the windows bulged from the intense heat, burst outward, and sprayed shards of hot glass on the crowd below. The people retreated momentarily, regrouped, and surged in again.

Noel pulled at Al's sleeve. "I'm cuttin' out, man . . . wanna see 'bout Frieda."

He turned and nearly fell over the small boy standing directly behind him.

"Jim-Boy!"

"Please, Mistuh Noel . . ." The rest was lost in the uproar.

Noel crouched down, gathering the child in his arms. "Whut you doin' out here in all this mess??"

For answer, the boy clung to Noel so tightly that Noel could feel, almost hear, the wild beating of the child's heart.

Jim-Boy and Noel had a special friendship, begun last summer, when Noel had retrieved a ball thrown wild. "Better be careful with that traffic, sonny," Noel had said, "them cars don't stop on a dime, you know. . . ."

"—name ain't Sonny, it's Jonrobert, but Grandma call me Jim-Boy."

"Well, it don't matter who calls you what, you go after that ball and traffic catch you the wrong way, you won't have no name at all, understand?"

Every evening after that, Jim-Boy sat on the stoop and waited, his small, round face dark and expressionless except for the lemon-yellow mark above his eyelid. When Noel appeared, Jim-Boy smiled, waved, and disappeared into the house. The house was now on fire.

"Where's your mama?"

"She down South, but Grandma . . . she . . . she . . ."

"Where's your grandma—"

The boy was pointing to the top floor. "—in 'er wheelchair . . ."

Noel could not bring himself to look at the building. He concentrated on the boy's shaking finger instead and fought the urge to run, to push Jim-Boy away from him and run, screaming, from this nightmare.

Here it is all over again, he thought. All over again. He wanted to rock back on his heels and laugh and shout and demand of God how something like this could happen twice in the lifetime of one man.

But the crowd milled around him, pressing him in the awkward crouching position. He felt the boy's heart beating against his own and, unbidden, the nightmare memory flashed in, obliterating present sight and sound. He heard his father's cry, strange and strangled behind the sheet of flame.

. . . curse all you . . . curse all your . . . children's children . . . and the cursing dissolving into a screaming, gurgling sound, then nothing save the crackling flames. And he, unobserved, creeping upon that scene too late, not knowing it was his own father until one of the mob laughed.

". . . this'll teach 'im . . . this'll teach 'im. Wavin' that shotgun . . . Now. We gotta git that no-'count nigger gal . . ."

That no-'count nigger gal. Frieda.

The yellow flames tore at the body against the tree, until the man no longer looked like a man and even the tree turned a dull crimson in the dark.

. . . daddy . . . daddy . . . daddy . . . He had shut his eyes to keep from screaming, and the flames leaped orange against his closed lids.

. . . daddy . . . daddy . . . daddy . . .

"Noel! For God's sake, you okay? You gonna squeeze the life outta that kid!" Al's hand shook him, and Noel blinked Jim-Boy back into focus.

"Your grandma—she in there and you ain't said nuthin'?"

"But I did, I did . . . oh! . . . I tol' 'em . . ." The child pointed to the firemen, and his voice, drained by fright, sank to a whisper.

Noel felt the constriction in his own voice and spoke rapidly. "Now listen, boy. You sure nobody got her out . . ."

"She's still there, Mistuh Noel, I know she is. . . ."

"Top floor?"

"Top floor . . . near the roof. Sometimes I go play on the roof, but Grandma don't like it. She like for me to be in the street where she can watch me . . . but the roof . . ."

"How you git down—"

"Over the roof . . . I tol' you—"

Al followed Noel as he pushed his way through the crowd.

"What you gonna do, man? You can't do nuthin' . . . come back!"

Noel reached the core of the crowd, and a fireman working the pump yelled, "Keep outta the way!"

"There's a woman up there!" Noel shouted. "On the top floor!"

"No, there ain't," another fireman replied. "They're all out. Out stealin' . . ."

The fireman's laughter was heavy and their movements, though coordinated from years of routine, were extremely slow. Noel was perplexed. Then he realized that they were all drunk. Without another thought, he left the crowd, skipped over the scattered hose, and raced into the adjoining building.

"Where you goin', you crazy nigger??" yelled another fireman at Noel's retreating figure.

Al, who had been behind Noel, grabbed the man by his throat and lifted him off the ground. "Who you callin' nigger, motherfucker?"

His arm shot out like a piston and the fireman went down under the blows. The crowd had heard the word, and the roar reached a deafening level as the people surged forward. The remaining firemen grabbed hatchets, pikes, and picks and crowded together in a tight circle to defend themselves. The few policemen at the scene joined the firemen.

"Get back! Back, or we open fire!"

The order came from a red-faced sergeant, frightened into sobriety and frightened beyond reason.

Inside was black with smoke. Noel reached the third floor, smashed a rear window, and leaned out. On the fifth floor he tripped over some debris and lost his footing. He went down and continued on his hands and knees until he reached the roof.

The two buildings were separated by a brick hedgelike barrier three feet high. He swung his legs over and the tar stuck to his shoes as he moved.

"Stairway's out," he said aloud to himself, surprised by the calm in his voice. "She watched him on the street, so she gotta be in the front."

The smoke was thick and smelled of old rugs. He could not see in front of him but knew that he had reached the edge when he felt the sharp rise under his foot. The railing leading down the fire escape was warm. As he descended, the metal felt hotter. The entire right side of the building was now enveloped, and the heat hit Noel in the face like a hammer, taking his breath away.

He was suddenly fatigued and thought of turning back, when a loud roar went up from the crowd below. They had seen him and, not knowing his mission, shouted for him to come down.

Al looked up with tears in his eyes. "Noel! You damn fool! Noooeelll . . ."

The name buzzed in circles.

"Noel . . ."

"Who . . . ?"

"Some damn fool name Noel . . ."

It reached the ears of a pregnant girl who had been caught in the crowd.

She began to scream and claw her way to the front. Two big men, who stood head and shoulders above the rest, spotted her and plowed forward, shouting her name.

Inside the burning building, the heat was not half as intense as it had been outside, but the smoke was worse. Noel crawled only a few inches before he touched the wheel of the overturned chair. The woman lay beside it.

"Lady . . ." He barely whispered. He wondered what he would do if she was dead. Bring her out anyway. Leave her. He could move faster if he left her. He wondered if he could leave another body burning. Smell the smell again. And who was to blame now? Last time it was different.

"Lady," he called again.

With great effort, he placed his hand on her chest. His fingers touched a double-strand rope of pearls, rising up and down in slow, laborious rhythm. He found her shoulders and began to pull her toward the window. From the ease with which she moved, he knew that she didn't weigh more than a hundred pounds.

Out on the fire escape, he saw that he was right. She hung in his arms like a frail gray doll, eyes closed, breath coming in shallow, irregular impulses.

The ladder had grown hotter, and he wrapped the hem of the woman's dress around his hands before climbing up. On the roof his shoes sank deeper into the tar, and he noticed that it had begun to bubble in some places.

He made it to the second floor of the adjoining building before the flames spread laterally and engulfed the stairwell above him. The intensity of the heat staggered him so that the old woman nearly slipped from his grasp. He clawed at her shoulders and drew her up again.

A terrible crackling roar filled his ears, and he began to run blindly down the last flight of stairs. He did not know where he was. He felt the heat behind and around him. A tight band squeezed against his chest, emptying his lungs.

Suddenly he felt the flow of air. Through the smoke and tears, he could make out a doorway and the street beyond. It was only a glimpse before he was blinded again by the smoke. He moved forward by sheer force of will.

A keen eye in the crowd noticed that the sergeant's arm was shaking.

"Hey, sucker, whyn't you rest that piece?"

"Mebbe he need a little help . . ."

"He gonna need a lotta help . . ."

"Get back, I'm telling you!!"

". . . *been* gittin' back, motherfucker. All our lives, matta fact . . ."

The crowd, bold, pressed nearer. The white man was in their territory now. Familiar ground and strange circumstance. His uniform, soaked and stained, smelled of a mouth-drying, gut-turning, ball-shrinking fear. The smell floated out and touched those in the crowd nearest him, and they were amazed. It was no different from the way they had felt every minute of every day of their lives as they floundered in unfamiliar, dangerous, downtown territory, their only protection being a flimsy waiter's apron or doorman's uniform.

The shouts and threats melted into thick, ominous silence. Everyone was waiting, but no one saw the bottle sail out of the darkness until it actually hit the sergeant in the eye. He got off a single wild shot before he went down; the crowd, hungry in its hatred, seized the moment and closed in screaming.

"Git 'em, git 'em, giii . . ."

The roar reached a pitch too high to hear.

Switchblades and straight razors flashed open as axes and picks swung in wide, furious arcs. Fighters grappled and grunted and slipped in their own blood. Two firemen grabbed a high-powered hose and focused, scatter-shot fashion, on anything that moved.

The tremendous force of the water hit Noel as he staggered from the building, the flames at his back. The force struck him, catapulting him back into the heart of the inferno where the wall collapsed on him and his frail burden.

Frieda fell to the ground screaming. The twins leaped over her, tore the two men from the hose and tossed them, like sticks of kindling, into the flames. They watched as the flames licked at the rubber slickers, the bodies inside performing grotesque gyrations, snapping and jerking like dancers in a film gone awry.

"We oughtta fry all these motherfuckers . . ."

"Later . . . we gotta git this girl to a hospital quick."

Halfway from the scene, halfway to the hospital, the twins stopped. Frieda had made no outcry—she was beyond that—but there was a sudden convulsion. They laid her down in the shattered street, but before they could summon help, they heard a crying so faint they might have imagined it.

The twins looked at each other.

"How could she—how could anybody—bring a kid into this—this goddamn mess," Sam cried.

Dan turned away from him to kneel beside Frieda. He did not want to see his brother's tears. "She didn't know, man. She just didn't know it was gonna turn out this way. . . ."

PLATITUDES

Trey Ellis

The digital alarm clock rolls little 7, 0, and 0 cards, white on black, over the 6, the 5, and the 9.

WAAA—

Off. Waffle-colored fingers have crawled from under both the regular and the fitted sheets, which have been detached from the bed, twisting around his waist, between his legs. Earle's finger has pressed the white clock button in to free it to poke farther out. Light pours through the apartment window over the large schefflera leaves; it filters past the P38 Mustang and the four-stage Estes Saturn 5 rocket (one nose-diving, the other rising, but both from monofilament fishing line lashed to the curtain rod, and both stream red-dyed cotton-ball flames). Quivering shadows dapple the room's far wall and Earle's collection of college pennants and the large map of the world voo-dooed with redheaded pins through the heart of every city Earle will visit on his sabbatical from Cal Tech or M.I.T. or someplace like that. He peels his face off the plastic mattress cover—a bumper sticker separating from its backing.

Errrrrrrrrr-rle, croons a too sweet voice from outside his door. It's time to wake uhhhhhhhhhh-up.

Oh-kaaaaaaaaaaa-ay.

His penis now makes a small white tent of his underwear, so Earle walks to his room's bathroom slowly, in place more than forward. Through the plant, the plane, and the rocket there she is, the wife in 10A, in the building's other wing, back already from her early-morning aerobics. She begins her cool-down pre-shower stretches; she sports a sport bra and Lycra knickers, a yellow ponytail, a sweatband/chronometer. Earle runs to his bed, pulls a small wooden wedge from under his mattress, runs to his room's door, wedges it closed (Mom! One second, don't try and force it. It must be swollen from the humidity. Yeah, swollen, he would say if he had to). Behind the large leaves, with his free hand, he tries to unscrew the toothpaste top, pinning it on the sink for leverage, finally opens it, but with an inadvertent ooze into his fingers. He licks off the gel, reaches, wets and puts his toothbrush into his mouth, brushes. Since he is now naked, no one can prove who is the Peeping, who the Tom.

Earle is soon spooning Cream of Wheat into his mouth in the kitchenette.

While his mother reminds him his suit for the B'nai B'rith/NAACP dance at the Copa this evening is back from the cleaners, hanging on her closet hook, I'll tell you what she does not look like:

She is neither fat (her breasts don't swell the lace top of the apron she has never owned), nor has she any gold teeth. She cannot sing, nor is she ever called "Mama" (though that is what she calls her own mother). She does not, not work in public relations and her two-handed backhand is not, not envied by her peers.

. . . should be here any minute. I told him we'd go to the zoo.

Yes, I do realize you are sixteen years old, smarty pants, but there's no law against sixteen-year-olds going to the zoo. You used to love the zoo. Your father and I would leave you for just one hot second and off you'd go to the monkey house, scratching your armpit and jumping up and down. One time you ran off and grabbed this balloon seller's bouquet of zoo balloons and were already a foot or two off the ground before your father could pull you back down, remember?

Oh, that must be Solomon. Be nice to Mr. Levitt even if you decide not to go with us, okay, sweetie?

Darling, you look like a million bucks, you always look like a million bucks, do you know that? In one of my buildings just the other day I was saying to the super, a lazy worthless EssOhhBee but he's been with me for years, I was saying, I know this woman who looks like a million bucks, says Mr. Levitt, rotating the last half of a cigar between thumb and forefinger before chomping on it again in the side of his mouth. Hey, kid, how they hanging?

Answer him, Earle, answer Mr. Levitt.

After the zoo, we'll get a bite to eat at this four-star joint I know in City Island, you wouldn't believe the crab cakes they got up there, as big as basketballs, then who knows? maybe a movie. My treat. What do you say?

Oh, let's just go on without him, Sol. When Earle gets in one of his moods, I swear. He even skipped school yesterday. I just don't know sometimes.

Solomon Levitt lays his briefcase flat on the dining-room table, fingers the wheels of the combination lock, then thumbs outward the triggers that free the latches to spring. Too bad, sport, but here's a little present. Your ma told me you was into that electronics stuff. He hands Earle a shrink-wrapped Heathkit U-Build-It multitester. And here's ten bucks for the batteries or something.

When Earle's mother says, What do you say, Earle says, Thank you, sir.

. . . and did I remind you to rinse your Cream of Wheat bowl, says his mother, now downstairs, calling on the doorman's house phone. You know how it gets glued to the bowl and spoon like sandpaper if you don't do it right away, and the dishwasher only bakes it in. . . . Promise me you'll get out of the house today. It's lovely outside, not too hot yet or muggy. . . .

The instructions for the multitester say it will take nineteen hours for people seventeen years old and older to assemble. It is now ten o'clock in the morning and I'm sure Earle's planning to finish the kit long before tonight's nine o'clock dance.

 The taxi's quick lean to the stop lifts Earle off the seat as he stuffs the folded dollars into the cab's money slot. She's got to come, Earle says to himself, reaching and reaching again for the car-door handle he only eventually finds.

Thumping interrupts Earle's words. A doorman holding a clipboard caps the disco's entrance. A group of pretty, light-skinned young black women and expensively dressed young white men hurl their names at the man at the door. They walk into the dark, into the beat. Earle speaks his name to the clipboard, twice.

There she is, alone.

A hostess approaching in a short, red, starched dress and emotionproof makeup sways between him and her. The hostess offers, then distributes, tiny scrolls from a tray yoked around her neck by a strap:

THE COPA

It makes their bodies throb.
The Beat, it thumps, the Beat.
Its pulse still makes them bob
Through melodies and sweating feet.

Reds criss and cross the blues,
They skim the crowds, these discs of light,
Finding mixed heads, yet they lose
The stuff beneath that height.

The strobe flash, hard flash.
Explode. Black. Room. In. The. Thump.
A simple thrust is seen a slash.
A sexy grind becomes a hump.

The chains drop from his throat
Like golden, frozen falls,
He undulates, appears to float,
His pants constrict his balls.

Her miniskirt is more a belt,
A narrow, leather thing.
It rubs her bone, will force a welt,
All just for a fling.

—Bill DePopulaire

Inside the club Earle's pupils expand with the ripples in the punch, responding to the beat on the punch bowl. A Jewish mother with a silk flower on her bosom and a heavy smile scoops fluid into Earle's two glasses and onto his hand. In this light the drink is black but tastes red. A black woman mans the hors d'oeuvres table.

There she is again, dancing with some girls. The crazy lights darken her hair. Another black young man nears Janey Rosebloom to the beat, groin first. She turns to him to the beat. They dance at each other.

The bathroom is warm and clean and empty and quiet. Earle turns the handle that turns the bolt into the hole in the stall door, shakes the stall door, wipes the seat with a pillow of tissue, and sits. The stall wall is patterned with jagged Magic Marker ink (see table 2.1), some of it still wet and thick-smelling. Yet even this doesn't help, so Earle exhales noisily, screws shut his eyes, wrenches tufts of hair, grits his teeth, and stamps his feet.

TABLE 2.1

Samples of Bathroom Graffiti

The color of chocolate and also of shit.
Vidi, Vici, Veni
Janey Rosebloom is Hot to Trot and I know it for a fact, Jack.

The men's room attendant, a wizened soul whose ebony skin is cracked and creased like some ancient Nubian riverbed that long ago suckled a thriving metropolis, nods toward an empty stall, and several high school boys scamper to line up in front of it.

Earle now stands at the sink, along with nerd after nerd, pressing forehead zits from the left and from the right.

Did you see Mary/Naomi/Laraine?/She's so incredibly beautiful, even better than her sister, but I was such a stu-nod saying, Hi, Darryl, this is Ramona—I mean you're Ramona, I'm Darryl! I could've just died right there/Heather pressed her leg into mine for a good minute and a half, she's got to want it/I just said to the pharmacist, They're for Mike, my big brother. You fill them up with water and throw them off the roof, right?

Earle tries to strut from the bathroom. Seeing Deborah adjusting herself so near, Earle stops and turns. Hey, foxy baby, would you care to dance, he mouths to himself.

T minus ten seconds and counting.

Earle brushes off his lapel lint.

Earle growls, revving up the vocal cords to prevent voice cracking.

T minus five.

Earle swishes a mouthful of air in his mouth to kill the anaerobic halitosis microbes.

Earle swishes his hands over his head to press down any uneven nuts of hair.

Hey, baby, I could not help but notice you are alone here. May I suggest we too start our own party? I've got some wicked weed with me, says Jamil in gold chains and tight pants. Deborah smiles, pulls him away.

Earle lifts a toast point and tilts it toward the dance floor—the only light in the room. He seems to be guessing the pâté's true color by its red, blue, and strobe-light forms. Shawna tells him he is about to eat *pâté de foie gras*, goose liver. They make it by strapping large wooden funnels to geese throats and force-feeding them until they vomit, then force-feeding them the vomit. Earle asks her to dance. She says she would rather eat goose liver. Earle gags and gags again, grips her shoulder.

The pâté on the toast at first sticks to his nose, then the bread dangles and falls face down to the floor. Leaving, Shawna rubs the remaining smudges of wet gray from her fingers onto the wall, her legs chopping through the slits up the back and front of her dress, calling, Bouncer. Bouncer.

The nerds see Shawna, see Earle; joyously they shovel their hands into the pile of liver and the nearby tub of California onion dip.

 Well, Earle's story so far has degenerated pretty quickly, now hasn't it? If you ask me it's got "No Sale" written all over it. But girls, women? Now black women *sell*, according to a friend of mine who works in publishing.

 From St. Rita's School for Girls, the young women flood, then dribble out the imposing and ornate Gothic gates.

Their kilts short, their socks tall, their loafers brown, their blouses yellow or white, from way up here they always look like little candies, delicate balls of assorted deliciousness. In one group of four, walking arm in arm in (etc.), the prettiest is dark brown and semisweet—Dorothy and friends in *The Wizard of Oz*. At the corner, from deep inside their jumbo athletic jacket sleeves that tunnel well after their fingertips, packs of cigarettes appear and are passed around. Ponytails are freed and shaken tangled. Dorothy lays her *Barron's Guide to the PSAT* on the sidewalk before her, bending over, but knees ever locked. Her friends also bend and stretch, press the sidewalk with their palms; pull up legs extending to pointed feet high above their heads. Obviously they are dancers.

When the limousine arrives, they quickly snap their cigarettes onto West Ninetieth Street. And though it is now out of sight, I see the long car stopping on Ninety-sixth, where Dorothy pecks her affluent friends, steps out, then down the subway stairs, and into a filthy uptown train.

Out of the subway stairway she rises, and rises well. Her bottom doesn't swing too much to be vulgar, just enough to provoke. Her skirt (that skirt! I can't imagine what was going through the mind of the nun who designed that plaid ultramini as the uniform for all Catholic girls. . . . *Now let me see, one more stitch and yes! Lovely! Mother Superior will be so proud of me. Why, it will almost even cover their little derrieres. Now surely the dear, sweet, precious young things will be certain of going to heaven. For as Augustine teaches us, "No girl shall find that pie-in-the-sky without exposing a whole lot of thigh."*) is unique this afternoon on Lenox Avenue. Harlem.

Girl, you better get your black ass out that street and in behind my register like you got good sense, says Dorothy's mother, Darcelle. She will be one of those fundamentalist, tough-as-nails black women who, underneath, are pussycats.

Moms, have I ever let you down, says Dorothy.

Behind the yellowed Formica counter, Dorothy crouches a bit, steps into the orange rayon jumper, and rises, an employee.

Darcelle sucks her teeth as she opens the thick Plexiglas cash-register stall and releases a woman under a hairnet. She says to her daughter, locking her inside the booth, And I want to see you studying them books in between customers. I'll have my eye on you, girl.

Thank you, sir, but no, I don't get off work until *very* late, Dorothy explains to a police officer through the circle of bored holes at her mouth level in the booth. My *mother* needs me here and I have to study *every* night. She eyes him as she plucks from him his bill, spikes it on the spindle tip that is so sharp it twinkles when the light hits right.

I didn't think that birthday party would ever leave, Darcelle says to Dorothy. You finish all your homework? 'Cause I don't have to be explaining the consequences if you didn't. Come on out the box and get yourself something to eat. We got some ribs still. They turned out good.

Yes, Mama, says Dorothy, folding closed the PSAT study guide on Part IV, Antonyms. Darcelle unlocks the booth door, and the mother and the daughter grab the long, iron, hooked poles leaning on the dining room's far corner and, outside, hook the heavy steel shades' ends, unroll them over the windows noisily. The narrow metal gate over just the restaurant door Dorothy closes only half down. Her mother, then herself, stoops back under the steel. Dorothy, inside, locks the front door behind them, leaves the key in the lock.

Mommy. Do you think I could head back downtown now? Julie's having some kids over and . . .

Darcelle walks to her office off the kitchen, pulls the top file open, dips in her hand. She slowly presses the silver bowl of the thermometer end toward Dorothy's pressed lips.

Mama! Dorothy's head dances around the thermometer. I ain't sick.

You must be sick asking me if you can go off downtown on a Monday school night.

That ain't funny. You aren't funny, Mother. It's just some friends. No boys or anything. Just a little study group for the PSATs. The girls I have dance class with.

Lord knows, if boys weren't going to be around, you wouldn't be calling me Mommy, wanting to go on down there so. You bad as Shawniqua, spend all that money to send her off to Yale University just so she can engage herself to some greasy Frenchman. Besides, Mr. Jefferson's taking me to studies tonight, so I need you to look after the twins. He says you just tell him your size and width and he'll get you all the Fayvas you want. I can't understand why you don't like him.

I'll have to call Julie then and tell her my mother's too mean to let me go study with her. You don't care if I fail the test or not.

You can tell that little rich girl to kiss my big black behind is what you can tell her.

Mama, you can be so street sometimes. Dorothy drags down the zipper of her jumpsuit, steps out, leaving the orange rayon shell slouched over her metal chair in front of the plate of ribs.

Darcelle stretches behind the bag of flour, pulls out the bottle of cooking sherry, then looks to the corner from where Dorothy will reappear, and swigs.

 From her throat, past her open lips, scratchy, wet sounds grind out Darcelle's mouth—an orthodontist's saliva pump hooked over your lip, sucking. The shrink-wrapped couch falls in around her; the corns on her feet, which flop on the coffee table, lump her knee-high stockings. From her left hand dangles the TV's remote control. The TV itself glows electronic static. It's crackling/the mother's snores: harmelodic.

Hanging her pumps from her fingers, Dorothy walks barefoot through the white wall-to-wall. Her calves ball tense over tiptoes as the black mini rubs a line in her thighs. The notes from her mother's throat descend as she laps at her own loose saliva. Dorothy stops, starts, watches Darcelle's eyelids. Dorothy squeezes the front doorknob before turning it, turning it, just till the lock is freed; then she inhales and squeezes around the door.

 I'm sorry. I don't know what more to write. This story's just as forced. It's embarrassing to stumble so obviously in so public a forum, but I guess sometimes you just have to throw it up the old flagpole and see who salutes. Things were going pretty well for a while, then somewhere along the line I got sidetracked again. I don't know. It's been almost twenty years since I was a teenager, but I thought it would all come back to me. I was also trying to remember my ex-nieces and nephews (my ex-wife's sister's children)—bourgeois, materialistic miscreants to the one, but I must have blocked them forever out of my mind. I swear that whole family is worth at least a thousand-page historical novel. Summers on the Vineyard, liposuction, tennis, analyses, golf, BMWs, and the Bahamas. If I were John Jakes I'd be laughing all the way to my made-for-TV-movie deal.

But as you can see, both story lines—Earle's and Dorothy's—have their problems. Obviously enough, folks, I need help. Anybody out there who's inspired, please write in and tell me which story you like better; and what are your favorite (and least favorite) characters, witticisms, grammatical devices, etc. I promise to incorporate your suggestions and keep the ship sailing smoothly from here on in. Just write to:

"Which Ones Do I Kill?"
c/o Dewayne Wellington
572 West 90th Street, Apt. 10E
New York, New York 10024

I'll stop writing until I hear from you good folks. Luckily, I have to take a breather anyway. Bills are stacking up, so I'm going back to Klein, Klein and Feldman to do some legal proofreading for a while. Most months I can squeak by, albeit by the skin of my teeth, but Rosa Luxemburg's developed this nasty heart condition (too much ash in the Fisherman's Platter with

Cheese Bits) and it looks as if they'll have to operate. Yet it's not nearly as degrading as you might think, becoming progressively myopic scrutinizing the briefs of $400K/yr partners almost a decade your junior. Joyce worked in a Trieste bank, Faulkner was the postmaster at Ol' Miss, and Ellison shined shoes.

September 20, 1984

Dear Freak,

What genus of disturbed, DT-ridden Muse rattles through the chambers of your vacant head? What, oh, what can evoke such a perverse perversion of pen and ink? Is it that you were encouraged to lick squids as a child? Told it was all right to play with yourself at the school assembly?

Yet enough. For me to further ponder your twisted and undoubtedly sordid beginning causes a sea of revulsion to well within me more thick and putrid than that evoked by any car-smashed rodent or Port-a-John.

"Which ones do I kill?" you so needlessly and smugly ask. My answer shall be as brief and as precise as the turbulent storm of my incensed thoughts will allow.

Yet I will not answer with the word you probably expect—"Yourself." Nay, instead I say all the women in your grotesque menagerie should be "killed"—liberated from your sweaty and pitiful grasp.

No, we women of color do not need your atavistic brand of representation, thank you.

Isshee Ayam

P.S. Here is how you should have commenced your "work."

Earle awakened to a day as new and as fresh as Mama's hand-starched and sun-dried petticoat, a huge, plain garment as large and as fresh-smelling as the revival tents that bloomed every summer along Route 49 in Lowndes County, Georgia. Yes, from out of those wide Baptist thighs, thighs that shook with the centuries of injustice and degradation, thighs that twitched with the hope of generations yet unplanted, thighs that quivered with the friction of jubilant, bed-thumping, and funky-smelling lovemaking, emerged Earle.

SUDER

Percival L. Everett

I sure as hell hope that craziness ain't passed from parents to children by way of the blood. I say this because my mother was out-and-out raving insane. When I was ten and my brother, Martin, was twelve, my folks called the two of us in to the kitchen. It was one of those hot North Carolina summer days when even the flies are moving slow. Daddy was sitting at the table in his underwear, and Ma was wearing her cloth coat with the dog fur around the collar. Sweat was dripping off Ma's face, and Martin and I moved slowly to our chairs at the table. There was a great big glass of iced tea in Daddy's left hand and a handkerchief in his right.

"Sit down, boys," Daddy said.

We were already sitting and we looked at him, puzzledlike.

"Oh," he said and gulped down some tea. "Boys . . ." He stopped.

Ma cleared her throat and sat up. A bead of sweat was hanging off the tip of her nose. "Your father has something he wants to tell you."

We looked back at Daddy.

Daddy's eyes were locked on Ma and then sorta snapped to and said, "Boys, your mother is crazy."

We looked over at Ma, and she nodded and smiled.

"Huh?" Martin was shaking his head. "I don't understand."

"Yes, son," said Ma, "I'm crazy."

Martin and I just sat there at the table staring at each other. We stared at each other for a good long while, and then Ma got up and walked out into the yard. Daddy rubbed his handkerchief across his forehead.

"Maybe it's the heat," Daddy said.

"Why is she wearing that coat?" I asked.

Daddy looked at me and wiped the back of his neck. "She's crazy, Craig."

"You're a doctor, Daddy," Martin said. "Fix her."

"I can't help her," Daddy said and got up and walked to the screen door. He looked out into the yard at Ma. She was now hoeing in the garden. "Ain't nothing I can do." He stood there leaning against the doorframe, drinking his tea and wiping his face and neck.

"Why is she wearing that coat?" I asked again.

"Maybe it's the heat," Daddy said, eyes fixed on Ma. He turned to my brother and me. He picked the newspaper up off the counter and walked out of the kitchen.

"What do you think?" Martin asked.

"I'm only ten years old."

Martin got up and walked over to the door and stared through the screen at Ma.

I started crying.

"Hush that noise up," Martin said.

"Our mama's crazy," I cried.

He just looked back out into the yard at her, and I heard him sniff a little, but I didn't say anything.

Martin and I went down to the pond and threw rocks at the ducks. Martin hit one of the birds in the head and it flapped away screaming.

"Maybe we could hit her in the head and knock some sense into her," Martin said.

"You think so?"

"How the hell should I know?" Martin looked up at the telephone lines and stared at the sparrows. "Go get my BB gun."

"I don't want to."

"Just get it."

I ran back home and when I walked into Martin's and my room I found Ma sitting on Martin's bed looking at the girlie magazines that he kept hidden between the mattress and box spring. I stopped in my tracks.

"Come here, Craigie," she said, patting a spot on the bed beside her.

I walked over and sat down. I was scared. She was crazy.

She put her arm around me and pulled me close and with her free hand grabbed the meat of my cheek. "You're a good boy, Craigie."

I tried to get up, but she pulled me down. "I've gotta take Martin his BB gun."

"You see this?" she asked, showing me a couple of pages stuck together. "You see this? Your brother is a bad boy." She dropped the magazine on the floor.

Just being so close to her coat was making me hot and sweaty and itchy. "Why are you wearing a coat, Ma?"

"I'm not wearing a coat, silly." She looked at me and pulled her mouth tight. "It's called masturbation."

I just looked at her.

"What he does with these pictures . . ." She moved her fist up and down over her lap. "Don't you ever do that. You'll go blind."

I started to get up again and she pulled me back. She started unbuttoning my shirt and I reached up and folded my arms over my chest.

"I want you to take a bath," she said.

"It's the afternoon," I complained.

"Take your clothes off!" she screamed through her teeth. Her eyes had a real strange sparkle.

"But—"

"Now!"

I undressed. She was crazy. She pulled me by the hand into the bathroom. "Get in the tub!"

I stepped into the tub.

"Sit down!"

I sat down and she began to pull a dry washcloth over my body.

"Ma," I said, "there ain't no water."

"The water is *not* too hot!" she screamed, and then she stood up. "The water is *not* too hot." She walked out.

It was Sunday, right after church, and Martin and I were out by the pond, still dressed in our powder-blue suits. Martin was trying to pick birds off the telephone line and I was watching tadpoles.

"You know," I said, "Ma didn't seem so crazy this morning."

Martin looked away from his target and at me. "Asking everybody to move out of the first three rows was pretty crazy."

I looked at my reflection in the pond and thought about Ma.

"Got him," said Martin. He started off toward his kill and I followed him. We stood over the sparrow and looked at the little red spot on his head. "Got him in the head."

I looked at Martin's face. We didn't say anything else. We just walked back to the house. We walked through the back door into the kitchen. All of Martin's dirty magazines were on the table and open to the fold-out pictures.

"Not again." Martin sighed.

"You filthy boy." Ma pulled her hair, wet from perspiration, out of her face. "You pull on yourself."

Martin turned and walked out.

"Don't you leave this house!"

Martin stopped and turned around.

Ma walked to me and put her arm around me. "Why can't you be a good boy like Craig?"

Martin sighed again.

"Oh, Martin, you're just like your father. He's out now, up to no good. The mighty Dr. Suder. He says he's gotta go see if Sara Harris is about to have her baby, but I know better. He's with that Lou Ann Narramore from down at the drugstore."

"That's not true," Martin said.

"Why can't you be a good boy like Craig, here?"

Martin looked at me real hardlike. His lower lip was pushed out slightly and his cheeks were puffed. He turned and walked out.

"You are a good boy, Craigie," Ma said and hugged me tight. "You're not like your father. You're like me. You're just like your mother, just like your mother."

She hugged me tighter and I tried to pull away. I fell back and to the floor. I pulled myself up by grabbing the table, and I knocked some magazines to the floor. Ma got down on her knees and started pulling them together.

As I stood over her, looking at the bald spot on top of her head where she'd tried to shave, I thought about what Martin had said about knocking sense into her. I picked up a china bowl from the dish rack and broke it over her head. She fell on her face. I let out a scream.

Martin came running in and saw Ma stretched out on the floor. "What happened?"

"I broke a bowl over her head."

Martin kneeled down and picked up Ma's head and let it drop. He closed his eyes for a second. "You can't tell anyone."

"What do you mean?"

"You can't tell anyone you hit her."

"I have to tell Daddy."

"No. We'll just say she passed out. Just like that. Do you hear me?"

"I don't know, Martin."

"Look here." He pointed at Ma. "She's out cold, maybe dead. Do you want to go to jail?"

"No!"

"Then what are you going to tell Daddy?"

"She passed out. Just like that." I paused. "She's not dead, is shc?"

———————————

Martin and I were standing at the foot of the bed looking at Ma, and Daddy was standing on her right, holding her hand. The curtains were open and the hospital room was flooded with light and it kinda made Ma look like she had a halo. The old lady in the bed on the other side of the room divider was moaning something awful.

"Oh, shut up, you old hag!" my mother yelled.

"Okay, dear, settle down," Daddy said.

Ma looked down along her body and over her feet at me. "Come here, Craigie." She held up her left hand.

I walked over to her left side and took her hand. The sun was hot on my back through the window. I looked closely at the wrapping on her head.

"Craigie."

"Yeah, Ma?"

She looked at Martin and then at Daddy. "I'd like to be alone with Craig." Her eyes moved again to me.

Daddy and Martin left the room, and I watched the big door swing slowly closed.

"Craigie," Ma said, "you're a good boy. You've got to be careful in life. Don't trust anyone. Trust not a living soul and walk cautiously amongst the dead."

"Yes, Ma."

She narrowed her eyes to slits and I got scared. "You know, your daddy's been a bad boy. He's been running around with that Lou Ann Narramore down at the drugstore."

"No, Ma."

She sat up and leaned toward me. The sun had made me hot and sticky, so I was scared and uncomfortable. "He is and I don't want to hear another word out of you about it. Your daddy is running around and we're going to catch him. You and me. You hear me?"

I nodded.

Daddy pushed his head into the room. "Craig, we're about ready to go."

"Get out!" Ma screamed.

Daddy's head disappeared.

"Okay, Craigie." She pulled me down and kissed my forehead. "Go on, but remember what we talked about." She stroked my face.

I nodded and turned and started out.

"Craigie." She called me back. "I love you the most. You were a breech baby. You were difficult. I almost died having you. That's why I love you the most. You and me. We're going to catch the two of them in the act, your father and that Lou Ann Narramore." She fell back into her pillow. "From down at the drugstore."

I started out again.

"Hey, psssst," called the old lady in the other bed. I stopped and looked at her.

She summoned me with her finger. "Come here, little boy."

I walked slowly toward her and looked into her face, which was contorted with pain.

"Look around," she said, "and see if you can find my pills. They're yellow. They're for the pain. Please, little boy."

"Huh?"

"Your mother took my pills and hid them. I don't know why, but she did. And now the nurse won't give me any more. Please, the pain is real bad."

Ma snatched the divider back and yelled, "Go home, Craig!"

I ran out. In the hallway Daddy looked at me and said, "She is still your mother."

Ma spent one night in the hospital, and Martin and I waited in the living room for Daddy to bring her home the next day.

"Daddy thinks it might be the heat," Martin said, "that's got Ma acting this way."

"Martin, I'm scared."

"Why should you be scared? She likes you. I'm the one who should be scared."

"Do you think Daddy is running around with Lou Ann Narramore?"

Martin thought. "I don't know. I don't think so."

The front screen door pushed open and Ma and Daddy walked in. Ma didn't say anything. She just walked past us and into her bedroom. She came out wearing her coat.

"Dinner," she said. "Dinner, dinner, dinner . . ." She walked into the kitchen.

———————

"Ma says doing that will make you go blind," I said to Martin as I watched the sheet above his middle move up and down.

"She's crazy," he said. He moved his flashlight beam to another open magazine.

"I don't know, I've heard other people say the same thing. Reverend Austin from the candy store told Virgil Wallace that doing it would put hair on his palms."

"He's crazy, too," Martin said.

"Why?"

"Because he just is."

"No, I mean, why do you pull on yourself?" I asked.

"Because it feels good."

"But why?"

He stopped and turned off his flashlight. "Sometimes you just feel like you have to do it."

"Virgil Wallace does it all the time out behind the old school. I've seen him."

"Just who is this Virgil Wallace?" Martin hit me with the beam of his flashlight.

I put my arms in front of my face. "Turn that off."

He turned it off. "Who is he?"

"You've seen him. He's that waterhead fella, wears them bright socks."

"Oh, you're talking about Moe."

"Moe?"

"The guys call him Moe."

"Why do they call him that?" I asked.

Martin didn't say anything. We were silent for a while and then the silence was broken by the barking of a dog.

"I'll bet that's Dr. Counts's hound," Martin said.

"Have you ever seen Lou Ann Narramore?" I asked.

"Yeah, I've seen her."

"What's she look like? Is she pretty?" I pulled my head up and rested it on my palm, my elbow stabbing my pillow.

"Yeah, she's pretty," Martin said. "She's real skinny and she's got big . . . big . . . hey, you're too young to hear this."

I didn't say anything. I just looked past Martin and out the window at the moon. The dog had stopped barking and the night became still and very quiet. Then Martin started up again, his flashlight panning from picture to picture.

The next morning I woke up early, got dressed, and went downstairs. I had plans to visit the pond and when I walked into the kitchen I found Ma at the counter, stirring the contents of a bowl and running in place. She was wearing her heavy coat and a brand-new pair of black high-top sneakers. Perspiration was pouring off her face and the fur about her collar looked matted in places.

"What are you doing, Ma?"

"Running . . . to lose weight. . . . Lou Ann . . . Narramore . . . skinny
. . . lose weight. . . ."

I started out.

"Where . . . you going?" she asked, still running.

"The pond."

She stopped running and looked at me. She wiped her forehead with
the back of her hand. "Be careful," she said.

━━━━━━

All over the ground by the pond were dead sparrows with BBs deep in their
bodies. I don't know what came over me, but I started picking them up. I
pulled the bottom of my T-shirt out and away from my belly and put the
birds in the net it formed. With my shirt full of dead sparrows I headed back
toward the house. I ducked behind a bush when I saw Martin coming my
way. He walked past me and on toward the pond. He was carrying his BB
rifle. I ran home and managed to sneak up to my room without being seen.
I dumped the birds onto my bed and counted them. Thirteen. I picked up
one of the sparrows and sat silently, bouncing it on my fingers. I dropped
the bird on my bed and went to the hall closet. I pulled down a hatbox and
went back into my room and put the sparrows in it. I put the top on the
box and slid it under my bed. I stretched out across the bed and imagined
the lives of those birds passing up through the box spring and the mattress
and into me.

Later, I walked over to the old school building and saw Virgil Wallace.
He was sitting with his back against the pole of a basketball goal which no
longer had a hoop. Virgil Wallace was about eighteen and real long and
skinny. One of his legs was bent and the other was straight out. He was
wearing one bright red sock and one bright yellow one. His hand was in his
lap and he tossed his head back and looked up at the sky. I moved toward
him. I noticed the ringworm on his head.

"Virgil?" I said. I was standing off to his side and slightly behind him.

He didn't notice me.

I walked around and stood right in front of him and I looked at the hand
that was in his lap. He was holding the head of his penis in his hand and
it was covered with a milky substance. "Virgil?"

He looked at me. His eyes were half-closed.

"Can I ask you a question?"

He nodded.

"Why do you pull on yourself?"

He held up his hand dripping with the stuff. "For this here."

"What is it?"

He looked at the stuff on his hand and then, without looking at me, he said, "Life." He laughed out loud. "Life," he repeated, looking up at me, the corners of his mouth curled slightly up. He pushed his messy hand toward me: an offer.

I ran all the way home. When I walked into my bedroom, Martin was pacing around, sniffing.

"Come in here," he said. "Tell me if you smell something."

I inhaled deeply. "No," I lied to him.

"You didn't even breathe."

"I did, too. I just don't smell anything. Maybe it's your lip."

Martin shook his head and left the room.

I pulled the hatbox from beneath my bed and looked inside at my birds. There were a few maggots moving around. I sneaked the box down into the garage and hid it behind a couple of tires in the corner.

———

Ma never knew that it was her younger-born that knocked her into uncon- sciousness in the kitchen. So she read it as a revelation from the Almighty. She figured it was God who slammed her face into the linoleum. When she came home from the hospital she began to mention God a little more often than usual and gradually she spoke of Him quite a bit, except she referred to Him as Max.

"Maxdammit," Ma said. "You will too go to the dentist."

I didn't say anything. I just stared at her, scared.

"And this dentist is a good Christian dentist," she added, wiping the perspiration from her face with the coat sleeve.

Martin must have seen it coming because he managed to slip far away from the house early, long before Ma mentioned the dentist. So it was just Ma and me in the car, silent from driveway to dentist, Dr. McCoy. The waiting room of Dr. McCoy's office was done all in white, and there was a picture of Jesus on each wall. Already seated in the waiting room were several other children and their mothers, all white. The white mothers all stared at Ma in her heavy coat and her black high-top sneakers. We sat down and Ma pulled a tissue from her pocketbook and dabbed at the corners of her nose.

A tall man, a white man all dressed in white, stepped into the room. His complexion was pale, his eyes were powder-blue, and his hair was white. He pulled his palms together in front of his chest. "Let us pray," he said in a soothing tenor voice. All the white people bowed their heads. I looked at Ma to see her head also lowered. "Our heavenly Father, give us strength to endure the dental trials which lie before us. Give us a steady hand in the wake of deep cavities and let us wade safely through the drainage of abscesses, God, and let us be good little patients, sitting still through every step of the procedure. Amen."

"Amen," the voices in the room mumbled.

The dentist pointed a long crooked white finger at me. Ma put her palm against my back and pushed me into standing. I followed Dr. McCoy through a white hallway, past white nurses dressed all in white, and into an examination room all done in white except for the bright silver of the instruments resting on the counter and hanging above and beside the chair. I sat down, and the nurse fastened a white bib around my neck and handed me a tissue.

I looked over at the nurse to find her head lowered and her eyes closed. I turned to see that once again the dentist had placed his palms together. "Let us pray," he said. "Dear God, please let everything go well with this little colored boy." He switched on the light above my face and looked into my mouth. He pulled back and stood erect. "Lord God, this boy has a cavity that must be filled. Give us a steady hand." I looked at the nurse. Her eyes were still closed. "Amen." Dr. McCoy opened his eyes, grabbed the drill, and gave it a couple of whirs.

"Ain't you gonna give me a shot?" I asked.

"No shots here, son. This is a dental office of the Lord. No shots here." He put his fingers in my mouth and pried it open. He pushed cotton into my cheeks and hung this metal thing over my lip which sucked up my spit. Then he started drilling. I closed my eyes. It all hurt very much and he was none too fast. I gripped the arms of the chair tightly, digging my nails into the vinyl. He stood up, finished. "Thank you, Lord."

The nurse pulled the cotton from my mouth. I was breathing rapidly.

"You drink Coke?" Dr. McCoy asked me.

"Huh?"

"Coke is real bad for your teeth. I put a tooth in a glass of Coke once and left it overnight. Next morning the tooth wasn't nothing but dust."

I just looked at him.

"Drink milk, boy. Lots of milk."

———

I looked out the window in the living room at the front yard. Ma was resting on her knuckles at the edge of the driveway. Martin came and stood beside me. Ma pushed her butt into the air, leaned forward, and took off in a sprint across the yard. Her coat became full with the wind as she dashed. Daddy came and stood behind us.

"What do you think?" Daddy asked.

Martin and I turned to face Daddy.

"I want to talk to you boys about something." He paused. "Do you think that your mother would be better off in a hospital?"

Martin looked back out the window.

"She's not sick," I said.

"Not that kind of hospital," Martin said.

"You mean the crazy house?" I opened my eyes wide.

Daddy nodded.

"No," I said. "No." I got real excited and my eyes watered up.

"Okay," Daddy said, calming me down.

Then Ma came running in. She was really sweaty and her coat was soaked. She was panting. "Around the city," she said. "I'm going to run around Fayetteville. It's twenty-three miles." She pulled her hair out of her face. "And I'm going to do it."

———————

Daddy was standing in the garage with his hands on his hips, looking around, sniffing the air. I was just outside, peering at him from the corner of the house. Martin was coming up the driveway on his bike.

"Martin," Daddy called.

Martin hopped off his bike and ran to Daddy's side.

"Martin, take a sniff."

Martin sniffed and frowned.

"Smells like something dead in here," Daddy said, "and we're going to find it." He paused. "Well, start looking."

We looked around for a good while, and then Martin found my hatbox full of dead sparrows. "Over here, Daddy," Martin cried.

Daddy looked at the decaying birds. "Jesus. Put the lid back on the box." He looked at the door to the house. "If your mother put them there, we should leave them there."

"Ma?" Martin asked.

"Yeah," said Daddy. "I'd say that's pretty crazy."

I didn't say anything.

"So you want me just to leave it here?" Martin asked.

"I suppose so." Daddy scratched his head. "I'll drop a little charcoal in the box and try to soak up some of the stench."

Martin pushed the box back behind the tires.

"Your mother must be pretty sick to keep stuff like this around. You boys stay away from this." Daddy headed out of the garage. Martin followed him.

I stood there for a long time, smelling the stench of the birds, feeling afraid because I thought I was crazy. Daddy just assumed the birds were Ma's, so he must have thought putting the birds in the box was crazy. But I put the birds in the box, so I figured I was crazy.

DE MOJO BLUES

Arthur Flowers

The receding blue ridges of Tennessee's Smoky Mountains lumbered slug-
gishly along the side of the highway. Tucept had made this Nashville run
a million times, but this time the scenery was new and narcotic. Smoky
blued mountain ridges lined with scrub trees, muddy lakes, and blue crystal
streams. He drove slowly, less careful than stalling. He hadn't called her.
Another surprise. What if he was the one surprised? What if she was with
somebody? His almost relieved mind ran through the scenario, forced her
to choose, him or me, or them, dammit, choose.

He felt for the ragged scrap of a letter in his pocket. The last one he had
received from her before leaving Nam. He didn't get them regular like when
he first got incountry. He had gotten in the habit of carrying the latest with
him, reading it whenever he got a chance, dogging it until the next one
came and he would put the tattered one away.

What if she had found somebody else? The thought that had haunted
him in Nam, lying in some godforsaken rice paddy trying to figure out what
time was it back in the World, what was Ruby doing now, out partying, in
school, fucking?

When he reached Nashville he sped through the tiny winding streets to the Tennessee State campus. Nashville's narrow little twisted streets always depressed him. Student apartments up on the Hill. At her door he hesitated, took a breath, rang the bell.

A tall pretty boy answered. It was a few seconds before Tucept could say anything.

Uh, is this Ruby's address?

Yeah.

The brother stood, waiting, tall, well-formed, pretty petulant lips, smooth brown skin, a frat cap. Qs. He stood in the door with the proprietary air of a man who feels that being a woman's lover gives him say-so in her affairs.

Is she in?

Who wants her?

Tucept HighJohn, said Tucept flatly. Voice grating, jaws tight, pissed. Just a minute.

He closed the door. Tucept fumed. He wanted to get in his car and go for home, but he would be damned if he would just walk off. Fuck this motherfucker.

Ruby came to the door and threw it open. Tucept! she yelled. They came together and hugged. Tucept's tension unwound like a taut spring sprung.

The feel of her body next to him was heaven, and her breath on his chest sent tingles up and down his spine. Ruby, Ruby, been gone so long. She made him breathless with pleasure, an effect that she had had on him since he first met her, when he was a practicing college militant, when she was a senior graduating from high school and he was her ideal of what college was about.

He saw the brother watching and closed him out. Her hug was his claim. Her hands in the small of his back pulled him to her, and the smell of her was in his nostrils. Damn, she felt good next to him like this. He could feel her against him, her breasts against him, her hips and legs; wisps of her hair tickled his nostrils. He grinned. He had not hugged in over a year. He couldn't believe it was really happening. Finally.

Hey, baby, he said, choking, how you doing?

What are you doing here? she pouted. You didn't tell me, what are you doing home, are you all right?

I'm fine, he said, feeling good.

They went to the living room. Two more dudes sitting in front of the TV. A college apartment, a TV, Day-Glo prints and textbooks. White lace lamp shades. Bright red throw pillows on a beige rug. The sharp bite of incense.

Ruby had Tucept about his waist, hugging him. Oh, Tucept, she said, it's so nice to see you. You should have called me, though.

This is Tucept HighJohn, she told everybody. He's the one I told you about.

Tucept, this is Joe Dyer, you met him at the door, and this is Sam and Ramon.

He shook the other brothers' hands. Joe Dyer nodded at him and they shook, not bothering to hide their animosity.

Ruby sat him on the couch and asked him if he wanted anything to drink.

He just wanted to look at her, short, firm, fine, a pixie face with a bird's nest of a 'fro, glittering eyes that looked right at you, wide and questioning. Cocoa-brown woman with big eyes and bigger ideas. He sensed a difference in her, in the way her eye fell on him with a new directness.

She sat on the couch next to him, and he realized that he was perched on the edge. He sat back, suddenly conscious of the field jacket and the floppy boonie hat he wore. Relax, he told himself angrily.

On the little black-and-white screen a newscaster spoke of Nixon's troop withdrawals. Clips of Vietnam. Ruby stared at the screen. He watched her surreptitiously. He wished these boys would leave, specially this Dyer fellow. Wonder what his role was. Tucept glanced at him. Dyer was watching him. Held Tucept's eye just long enough to be a challenge.

Ruby stroked his shoulder.

How long have you been home, Tucept? Why didn't you call me?

I wanted to surprise you.

Well, she said, laughing, okay, I'm surprised.

It embarrassed Tucept to be going through all this in front of the other three. Why doesn't she tell them to leave? He hasn't seen her in a year.

How are your folks? she said.

Everybody's fine, how have things been up here on the Hill?

You know the Hill, she said. It keeps you going.

Hey, Ruby, said Joe Dyer, you hear about Tadpole?

They laughed, an insider's joke. Tucept smiled uncertainly. He should pack up and get the hell out of here. Instead he sat uncomfortable but determined to last it out. Ruby stood, and fat nipples traced erotic designs on her blue blouse. Tucept glared at the brothers, daring them to look. They looked.

A chopper *whopwhopwhopp*ed across the screen. Vietnam. Tucept's eye was drawn to the newscast.

You just got back from Vietnam, didn't you, man? asked Joe Dyer.

Ambush, Tucept thought and nodded slowly.

So how was it, man? Tell us about it.

You know, basic garden variety war, he said in a low mumble of shrugged shoulders.

Joe Dyer leaned forward, face sharp and alert. Smelling blood.

Tell me about it, he said, I didn't go, they tried to draft me, but I told them what they could do with that hokey shit.

Sho did, didn't he? said one of the frat brothers. Tucept didn't remember names.

And kept on telling them, the other commented.

They hooted and slapped five.

So tell me, asked Joe, what was it like?

Tucept shrugged again.

Like on TV? asked Ruby, still looking at the newscast. The newscaster gave a body count.

You got drafted? asked Dyer.

Tucept considered lying. No, he said finally, I volunteered.

Dyer leaped on it, spinning his chair around to face Tucept. Hey, Hey, Hey, he said, Gung ho. Sergeant Fury and his howling commando.

The room laughed

You volunteered for Vietnam? said Dyer.

Well, you know, said Tucept, I didn't really think about Nam when I volunteered.

Which was a lie, he had wanted to war.

Oh, said Dyer, you thought maybe they were going to send your black ass to the Pentagon. Doesn't sound like you were thinking period.

Shamed, Tucept could only shrug.

So tell me about it, man, said one of the frat brothers. My main man he went to Nam and he came back wasted.

I hear the brothers went on a funny trip, said Dyer.

Tucept fumbled it. We, uh . . .

He remembered a blues that Jethro sang one guard duty night in a perimeter bunker.

> Me 'n' my brothers, we had to throw down
> We went to the war, we caught hell all around
> And now I've learned to watch my brother's back
> Ain't nothing we can't do if we be bold and black
> We learned how to throw down, we learned how to throw down
> On Firebase Sin Loi

How could he explain it? A brother looking out for another brother's back.

You know, we learned that, uh, the brothers, you know, uh we stood together. Tucept stumbled and lamely finished . . . we survived.

Wait a minute, man, said Joe Dyer, what you trying to tell us is that you felt like a man 'cause you were over there playing soldier for these white folks, a nigger killing gooks for crackers.

Tucept flushed. Smash this motherfucker. Empty a M16 clip into this motherfucker's face. Watch it shred away in a red angry spray.

That's not what I was saying, said Tucept angrily, I was just trying to . . . fuck it.

He wasn't going to keep playing Dyer's game. He wasn't walking into an ambush with his eyes open.

Ruby leaned forward, her face lit with a sudden question.

Did you ever kill anybody, Tucept?

Ruby, Ruby, oh, Ruby . . .

Tucept looked at her blankly, running the words back in his head, feeling the texture of them for booby traps, pungi sticks, bouncing bettys that strip a man of his balls.

Dyer grinned. Sure you did, didn't you, brother? I hear some dudes get to nutting off when they get to killing gooks.

Joe! said Ruby sharply.

Tucept withdrew from the conversation, eyes narrowed, face closed, attention to the TV screen. Like he was watching the movie. Sensing his discomfort, Ruby shifted the conversation back to the randy fool Tadpole. The screen threw restless shadows across their faces in the dark and they spoke of school while Tucept watched golden memories. He wanted to leave, but he was determined to be there when these other motherfuckers left. Finally Ruby put them out. The frat brothers told him welcome back and good-bye. Tucept and Joe Dyer didn't even try to be civil.

As soon as the door closed, he turned on Ruby. Don't you ever go against me again, woman.

His voice was nasty and dangerous.

Surprised, Ruby took a minute to respond. Wait a minute, she said. I'm sorry if you got your feelings hurt, but it wasn't my fault. It wasn't Joe's either.

She was defending that motherfucker. Yeah, well fuck her, too.

You fucking him? he asked.

She hesitated only a minute, but that was all he needed to hang her.

He's a friend, Tucept, and I do date, she said, her voice saying that she could do damn well what she pleased.

So what's the deal? he insisted. Him or me?

Oh, come off it, Tucept, she said, getting up and sitting on the couch where she didn't have to face him. There isn't any you or him, I'm concerned with me.

Her voice patronized an unruly child. His voice grated ominously, You saying he's more to you than me.

Her face soured. Oh, be real, Tucept.

I thought you were my woman, he said, I thought you were waiting on me.

He sounded like a fool and knew it.

I'm just tired, Tucept, she told him, that's all.

She sounded like she was tired of this shit. He was blowing it. He caught himself, nodded, and acted as if that really was all that was wrong. Yeah, he said, I guess I'm tired, too. He yawned. It was a long drive.

She busied herself picking up items in the living room, putting them into stacks and places.

Are you staying or are you going back to Memphis? she asked without stopping what she was doing or looking at him.

His insecurity radar told him she was saying go back to Memphis. He started to cop an attitude and go. The strong move. But he couldn't do it. That would be it, all over, and he wanted her. He wanted to be with her tomorrow and next year, forever.

I'm leaving in the morning, he said assertively, casually adding as if an afterthought, if that's all right with you?

That night she came to bed in a blue nightgown, thick, cotton, and functional. Silently she lay beside him, and their tentative caresses grew cautiously into passion.

Soon her palm was fever on his skin, and his tongue was full of the taste of her heat. But his dick stayed soft. He became aware of it. Panic seeped in as he sent urgent messages downriver. What the hell was happening down there? Let's get on the job gang. Everybody has to do their part. Sweat popped out on his forehead, and he took a moment to wipe it off, like that might be the answer. God, she would think it happened all the time. Tucept concentrated on a hard dick, didn't feel even a twinge. Damned thing felt like it was curling up on him. He concentrated on her firm breasts, her wet tight sheath. Not with Ruby, not now. Her warm heated palm circled his dick. He could feel the passionate pressure of her hand turn questioning. He felt her firm lips slacken under his. Her eyes opened, and she looked up at him.

He wanted to explain it away, but what could he say; his dick was saying it all. He wanted to cut the motherfucker off; what good was it?

You don't want to? she asked him.

I want to, he said, attempting levity, my dick doesn't.

He rolled off and lay down beside her, disgusted with himself. Driven to distraction by the feel of her warm, still undulating flesh, anguishing silently, This has never happened before. Why now, why with Ruby?

Don't worry about it, she said.

I don't know what's happening, he said, it's never happened before. I swear.

He picked the limp dick up in his hand and studied it, as if he would be able to see the problem.

Don't worry about it, she repeated. She pecked at his cheek and went to sleep. He lay there, pissed at the world long before sleep came. Nothing was going right, he thought with real anguish. How many times had he thought about Ruby, about seeing her again, how many scripts had he run through his head. His scripts had gone fine. It was life that was perverse.

His sleep was restlessness. She felt it and woke in the night. A contoured brown breast settled sensuously as she flicked on the bedside table lamp. She studied him under the lamp's lit circle. Her matted 'fro threw uneven shadows on his back. He lay on his belly, facing her, lips slightly parted, beads of sweat dotting his forehead.

He twitched and moaned, and she leaned closer, trying to listen.

Choppers fall from a leaden sky and spit Buffalo soldiers into a muddy gold rice paddy. Puppets on a string, buck-dancing minstrels dodging slow motion bullets to the tune of "Yankee Doodle Dandy." You dance on gossamer strings sometimes seen, sometimes not. They move your arms like jerky windmills and buck-dance your feet, you fight and strain but still you dance, what a dance do they do.

Tucept shifted, his head leaving a damp spot on the pillow. She frowned and placed her hand on his back. His skin was damp, the rhythmic rise and fall of his deep breathing pleasing to her touch. Her hand stroked his back in small concerned circles. She frowned, her smooth brow furrowed in thought. When he was in Nam she had used him to keep others at an emotional distance, her man in the war. She didn't really feel anything for him. There had been a certain glamour, a sense of romance about her man in Nam, her soldier boy, but now he was back, making demands and being a problem. Well. It just wasn't fair for him to act like she owed him something. To make her feel for him. She stilled herself to see if she could detect something in her for him and shrugged.

She had felt for him once, loved him even, but since she'd been on the Hill she'd already loved others.

Seven little yellow puppets in black pajamas and conical black straw hats walk into the bright gold killing zone. Seven little puppets in black pajamas tell jokes and laugh and dance and sing. Tucept empties an automatic clip from his M16. They die laughing, jerking grotesquely on strings suddenly cut. After lying dead, they pick themselves up and laughingly dust themselves off. A joke by Mattel. They begin again, string-jerked back into position. This time they get to wear the white hats. This time the Americans get ambushed. Tucept's strings jerk him onto the trail. Tucept tells the man behind him a joke. And they walk into the killing zone.

The muscles of his back knotted spasmodically, and she jerked her hand back. Lines bunched on his forehead and moved in fitful twitches. He cried out. She reached for his shoulder. At her touch he jumped up, arm flung out and knocking her back. His eyes snapped open. She scooted out of range. Tucept registered the move and focused. He lay back down on the bed.

What happened? he asked.

A dream? she ventured.

He didn't answer. It wasn't until she heard his breathing regulate itself that she realized he had fallen asleep.

That morning their conversation was plastic, bland, uninspiring. Neither spoke of last night, yesterdays, or tomorrows.

Coffee?

Please.

Weatherman said it would be nice today. Not too cold.

Good.

Tucept watched her with a certain regret. He'd blown it. He'd lost the slightest semblance of confidence, and in the harsh light of morning his defeat could only irritate her. He watched her eyes focus on everything but him, and he realized that he didn't know her. A year of dreaming about her in Vietnam had warped his idea of who she was beyond all sense of human possibility.

Finally he said he was leaving. At the door he stood for a moment of uncertainty and hope unrealized.

She could have been his, he thought bitterly. All the plans he had made were cold and sour. He felt like a fool for dreaming, a fullness threatened to rise up in his throat, but he's cool. He locked it back and smiled a lopsided ain't-no-big-thing smile. He studied her face. He had learned in Nam the value of having clear, well-etched memories of people you wanted to re-member. They kissed and went through the motions of I'll be in touch, come back soon, please do.

He rode home hard, pedal to the metal, bogarting cars in front of him, creeping up bumpers, evil red eyes challenging drivers when they glanced in their rearview mirror. He almost lost a curve, tires screeching for traction, the back of the Toyota fishtailing the highway. He pulled over to the side of the road and calmed himself. Standing beside the car, he kicked tufts of the dirt from the gravel-covered roadbed. He wouldn't be going back to Nashville for a while. Moisture gathered in the corner of an eye, and wiping at it angrily, he got back into the car and drove home.

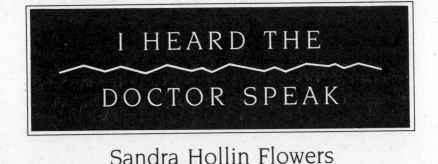

I HEARD THE DOCTOR SPEAK

Sandra Hollin Flowers

After the policeman told me I had the right to remain silent, that's what I decided to do.

That would simplify things. In these last few days since Huey got shot, I have been needing to talk about people I knew when they were like Huey was long before he became whatever he was when he died. But who would I talk to? There was a time when my girlfriends and I would tell each other everything about the people in our lives, the men in our lives. As we got older, we were less inclined to tell everything. We had our reasons. Some of us told nothing anymore. And nobody cared at all about unfinished business hanging on from the past. People have too hard a time hanging on to the present to get into your past in an intense way. But I am intense about my past, and if I talked about it, I probably would cry and not be able to stop for a while because this would be twenty years' worth of crying. Then I would have to tell my husband. You can't live with a person, especially not a person who is always telling you to *be practical*, and not tell him why you're crying all the time.

The cop had stopped me for speeding on Cascade. "I don't have one," I told him when he asked for my license.

Which I thought was true, because it seemed like I had lost my wallet when I was burying Rasool. Or whatever I did with him. Rasool is one of those people I needed to talk about. I tried to explain to the cop that I had just killed a man and was sort of disoriented.

The cop: Well, where is his body?

Me: I don't know, I can't remember.

The cop: Um-hmm. And how did you kill him?

Me: I guess I must have shot him. That's how he killed Jamaal, so I probably shot him.

Everybody wants to know why I said these things to the cop. *I* want to know why I said these things to the cop. As far as I know, Rasool is still alive. Jamaal is not, but Rasool probably is. Jamaal was the other person I needed to talk about. Mainly Rasool and Jamaal.

I got out of the car like the cop told me to. Opened the trunk, let him look in the glove compartment, under the seats, in the door pockets. But when he put his hands on me for the search, I kicked him. I guess there might have been some kind of struggle. I don't remember. All I know is that he told me I had the right to remain silent and then he got on his radio and called a wagon to take me to the detention center. Assaulting an officer of the law.

There were all kinds of people at the detention center. Drunk ones, slick ones, sick ones, high ones, mad ones, hustling ones, crying ones. Most of us, including the cops, to give the devil his due, were black. I had to sit on a bench next to one wearing musk oil. I can't stand that stuff. The rotten-meat smell of it would have made me puke several times under normal circumstances. But I talked myself out of it because there was no use in the two of us sitting there stinking together. And we did have to sit together. Obviously we were sitting in line. Figuring that if I tried to get up, a cop would yell at me, I just stayed in my place and slid along the bench with her like a two-person chain gang. She didn't seem to like the hostile teenage boy sitting on the other side of her, so she tried to strike up a conversation with me once or twice. Obviously that was a waste of her time and mine. But we understood each other and what we were supposed to do. Every time somebody farther up the line got called to a desk to be typed about, the two of us would silently slide over so another body could get on the bench.

Finally she got called to the typewriter. I took deeper and deeper breaths as her musk oil faded out of my air. Then my turn came. At the desk I kept on remaining silent until finally the cop said, "Look, lady, I can *arrest* you *without* a name, but if you ever want to go home again, you got to have one."

Did I want to go *home?* Did I *want* to go home? Did *I* want to go home?

The cop was giving me a choice. I wanted to think it over carefully instead of just doing what was expected of me. I thought about it a while, decided that yeah, I guess I did want to go home. Anyway, I didn't want to stay *there*. I told the cop what he wanted to know, and he told me what I already knew, which was that I didn't have to talk about the circumstances of my arrest without a lawyer, which my husband was, so I called him. Naturally he was on the tennis court. A couple of the kids said they would go get him. Any excuse to drive the car.

The cop had said that he didn't have to let me use his phone, but since I clearly didn't belong there, he would. He left me alone at his desk, so I moved around to his chair, picked up the phone, opened my folder while I was waiting for the call to go through. The picture was pretty good, actually. Made my complexion look better than it really is. Brought out the chocolaty tones. My Afro, still sharp from last week's cut, was about an inch long, framing my face just right, the gray streak slightly left of center. I was looking straight into the camera like I look into people's eyes, with that serious "so what" look my friends tease me about. Eyebrows needed shaping, forehead was creased into the frown I couldn't seem to get rid of lately. But all in all, it wasn't a bad picture. I mean, I've taken worse.

The cop still hadn't come back by the time I finished calling home, so I started proofreading what he had typed about me. Name spelled right, but I penciled in an accent mark over the first A to help them get the stress right. They would probably still pronounce it wrong, as most people did, saying A-kilah instead of Ah-kilah. That would drive me crazy, since I wasn't going to be talking and couldn't correct them. Birth date, November 13, 1946, that was right. Weight, 126. I wondered if I should change it to 133, decided not to. Height 5′6″. I don't know. That's what it was the last time I had a physical. HANDICAPPING CONDITIONS was left blank, so I wrote in "Doesn't talk."

I was just starting on the arresting officer's report when my cop came back and said, "Do you mind?"

Then he had a lady cop take me down the hall for a physical because if my husband wouldn't bail me out—ha!—and if I had to stay at the detention center until my hearing—ha!—they didn't want to put me in a cell until they were sure I wasn't dying or contagious.

My husband was there by the time the physical was over. I had been so caught up in the act of remaining silent and in observing the orderly disorder of the detention center that I had forgotten about him, about how he must be feeling. But when I saw him standing at the end of the hallway the lady cop was walking me down, I realized several things all at once. First it occurred to me that before today I never had any real sense of what his professional life was like beyond the supposed glamour of being an attorney. I mean, I never went to work with him. How would I know? Now I saw another side of him, one that added rather than took away from him. He was part of this orderly disorder, passing into and out of it all the time with his clients. He knew something about life that I had lost touch with, and the fact that he continued to expose himself to it when he really didn't have to was something to respect.

The second thing I realized was that I wasn't sure how I felt about him personally in a one-on-one way. What made me realize that I wasn't sure was the fact that I knew without having to agonize over it that I was going to remain silent with him just like I had been doing with the people in the detention center. He would be hurt. And I was willing to let him be hurt. How do you feel about somebody if you're willing to let them be hurt? Maybe what you feel is better about yourself. Or so bad about yourself that you can't worry about how they feel. As I drew closer to him, I kept telling myself over and over, You have the right to remain silent. You have the *right* to remain silent. *You* have the right to remain silent.

The third thing I realized was that I was still attracted to him, though since the last baby two years ago, there had been a lot of doubt about that. I hadn't wanted that fourth child. And when I found myself pregnant again, going on forty, it was like for the first time I realized that, given a little carelessness on my part, he had the power to impregnate as well as please my body, whether it wanted to be pleased or not, whether it wanted to be impregnated or not. I had had my tubes tied before I left the hospital. It seemed like something I had done for his convenience, since he refused to have a vasectomy. Afterwards I withdrew. Chilled out in what has to be the most chilling sense of the word. But now there he was at the end of the hall. Looking sexy and manly and capable in his tennis whites, the shorts hugging and drawing the eye to rippling thigh muscles, the knit shirt clinging to the contours of chest, arm, and shoulder, the dark skin glowing against the whites like it had sunlight trapped inside it, the silvered crispness of natural-state hair that, well into his middle age, was still thick and carefully, vainly, brushed close to the scalp. I noticed with satisfaction that women were staring at him, with less satisfaction that men were, too. But that was his body, not mine, a distinction I used to have trouble making when I was in love with a man who was supposed to be in love with me, too. I fought back possessiveness and my own vanity long enough to restart the you-have-the-right-to-remain-silent routine.

He came up to me with a worried, questioning look. Hugged me. Drew back and looked at me, the beginnings of hurt already moving across his face. He was not mad, but he was not happy. They must have told him that

I wasn't talking. Even if he hadn't known, he wouldn't have questioned me there. He put up the five hundred cash and got me out on bail.

On the sidewalk he asked, "What is this all about?"

I told him I had some thinking to do and for the time being was going to exercise my right to remain silent and that I would appreciate it if he would tell that to the children, handle their affairs, and see to it that he and they honored my wishes and respected my privacy. Period. End of conversations.

At the hearing the next day, the judge set the court date for ten days away to give my husband time to take me in for psychiatric evaluation. I hadn't gone to the hearing because my husband, in his summing-up voice, had said it was neither necessary nor advisable that I be there, since my presence would be more of a hindrance than a help. Of course since I was still remaining silent, I didn't ask him what he had said on my behalf that made a judge who had never even laid eyes on me decide that I needed psychiatric evaluation. In my opinion, my husband was the one who wanted me psychiatrically evaluated. I am becoming more and more convinced of that as I sit here in this shrink's office listening to him and my husband talk about me.

My husband: I can't buy that. My wife hasn't said a word for six days, and all you can tell me is that the way she's acting is *not uncommon?* Hell, man, this woman talks *all* the time. She talks to people she doesn't know, there's no such thing as a moment of silence in my house, she stays on the telephone, she . . .

The shrink: I'm not saying it's common for her specifically, Mr. Styles. But whatever's bothering her . . .

My husband: I'll tell you what's *bothering* her. *She told the police she killed a man, dammit.* And that he killed somebody else. For the last week every time a fresh male corpse turns up, somebody calls to ask me where my wife was at such-and-such a time. And all you can say is that it's not *uncommon?*

The shrink: These things take time.

They didn't say anything for a while. My husband was not taking this well. Seeing him in the shrink's office in the last few days, a person would never think that he could sit in a courtroom day after day, sometimes for weeks, showing no sign of emotion. Now days, his eyes had the look of a fugitive's, his voice often left the bass register and sailed into the treble, he had developed a habit of stroking his mustache or running his hand over his hair every few minutes, and, most annoying to me, instead of sitting with his feet flat on the floor or in some other natural posture, he sat forward in chairs, his ankles bent so that the weight rested on the ball of his foot while one heel or the other constantly bounced like he was having muscle spasms.

He had been torn between getting a black shrink or a white one. There were only two black ones in town. They weren't exactly friends of ours, but we knew them socially. My husband was afraid that if we went to one of them, our business—my business—would end up in the street. But he figured that a white shrink would be culturally deprived, which would mean that he, my husband, would have to spend most of the sessions interpreting the black experience to him, the shrink. *Spending MY money*, my husband said, *to buy HIS time to teach him what he should have learned in school!* Then he digressed, as he will do, to lecture me, like I was one of the kids or something, about the underlying racism of a society that in the face of all the evidence to the contrary insisted that the Anglo-centric view was the norm. For the first day or so, I had felt embarrassed for him, being committed to silence, trying to decide how to react and behave while he explained and justified his thinking and actions. But he insisted on explaining everything. Said he was just going to act normal so I would know that whatever my problem was, he would be there for me. He was always "there for me," more, I guess, than I was "there for him." Whenever "being there" came up, it made me uncomfortable. I wanted to know the limits of "there." What his limits were and what he expected mine to be.

After a day of agonizing he had compromised on this Hispanic shrink. Actually he was Afro–Cuban. He looked black enough to identify with. But he sounded white enough to make you feel some distance from him, so I guess my husband was satisfied.

Whether he was or not, I liked this shrink. My husband had to be right all the time, which was probably why he was always explaining and justifying. Being right all the time, he went off on people a lot. "My God, man!" or "Goddammit, woman!" And then he would tell you what was right. The only people he didn't do this to, other than his parents, were judges, though he had a diluted version for both the judges and his parents. When he went off on the shrink, the shrink usually answered him without words. Realigning his spine with the back of the chair. Gracefully shifting all that weight around. Tapping his fingertips together. Swiveling in his oversized chair. Smiling the whole time. Then when my husband got through, the shrink would clear his throat and say something like, "Now. As I was saying . . ."

My husband: Do you think she did it? Killed a man?

The shrink: I won't have an answer to that until she decides to talk again. From what you've told me, though, I would say it's not altogether out of the question.

My husband: You think she's violent? Like she's got latent violent potentials?

The shrink: What are latent violent potentials?

My husband: I don't know.

The shrink: Neither do I. Stop trying to second-guess me, Mr. Styles. When I can give you some intelligent answers, I will. Same time tomorrow?

The shrink stood up. So did my husband. The shrink turned to me with his hand out. He had soft-looking hands, like he spent all day pampering them. And a manicure. He must have had his manicure redone every other day or so.

"Would you like to leave those in the trash?" the shrink asked, nodding toward my hand.

I was holding some of his business cards. Five or six of them. Every day when the shrink and my husband started talking, I would get one of his cards out of the little holder and start drawing and scribbling words and names and places that I wanted to think about later. When I filled the card up, I would get another one. Then another one. The more the shrink made my husband talk about me, the more cards I needed.

He said, "Hmm?" and motioned to the cards.

I balled them up and put them in my pocket.

The shrink: I think she's suffering from sixties psychoneurosis.

This was Wednesday, the fourth session. We had been meeting the shrink every day except Saturday and Sunday, two hours each time, since Friday.

My husband: Sixties *what*?

The shrink: Psychoneurosis. This could very well be the first documented case.

My husband: You mean you made it up.

The shrink: I gave a name to a set of symptoms I'm seeing in your wife and which I've seen in other clients about her age.

My husband sighed and looked out the window like he was real tired. He should have been. Hadn't been on the tennis court or to his office since he bailed me out. When he wasn't fussing at me and trying to get me to talk, he was fussing at the kids and trying to get them to shut up. I reached for one of the shrink's business cards, but where the card holder had been there was a stack of paper, like typing paper cut in half. Crooked cutting, too. Ragged edges stuck together where the scissors had passed across them. I drew my hand back and looked at the shrink. He was tapping his fingers, swiveling, smiling.

My husband: So what does it mean?

The shrink: To put it in familiar terms, it's a sort of civilian parallel to the post-traumatic stress disorder that Vietnam vets experience.

My husband: I told you I wasn't in the war.

The shrink: But you know about it. You probably have buddies suffering from it. You might have prosecuted some of its victims.

My husband: Okay, yeah, all right. So now I got a wife suffering from something like it. Only you made it up. What the hell am I supposed to do with that?

The shrink: Don't you want to know something about it before you start getting . . .

My husband: Getting *what*, man? This woman has been mute for going on two weeks. When we go to court . . .

The shrink: I'll go with you, naturally.

My husband: Maybe you won't. Right now I'm thinking that I need to find somebody with some *real* answers. All you can do is make up something. Meanwhile, I've got four kids at home wanting to know why their mother won't talk to them or me. My God, man . . .

While my husband was going off on the shrink, I snuck some of the raggedy paper off the desk. God, it felt good to have that paper in my hands! I started drawing, just drawing. Peacock feathers. A door with wrought-iron bars. My husband was firing on the shrink: *Shrink, do you realize how much time this is taking from my practice? Time is money, and I have kids needing that money for college since my wife and I don't qualify for financial aid, and I'll be damned if I'll have MY kids coming out of college with debt from tuition loans up to their asses. And, shrink, do you have any idea, any idea at all what my home life is like these days? I need something that somebody has heard of, something somebody will believe, something that will hold up in court and get my wife back to normal.* He said "sixties psychoneurosis." I wrote it down and started drawing a gun with "sixties psychoneurosis" as the barrel. My husband kept blasting until the doctor interrupted.

The shrink: I am *not* making a guinea pig out of her, Mr. Styles. From what you've told me, she's definitely got some kind of disorder that's rooted in the nineteen sixties.

My husband: Then why don't I have it? We're practically the same age.

The shrink: Yes, but the sixties didn't mean as much to some people as they did to others. Like a love affair. Usually it means more to one party than to the other, right? Anyway, what makes you so sure you don't?

My husband: I'm talking, she's not.

The shrink: The absence of speech is simply the manifestation of the advanced nature of her case. After all, she was talking, too, up until last week.

My husband didn't say anything. The shrink opened a folder, shuffled through some papers, pulled one sheet out, studied it a moment while my husband fumed like a volcano trying to hold itself back. The shrink put the sheet aside and started talking, swiveling and tapping his fingers together as he glanced from me to my husband. He sounded happy. Excited.

The shrink: You see, over the last four or five years I've had a number of clients and friends whose behavior has many similarities to your wife's. Oh, they don't stop talking, you know. There was one who did for a session or two, but that's because he was angry at me.

My husband: So who is my wife angry at?

The shrink: Well, I didn't say that cessation of speech is necessarily an indication of anger. If that's the case with her, I don't yet know who the target is. Maybe you, maybe this man she claimed to have killed, the one who killed—what was the name she gave the arresting officer?—Jamaal. Or maybe she's mad at Jamaal and in her mind the killing of the other man was equivalent to killing him.

My husband: Then you *do* think she killed somebody?

The shrink: I didn't say that. Look, why don't you just let me tell you my theory and explain the approach I want to take.

My husband waved his hand, said for him to go on. Based on what my husband had told him, the shrink said, I was exhibiting the classic symptoms of repressed mourning of the passing of the sixties. Distorted perceptions of the past, probably alternating between glorifying and maligning the sixties, whether or not I actually ever talked about them. That could explain what my husband considered my unexplained depression and anger. Alienation from the present. As an example he reminded my husband of what he had told him about my inordinate fondness for the music of the period, the way I listened to nothing but that—in my car, as I worked, while I cooked or cleaned house.

My husband: Get serious, man. With all these oldies stations? It's not like she has to go looking for the stuff.

The shrink: Yes, yes, exactly! Who do you think owns those stations and does the programming? Her—our—peers.

My husband: And they're sick, too?

The shrink: Not necessarily. Some people might call it an obsession. I'm looking for a better word because that one connotes sickness, and I don't mean to imply that the whole generation is sick. But let's say, for the sake of argument, that it is an obsession. All right. Some people find creative ways to express that obsession. Oldies stations. Albums of original sixties songs or new versions of certain songs. TV series and movies based on the sixties. Commercials set to the tune of sixties music. Others, trying to satisfy their obsession, become consumers of these products. Some consumers, like your wife, become addicts. In extreme cases, they could become disoriented and socially dysfunctional. Withdrawing from reality, fantasizing excessively.

All through this, my husband had been fidgeting. Stroking his mustache. Smoothing his hair. Bouncing one heel. I had started a new sheet of writings and drawings. This session had just taken a turn for the worse, as far as I was concerned. Where had the shrink gotten this stuff? Evidently my husband had been talking to him on his own, speculating and hypothesizing like he does when he's preparing a case. It had to be that. The shrink couldn't have invented something as silly as this on the basis of the boring discussions he and my husband had been having in *my* presence.

The shrink was really wound up now. People suffering from sixties psychoneurosis, he said, have a sixties profile similar to mine. Their politics had taught them what it was like to live at the edge of annihilation. To stave off the threat, they had devised various coping mechanisms. In the white culture they were flower children and peaceniks and hippies and Young Socialist Democrats. In the black culture they were nationalists or, if they weren't political, they were into drugs and alternate life-styles. In all cultures there were those who turned the political and social climate to their own advantage. An excuse to unleash inhibitions. Especially in California.

I glanced at my husband. Yes, he had been up to his speculations and hypotheses. He had spent all his life in the South and would forever be confused about people from California. My husband looked at me. Raised his eyebrows. Shrugged. I fixed my expression to say, "Go to hell!"

The shrink stopped swiveling, leaned forward, hands flat on his desk. Did you want to say something, Mrs. Styles?

I went back to the drawing I was working on. A brother with a big 'fro with his hands tied behind his back staring at another brother who had a huge handgun pointed at his genitals.

The shrink: Am I on the right track, Mr. Styles?

My husband: Maybe.

The shrink: Well, I'll give it some more thought before our next session. Fascinating, isn't it?

My husband had enough sense not to say anything.

The shrink: By the way, I'm thinking about asking the judge to reschedule the hearing for a later date. I think we need some more time. Do you have any objections?

My husband: It depends on what you intend to do with the time.

The shrink hesitated. Swiveled away. Looked out the window. Swiveled back.

The shrink: I'm going to need your cooperation, Mr. Styles. I need you to trust me, keep an open mind. Would you be willing to let me put your wife in the hospital for observation? A private hospital, of course.

He wanted to have me committed.

I walked out. The little fat shrink had swiveled too far to the right. Who did he think he was? Who did he think *we* were? My husband would never consent to anything so degrading, treating me like a crazy person. I just walked out, my husband right behind me, yelling over his shoulder, "Forget it, man, we're outta here! I'm going for a second opinion!"

Two days later my husband checked me into the shrink's private hospital. It had bars on the windows and security guards for nurses.

TOMORROW

Bill Williams Forde

Cocooned from head to toe in newspapers and cardboard, Magdelena, also known as Miss Lady, or Twin's woman, has fallen asleep. The foul subway air and purple grease do not disturb her, nor is she awakened by the trembling earth or the sound of alligators. Occasionally the approaching and departing trains spark and bellow like elephants on roller skates, but her dreams are impenetrable. At times she is convinced she has soared across continents and discovered Magic Water; in another second she is positive that she and not Mary is the true mother of Jesus. Then, now a giggly young girl, she is sailing toward a silver-blue sky upon the uppermost peak of a Ferris wheel, from where she descends in search of flowers and the enchanting promise of her first embrace. . . . She begins to toss and turn upon the cold gray concrete only when the flowers, losing their caressing fragrance, begin to wilt, and weep like children, blood and pus suddenly gushing from dying buds, while she, while that misty self of herself—astonished at the cruel impact of knife-sharp knees, now sees herself being bounced even higher than the Ferris wheel, so high she can nearly touch the burning sun. But though she recoils and grinds her teeth into newspapers and against the concrete itself, the fiery ball does not vanquish sleep either. She continues to groan and toss and turn. Not until the sun, itself yearning for adventure and perhaps even love, sticks out its finger and hitches a ride aboard one of the noisy and graffitied trains, from whose smoking wheels lightning flashes and glints as it jumps the tracks and gains the platform and hurls itself toward her knees, does she gasp and grab for the wall and blink herself awake.

I must've dozed, she thought, bewildered. When she certainly hadn't intended to—not on this important night—especially this important night— not often you got the chance to confirm your worst suspicions. . . . To hold a mirror before the face of another and demand: truth. Truth! And wouldn't the truth set you free?

But was she too late? She thought she was much too late until she heard the harmonica. A fragmented and yet haunting melody came from the farthermost end of the platform and vied with the raucous sound of a saxophone erupting from some hidden place among the crowd of people waiting for trains. Then she glimpsed his white hat, emerging from the gloom, looking at once gray and then off-white and even yellow and then white again, floating toward her as if without an owner. She leaned up on one elbow and squinted, searching for his face, but so far could only distinguish his lips—thin, white, nervous, sucking his golden harp, while his slight chin faded into his long, slender fingers. He came out of the semidarkness at a loping trot, a seedy gray coat flapping about his kneeless blue jeans and scuffled brown boots, and she turned her face to the wall and hid behind the newspapers, looking around again only when she knew his boots were no longer pounding in her direction. The odor of dying flowers, still clinging to the air, sweetly, and even seductively, followed him toward the knot of people. From there, the saxophone burst into a shower of exuberant melodies.

She eased into position to watch him, careful not to rustle the newspaper and cardboard, and except for the thumping of her heart she felt she had blended herself into the concrete. He had slowed and was scanning the crowd, especially the women, which did not surprise her. Each time he tooted a few humorous notes on his harmonica in accompanying the saxophone, a sprinkling of people turned and regarded him and smiled.

He was scrutinizing breasts, hips, ankles, covertly circling the women like a famished animal. The late theater hour had released the crowd into the subway. But what precisely was he looking for? she wondered, the tips of her cold fingers rising to her throat, remembering that truth did not always set you free, not always—was he looking for an elderly woman? A young woman? A very, very young woman—Eurydice, for example? When he paused a short distance from a young woman—hardly more than a teenager— a swift surge of panic gripped her chest, and she had difficulty breathing for a moment. But the young lady was in the company of others, and tightly guarded, and he turned away, frustration shining on his narrow forehead and angular jaws.

He circled the clot of people again. Soon his attention shifted to an older woman, and he appeared to make up his mind, and propped halfway up from the pallet, she relaxed a little. The lady seemed old enough to be his mother. . . . Good!

He followed the woman into the last subway coach. Just before the train closed its doors, she bounded up from the newspapers and cardboard and flung herself aboard, choosing the coach just ahead of the one into which he'd trailed the woman. Her knees shaking and her heart still galloping in her chest, she advanced to the door that separated the two cars. As she changed her wig, from a disheveled brunette headpiece stained by purple grease to a clean youthful-looking one—a magnificent strawberry, with fiery gold bangs that drew her fingers in helpless caresses—she peered into their car. They were alone. He sat a reasonable distance from her, the silent mouth organ strapped around his throat, as he peeped nervously at her from beneath his massive white hat. Otherwise he didn't move. For a second she was assailed by confusion—halfway hoping she'd been wrong, that he'd been wrong, and that this woman, too, wouldn't fit his dreams. . . . But what had been the alternative? Someone younger . . . much younger!

Still, so stupid of this one to ride the car alone, she thought. So stupid to trust the footsteps of—of—She lost her train of thought. Sweat had popped from her eyelids and was fogging her vision. For an instant the woman, seated there under the flickering lights, smiling into her playbill, appeared youthful—almost girlish—Flying toward the sun—far above the dying scent of chrysanthemums and honeysuckle and roses—across continents where she'd found the Magic Water—but was that true? God, what had she been thinking? Stupid to ride the car alone—and to trust—trust the footsteps of strangers—while you lay curled in doorways or huddled on lonesome stair-wells dreaming, or most likely dreamless, but trusting yourself to the footsteps of strangers, any one of whom might strike matches and toss the flames into your eyes—how well she knew!

She stroked the opulent strawberry hair, her brow furrowed uncertainly. She couldn't always rely on her thoughts—but who could? Sweat drenched her armpits. She pushed her face toward the glass. Surrounded by the grim world of graffiti, the woman kept smiling into her playbill, both youthful and elderly—Older than herself? Flabbier than herself? The train rocked and slowed. Yes, she was a handsome woman, she had to admit that—who loved the theater and perhaps even solitude. A cultured, good, decent woman, with a beautiful home somewhere out there in the city, and perhaps a family. Such a good woman, and should neither incur trepidation nor

envy nor jealousy, for the man hadn't moved even yet. Suspicions had been
unwarranted. He could be a faithful man, not a two-timing dog—why embarrass herself by remaining on the car with unjustified suspicions? She could
get off—the brakes screamed like the bellow of elephants.

Then, now that she was no longer exactly sure what she preferred him
to do, and yet almost sure he'd never stand, he stood. One hand remained
concealed inside his shabby gray coat. He edged closer to the woman, who
now wore a smile as beautiful as a new moon as she flipped the pages of
her playbill: actors living again on the stage, endearing words of love, tragedy,
tearful resolutions. But if she was momentarily an actor herself, so was the
man entering her dream.

He smiled, a thin white grimace, and yet not without a certain charm.
When she looked up, a silver light swept from his coat and encircled her
neck. Happiness vanished from her face as the train jerked to a halt, and
the man compelled her to walk from the car at his side as if they were lovers.

She followed them off, shivering with outrage as well as a giddy irres-
olution. Just when she'd thought she could be wrong—just when she'd
thought or hoped that—Though suddenly repelled by the touch of her strawberry wig, she continued to press her fingers into the fine red-gold hairs,
and trailed the two into the semidarkness. Their footsteps tapped down the
iron ladder, going deeper underground. No one had turned to regard them.
Now, climbing deeper still into the bottom of the earth, all but enveloped
by gloom, save for the spattering of sparks drifting from the rails above, no
one there but the three of them.

She afforded herself the risk of tailing them closely, and even thought
she could hear them breathing, and the woman murmuring over and over
something like, ". . . No. No. Don't! Help, somebody, please . . . !" Even
in fear, a refined and cultured voice. Sensitive.

Yes, I will help! she thought. Then she heard the man's chilling voice,
reverberating back up the ladder, crueler than any tone she would've suspected him of possessing: "You want to live?"

"Please don't. Somebody, help. . . ."

"Then shut up!"

She shivered again and clung to the ladder, descending into the gloom
without certainty. Now they'd reached the cavern beneath the subway, what
may have been a subway passage itself years before, and the trains up above
were but distant echoes. To the left flowed the sewage. To the right a path
that led more directly toward the river and therefore the ocean. From an
angle upstairs, she figured they might be viewed as below the train terminal
or even City Hall, and she eased after them through the fetid air, thinking
she could hear somewhere out there in the crepuscule world the thrashing
and rasping cries of alligators.

Predictably, he stopped before the stone wall of the house where he lived. Silence wafted from the adjacent makeshift homes, some composed of no more than strips of cardboard and old mattresses and bundles of rags, and a few candles flickered here and there.

No one stepped from their home to challenge him, and he half-dragged the woman through the stone door. Incensed, she followed through the door, and past the aluminum and bamboo room dividers, and into a living room of stolen TVs and VCRs and record players, and a blond sofa and prints of Andy Warhol and Picasso adorning the leaky walls.

He had continued into the bedroom. She took a deep breath and didn't move for a time, the odor of wilting flowers seeping into her nostrils. From beyond the partition she didn't hear anything yet. She waited, undecided, glancing into the kitchen where there would be knives, but still didn't move. Then the low mournful cry erupted again, "Please, don't. . . ." Then the aborted sound of a struggle, and then the woman screaming her outrage: "Don't, you bastard! You bastard!"

"Shut up!"

The new prolonged silence which was not altogether a silence lasted for all of thirty minutes; she was aware of time, for occasionally she gazed at the huge stolen clock propped between the bookcase and blue vase of artificial flowers. Still she waited, grinding her teeth into her tongue, conscious of her magnificent wig gripping her skull like iron fingers. Racked by indecision, the thought of knives crossed her mind again, but she doubted she'd use one. A rodent that seemed as massive as a pit bulldog strolled across the carpet and scurried out the door. Then the fragmented silence echoed around her once more. After a time, trembly, and even unaccountably fatigued, she stepped into the kitchen and turned on an eye of the hot plate and heated a cup of coffee. In less than another five minutes she heard him dragging the woman from the bedroom and through the living room and out the door. The scalding coffee burned her tongue, and when she leaned over the plastic garbage bag to spit, she noticed she'd begun to retch, her spittle dotted by tiny specks of blood.

Finally she wiped her mouth and went out, struggling to control both her breath and her temper. Nauseated by the abominable odors, she circled the house and took the slippery path and then the steps toward the sewage, and saw him where he had paused; where he stood above the woman, as if as undecided and bewildered now as she'd been earlier. She wouldn't have been surprised if he'd lifted his golden harp to his lips and begun to play, but he didn't.

Conscious of the rasping and fermenting sewage below, she balanced herself against the wall and approached his turned back. Once she'd cleared her throat and pressed a half-smile onto her lips, she was amazed at the nonchalant note she managed to infuse into her voice. "Hello," she said. "What do we have here?"

He spun around, his youthfully baffled face suddenly twitching dangerously, and then he gave her an uncertain smile from beneath his prodigious white hat. He hesitated, then announced unhappily: "This woman wandered into the subway . . . and . . . and fell. . . ."

"Oh," she said.

"Not very intelligent to leave the platform upstairs and wander about."

She peered through the gloom, seeking to maintain a neutral tone. She couldn't pull her eyes back from the woman. —Soaring toward the sun. — Scent of dying flowers. Magic water—? An intelligent, sensitive woman who loved—"She looks hurt," she said. "Real bad. Worse than hurt . . ."

"I found her like this," he said. "Right where you see her now."

For a time she said nothing, simply staring at him again now, but unsmiling, unable to smile; then she said: "Somebody killed her. Somebody did. She didn't wander around. She was abducted. Somebody dragged her down here and killed her. . . ."

He was uncertain again; he'd begun biting his fingers and even his wrist, cringing away from the woman. He eyed her. He didn't like her tone. "Yes," he admitted. "That's possible. In fact . . . in fact . . . I saw a man in a gray coat. . . . I tried to . . . save her."

"Gray coat?" she said. "So you saw a gray coat? Like the one you're wearing?"

He frowned and glanced away from her eyes. "No. No. The man might have been wearing a blue coat. . . ."

Again she looked down at the poor woman. The feeble fingers of light had turned her a ghastly blue. What about her family? Did she have children? No matter if she seemed older now, still too young to have—

"You did it," she finally said, tiredly. "You sick-in-the-head sick bastard!"

"No. No. No. No!" he said.

"Don't hide your face! I saw it. This time I saw it. And this is the second, maybe even the third time, maybe even more . . ."

"No. No. No."

"I saw it this time."

"A man in a gray coat; I mean, a blue coat . . ."

"You're the man in the gray coat!"

"No. No. So now you hate me—"

"Don't you think I should?" she all but shouted. "The second or third or maybe even the fourth time!"

"I don't remember the others. I don't remember this one either."

"Oh, you sick, sick bastard."

"I don't remember. . . ."

"Oh, God. And you would've picked a younger one if you'd found one alone!"

"Take the knife," he said, and gave it to her, and swept off his beautiful hat and dropped to his knees and pushed his arms around her waist. "Kill me!"

She uncoiled her muscles and breathed again and could again taste the blood in her mouth and smell the stale flowers. She looked down at his hairless head, as round and smooth as that of a baby. She could even envision the knife sinking into his throat, but shuddered and shelved him away. "God knows you deserve to. . . . And if this one had been younger, maybe then I'd . . . I'd . . . But what about me? I put trust in you. All my trust. And now I could be left down here alone. Alone."

He remained upon his knees, weeping—sobs that echoed through the underground—but she vaguely noticed he didn't hesitate to take the knife from her hand and stick it back into his coat. "What are we going to do?" he said.

"We?" she said, refusing to look at him, but feeling her own eyes misting with tears. "Not we. You! As usual, clean up your own mess."

She lay in bed with him. At moments she thought she could smell purple grease dripping from his fingers. She closed her eyes and listened to his erratic breath whispering across her chest. Once, perhaps not so long ago, she'd pushed a tram through the sun-swept city park, joined other mothers—attempted to join them, in any case—some of them had avoided her. She sat upon the benches and fed the pigeons. No matter whose child squirmed about in a tram and broke into fretful cries, she was swept by an urge to feed and comfort it. Why was she being avoided?

Now she fed grown men and women—at least she did the cooking—and they seemed grateful. Outside in the kitchen atop the giant hot plate stood each day a pot of red beans and rice or spaghetti and meatballs or sometimes a stew. Neighbors felt free to drop in, and though she didn't ask, they might leave a present—a stolen vacuum cleaner, another TV set, a car radio, a side of beef, or even a fur coat or a piece of jewelry. They possessed only vague memories of home, so home for some of them became wherever she was.

While her knees suddenly ached to share his scalding breath, he lingered, as usual, at the tips of her bosom. He pulled at her nipples until pain rushed into her skull, and she grasped the sheets. He seemed as baffled as a child when milk refused to flow, or was he thinking blood? Before losing control of his trembling fingers, he had the habit of jumping from the bed and fleeing into the bathroom or kitchen; when he came back, he smelled of real milk or urine, or sometimes both.

Oh, God, kiss me! she thought. Kiss me. Push deep into my heart—But he remained frozen on the other side of the world, might as well have been at the North Pole. What he'd already shared with her, she knew, was all he could afford, all he seemed to have, had ever had. She was fortunate if he managed to lift himself briefly and fling his legs across her hips, even then leaving only a fleeting memory of his belly and knees.

Irritably, she opened her eyes and gazed at the watermarked ceiling where a colony of water bugs lumbered toward the air conditioner. The aroma of red beans and rice sifted from the kitchen. News from upstairs blared from the radio. The mayor was all set to give a press conference. Some new president had been elected. A man and his briefcase had been pushed from a subway platform, and the man had bounded to his feet, alive, but an arm missing. . . .

"Stop!" she said sharply. "Enough! That's enough. You never learn. . . ."

"Oh, Miss Lady!"

"You never learn. That's enough. I'm hungry. Others will be arriving soon."

"I brought you a present. Real pearls, I think."

"Thanks. But you got to get up. Others will be arriving soon."

He gripped her chest and began sobbing again, and she fought the impulse to strike him as if he were indeed a baby, and instead pushed him to the side of the bed and stepped over him. Behind the curtain, in the shower, she scrubbed vigorously, aiming at what seemed like spots of purple grease, stubbornly clinging to her skin, not for lack of soap but because the hot water often suddenly vanished. When she came out, wearing sweat pants and two skirts and sweaters against the chill, and sporting her strawberry wig again, neighbors had begun arriving in the kitchen.

"Dress," she told him. "Quit crying. And come out and welcome company."

Pickpocket and Bouncer were already hovering above the pots. The odor of Black Flag spray, ammonia and boric acid had stunned most of the water bugs and roaches and discouraged their attempts to share in the meal. Pickpocket, a skeleton of a man, with eyes the size of floodlights, and long, delicate fingers, had heaped his plate with steaming rice and beans. He pushed the burning food down his throat.

"Miss Lady, you've outdone yo'self! As a man from New Orleans I don't hesitate to say yo cooking reminds me of the food I cut my teeth on. Mama herself would have to compliment you!"

"Sure good," Bouncer agreed, though he hadn't tasted his food yet and was blowing on it. Like his brother, Buddy, he was a tall, broad-shouldered man, with fists as big as air hammers, and neither he nor his brother would allow anyone to bother her. But they didn't much like her friend.

"Where's Millie?" she said.

"Upstairs around the train station," Bouncer said. He had a deep, melodious voice and had once thought of becoming a professional singer before he went to the war. Except that his eyes batted rapidly and his lips appeared to be eating when they weren't, no one would assume he'd been wounded on a faraway battlefield. "Sometimes she's lucky if she gets as much as a quarter thrown into her cup. Folks stingy these days."

"She ought to come down and have a bite. Did I hear her coughing again last night?"

Both men went silent. They knew this was not the question she'd most like an answer to. Their eyes drifted toward the bedroom divider, and Bouncer stuck beans and rice into his ravenous mouth and looked away.

"I didn't hear her," Pickpocket said. "I know she got a bad cold, caught in the last cold snap up there, but I didn't hear her coughing."

She went to the hot plate and dipped a modest helping onto her dish. The steam rose and nauseated her. The ketchup looked like blood. She was happy she hadn't attempted to cook hamburger. Seasoning, sticking her fingers into—

"Where's he?" Bouncer said. "Asleep?"

"He's not feeling well," she said at once. "He had a fight last night. Earlier in the day he went into Bloomingdale's and did good, brought me some real pearls from there, but coming back home he ran into a man wearing a gray coat and had a fight. . . ."

They didn't meet her eyes.

Her voice rose. "He had a fight."

"Sure, Miss Lady," Bouncer said.

Why didn't they look at her? What were they thinking? Had one of them or both of them seen the woman, the last woman, who'd loved the theater, and who'd been rather beautiful if not young—and seen maybe the other ones, too? Had they heard her cries in the middle of the night?

She hugged her stomach and looked around the underground home, the new gleaming plastic chairs that bordered the chromium glass-topped kitchen table, the sparkling copper pots and pans and utensils, the blue-and-white china, the crystal glassware, and the prodigious refrigerator packed with frozen steaks and chickens. Everything she'd once longed for—though the microwave and the stove no longer worked, had gone kaput. . . . And out there in the living room Persian rugs that swept from one wall to the other.

"He provides well," she said. "Before he came down here, I slept on cardboard and newspapers. Went hungry nearly every day. I had a knee infection from where I'd fallen, and I needed to see a dentist badly, but I had no money. Now all of that is taken care of. Sometimes I've even thought I could send for my children—"

"Oh, he's a wonderful provider," Bouncer hurriedly admitted.

"Does anyone live in perfect bliss?" she rushed on. "I don't know anyone who does—I surely didn't know such a couple when I was married upstairs."

"Uh-huh," Bouncer said evasily, swallowing beans and rice. "You right. Bound to be domestic squabbles and differences now and then. Nothing ever goes smooth in this life."

"I hear that," Pickpocket said. "I ain't never found no bed of roses either."

"But him . . . he . . . well . . . Miss Lady," Bouncer said, but then decided not to say anything more and walked back to the pot; he piled another heaping of beans and rice on top of the food he hadn't finished yet.

She regarded her two friends. Why did they keep tipping around her as if walking in a pot of glue? An unreasonable guilt, and even shame, surged up in her chest. She caught herself suddenly blabbering and apologizing. "Please. I don't mean to belittle your gifts to me—I appreciate the air conditioner and the vacuum cleaner. And, Pickpocket, you just can't imagine how much I loved the fur coat. And I certainly would've worn it already if I could find somewhere to—"

"Miss Lady. Miss Lady," Pickpocket said. "We happy at anything we can do for you. I miss New Orleans. . . . I miss the family I ain't got no more. When I walk into yo kitchen, I feel like I'm at home again."

"Please. Have some more beans and rice," she insisted. "Have all you want. Bouncer, did you get enough? I'm sorry I don't have any dessert today, but when the stove broke down and then the microwave shorted out, no way I could make a pie or cake or anything."

"Don't worry about it," Bouncer said. "Buddy is still upstairs looking around. It's just a question of what brands he decides to bring you."

"Ummmm. Ummmmm," Pickpocket said. "I can already taste yo chocolate cake and coconut pie, Miss Lady!"

"If I only knew how to make sweet potato pie like you said your mother did," she said with enthusiasm, "I'd make that, too." For a moment everyone seemed happy again and uncritical, and she smiled, and the day began to feel good and normal, but Bouncer couldn't contain himself, wouldn't leave well enough alone. She watched the question jump out of his hungry mouth. "Police looking for him yet?"

She flushed. "For what?"

"Well, just thought I heard something on the news or read in the papers where they looking for somebody that fits his general description. . . ."

"I heard nothing about that. Didn't read it either. The news was only talking about the mayor and the new president. And the man who got pushed into the path of the train."

"Rotten thing to do!" Bouncer said, shaking his head. "Pushing a human being into a subway train. No profit in it, either. Didn't even grab the man's briefcase first. Buddy and me would never do a thing like that. Sick, I'd say."

"Sick. Sick," Pickpocket said. "So many sickies everywhere you look. So many kicked out of hospitals while they still raving nuts."

"So many," Bouncer agreed. "I'm glad I'm healthy, but I don't know about Buddy. . . ." He kept on looking at her with his furiously batting eyes. "And I understand yo friend spent a little time in a hospital, too, didn't he, Miss Lady?"

She looked down at her plate and stabbed her fork into the blue-and-white china. The smell of Black Flag was suddenly overwhelming. "Merely a few months," she said. "When his mother died. When she went to sleep and didn't wake up. He told the police the truth about that, but they continued badgering him with questions—His nerves went bad for a little while, which could happen to anybody. So he spent just a few months in the hospital where they watched over him and helped him. . . ."

"I don't know about helped," Bouncer said. "They just told Buddy to pick up his socks and go."

The aluminum divider trembled open, and he appeared. His cheeks looked green and his fingernails, that had been eaten to the quick, as red as the ketchup. The harmonica dangled around his neck. He still smelled of urine if not milk. He stuck his knuckles into his reddened eyes and grinned boyishly at everyone. "Any food left?"

Silence greeted him. He was almost as thin as Pickpocket, but taller and younger; at least several years younger than herself. His overly bright eyes under the wide brim of his white hat clouded at the less than enthusiastic reception.

"Come on in, Twin," she said hurriedly. "Been saving food for you. And Millie and Buddy, too, if they ever gets down here."

"Something is wrong with the shower," he complained. "Sometimes the water is hotter than a steam bath, and then it is suddenly like standing under ice."

"I tried to fix it once," Pickpocket decided to remind everyone. "But I'm no plumber."

"I'm not very mechanical either," Bouncer joined in. "Buddy neither. Maybe we got to find us a plumber upstairs somewhere and get him down here to fix the things we can't handle."

"Most journeymen plumbers got good jobs upstairs," Pickpocket said. "Never have anything to do with us. So we got to content ourselves with jacklegs."

"Well, I hope nobody expects me to know about fixing pipes," Twin said irritably. "And the stove. And the oven. I can't be expected to know and do everything around here."

"No one is blaming you for the shower, Twin," she said hastily. "Or the oven and the stove. Come on. Sit down. Have something to eat. Everyone be sociable now, please."

"I got to go," Bouncer said. "Got to get in a day's work."

"Me, too," said Pickpocket. "Get upstairs for the rush hours. Around the City Hall the mayor is suppose' to be speaking today. That don't attract much of a crowd, but they got some kind of rally marching on City Hall and that ought to add some customers."

"If you see Buddy or Millie, tell them there's still something on the stove down here," she said.

"Ain't you coming up soon?" Bouncer said, stepping toward the door.

"Soon," she said. "I guess you all can find me in the park if I don't come to see the mayor and listen to the speeches."

Bouncer and Pickpocket hurried out, leaving a wall of stony silence. Twin sat down at the table and cradled his hat upon his knee and idly ran his tongue over his harp and waited for her to serve him. An abrupt surge of resentment ringed her heart, and she stood looking down at his shining skull. Rather than go to City Hall where she might encounter friends she hadn't seen in years or into the park where, in her poorer days, she used to lift her palm before the face of strangers, it vaguely occurred to her she ought to stop in and see the police today. . . . Tell them about Twin! Tell somebody. Tell somebody so that the woman who loved the theater would stop plaguing her mind. But like yesterday and the days before, she picked up a blue-and-white plate and filled it with a generous helping and pushed it upon the table before Twin's melancholy eyes.

IN MY FATHER'S HOUSE

Ernest Gaines

Elijah had put away his tray of cups and glasses, and now he stood in the center of the room, clapping his hands for silence. The people were making too much noise to hear him, and he clapped again and stamped his foot. When everyone had quieted down, he told them that Reverend Martin wished to say a few words to them. The people turned to Phillip, who was already surrounded by a small crowd.

Phillip Martin wore a black pin-striped suit, a light gray shirt, and a red polka-dot tie. He was sixty years old, just over six feet tall, and he weighed around two hundred pounds. His thick black hair and thick well-trimmed mustache were just beginning to show some gray. Phillip was a very handsome dark-brown-skinned man, admired by women, black and white. The black women spoke openly of their admiration for him, the white women said it around people they could trust. There were rumors that he was involved with women other than his wife, but whether these rumors were true or not, he was very much respected by most of the people who knew him. And no one ever questioned his position as leader of the civil rights movement in the parish.

The people had begun to applaud Phillip, and he raised his hands for silence. Shepherd, who stood next to Virginia's new tenant in the back of the room, could see the two big rings on his fingers, and the gold watchband around his wrist. The people would not stop applauding him, and Shepherd could see how the gold watchband sparkled in the light as Phillip shook his hands for silence.

Phillip told his audience that he didn't have a speech to give, that he only wanted to remind them about next Friday when the committee would meet with Albert Chenal.

"It took us years to get Mr. Chenal to hire black people in the first place," he said. "Now, after he hires them he don't want to pay them nothing. When we go up there Friday we go'n make it clear. Either he pay the black workers the same he pay the white, or we march before the door. Now, we spend more money in that store than white people do—the white people go to Baton Rouge and New Orleans—some of them even go up North and 'way to Europe. Poor black people don't have that kind of money to do all that traveling; we spend ours here in St. Adrienne. Therefore, we want our black workers to get the same pay, the same treatment, or we close down shop. We'll see how long he can last if no blacks go in his store. Mr. Chenal—"

Elijah, standing in the center of the room, led the applause. He clapped his hands over his head and turned completely around so others would see him and join him. Phillip waited until he had quiet again.

"But Mr. Chenal will challenge us," he went on. "Sure as I'm standing here talking to you, Mr. Chenal will challenge us. First, he'll offer us pennies. When we turn that down, he'll make it nickels. Turn that down, then dimes. When we turn all of this down, he go'n tell us to get out. See how long we can take the cold. You may recall he did the same thing before—not when it was cold, when it was hot. He beat us when it was hot. Yes, when it was hot. And you know how much black people love hot weather—we thrive on hot weather."

The people started laughing, and Phillip held up his hands.

"Just why d'you think so many our people leaving the North and coming back home?" he asked them. "Our good old Southern hot weather, that's why. Still, we let Mr. Chenal beat us on the hottest day. Took the crumbs he offered us and said thanks. So what will he do now, knowing how much black people hate cold weather? He go'n offer us crumbs again, and when we turn it down, he go'n tell us to get out his store. In the back his mind he go'n be thinking, They can't take cold weather. Ten minutes out there with Mr. Jack Frost, they go'n run home and drink hot toddy. He-he-he. Well, Mr. Chenal is wrong, deadly wrong, we can take cold weather." Phillip looked across the room. "What you say, Mills?"

Tall, gray-headed Howard Mills standing against the wall raised one big fist up in the air.

"Got my overcoat cleaned this week," he said. "And got me some new rubber boots to hit that rain."

The people laughed at Howard Mills.

"Jonathan, ain't you ready?" Phillip asked.

Jonathan, who stood next to Mills, raised both fists high up over his head.

"I'm ready to walk till next year this time," he said. "And I hope every last person in here is ready to do the same."

The people applauded Jonathan. Phillip waited for silence.

"Poor Albert Chenal," he said. "Poor, poor Albert Chenal. I don't hate Albert Chenal. I don't want you to hate Albert Chenal. I want you to pray for Albert Chenal. Tomorrow in church pray for Albert Chenal. Before you go to bed tonight, pray for Albert Chenal. Remember, love thy neighbor as thyself."

One of the two white women in the room applauded quietly. But when no one else joined her in support of praying for Albert Chenal, she brought her applause to an abrupt end.

Phillip went on. "Love is the only thing. Understanding, the only thing. Persistence, the only thing. Getting up tomorrow, trying again, the only thing. Keep on pushing, the only thing. You got some out there screaming Black Power. I say, what is Black Power but what we already doing and what we been trying to do all these years? Then you have that other crowd sitting in the bars—they even worse than the Black Power screamers—they saying, 'What's the use? Nothing will ever change. Hey, Mr. Wrigley, pour me another drink.' I'll call on Brother Mills again. What you say, Mills? You seen any changes around here?"

Mills nodded his gray head. "I'm a witness to it," he said.

"Jonathan?" Phillip said. "You been there, too. Well?"

"I've seen progress," Jonathan said. "But we have a long way to go, a long way to go."

"Amen," Phillip said.

But Jonathan was not through. He raised both fists over his head and looked around at the people in the room. "We need more people," he said. "More young people. More old people. We need the ones in the bars. We need the schoolteachers. We need them who go to work for the white people every day of their lives. We need them all. All, all, all. No reason to stay back, no reason at all. The wall is crumbling—let's finish tearing it down."

"Amen, amen," Phillip said, as the people applauded Jonathan.

Jonathan wanted to say more, but Phillip didn't give him a chance to go on.

"I'll call on a sister now," Phillip said. "Remember our sisters was out there first. Miss Daisy Bates, Miss Autherine Lucy, and countless more. And there's Sister Claiborne standing over there with her fine foxy self—you seen any changes, Sister Claiborne?"

A small gray-haired woman dressed entirely in black nodded to Phillip.

"Sister Jackson?" Phillip said. "Don't that bus run back of town now? And don't we even have a little bench there for you to sit on when you tired?"

Sister Jackson, who was about the same age as Sister Claiborne, also wearing black, and a red bouquet, nodded as Sister Claiborne had done.

"If you want to know about changes, talk to a couple of these sisters around here," Phillip went on. "Sister Aaron, can't you vote today for the mayor of St. Adrienne, the governor of Louisiana, the President of the United States?"

"Yes," Sister Aaron said. "And I'm go'n vote for the first black congressman from Louisiana, too, who will be no one other than our own Reverend Phillip J. Martin."

The people started to applaud, and Phillip raised his hands for silence. But the people would not be silent. Anthony McVay, the white attorney, standing on one side of Phillip, and Octave Bacheron, a white pharmacist, standing on the other side of him, each took one of his hands and held them high up in the air. And the applause was deafening.

After things had quieted down some, Howard Mills put on his overcoat and left the house. About a dozen other people left at the same time. But still the big living room remained noisy and crowded. Half the people were gathered around Phillip on one side of the room; the rest were in smaller groups throughout the house. Virginia's new tenant had moved. Now he was standing near the door that led out of the living room down the hall. But even when he moved, he never took his eyes off Phillip Martin. Whenever someone got between them he would move again, never getting any closer, but always keeping Phillip in sight. Yet he did it so discreetly that no one, not even Shepherd, who stood next to him most of the time, was suspicious of anything. Beverly had joined them, and both Shepherd and she moved about the room with Virginia's tenant. They were never aware that he was doing this on purpose. They felt that it was the crowd pushing them into different places.

For the past few minutes Joyce Anne, Phillip's ten-year-old daughter, had been playing the piano. But there was so much noise in the room that no one paid any attention to her until Crystal McVay, the wife of the attorney, moved away from the crowd around Phillip and turned to the girl at the piano. Others in the room soon joined her. Elijah, who was Joyce Anne's teacher, stood behind the crowd with his tray of cups and glasses. Each time she played a difficult piece well he would shut his eyes and shake his head from side to side. But when she came to a part that might give her some trouble, he would catch his breath and wait. Then when it was over, when she had done it in good form, he would sigh deeply (loud enough for others to hear), nod, and continue on through the crowd with his tray.

But not everyone near the piano was listening to the music. Phillip Martin was not. Neither to the music nor to the people around him. For the past couple of minutes he had been looking across the room where Shepherd, Beverly, and Virginia's tenant were standing. Shepherd, who had noticed it, didn't think Phillip was looking at them in particular. They were at opposite ends of the room, there were at least three dozen people between them, so he could have been looking at anyone in that direction. Still, he looked nowhere else. And even when someone would speak to him or touch him on the arm, he would give that person his attention only a moment, then look back across the room again. He looked puzzled, confused; a deep furrow came into his forehead, and he raised his hand up to his temple as if he were in pain. Shepherd continued to watch him watching them. Suddenly he became very jealous. He knew of the minister's past reputation with women, so maybe he was eyeing Beverly now. Shepherd was angry for a moment, then he thought better of it, and he grinned at Phillip to let him know that he knew what was going on in his mind. But if Phillip saw him grin, he showed no sign that he did. Yet he looked only in that direction. When someone got between him and them, he craned his neck to see them better. Shepherd told Beverly what was going on.

"He's a handsome man, isn't he?" she said.

"Yes," Shepherd said. "And if I ever catch you anywhere near him, somebody's getting hurt."

"Really?" she teased him.

"Really," he told her.

Phillip was not aware that they were talking about him, he was not aware that they were even looking at him; yet he continued to stare at them, the expression on his face still showing confusion.

Joyce Anne was bringing her third song to an end now, and the people were applauding her performance. But Phillip Martin was not hearing a thing. He pushed his way out of the crowd and started across the room. He had taken only two or three steps when he suddenly staggered and fell heavily to the floor.

The pharmacist, Octave Bacheron, was the first to reach him and told everyone else to stay back. But the people did not get back, they pressed in closer. Sister Aaron, whom Phillip had called on during his short speech, cried out that he had been poisoned, and soon the word was all over the house that he had been drugged. The little wife of Octave Bacheron, who was hard of hearing, kept asking who had fallen. The other white woman, the attorney's wife, told her that it was Phillip.

"Phillip drunk?" Phoebe Bacheron asked. "Phillip drunk?" She was a very small woman, and she had to lean her head back to look up at the people around her. "Phillip drunk?" she asked. "Phillip drunk?"

No one answered her. They moved in to look at Phillip on the floor. Virginia's new tenant was there with all the others. His reddish eyes narrowed, his face trembled as he stared down at him. It seemed for a moment that he might say something, maybe even scream, but he jerked away from the crowd and went out. He was the only one who left, but there was so much confusion in the room that no one paid him any attention.

Alma, who had rushed to Phillip when he fell, now knelt beside him holding his head up off the floor in her lap. He had lost consciousness only a moment, as a fighter might who has been hit hard on the jaw, but now he began recognizing people around him again, and he tried quickly, desperately, to push himself up. Octave Bacheron, who knelt on the other side of him, put his small white hand on Phillip's chest and told him to lie still a moment.

"I'm all right," he said to Octave Bacheron. "I'm all right," he said to Alma. He looked up at all the people standing over him. "I'm all right, I'm all right," he said to them.

"No," Octave Bacheron said, pressing his small white hand on his chest. "Be quiet a moment. Listen to me. Can you hear me, Phillip? Be quiet. Lie still a moment."

"I'm all right," Phillip said. The people who stood over him canopylike could see tears in his eyes. "I'm all right. Please let me up. I have to get up. Don't let me deny him again."

No one knew what he was talking about. No one asked him what he was talking about.

"You don't feel well, Phillip," Octave Bacheron said. "Listen, you don't feel well."

"Alma?" Phillip said. "Alma, please," he begged her. "I'm on the floor. I'm on the floor."

Octave Bacheron nodded to Anthony to help him get Phillip to his feet. Jonathan, who was closer to Phillip, took his arm, but Anthony pushed him roughly aside.

"What you think you doing?" Jonathan asked him.

"Helping your pastor," Anthony said.

"Ain't y'all done enough helping for one day?" Jonathan said. "That's why he's on his back now."

"Watch it, boy," Anthony said. "Watch your tongue there, now."

"Boy?" Jonathan said. "Boy?" He turned to the others in the room. "Y'all hear that, don't you? It's boy now. It's boy all over again."

"Please, Jonathan," Alma said. "Please. Phillip's on his back. Please."

Jonathan and Anthony glared at each other a moment, then Anthony turned to Phillip. Phillip told them again that he was all right and he could stand on his own. But the two white men insisted on helping him to his feet, and they made him lean on them as they followed Alma down the hall to the bedroom. Elijah, Joyce Anne, and another woman followed after them.

Everyone had deserted the two white women now. The smaller one, Phoebe, was crying and asking why was Phillip drunk. Why did he drink? Didn't he know drinking was no good? The other white woman did not try to explain but took Phoebe in her arms and patted her shoulders. The rest of the people watched the door and waited for some kind of news from the bedroom.

After about ten minutes Octave Bacheron came back into the front. He told the people he believed that Phillip had fallen from exhaustion, but he was calling the doctor to be sure. He told them that both he and Alma would appreciate it if they did not take the rumor out of here that Phillip had been poisoned. Now, he wished that they would all get their coats and leave quietly, because their pastor needed rest more than anything else.

The doctor, a small clean-shaven bald man wearing a trench coat over a brown tweed suit, came to the house a half hour later. He was in the bedroom only a couple of minutes, then he wrote out a prescription for two bottles of pills. Elijah followed the pharmacist uptown and brought back the medicine.

Now that everyone else had gone, the house was deadly quiet. The doctor, repeating exactly what the pharmacist had said earlier, told Alma that what Phillip needed most was rest—quiet and rest. Alma, Elijah, and Joyce Anne sat in the living room talking so softly among themselves that they could hardly hear each other.

But things were quiet and peaceful only a short while, then the telephone started ringing. Elijah, who sat nearest the telephone, would try to reach it before it rang a second time. Everyone wanted to know what the doctor had said about Phillip. "He's tired and needs rest," Elijah told them. "Other than that he's fine. Fine. Fine. He just needs his rest." Elijah would hang up the telephone, but no sooner had he sat down than it would ring again. Several people had heard that Phillip had been poisoned. "It's nothing like that," Elijah assured them. "Nothing like that. That's the kind of rumor we don't want out." Virginia Colar called from the boardinghouse. "You sure he's just tired?" she asked. "You sure he wasn't poisoned? You know how these white folks are. Remember President Kennedy, don't you? They ain't straightened that mess out yet—putting it all on poor Oswald. Remember King, don't you? Remember Long, don't you?"

"I remember all of them," Elijah told her. "But Reverend Martin is just tired. Everybody ate the same food. Everybody drank out the same pot of eggnog, which I made myself. Mr. Octave drank out the same cup Reverend Martin drank from. Nothing happened to him."

"And how you know it was the same cup?" Virginia asked. "You got to watch white folks. They sharp, them. Can switch a cup right 'fore your eyes and you'll never see it."

"It was the same cup," Elijah said. "Reverend Martin's little blue-and-white china cup from Maison Blanche. I know that little cup like I know my name. He drinks out the same cup every day."

"That's the trouble right there," Virginia said. "He drinks out the same little blue-and-white cup, and everybody know it. Can't they go to Maison Blanche and buy another little blue-and-white cup just like his?"

"Listen, Virginia, now listen," Elijah said. "It was his little blue-and-white cup. His. Now, good night. I'll see you in church tomorrow."

Elijah sat up answering the telephone long after Alma and Joyce Anne had gone to bed. Then around midnight he went down the hall to his own room. He had been lying in bed wide-awake for about an hour when he heard Alma and Phillip arguing out in the hall. Phillip had gotten out of bed and gone into his office, and Alma was trying to get him out of there. Elijah could hear her saying that she was going into the kitchen to warm up a glass of milk, because those pills weren't doing any good. He heard her passing by his room on her way into the kitchen, and a few minutes later he heard her going back up the hall again. It was quiet another hour, then more footsteps. Elijah listened for Alma's voice but didn't hear it. Now he called her, calling quietly: "Alma? Alma?" When she didn't answer, he got up and went to Phillip's office and knocked. It was quiet in the office, and Elijah pushed the door open and went in. Phillip sat behind his desk in the dark, facing the curtains over the window.

"Something the matter?" Elijah asked him.

"Thinking about service tomorrow," Phillip said without looking around.

"You ought to be in bed," Elijah said. "Let Jonathan conduct service tomorrow."

"I'm all right," Phillip said, still facing the curtains.

"The doctor want you to stay in bed," Elijah said.

Phillip didn't answer him.

"Reverend Martin, sir?"

"Leave me alone, will you?" Phillip said, looking back over his shoulder. "I just want to sit here and think a while."

Elijah went back to his room and lay on top of the covers, but a few minutes later he was knocking on the office door again.

"Reverend Martin? Reverend Martin, sir?"

"All right," Phillip said, coming out. "Good night, Elijah."

⸻

Phillip Martin went back to bed, but he couldn't sleep. He lay wide-awake for hours, listening to his wife snoring quietly beside him. He was trying not to think about the boy. He didn't want to think about him in here because he couldn't think clearly enough in here. The only place where he could think at all was in his office, but they came and got him out each time he went in there. He lay wide-awake, hoping for tomorrow to hurry up and get here. Alma, Elijah, and Joyce Anne would go to church, and he would have the entire house to himself.

Phillip lay on his side facing the wall. He wondered about the boy. But, no, how could it be? If anyone had known who the boy was, they would have brought it up yesterday.

Again in his mind's eye he saw the boy's thin, bearded face watching him from across the room. At first he paid it little attention, but after noticing it each time he looked in that direction, he began to ask himself why. Who was he? How did he get in here? Who invited him? He was sure he had never seen him anywhere before. He would look away a moment to answer someone's question, but when he looked back across the room he would find the boy still watching him as if no time whatever had passed. Why? he asked himself. Why? Who is he?

Then he remembered having heard about a stranger in St. Adrienne. The stranger had sat behind his church door the first night that he was here. Several people had seen him passing by the house. One or two had even seen him standing out in the street watching the house. Yes, and now that he remembered, Elijah had said something about inviting him to the party. But why was he standing there watching him? Why?

Then he knew. Even when he told himself no, it couldn't be so, he knew definitely that it was. The dream that he had a night or two before the boy got here was more than a dream; it was a vision, an omen, a warning.

Phillip pressed his face down against the sheet and tried not to think about it anymore. Let him think about anything else but not about this. Think about Chenal. Chenal wasn't going to be easy. Chenal knew the people needed work. Even if he paid them less than minimum they still had to work for him, because there weren't any other jobs. Phillip wondered what he would do if Chenal said no to their demands. Demonstrate against the store? Yes. What else? But suppose Chenal fired the people working for him, then what? They could eventually close down Chenal if the people demonstrated long enough against the store, but where would they work during that time?

Phillip started thinking about the boy again. Why? he asked himself. Why after all these years—why? And how did he know where to find me? Did she send him-here? And if she did, why this game? Why sit behind the church door? Why for a week walk the street and watch the house? Come into the house, watch me, but say nothing—why? What's he want? What's he up to? He's got to be up to something. What?

Phillip Martin felt tired and confused. He looked at the two little bottles of pills and the glass of water on the small lamp table by the bed. He picked up one of the bottles and started to unscrew the cap, then threw it back. He wanted to knock everything on the floor, but he knew Alma would hear the noise and come into the room.

A WOMAN'S PLACE

Marita Golden

Rasheed

She reminds me of my first wife, Lena. Even looks like her and carries herself with that same kind of delicate style. But I wanted Lena because she was a woman; I desire Aisha because she's a child. A child who can neither entrap nor fool me. Who does not know how complex and unreliable love can be. Like Aisha, Lena inspired an openness in me that is not my true nature. I told Lena things I didn't even know I felt. She was five years older. Had been married once before. And I planned to give her everything. So I worked two jobs to earn the money to set up my hardware stores. She made me a father twice, and I was proud, but I only associated the children with christenings and birthdays. I spent so much time working that the passing of their days into years I only witnessed now and then, helping them with homework sometimes and looking in on them when I came home at two A.M., or falling asleep as I read them a bedtime story.

And when I had made the money, opened the first store, I looked around

and I had lost them. I was unsure around the children. They were uncomfortable with me, didn't know how to accept my affection. Challenged my
authority while accepting Lena's because she'd always been there. And she
had friends, interests, a promotion on her job, that I knew nothing about.
I had been too tired to ask, too obsessed with my business to care. I tried to
find an explanation for the emptiness that had sprung up where feelings used
to be. But I saw no crime, only her unhappiness.

One of the men I'd known when I worked at the Post Office had become
a Muslim. I was always skeptical about most religions. But one day, out of
curiosity, I attended a service with Guy and met his wife and children. The
reverence of his wife around him, the obedience of the children impressed
me. The order I saw in his family made the chaos of my own seem all the
greater. I thought Islam would give me back the family I'd lost. But Lena
resisted. Even refused to allow me to take the children to the mosque. I
joined the faith anyway, and soon it was over between us.

After we separated, more than once I stopped by her apartment to visit
the children and ended up staying the night. Lying in her arms, I told her
new secrets, more revealing than the old ones. Then one day I came to the
apartment and the landlord told me she'd moved. What did all those words
earn me? All the pleas, the confessions? And since then loneliness has lived
with me. Took over this house, staring at me as I ate dinner alone in the
kitchen. Mocked me when I left in the morning or pulled into the driveway
at night.

I've heard this house laugh at me as it watched me eat too much, then
felt depression sink into my spirit and steal my appetite for anything other
than grief. And the house has seen me, tongue-tied with the children I no
longer knew, when they still used to visit on the weekends before Lena
married again. And so I promised myself there would be few words next
time. There would be possession and there would be control. I want this
house to be filled with all the things I lost. And this time I'll protect them.
I won't let them get away.

In the beginning we used
to talk a lot. He asked me to tell him things about myself. But we don't do
that so much anymore. It's like he has learned already all he needs to know.
I know there won't be any denying him. And he is now as confident of me
as he seems of himself. After Jummah he comes to the back of the mosque

and gives me a look that asks me to come and stand with him. He squeezes my hand and then just wants me to be near him. Like us standing together completes a picture he has of himself. We don't talk so much like before, but there's a bond between us that maybe makes words unnecessary. The things we do are ordinary, simple things. We signed up with some people in the mosque to take an Arabic class at the Y. We study the Hadith together, at my house. And on Wednesday nights at his house there's a Qur'anic study group. I come early and help him make refreshments. He's assuming something very important about us. So am I. But neither one of us knows how to say what it is.

Rasheed

I told sister Khadija I've been seeing her. And I hinted at how deeply I feel for the girl. Khadija is one of the few women I really respect. She carries herself with dignity, and that's rare these days, even among the women in Islam. I've taken her boys out to the park, the movies, or on errands with me, just so they could be around a man. I've spent evenings at her house discussing the Qur'an, people in the mosque, and anything under the sun. I thought we were friends. So I was surprised when she let me know she had doubts about my wanting Aisha.

I was sitting in her kitchen watching her wash her daughter's hair in the sink. When I told her, she didn't even look at me, just said, "I knew something was up. Everybody in the mosque does."

"Well, what do you think?"

"Why should it matter, what I think?"

"You're right. It shouldn't. But it does." She was drying Amina's hair and trying, I could tell, not to look at me.

"You know me, I do what I want," I said. "But I was just curious. It's not like what you think will change my mind."

"I wish it could," she said, wrapping the towel around Amina's head and telling her to go into her bedroom. "I just have a fearful feeling, that's all."

"Fearful? You act like I'm some madman, somebody with nothing to offer her."

"Calm down . . . Rasheed, calm down." She poured a cup of tea and sat down across from me at the table. One of the things I like about Khadija is, she won't shrink before you. Right or wrong, she stands up for what she believes. But I could tell what was coming, and for the first time since I'd known her, I wished I could sway her.

"You've had so much more experience." She was finally looking at me. "I wonder if you might not ask her for too much. More than she can give."

"What am I asking for but a wife, a family. Not to be alone."

"I know that sounds very simple to you. But depending on how you want her to fulfill all that, it could be harder than it seems."

I got up and looked out the window, just to avoid her stare.

"A man like you, I never understood why none of the other women in the mosque ever attracted you. You been living like a monk, from what I can see."

"Can you believe I was scared? Scared of choosing with my heart instead of my head. I did that the first time around, and I'm still paying for it. I never let a woman get too close because I hadn't met anybody I could have on my terms."

"And you think you can have Aisha, as you say, on your terms?"

"I do. And if I didn't know better, I'd almost say you don't want me to be happy."

"Sure I do. It's just that I want Aisha to be happy, too."

"And so I can't . . ."

"I'm not saying that. I'm saying you've decided already what she's got to be, who she's got to become to please you. What'll you do if she can't do it? If she wants to be someone else? She's yet to be tested. How do you know she can make a commitment to the kind of marriage the faith requires?"

"She's got more conviction than lots of people who *live* in the mosque."

"I don't doubt her belief. I just know she's got some growing still to do that's got nothing to do with Allah."

"Everything has to do with Allah."

"You sound like a man who's made up his mind not to listen."

"I sound like a man who's decided what he wants."

"Maybe you're right. Maybe she'll stay the way she is now. But I wouldn't wish that on her or you."

"Anyway, I haven't even asked her yet to be my wife."

"What do you think she'll say?"

"It's been enough just trying to live with the question. I don't yet have the nerve to imagine the answer."

Aisha

His house is large. Too big
for one person. And in it there are the ghosts of the people who once lived
there with him. It's a house that's been lived in too much and too little. All
at the same time. Last night after everybody had left to go home after the
study group, we were sitting in the kitchen drinking tea. I looked around
and thought about the three bedrooms and the study upstairs and the large
front and back yards. I thought about all the space in the house, and it struck
me as maybe not as much of a blessing as it seemed.

So I asked him, "What's it like, to live alone in a big house like this?"

"There are days and nights when it's a pleasure and times when it almost
drives me crazy."

"Does it make a difference that you built it?"

"That's why I've stayed in it so long. It's like a second skin."

"I never lived in a house," I told him. "Only apartments. Houses I saw
in magazines or on television. My grandmother has a house in the country
in Maryland, but it's not anything special."

"I've thought of moving out. But I put too much into it," he said. "It
meant too much to me, building it with my own hands. This isn't just a
house, it's everything I believe in. Everything I am."

"Would you ever sell it?"

"No. Never. I'd rent it out, but it'll always belong to me. Could you live
in a house like this?" he asked me.

"Alone or with somebody?"

"Could you live in this house with me?"

"I don't think at this point there's any other place I'd rather live." I
reached out to touch his hand, but he stood up real quick and went over to
the refrigerator and leaned against it with his hands folded across his chest.
He was talking to me but looking at his shoes. And he asked me to marry
him like he was asking me to do a favor he was afraid might inconvenience
me. "I want a wife and a family I can be sure I won't lose. But I've been
alone too long for it to be easy to live with me. You're so young. Just looking
at you makes me think about starting all over. Fresh. With no mistakes this
time." Finally he looked at me and said, "Maybe that's why I'm scared, too,
of my own desire. And whether or not it'll give me a second chance."

Aisha

He didn't say anything about love. When I told Mama, she said love wasn't the most important thing in a marriage, that it wasn't even always necessary. She said respect was the thing that mattered most. And anyway, "Just because he didn't say it don't mean he don't feel it," she told me. Then she said, "I don't know nothing about you-all's religion and all that. But he strikes me as a decent man." That's about what I'd expect Mama to say. There wasn't too much for me to think about, really; it had already been decided. Because I like what he's done with his life. And I want to see what he'll do with mine.

Last night he gave me my dowry. I had asked him for a ring, a prayer rug, and a copy of the Qur'an. He brought everything all wrapped up in a box and gave it to me, with Mama standing right there watching us. Then he brought out another box from his pocket and opened it. Inside were three gold bracelets. He put them on my wrist and told me I was more beautiful than any jewelry and more precious than any stone, because I was a woman who had submitted herself to the will of Allah. I could feel his hands warm, and though we weren't that close to each other, his body wanting me. The urge just came down on him like a fever, but before that feeling could possess us, he dropped my hand and just said real softly, "I took you as my wife the first day I saw you."

Almost everybody in the mosque came to our wedding. Mama made me a long beautiful dress of lace and silk. And Crystal and Serena came, looking like they didn't quite believe what I was doing, but happy for me anyway. After the Imam talked about the meaning and importance of marriage, he joined my and Rasheed's hands and placed a white handkerchief over them. Then I knew I was Rasheed's wife. Then I knew Allah had answered my prayers.

He tells me, when we make love, that my hands feel like dove feathers against his skin. But it took me a long time to learn how to please him. And I'm still learning. The first few weeks after we got married, I was nervous and shy. He'd have to pull me close to him and guide my hands over his neck, chest, along his thighs and between his legs. After a while I relaxed and could do it naturally.

I like it when we do the same things to each other together. And he has a strange, funny taste. I never did that with anybody before. His skin is warm and salty on my lips, and his penis brushes against my teeth, resting on my tongue. And then sometimes he smells a little like antiseptic, and the scent fills my nostrils. His hairs get inside my nose while he's pushing harder and harder against the walls of my mouth. When he's real excited his fingertips knead my scalp and hold on to my curls. He starts whimpering, and it sounds like a baby getting ready to cry. I want to tell him it hurts, and just then he pulls himself out and comes inside me. He lays on me for a while, his breath hot and raspy in my ears, his fingers playing with my hair. Then he rolls onto his side of the bed and pulls me close. This time just to hold me. Almost all the time I fall asleep in his arms.

One night I told him about Jessica. We were laying on our backs, just staring at the ceiling. The dark and the things we had just done made me tell him. And when I did, I said, "I didn't expect to grieve. I didn't think it would hurt so much. I missed that baby just like it was a friend instead of a promise." He squeezed my hand and said, "We'll have babies of our own. Babies for you to love and to ensure I'll never die."

Rasheed

I never get tired of looking at her when she's pregnant. Her skin starts to glow around the fifth month, and for the whole time her eyes sparkle. When she is carrying my child and I make love to her, her body's filled with surprises. It becomes the body of the woman she's going to be one day.

I'm a father now, really for the first time. With Tameka and Tariq, we'd both get up at night to feed them. Aisha from her breast. Me with a bottle of her milk. At first I was so amazed we had twins, I didn't know what to do, where to begin, which child to look at or hold. The first month I let Randolph run the stores for me, and I stayed home with Aisha. I'd waited so long to have children in this house again I didn't even mind that for weeks seemed like all I smelled was dirty diapers and sour milk, or that me and Carrie kept up the house while Aisha dealt with the babies. None of that bothered me at all. Because I'd missed even this with my other kids. I got so good I could change diapers in a flash, and even feed them without being scared they'd choke. When they started crawling and getting into things, Aisha was always telling them no, taking things out of their hands. But I told her to leave them alone, let them have the run of the house as long as they didn't touch nothing that could hurt them. I'd just sit and watch them. They'd be pulling down magazines from the bottom shelves of the bookcases and knocking over trash cans and squealing every time they found out a new thing to do. I could see my children growing right before my eyes.

I don't much care whether this child is a girl or a boy. Everybody says from the way Aisha's carrying it, that it's a girl. If it is, one of her names will be Rose, that of my mother, to ensure that she's got the same kind of strength she had. We didn't have much, not sharecropping in Macon, Georgia. And it was the kind of life guaranteed you'd never have nothing either. But my mother'd bring home old magazines from the house of the people she worked for. The *Saturday Evening Post* especially. Almost every night we'd look through the magazine after dinner, and looking at those pictures was better than any fairy tale. Mama'd always tell us, "Just 'cause you don't see your face here, don't mean your name ain't on these cars and houses and clothes. There's good things waiting for you to come and claim 'em. Got your name on 'em right now. Always look farther," she told us, "than you can see." And the older I get the more important I think names are. That's why I told Aisha we'll give each of the children one name that comes out of our faith and another name of someone in the family. Those are the two most important things, and without one or the other you don't have very much, in this life or the next.

Aisha

The houses on our street are well tended and sturdy. The lawns are neat and most of the driveways have two cars, some even three. Christmastime everybody's house but ours is dressed up in lights, wreaths and holly. It's as if the people inside were surprised that they had gotten through another year and wanted everybody to know they could afford the year to come. Everybody knows Rasheed, he's lived in the neighborhood so long. When we first got married, the other women on the block were kind of distant. They'd stare at me, not even trying to hide their curiosity. I think they were trying to figure out how young I really am. Then when I had the twins, they became friendlier, stopping to talk when they passed me on the street or saw me at the shopping center with the babies in the double stroller. Seems like a child can win over anybody.

Some of our neighbors are from the islands—Trinidad, Jamaica, Haiti. I've seen pictures of those places, and I can't imagine ever wanting to leave them. But Rasheed told me that the islands, despite their beauty, had betrayed the people, given them lives that were meager and secondhand. We were in his study, and he pointed to the Caribbean on his globe. He told me

about the history of that part of the world, about slavery and sugar cane and
the British and the French revolutions. And why all the people think about
America when they want to flee.

In the afternoons I put the twins in bed for a nap, and after they've gone to
sleep, I tiptoe back into the room and just look at them sleeping. I study
them best when they're asleep, see things about them that I can't when
they're laughing or crying. In sleep they don't resist me. And I never look
at them long or hard enough to see everything they are.

Today Serena came over to tell me she's going to Africa next month, and
that she might stay for a while. She said that she envied me because, as she
put it, I had "defined my borders narrowly but found in them a whole
world." She sounded excited and a little scared. Her voice had an urgent
sound, and she was talking real fast, the way she always does when she's got
a plan or has made up her mind to do something. She told me about the
closing of the center where she'd been working and said that even if it hadn't
run out of funds, she'd probably have left.

"I'd done what I came there to do," she said. "I helped some women
who needed training and jobs find both, gave them support and encouragement, and met some people I'll never forget. But it wasn't enough. I wanted
to do something more. I wonder if I'll ever find a job or an endeavor big
enough for me." She talked about wanting to learn French and maybe
Swahili while she's in Africa and maybe work with some UN project and
go to see Victoria Falls. Just listening to her talk made my heart beat a little
faster, made me smile for no reason, made me think maybe I could do
anything I wanted to.

It was nice outside, so we took the kids into the backyard and put them
in the swings. Serena looked around the yard, at the two huge oak trees and
the screened-in patio. The air smelled like October—crisp and cold and
maybe even snow. "This is so perfect," she said.

"And it's too small for you," I told her.

"Some people have to leave everything they know to discover who they
are," she said, giving Tariq a hard push in his swing.

"I don't think you ever leave everything you are," I told her. "Maybe
you didn't pack it in your suitcases, but believe me it's right there with you."
Serena looked at me like she didn't expect me to say something like that,
and I told her, "There's nights when I still hear my mama giving me a
lecture about why I have to go to college. And warning me to trust myself
before any man. And sometimes I think about Jessica, especially when I see
how healthy the twins are. You know, I've even thought about that boy who
made me pregnant? Wondered what he was doing, where he is, and if he's

found as much peace as I have. The past never lets you go, never sets you free," I told her. "One way or another you're going to bump into it, trip over it, or feel it like a shadow." I pushed Tameka and said, "Remember when I told you that time at Winthrop that I didn't like who I was, that's why I wanted to keep the baby. Now I can see I was so young then I thought that girl was who I'd always be."

We pushed the kids in the swings a few more minutes and then went inside. We drank hot cider, and even though all Serena was talking about was leaving, I didn't feel sad, or like I'd miss her. She left around four o'clock, and I couldn't figure out why I felt so happy, so excited the next couple of days. I felt so good, even when I thought about not seeing her for a long time. Then I realized that it was because she'd left behind a little spark of her imagination, a little bit of her courage for me to live on while she's gone.

We named the baby Malika Rose. She was born right in this house, in the same bed where she was conceived. Sister Khadija is a midwife, and during the pregnancy she had me drinking special teas for anything that ailed me. We didn't use any medicines or drugs at all. This time I didn't feel like I was giving myself over to people who didn't really care about me, like when I had the twins in the hospital. This time my baby was born where she's going to live. Rasheed took Tameka and Tariq over to stay with Mama during my labor. And when he came back he sat in the bedroom to see his child being born. There were times with this baby I wanted to give up, my labor was so long. And it hurt real bad because we weren't using any drugs.

I kept thinking on the things Sister Khadija had told me to and praying to Allah. I could even see how beautiful my baby's face would be when I finally saw it. But it hurt. It didn't feel like there was much difference in the pains when they came. They were all sharp and long. Hard pains that dug into me and didn't want to let go, that made all the breathing exercises useless. And I didn't want to cry or scream because Rasheed was watching and I wanted him to be proud. And to think I'm strong. He was looking at me with no emotion on his face that I could see. Like he was trying as hard as me to control what he felt.

And then the pains stopped for a while and that was when I cried, because I was so tired and felt like my baby was holding me hostage to pain. The only thing I could see very well or hear was the clock, and I knew it had been fifteen hours since my baby started trying to move into this world. Rasheed wiped my forehead with a damp cloth, and because he was so close to me I got to see him clearly, and I saw that he'd been crying, too. I saw that even as he put a dry towel over the pillow beneath my head and tried to make me more comfortable, tears were streaming down his cheeks. I knew not to say anything. I couldn't even think of what to say if I'd had the strength right then. Maybe I'd have just said thank you. And when Sister Khadija came back into the room, my own tears had dried. And I was ready to bring my baby into the world. And two hours later I did.

Malika Rose is a good baby. She sleeps straight through the night and has an even, friendly disposition. Rasheed has shown me pictures of his mother, and Malika has her eyes. She's not like some babies who stare and stare and you can't tell if they really see or understand what they're looking at. When Malika Rose looks at you, you know she sees you. And her gaze kind of warms you up. She was chubby and very round when she was first born. Even had a double chin. But now she's slimming down and we can see she's going to be tall. Malika Rose has the eyes of a seer. Maybe that's what she will be.

I like children best when they're babies. I look at them then and think everything is possible. But as they get older, I fear for them and am filled with regrets for all the things they will want and never have, the things they will yearn for and lose before they are in their grasp. Then, too, I'm more confident of myself as mother to a baby than an older child. A baby's needs are so basic. The twins will be four next year. They're moving into a child-hood that is a never-ending change. And they are so many different children all at once—just when I feel like I know them, they become strangers quite suddenly again.

 I asked her to dye my hair the other night. Every time I look in the mirror these days, all I see is gray—in my beard, my mustache, my hair. She asked me why I wanted to dye it. Said she thought it was beautiful. "When I was your age I thought gray hair was pretty, too," I told her. "But that's 'cause it was on somebody else's head."

She laughed and looked at my hair like it was something she couldn't resist, saying, "Those silver strands make me imagine all the things you've done and seen."

"All I see in the mirror is endings and things I may never get a chance to do," I told her.

"I wanted you *because* you're older than me," she said, all serious and agitated. "Because I thought you'd teach me everything I figured you must know."

Her eyes were pleading in a quiet way. But they didn't stop me from telling her, "I know what I'm doing."

"You want to dye your hair because it makes you think about death."

"That's not true," I said, uncomfortable because she read me so well. "Mostly it makes me think about being helpless and needy and pitied the way my father was when he got old. It makes me feel angry, like the day I was in the park with the kids and this woman sits beside me and starts talking about how cute Tariq and Tameka are, and then says, 'I've got grandchildren, too.' If I dyed my hair maybe I wouldn't feel like every birthday just meant you becoming more of a woman and me becoming less of a man."

"But how will it change anything?"

"I'll feel like maybe I could live long enough to see my children grow up. Like I could live long enough to give you what you desire *and* what you need. Long enough for us to have a life, not just an interlude."

I don't know if she understood everything I said. I mean *really* understood. Understood as deeply as I felt everything I told her. But she must have because she stood up and draped the towel over my shoulders and started rubbing the dye in. I was surprised even to hear myself saying all those things. I'd told her what I'd sworn never to tell anybody. But because she's my wife, she'd know what I felt even if I never said a word.

I showed her the drawings I've done for the next house. It's gonna be another year or two before I start on it, but I'm thinking about it now. We're running out of rooms in this house already. And what with us wanting to have another child, we're going to need more space. I've been working on the drawings for the last couple of months, almost every night. I'll be sitting right here in my study and Aisha's over there in the corner feeding Malika Rose or maybe crocheting. She was rocking Malika Rose to sleep on her back when I asked her to look at what I'd done. I explained where everything would be. We talked about how many bedrooms we'd need and then about where I'd build it. We sat up a couple of hours talking about all that. Then I rolled up the drawings and told her I was going to build a house where we could be happy. "I just want a house," she said, "that's big enough for all of us to grow in. Build us a house where our children can become the people we want them to be," she said. "Build us a house where you can be their father and their friend. Where I can be their mother, your wife, and anything else I need to be."

Then she said she was tired and was going to bed. It was past midnight. I told her I'd be upstairs soon. But after she left the room I just sat there, afraid to go to bed, terrified of going to sleep because lately I've been having dreams about suddenly dying, or having a heart attack, getting real sick right in the midst of everything I wanted, losing it all before I could really call it mine.

THE VAMPIRE WHO DRINKS GOSPEL MUSIC

Peter Harris

"Psst . . . watch this man, this the good part. Watch how he sneak up on these bloods." In the glow from the movie screen, his silhouette swallows a handful of Jujy Fruits.

"Shhh! Man! I don't like nobody telling me the movie just 'cause they already seen it!"

"Okay, okay . . . don't get high blood pressure! I was just gonna describe him for you."

Across the theater a voice leaps from the dark toward the screen: "Don't trip on that sweet cape, you blood-sucking mama jamma!"

Everybody watching laughs, then screams, whistles, and applauds as the vampire stalks into the left side of the screen and starts silently toward the couple.

He wears a deep-green cape. With each step it puffs, as if a forest were breathing. A gold cross, hanging on a chain around his neck, bounces lightly against his chest. He walks like all vampires walk: smooth as Michael Jackson camel-walking, ghost-gliding, you know, like on their own self-cleaning conveyor belts. Camera cuts to shot of teenaged man and woman, standing at a bus stop. Naturally, they don't hear him. And even if they had seen him, they might have waited a heartbeat or two before screaming, in appreciation of his hip but tasteful rags (what vampire you know that don't dress his ass off? Cut to head-on full shot of the vampire.)

(He wears sharply creased, burgundy-colored gabardines. His shirt, tan, is buttoned all the way up. His tie, matching his pants and knotted with care, hangs evenly and is pinned by a gold tie clasp. And the cape—well, is a cape—has to be silk, maybe mixed with velvet, but definitely *silky*, because vampires simply do not wear rayon or Dacron or nylon or any other *tryons*. . . . His shoes are handmade of high-glossed leather, soft and ever so comfortable after centuries of creeping up on his victims. His 'fro is short, so it doesn't push at the wine-colored wool beret cocked right on his head. His beard is short and well kept. He is fairly handsome, in that grand William Marshall sort of way, except that his eyes are bloodshot and narrowed; his eyeballs are red, which throws off even the most admiring victim. Anyway, he only pauses long enough to size up his supper and give the audience in the theater the chance to check out his wardrobe. That done, he starts easing again. Cut to shot from behind vampire, toward the couple.)

"Turn around, fools! Turn around!" a girl hollers at the young couple on the screen, who are now kissing like they got all the time in the world. "Y'all can get that play later," she yells again. "And you better forget that bus; they ain't never on time no way!"

(The vampire grins, as if on cue, showing his fangs, of course they ivory-gleam. He pauses, feline and ready to wrap up this stalk. Suddenly gospel piano chords—low like when the preacher asks new members to come—begins playing in the background. The music plays louder. Then a choir—fifty voices compressed into one—sings.)

>　　　Ohhh . . . the evil we fear
>　　　from the depths of our soul
>　　　swallows our tears
>　　　leaves us old and cold
>　　　leaves us old and cold.
>
>　　　Ohhh . . . the evil we fear
>　　　from the depths of our soul
>　　　swallows our tears
>　　　leaves us old and cold
>　　　leaves us old and cold.

A boy sitting in the right wing of seats hollers: "They ass is grass now—here come that church music!"

"Well!" somebody yells from the other side.

(The vampire begins walking again, and the piano chunks with each step. The choir is moaning low. Everybody is holding their breath. The vampire spreads his cape. The light from the streetlight glints off his cross. Cut to close up of the couple. Smiling, they glance behind them, checking to see if anybody saw them kissing. Somebody saw them. Their eyes widen. Their jaws drop. They don't scream, though, having watched too many horror flicks of their own to know that screams don't work. They bolt, knowing also that neither one is religious enough to work no pure-d-goodness-magic on the brother, plus, observant as they are, they see that this cat already wears his own cross, and probably could quote Scripture, chapter, verse, and line, if asked.)

(So they don't waste time in panic; they just take the advice of the young narrator in the right wing of seats and turn to run. But of course it is too late. A shadow descends on them. Cut to close-up of vampire. He accelerates his glide into a sprint and clutches the couple before they can really rev up, and as the dude down front of the screen screams.)

"I bet he wish he lost that sister's phone number!"

(Cut to a meeting between our heroes: Candace Stallings, anthropologist and expert on African vampires; Shelby Holdin, sculptor of wood and metal, and friend of Candace, who's agreed to create sharp knives according to Candace's specifications, and Roger Dabney, Director of Public Relations for the police department. Candace is telling them the history of the vampire cult in Africa, whose members decided to check out where all those ships carrying so many men and women were going. They nominated Sechaba, the strongest of the young initiates, to be captured and travel on one of the ships. Cut to close-up on Candace.)

CANDACE: When he arrived in the Strange Land, he allowed himself to be enslaved. He learned the new customs of his people, and those of the people who thought they were his masters.

(Camera pans faces of Shelby and Roger. Cuts back to Candace.)

CANDACE (speaking quietly): Sechaba laughed at the masters' beliefs that vampires could be killed with sunlight and crosses. He became a preacher himself, and began wearing a gold cross, which he still wears.

(Cut to Roger.)

ROGER (who speaks hysterically): So how do we destroy him? If we can't hold a cross up in his face, if we can't open his coffin in the sunlight, how do we even know if he sleeps? And if he doesn't sleep, how are we going to slam one of Shelby's stakes into his chest?

(Close-up on Candace.)

CANDACE (in a warning voice): This is why Sechaba is such a menace. . . . But there is more than one way to destroy him. Remember I said he became a preacher. He was so inspiring, urging his people to remember Africa and resist slavery, that hundreds, thousands flocked to hear him speak.

He lived well, as a preacher, and as a vampire. But he developed a passion, a *need*, for the music of his choir.

(Cut to shot from behind Candace toward Roger and Shelby, who look at each other in surprise. Hold shot as they stare at Candace.)

CANDACE: He has grown dependent on gospel music. Literally it sustains him, as much as the blood he drinks. If he does not meditate on gospel music at least once a day, then he weakens and must sleep for twenty-four hours. If we can deny him that session, if we keep him from drinking the music, we can wrestle him to the ground and drive Shelby's knife through his heart. But remember . . .

(Camera pans to her face as she pauses.)

CANDACE: . . . we must be careful, because no doubt he has set up an elaborate sound system wherever he rests, complete with backup generators in case of power failures. Or in case someone—like us—discovers his secret and attempts to silence his sounds. . . .

"Psst . . . listen, I know you don't want to hear this. . . ."

"You right, man—"

". . . But ain't he bad? Almost make me want to be a vampire. Look at his crib. Listen to that system. Shit, he got speakers up the ying yang!"

"I know. I know. I can hear. Just don't be telling me what's coming next!"

(Sound of Shirley Caesar singing a gut-wrenching "No Charge" fills the room. Shot from the ceiling looks down onto the vampire sitting in a comfortable padded chair. Cut to close-up of a reel-to-reel tape recorder turning, then to the serene face of the vampire, eyes closed. Camera pans the room, stopping for a beat on original art by Romare Bearden, Elizabeth Catlett, Varnette Honeywood, Jeff Donaldson, sculpture by Winnie Owens, Joyce Scott, Ed Love, and photographs by James Van Der Zee, Jean Moutoussamy-Ashe, Gordon Parks, Roy Lewis. Music fades. Cut to vampire opening his eyes, a look of hazy, smiling satisfaction on his face. He gets up (camera pulls back). He walks over to the recorder and turns the off switch (camera faces his back).

SECHABA: Hmph . . . hmph . . . hmph.

(He turns to face the camera, which zooms.)

SECHABA (with conviction): I must get to Chicago soon and tell that woman how much I love that song.

(Fade.)

(Sound track: fiery gospel piano solo. Tambourines and organ chime in, stoking the pace. Camera is high over the highway, tracking a blue van, which exits and follows a winding road up a wooded hill. In the distance sits a compound of domed houses, which are enclosed in a fence made of stone shipped from Tanzania. The van pulls off the road about a mile from the compound. Cut to shot from inside rear of the van. Candace is behind the steering wheel. Shelby rides shotgun. Roger sits in the bench seat behind them. Candace cuts motor. Piano chords sound quietly. Cut to shot of all three of them through the right window. Candace looks at Shelby.)

CANDACE: Okay, hand me my knife and give Roger his.

(Candace flattens the sharp knife against her right cheek and holds it there.)

CANDACE: Sechaba is attending church in the city this morning. There's a Gospel Invitational Festival at the Real Glory Pentecostal Temple this weekend.

ROGER: My officers are there, but how will they know what he looks like?

CANDACE: Remember the gold cross. He always wears it outside his clothes.

ROGER: Hell, in a *church!* Everybody and their mothers wear crosses!

CANDACE: But not everybody's cross glows as the music gets louder. Your officers will be able to see the gleam. When they pick it up, they must radio us so we can be sure of his movements while we try to rip off his sound system.

(Cut to Real Glory Temple, which is rocking. Two choirs swaying behind the pulpit sing full blast. Pan the congregation. Stop on a sharp golden reflection from the front row. Sechaba sits, eyes closed, a cassette tape recorder sitting on his lap. He raises his right hand to testify.)

(Cut back to heroes standing outside of the locked gate in the fence. Shot is high behind them and includes the compound. The biggest domed house sits in the center of a grassy lawn. Smaller domes sit to right, left, and rear of the main house. Cut to close-up of Roger's hands on lock.)

ROGER (as he jiggles the lock): My officers say he's sitting right on the front row, swilling that sound like a baby breast-feeding.

(He pushes the gate and it swings open. He walks through, followed by Candace and Shelby, who closes the gate. Cut to shot facing them as they walk toward the domes.)

SHELBY: By the way, since when does a public relations expert know how to jimmy locks?

ROGER: Look, I haven't always typed seventy-five words a minute. When I was growing up, I had friends who had keys for fingers.

SHELBY: Well, your hands must be made from the same locksmith. Candace . . . won't Sechaba be taping the concert?

CANDACE: I'm sure. Even so, if we rip out his system here and leave enough of a mess, he'll get so mad he'll blow his high trying to figure out who busted him, and—

ROGER: And I intend to leave enough mess even Hattie McDaniel won't be able to clean up the pieces.

CANDACE: Wondering how he'll fix it will panic him more. We'll have to be patient, but in a few hours he'll be weak enough for us to confront him. Let's try that small dome there first.

(Cut to shot of dome to the right of the main house. It is made of the same stone as the fence. It has one wooden door and red-stained wooden slats on the roof. Round stained-glass windows are spaced evenly around the walls. The dome is as big as a two-car garage. Cut to head-on of our heroes striding toward the dome.)

SHELBY: That looks like his own chapel.

ROGER (sarcastically): Should we genuflect?

CANDACE: Sechaba is hardly a pope.

SHELBY: Look how he has designed his home. It must come from his memories of home.

(They reach the door, which Roger also opens. Camera stares into Sechaba's music study. The angle widens as they walk into the room. Utter quiet. Cut to tight shot of their faces.)

ROGER: Damn!

SHELBY: How can anybody with art like this suck people's blood?

CANDACE: This is the room. Roger, close the door and keep that walkie-talkie turned on.

(Roger closes the door. Camera backs off for a shot from their waists up.)

CANDACE: Roger, you do the walls. Rip off paneling. Smash speakers. Yank out wiring. I will find the tapes and unwind them and light matches to them in that fireplace. Shelby, you slice up the art and photos—

(Cut to close-up of the surprised artist.)

SHELBY: Candace! These are priceless.

(Cut to Candace.)

CANDACE: I'm sorry. You know I understand, too, but we've got to mess up the art to distract him and anger him even more. If you can't, I'll do it and you smash his tape recorders and turntables. But if you'd rather admire his collection . . .

(Cut to Roger walking toward one wall. He snatches a Bearden collage and kicks a hole into it.)

ROGER: Admire this!

(He turns to Shelby.)

ROGER: Listen, we aren't writing term papers here. This is a vampire's house we're in, not some art professor's.

(He turns and begins pulling at the paneling with the hammer he pulls from his sports coat pocket. Camera holds on his back momentarily. Cuts to Shelby staring at him. Then (as camera cuts to Candace) at the anthropologist, who does not smile. Camera follows Shelby's eyes to the cabinets holding the tape players and turntables and stacks of cassettes and reels.)

CANDACE (off camera): All right then. Those choirs will get hoarse soon enough.

(Cut to shot from ceiling, showing them ripping out walls, cracking tape casings, slashing art (except Shelby), flinging albums against the walls, stomping on tape players, yanking out wires from walls behind paneling, grinding unwound tape into the floor.)

(The bass of an organ is pumping loudly, slowly. The choir grunts in unison on the downbeat. Camera fades to Real Glory Temple, and there is an overlay of images: Roger, Candace, and Shelby careening throughout Sechaba's precious study, and the serene face of the vampire nodding to the music of the Gospel quartet shouting out an ad lib, which mixes with the slower music of the sound track. Finally the scene dissolves into a shot of the wrecked study, from the door. The music fades. The last sound is the quartet at Real Glory shouting, "Thank you, Jesus," and "Praise Him," clapping and sounding off of the appreciative testifying from the congregation. Voice of the preacher at Real Glory overlays the scene of Sechaba's study: "And if we all can't sing, my friends, we can all say Amen, can't we! We can all say yes, yes, yes, for the good music He can play through us. . . . (Camera pans the debris in the study.) . . . And what a perfect ending to our celebration. We, of course, want to invite anyone, who is not already, to become a member of Real Glory Temple. Please come now. Let the Lord glue all your pieces back together. Let Him, the Master Builder, reconstruct you into some blessed Temple yourself. . . .

(Fade.)

(Dark shot from the rear of Sechaba facing the door to his listening room. Choir sings low on the sound track.)

"Ding dong . . . Avon calling!" some dude yells from the left side of the movie house.

"He gon' need more than perfume when he see that room!" another voice on the right answers.

"Yeah . . . a dump truck!" somebody in the back suggests.

(Sechaba pushes open the door. The camera pans the wreckage. Cuts to close-up of his face. His eyes widen in surprise. He steps in and quickly looks to the shelves where he sees the cracked consoles and machines. He walks over to the shelves and cabinets. He bends to pick up a cracked reel, twisted tape dangling. Close-up on his slit eyes. The choir begins to moan.)

SECHABA: My Lord!

"He going to bite a whole choir now, behind all that mess," a deep voice cracks from the darkness in the middle of the movie theater.

SECHABA: My music . . . who desecrates my music?

(The vampire whirls toward the open door. He whimpers.)

SECHABA: My art . . . my art. . . .

(He steps toward the door and stumbles over the bent chassis of his amplifier and falls to one knee. He bows his head to his chest and clutches his cross.)

SECHABA: How evil can my people be? Who are they to raid my house and destroy priceless art and silence the sounds of my life? I deserve to live! I deserve to live!

(Camera cuts to shot from the door. Sechaba looks up into the camera. He rises and walks toward the door. He steps outside into dusk. Camera follows his look toward the orange sunset.)

SECHABA (voice rising in intensity): If you are out there—you who invaded my very history, disturbed my sacred communion with my ancestors— you . . . I will savor every sip of your life!

(Sechaba walks toward his home.)

(Camera cuts to Candace, Roger, and Shelby crouching in the bushes near the front gate of Sechaba's compound. They watch the vampire walk into the large domed building.)

CANDACE: I hoped he would be too angry and shocked to stalk tonight, once he saw his room. Roger, tell your officers to come and come strong, but come quietly.

ROGER (into his walkie-talkie): All units advance.

(Camera cuts to hundreds of officers, all carrying wooden stakes. They come through the gate and meet with the public relations director, the anthropologist, and the artist.)

CANDACE (in a low voice): Remember he is weakened but will struggle. We don't need heroes. So stay in groups of five.

(Cut to faces of the cops, then back to Candace.)

CANDACE: This is a real-life vampire who will suck your blood. This ain't the movies. Attack only in your groups.

(They begin walking quietly toward the vampire's house. Camera cuts to close-up of Sechaba staring at them through a crack in the curtains of his window. He's wearing the headphones of a Walkman tape recorder.)

"Still grooving on that gospel!" remarks a girl up close to the screen.

"He getting hungry, too!" a voice says from the back.

"Yeah, he only chipping on that tape!" she answers.

"Here come the main course then, walking right into the microwave."

(The camera remains on the vampire's face, as he hears the sound of the cops bashing in the front door. He turns around and faces the door of his room. Camera pans as he turns. Seconds later that door bursts open and the first five officers, waving sticks, rush toward him. Cut to Sechaba's hands turning up the volume on the cassette player attached to the waistband of his pants. Cut to his face. He bares his fangs, causing two of the cops to pause. Sechaba quickly grabs them and pushes them into the three others. Sound track is fast and furious. Quickly the vampire punctures the officer he holds in his right hand; the cop in his left hand faints. Sechaba lets them drop and stares at the other stunned cops surrounding him. Sound track drops to solo piano chording quietly.)

CANDACE (off camera): Grab his Walkman!

(Sechaba looks toward her face.)

SECHABA: So you . . . how do you know?

(He starts toward Candace, but the officers block his path. Sechaba stops. The cops stop, pointing their sticks at him. Camera cuts to Candace's face, framed through the shoulders of the cops.)

CANDACE: How long could you fight us, Sechaba? How long before the tape runs out, before you'd tire?

(Cut to vampire's hands turning down the volume on his tape player.)

SECHABA: I didn't catch that. What did you say?

CANDACE (exasperated): I *said* how long could you fight us, chump! How long before your music wears out?

SECHABA (smiling mysteriously): That would be quite a gamble, don't you think? Surely you don't think they could hold me for long.

(Cut to Roger.)

ROGER: Let's stop wasting time. I got a deadline to meet or my press release won't make tomorrow's paper.

(Cut to vampire.)

SECHABA: And would you volunteer to confront me?

(Cut to Roger, who trembles silently.)

(Cut to Candace.)

SECHABA (off camera): So we are stalled. Who are you, may I ask?

CANDACE: You may ask. . . .

"*Don't be so cold, girl,*" *a sister signifies from the back of the theater.*

CANDACE: But I am no fool. My name is unimportant. I know *your* name. And your secrets. And I'm prepared to become your nightmares.

(Cut to vampire snarling.)

SECHABA: My *nightmares?*

(He fakes a step toward Candace. The sound track blasts into action. The officers protecting her jab their sticks. But Sechaba whirls and surprises the cops behind him. He grabs two of their sticks, pulling the cops forward. He grabs their jackets. He throws one of the sticks into the cops in front of Candace. He uses the other one to batter the officers he now faces, pushing his way to the wall, where he turns and uses the cop as his shield. The action and sound track stop. Close-up of faces of the cop and vampire.)

SECHABA: Step forward, woman who is my nightmare. Or he dies sooner than later.

SHELBY (off camera): No, Candace. We have him now. You said he would weaken. Wait him out.

(The cop's sweaty eyes beg for rescue.)

SECHABA: Yes, *Candace!* Wait until I weaken. Then you can deliver my final blow. You alone know all my secrets—don't you?

(Cut to Candace)

CANDACE: I know what I need to know. The rest I'll learn watching you wither into dust!

(She steps forward and stands shoulder to shoulder with the officers who'd stood in front of her. Silence.)

(Cut to Sechaba. He jerks the cop's head to one side and stares at his neck.)

SECHABA (as he prepares to bite the cop): Can you learn from this?

(Close-up on cop's face. He's trembling, whimpering. Cut to his right hand, which moves along the vampire's waistband, finding the cassette player. He yanks it free and pulls till the headphones slide off Sechaba's ears. Cut to vampire. His eyes widen. He drops the cop, grabbing for his headphones. Sound track heats up. The cop falls and rolls toward the Walkman. He grabs it and flips it blindly into the advancing officers. Cut to vampire. His face shows fear, anger, desperation. He grabs two more cops but is quickly overrun by others. They sit on his arms and legs and clamp a stick crossways into the vampire's mouth. Cut to Candace standing over the vampire, who strains to push off the cops. Theme music quiets; solo piano plays in the background.)

CANDACE: Shelby, bring me your knife.

(Cut to Shelby, walking shakily toward the anthropologist.)

SHELBY: Let me use my own knife, Candace. I made it.

(Cut to Candace.)

CANDACE: This is not chemistry lab, you know. We aren't about to dissect a frog. You could barely break a vase.

SHELBY (beside Candace, staring at the vampire with awed disgust and fear): He's no statue. Just tell me what to do.

CANDACE: We must stab his heart together. But first . . .

(Candace reaches into the pocket of her jacket. She pulls out another cassette tape and a portable cassette player. She puts the tape in and presses the play button. In the silence before the sound, cut rapidly to Shelby, Roger, Sechaba, randomly from cop to cop, then back to Candace. Camera follows her look into the vampire's face as her voice comes out of the tape recorder.)

VOICE OF CANDACE: When face to face with evil, who is fearless? Who does not wish for the safety of childhood or the embrace of a lover? We face evil now, evil so powerful it finds nourishment on sound that we make to honor all we believe is most sacred. But we stop the music right now. And replace it, replace it with a strong antidote, replace it right now with the sound of . . . funk. . . .

(Cut tight to Sechaba's face, as the finger-popping bass line jumps out of the tape, followed by rap lyrics.)

> I say hey hey hey
> say a brand-new day is here
> I say hey hey hey
> heard there's beaucoup evil here
>
> But we come right now
> 'cause we got to get down
> on ghosts, devils, and fear
>
> don't even mind
> not one little bit
> if there's a jivetime vampire here
>
> when goblins, pimps/other nasty fools
> decide to come around
> count on us
> to be on the scene
> making everything safe and sound
>
> ain't nothing on earth
> we like better
> that'll make us rap and shout
>
> than breaking down
> with any kind of fellas
> that's turning vampire lights out
> that's turning vampire lights out

(Cut to Candace, who's nodding and moving her shoulders in time to the music, her eyes closed in private prayer. Cut to vampire, who's shouting to drown out the rap music. Cut back to Candace and Shelby from chest up.)

CANDACE: Now, Shelby . . . now!

(They raise their knives and slam into the vampire. Sound track: driving gospel organ, tambourines, drums, choirs screaming, then fading, and the sound of the choirs at the Real Glory revival mix in. Cut to vampire, his face first in pain, then serene. Sound track quiets to choir moaning and organ droning. Candace looks at Shelby.)

SHELBY: Candace, I thought you hated rap music.

CANDACE (pausing and smiling slowly): Maybe I won't buy it . . . but when you plan a party, if you're going to party to *death*, you got to play the right music. . . .

(Freeze on her smile/up rap music.)

"You wait," a dude bent on the last word pronounces from down front. "The next flick, the vampire be rappin' hisself, once he get his teeth fixed!"

Laughter ripples across the theater. The lights brighten.

SNAPSHOTS OF

GRACE

Safiya Henderson-Holmes

First picture: black and white, slightly out of focus

A white room, white sheets on three narrow white beds, a black female's body on the third bed, a white light in a black window, a long black arm lifting toward a white ceiling, a long white tube running beside the long black arm; no resistance from the attached black hand. The hand is swollen, black fingers bent, as if begging to come down. A black face slightly out of focus.

Second picture: color, close-up

Grace is five, tall, cinnamon-brown, black eyes, head full of thick black hair. Grace looks at herself in her mama's bedroom mirror. She smiles, sticks out her tongue, puffs her cheeks, lifts her arms over her head, spins, stops, shakes herself out, puts her hands on her waist, spins, stops, picks up the hem of her blouse, holds it tightly, then, slowly, as if not at all, she raises her blouse over her navel, slowly, feeling her mama's Florida water scent touch her stomach, slowly rise to her ribs. Grace smiles, her blouse is above her chest, two perfectly round, perfectly mahogany-brown circles stare at her. Grace touches the left, then the right; she giggles in her hands and runs from her mama's bedroom mirror.

Third picture: black and white, overexposed

White walls, black metal doors, fifty black metal chairs in ten neat rows. A handsome black woman dressed in black, white lace shawl around her shoulders, white beaded barrette in her black hair, sits in the third row, third seat. Every now and then she looks up from her newspaper to smile at an old black man dressed in white, who is humming in the seat next to her.

"Number twenty-nine?"

The handsome black woman pulls her shawl closer, opens her left hand, looks at a folded white card that she's held for an hour.

"Number twenty-nine?"

The handsome black woman stands, excuses herself by the humming black man dressed in white, and a sleeping white woman dressed in black.

"Number twenty-nine?"

"Yes."

"Medicaid, Medicare?"

"No."

"Blue Cross, Blue Shield?"

"Ah, I'm under my husband's plan and . . ."

"Have you been here before?"

"Ah, yes."

"You have your clinic card?"

"No."

"You know the number?"

"I'm sorry, I really didn't plan on coming here today."

"I know the feeling. Go into the third room on your left, a doctor should be with you shortly."

"The third room?"

"Yes."

"Good, three's my lucky number."

"You should play it."

Fourth picture: color, group shot

"Mama, am I gonna have real big titties like you and Mrs. Warren?"

"Don't be so loose with your mouth, Grace, say breast. Cows got titties, dogs, cats, pigs, goats, human bein' women have breasts. Say breast, chile."

"Everybody else say titties, Mama. Geraldine's mama lets her say titties and a lot of other stuff, you shoulda heard what Geraldine said about Mrs. Warren's titties."

"Grace, what did I say, and hold your head still so I get this part straight."

"Geraldine said that her mama said that Mrs. Warren use to have itty-bitty breast, but too many men sucked on them and made them just too big."

"Grace Bowman! If you don't stop with that kind of talk around here, this mornin', so help me, I'll beat you blue with this hairbrush!"

"Yes, ma'am, but, Mama, I don't want real big breast hangin' down to my feet and stuff. I won't be able to sleep like that, Mama."

Fifth picture: color, group shot

Grace is hot. Sweat and watermelon mix with the spit and bubble gum in her mouth.

It will soon be her turn on the swing. Grace is going to pump Charlene. Charlene is fat, olive-brown, silver wires on her teeth. Grace is the only willing pumper Charlene has. Grace can take the weight.

"Your turn, Gee."

Grace takes a big bite of watermelon; it's sweet, juicy, running all over her blouse. She feels cool. Her friends call her Gee, her mama calls her Grace, her daddy died before she was named.

"Gee, you gotta go way pas' that fence and make your head touch the middle branches of that big tree. Paulette did it already, so you gotta do it, or else she's the winner and you gotta give her a nickel to buy an icy."

"I don't have to give her nothin'." Grace licks her lips, wipes her hands on her blouse, spits, takes Charlene's hand, and they mount the swing.

"You ready, Charlene?"

"Uh-huh, but ain't you gonna button your blouse?"

Grace bends her knees, the swing sways, she bends again, harder, coming up straighter, going down real low, up again. Grace and Charlene are part of the sky. Grace's blouse splays behind her like wings.

"Hey, Geeeeee!" from far, far away.

Grace bends, straightens, bends, straightens.

"Hey, button your blouse, girl, we can see all your titties!"

Grace squeezes the chains of the swing tight, squints at a sea of pointing fingers and wide laughing mouths; throwing her head back, she bends, straightens, bends, shouts, "Your mama's!" and flies away.

Sixth picture: black and white, I.D.-sized photo

A young white female doctor dressed in white, a black stethoscope and white pearls around her neck, a black pen in her blouse pocket, a white ribbon in her black hair, white hands holding a black folder, smile needing lipstick but settling for importance, enters a small white room where a handsome black woman dressed in black, white lace shawl around her shoulders, white beaded barrette in her hair, sits.

"I'm Dr. Friedman, and you're?"

"Grace, Grace Williams."

"Great, I have the right chart."

"We're in business." The handsome black woman sits in a soft black chair next to a black metal desk; the chair has a high, reclining back, but she doesn't lean. She removes her shawl, folds it on her lap, places her newspaper on top, crosses her legs, ignores a fly on her left wrist.

The young white doctor removes her stethoscope, reads the white papers in the black folder, sits in a small white metal chair. "So, you were here a year ago?"

"Yes, about that."

"It says here that you were examined last February by Dr. Brewster."

"Yes, February."

"He wanted you to come right back in for some test."

"Yes, a biopsy."

"Right, but you didn't come back?"

"Ah, no."

"Did you have it done elsewhere?"

"Ah, no, I didn't." The handsome black woman leans into the soft black chair, waves a fly from her eyes.

The young white doctor taps the black metal desk with her pen, replaces her stethoscope, stands, walks over to a white sink, washes her hands, then each finger, shakes them dry. "A year, huh. Any pain, discomfort?"

"A dull kind of pain, just sometimes."

"Discharge?"

"It's probably nerves, but last month I noticed a slight something coming from the left one. I don't know."

Seventh picture: color

"Grace, baby, you shouldn't be ashamed or afraid, it's the cycle of a woman's life, it helps clean you out."

"I ain't a woman, and I ain't dirty."

"Don't say *ain't*, Grace."

"But I'm not."

"Sugar pie, not like street dirt, like inside your body dirt, Grace, like when you have dirty blood or dirty body juices, yeah, like dirty body juices; that body cycle thing just comes on down like a big rain and washes all that bad, dirty blood away and that keeps you healthy."

"But I'm not sick, Mama. And you know how sometimes you tell me to wash my mouth out with soap, I do it, and how you tell me to scrub real good down there with plenty of warm sudsy water, I do that, Mama."

"I know, Grace, but this is somethin' else altogether."

"I change my underwears every day, I ain't sick or dirty nowhere down there, Mama, so I don't need it."

"You do need it, sugar pie."

"How come Charlene don't need it?"

"Charlene needs it, she just don't have it yet."

"God, that ain't fair."

"Don't use the Lord's name in vain, Grace."

"I ain't, Mama, I really mean, Dear God, it ain't fair for me to bleed and for Charlene not to, and I'm not tellin' anybody. . . . Please, Mama, don't tell anybody."

Eighth picture: black and white

A young white female doctor dressed in white examines the soft black breast of a handsome black woman dressed in black. The doctor cups each breast, walks her white fingers gently around the soft black breast.

The handsome black woman follows the doctor's fingers with her breath.

"Can I ask you something?" A perfectly white pearl rests atop a perfectly black breast.

"Yes."

"Why didn't you come back in and see about yourself?"

The handsome black woman holds her breath, releases it. "It was a busy year, work, my mother was very ill."

"Oh, I'm sorry, is she better now?" The white fingers stop underneath the left breast.

"She died in August."

"I'm sorry." The white fingers lie quietly beside the soft black breast on the left.

Ninth picture: color, flowers in a vase

Grace looks at herself in her mama's bedroom mirror, puts her hands on her waist, turns left, right, drops her hands, sucks her teeth and slowly unbuttons her blouse. "Mama? Mama? Ooooh, Mama, I really, really need a bra."

Tenth picture: color, birds in a park

"Geraldine's is padded, I seen it."

"Well, mines ain't, I don't need pads."

"Me neither."

"You sleep in yours?"

"Uh-uh. You?"

"Uh-huh. My mama does, too. She says that way they'll never sag and you'll look good for your man."

"Really?"

"Uh-huh. My mama even got some with wires in 'em, those are real good."

"Wires where?"

"Right under the titties and on the side. When my mama wears that, look out! She be standin' right up there."

"God! Charlene, what will happen if one grows crooked or bigger than the other or somethin'?"

"I don't know."

"God, I sure don't want crooked titties."

"Me neither. How would we get a husband then?"

"I don't know."

"Stuff our bras with somethin'?"

"Yeah, I guess."

"Yeah!"

Eleventh picture: black and white

A white narrow bed, a black female body on a white narrow bed, a white sheet over the black body, a black breast exposed. Six white hands walk gently around the exposed black breast, one white hand holds a thin white blade, the blade cuts the soft black breast, making it cry.

Twelfth picture: color

"Grace Louise! You get your tail in this house right this minute!"

"He started it!"

"I don't care if Satan himself started it. You don't be fightin' with boys! Now get in here!"

"But, Mama, he . . . !"

"No *buts!* Next thing you know he will have knocked you in your chest or stomach and messed you up for life. Now get in here!"

Thirteenth picture: black and white, overexposed

A soft black breast is crying, its tears are icy white, thick. Two white hands catch the tears in an icy white bowl, place the bowl under an icy white light, examine the tears with the point of a long, shiny black pen. The soft black breast is still crying.

Fourteenth picture: black and white

A young white female doctor dressed in white stands over a handsome black woman's body dressed in black, on a narrow white bed. The young doctor rubs the cheek of the handsome black woman. "Mrs. Williams, you've got a rather large mass in your left breast."

The handsome black woman closes her eyes. "That's what they told me last year. I guess—I guess all year I was hoping it would disappear or move down to my big toe or something."

The doctor sits on the narrow bed. "Grace, you have a smaller one in your right breast, too."

"So what did it have, a baby?" The handsome black woman covers her face with her white lace shawl. The doctor holds her hand.

Fifteenth picture: color, glossy finish

"How do I look, Mama?"

"Oh, Grace, honey, you look just like one of them models."

"Mama, this is the prettiest dress you've ever made for anybody!" Grace turns on her toes in front of her mama; two purple beaded barrettes in her hair, a dress of lavender lace, black patent-leather shoes, pearl earrings, pearl necklace. "I swear, Mama, I never imagined lookin' this pretty, ever!"

"You'll be the prettiest girl at the prom."

"Oh, Mama."

"And I like the way that bra carries you."

"Uh-huh."

"Sometimes us full girls have a problem gettin' a good fit, but we got one this time."

Grace turns on her toes. "Oh, Mama."

"You make sure one of them picture-takin' people get some good pictures of you. I'll put it up on the dresser, and when folks come in for their fittin' and things, they'll see you, sittin' there next to all those spools of thread, and say, 'Why, Gloria, you make beautiful children, too!' "

Sixteenth picture: black and white

A soft black breast cries icy white tears onto a whiter sheet; the tears are many, falling onto a narrow white bed, then onto a shiny black floor. Two white hands pick up the tearful breast, a third white hand holding a white light enters the soft black breast, exits, enters again with a thin white blade. The blade goes deep into the soft breast, pricking its inner edges. Many icy tears cover the thin white blade and hand, the hand exits, enters again with a tiny white straw. The straw sucks up the icy white tears of the soft black breast, puts them into a small white jar, leaving the crying breast wide open, exposing a bit of its nerves and muscles.

Seventeenth picture: color

Grace is sixteen; she has a friend named Ben. Ben is seventeen, copper-brown, taller, more muscle in his arms, more time in his eyes, more gut in his strut than any other young man Grace has known. Ben is grown and Grace fries chicken for him, bakes him apple pies, has made him seven shirts, knitted him three wool scarves and two wool caps. Grace loves Ben.

Ben buys Grace roses and fancy beads and barrettes for her hair, has taught her how to whistle, throw a dart, and spin a basketball on her finger. He has made her two sewing boxes, three stools, a bookshelf, and has carved her a small wooden comb. Ben loves Grace.

One day after school Ben and Grace meet. Ben puts a red beaded barrette in Grace's hair. Grace gives him a pie. They walk three blocks to Ben's older brother's house, climb three flights of stairs to a room that smells of peaches; a mattress covered with a yellow sheet is on the floor, a red radio and a black Bible sit on a blue glass table, the walls are pale pink and the windows look out upon a park.

"This is our place, Grace."

"God, Ben."

Ben sits on the mattress, holds out his arms for Grace. Grace folds her arms across her chest, looks at the red radio, black Bible, blue glass table, smiles, sits in Ben's arms.

Ben kisses the nape of Grace's neck, tip of each shoulder, lobe of each ear, cheeks, lips. Grace closes her eyes. Ben's kisses find Grace's breast, and the smell of peaches is everywhere.

Eighteenth picture: black and white, still life

"C'mon, put your clothes on and let's just talk about a few things."

"Well, I know now I'll need some sort of surgery, which means I'll need time off from work again. I'm sure my department head will love that, and Sarah, poor Sarah, she's the only one whose hours seem to work well with mine."

"Ah, Grace . . ."

"Now, Marilyn may do it, but, I don't know, she's been acting strange ever since I got this bit of a promotion."

"Can I help with your zipper or something."

"No! I—I can do it, this is my favorite dress, but it always gets stuck."

The handsome black woman puts her long black arms into the sleeves of a black dress. "Maybe Harriet, but she's not very good with large classes, and I hate the way she teaches biology! Hey, I've never said that before!"

"Grace, please, let's sit down and talk."

"When do I have to come in? Could we schedule the whatever for, say, for Thursday, then with a couple of days' rest I can go back in on Monday."

"I know it's a lot to think about, but we . . ."

"God! Ben's birthday party, I haven't even called the first person yet." The handsome black woman bites her lips, walks toward a black chair, sits. "And my daughter—ah, she graduates from college in three days. I really can't come in before that, not even if they're malignant." The handsome black woman, dressed in black, white lace shawl around her shoulders, white beaded barrette in her hair, sits in a high-back black chair, tracing the lacy pattern of her white shawl with her fingers. "I never felt anything in the right one."

"Grace, we can do the biopsy today."

"My dissertation is on women and—"

"Grace."

"Oh, God, why can't I scream about this."

Nineteenth picture: color, group shot, fading handwriting around a narrow white border

"Black people in this country have every right to the full benefits of this country," Grace shouts into a bullhorn. Ben and Charlene encourage passersby to join a picket line. "We cleared this land, probably this very spot that this Jewels' Department Store occupies was plowed and planted and picked by some of y'all's family, maybe Mr. Jewels himself had a black woman in his home, cookin' and cleanin' for him and his family." Grace walks among a large black crowd in Birmingham, Alabama; she wipes sweat from her lips, neck. Ben takes her picture, kisses her, gives her a cup of water, a pat on the back. "Now this here Jewels' Department Store boasts about bein' the store with the most black workers, but good ol' Jewels' doesn't let a single one of those black workers eat their lunch in the store, or wash their hands, or use the phones, or use the toilets. The black workers of Jewels' got to go elsewhere for all that. And we're here today to say that those ways cannot stay."

Policemen with helmets, guns, water hoses, and dogs surround the large black crowd.

Charlene motions for Grace to be quiet.

Grace shouts, "This here Jewels' Department Store is not worth the pot that it refuses to let black people piss in!"

Barking dogs, screams, blood cover Grace.

Twentieth picture: black and white

A soft black breast with its nerves and muscles exposed lies on a white sheet. A white hand with a long, thin black needle approaches the soft black breast, the needle finds a nerve and pierces it. The breast becomes flat, a white hand holding a pair of long white scissors begins cutting away the skin of the soft black breast.

Twenty-first picture: black and white

A handsome black woman dressed in black, white lace shawl around her shoulders, white beaded barrette in her hair, sits in a black chair, in a small white room, tracing the lacy pattern of her shawl with her fingers, wondering how many women have sat in the same chair, same room, what colors were they, what colors did they wear, ages, sizes, names.

"Grace, we can do the test today. That way we can know what's up." A young white female doctor dressed in white chews on a black pen. "I mean, I will take the specimen to the lab myself, wait on it, and maybe you could be home in a few hours."

"A few hours?"

"At least we'll know something then, Grace."

"Yes, today."

Twenty-second picture: color, roses everywhere

"Ben Williams, do you take this woman, Grace Bowman, to be your lawfully wedded wife, to have and to hold, for better or worse, for richer or poorer, in sickness and in health, for as long as you both shall live?"

"I do."

Twenty-third picture: color, more roses

"I sure love snugglin' right here in the middle of 'em."

"You sure do."

"Like to feel 'em on my cheeks and nose, so soft and warm."

"I like it best when you touch 'em with your fingertips real slow, like . . ."

"Like this?"

"Yeah, especially the left one."

Twenty-fourth picture: black and white

A handsome black woman dressed in black sits alone in a small white room; her legs are crossed, hands folded on her lap. She watches the walls move and listens to her breath as it dries her lips.

Twenty-fifth picture: black and white

The skin of a soft black breast lies on a white sheet. Two white hands, one holding a white light, the other a thin black blade, encircle the soft black breast. The thin black blade begins to cut muscle away from bone.

Twenty-sixth picture: color, butterflies in a net

"C'mon, sugar, you can do it, you can do it, push that baby out, c'mon now, c'mon, we wanna see what you been hidin' in there."

"You're doing fine, Grace."

"Am I—oh, God, another one! Aheeeeee!"

"Breathe it through, no screaming, just breathe it through."

"Yeah, honey, you can do it. C'mon, I don't care what you give me."

"Aghhhhh!"

"Push with this one, Grace."

"Go on, sugar."

"Aghhhhh!"

"Good, Grace, one more push like that, and I think you and your husband will have yourselves a baby."

"Oh, God. Aha, ah, ah, ah, ah, aghhhhhh!"

"C'mon, sugar, oooh, Grace baby, I see the head, I see the head!"

"Great, now just keep pushing, Grace, don't let the baby slip back up. Keep pushing, Grace, c'mon, c'mon, c'mon, okay, here comes your baby!"

"Ben?"

"It's a girl, sugar, a pretty, fat, healthy girl, she's fine, Grace."

"Here, Grace, let your baby nurse while I look and see what the damage is, if any."

"Oh, my God, my breasts are bigger than her head!"

Twenty-seventh picture: black and white

Underneath the muscle of a soft, black breast are rows of porcelain white bones, underneath the bones a fast-beating heart.

Twenty-eighth picture: black and white, underexposed

A handsome black woman dressed in black, white lace shawl around her shoulders, sits in a black chair, in a small white room. The walls of the room have gone around her several times.

A young white female doctor dressed in white, a black stethoscope and white pearls around her neck, a black pen in her blouse pocket, white ribbon in her black hair, her smiles needing lipstick to hide a dark spot, settles for sigh, enters the small white room where the handsome black woman sits. "Grace, I got the results back, and I'm sorry, the . . ."

"Shhhhh!" The handsome black woman stands, walks quickly toward a white sink, opens her mouth wide, filling the sink with tiny black pieces of herself.

Twenty-ninth picture: color, roses in a vase
"Daddy sure loves buying people flowers."
"He's gonna go broke one day from the roses alone."
"If you think this is something, wait till you see the house, and at graduation, I needed a shopping bag just to bring home Daddy's flowers."
"I'm sorry I missed your graduation."
"Oh, Mama, c'mon, you see one graduation, you've seen them all."
"But I know your father sat right up front and took a zillion pictures."
"Yep, and I did miss taking one with you."
"Oh, you did, did you? I guess some graduations are different?"
"Yeah, I guess."
"Aisha, now you know what I'm gonna ask, so don't go getting upset."
"Oh, Mama."
"Don't 'Oh, Mama' me either. Did you wear a bra? Your father is going to send some of those pictures to his folks, and you know how they are."
"I bet you been sittin' here in this bed the whole time worrying about that."
"Never mind what I been worrying about. Did you?"
"Yes, Mama, I did. Now, do you think you can relax, please?"

Thirtieth picture: black and white
Two soft black breasts lie on a white sheet, one is flat and quiet like a closed eye, the other, full, staring at a white light in a black window as if to challenge it, to a fight.

SURVIVING

CHRISTMAS

Kristin Hunter

Boldly she wore the ring to her shop the next morning on her right hand.

It was conspicuous as a spotlight, but B.J., bent over her worktable and writing with painful concentration, did not notice it. She picked up the top envelope from the completed stack at his left, turned it over and studied it critically. It was neatly addressed, in a round, clear, childish hand, to Mrs. Edward Cosgrove at the Valley View Apartments.

"Those are the thank-you cards," he said without looking up through his thick lashes. "They're all finished. I left 'em unsealed in case you wanted to write something on 'em. I'm doing the Christmas cards now."

"Christmas cards?" she asked blankly, as if she had never heard of such things.

His hand darted into an opened box on his right, plucked out an envelope, then shoved the box toward her for inspection.

B.J. had chosen well. The card was not gaudy and not ordinary either, yet it was clearly not cheap. It pictured a golden partridge in a tree dripping with golden pears, and was suggestive of opulence and sophistication, but not blatantly so.

Inside its single fold was a one-word message: *Greetings*. Nothing more; nothing religious to offend the various creeds of her customers.

"You like it?" he asked without looking up.

"Very much. I couldn't have chosen a better one myself."

Her next remark was a surprise attack. "How much money do you have left in your bank now, B.J.?"

"Enough," was his non-answer.

"How much money did you have before I went to the hospital?"

"Hey, look what you made me do, asking all them questions." He held up a smeared envelope, then tore it up. "Now I got to write this one all over again."

He was trying to distract her, and she knew it. "Stop writing a minute, B.J. I want to talk to you."

"I got to get these done in time to take 'em to the post office. It's December twenty-first *already*," he grumbled.

"B.J., *they can wait*," she said in her no-more-nonsense tone of voice.

"Okay," he said reluctantly, and swiveled in the chair to face her.

"I asked you how much money you had left in your bank, and how much you'd spent."

"I don't know exactly. I had a lot once. Now I got five or six dollars left, I guess. The cards were twelve-fifty. Ten for the Christmas cards and two-fifty for the thank-yous. I bought 'em with your money, but if you think they cost too much, tell me what you wanted to spend and I'll make up the difference."

"I'm not worried about the cards," she said, conscious that he was dodging the issue. "They're worth whatever they cost. What I'm wondering is where you got the money to buy this."

She threw her fist at his face so suddenly he ducked. Then he saw the diamond.

His face contorted with rage. "But you promised!" he screamed. "You promised not to open it till Christmas!"

"You won't be around at Christmas, remember?"

"I know you mad about that, Miss Lena. Mom Boggs and Pop Earl would have invited you, but they was afraid you'd say no. They ain't got a nice house or nothing fancy. You're a high-class, refined lady, and they're just ordinary people."

"We're all ordinary people around here, B.J. Ordinary people who can't afford diamond solitaires."

"How you know it's a real diamond?"

"I know," she said quietly. "I've seen enough real jewels to tell them from fakes. Where did you get it?"

"I bought it."

"Where?"

"I promised I wouldn't tell. But I bought it with my own money."

"I don't believe you. Prove me wrong. Show me the sales slip."

He shook his head. "I can't. I ain't got none."

"Of course not, because you didn't buy it."

"I didn't buy it in a *store!*" he shouted.

"Where did you buy it, then?"

He was silent.

"I think you stole it, and you know how I feel about stealing. If you don't tell me who you stole it from right now, I'm going to call the police, and they'll *make* you tell."

His face, faded from black to ashen gray, looked older than when she had first seen it. His voice was choking. "I just wanted to give you something nice instead of some old dumb junk like toilet water or costume jewelry. But the trouble is, you don't trust nobody. Maybe you can tell real jewelry, but you can't tell when people are faking and when they're real." Looking up at the ceiling as if addressing an invisible third party, he complained, "Aah, what's the use talkin' to somebody who don't believe nothin' you say? Ain't no use. No use at all."

She thought he was crying as he ran out the door, but he moved so swiftly she could not be sure if she had seen wet spots on his ashy cheeks.

She followed him, holding his hat and coat. "It's cold out, B.J.!" she called. "Come back! You forgot your jacket."

But the street was empty of both pedestrians and traffic, and eerily silent as it whitened swiftly with the winter's first snow. No one answered.

Well, good riddance, she said to herself. He was nothing but trouble anyway.

But the echo of her own lecture was still ringing in her ears as it must have sounded to his. Already it seemed pompous, self-righteous, perhaps even grossly unfair. She was still standing just inside the door, foolishly holding the hat with its earflaps and the warm plaid jacket. She laid them carefully on a chair. He would be back for them, she told herself, as soon as his temper cooled. She would apologize for her barrage of accusations and ask him again, gently this time, to explain about the ring. This time he would tell her the whole story, and she would believe him. She twisted the ring on her finger as if it had magic powers to bring him back and make it happen.

But the day lengthened and grew even quieter, the snow continued to fall, and B.J. did not appear. Nor did anyone else. She peered at the calendar, saw no squiggles or doodles in the block labeled Friday, and concluded that she had no appointments today. She might as well leave.

But there *was* that stack of cards to be finished and mailed. Calling on her self-discipline not to desert her now that B.J. had, she sat down and resolutely addressed herself to the task.

Almost immediately she knew she needed B.J. She spread out the thank-you cards and stared at them. She could not remember which women had brought her which gifts. She had to settle for an all-inclusive phrase—"Thank you for your thoughtfulness"—which she wrote on each card before signing her name.

Addressing the Christmas cards required even more discipline. For her, it was always the most depressing chore imaginable, but this year it shrouded her in an extra blanket of gloom. Her reluctance made it slow work. When the last envelope was sealed, the room had begun to grow dark, and there was still no sign of B.J. She had just enough time to mail the cards. She pulled on her boots, closed up her shop, and headed toward the post office. Afterward she would go straight home and make some cheerful holiday plans. She would not waste another minute of her life running after that wayward child.

But it seemed she had forgotten how to enjoy herself alone. It had happened so insidiously, she had not realized she was growing accustomed to constant companionship, to lively questions that required answers, to keen ears that listened, and a quick mind that responded even when she was talking to herself. Her cozy apartment no longer comforted her, and her gadgets did not invite her to pleasure. Side by side, the television and the eye-level oven stared at her with blank, doleful eyes like an idiot's. Before she might begin to cry.

She dialed the hospital and asked for Mamie. It seemed that Mamie was out to lunch. On the Friday before Christmas, everyone was always out to lunch. Whenever you really needed people in this world, they were out to lunch. Or out to shop, or celebrate, or fornicate, or something.

Feeling herself grow hysterical, Miss Lena pulled herself up rigidly and asked herself: since when had she needed anyone? People were nothing but a plague. If she didn't keep them at a distance, they'd infect her with their idiocy.

But that philosophy, which worked for her so well the rest of the year, would not help her get through the dreadful, artificially cheerful holidays. She called Leroy at home.

He was just finishing his packing. "Child, why didn't you call me sooner? I might have been able to do something even last night, but today there isn't a seat left on any plane. I just tried to get one for another friend of mine. I'm so sorry, but I've got to dash to the airport now."

He'd tried to sound disappointed and sympathetic, but there was no disguising the undertone of elation in his voice. In an hour he'd be airborne, his plane nosing toward the coast of another continent. He was already anticipating a week of new experiences: new scenery, a new climate, new foods, new friends.

As for the other so-called friends who had crowded into her shop a few weeks ago, where were they now? Packing for honeymoons, rehearsing their weddings, or busy decorating and provisioning their already cozy nests. Buying gifts to stuff like pack rats into the void of loneliness that ached worse on December 25th than on any other day of the year. Filling that hollow place to the brim would insure that on this one day they would be surrounded by a close circle of love and gratitude, however distant and indifferent the circle might be on all the other days. Any other time, people could stand loneliness, indifference, even hostility. But on December 25th, when happiness was practically required by law, even a circle of greed was better than none at all. If she called her married friends, they might take pity and make room for her at their holiday tables. But Miss Lena did not want charity. She was too proud to admit she was desperate—except to someone likely to be as lonely as she was.

She dialed Mamie at home and, miraculously, connected. The husky, familiar voice said, "Hello," as if it were saying, "Go to hell," on the third ring.

"What are you doing over the holidays?" Miss Lena asked.

"Trying to live through them, just like all the other lonely old bags. What else? I tried to get work straight through New Year's, but they didn't need me. So I'll just have to sit here and endure it. They'll need me after the first, though. The place always fills up with attempted suicides over Christmas. I just have to hang on for ten days and try not to be one of 'em."

"I thought you said you had children."

"*Grown* children, honey! The boys are overseas in the Army, and the girl's in California. They ain't about to fly all this way just to see an old lady."

"What about your gentleman friend?"

"Christmas is one time a married man's got to spend every minute with his family. Leaving me high and dry." She chuckled with the rich humor Miss Lena was sure would always keep Mamie from becoming a suicide statistic. "If I'm dry, how the hell can I be high? I sure wish I could afford to stay drunk the next ten days."

"How'd you like to get drunk with some company?"

"Who?"

"Another lonely old bag. Me."

Mamie pretended to hesitate. "You ain't exactly my type." There was a long pause, then a hearty chuckle. "But you'll do. Listen, no offense, I just meant I'd prefer to be with a man. You understand. The truth is, I'd go out with King Kong tonight, or *Mrs.* King Kong, for that matter, but I ain't had no offers from either of 'em. You look better than they do. Act better, too. Stay where you are. I'll be over as soon as I put on some glad rags."

Miss Lena had not planned to go out, only to offer Mamie the hospitality of her apartment and her food and wine hoard. But to keep her Christmas depression at bay, she was ready to do almost anything, even break one of her most basic survival rules: always stay home after dark, especially on weekends and holidays.

"Put on the finest thing in your closet. Maybe we can go out and stir up some action. If we can't, at least we ain't too old to dream."

Miss Lena searched her closets for something that would come up to Mamie's expectations. Though many of her neatly tailored business dresses were colorful, she was sure none of them would do. "Fine" meant sexy, gaudy, eye-catching. *Male* eye-catching.

She rooted in the box at the bottom of her closet where she kept her samples and pulled out the purple velvet minidress and matching shorts that had spent last October in her window. Well, why not? she thought recklessly. Her legs were at least as good as Mrs. Lewis's, if not better. Mrs. Lewis had borne children and was a quarter-century older besides. She hung the velvet outfit in the bathroom and turned the hot shower on full to steam out the wrinkles. Then, with wild inspiration, she used grape juice to dye a pair of panty hose to match and dried them in the cap of her hair dryer.

She was already so far out of character she decided to go all the way. She smeared her eyelids with purple shadow and purpled her lips as well. Then she doused herself with the gardenia cologne Miss Everett had given her.

When she opened the door for Mamie, both of them burst into spontaneous, mutually self-deprecating laughter. Mamie's large swollen feet were crammed into gold sandals, and her body was bursting the seams of an orange satin sheath that was so shiny it seemed fluorescent. Her breasts rose above its scoop neckline like a pair of floating coconuts, and she smelled like a hothouse full of gardenias.

"Lord, girl, I sure hope we can find us a couple of things in pants to pair off with quick! At least we smell the same. But—purple and orange! I never saw a worse clash of colors in my life.—Oh, what the hell, who's going to see us? It's dark as a cave in Susie's anyway."

"What's Susie's?"

"A nice place. You'll like it. Let's go." And here she went, blithely breaking another of her cardinal survival rules: *Never go into a bar unless escorted. And never, even then, unless it's a nice bar.*

Susie's met Mamie's criterion of a nice bar, but not Miss Lena's. She could hardly complain, since she had already broken Rule Number One: *Never be so desperate for company you're forced to lower your standards.*

Miss Lena's standards did not condone loud conversation; a jukebox that was just as loud, but drowned out none of the more offensive words; ragged linoleum floors with curling edges that provided a dangerous footing for high heels; or loose, tilted bar stools that threatened to dump their occupants. Not that her code let her sit on a bar stool anyway. Ladies, she believed, always sat at tables. Females who sat on bar stools were not ladies, she explained to Mamie. They were women asking to be picked up.

"Well?" Mamie demanded. "Why you think I brought you here?"

When Mamie also pointed out that most of the booths were already occupied by men sleeping off too many drinks, Miss Lena rapidly shed her ladyhood, climbed aboard a shaky stool, and tightly wound her purple-clad legs around its pedestal.

"What you drinking?" the young, sweet-faced barmaid asked.

Miss Lena, never a big drinker, said, "A glass of white wine."

"We ain't got nothin' but Tokay, sherry, and muscatel."

"We're both drinking champagne," Mamie declared imperiously.

Miss Lena reached hesitantly for her purse. Champagne was expensive. "I didn't bring much money with me, Mamie. I never carry much cash."

"You ain't s'posed to. Put that pocketbook away, fool. Don't you know those men down there are buying our drinks?"

"What men down where?"

Mamie nodded her massively bewigged head to the right. "Those two at the far end. They'll probably be over in a minute."

"That's what I'm afraid of."

"Afraid? Why? Don't tell me I'm out with a fifty-four-year-old virgin."

"Not exactly," Miss Lena said with a smile. "I've just lived like one for twenty years."

"Well, you better relax and act like you thirty-four again. 'Cause that's what age you look, and they been starin' at you ever since you walked in. It's them legs that did it, I think. Them crazy purple legs."

As her eyes grew accustomed to the dim lighting, Miss Lena recognized the two men: one of them tall, broad-shouldered, and lean-waisted, the other shorter, and as wide below as he was above. Earl Junior and his father.

She returned their raised-glass salutes and whispered, "I know them, Mamie."

"Well, that always helps. They don't look too bad. They favor each other. Are they brothers?"

"Father and son," Miss Lena said.

"No kidding. They both look to be in their forties."

"It's dark in here."

"Not too dark for them to see you. What ages are they, then?"

"I don't know them that well, but I'd say one's in his early thirties, and the other one's in his early fifties."

"Married?"

Miss Lena shrugged. "I think the father is. I don't know about the son."

"Who cares?" Mamie said gaily, draining her champagne glass. "They men, ain't they? Listen, girl, I play, you know that, but I play fair. They saw you first, and you knew them first. You can have the young one. I'll take the old one."

"Take them both," Miss Lena said, too late. Pop Earl had slid onto the stool at Mamie's right, and she had already turned her back on Miss Lena to greet him.

And on her own left, Earl Junior was snaking an arm around her shoulders as if he had paid for that privilege along with the champagne. She did not draw away from his touch because she was repelled, however. She drew away because she was attracted.

Trying to turn off the disturbing feelings she thought her nerves had forgotten how to produce, she reminded him that she was old enough to be his mother.

He laughed easily, revealing a full mouth of perfect, even teeth. Miss Lena wished he had not smiled. Miss Lena found perfect white smiles against dark lips nearly irresistible. Black men—and women, too—with full sets of teeth were so rare.

"I already got a mother," he said. "And you already got a son."

"I wish you had a few missing teeth," she mumbled, and took a nervous sip of her champagne.

"What was that?" he asked, and leaned closer.

"Never mind. Have you seen him?"

"Who?"

"The boy you call my son."

"Oh, he was by for a few minutes tonight, to grab a bite and get a sweater he left at our house. But then he had to make a run. Said he might be back later." He chuckled. "Smart for his age, that kid. A regular little man. Always wheeling and dealing. I see you're wearing your ring." He stroked her hand sensually, letting his fingertip linger just above the ring. "You must like it. I'm glad."

She jerked her hand away in sudden surprise. "Did he get it from you?"

"Not exactly. Hey, why you so jumpy?"

"What does 'not exactly' mean?" she asked crisply.

"You've hardly touched your champagne, lady. Don't worry, there's plenty more. We bought a whole bottle. And when that's gone, there's more in Susie's icebox."

They were big spenders, then. How could they afford it? Warily, she sipped from her glass. She didn't want to get drunk. If she had ever needed to be alert, this was the time. As soon as she set down the empty glass, it was refilled like magic.

His fingers were stroking her left hand now, stimulating feelings she had thought long dead. "You ought to have another ring for this hand."

She had downed only one drink, and her head was swimming. Was this suave street bandit proposing to her? In the dim light, he was handsome; his scars invisible, his hair well combed, his eyes clear and sparkling.

"I might like one," she said.

"You can have it for the same price he paid. Twenty-five dollars."

In spite of the champagne, Miss Lena instantly became as alert as if ice water had been thrown in her face. Earl Junior was not wooing her. She had been an old fool to think so. He was merely using his considerable charm to persuade her to buy. But she toyed with her ring, pretending to be deceived. She needed to find out what B.J. was mixed up in.

Earl Junior seemed to sense her indignant feelings from the sudden rigidity of her back. He began to stroke it. "You know, I'm not just interested in selling you jewelry. A man my age gets tired of living with his folks. He'd rather have a place of his own, and his own woman." He ran his fingertip down the line of her jaw, from earlobe to chin, as if to remind her that she, too, was scarred now, and it did not spoil her appearance for him. "His own *beautiful* little woman."

It was a little easier not to respond to him now that she knew his attentions were all salesmanship, but not much. "I don't understand how these rings can be so cheap. Are they hot?"

He smiled again, lighting up the room. "Do I really have to answer that question? My parents and I, we have a lot of friends who bring us nice things. And we have a lot of other friends who want nice things. We just help them get together, that's all. You might say we're in the retail business."

"Where do your friends get these things?" she persisted.

"Why do you ask so many questions, pretty lady? I never ask questions like that. I just accept the good things that come my way, like manna from heaven. The good Lord provides, and I thank Him." He raised his arms to illustrate his pious speech. "It's getting cold out. Couldn't you use a nice, warm fur coat?"

Miss Lena was sure the good Lord had nothing to do with it. "No," she said, trying not to react to the warm, steady pressure of his hand against her back.

"Oh, come on. Every woman wants a fur coat. Every woman *needs* one.

When your lover's arm isn't around you, like mine is now, you can snuggle into your fur and feel just as good. I'm not talking about something cheap, now. I would never suggest something cheap to a high-class woman like you. I'm talking about something nice, something that would suit your personality. Come on, now. What's your favorite fur? Sable? Ermine? How about a beautiful jet-black mink? I could get you one, brand-new, for only four hundred dollars."

He was breathing in her ear. He was brushing her ear with his lips. In spite of knowing it was all part of the sales talk, she was reacting as any woman would. Enough was enough, Miss Lena decided. "You mean a coat with sleeves, or one without?" she asked boldly. The remark made him flinch, but not withdraw. He only tightened the pressure of his arm.

She nudged Mamie so violently she almost toppled from her stool.

"Hey, ouch! What's wrong with you, girl?"

"I want to leave. I know a nicer place."

"Just when I was getting comfortable," Mamie grumbled. But something on Miss Lena's face stopped her from more complaining. She said something to Pop Earl, stuffed an object in her purse, snapped it shut, and climbed down awkwardly from the stool.

"Leaving so soon?" Earl Junior asked with a semblance of a stricken face.

"The night's young, and so are we. We'll be back later," Mamie promised with a wink, and followed Miss Lena to the street.

She was panting when she caught up with her. "Hey, what's the hurry? What'd that cute young stuff do to make you so mad?"

"He was trying to sell me something. Furs. What did his father try to sell you?"

"French perfume." Mamie opened her bag to reveal a frosted glass bottle, then snapped it shut. "We didn't agree on a price, though. I said I'd pay him when I see him. That's one way to make sure I *do* see him."

"I hope you don't," Miss Lena said grimly.

"Oh, I get it. You thought you was getting all that attention for free. When you found out it wasn't free you got mad. You too proud to pay for it. Right?"

"Aren't you?"

"Sometimes. But sometimes I ain't too proud," Mamie admitted humbly.

TREEMONT STONE

Angela Jackson

It was Halloween.

Spirits were being loosed, crossing bridges into matter and climbing stairs. Windows were opening and veils were lifted. Ether-kittens mewed deep within the plaster broken walls. Ghosts came, and my mother would wash them clear in her smiles. Yet there was a witch who was in our house. We swore that evil incantations were hidden beneath her breath and between her moving lips. She drew her eyes against us blankly. She rode no broom; she wore one, more or less, upon her head.

That Friday we came home from school, and she was there. The worn couch waiting, facing the front door for her to sit there sometime like that time. And she would sit like she been forever in the center of the sag where the pillows pull apart. And she would never be busy save for her unfinishing hands.

I could not understand the fidgeting of her hands. They made nothing. They suggested chaos.

She pushed the blond hair from her neck where it lay like Desdemona, the watermelon man's horse's mane lay on her strong chestnut neck. The watermelon man would beat his mare for being so slow, so slumped, so pitiable, then take her strong neck in his hands and stroke her matty mane so like Charlotte's store-bought hair. Charlotte would push the slush-colored yellow wig back from her forehead and actual hair would inch out blackly, burned down around the edges and tangle-haunted by no comb. Her hair might have been in braids so she three-finger snatched a stump and twisted and mistreated it and twisted and picked at it like her hands were not her own and were about some figurative occult business. Charlotte would smile.

We came through the door, and her legs were loose, astraddle the air from the opening door. As if to unspecifically embrace. She wore a dead brown short dress, and she was very tall. Her tallness, her presence, and her pretty yellow face with its blank eyes found her modeling jobs on weekends, sometimes strolling down makeshift ramps.

She would ignore us as we filed through the door in our shiny blue jumpers and white blouses. We would ignore her; costumed in inexplicable childish hostility. Marching toward the kitchen like an enemy army. I would mutter in the ranks.

"I bet she stink," I'd say. "You know Charlotte stink."

Pearl, demonstrating her maturity, would push me.

"Why she go and say Littleson steal her underwear?" I asked, enraged. "Why she say that? Who would want her underwear?"

Pearl pinched me.

"You know Charlotte ain't right in her head," she said.

I scowled and peeked back around the corner between the two rooms to where Charlotte sat like a Hindu Kali with her feet crossed on the couch pillows. Her legs wide. Her smile wide. A joke at that time jumped up inside her to light up her eyes. She leaned forward, rocked and hugged herself. Laughed wide and spread her legs open more. She sat and rocked, rocking that joke inside her.

"She got her feet on Mama's couch," I said in sour amazement.

Pearl had put the salt pork into water for pinto beans. I have always loved pinto beans seasoned like Mama seasons with her secret sweetening. But that night it was clear that I would feast only on the plunders of trick or treat. So Pearl was aproned and at the stove wearing our mother's expressions, but I knew her seasonings were quasi, poor substitutes in a pathetically aromatic disguise.

I had braved the cluttered pantry beside the kitchen to find old shoes for a childish masquerade. Charlotte was content in her joke in the front room. I tensed my spine to enter that tiny room where a kitten had died a gutty death beneath a boot. MySun, the yellow kitten, had died in innocence on a bed of rags where the sibling kittens lived in our pantry. I knew the pantry was haunted by her cries, so I put my hands to my ears as best I could while fumbling through a box of battered shoes.

I picked out a pair of Mama's high-heeled shoes for Ernestine; the pointed toes oppressed my feet. Madaddy's workman boots with the brown mud paint splashed across the buckles I chose for Shirley, because the paint matched her jacket that used to be mine. I threw everything out of the box but could not find anything that expressed me. All the women's shoes (Honeybabe's, Mama's, Pearl's) were too small. "Bigfoot. Birdlegs. Nappyhead." Sam Junior always called me. All the men's shoes had no mates.

In a huff I went into the kitchen. Pearl turned from our mother's stove. Wet speckled pinto beans in her hands. "You gone leave them shoes all over the pantry floor?"

I said, "I might." And walked away.

I went to the front closet in the room next to the one where Charlotte had been sitting. Charlotte had moved. I could hardly get into the closet for her. She was standing in the full-length mirror that hung on the outside of the closet door. The crack in the mirror was zigzagging across her stomach. She was smoothing down her blond stringy hair to no avail. An evil thought was in my head. "She look like a witch with that witch-wig on. . . ."

I tried to open the closet door so I could squeeze inside, and she shut it so her mirror would stay straight. She looked at me. Daring me to move. I was still, just staring at her. She went back to the mirror. Grinning at herself. She patted her stomach. She slapped her behind the way one slaps a prize mare. A fine piece of flesh. She looked at me with cool eyes. "Don't you wish you grow up thin enough to be a model like me?"

I was silent, sullen and plotting. Pushing the door open a little at a time. She smiled at her mirror-face. Make-up chalky on her yellow skin. "But then you'd still be a little chocolate drop, Pearl."

"My name ain't no Pearl."

She looked at me but still noticed no difference. "You probably be a chub. Like yo mama be soon. She coulda had a nice figure. She coulda been somebody if it hadna been for all you babies. Why, I saw a picture of yo mama, and she had long nat-u-rally red hair flowing down her back like a Indian maiden. She coulda been somebody. Did somethin' with herself. If it hadna been for all you babies." Reaching, she moved toward me. I slammed the door open and jumped inside the dark. Safe.

I rumbled around for the shoe box. Felt inside for Littleson's old brogans. I jerked on the door string. It stuck. I jerked again. Charlotte was laughing. I was locked in the dark.

I waited a minute without moving. Then I pulled very quickly. The door flew open. I came out and she was laughing. Wrapping her arms around her stomach.

"Whatchu do that for?" I was fire. She stopped and looked at me with blank eyes, holding her stomach tight. In the mirror she was broken across her fattening middle on her slim frame.

In the beauty shop in Mrs. Wilson's apartment they had spoken of Charlotte and her family. It was the day before Easter. Easter was late that year, but I was still late getting my hair done. Mrs. Wilson berated me for my genes and the hopelessness of my head always dipped into a book, always turning back. Hair so soft it would not hold enough heat to curl hard. A head full of books and pictures and framed in soft, persistent shells.

The hot smell of hair, Mrs. Wilson's sweat, Dixie Peach, and the grapevine bursting in its heady gossip-wine made me drowsy. In the sluggish heat I missed the origins of much of Charlotte's story.

Mrs. Wilson's glasses pressed her nostrils together so that her nose seemed a low bridge with one hole. She was not a pretty woman, though her hair was always "did" so nice. She slept alone in the back room of her shop. (Was there ever a Mr. Wilson?) She was a managing woman. She managed the heads of the neighborhood women and girls. She managed the heart of the neighborhood, her hot curlers and straightening combs and her pomades working against the chaos that ever returned. She was the connective spoke in a wheel of women. Trifling menfolk would go cold to tread on Mrs. Wilson's salon steps. Hardworking men touched their hats and waved to her through her frosted windowpanes. She knew the story of every visitor and the changes of the weather passing by.

That day before Easter, Otis Rucker, a trifling man, came into Mrs. Wilson's shop with much bowing and courtesy embellished with whiskey scents. He wore his workman clothes for his odd-job business, to fix a faulty lock. He kept dropping his tools. His palms must have been sweaty with nervous sweat. Criminals sweat under a righteous eye. Mrs. Wilson knew his laziness was a crime. His noises brought me to the edge of wakefulness. With my eyes closed I listened to their adult rituals: the clang of curlers, the clash of his hammers and screwdrivers.

Mr. Rucker had forgotten a tool. He left the shop, and Mrs. Wilson talked about him, his wife Cynthia, and their daughter Charlotte.

"He drink the money," Mrs. Wilson censured that trifling man. "That good woman work herself half to death for him, and that long-legged girl and he drink up the money." My eyes were closed, but I could see the images of their outraged silences and sentences: liquid money in a shot glass, a drinking man, a long-legged girl, and a woman work-worn and stricken.

"Now, the girl I know she got some looks, went up to one of them charm schools payin' out all her mama's good money, maybe she get something in her line. But shoots! You got to be more secure. She too spoiled. She too pretty and spoiled for good luck. You mark my words."

And I did.

I fell asleep on Mrs. Wilson's warning: there was trouble afoot. The ingredients for tragedy were brewing in a cup spiked with Mr. Rucker's spirits. Time would stir. Time has a hand of its own.

So something had driven a long-legged girl named Charlotte to seek solace in the home of her friend who was my oldest sister, Honore Grace, called Honeybabe: Cynthia, Charlotte's mother, had died.

Charlotte's mother worked herself to death, all the women said. I heard about it in the shop when I brought the chicken dinner Mrs. Wilson had sent me and Jeannie for. Mrs. Wilson had told Miss Rose that Mrs. Rucker had passed. Jeannie told me she didn't know Mrs. Rucker had gone to school. Mrs. Wilson slapped us both with a big black comb and sent us out the door.

One week before Halloween when Charlotte had been in our house for two weeks, when her presence had sat like a crimson aura upon Littleson and me and the impassive Pearl, one week we labeled some of the ingredients of Charlotte's story. The label was made of religious words like *man*, *woman*, *want*, *need*, and *sex*.

Mr. Rucker had come to our house accompanied by a friend. Miss Rose and our mama were sitting in the front room. Mama in Madaddy's big chair. Miss Rose on the couch where Charlotte usually sat. Charlotte, weeping under her ineffectual blond wig, had secreted herself in the bathroom.

Mr. Rucker had told Mama she "better get the girl's clothes together now 'cause she comin' with me."

My mother answered him in her most refined voice generally reserved for the insurance man and other white people. She said that her husband would be home later and perhaps they would care to wait and speak with him. They wrangled for a time. Mr. Rucker yelling that Charlotte was his blood and Miss Rose yelling back that the blood needed letting now or never. Mama and Miss Rose looked at the two men as if they were watching a stockyard truck go by.

In the face of their feminine disdain so like the dead Cynthia's, Mr. Rucker thrust his companion forward, forming an articulate barrier between himself and such entrenched opposition.

Mr. Rucker's friend was wearing an old gray suit, the pants with a shiny seat. He was carrying a greasy gray hat, and he handed Mama a card she read aloud and passed to Miss Rose: Reverend Doctor Tobias Jessuah Hill: Spiritual and Metaphysical Advisor: Psychological Physician.

"Madams," he announced, "allow me to introduce myself; my name is

Tobias Hill. Reverent Doctor Tobias Hill. As you will see written on my calling card I am a psychological physician and a philosophical colleague of Mr. Rucker. Miss Charlotte Rucker is under my medicinal supervision." My mother's face was a study of stockyard odors.

Then Littleson pulled me from the door, saying, "I cain't hear."

I said, "I was here first." Littleson and I skirmished.

Then he said, "You don't know what's happenin'. Let me explain it to you, Maggie." He leaned into the front room to be eyes for both of us. I watched over the curve of his back. Pearl was in the thick of the action, beside Mama's chair as inconspicuous as possible. Her head turning from adult mouth to adult mouth, like somebody watching a tennis game. There was nothing she would miss. My attention was diverted by envy. I missed a portion of the exchange. Their voices had grown louder, I knew Charlotte could hear even in the bathroom.

Dr. Hill was telling my mother exactly what Charlotte needed, what he prescribed.

"She need a man!" he bellowed. Pearl's eyes flew open.

"I beg your pardon," Mama said in a stunned voice. Miss Rose coughed.

"She nine and ten and ain't never been had."

"And you intend to know her?" Mama asked, and her voice was dangerous in its innocence.

"We will find someone for the girl in due time. Whoever prove to be a suitable body, madam," he replied.

My mother nodded toward Mr. Rucker, "Was the old drunk buddy he locked his own daughter in a room with suitable or fit to be known in any way?" she asked softly. "If he was so much of what Charlotte needed, why did she scratch his face up and break down the bedroom door to get away from him?"

"The girl has been behaving hysterically since her mother's sudden demise—" Dr. Hill began to explain.

"Exactly," Mama cut in. "She was downright hysterical when she first came here. Knocking on this door in the middle of the night. That's why she needs to be around responsible people, especially other women, at this point. She need some peace and quiet, too."

"She need a man!" the physician thundered. At which point Miss Rose got up from the sagging couch. She passed by Littleson and me on her way to the kitchen. I thought she was going to comfort Charlotte, to keep her from being so afraid.

Miss Rose came back through the hall, in the doorway winking at Littleson and me. She carried a stiff-bristled broom. Littleson asked her if she was going to sweep our house. She smiled. "I most certainly am, honey."

She entered the front room like a righteous witch. Mama was chanting reason. "Well, it seems to me as Charlotte is now a legal adult she can makes these decisions for herself."

There was uproar then. Otis Rucker boxing his arms in the air. The psychological physician raging in words of more than three syllables. He made no sense but noise. Neither man made an actual physical threat lest word go back to our father, Sam Grace.

The words and sights were horrendous. In the center of it all Miss Rose was wielding her broom. She swept them out the front door and down the steps into the street. From the window we watched the shiny seat of Dr. Hill's pants disappear into the evening.

Charlotte stayed in the bathroom all evening. I loved the excitement, but that—the rituals she generated, the forbidden words surrounding her— could be held for longer than I could hold my water. I hated her. I had to go downstairs to our neighbor's to use the bathroom.

Littleson was my ace boon coon. But, well, I think now I was never so dear to him. Or do I deprive him of his loving credentials? Eddie was, at that time, his best running buddy. They were as thick as thieves. Acrobatic in their intrigues. I was never so able. Where once Littleson and I had been inseparable, he had grown increasingly aloof. I was losing my brother to the sealed camaraderie of males. So I found myself embarking into All Hallows' Eve evening with Ernee and Shir, the two sisters just younger than me.

Each of us was dressed in collages of feminine and masculine para- phernalia. They were waving excited sounds above their heads, while swing- ing their, then, empty bags. I was in a muted mood, feeling as mix-matched as my costume.

Everything outside was in its season; the trees were speaking their autumn for trick or treat. The leaves were withering brittle. Blazing orange and brown and falling to the ground just so we could tramp through them in somebody else's boots. "Walk in someone else's moccasins . . . and what happen to you?" Subdued and semihostile, I could not fit into the season.

I longed for the summer all crazy with leftover sweat and our child-faces wet with the Watermelon Rind Wars, where we scrubbed our enemies' faces in the used whites of summer fruit. We would be tired from running and playing "werewolf" where Littleson was always the monster because he had two long dogteeth in his mouth. He could jump from the side porch railing of the house next door right onto his victim's back. Just like a real werewolf.

In flashes I would fear, moon or no moon, that perhaps Littleson had been transformed into the werewolf like Larry Tolbert or Lon Chaney, Jr. He would kick and claw and scratch and bite just like a real werewolf. I liked it best when he did all those things to Jeannie. I was safe, I soothed myself with my secure position as the witchcrafting gypsy woman who poured a comforting chant over the tormented wolfman.

Littleson would lay in the yard under the intense summer sun and give himself to torment after having mauled the other children. The gypsy woman would bless the wolfman and repeat a verse I half remembered and mostly invented. I would say, holding Littleson in my arms, "The way you walk is thorny, my son. A wolf does pick no roses, yet searches for meat. Dust to dust. Ashes to ashes. One to one. As the river flows to the sea you will find peace, my son."

The curse would be broken for a time and all of us could begin a new, less painful game.

I was not always Littleson's comfort, his savior from the fates of his full moon. There was one time a huge sun fell in all our bones. We were heavy and too tired for monsters. Yet it was a summer day made for mischief. The air was high with laughter, and I had been looking for something to do. Because the sun was saying something hot and wicked like "being bad." You know? So I had a devil inside of me and I looked for a forbidden rite to perform. For once I scraped The Word in chalk on the next-door garage. I felt a sense of evil completion when I finished. Littleson was sudden as conscience at my elbow. He made me get a rag and water and wipe The Word off.

It did not remove well. I was crying with shame and fury. "Ol' high butt self, just makin' me just like you so doggone good. Ol' booty set so high in the sky I bet it's a stepladder to heaven." In short rough strokes I wiped off the *p* and it came off clean, and *u* left a faint impression. The *ss* I scrubbed and scrubbed, and Mama called us to eat on the last letter so I left it. It is still there like a question *y*, forever reminding me of Littleson with his mouth teacher-tight going, "Maggie, now just what do that mean?" Pointing to my sin as a nun points. I said, "I own know."

He snapped, "You fool. I knowed you ain' know what it mean so you just get it off. Get it off now." Shame heavy in my eyes. The sugar of resentment in my mouth.

When Pearl had told me to pick up the shoes in the pantry, I ignored her. In slow motion I threw the boots and shoes into the box. She must not think she made me.

I ignored her pseudo-maternal admonitions as we trooped out the door to our trick or treat. Be home before dark. Be careful crossing streets. Don't eat no loose candy. Watch for razors in those apples.

"How somebody push a great big ol' razor up in a apple and you don't see it?" I asked in disgust.

Ernee and Shir had gotten out of school late because Sister Veronica and Sister Irene wanted to impress on their good young clay minds how Halloween was a pagan rite that they must not practice. They must not maraud, but must blow out their candle early and rise for mass on the Holy Day of Obligation, All Saints' Day. They had told me what the nuns had said while I helped them into their costumes. They twisted their faces as sour as Sister Irene's. I put white shoe polish on their faces. They looked like alabaster saints. They were still half-baby.

Pearl was leaning over the railing, screaming warnings after us, trying to put Mama's music into her voice. So Mama would be proud of her when she came home from work.

"I ain't no dummy," I muttered.

Littleson had said he was too old for trick or treat. The year before, the women who had opened their doors had looked at him with censorious eyes. They dropped broken candy into his bag. They gave whole candy bars to the smallest children who could not eat them—Butterfingers and Baby Ruths. Littleson refused to beg again.

We met him and Eddie and Leave-ma-be at the corner of our block. I asked Leave-ma-be if Jeannie was doing better. He grunted. I asked him what was wrong with her. He answered, "You oughtta know." They walked with us for a while.

Ernee and Shir stumbled in their ill-fitting shoes in front of us. I was in the middle. The three male guards brought up the rear. We would confront our victims in this manner. Ernee and Shir would advance to the closed door and beguile and beget sugar. My reward came capriciously. The boys stood at a disdainful distance.

We turned from each shutting door, our faces shelving sugar for another occasion. At a brick two flat a smiling woman passed out apples. Walking down the street, I inspected mine. Littleson had something to say.

"Don't eat none a them apples. They might got razor blades in 'em."

"Ain' no razor blades in these apples, honey."

"Well, they dirty, so don't eat them."

I told him that from here on I'd be glad to take care of myself. He, Eddie, and Leave-ma-be left us, saying they'd meet us at the corner in an hour. I watched them run wildly up the skinny street under the low lights.

Mr. Rucker under the streetlights. He was riding the fire hydrant and whiskey riding him. His dirty gray workclothes crumpled on him. When we got past him, he said, "Where my daughter? Ain'chu some of them got her?"

We rolled our eyes at him and shot around the corner. We could smell him. We hated his smell. He stank, and Charlotte was out her mind. I explained the logistics of it to Ernee and Shir. "Miss Rose say that Mr. Rucker ran Charlotte out her mind. That's why she ain't there no more and going to a nervous breakdown. That's why she wear a blond wig and whisper and laugh under breath to herself."

Mr. Rucker shouted for us to come here to him so we could get some trick or treat.

Within an hour we were walking in the Halloween-walk, an old woman walk, leaning to one side with our heavy candy and used fruit.

The moon was complete, clear as a fine china plate. White as a kitten's skull.

Night was a gray gossamer veil falling over a city woman's shabby face. We were children painted on the city woman frivolously like cinnamon lipstick and rouge.

Some boys were coming toward us. They moved like scars beneath the city woman's net. They wore the baggy pants, berets, and funky knits of gangster boys. They were who they appeared to be.

"Gimme that candy, bitch."

"Gimme that trick-or-treat shit 'fore I kick yo ass."

I was weighing my umbrella, thinking how weak and fragile it was, like a baby's limb. There were three of them.

One of the boys had the pinkeye. I remember thinking how old he was to have that. That was for babies. What kind of baby was he?

Ernee and Shir were born in the city. They grit their teeth and squared off in their flobby clothes. I was crying and ready to go crazy.

One of the boys grabbed me, and they started yanking. Six pairs of hands on one trick-or-treat bag.

Ernestine started screaming, "Help! Help! Polease! Polease!"

And Shirley going, "Leave a alone, you heifer. Leave a alone, you heifer." And I was too busy to tell her it's only girls that're heifers.

"Help! Help! Polease. Polease. Arrest these mens!"

"Robry! Robry! Help! Help!"

Littleson, Eddie, and Leave-ma-be arose through the clouds in my eyes like the cavalry. Rescue music. Everything was frozen askew. The gangster boys withdrew and smiled friendlylike. There was a pause.

Littleson looking like he looked when Mama told him to empty the garbage, and it was Junior's turn, and Mama would tell Littleson the garbage runnin' all over the back porch, don't go to bed till the garbage is emptied, and Littleson would stay up all night on the living-room couch with his arms folded across his chest, looking his rocklike, because it wasn't his turn. The same way he faced the gangster boys.

Pinkeye, smiling, said, "Gimme."

Littleson said, "Take it," pushing me behind him, slinging me by one arm, and my other arm lashing out with the umbrella. All hands were moving quick as dust.

We fought tough enough to break the china plate moon, or at least to leave a film of grime on it. Ernee and Shir fought blind as windmills with their heads down. One of the trick-or-treat bags broke, and a sweet roll wobbled across the sidewalk, and the gangster boys fell away. Defeated.

Maybe it was never candy or sweet things they had wanted from us. Maybe they wanted our contentment, our guilessness, our attainable joy, our innocence.

Walking, we should have known. We had been full as balloons; they had had to burst.

Ernee and Shir and I were tired. Shir had begun to whimper. Littleson began to swagger down the street. Eddie, Leave-ma-be, and he were talking loud, reliving the great siege.

"Shoot, man, they'da whipped them girls' behines."

"Yeah, man, them girls was runnin'. . . ."

All the way home I was silent with this new salt inside my wounds. What had been a superficial excitement now cut, grinded against bone.

They left me and Ernee and Shir in the front of our house. Mama called downstairs for us all to come inside. "Littleson, too," she said.

"Mama said," I said, somewhat satisfied.

Me and Littleson were laying across Mama and Madaddy's bed on top of Mama's good green spread. I was stuffed with miscellaneous junks. Littleson had thrown away all the apples.

Littleson was reading the newspaper. I had been reading a Nancy Drew book until she had sat on her daddy's lap with her grown eighteen-year-old self and kissed him on his cheek and went, "Dad, you're a peach." Because he had just given her her own roadster. I threw the book against the radiator. I did not known the just why I was so furious. I was lying on the bed thinking about this when Littleson looked up into my face. He dipped his head back into the paper spread open across two pages.

He looked at me. My hand under my chin. He pointed to the page he had been studying.

"What's this?"

I leaned over and looked at a lady's ad. It was about a box of the secret. "Lady napkins." Jeannie was wearing them. She'd told me her stomach felt like somebody twisted a screwdriver in her and somebody worked a blood-rite and nasty smells inside her body.

"What is it?" I'd asked her.

"It's a secret," she'd said. I must never tell a man or a curse would fall on me and I would have a baby. So I was afraid Littleson would find out the secret from me.

"I own know. I own know what that's for."

Littleson half-shut his eyes. He squeezed his lips together. He wanted me to know he was suspicious.

He lifted his chin, then dipped his head back up in the paper, still looking at my guilty face out the corner of his eye.

I fled from Littleson's scrutiny and went about the house looking for something to interest me. I settled down to make pictures on the scrap paper my mother saved for me.

Honeybabe and Charlotte were in the bathroom. Honeybabe had on a lemon-yellow flared-skirt dress, Charlotte wore the brown dress she had worn since the first day she had come to our house. Even Mama could not get her to part with it. It was a loose knit dress; for work and dressy occasions such as that Friday night she wore the matching short jacket.

Honeybabe was reworking her face with an eyebrow pencil: thickening brows, outlining her eyes, marking an imaginary mole high on her right cheekbone.

Charlotte, taller than Honey, was behind her in the mirror, applying a pale pink powder to her face. Her hand was heavy and unsteady, so she made her face warlike and whorish. Her lipstick she wore lopsided and smeared.

She split her mouth to giggle. Her mouth moved like a machine. She amazed me. I hid myself around the doorway.

Charlotte was running a monologue in the mirror and the back of Honeybabe's hair.

"I cain't stand nothin' ugly and stanky. And that include all them Africans."

Honeybabe raised one of her thickened eyebrows ironically. She sniffed.

Honeybabe combed all her hair back from her face, then pushed it forward with her hand until it lay in waves about her head and ruffled at each temple. She was silent.

"They all got them white little teeth like they been chewing on barbecue bones." Charlotte laughed. Honeybabe smiled tightly while laying on her orange lipstick.

"They skin so black they look like charcoal grinded up in it. They be so strong they light up the room."

"They hair like little steel balls. . . . Now Frederico, Frederico, he look like a human being. He got good hair. It so curly." She moved into the mirror.

"Frederico? You mean Fred Bates?" Honey said. "That nigger ain't got no good hair."

Charlotte laughed and brushed the surface of her wig. "You just jealous. Frederico say he gon' be rich. And I will be rich with him. I'm his good luck."

"What's bad luck, Charlotte?"

"You just jealous."

"You sure want somebody to be jealous of you."

"Well, I guess you happy. You and yo little pygmies."

"Charlotte," Honeybabe said, and I knew Charlotte better be careful, "Charlotte, if my Africans too ugly to go out with, stay here. They'll keep they ugly money. Plus, Fred Frederico Bates, good hair or no good hair, model agency or no model agency, he ain't making nobody famous except for being a fool."

"We'll see." Charlotte smoothed the dress over her hips.

"Yeah. We will. You gon' find out ain't nothin in your hand."

"We'll see."

"Uh-huh. Keep on lookin'. Better say some magic words and I'll put spit on it."

Charlotte began to hum. She patted her dress over her tummy and her expression was fugitive and puzzled, only I could see.

Then, for no apparent reason, Charlotte just laughed and laughed.

Honeybabe was bent, smoothing her stockings along her calves. She said her big legs were her most potent attribute.

Honeybabe laughed like a charm bracelet fading into steps. Charlotte's voice was an echo that had no beginning, or rather it arose out of sounds of things forever breaking. Charlotte wore cologne as strong as church incense. It clouded my stomach, and I moved from her.

Mama told Honey not to stay out too late since she knew the way our father is. Honey rattled her age in Mama's face, the way eighteen-year-olds do.

Littleson was playing war on the dining room table, moving his soldiers in and out of cannon fire and tank tracks. He was talking about "amphibious forces." Because he liked to say that phrase. It lulled his tongue, untangled his tendency to stutter.

Pearl was reading a mystery to everybody but me, I listened tentatively. We were each in our way when the Africans came; we were each in our way when they left.

They wore business suits and spoke in British accents with lovely herbs ground into certain syllables. I closed my eyes and was enchanted with the

melodies they made. Eyes open, I could see Honey shoulder to shoulder
with Wally. Charlotte was a painted tree casting a pale shadow over Charles
Aduba's dark bush.

I watched them float away in engine smoke. On the front steps I sucked
in the gas fumes. Honey saw that I had trailed them down the steps. She
promised, at last, to bring me something back if I was a good girl.

My father is a man who thinks that things are generally what they seem.
At least for other people: I was in bed with Littleson so we were sleeping
half-submerged in covers.

Mama would have known by the shape of my spine and my head under
cover and by the texture of our breathing, Littleson's deep and slow, mine
quick and ethereal, that I was wide awake and reading Trixie Belden by
flashlight. My father's mind believes that what exists lives. He knows no
nuances but his own. So he closed his bedroom door, satisfied that the one
child of his not accounted for was Honeybabe, the other child missing was
a foreigner and incomprehensible and preposterous in her pain.

I could hear his steps and stopping when he interrogated Mama about
the absence of Honey. Mama's replies were sleepy and half-annoyed. Then
a silence took the house save for boards and springs that cried out thinly and
always suddenly in sounds a kitten's ghost would make.

I gave up reading and went into restless sleep, the ghost of a kitten walking
on my nerves.

My face was in the moon in the window. Sleeping at the foot of the bed.
Littleson wiggled his feet in my chest. My chest was just a chest like his still.
The day before I'd practiced wearing a bra in the mirror. Mama'd come in
to say don't be in no hurry; it be there directly.

So my chest was bare. And my throat was dry. I was drinking spit from
my mouth.

I had to walk in the dark. Last week a werewolf I had seen on the dresser
had been just dried clothes from the line, bundled and rough. I walked past
the mirror, and eyes were blinking at me. I didn't see the beast they were
attached to. A familiar? It was there. Waiting to grab, and the kitchen a
long way off. I had to travel through my dangerous imagination.

I could hear Honeybabe and Charlotte in the kitchen. The oven door
slapped down. I knew Honeybabe toasted her feet in the oven. Littleson said
once the oven is like a lion's mouth; he put his head in one time. He took
all the racks out. The oven roared. Mama had seen him with his head stuck
up in the oven and she jerked him out. She asked him if he was a fool,
stickin' his head in that leaky oven.

Honeybabe was toasting her feet. Her mouth was running steadily. Charlotte was walking back and forth, her skinny heels drilling on the kitchen
linoleum. I cain't stand her ol' stinky butt. I hope she trip on that crack that

stick up sneaky in the air right in front the sink. Hope she bust her lip. She think she cute anyway.

Charlotte was talking. Her words carried heat and nastiness.

"I don't be letting no man hold my hand in public, girl. What was that nigger whispering in yo ear? I don't be letting no nigger talk all up in my ear. Breathing on my neck."

"Oh, Charlotte, that's some stuff. They were being friendly."

Charlotte howled.

"Friendly! With his sweaty African hand on my knee. He ain't giving me no money!"

"Frederico givin' you some money?"

"Frederico giving me other things."

"He come to yo mama's funeral?"

"I don't want to talk about her."

"I ain't talking about your mother, Charlotte. I'm trying to make you see this nigger ain't even pay her no respect. So how he ever going to respect you? He ain't worry about you when you needed him. You have to face facts, Charlotte." Honeybabe's bracelets jangled and her chair scraped and she moved to Charlotte.

Charlotte was laughing and laughing. "I want pretty things. Honey. I want pretty things. My daddy, where I be, so ugly. So ugly. I'm pretty. I was made for pretty things. I want to make pretty things. I want to wear pretty clothes." She rubbing her wig more securely on her head in long, desperate gestures.

Suddenly she shoved Honeybabe. She was not shouting in the quiet house, but her voice could have broken things. "I'm a nice girl. I'm a virgin. I'm a nice girl. I'm a nice girl. My mama raised me to be nice. Men respect me. I'm a nice girl."

Strange, I was shaking and hiding in the dark. Honeybabe went past me like a storm of pity and futility. Charlotte was alone in the kitchen. My water was forgotten, but I could hear her moving around in the kitchen.

She scuffled on the radiator in the kitchen. Next to the stove. The oven door was still open. Radiator must have been too intense on her behind so she moved around. She moved.

Water was running. I listened at her. Reaching with her breath trying to pull back some night-crying.

I listened at her night-crying, and her lips splashing together like wet glass, calling lips moving like she was gripping, pleading, invoking some god, placating some god with a sacrificial bowl of salty beggings.

I listened at her, then she said, "God. Jesus." Then, "Oh, Mercy."

Her voice torn out of her like the wail of the yellow kitten when Uncle Blackstrap lay then lifted his big boot and dragged some of MySun's guts out onto her yellow crayon fur. MySun had been playing, rolling belly up and beautiful and new.

"MySun, MySun," she moaned in her kitten voice. Me and Littleson were screaming. My Uncle Blackstrap was trying to take our baby, and the other little kittens were crying. And Littleson and I wanted to hold MySun forever, and MySun was crying from way inside her tore stomach, and she cried, she cried so long, so long, until Mama came home and took her and held cotton with an incense on it over her face. MySun. MySun.

We'd called Uncle Blackstrap a murderer, and he had gone away to a quiet place and wept into his calloused hands. He wept softly the way Charlotte began to weep. The way grown people weep.

I had forgotten water. It was on my face.

Charlotte cried and rocked herself. And rocked the pantheon inside her head. And soothed the savage deity in her stomach for it was tiny and curved like a shrimp.

Over a jar of pomade and hot irons, Mrs. Wilson would make a tragic mythology. It would go down for years and years. Even while each year marked Charlotte's pretty face in scarifications. The shrimp would uncurl and be eaten by eyes; would bloom into a brown and love-turned joke, a Jesus of a public virgin's joke. I would begin to bleed a bowl of blood and mark my mouth in soft sweet chalks.

I was very tired.

I left Charlotte alone. Walked through my imagination with no worry.

I took the extra blanket from the foot of the bed.

Littleson. He didn't notice. I covered up his leg sticking out from his blanket tube. It get kinda cool in the middle of the night, you know.

"Huh," he said, and lifted his head. His eyes were like two pearls with ink spilled on them.

"What you doin' up, Maggie?" Littleson asked me, but he didn't wait for no answer. He was sleep-blind. He just rolled himself up more in the covers. Till he was the mummy. And I couldn't see nothing but moonlight falling across his hide-and-seek body.

"You a boy, Littleson," I told him like this some sudden magic I knew that hurt, but he didn't hear me.

I went to the door and opened it a piece, and he raised up like Jesus.

"Where you goin', Maggie?"

No use in me answering. I knew I could not get away from the moon. It filled the whole little room then. It split the dark. Made my life a bowl. So I just stepped and closed the door. With my own blanket in my arms. I went out in the pitch dark looking to sleep where Pearl slept. Pearl, who hates my reading in the dark.

CHINA

Charles Johnson

If one man conquer in battle a thousand men, and if another conquers himself, he is the greatest of conquerors.

—*The Dharmapada*

Evelyn's problems with her husband, Rudolph, began one evening in early March—a dreary winter evening in Seattle—when he complained after a heavy meal of pig's feet and mashed potatoes of shortness of breath, an allergy to something she put in his food perhaps, or brought on by the first signs of wild flowers around them. She suggested they get out of the house for the evening, go to a movie. He was fifty-four, a postman for thirty-three years now, with high blood pressure, emphysema, flat feet, and, as Evelyn told her friend Shelberdine Lewis, the lingering fear that he had cancer. Getting old, he was also getting hard to live with. He told her never to salt his dinners, to keep their Lincoln Continental at a crawl, and never run her fingers along his inner thigh when they sat in Reverend William Merrill's church, because anything, even sex, or laughing too loud—Rudolph was serious—might bring on heart failure.

So she chose for their Saturday night outing a peaceful movie, a mildly funny comedy a *Seattle Times* reviewer said was fit only for titters and nasal snorts, a low-key satire that made Rudolph's eyelids droop as he shoveled

369

down unbuttered popcorn in the darkened, half-empty theater. Sticky fluids cemented Evelyn's feet to the floor. A man in the last row laughed at all the wrong places. She kept the popcorn on her lap, though she hated the unsalted stuff and wouldn't touch it, sighing as Rudolph pawed across her to shove his fingers inside the cup.

She followed the film as best she could, but occasionally her eyes frosted over, flashed white. She went blind like this now and then. The fibers of her eyes were failing; her retinas were tearing like soft tissue. At these times the world was a canvas with whiteout spilling from the far left corner toward the center; it was the sudden shock of an empty frame in a series of slides. Someday, she knew, the snow on her eyes would stay. Winter eternally: her eyes split like her walking stick. She groped along the fractured surface, waiting for her sight to thaw, listening to the film she couldn't see. Her only comfort was knowing that, despite her infirmity, her Rudolph was in even worse health.

He slid back and forth from sleep during the film (she elbowed him occasionally, or pinched his leg), then came full awake, sitting up suddenly when the movie ended and a "Coming Attractions" trailer began. It was some sort of gladiator movie, Evelyn thought, blinking, and it was pretty trashy stuff at that. The plot's revenge theme was a poor excuse for Chinese actors or Japanese (she couldn't tell those people apart) to flail the air with their hands and feet, take on fifty costumed extras at once, and leap twenty feet through the air in perfect defiance of gravity. Rudolph's mouth hung open.

"Can people really do that?" He did not take his eyes off the screen, but talked at her from the right side of his mouth. "Leap that high?"

"It's a *movie*," sighed Evelyn. "A *bad* movie."

He nodded, then asked again, "But can they?"

"Oh, Rudolph, for God's sake!" She stood up to leave, her seat slapping back loudly. "They're on *trampolines!* You can see them in the corner—there!—if you open your eyes!"

He did see them, once Evelyn twisted his head to the lower left corner of the screen, and it seemed to her that her husband looked disappointed—looked, in fact, the way he did the afternoon Dr. Guylee told Rudolph he'd developed an extrasystolic reaction, a faint, moaning sound from his heart whenever it relaxed. He said no more and, after the trailer finished, stood—there was chewing gum stuck to his trouser seat—dragged on his heavy coat with her help, and followed Evelyn up the long, carpeted aisle, through the exit of the Coronet Theater, and to their car. He said nothing as she chattered on the way home, reminding him that he could not stay up all night puttering in his basement shop because the next evening they were to attend the church's revival meeting.

Rudolph, however, did not attend the revival. He complained after lunch of a light, dancing pain in his chest, which he had conveniently whenever Mount Zion Baptist Church held revivals, and she went alone, sitting with her friend Shelberdine, a beautician. She was forty-one; Evelyn, fifty-two. That evening Evelyn wore spotless white gloves, tan therapeutic stockings for the swelling in her ankles, and a white dress that brought out nicely the brown color of her skin, the most beautiful cedar brown, Rudolph said when they were courting thirty-five years ago in South Carolina. But then Evelyn had worn a matching checkered skirt and coat to meeting. With her jet-black hair pinned behind her neck by a simple wooden comb, she looked as if she might have been Andrew Wyeth's starkly beautiful model for *Day of the Fair*. Rudolph, she remembered, wore black business suits, black ties, black wing tips, but he also wore white gloves because he was a senior usher—this was how she first noticed him. He was one of four young men dressed like deacons (or blackbirds), their left hands tucked into the hollow of their backs, their right carrying silver plates for the offering as they marched in almost military fashion down each aisle: Christian soldiers, she'd thought, the cream of black manhood, and to get his attention she placed not her white envelope or coins in Rudolph's plate but instead a note that said: "You have a beautiful smile." It was, for all her innocence, a daring thing to do, according to Evelyn's mother—flirting with a randy young man like Rudolph Lee Jackson, but he did have nice, tigerish teeth. A killer smile, people called it, like all the boys in the Jackson family: a killer smile and good hair that needed no more than one stroke of his palm to bring out Quo Vadis rows pomaded sweetly with the scent of Murray's.

And, of course, Rudolph was no dummy. Not a total dummy, at least. He pretended nothing extraordinary had happened as the congregation left the little whitewashed church. He stood, the youngest son, between his father and mother, and let old Deacon Adcock remark, "Oh, how strong he's looking now," which was a lie. Rudolph was the weakest of the Jackson boys, the pale, bookish, spiritual child born when his parents were well past forty. His brothers played football, they went into the navy; Rudolph lived in Scripture, was labeled 4-F, and hoped to attend Moody Bible Institute in Chicago, if he could ever find the money. Evelyn could tell Rudolph knew exactly where she was in the crowd, that he could feel her as she and her sister, Debbie, waited for their father to bring his DeSoto—the family prize—closer to the front steps. When the crowd thinned, he shambled over in his slow, ministerial walk, introduced himself, and unfolded her note.

"You write this?" he asked. "It's not right to play with the Lord's money, you know."

"I like to play," she said.

"You do, huh?" He never looked directly at people. Women, she guessed, terrified him. Or, to be exact, the powerful emotions they caused in him terrified Rudolph. He was a pud puller if she ever saw one. He kept his eyes on a spot left of her face. "You're Joe Montgomery's daughter, aren't you?"

"Maybe," teased Evelyn.

He trousered the note and stood marking the ground with his toe. "And just what you expect to get, Miss Playful, by fooling with people during collection time?"

She waited, let him look away, and, when the back-and-forth swing of his gaze crossed her again, said in her most melic, soft-breathing voice: "*You*."

Up front, portly Reverend Merrill concluded his sermon. Evelyn tipped her head slightly, smiling into memory; her hand reached left to pat Rudolph's leg gently; then she remembered it was Shelberdine beside her, and lifted her hand to the seat in front of her. She said a prayer for Rudolph's health, but mainly it was for herself, a hedge against her fear that their childless years had slipped by like wind, that she might return home one day and find him—as she had found her father—on the floor, bellied up, one arm twisted behind him where he fell, alone, his fingers locked against his chest. Rudolph had begun to run down, Evelyn decided, the minute he was turned down by Moody Bible Institute. They moved to Seattle in 1956—his brother Eli was stationed nearby and said Boeing was hiring black men. But they didn't hire Rudolph. He had kidney trouble on and off before he landed the job at the Post Office. Whenever he bent forward, he felt dizzy. Liver, heart, and lungs—they'd worn down gradually as his belly grew, but none of this was as bad as what he called "the Problem." His pecker shrank to no bigger than a pencil eraser each time he saw her undress. Or when Evelyn, as was her habit when talking, touched his arm. Was she the cause of this? Well, she knew she wasn't much to look at anymore. She'd seen the bottom of a few too many candy wrappers. Evelyn was nothing to make a man pant and jump her bones, pulling her fully clothed onto the davenport, as Rudolph had done years before, but wasn't sex something else you surrendered with age? It never seemed all that good to her anyway. And besides, he'd wanted oral sex, which Evelyn—if she knew nothing else— thought was a nasty, unsanitary thing to do with your mouth. She glanced up from under her spring hat past the pulpit, past the choir of black and brown faces to the agonized beauty of a bearded white carpenter impaled on a rood, and in this timeless image she felt comforted that suffering was inescapable, the loss of vitality inevitable, even a good thing maybe, and that she had to steel herself—yes—for someday opening her bedroom door and finding her Rudolph facedown in his breakfast oatmeal. He would die before her, she knew that in her bones.

And so, after service, Sanka, and a slice of meat pie with Shelberdine downstairs in the brightly lit church basement, Evelyn returned home to tell her husband how lovely the Griffin girls had sung that day, that their neighbor Rod Kenner had been saved, and to listen, if necessary, to Rudolph's fear that the lump on his shoulder was an early-warning sign of something evil. As it turned out, Evelyn found that except for their cat, Mr. Miller, the little A-frame house was empty. She looked in his bedroom. No Rudolph. The unnaturally still house made Evelyn uneasy, and she took the excruciatingly painful twenty stairs into the basement to peer into a workroom littered with power tools, planks of wood, and the blueprints her husband used to make bookshelves and cabinets. No Rudolph. Frightened, Evelyn called the eight hospitals in Seattle, but no one had a Rudolph Lee Jackson on his books. After her last call the starburst clock in the living room read twelve-thirty. Putting down the wall phone, she felt a familiar pain in her abdomen. Another attack of Hershey squirts, probably from the meat pie. She hurried into the bathroom, lifted her skirt, and lowered her underwear around her ankles, but kept the door wide open, something impossible to do if Rudolph was home. Actually, it felt good not to have him underfoot, a little like he was dead already. But the last thing Evelyn wanted was that or, as she lay down against her lumpy backrest, to fall asleep, though she did, nodding off and dreaming until something shifted down her weight on the side of her bed away from the wall.

"Evelyn," said Rudolph, "look at this." She blinked back sleep and squinted at the cover of a magazine called *Inside Kung-Fu*, which Rudolph waved under her nose. On the cover a man stood bowlegged, one hand cocked under his armpit, the other corkscrewing straight at Evelyn's nose.

"Rudolph!" She batted the magazine aside, then swung her eyes toward the cluttered nightstand, focusing on the electric clock beside her water glass from McDonald's, Preparation H suppositories, and Harlequin romances. "It's morning!" Now she was mad. At least working at it. "Where have you been?"

Her husband inhaled, a wheezing, whistlelike breath. He rolled the magazine into a cylinder and, as he spoke, struck his left palm with it. "That movie we saw advertised? You remember—it was called *The Five Fingers of Death*. I just saw that and one called *Deep Thrust*."

"Wonderful." Evelyn screwed up her lips. "I'm calling hospitals and you're at a Hong Kong double feature."

"Listen," said Rudolph. "You don't understand." He seemed at that moment as if he did not understand either. "It was a Seattle movie premiere. The Northwest is crawling with fighters. It has something to do with all the Asians out here. Before they showed the movie, four students from a kwoon in Chinatown went onstage—"

"A what?" asked Evelyn.

"A kwoon—it's a place to study fighting, a meditation hall." He looked at her but was really watching, Evelyn realized, something exciting she had missed. "They did a demonstration to drum up their membership. They broke boards and bricks, Evelyn. They went through what's called kata and kumite and . . ." He stopped again to breathe. "I've never seen anything so beautiful. The reason I'm late is because I wanted to talk with them after the movie."

Evelyn, suspicious, took a Valium and waited.

"I signed up for lessons," he said.

She gave a glacial look at Rudolph, then at his magazine, and said in the voice she had used five years ago when he wanted to take a vacation to Upper Volta or, before that, invest in a British car she knew they couldn't afford:

"You're fifty-*four* years old, Rudolph."

"I know that."

"You're no Muhammad Ali."

"I know that," he said.

"You're no Bruce Lee. Do you want to be Bruce Lee? Do you know where he is now, Rudolph? He'd dead—dead here in a Seattle cemetery and buried up on Capitol Hill."

His shoulders slumped a little. Silently Rudolph began undressing, his beefy backside turned toward her, slipping his pajama bottoms on before taking off his shirt so his scrawny lower body would not be fully exposed. He picked up his magazine, said, "I'm sorry if I worried you," and huffed upstairs to his bedroom. Evelyn clicked off the mushroom-shaped lamp on her nightstand. She lay on her side, listening to his slow footsteps strike the stairs, then heard his mattress creak above her—his bedroom was directly above hers—but she did not hear him click off his own light. From time to time she heard his shifting weight squeak the mattress springs. He was reading that foolish magazine, she guessed; then she grew tired and gave this impossible man up to God. With a copy of *The Thorn Birds* open on her lap, Evelyn fell heavily asleep again.

At breakfast the next morning any mention of the lessons gave Rudolph lockjaw. He kissed her forehead, as always, before going to work, and simply said he might be home late. Climbing the stairs to his bedroom was painful for Evelyn, but she hauled herself up, pausing at each step to huff, then sat on his bed and looked over his copy of *Inside Kung-Fu*. There were articles on empty-hand combat, soft-focus photos of ferocious-looking men in funny suits, parables about legendary Zen masters, an interview with someone named Bernie Bernheim, who began to study karate at age fifty-seven and became a black belt at age sixty-one, and page after page of advertisements for exotic Asian weapons: nunchaku, shuriken, sai swords, tonfa, bo staffs, training bags of all sorts, a wooden dummy shaped like a man and called a Mook Jong, and weights. Rudolph had circled them all. He had torn the order form from the last page of the magazine. The total cost of the things he'd circled—Evelyn added them furiously, rounding off the figures—was $800.

Two minutes later she was on the telephone to Shelberdine.

"Let him tire of it," said her friend. "Didn't you tell me Rudolph had Lower Lombard Strain?"

Evelyn's nose clogged with tears.

"Why is he doing this? Is it me, do you think?"

"It's the Problem," said Shelberdine. "He wants his manhood back. Before he died, Arthur did the same. Someone at the plant told him he could get it back if he did twenty-yard sprints. He went into convulsions while running around the lake."

Evelyn felt something turn in her chest. "You don't think he'll hurt himself, do you?"

"Of course not."

"Do you think he'll hurt *me?*"

Her friend reassured Evelyn that Mid-Life Crisis brought out these shenanigans in men. Evelyn replied that she thought Mid-Life Crisis started around age forty, to which Shelberdine said, "Honey, I don't mean no harm, but Rudolph always was a little on the slow side," and Evelyn agreed. She would wait until he worked this thing out of his system, until Nature defeated him and he surrendered, as any right-thinking person would, to the breakdown of the body, the brutal fact of decay, which could only be blunted, it seemed to her, by decaying *with* someone, the comfort every Negro couple felt when, aging, they knew enough to let things wind down.

Her patience was rewarded in the beginning. Rudolph crawled home from his first lesson, hunched over, hardly able to stand, afraid he had permanently ruptured something. He collapsed facedown on the living room sofa, his feet on the floor. She helped him change into his pajamas and fingered Ben-Gay into his back muscles. Evelyn had never seen her husband so close to tears.

"I can't *do* push-ups," he moaned. "Or sit-ups. I'm so stiff—I don't know my body." He lifted his head, looking up pitifully, his eyes pleading. "Call Dr. Guylee. Make an appointment for Thursday, okay?"

"Yes, dear." Evelyn hid her smile with one hand. "You shouldn't push yourself so hard."

At that, he sat up, bare-chested, his stomach bubbling over his pajama bottoms. "That's what it means. *Gung-fu* means 'hard work' in Chinese.

Evelyn"—he lowered his voice—"I don't think I've ever really done hard work in my life. Not like this, something that asks me to give *every*thing, body and soul, spirit and flesh. I've always felt . . ." He looked down, his dark hands dangling between his thighs. "I've never been able to give *every*thing to *any*thing. The world never let me. It won't let me put all of myself into play. Do you know what I'm saying? Every job I've ever had, everything I've ever done, it only demanded part of me. It was like there was so much *more* of me that went unused after the job was over. I get that feeling in church sometimes." He lay back down, talking now into the sofa cushion. "Sometimes I get that feeling with you."

Her hand stopped on his shoulder. She wasn't sure she'd heard him right, his voice was so muffled. "That I've never used all of you?"

Rudolph nodded, rubbing his right knuckle where, at the kwoon, he'd lost a stretch of skin on a speed bag. "There's still part of me left over. You never tried to touch all of me, to take everything. Maybe you can't. Maybe no one can. But sometimes I get the feeling that the unused part—the unlived life—*spoils*, that you get cancer because it sits like fruit on the ground and rots." Rudolph shook his head; he'd said too much and knew it, perhaps had not even put it the way he felt inside. Stiffly, he got to his feet. "Don't ask me to stop training." His eyebrows spread inward. "If I stop, I'll die."

Evelyn twisted the cap back onto the Ben-Gay. She held out her hand, which Rudolph took. Veins on the back of his hand burgeoned abnormally like dough. Once when she was shopping at the Public Market she'd seen monstrous plastic gloves shaped like hands in a magic store window. His hand looked like that. It belonged on Lon Chaney. Her voice shook a little, panicky. "I'll call Dr. Guylee in the morning."

Evelyn knew—or thought she knew—his trouble. He'd never come to terms with the disagreeableness of things. Rudolph had always been too serious for some people, even in South Carolina. It was the thing, strange to say, that drew her to him, this crimped-browed tendency in Rudolph to listen with every atom of his life when their minister in Hodges, quoting Marcus Aurelius to give his sermon flash, said, "Live with the gods," or later in Seattle, the habit of working himself up over Reverend Merrill's reading from Ecclesiastes 9:10: "Whatsoever thy hand findeth to do, do it with thy might." Now, he didn't *really* mean that, Evelyn knew. Nothing in the world could be taken that seriously; that's *why* this was the world. And, as all Mount Zion knew, Reverend Merrill had a weakness for high-yellow choir girls and gin, and was forever complaining that his salary was too small for his family. People made compromises, nodded at spiritual commonplaces—the high seriousness of Biblical verses that demanded nearly superhuman duty and self-denial—and laughed off their lapses into sloth, envy, and the other deadly sins. It was what made living so enjoyably *human*: this built-in inability of man to square his performance with perfection. People were naturally soft on themselves. But not her Rudolph.

Of course, he seldom complained. It was not in his nature to complain when, looking for "gods," he found only ruin and wreckage. What did he expect? Evelyn wondered. Man was evil—she'd told him that a thousand times—or, if not evil, hopelessly flawed. Everything failed; it was some sort of law. But at least there was laughter, and lovers clinging to one another against the cliff; there were novels—wonderful tales of how things should be—and perfection promised in the afterworld. He'd sit and listen, her Rudolph, when she put things this way, nodding because he knew that in his persistent hunger for perfection in the here and now he was, at best, in the minority. He kept his dissatisfaction to himself, but occasionally Evelyn would glimpse in his eyes that look, that distant, pained expression that asked: *Is this all?* She saw it after her first miscarriage, then her second; saw it when he stopped searching the want ads and settled on the Post Office as the fulfillment of his potential in the marketplace. It was always there, that look, after he turned forty, and no new, lavishly praised novel from the Book-of-the-Month Club, no feature-length movie, prayer meeting, or meal she fixed for him wiped it from Rudolph's eyes. He was, at least, this sort of man before he saw that martial-arts B movie. It was a dark vision, Evelyn decided, a dangerous vision, and in it she whiffed something that might destroy her. What that was she couldn't say, but she knew her Rudolph better than he knew himself. He would see the error—the waste of time—in his new hobby, and she was sure he would mend his ways.

In the weeks, then months, that followed, Evelyn waited, watching her husband for a flag of surrender. There was no such sign. He became worse than before. He cooked his own meals, called her heavy soul-food dishes "too acidic," lived on raw vegetables, seaweed, nuts, and fruit to make his body "more alkaline," and fasted on Sundays. He ordered books on something called Shaolin fighting and meditation from a store in California, and when his equipment arrived UPS from Dolan's Sports in New Jersey, he ordered more—in consternation, Evelyn read the list—leg stretchers, makiwara boards, air shields, hand grips, bokken, focus mitts, a full-length mirror (for Heaven's sake) so he could correct his form, and protective equipment. For proper use of his headgear and gloves, however, he said he needed a sparring partner—an opponent—he said, to help him instinctively understand "combat strategy," how to "flow" and "close the Gap" between himself and an adversary, how to create by his movements a negative space in which the other would be neutralized.

"Well," crabbed Evelyn, "if you need a punching bag, don't look at *me*."

He sat across the kitchen table from her, doing dynamic-tension exercises as she read a new magazine called *Self*. "Did I ever tell you what a black belt means?" he asked.

"You told me."

"Sifu Chan doesn't use belts for ranking. They were introduced seventy years ago because Westerners were impatient, you know, needed signposts and all that."

"You told me," said Evelyn.

"Originally, all you got was a white belt. It symbolized innocence. Virginity." His face was immensely serious, like a preacher's. "As you worked, it got darker, dirtier, and turned brown. Then black. You were a master then. With even more work, the belt became frayed, the threads came loose, you see, and the belt showed white again."

"Rudolph, I've heard this before!" Evelyn picked up her magazine and took it into her bedroom. From there, with her legs drawn up under the blankets, she shouted: "I *won't* be your punching bag!"

So he brought friends from his kwoon, friends she wanted nothing to do with. There was something unsettling about them. Some were street fighters. Young. They wore tank-top shirts and motorcycle jackets. After drinking racks of Rainier beer on the front porch, they tossed their crumpled empties next door into Rod Kenner's yard. Together, two of Rudolph's new friends—Truck and Tuco—weighed a quarter of a ton. Evelyn kept a rolling pin under her pillow when they came, but she knew they could eat that along with her. But some of his new friends were students at the University of Washington. Truck, a Vietnamese only two years in America, planned to apply to the Police Academy once his training ended; and Tuco, who was Puerto Rican, had been fighting since he could make a fist; but a delicate young man named Andrea, a blue sash, was an actor in the drama department at the university. His kwoon training, he said, was less for self-defense than helping him understand his movements onstage—how, for example, to convincingly explode across a room in anger. Her husband liked them, Evelyn realized in horror. And they liked him. They were separated by money, background, and religion, but something she could not identify made them seem, those nights on the porch after his class, like a single body. They called Rudolph "Older Brother" or, less politely, "Pop."

His sifu, a short, smooth-figured boy named Douglas Chan, who, Evelyn figured, couldn't be over eighteen, sat like the Dalai Lama in their tiny kitchen as if he owned it, sipping her tea, which Rudolph laced with Korean ginseng. Her husband lit Chan's cigarettes as if he were President Carter come to visit the common man. He recommended that Rudolph study T'ai Chi, "soft" fighting systems, ki, and something called Tao. He told him to study, as well, Newton's three laws of physics and apply them to his own body during kumite. What she remembered most about Chan were his wrist braces, ornamental weapons that had three straps and, along the black leather, highly polished studs like those worn by Steve Reeves in a movie she'd seen about Hercules. In a voice she thought girlish, he spoke of eye gouges and groin-tearing techniques, exercises called the Delayed Touch of Death and Dim Mak, with the casualness she and Shelberdine talked about bargains at Thriftway. And then they suited up, the boyish Sifu, who looked like Maharaj-ji's rougher brother, and her clumsy husband; they went out back, pushed aside the aluminum lawn furniture, and pommeled each other for half an hour. More precisely, her Rudolph was on the receiving end of hook kicks, spinning back fists faster than thought, and foot sweeps that left his body purpled for weeks. A sensible man would have known enough to drive to Swedish Hospital pronto. Rudolph, never known as a profound thinker, pushed on after Sifu Chan left, practicing his flying kicks by leaping to ground level from a four-foot hole he'd dug by their cyclone fence.

Evelyn, nibbling a Van de Kamp's pastry from Safeway—she was always nibbling, these days—watched from the kitchen window until twilight, then brought out the Ben-Gay, a cold beer, and rubbing alcohol on a tray. She figured he needed it. Instead, Rudolph, stretching under the far-reaching cedar in the backyard, politely refused, pushed the tray aside, and rubbed himself with Dit-Da-Jow, "iron-hitting wine," which smelled like the open door of an opium factory on a hot summer day. Yet this ancient potion not only instantly healed his wounds (said Rudolph) but prevented arthritis as well. She was tempted to see if it healed brain damage by pouring it into Rudolph's ears, but apparently he was doing something right. Dr. Guylee's examination had been glowing; he said Rudolph's muscle tone, whatever that was, was better. His cardiovascular system was healthier. His erections were outstanding—or upstanding—though lately he seemed to have no in- terest in sex. Evelyn, even she, saw in the crepuscular light changes in Rudolph's upper body as he stretched: Muscles like globes of light rippled along his shoulders; larval currents moved on his belly. The language of his new, developing body eluded her. He was not always like this. After a cold shower and sleep his muscles shrank back a little. It was only after his workouts, his weight lifting, that his body expanded like baking bread, filling out in a way that obliterated the soft Rudolph-body she knew. This new flesh had the contours of the silhouetted figures on medical charts: the body as it must be in the mind of God. Glistening with perspiration, his muscles took on the properties of the free weights he pumped relentlessly. They were profoundly tragic, too, because their beauty was earthbound. It would vanish with the world. You are ugly, his new muscles said to Evelyn; old and ugly.

His self-punishment made her feel sick. She was afraid of his hard, cold weights. She hated them. Yet she wanted them, too. They had a certain monastic beauty. She thought: He's doing this to hurt me. She wondered: What was it like to be powerful? Was clever cynicism—even comedy—the byproduct of bulging bellies, weak nerves, bad posture? Her only defense against the dumbbells that stood between them—she meant both his weights and his friends—was, as always, her acid Southern tongue:

"They're all fairies, right?"

Rudolph looked dreamily her way. These post-workout periods made him feel, he said, as if there were no interval between himself and what he saw. His face was vacant, his eyes—like smoke. In this afterglow (he said) he saw without judging. Without judgment, there were no distinctions. Without distinctions, there was no desire. Without desire . . .

He smiled sideways at her. "Who?"

"The people in your kwoon." Evelyn crossed her arms. "I read somewhere that most body builders are homosexual."

He refused to answer her.

"If they're not gay, then maybe I should take lessons. It's been good for you, right?" Her voice grew sharp. "I mean, isn't that what you're saying? That you and your friends are better'n everybody else?"

Rudolph's head dropped; he drew a long breath. Lately his responses to her took the form of quietly clearing his lungs.

"You should do what you *have* to, Evelyn. You don't have to do what anybody else does." He stood up, touched his toes, then brought his forehead straight down against his unbent knees, which was physically impossible, Evelyn would have said—and faintly obscene.

It was a nightmare to watch him each evening after dinner. He walked around the house in his Everlast leg weights, tried push-ups on his fingertips and wrists, and, as she sat trying to watch "The Jeffersons," stood in a ready stance before the flickering screen, throwing punches each time the scene, or shot, changed to improve his timing. It took the fun out of watching TV, him doing that—she preferred him falling asleep in his chair beside her, as he used to. But what truly frightened Evelyn was his "doing nothing." Sitting in meditation, planted cross-legged in a full lotus on their front porch, with Mr. Miller blissfully curled on his lap, a bodhisattva in the middle of house-plants she set out for the sun. Looking at him, you'd have thought he was dead. The whole thing smelled like self-hypnosis. He breathed too slowly, in Evelyn's view—only three breaths per minute, he claimed. He wore his gi, splotchy with dried blood and sweat, his calloused hands on his knees, the forefingers on each tipped against his thumbs, his eyes screwed shut.

During his eighth month at the kwoon, she stood watching him as he sat, wondering over the vivid changes in his body, the grim firmness where before there was jolly fat, the disquieting steadiness of his posture, where before Rudolph could not sit still in church for five minutes without fidgeting. Now he sat in zazen for forty-five minutes a day, fifteen when he awoke, fifteen (he said) at work in the mailroom during his lunch break, fifteen before going to bed. He called this withdrawal (how she hated his fancy language) similar to the necessary silences in music, "a stillness that prepared him for busyness and sound." He'd never breathed before, he told her. Not once. Not clear to the floor of himself. Never breathed and emptied himself as he did now, picturing himself sitting on the bottom of Lake Washington: himself, Rudolph Lee Jackson, at the center of the universe; for if the universe was infinite, any point where he stood would be at its center—it would shift and move with him. (That saying, Evelyn knew, was minted in Douglas Chan's mind. No Negro preacher worth the name would speak that way.) He told her that in zazen, at the bottom of the lake, he worked to discipline his mind and maintain one point of concentration; each thought, each feeling that overcame him he saw as a fragile bubble, which he could inspect passionlessly from all sides; then he let it float gently to the surface, and soon—as he slipped deeper into the vortices of himself, into the Void—even the image of himself on the lake floor vanished.

Evelyn stifled a scream.

Was she one of Rudolph's bubbles, something to detach himself from? On the porch Evelyn watched him narrowly, sitting in a rain-whitened chair, her chin on her left fist. She snapped the fingers on her right hand under his nose. Nothing. She knocked her knuckles lightly on his forehead. Nothing. (Faker, she thought.) For another five minutes he sat and breathed, sat and breathed, then opened his eyes slowly as if he'd slept as long as Rip Van Winkle. "It's dark," he said, stunned. When he began, it was twilight. Evelyn realized something new: he was not living time as she was, not even that anymore. Things, she saw, were slower for him; to him she must seem like a woman stuck in fast-forward. She asked:

"What do you see when you go in there?"

Rudolph rubbed his eyes. "Nothing."

"Then *why* do you do it? The world's out here!"

He seemed unable to say, as if the question were senseless. His eyes angled up, like a child's, toward her face. "Nothing is peaceful sometimes. The emptiness is full. I'm not afraid of it now."

"You empty yourself?" she asked. "Of me, too?"

"Yes."

Evelyn's hand shot up to cover her face. She let fly with a whimper. Rudolph rose instantly—he sent Mr. Miller flying—then fell back hard on his buttocks; the lotus cut off blood to his lower body—which provided more to his brain, he claimed—and it always took him a few seconds before he could stand again. He reached up, pulled her hand down, and stroked it.

"What've I done?"

"That's it," sobbed Evelyn. "I don't know what you're doing." She lifted the end of her bathrobe, blew her nose, then looked at him through streaming, unseeing eyes. "And you don't either. I wish you'd never seen that movie. I'm sick of all your weights and workouts—sick of them, do you hear? Rudolph, I want you back the way you were: *sick*." No sooner than she said this Evelyn was sorry. But she'd done no harm. Rudolph, she saw, didn't want anything; everything, Evelyn included, delighted him, but as far as Rudolph was concerned, it was all shadows in a phantom history. He was humbler now, more patient, but he'd lost touch with everything she knew was normal in people: weakness, fear, guilt, self-doubt, the very things that gave the world thickness and made people do things. She *did* want him to desire her. No, she didn't. Not if it meant oral sex. Evelyn didn't know, really, what she wanted anymore. She felt, suddenly, as if she might dissolve before his eyes. "Rudolph, if you're 'empty,' like you say, you don't know who—or what—is talking to you. If you said you were praying, I'd understand. It would be God talking to you. But this way . . ." She pounded her fist four, five times on her thigh. "It could be *evil* spirits, you know! There *are* evil spirits, Rudolph. It could be the Devil."

Rudolph thought for a second. His chest lowered after another long breath. "Evelyn, this is going to sound funny, but I don't believe in the Devil."

Evelyn swallowed. It had come to that.

"Or God—unless we are gods."

She could tell he was at pains to pick his words carefully, afraid he might offend. Since joining the kwoon and studying ways to kill, he seemed particularly careful to avoid her own most effective weapon: the wry, cutting remark, the put-down, the direct, ego-deflating slash. Oh, he was becoming a real saint. At times it made her want to hit him.

"Whatever is just *is*," he said. "That's all I know. Instead of worrying about whether it's good or bad, God or the Devil, I just want to be quiet, work on myself, and interfere with things as little as possible. Evelyn," he asked suddenly, "how can there be *two* things?" His brow wrinkled; he chewed his lip. "You think what I'm saying is evil, don't you?"

"I think it's strange! Rudolph, you didn't grow up in China," she said. "They can't breathe in China! I saw that today on the news. They burn soft coal, which gets into the air and turns into acid rain. They wear face masks over there, like the ones we bought when Mount St. Helens blew up. They all ride bicycles, for Christ's sake! They want what we have." Evelyn heard Rod Kenner step onto his screened porch, perhaps to listen from his rocker. She dropped her voice a little. "You grew up in Hodges, South Carolina, same as me, in a right and proper colored church. If you'd *been* to China, maybe I'd understand."

"I can only be what I've been?" This he asked softly, but his voice trembled. "Only what I was in Hodges?"

"You can't be Chinese."

"I don't want to be Chinese!" The thought made Rudolph smile and shake his head. Because she did not understand, and because he was tired of talking, Rudolph stepped back a few feet from her, stretching again, always stretching. "I only want to be what I *can* be, which isn't the greatest fighter in the world, only the fighter *I* can be. Lord knows, I'll probably get creamed in the tournament this Saturday." He added, before she could reply, "Doug asked me if I'd like to compete this weekend in full-contact matches with some people from the kwoon. I have to." He opened the screen door. "I will."

"You'll be killed—you know that, Rudolph." She dug her fingernails into her bathrobe, and dug this into him: "You know, you never were very strong. Six months ago you couldn't open a pickle jar for me."

He did not seem to hear her. "I bought a ticket for you." He held the screen door open, waiting for her to come inside. "I'll fight better if you're there."

She spent the better part of that week at Shelberdine's mornings and Reverend Merrill's church evenings, rinsing her mouth with prayer, sitting most often alone in the front row so she would not have to hear Rudolph talking to himself from the musty basement as he pounded out bench presses, skipped rope for thirty minutes in the backyard, or shadowboxed in preparation for a fight made inevitable by his new muscles. She had married a fool, that was clear, and if he expected her to sit on a bench at the Kingdome while some equally stupid brute spilled the rest of his brains—probably not enough left now to fill a teaspoon—then he was wrong. How could he see the world as "perfect"? That was his claim. There were poverty, unemployment, twenty-one children dying every minute, every day, every year from hunger and malnutrition, more than twenty murdered in Atlanta; there were sixty thousand nuclear weapons in the world, which was dreadful, what with Seattle so close to Boeing; there were far-right Republicans in the White House: *good* reasons, Evelyn thought, to be "negative and life-denying," as Rudolph would put it. It was almost sin to see harmony in an earthly hell, and in a fit of spleen she prayed God would dislocate his shoulder, do some minor damage to humble him, bring him home, and remind him that the body was vanity, a violation of every verse in the Bible. But Evelyn could not sustain her thoughts as long as he could. Not for more than a few seconds. Her mind never settled, never rested, and finally on Saturday morning, when she awoke on Shelberdine's sofa, it would not stay away from the image of her Rudolph dead before hundreds of indifferent spectators, paramedics pounding on his chest, bursting his rib cage in an effort to keep him alive.

From Shelberdine's house she called a taxi and, in the steady rain that northwesterners love, arrived at the Kingdome by noon. It's over already, Evelyn thought, walking the circular stairs to her seat, clamping shut her wet umbrella. She heard cheers, booing, an Asian voice with an accent over a microphone. The tournament began at ten, which was enough time for her white belt husband to be in the emergency ward at Harborview Hospital by now, but she had to see. At first, as she stepped down to her seat through the crowd, she could only hear—her mind grappled for the word, then remembered—kiais, or "spirit shouts," from the great floor of the stadium, many shouts, for contests were progressing in three rings simultaneously. It felt like a circus. It smelled like a locker room. Here two children stood toe to toe until one landed a front kick that sent the other child flying fifteen feet. There two lean-muscled female black belts were interlocked in a delicate ballet, like dance or a chess game, of continual motion. They had a kind of sense, these women—she noticed it immediately—a feel for space and their place in it. (Evelyn hated them immediately.) And in the farthest circle she saw, or rather felt, Rudolph, the oldest thing on the deck, who, sparring in the adult division, was squared off with another white belt, not a boy who might hurt him—the other man was middle-aged, graying, maybe only a few years younger than Rudolph—but they were sparring just the same.

Yet it was not truly him that Evelyn, sitting down, saw. Acoustics in the Kingdome whirlpooled the noise of the crowd, a rivering of voices that affected her, suddenly, like the pitch and roll of voices during service. It affected the way she watched Rudolph. She wondered: who are these people? She caught her breath when, miscalculating his distance from his opponent, her husband stepped sideways into a roundhouse kick with lots of snap— she heard the cloth of his opponent's gi crack like a gunshot when he threw the technique. She leaned forward, gripping the huge purse on her lap when Rudolph recovered and retreated from the killing to the neutral zone, and then, in a wide stance, rethought strategy. This was not the man she'd slept with for twenty years. Not her hypochondriac Rudolph who had to rest and run cold water on his wrists after walking from the front stairs to the fence to pick up the *Seattle Times*. She did not know him, perhaps had never known him, and now she never would, for the man on the floor, the man splashed with sweat, rising on the ball of his rear foot for a flying kick—was he so foolish he still thought he could fly?—would outlive her; he'd stand healthy and strong and think of her in a bubble, one hand on her headstone, and it was all right, she thought, weeping uncontrollably, it was all right that Rudolph would return home after visiting her wet grave, clean out her bedroom, the pillboxes and paperback books, and throw open her windows to let her sour, rotting smell escape, then move a younger woman's things onto the floor space darkened by her color television, her porcelain chamber pot, her antique sewing machine. And then Evelyn was on her feet, unsure why, but the crowd had stood suddenly to clap, and Evelyn clapped, too, though for an instant she pounded her gloved hands together instinctively until her vision cleared, the momentary flash of retinal blindness giving way to a frame of her husband, the postman, twenty feet off the ground in a perfect flying kick that floored his opponent and made a Japanese judge who looked like Oddjob shout "ippon"—one point—and the fighting in the farthest ring, in herself, perhaps in all the world, was over.

EVA'S MAN

Gayl Jones

The police came and found arsenic in the glass, but I was gone by then. The landlady in the hotel found him. She went in bringing him the Sunday's paper, and wanting the bill paid. They say she screamed and screamed and woke up the whole house. It's got a bad name now, especially that room. They tell me a lot of people like to go and look at it, and see where the crime happened. They even wrote an article about it in one of these police magazines. That's the way they do, though. I never did see the article. It bothered me at first when I found out they'd used his picture in there, one showing what I did. It didn't bother me so much having mine in there. Elvira said they had my picture in there and my hair was all uncombed and they had me looking like a wild woman.

Elvira's the woman in the same cell with me down at the psychiatric prison. They let her go out more than they do me because they say she's got more control than I have. It ain't nothing I've done since I've been in here. It's what I did before I came, the nature of my crime that makes them keep me in here. The way they look at me. They don't let me out with the other women. When Elvira goes out, she reads the papers and comes back and tells me what's in them. She wanted to bring me that article but they wouldn't let her bring it to me. I wanted to see it at first, but then when she sneaked it in with her down in her underwear, I wouldn't look at it. I made her tear it up and flush it down the toilet.

"You know, they thought you was going to give that hotel a bad name," she said. "I mean, a bad name where wouldn't nobody want to come and stay in it. But now it turns out that they's some queer people in this world."

"What do you mean?" I was frowning.

"I mean, they's people that go there just so they can sleep in the same place where it happened, bring their whores up there and all. Sleep in the same bed where you killed him at. Some peoples think that's what you was. A whore."

I kept frowning.

"It ain't me saying it."

I lay on my cot and stared up at the ceiling. There were also people saying I did it because I found out about his wife. That's what they tried to say at the trial because that was the easiest answer they could get. I've seen his wife, though. I didn't want to see her because I didn't know how I was going to feel. She came in to see me only one time during the trial. She was a skinny, run-down-looking woman in a black hat. For some reason, I had expected her to be a big, handsome-looking woman. She didn't say anything. She just stood there outside the cell and stared at me, and I stared back. The only thing I kept wondering is how did he treat *her*. Because it looked like he made her worse than he made me. I mean, if she was as bad-off on the inside as she looked on the outside. She must've stood there for close to fifteen minutes, and then left. She didn't have anything at all in her eyes—not hate not nothing. Or whatever she did have, I couldn't see it. When she left, I wondered what she saw in mine.

Even now people come in here and ask me how it happened. They want me to tell it over and over again. I don't mean just the psychiatrists, but people from newspapers and things. They read about it or hear about it someplace and just want to keep it living. At first I wouldn't talk to anybody. All during the trial I wouldn't talk to anybody. But then, after I came in here, I started talking. I tell them so much I don't even get it straight anymore. I tell them things that don't even have to do with what I did, but they say they want to hear that, too. They want to hear about what happened between my mother and father as well as what happened between me and that man. One of them came in here and even wanted to know about my grandmother and grandfather. I know when I'm not getting things straight, and I tell them I'm not getting this straight, but they say that's all right, to go ahead talking. Sometimes they think I'm lying to them, though. I tell them it ain't me lying, it's memory lying. I don't believe that, because the past is still as hard on me as the present, but I tell them that anyway. They say they're helping me. I'm forty-three years old, and I ain't seen none of their help yet.

I was thirty-eight when it happened. It don't seem like five years ago, but it was. It don't even seem like five months ago. I can still taste that cabbage I was eating. I was sitting in this place eating cabbage and sausage, drinking beer and listening to this woman onstage singing blues. I was in upstate New York then. I've lived in Kentucky. I've lived in New York City. I been in West Virginia, New Orleans. I just came from out in New Mexico. I just up and went down to New Mexico after I got laid off in Wheeling. They've got tobacco farms in Connecticut. I been there, too. I didn't travel so much until after I was married, and that went wrong, and then I said I would just stay alone. It's easier being a woman and alone in different places than it is in the same place. It had been a long time since I'd even said anything to a man. . . . The cabbage was good, kind of greasy. They cooked it right with the sausage. I was sitting in the darkest corner. I saw him before he saw me. Tall, dark-skinned, good-looking man. Remind me a little bit of the way my husband might have looked when he was young. I didn't know him when he was young. He was old when I knew him. But it might've been why I wanted him over there—I mean, reminding me of a man I used to be married to. He just reminded me of him up to the point he came to the table, though, because after that he was just himself. He'd been looking for a place where to sit, and then when he saw me he came over where I was.

"You alone?" he asked.

I could tell he was from down South. I was from the South, too. I'd sort of thought it before he opened his mouth.

"Not if you join me," I said.

He pulled back the chair and sat down. I was nervous, but I tried not to show it.

"What's your name?" he asked.

"Medina. Eva Medina."

"Medina your last name?"

"Naw. It's my middle name."

"You ain't scared of me, are you?"

"Naw."

"I'm Davis. Where you from?"

"Any place the train takes me."

"What do you do?"

"Nothing right now."

"You hard to get next to, you know that?"

"Not so hard."

I had sweat in my hands. I put one hand under the table and held the fork with the other. I wasn't eating.

"You on the road now?" he asked.

I said, "Naw, I'm here."

He laughed. The blues singer came out onstage again. It was a little narrow stage close to the tables. He stopped talking and we listened. She sang "The Evil Mama Blues" and "Stingaree Man," "See See Rider" and "Wild Women Don't Get the Blues." While she was singing, he looked over at me and said, "She's fine, ain't she?" I nodded. She was still singing when he started talking again. He said he was from somewhere down in Kentucky. He worked with horses. He spent all his life working with horses. It was horses that brought him this way North.

I didn't tell him that I knew all about men that worked with horses, that I'd spent three years of my life in Kentucky. I let him go on talking.

"I seen this ad in the paper these people wanted you to bring some horses up to New Hampshire, so I did. And now I ain't been home in almost a year. Do you follow the races?"

"Naw."

"I don't bet on the horses myself," he went on. "The last time I bet on a horse, I didn't make nothing but a hundred and eighty dollars. Now that ain't no kind of money. You know what I wanted to do was send some money home, but then all I had to send was that paycheck and a hundred and eighty dollars, but you know that ain't no kind of money. When you send money home, you don't want to send just a little taste, you know what I mean? You want to wait till you get some real money."

"I know what you mean," I said.

"They call it the devil blues," the woman was singing, low now. Davis looked back. "She real fine," he said, then he looked at me. "I can tell you something about you," he said. "You ain't been getting it, have you?"

I didn't think he'd said that, but he had. I didn't know what to answer.

He looked at me. "I don't expect you to say nothing. I can read your eyes."

"Can you?"

"Yeah, that's why I came over."

"You couldn't see my eyes then."

He nodded. "Yes I could."

The waitress came over and asked him if he wanted something.

"I'll have the same," he said, pointing to my plate. "But don't put any mustard on the sausage."

When the waitress left, he told me mustard always looked like turd to

him, baby's turd, and then he smiled and said he hoped he hadn't spoiled
my stomach.

"No, my stomach's hard."

"I'll bet it is," he said. He looked at me carefully. "A woman like you.
What do you do to yourself?" he asked.

I said nothing, then I said, "Nothing you wouldn't know about."

He laughed. "A mean, tight mama, ain't you? A old woman got me
started. Old to me then. She was thirty-nine and I was fourteen and she
lived next door and she got me started."

I was silent. "I'd've thought you got yourself started," I said finally.

"You a hard woman, too, ain't you? I *know* you got yourself started."

I didn't answer him. I was thinking of a boy with a dirty popsicle stick
digging up in my pussy, and then he let me feel his dick, and it was like
squeezing a soft milkweed.

"I got started like everyone else does," I told him. "I opened my legs.
My mother said after you've done it the first time, you won't be satisfied till
you've done it again."

"Have you ever been satisfied?"

"What do you think?"

"Let's get out of here."

"Where do we go?"

"Come home with me."

"I won't be good tonight. I'm bleeding."

"Then we'll wait."

His hand scraped my hair and he ate his food, then paid the bill and
we left.

What Elvira said those people think I am, Davis probably thought so, too.
It's funny how somebody can remind you of somebody you didn't like, or
ended up not liking and fearing—fearing is a better word—but . . . I hadn't
said anything to any man in a long time. And I'd never said Join me before.
He probably thought I was in the habit of sitting there in that dark corner
just so men would . . . Yeah, they'd come where I was. "Shit, bitch. Why
don't you stay in the house if you don't want a man to say nothing to you."
"Where you from, sweetheart?" "Shit, I know you got a tongue. I ain't never
met a bitch that didn't have a tongue." And then when I was standing at
the corner that time that man drove his car real close to the curb and opened
the door. I just stood there looking at him, and then he slammed the door
and went around the curb real quick. "Shit, you the coldest-ass bitch I ever
seen in my life." "If you don't want a man to talk to you you ought to . . ."

"Are you lonely?"

"Naw."

"You want a ride?"

"Naw."

"You think I'm gon' bother you. I ain't gon' bother you. I was just askin' if you want a ride. Shit."

That was when the buses were on strike.

"Shit, you the coldest-ass bitch I ever seen in my life."

"Are you lonely?"

"Naw."

"Why you so cold?"

"You a evil ol' bitch. Your name ain't Eva it's Evil. I wasn't doing nothing but trying to . . ."

Before Elvira went to flush the article down the toilet, she wanted to show me the picture they had of me. She folded it so that I could see the top of my wild head. Then she stuffed it in her bloomers and called them to let her be excused. He wouldn't let me comb my hair. I don't know why, but he kept me in that room and wouldn't let me comb my hair. Took my comb and kept it in his pocket.

"What the shit you want to comb your hair for. Ain't nobody see you but me."

"I don't want you to see me like this all the time."

"Shit."

I looked at him. I remember just looking at him. I said nothing.

I tell the psychiatrist what I remember. He tells me I do not know how to separate the imagined memories from the real ones.

"You know what I told you," Elvira says from her cot now.

I keep staring at the ceiling.

"The first man after you get out. The first man who does you wrong."

"Maybe I won't let no other man get close enough to do me wrong."

She laughed hard. I looked over at her ankles.

I was sitting up on the bed watching him. We were in his hotel room now. I had my shoes off and my feet up on the bed. I was hugging my legs.

"What's wrong?" he asked.

"I'll be okay after tonight. It's the first couple of days I get the cramps, and then I'm okay."

"Ain't you got nothing to take?"

"Naw."

He reached in his pocket and threw me a little tin of aspirins. He kept a jar of water on the night table. It had little bubbles in it. I poured a little in a glass. I handed him back the aspirin, but he said to put them on the table, I might need them again.

He was looking at me and then he came and rubbed his hand across my forehead. "Your forehead is like butter," he said.

I said nothing. I'd never liked for anyone to touch me around the head, but I let him. I reached up and touched his wrist.

"How long?" he asked.

"Three days," I said.

"She ain't nothing but a whore," Elvira said about one of the women in the psychiatric ward.

"She don't look like one," I said.

"Don't none of them look like none," she said.

"I only knew one whore," I said. "Some woman that lived in the same building we did."

"Did she look like one?"

"Naw. Mama said she was."

Elvira laughed.

"Once you open your legs, Miss Billie said, it seem like you cain't close them."

"What you say?" Elvira asked.

"I said what they used to say when I was a little girl."

She asked me and I told her.

She looked at me hard. "What about once you close them?" she asked.

I sat squeezing my legs together, holding my knees. I had on a long skirt.

"You look like a lion," Davis said.

He was standing at the table peeling onions. He was going to make me his favorite salad, he said. Tomatoes, onions, cucumbers, lettuce, hard-boiled eggs. Sometimes bits of ham and cheese, if he had ham and cheese. Today he didn't have ham and cheese.

"You look like a lion, all that hair."

"It's the male lions that have a lot of hair."

"Then you look like a male lion," he said, laughing. "Eva Medusa's a lion."

"Medina," I said.

"Medina," he said. "How'd you get a name like that?"

"It was my grandmother's name."

"How'd she get that name?"

"I don't know. I think one time some gypsies came by their house, and one of them's name was Medina, and her mama thought it was a pretty name."

"Aw."

The onions made tears in the corners of his eyes. He wiped them on his sleeve.

"I don't know if it's true or not. That's what they told me."

"If they told you, then it's true."

"I can help," I said.

"Naw, you still got the cramps, ain't you?"

"Yes."

Elvira laughed. "Once you close them, do you keep them closed?" she asked.

I stared at the ceiling.

"I knew a man once," Elvira said. "He drove every woman he had crazy. I don't mean easy crazy, I mean hard crazy. Had some of 'em committing suicide and stuff, and even when these women knew how he'd done all these other women, they still wanted him. I guess they figured he wouldn't get them, figured they was different or something. He was good-looking, too. But every one of 'em that went with him just got plain messed up. He messed up every woman he went with. That's the way I think of that nigger you had. That's why you killed him cause . . ."

"Shut up."

"Or maybe you that kind of a woman. Do you kill every man you go with?"

I stared at her.

I had on a skirt with an elastic waistband. He put his hand inside my underwear until he touched the edge of the pad.

"Some women wear these so they won't have to do anything."

"I wouldn't be here if I didn't want to do anything."

"Now all I got to put on this is vinegar," he said, going back to the salad. "When the vinegar touches the egg it smells like . . . a woman's smell."

"What were you going to say?"

He didn't answer. He had a sack full of paper plates. He got out two, and two plastic forks. He dished himself up a plateful and me a plateful. I stayed on the bed, but put my feet on the floor. He put my plate in my lap. He sat down beside me on the bed. He ate the lettuce and onions with his fingers and the bits of egg and tomato and cucumber with his fork.

"Egg's the same thing a woman's got up inside her," he said. "That's why it smells that way. It smells like fuck."

I frowned.

He said, "Excuse me." He took a bit of my egg on his fork, and gave me a bit of tomato from his plate.

"You don't wear earrings," he said.

"Naw."

"Most women who look like you do wear earrings."

"What's that suppose to mean?"

He didn't answer.

Davis saved most of his egg and ate it last, and then he folded my plate and his and put them in the sack he used for a trashcan.

"That was good," I said.

"It'll take a age for this room to air out," he said, then he put his arm around my waist and kissed me.

The light was swelling from the ceiling. Davis said I was pretty. He put my chin in his palm. "You so pretty," he said. "Come lay on the bed with me, honey. I won't do nothing."

But his hands made rhythms in my belly. I could feel I wanted him already.

"Who are you? Where did you come from?" he asked playfully, stretched out beside me. He'd taken off his trousers. I was down to my panties, the sanitary kind, with the plastic strip in the crotch. I was still afraid I'd stain the bedspread, so he put a towel under me. He stroked my thighs.

"Sometimes I wonder myself," I said.

He said he could smell perfume and menstruation. He said he didn't like it. I kissed his mouth.

"I got all that egg smell out, and now you smelling up my room again." He laughed.

I laughed back at him.

"Now if it was another smell . . ." he said.

I sat up in bed and started singing, the song about staying until it was time for going. He said he liked the song. I lay down beside him again, scratching under my breasts. I could tell he wanted to suck them, but he didn't. I asked him to get closer because it helped the cramps.

"All that blood," he said. "I never could help feeling it was something nasty, even with . . ."

"What's wrong?"

He got up against my belly.

Elvira asked, "What about when you close them? Do they stay closed?"

I asked her if she had another cigarette. She was going to light it for me, but I said I'd light it myself. She'd wanted to light it in her mouth and then pass it to mine.

I usually didn't smoke, but every now and then I'd want one to give me something to do. At first they wouldn't let Elvira have any cigarettes, and then when she started improving, they'd let her have cigarettes.

"Yeah, they thought I was too crazy to even have my own cigarettes," she said, stuffing them back in the pocket of her dress.

She asked me again if once you closed your legs, did you keep them closed. I asked her what did she think.

He was up against my belly. "I ain't never got in no trouble over no woman," he said. "I know mens that kill on account of a woman. I ain't even fought over no woman."

"What would you do, just let her go?" I asked.

"Yeah, I'd just let her go. If she wanted to go, I'd let her go." He started laughing, and squeezed my waist. "Now, if she didn't want to go, that's another story. If some man was trying to take her somewhere and she didn't want to go, that would be different."

"I knew a man that killed another man on account of a woman."

"Was you the woman?"

"Naw. I didn't know her. I just knew the man. . . . My cousin told me about how this man killed another man and they put him in jail for seven years. He killed him in the same restaurant we used to go in. He said they wouldn't even let him in that restaurant no more. He could come and peek in or he could send somebody in there and get him something, but he couldn't come in. Alfonso—that's my cousin—Alfonso said it was all on account of his temper. People were scared of him just on account of his temper. Alfonso said he wouldn't bother people he liked. Alfonso said he wouldn't bother me."

"He didn't kill nobody on account of you?" Davis asked.

I said nothing.

"Alfonso said he wasn't a bad man, he just had a bad temper," I said finally.

"Alfonso shit. I can feel you want me now, don't you? I can smell you want me."

"I can't now, Davis."

He got away from me.

"I'd like to, but I start getting pains afterward if I don't wait."

"Yeah, some women are like that," he said.

HOMESICK BLUES

William Melvin Kelley

Sweaty H. L. Mencken is climbing a steep rocky hill on an island in the Caribbean. Several dark-brown boys (aged eleven) playing cricket with a palm branch and scuffed red ball stop to study H. L. Mencken. He calls them over to ask questions. Opens his attaché case and produces a photo. One dreadlocked youth points toward a cluster of zinc-roofed board houses. In thanks, H. L. Mencken gives each boy a tiny sample bottle of bourbon. All but the dreadlocked youth tear into the booze. Immediately aggression comes into each innocent face. They begin to fight. One hits another in the head with the palm branch cricket bat. Blood flows.

Sweaty H. L. Mencken trudges toward the zinc-roofed houses. An old lady (thin and black) in a porch rocker watches his progress. She continues her sewing. Says something over her shoulder. H. L. Mencken trudges closer. A medium-brown, medium-height dreadlocksman comes around from the side of the old lady's house, shades his eyes, watches H. L. Mencken for a beat, goes back around the house.

A pride of dreadlocksmen sitting in the shade of low trees, playing dominoes, smoking cannabis sativa (Indian hemp) in giant goat-horn pipes. The smoke all but obscures them. Beyond them, an acre of cannabis sways and shines in the blinding sun. The first dreadlocksman penetrates the cloud of smoke.

A smoking pipe makes the rounds, reaching Clive Fairchild (played by Richard Pryor, dreader than dread, barefoot in bathing trunks and T-shirt). The first dreadlocksman alerts Clive Fairchild, who continues to smoke the pipe.

H. L. Mencken comes around the house corner, approaches the men. "Does Clive Fairchild live in this . . . ah . . . field?"

Clive Fairchild gets up and motions to H. L. Mencken to follow him. They squeeze between two cabins, climb a zinc fence, and enter a one-room cabin on stilts. A bed, a table, a chair. On the wall a photo of Haile Selassie and one of Clive Fairchild standing beside a giant oyster shell. On the table a Bible, on the bed an enormous plastic bag filled with cannabis, on the chair a black cat. Clive Fairchild sits on the bed and starts to roll a six-inch spliff.

H. L. Mencken sits on a chair. Cat does not move. Shares chair with black cat. "Are you really *the* Clive Fairchild?"

"You vas expecting maybe Mr. Kitzel?" Clive Fairchild lights the spliff, passes it to H. L. Mencken.

"But how—?"

Cut to huge, closed oyster shell floating in the blue, blue sea. In the distance a seagoing rowboat manned by six dreadlocksmen inches over the swells, approaching. Boat and shell come together. Straining, they haul the shell (diameter: five feet) into their boat. They try to open it. Their knives and cutlasses break. They row the shell ashore, carry it up the steep rocky hill to the village. Sun goes down below horizon. Suddenly night.

Quickly they collect dry wood for a bonfire and get it blazing. Three men carry and rest the shell on top of the blazing fire. The oyster shell begins to emit steam, slowly yawns open.

Clive Fairchild (Richard Pryor dressed in a diaper, shaved bald like baby) sits up in the shell. (By technical means, he appears to measure only eighteen inches from toes to top of head.) He stretches, stands up, climbs out of oyster shell. Takes a few baby steps away from the shell and the fire. Begins to grow, growing until the diaper barely covers his jewels. Stops growing when he reaches man size.

General hubbub and rumbling stops. Then stampeding with much uproar, throng disappearing into houses and up trees and down shadowy alleyways. Except one diminutive, fearless dreadlocksman. He confronts the tall, diapered stranger.

Dread Nyah: "Is this man acome directly from the Father?"

"Sheet, no, brothermucker!" Clive Fairchild answers contemptuously. "Ain't you never seed natural childbirth before?"

Dread Nyah persists. "Then the man is flesh and blood like I, man?"

Clive Fairchild sucks his tongue, cuts his eyes to the star-embedded skies. "Is I look like a brothermucking cucumber to you?"

"No, the man resemble man, true. But then is why the man not talk like man? The man have strange twang."

Recognition crosses Clive Fairchild's face. His hand moves to his belly button, a smooth black button built into his navel. He presses the button. His fingers aimlessly strum his stomach, waiting for an answer. "Wonder if they out to lunch?"

Clive Fairchild's forehead begins to glow. Lights up. A small square screen appears.

On small square screen appears Top Supreme Commodore (Redd Foxx dressed in space jumpsuit and made up to look one hundred twenty years old) sitting behind a desk.

Clive Fairchild: "9-2-1-7-2 reporting to Top Supreme Commodore, sir. I got here. All right except for the cold weather. I need a temperature adjustment. And you brothermuckers programmed my ass to brothermucking speak the wrong brothermucking language."

Top Supreme Commodore promises to adjust his computer bank. Henceforth, Clive Fairchild will automatically answer in the language spoken to him. T.S.C. signs off. Screen fades. Clive Fairchild's forehead returns to normal.

Dread Nyah has not budged. "Is sweet trick the man a have with the portable TV in him head front. Can the man teach I man that one?"

Clive Fairchild's eyes glinting. "That, me bredda, and a whole heap more." He puts his arm around Dread Nyah's shoulder. They stroll into the shadows. Follow their silhouettes down dark alleyway. Pass light in window. (By technical means.) Seeing Clive Fairchild's face rearranging itself. (Left side of face like Richard Pryor. Right side like O. J. Simpson.) Darkness again. A next window with lantern. (For the moment O. J. Simpson replaces Richard Pryor as Clive Fairchild.)

Cut to Clive Fairchild (O. J. Simpson, dreader than dread, in bathing trunks and T-shirt) strolling at sundown along lovely beach. At anchor, a quarter mile offshore, a magnificent yacht. Sounds of woman's laughter across the smooth, silent, sunset sea. Clive Fairchild stops, listens, smiles, strolls on. Then screams come over the waters. "Help!" Bubble bubbles. A woman drowning.

Clive Fairchild shattering the sea stillness, swimming toward the bubbling screams. Shark-swift through still waters.

From the yacht's bridge Sir Noel Coward (puffing a cigarette in holder) watches the swimming dreadlocksman through a spyglass, shifts his attention to the drowning woman.

Sir Noel Coward: "Wager you a week's wages he won't reach her in time, Desmond!"

Desmond (played by Sidney Poitier in Hitler mustache, white coat, and black trousers) steps forward with an ashtray. "Done, mein Herr!"

Blond tresses suspended, bubbles, in water. Breasts floating. A hand clutches at air, sinks. Clive Fairchild crashes into frame, dives. Still water. Water shatters. Clive Fairchild spitting a mouthful, smiling. (Theme music, uptempo.) Clive Fairchild levels out in the water, dragging Miss Fine Young Thing by long blond hair.

Sir Noel Coward to Desmond: "Oh, well, better throw them a line, dear boy."

Desmond hops to the task, throws life preserver. Clive Fairchild catches the ring. Desmond tows them through the dark green sea to the yacht. Lowers the portable stairs. Clive Fairchild carries Miss Fine Young Thing on board, lays her out on the deck. Her breasts sag sideways. A big red lobster has her by her big toe.

Miss Fine Young Thing looks d.e.a.d. Clive Fairchild kneels to offer mouth-to-mouth resuscitation. Close-up of face of Miss Fine Young Thing (played by Donna Summer in platinum blond wig).

Miss Fine Young Thing slowly recovers. Clive Fairchild and Desmond give each other elaborate Afro-American-style handshakes. Laugh with pink tongues.

Miss Fine etc. opens her eyes. "What Mammy said about heaven, it's true after all."

Sir Noel Coward calls down from the bridge. "Getting a little lonesome up here, chaps."

"Lobster for dinner this evening, mein Herr." Desmond prying the lobster's claw open.

Clive Fairchild lifts up Miss Fine and carries her below deck. Desmond packs the red lobster (obviously rubberoid) in ice and joins them, finding they have already begun to share each other's charms. Sheets jumping up and down with pumping and bumping.

"Heaven. Heaven. Heaven." Miss Fine repeating.

Desmond taps Clive Fairchild on the shoulder. "Your presence is requested in the captain's cabin, my dear schvartzer."

Cut to Clive Fairchild (O. J. Simpson in borrowed white bermudas and sport shirt) striding along a passageway, stopping, knocking at a door, waiting. Opens door. Steps over high sill into the captain's cabin.

Sir Noel Coward looks up from requisite papers. "I trust you found your accommodations satisfact'ry, Fairchild. Suppose you've wondered why I've done all this for you."

Sir Noel Coward unveils his plan. So to inflict the American People with the virus of feeling inferior that they will beg to abolish the Republic and ask to rejoin Her Majesty's Empire and Commonwealth. "After all, we've been the Mind of America from the first over. We've sent Tom Paine. Charles Chaplin. Bob Hope. Cary Grant. Richard Burton. The Beatles. Shirley Bassey." Hums a few bars of Harrison's "Something." "The weapon we'll use is corruption. Death before it begins to stink. We'll prove conclusively that absolutely every American has a price. Rupture the American Spirit once and for all! What a pool of cheap labor—pardon, labour—for the Mother Country!" Chuckles cynically, curling his lip.

Fairchild asks requisite dumb question. "What could your megalomaniacal plan possibly have to do with yours truly, this humble dreadlocks?"

Sir Noel Coward cocks his eyebrow. "I need a fearless man. A man with nothing to lose. An existential warrior. A superlative salesman, dear boy. You've come into my life precisely on time. But first you need a bit of gloss."

Cut to long shot of Fairchild crossing Cambridge Common going toward Harvard Square. Fairchild (library footage of O. J. Simpson) feinting and sprinting up and down the gridiron. Thousands cheering wildly. Cheerleaders making their boobs bounce, jumping in glee. Yalies disconsolate.

Medium shot of Fairchild studying in Widener Library. Then raising his hand in class, answering eagerly. Fairchild (in Ve.Ri.Tas sweatshirt and pants, A.Di.Das warm-up shoes) running around Soldier's Field track. Harvard head track coach (played by vintage Gary Cooper in baseball pants and maroon jacket) with stopwatch, nodding head in amazement. Close-up of stopwatch, symbol of time clapping irons on life, becomes close-up on end of rolled college diploma. Fairchild in cap and gown. Steps forward and shakes hand of president of the University (played by T. S. Eliot, in academic robes and pince-nez, pro.Keds sneaking out from under gown). Fairchild in his room in Winthrop House packing his collection of designer jock straps and radical literature.

Sir Noel Coward watches. Sitting astride a desk chair, spats flashing, elbows resting on chair back. "Proud of you, dear boy."

Desmond (Sidney Poitier in Hitler mustache and Brooks Bros. suit and two bulbs light-up his bow tie) takes monocle from left eye. "But has he learned the vays of evil? College is, after all, not life."

The three men turn to front and nod gravely.

Cut to Washington, D.C. (Montage). Washington Monument. Some men with attaché cases. Jefferson Memorial. Some men with briefcases. Stone Abraham Lincoln high on his throne. Some men with attaché cases. Supreme Court building. Some men with briefcases, climbing front steps. Congressional dome. Senate Chamber. Senator Daniel Webster rising from behind his little black school desk to request that the Senator from the great State of Affairs yield ourselves to mark well these signs for as the sky, deeply imbued with the spirit of reckless deliberation on all sides, can certainly in this hour of unrivaled in our e.r.a. All nod thoughtfully. Reverse zoom shows Senate Chamber as game on table. Medium shot of Sir Noel Coward spying on White House through his spyglass. Sir Noel Coward takes spyglass from his eye. Close-up of black ring around Sir Noel Coward's eye.

Fairchild and Desmond give each other elaborate Afro-American hand-shake, laughing with big pink tongues.

Sir Noel Coward spies himself in mirror and does a slow Edward Kennedy burn. "I am not in the least amused. I could easily have involved myself and resources with another set of bongos and avoided a great deal of mental fat.tee.gay."

Desmond snaps to attention, clicking heels of shiny black jackboots. "Of course he iss right, Fairchild. Time for Blacks, Leftists and Fascists alike to get serious."

Fairchild to Desmond: "And which are you, Desmond, Leftist or Fascist? I'm never quite certain."

Desmond to Sir Noel Coward: "Doesn't know us wary well, does he?" To Fairchild: "My dear schvartzer, the voild iss divided between two kinds, those who carry Whips and those who carry Shovels. I am a Whip. Some-times a Leftist Whip. Sometimes a Fascist Whip. But always a Whip."

Fairchild to Desmond: "And might I ask where women fit into your scheme of things?"

Desmond to Fairchild: "Why, females are born Shovels!" Lights his two-bulb bow tie.

(Kate Millet, Eleanor Holmes Norton, and Bella Abzug, stunningly done up as dance-hall girls, all breasts and bustles on ten-inch stiletto heels, tear out the upper left corner of the screen. They hiss and boo and give Bronx cheers: "Hissss! Boooo! Thpthptzzzz!")

Sir Noel Coward to all: "Gentlemen, gentlemen. Let's sit around the requisite planning table and plan our evil campaign. New York will be more difficult to conquer than Washington. All the best, the youngest and strong-est, collect there. The cream."

Desmond strikes a Jimmy Durante shuffling-off pose, eyes ashine. "Sour that cream, Clive Fairchild. Won't I have the time of my life strutting through the corridors of power! In my black knee-high boots and sweeping trench coat. Man, have I got nuts to get off!"

Fairchild contemptuously: "You whips are all alike. Theatrical! Let's get on with it. I've business elsewhere."

Sir Noel Coward to Fairchild: "Well, then, dear boy, is there anything new coming out of your laborat'ry?" Puts arm around Fairchild's shoulder, leads him from table toward leather sofa.

Cut to Clive Fairchild standing on the steps of the Harvard Club and chatting with Teddy Roosevelt. In unison, they turn to look west on Forty-fourth Street. Long shot of Ralph Waldo Emerson. He smiles, waves, quickens his pace. Meeting, they shake hands all around and enter the clubhouse, climb a circular staircase to a private meeting room on an upper floor. Fairchild's face undergoes transformation with a mosaic of quick microscopic close-ups of individual features (Pryor's mouth; Simpson's right ear; Pryor's left eye; Simpson's nose), changing from O. J. Simpson into R. Pryor with each step the three men climb. The change happens so smoothly and subtly that neither Teddy Roosevelt nor Ralph Waldo Emerson notices.

They reach the upper room. They enter. Clive Fairchild locks door behind them. They sit around a round table. Fairchild puts his attaché case on the table. Two locks spring open. Fairchild raises the case lid. Close-up of case insides. Sticky resinous bark-brown cannabis.

Teddy Roosevelt and Ralph Waldo Emerson sigh, nod approvingly, eyes alight. Fairchild puts a handful in front of each man. All produce personal Bambu papers and start to clean and roll. Fairchild uses bread-wrapper paper found only in Kingston to build himself a gigantic spliff. The three men light up. Take deep drags. Get well charged. Emerson cracks up everybody with his imitation of Henry Ward Beecher. Teddy Roosevelt captures center stage with a bloody good yarn about hunting in the Dakotas. Fairchild observes.

Ralph Waldo Emerson to all: "One of my many protégés cultivates a hemp like this in the woods near Walden Pond, though not so well cured."

Teddy Roosevelt, spliff clenched in teeth, pounds his palm with his fist. "Bully smoke! San Juan Gold can't compare!"

Fairchild to both: "You boys drop pills?"

They reply eagerly in the affirmative. Fairchild reaches into his suit-coat pocket and pulls out a large assortment of pills. Close-up of Fairchild's pill-piled palm. One pill appears larger than the round and oblong assortment. Zoom to tight close-up of strange pill. A tiny naked woman encased in the clear pill, mummy-like.

Teddy Roosevelt shows interest in the strange, coffin-shaped pill.

Fairchild cautions Teddy Roosevelt: "You don't take that one, sir. It takes you."

Teddy Roosevelt insists. Fairchild places the tiny pill on the oak table. He finds a carafe of water and splashes some into a glass, returns to table. Pours a few drops onto the pill.

Fairchild to all: "Ordinarily you do it in the bathtub."

Strange pill begins to disintegrate as form within grows, taking the shape of Miss Fine Young Thing stretched out on oaken table like Elsa Lanchester in *The Bride of Frankenstein*. Miss Fine Young Thing blinks. Sits up. (Disco music building behind.) Stands up on table. Gets down to boogie. The joint starts jumping.

Teddy Roosevelt pulls a magnum of champagne from a large inside pocket and drinks bubbly from Miss Fine's glass slipper. Ralph Waldo Emerson removes tons of Victorian clothes and vows to outdo Thoreau by spending five years at Walden Pond. Teddy Roosevelt asks if he might take some party pills home with him. Fairchild whispers into ear of Teddy Roosevelt. Ralph Waldo Emerson, wearing shoes but sockless, boxer shorts but shirtless, stuffs his jacket pockets with cannabis and wanders out. (Disco music fades.) Teddy Roosevelt rolls some smokes for the journey, straightens his tie. Fairchild hands him big bottle of pills. Close-up of bottle. All pills, each pill with sleeping princess inside, blonds, brunettes, redheads, some Orientals, some Hispanics, some Negresses. Hours of funnilingus uninterruptus. Teddy Roosevelt departs. Image of Miss Fine Young Thing starts to fade, calling plaintively to Fairchild, as if lost. "Fairchild? Fairchild! Where are you?"

Fairchild to fading image: "Shut up, witch. You said you wanted me to put you in show biz!" Image disappears.

Clive Fairchild sits in an official black Harvard chair. Leans back. Thinks. Fumbles with buttons on his button-down shirt and pushes his black belly button, relaxing deeper into the hard chair. Forehead starts glowing. Square of light comes on, grows more definite. Full-color three-inch TV screen.

Close-up of screen. Top Supreme Commodore sitting behind desk, smiling benignly. "So awfully glad you found me at home, 9-2-1-7-2. As a matter of fact, I do hope you will make this interview short and to the point. I've tickets for a Thru Time Theater presentation of the original production of Ira Aldridge as Othello. That's why you've found me in my British voice."

Fairchild, as if in meditation talking to himself: "Well, I didn't mean to . . ."

Top Supreme Commodore, reassuringly: "No, no, 9-2. You don't mind my using the familiar, do you? No, go ahead."

Fairchild: "It's this mission, sir. A bit nasty. I don't fancy the wicket. I don't like things I'm having to do, sir."

Top Supreme Commodore: "Such as? I haven't been watching your activities very closely."

Fairchild: "I've run into an evil man, sir. He's having me do the vilest things. Concerning some differences this species is having. Primitive political stuff, really. Anyway—"

"You shock me, 9-2!" Top Supreme Commodore's image burns brighter in Fairchild's forehead. "And, might I say, disappoint me. We've sent you on a delicate mission of universal significance and you're bloody crying in your bloody milk over some minor tribal doings. This is insupportable nonsense! Do the job, 9-2. Do the job. Accomplish your mission and return to base! Good night!"

Screen in Fairchild's forehead goes out abruptly, leaving the room dim. Close-up of Clive Fairchild's face. Eyes brim. One tear trickling. Close-up of tear. Glistens. Fades.

A VISITATION

OF SPIRITS

Randall Kenan

April 29, 1984
11:30 A.M.

. . . What to become?

At first Horace was sure he would turn himself into a rabbit. But then, no. Though they were swift as pebbles skipping across a pond, they were vulnerable, liable to be snatched up in a fox's jaws or a hawk's talons. Squirrels fell too easily into traps. And though mice and wood rats had a magical smallness, in the end they were much smaller than he wished to be. Snakes' heads were too easily crushed, and he didn't like the idea of his entire body slithering across all those twigs and feces and spit. Dogs lacked the physical grace he needed. More than anything else, he wanted to have grace. If he was going to the trouble of transforming himself, he might as well get exactly that. Butterflies were too frail, victims to wind. Cats had a physical freedom he loved to watch, the svelte, smooth, sliding motion of the great cats of Africa, but he could not see transforming himself into anything that would not fit the swampy woodlands of southeastern North Carolina. He had to stay here.

No, truth to tell, what he wanted more than anything else, he now realized, was to fly. A bird. He had known before, but he felt the need to sit down and ponder the possibilities. A ritual of choice, to make it real. A bird.

With that thought he rose, his stomach churning with excitement. A bird. Now to select the type. The species. The genus. He knew the very book to use in the school library; he knew the shelf, and could see the book there in its exact placement, now, slightly askew between a volume on bird-feeders no one ever moved and a treatise on egg collecting; he could see the exact angle at which it would be resting. Hadn't the librarian, Mrs. Stokes, always teased him that he knew the library better than she ever would? And wasn't she right?

He was sitting on the wall at the far end of the school campus, on the other side of the football field, beyond the gymnasium, beyond the main school building. He had wanted to be alone, to think undistracted. But now he was buoyed by the realization that he knew how he would spend the rest of his appointed time on this earth. Not as a tortured human, but as a bird free to swoop and dive, to dip and swerve over the cornfields and tobacco patches he had slaved in for what already seemed decades to his sixteen years. No longer would he be bound by human laws and human rules that he had constantly tripped over and frowned at. Now was his chance, for he had stumbled upon a passage by an ancient mystic, a monk, a man of God, and had found his salvation. It was so simple he wondered why no one had discovered it before. Yet how would anyone know? Suddenly poor old Jeremiah or poor old Julia disappears. Everybody's distraught; everybody worries. They search. They wait. Finally the missing person is declared dead. And the silly folk go on about their business and don't realize that old Julia turned herself into an eel and went to the bottom of the deep blue sea to see what she could see. There are no moral laws that say: You must remain human. And he would not.

His morning break was over. The other students were hustling back to third period. But he decided to skip. What did it matter? In a few days he would be transformed into a creature of the air. He could soar by his physics class and listen to Mrs. Hedgeson deliver her monotone lecture about electrons; he could perch on the ledge and watch the biology students dissect pickled frogs; hear the Spanish class tripping over their tongues; glide over the school band as they practiced their awkward maneuvers on the football field, squawking their gleaming instruments. All unfettered, unbound, and free.

As he walked down the hall, he suddenly realized he had no hall pass and that the vice-principal might walk by and demand it. But no. He was

Horace Thomas Cross, the Great Black Hope, as his friend John Anthony had called him. The Straight-A Kid. Or once, at least. Where most students would be pulled aside and severely reprimanded, he could walk unques- tioned. In his mind he could see his Cousin Ann smiling her cinnamon smile and hear her say in her small, raspy voice: But don't you know it yet, Horace? You the Chosen Nigger.

The library was empty except for old Mrs. Stokes, who stood by the card catalogue and smiled at him, nodding knowingly. If she only realized—her gray hair would turn white. He walked straight to the exact aisle, the exact shelf, selected the exact book, and took it to a table in the back of the library, even though he was the only other person in that large room. He sat by a window overlooking the long, sloping lawn, spring green, that dipped into the pine-filled woods.

It was a huge book. White cloth with elegant gold lettering: *Encyclopedia of North American Birds*, a book he had known since elementary school, with its crisp photographs and neat diagrams and its definitions upon defi- nitions upon definitions. Because it was a reference book he couldn't check it out, so for long hours he would sit and read about migratory paths, the use of tail feathers, the gestation periods of eggs. . . .

As he opened the book he felt the blood rush to his head, and the first color plates cranked up his imagination like a locomotive: gulls, cranes, owls, storks, turkeys, eagles. He flipped through the book, faster and faster. Which bird? Sparrow, wren, jay. No, *larger*. Mallard, grouse, pheasant. *Larger*. Goose, swan, cormorant. *Larger*. Egret, heron, condor. Pages flipped; his heart beat faster; his mind grew fuzzy with possibilities. Raven, rook, black- bird. Crow . . .

He slammed the book shut, realizing that he had been riffling through the pages like a madman. Mrs. Stokes looked up quickly, startled, then gave him that brief, knowing smile.

He closed his eyes and thought of the only way he could make his decision. He thought about the land: the soybean fields surrounding his grandfather's house, the woods that surrounded the fields, the tall, massive long-leaf pines. He thought of the miles and miles of highways, asphalt poured over mule trails that etched themselves into the North Carolina landscape, onto the beach, sandy white, the sea, a murky churning, the foam, spray, white, the smell of fish and rotting wood. He thought of winters, the floor of the woods a carpet of dry leaves, brown-and-black patchwork carpet. He thought of the sky, not a blue picture-book sky with a few thin clouds, but a storm sky, black and mean, full of wind and hate, God's wrath, thunder, pelting rain. He thought of houses, new and old, brick and wood, high and low, roofs mildewed and black, chimneys, lightning rods, TV antennas. He was trying to think like a bird, *the* bird, the only bird he could become. And when he saw a rabbit, dashing, darting through a field of brown rye grass, and when he saw talons sink into the soft brown fur, he knew.

But he had known before, had realized when he stumbled across the pact the old monk had made with the demon in the book, that if he were to transform himself, irrevocably, unconditionally, he would choose a red-tailed hawk. He opened the book to the hawk family—pausing at the eagle, but knowing that was too corny, too noticeable, not indigenous to North Carolina—and flipped to the picture of his future self. He could not help but smile. The creature sat perched on a fence post, its wings brought up about its neck, its eyes murderous. Many times he had admired the strong flight of the bird, the way it would circle the field like a buzzard, but not like a buzzard, since the rat or the rabbit or the coon it was after was not dead—yet. Talons would clutch the thrashing critter tighter than a vise, its little heart would beat in sixteenth notes, excited even more by the flapping wings that beat the air like hammers and blocked the sun like Armageddon. Then the piercing of the neck, the rush of hot, sticky blood. The taste of red flesh. He felt a touch of empathy for the small mammal, its tail caught in the violent twitching of death thralls, but he was still thrilled.

He turned and looked to the woods and sighed, the sigh of an old man, of resigned resolve and inevitable conclusion. A sigh too old for a sixteen-year-old boy. He rose and replaced the book. The bell rang, signaling the end of third period. He thought of never walking down this aisle and past that shelf again; he would read none of these volumes again. He allowed himself to swell up. Not with sadness, but with pride. He had found the escape route, of which they were all ignorant. Mrs. Stokes once again gave her knowing nod. He winked at her and did not look back.

He sat through the rest of his classes, taking no notes, not listening, more as a matter of form, a fare-thee-well. No one bothered him. He had noticed that for the last few weeks people had been staying away from him, whispering behind his back that he was acting strange. But it was no matter. Soon it would all be over.

He rode the bus home in peace. Track practice was over. There were only two weeks left before summer vacation, but he would have skipped practice anyway. He sat back and watched the other students in their horse-play and shenanigans, the girls lost in their gossip, the boys bragging and arm-wrestling, playing cards. From the window he watched the land, the land over which he would soon rise. Soon and very soon.

Looking out the window, he felt a brief wave of doubt flicker within. Had he gone mad? Somehow slipped beyond the veil of right reasoning and gone off into some deep, unsettled land of fantasy? The very thought made him cringe. Of course he was not crazy, he told himself; his was a very rational mind, acquainted with science and mathematics. But he was also a believer in an unseen world full of archangels and prophets and folk rising from the dead, a world preached to him from the cradle on, and a world he was powerless not to believe in as firmly as he believed in gravity and the times table. The two contradicting worlds were not contradictions in his mind. At the moment it was not the world of digits and decimal points he required, but the world of messiahs and miracles. It was faith, not facts he needed; magic, not math; salvation, not science. Belief would save him, not only belief, but belief in belief. Like Daniel, like Isaac, like the woman at the well. I am sane, he thought, smoothing over any kinks in his reasoning and clutching fear by the neck. He had no alternative, he kept saying to himself. No other way out.

When he got home, he went straight to his room and closed the door. His grandfather was out, but he didn't want to risk tipping his hand. His room, the entire house, smelled of hard pine and the lingering smell of paint and floor varnish, of cypress window frames and heavily oiled oak furniture and dust trapped in the curtains, the farmhouse dust from the dirt road and the fields—but more than anything else there was the ever-present smell of pine. Heart pine, the old folks called it. The hardest there is. Better than oak. A seventy-one-year-old smell he had smelled all his life, through the many coats of antique white paint, through the well-coated floors, through the dust. In his mind it was the smell of prayer, the smell of childbirth, the smell of laughter, the smell of tears, dancing, sweat, the smell of work, sex, death.

On the white walls of his room hung his many friends. Over the bed was the Sorcerer—the Conjurer, the Supreme Magician. His eyes were a mysterious blue, piercing and all-knowing. Over his eyes hung a great shock of black hair, showing his virility; the hair at his temples was snowy white, showing his wisdom. His great red cape was caught in a wind, making it billow as dramatically as a thunderclap. His stance—you could tell he was commencing to cast a spell because his hands were surrounded by an electric-blue glow—resembled a pouncing tiger's. His body was well muscled and lean, covered in skintight blue leggings and a blue tunic with an Egyptian ankh on its chest. A huge amulet was suspended from a chain about his neck, a half-open eye peering through.

On the other walls hung a huge green monster-man so muscled he appeared to be a green lump, with huge bare feet, clad only in tattered purple pants, giving an animal leer; a woman whirling a golden lasso, wearing a brassiere shaped like an eagle and zooming through the air atop an airplane made of glass; a Viking with long yellow hair and bulging muscles, swinging a hammer as large as he, his icy blue eyes flashing a solemn warning; a man dressed in a midnight-blue cowl with pointy ears like a cat and a midnight-blue cape to match, which billowed even more than the sorcerer's, the emblem of a bat planted across his chest. There were posters of little creatures with hair on their feet as thick as rugs, who possessed round bellies and smoked huge pipes. There were designs for starships, and diagrams of battlestars, star maps and star charts, a list of names of demons and pictures of gryphons and krakens and gorgons. . . .

Papers were scattered about the room; on the bed, on the floor, on the desk and the dresser and the nightstand. And the books. Books piled high, opened and marked. Old books, new books. Colorful and drab. Books half-read standing on their parted pages, the spines pointing toward the ceiling. Boy, his grandfather would say, cross and vexed, can't you keep your room no neater than this? What you gone do when they puts you in the army? They don't have no such foolishness there. But the A's and A-pluses on his report card would quiet his grandfather's commands—Clean up that room, boy—to mere grumbles, mild reproaches, disapproving shakes of his head.

The school library allowed Horace, or any other student, to check out only three books at a time. So he also belonged to both the county library in Crosstown and the local library in Sutton. Then there were the book clubs: the Book-of-the-Month Club, the History Book Club, the Science Fiction Book Club. . . . He borrowed books from his teachers, from his friends. When he went to larger cities—Wilmington, Kinston, Goldsboro —he would buy even more books, usually paperbacks. Most of them he had read, some more than once; in others, mostly the nonfiction, he read the parts that interested him most, from ancient Chinese history to shipbuilding to biographies of famous businessmen and great scientists. But that had been before; now he concentrated on the occult.

Littered about the room were books with titles like *Black Magic/White Magic, The Arcane Art, Witches, Voodoo, Essays on the Dark Arts, Third World Religions, A History of Magic, Magicians of the Bible, Gray's Index to the Bizarre and the Unusual, Demon Lore*. It was in one of these volumes that he found the key, and he had spent weeks checking and double-checking, cross-referencing, correlating, compiling his facts and perfecting the perfect spell. To him this room was not a high school lad's bedroom in an old farmhouse on a dirt road in the backwoods, but the secluded and mysterious lair of an apprentice sorcerer about to step into the realm of a true mystic. The walls were not wood; they were ancient and chipped stone. The books were not paperbacks and library loans; they were parched scrolls and musty tomes.

Simplicity. The simplicity alone swept him away. The very notion that the entire ordeal was no ordeal at all—not for those who read and thought and were unafraid. He looked at the list before him. On the surface it looked like a grocery list, but as you read it the oddity struck. What kind of cake could be baked from cat's urine and the whole head of a hummingbird? The list was long and complicated, each ingredient demanding its own special care and sometimes an ingenious method of collection. It had taken well over a month to compile this list. How do you capture the stale breath of a hag threescore and ten? Where could he possibly find the ground tooth of a leviathan? But after painfully checking and rechecking with similar recipes and rites, he was sure it was okay to substitute nail clippings for the breath. And a shark's tooth instead of a real sea monster's. He was confident the substitutions would work, except for one: the most powerful ingredient was the body of a babe, no older than three years. He could not decide if the "babe" had to be human or whether it could be any species of infant. The worry had caused him many a sleepless night and many dark dreams of sneaking into a house after midnight and stealthily snatching an infant who would look dolefully into his eyes, innocent and quiet, sucking its thumb in sweet contentment. In the dream he would sing to the child, singing: *Hush, little baby, don't you cry,* as he smothered it to its white death beneath a goose-stuffed pillow and when he raised the pillow in the dim starlight the silent child would still be staring at him, this time the eyes a little puzzled, unfocused, slobber rolling fresh from its still-smiling, slightly parted lips. He would wake from these dreams with a moan at the back of his throat, chill sweat beading his forehead, the fear of the wrath of the one true God beating in his breast, frantic to escape. But it would be madness to commit such a horrible sin to obtain his freedom. For was not this dipping, this dunking, this drowning in magic an attempt to escape from that sin he would surely commit if he remained human?

So, confident that his spells would work, he collected the sackcloth bag containing all the powerful talismans of his liberation and left the room, walking down the heart-of-pine floor and out the back door. In the backyard, beyond the lawn, was an apple orchard, begun with saplings his grandfather's mother had planted even before the house was built. Most of the yard had been a chicken pen, with bare dirt from their scratching. But when his grandmother died, his grandfather decided to get shed of the chickens and let the grass grow over the earth. Here he now cut the grass once a week, beginning in May, going almost into October, grass that grew greener and tougher with each summer rain.

The apple trees bore pale-green fruit no larger than his thumb this time of the year. By August they would be a little smaller than his fist and red like roses' red. They were what people called horse apples, sour and small, only good for making tart apple pies and cobblers. Come July he would pluck one off every now and again, remembering how as a little boy he would be so sternly reprimanded: Boy, them green apples will give you a stomachache. Make you sick as a dog. But he would eat them anyway. And miraculously he never got those green-apple bellyaches. He did so love that tart and sour taste that drew his mouth up the way a lemon would, the texture of the white flesh on the inside, even the crisp crunch it made when you bit into it. While thinking this a wave of sadness washed over him, for he realized birds can't really bite into an apple; they peck. And only chickens peck at barnyard apples. But he would feast on squirrel and rabbit—he would lose green apples for a real chance at eternal life.

Twilight was falling. The days were beginning to lengthen, so he had time to prepare; he knew his grandfather would be away until very late. The day before he had set up the pyre. A slab of metal to hold the ingredients. A few pieces of old pine, dripping strong with turpentine. Oak and hickory. A little tar, because one spell called for pitch. Then he spread the sack over the pyre and checked his grim ingredients against the list. The plastic bag that held the body of the kitten he had killed was thick with moisture, the animal's hair matted, black, and lank. Then with a strike-anywhere match he set it all afire. It was slow to blaze, but after a while—he had stuck some straw between also—its flames licked and belched and farted and sparked in a way that aroused him. The black smoke from the tar wisped up through the apple trees and danced high.

He began to chant some archaic words, most of whose meaning he had no notion of, but which he suspected had to be powerful, words he had spliced together from different rites and rituals from similar conjurings and acts of high sorcery. The words sounded German and French and Latin and Greek, and because he had no true knowledge of any other language than his high school Spanish, he created a special accent for this chant, which he fancied a cross between High German and French. And in the middle of his chant the smell of the burning cat struck him full in the face—a green, vile smell of guts and hair and dried urine and feces. But he continued, as he choked on the noxious fumes, to recite in his elegant accent.

When he had finished chanting the chant, thrice—an act that would make the ashes holy and protect him from the demon he would summon— he committed the paper with the chant and the paper with the list to the fire and went behind an apple tree and retched in violent spasms that brought tears to his eyes. Weakly he walked to the water spigot by the pump house that sat on top of the very well where once his great-grandmother had hauled up water in a wooden pail. The water was still well-sweet and well-bitter and tasted thick with iron. First he washed his mouth out and then he drank deeply of the sweet and bitter water, finally washing his face in its coolness. He sat on the back stoop, watching the fire die down and down. The sky, which had been high and blue earlier, streaked with thin white clouds, was now collecting clouds the color of tar smoke. His stomach began to knot for fear of what the gathering clouds could mean or should mean to a true mystic.

About an hour later, when the fire was no more than coals crackling with heat, he went to bank the smoldering ashes so they would be ready for the hour of his transfiguration. He went into the house, into his room, and began to tidy up, the neatest it had ever been. Books stacked in straight piles, papers filed away, clothes folded and put in a drawer. He did not worry about the library loans, for it would all be part of his disappearance. Now he was excited and restless. He considered leaving his grandfather a note: Granddaddy, I have been transformed. I will see you in the rapture. But no, his grandfather would think it a queer and peculiar joke. It would confound and confuse him and then, when his grandson did indeed actually disappear without a trace, it would leave him thinking strange and bizarre thoughts, because he would have no knowledge of the dazzling, wondrous truth.

He went back out to the pile of ashes, now all white and less hot. He stoked them yet higher and went back inside to complete the last leg of his conjuring. His grandfather had returned while he had been outside and asked why he had not touched the food his aunts had left. Horace complained of not being hungry and went into his neat room and lay down in the darkness, knowing he would not fall asleep. He set his alarm clock for fifteen minutes to twelve. Then, suddenly appearing in the doorway, his grandfather asked: What you been burning, boy? Smells like you been burning tires or something. He told his grandfather: Just some old planks that kept getting in my way when I cut grass. His grandfather stood silently for a while, peering into the black, silhouetted by the light from the kitchen. Rather than ask, as Horace was sure he would, if he was feeling sick, the old man turned and went back into the kitchen. Horace heard the sounds of his grandfather washing his one dish: the water pipes clunking; the water splashing; a plate being set in the dish rack to dry; the refrigerator door opening and closing. He heard the light go out—for his eyes were closed—and the sound of the metal chain chinking like a pendulum against the hollow light bulb; then he and the house were locked in one dark velvet quiet. He listened to his grandfather shuffle out to the porch where he sat in his rocking chair and rocked, the planks of the wooden porch beneath groaning in a slow rhythm. Had the doctor not made his grandfather give up chewing tobacco, he knew he would have heard the splat of juice, flawlessly aimed, hit the azalea bush.

Crickets and frogs and cicadas chirped the beating of a thousand tiny hearts. A turtledove cooed in the woods in the distance, and he did not think of birds and soaring and freedom as he had earlier, but of his humanity, his flesh, his blood, his soon-to-be-gone, soon-to-be-changed life. He considered the deep quiet called death and how different it was from this blue solitude, here, now, on his bed surrounded by thinly made sound and soft black.

After an hour or so his grandfather stopped rocking, stood, and walked into the house. The screen door banged behind him loudly. Well, his grandfather said, good night. After a pause his grandfather asked if he was all right. Quickly, too quickly, Horace said yes, in a voice that was almost puzzled. His grandfather said nothing more, shuffling softly to his room, turning on no light. Horace heard the old man remove his clothes and get into his pajamas—he was sure they were the light-blue pajamas he wore in summer, the ones his aunts ironed with too much starch—and ease into bed. Then the light came on and he heard the rustle of paper, the onionskin pages of a book. He knew it was the Bible his grandfather kept on his nightstand, for that was the only book his grandfather ever read, save the *Lady's Birthday Almanac* (which was really a magazine). Not long after the book went back on the nightstand, the light went out, and his grandfather sighed a long sigh, almost a sound of frustration. Once again there were only the other sounds, the natural, small music of the night.

He would not look at the clock—though, in truth, he had stolen a glance earlier to see if it was working. It was. So he just lay immobile, thinking of white ashes. At one point his grandfather rose to go to the bathroom. Sounds of the house, settling, sounds he once thought—and sometimes still thought—to be ghosts drifted in and out. But soon it was time, and five minutes before the alarm was to go off he rose, retrieved the candle from his drawer, and walked quietly out the front door.

The candle was a regular white affair, but he had placed it under the pulpit that past Sunday before the services and had snuck it out afterward, so he was confident it had been sufficiently blessed. Once outside, he struck a match and lit the candle. Its light was weak, but intense enough to blind his dark-adjusted eyes. A breeze played with the flame and finally blew it out. He stuffed it into his pocket and went on about his task.

Though the moon was not full—the rituals did not call for a full moon—there was a good-sized crescent peeking through the thick clouds to light his activity. The ashes were now only warm; there was but a faint glow in the very middle. With a trowel he stirred the center of the pile, and after he had a substantial heap of what he was sure was the mixture of powder he wanted, he carried a shovelful over to what was roughly the center of the apple orchard and began to design a pattern on the ground. It was a complicated and jagged pattern, a combination of the European Circle of Power and an American Indian figure he thought to be Hopi. After eleven trips with the trowel he was sure the design was complete. The breezes were strong, but his intensity was such that he barely noticed. Finally he sat in the center of the design—careful not to step on the ashes—and once again he lit the candle, blocking the wind with his body.

It was after twelve, he was sure. The time when demons walked the earth most freely. He tried to clear his mind of all except for the name of the High Demon confronted by the good monk, in the story, who forced the demon to do his bidding—the great and fierce demon who would ordinarily crush this puny child. But he was ready, armed not with the armor of righteousness and the shield of truth, but with the arcane knowledge that he firmly believed was the more powerful. It had chained the demon once, and he would be damned if he did not chain the demon again.

The breeze turned to gusts, which he took for a sign that his mojo was working. Some of the ashes blew in his face, but he was concentrating, concentrating, concentrating on the name of the name. Kneeling, he began to repeat the dread name aloud, his chest pounding as if his heart would jump out and run away. When the clouds covered what moon there was, he took it for His sinister presence. As he continued to chant the name of the demon, his eyes wide with fright, he wondered in part of his mind what the demon would look like. Tall, perhaps taller than the apple trees, the pine trees even. Red and fierce, with huge yellow teeth and foul breath. But no, this was a great demon, a member of Satan's High Court, the Inner Cabal. Maybe it would take the form of a centaur, of a gigantic fiery bird; mayhap it would come as a snake or a woolly beast. Or even in the form of a man, a devil like the one Reverend Hezekiah preached about, not with horns and a pitchfork, but in a white suit, with a handsome face and white teeth, smiling, as the devil is known to do.

He chanted. The name became a mantra, losing all meaning; it was a beautiful name with nice vowels and a foreign sound. He repeated and repeated and repeated. The intense fear that had crouched in his stomach started to fade, and for the first time he really allowed himself to think how silly this all was; how foolish and juvenile and desperate and impossible and insane; how there was no monk who saved a village by chaining a demon and releasing him only after he did his bidding; how there were, in fact, no such things as demons who walked the earth after midnight, or at any other time, for that matter; how if there were such things as demons he hadn't the slightest notion of how to force them to transform him, or even how to plead with them; how all those people who disappeared either really ran away or just died—the way he would.

Then, at first like a gentle kiss, here, there, light but unmistakable. Rain. Soon it was falling in a downpour. Water and water. The candle had long ago been doused. Now he sat with the water soaking him, streaming into his eyes and his mouth. A joke, he realized, this had been an elaborate joke he had played on himself. He was sixteen years of age and out in a rainstorm in the wee hours of the morning, calling on ancient demons to save him from—from what?—from himself? He noticed he was crying; hot tears stung his eyes. He shivered and slumped, and finally sprawled on the wet earth, cold not with the freezing cold of winter, but with a surface chill, like swimming in the ocean after dark in July.

He was not aware of the rain stopping or of the cloud drifting away from the crescent moon. He just lay there, wet and shivering; even the sobs had gone, leaving him with an empty feeling of exhaustion and confusion. His was the sudden feeling of falling down a well, knowing no one will come to the rescue for days. The dread of a horrible, inevitable, known future.

A voice. Where? In his head? In his mind? In his soul? It was the voice of a chorus, a host like the host that welcomed Jesus to the earth on that starry night in Bethlehem, and at the same time the voice of a wizened old man racked with pain, and the very voice of pain and anguish and sorrow itself, and the voice of lust and hate and war-torn plains with wind whistling and whispering through trees, the voice of wisdom, old and all-knowing, and the voice of foolishness, ignorance, and childish bliss. But a voice. One voice.

The voice said: Come.

The sky, now a classic spring sky after a quick rainstorm, seemed higher, wider, cleaner. The frogs, now happy and wet, sang joyous and raucous songs. He smiled and reached into the mud, into the soggy sod where the ashes had melted, and in one motion smeared his face with them, as though to reacquaint himself with the sensation of touch. Again he smiled, his face as vacant as his soul. The voice said rise, and he rose, stripping buck naked, as the voice told him, tearing off his clothing as though he were afire, wallowing like a hog where the ashes were, with innocent abandon. The voice told him to go into the house and get his grandfather's old rifle. He did, and turned and waited for the voice in his head, staring over the starlit fields toward the woods. The voice said merely, Walk. He did, his body mottled in clotted wood ash and mud, his skin cool but not cold, listening, listening for the voice that now seemed his only salvation. Salvation? Was that it, now? Beyond hope, beyond faith? Just to survive in some way. To live.

Did he see the low-swooping owl or the scurrying wood rat as it dashed into a gulley just by his bare foot? His mind was on spiritual things. For it was just as preachers had been preaching it all the years of his life, warning: There are wretched, wicked spirits that possess us and force us to commit unnatural acts. It was clear to him now: he had been possessed of just such a wicked spirit, and the rain was a sign to prove that he could not be purged. Why fight any longer? said his brain.

So he listened to the voice, the voice that was old and young, and mean and good. He put all his faith in that voice. The voice said march, so he marched, surrounded by hobgoblins and sprites and evil faeries and wargs—aberrations like himself, fierce and untamed, who frolicked about him with hellish glee at his acceptance of his doomed, delicious fate, and he was happy, oh, so happy, as he cradled the gun in his hand like a cool phallus, happy for the first time in so, so many months, for he knew the voice would take care of him and teach him and save him, and there was feeling, full and ribald and dangerous, and he reveled in the sensation and whatever felt good, and he marched leading his devilish crew, listening for the commands of the one voice, the only voice, which said, Go, and he went, surrounded by fiends who quaffed strong ales as they marched along through the fields, who danced about on the tree limbs and on the surfaces of streams all by the light of the crescent moon and fornicated and let blood from one another in bouts more violent than cockfights, smearing excrement on one another, jerking and touching and biting, shouting profanity and blasphemies, all with cheers and loud laughter, and he smiled and joined in, for this was his salvation, the way to final peace, and as he marched along, aware of the gun that he held tight in his hand, glad to be free, if *free* was a word to describe what he felt, he began to wonder—though it was much, much too late—as he pranced along alone down the road, somewhere in the small bit of his mind yet sane, he pondered: Perhaps I should have used, instead of a kitten, a babe.

LUSH LIFE

John McCluskey

Dayton, Ohio

Behind the dance hall the first of the car doors were banging shut, motors starting up, and from somewhere—a backyard, an alley—dogs barked. The band's bus was parked at one darkened corner of the parking lot. Empty, it was a mute and hulking barn in this hour. Along its side in slanted, bold-red letters was painted a sign: EARL FERGUSON AND AMERICA'S GREATEST BAND.

Suddenly the back door to the dance hall swung open and loud laughter rushed out on a thick pillow of cigarette smoke. Ahead of others, two men in suits—the taller one in plaids and the other in stripes—walked quickly, talking, smoking. They stopped at a convertible, a dark-red Buick, dew already sprouting across its canvas top. Other men, all members of the band, in twos or threes, would come up, slap their backs, share a joke or two, then drift toward the bus. In the light over the back door, moths played.

The shorter man, Billy Cox, took off his glasses, fogged the lenses twice, then cleaned them with his polka-dot silk square. He reached a hand toward Tommy, the bassist, approaching.

"I'm gone say, 'See y'all further up the road in Cleveland,' " Tommy said. "But after a night like tonight, it's gone be one hell of a struggle to tear ourselves from this town. Am I right about that, Billy C.?"

Tommy laughed, gold tooth showing, and patted his impeccable "do." More than once it had been said that Tommy sweated ice water. With his face dry, hair in place, tie straightened after three hours of furious work, no one could doubt it now.

Tommy spoke again, this time stern, wide-legged, and gesturing grandly. "Just you two don't get high and dry off into some damn ditch." His usual farewell slid toward a cackle. Billy waved him off.

In the Scout Car, Billy and Earl Ferguson would drive through the night to the next date. Throughout the night they would stay at least an hour or so ahead of the bus. They would breakfast and be nearly asleep by the time the bus pulled into the same hotel parking lot, the men emerging, looking stunned from a fitful sleep on a noisy bus.

From a nearby car a woman's throaty laugh lit up the night. They turned to see Pretty Horace leaning into a car, the passenger's side, smoothing down the back edges of his hair and rolling his rump as he ran his game.

"Man, stop your lying!" came her voice. She, too, was toying with the ends of her hair, dyed bright red and glowing in that light. Her friend from the driver's seat, with nothing better to do perhaps, leaned to hear, to signify, her face round as the moon's.

Moving with a pickpocket's stealth and slow grin spreading, Poo moved up to the driver's side of the car and whispered something. The driver jerked back, then gave him her best attention, smiling. One hand to her throat, she moistened her lips, glistened a smile.

In unison, Billy and Earl shook their heads while watching it all. Billy slid one hand down a lapel, pulled a cigarette from the corner of his mouth. "Some of the boys gone make a long night of this one."

Earl nodded. "Some mean mistreaters fixing to hit that bus late and do a whole lot of shucking, man."

Yes, some would dare the bus's deadline by tipping into an after-hours party, by following some smiling woman home. The rules were simple, however: if you missed the bus and could not make practice the next day, you were fined fifty dollars. If you missed the date because you missed the bus or train, you were fired. Daring these, you could seek adventure that broke the monotony of long road trips. You could bring stories that released bubbles of laughter throughout an overheated and smoke-filled bus.

Cars were rolling out of the side parking lot and, passing members of the band, the drivers honked in appreciation. Earl bowed slowly and waved an arm wide and high toward his men, some still walking out of the back door of the dance hall. Then he embraced Billy, mugged, and pointed to

Billy's chest as if branding there all the credit for a magnificent night. After all, they had done Basie and Ellington to perfection. Their own original tunes had been wonders to behold. From the very beginning the audience had been with them and danced and danced, heads bobbing and shoulders rocking, cheering every solo. The dancers had fun on the stair step of every melody; hugging tightly, they did the slow grind to the promise of every ballad. Now they thanked the band again with the toot of their horns, shouts, and the wave of their hands.

Within an hour the bus would start up, all the equipment packed and stored below. Then it would roll slowly out of the parking lot. Some of the men would already be snoring. By the outskirts of town, a car might catch up to it, tires squealing as the car rocked to a stop. One of the men—usually McTee or "Rabbit" Ousley, as myth might have it—would climb out and blow a kiss to some grinning woman behind the wheel and strut onto the bus like some wide-legged conqueror. The doors to the bus would close behind him, sealing his stories from any verification and sealing them against the long, long night.

But it was the Buick, Earl and Billy inside, pulling away first. They would leave before these tales of triumph, outright lies about quick and furious love in a drafty back room or tales of a young wife whispering, "Run! Run!" and the scramble for a window after the husband's key slid into the lock downstairs. Yes, before all that, Earl and Billy would pull from the parking lot and start away, slow at first, like they had all the time in the world.

Well before the edge of town, they would have checked for cigarettes, surely, and from some magical place on a side street, a jukebox blaring and the smell of fried chicken meeting them at the door with its judas hole, they would find their coffee in Mason jars, coffee heavily sugared and creamed, and steaming chicken sandwiches wrapped neatly in waxed paper.

Older women, who would do double duty at Sunday church dinners, would smile and wipe their hands on their aprons. And bless them, these good and prodigal sons with conked hair. Then, moving toward the door, Billy and Earl would be greeted by achingly beautiful women with late night joy lacing their hoarse voices. Billy and Earl would take turns joking and pulling each other away, then, outside and laughing, climb back into the car for the journey through the night.

For the first few minutes, the lights of Dayton thinning, used car lots and a roller rink as outposts, they were silent before nervous energy swept over them. It was that unsettling bath of exhaustion and exuberance, rising to a tingle at the base of the neck, so familiar at the end of a performance. With Earl at the wheel, they began to harmonize and scat their way through

"Take the A Train," "One O'Clock Jump," and their own wonderful collaboration, "October Mellow." In this way they would ride for a while. They would sing in ragged breaths before they gave out in laughter. The radio might go on, and there would be mostly the crackle of static, or, faintly, a late night gospel concert with harmonics rising and falling, like a prayer song tossed to the wind. Stray cars would rush past in the next lane, headed back toward Dayton. They passed a trailer groaning under its load, one or two squat Fords, then settled back. The night's first chapter was closed behind them with the noise from the motor, with smears of light.

Like a sudden tree in the car's lights, a sign sprouted and announced the city limits of Springfield.

Billy started nodding as if answering some ancient question. "Springfield got more fine women than they got in two St. Louises or five New Orleanses, I'm here to tell you."

"Wake up, Billy. Find me a place with women finer than they got in St. Louis or New Orleans or Harlem—think I'm gone let Harlem slide?—find me such a place and you got a easy one-hundred-dollar bill in your hand and I'll be in heaven. I'm talking serious now."

Billy snorted, sitting up straight and shaking his head. "I ain't hardly sleeping. Just remembering is all. See, I ain't been through here since 1952, but I can call some preacher's daughter right now—brown skin and about yeah-tall—yeah, at this very hour. Lord, she would be so fine that you and me both would run up the side of a mountain and holler like a mountain jack."

Then Earl blew a smoke ring and watched its rise; maybe it would halo the rearview mirror. "Well, okay, I'll take your word for it now, but if we're ever back through here, I definitely want to stop and see if these women are as pretty as you say."

"They pretty, they mamas pretty, they grandmamas pretty. . . ."

Earl laughed his high-pitched laugh. "You get crazier every day, Billy Cox." He pushed the accelerator, slamming them deeper into their seats.

Earl leveled off at sixty and for minutes was content to enjoy the regular beat of the wheels hitting the seams across the pavement, *pa-poom, pa-poom, pa-poom*. It was on the next stretch of road, ten miles outside of Springfield, that they truly sensed the flatness of the place. In the darkness there were no distant hills promising contour, variety, or perspective. Fields to the left? Woods to the right? They were silent for a minute or so. Crackling music flared up once again from the radio, then died.

"What do you think of the new boy's work tonight?" Billy asked.

"Who, 'Big City'? Not bad, man. Not bad at all." Earl snapped his fingers. "He's swinging more now. Matter of fact, he's driving the entire trumpet section, Big Joe included. You get the prize on that one, you brought him in. I remember you kept saying he could play the sweetest ballads, could curl up inside something like Strayhorn's 'Daydream' as easy as a cat curl up on a bed."

Billy nodded and looked out the side window. "I knew he had it in him the first time I heard him. His problem was hanging around Kansas City too long with that little jive band and just playing careful music. Sometimes you can't tell what's on the inside—just fast or slow, just hard or soft, just mean or laughing sweet. Can't never tell with some. But I had that feeling, know what I'm saying? Had the feeling that if we cut him loose, let him roam a little taste, that he could be all them combinations, that he could be what a tune needed him to be."

Earl tossed a cigarette stub out the window. He remembered the night he had met young Harold. The band was on break, and Harold walked up slowly, head down. The trumpet player had been nervous in his too-tight suit. Earl had later confided to Billy that he looked like he had just come in from plowing a cornfield and that if he joined the band he would have to learn how to dress, to coordinate his colors of his ties and suits, shine his shoes. When you joined the Ferguson band, you joined class. Style was more than your sound. It was your walk, the way you sat during the solos by others, the way you met the night. Earl had promptly nicknamed him "Big City."

"He said meeting you was like meeting God," Billy had said the next morning over hash browns and lukewarm coffee.

Earl smiled now. He was not God, true. He did know that among bandleaders roaming with their groups across this country, he was one of the best. He knew, too, that soft-spoken Billy Cox, five years younger, was the best composer in the business, period. Together they worked an easy magic. Few could weave sounds the way they could, few could get twelve voices, twelve rambunctious personalities, to shout or moan as one. And with it all was the trademark sound: the perfect blend of brass and reeds. Basie might have had a stronger reed section, with the force of a melodic hurricane; Ellington, a brass section with bite and unmatchable brightness. But they had the blend. Within the first few notes you knew that it was Earl Ferguson's band and nobody else's. Now and then players would leave to join other caravans inching across the continent, but the sound, their mix, stayed the same.

The scattered lights of Springfield were far behind them now, merged to a dull electric glow in the rearview mirror. And out from the town there were only occasional lights along State Route 42, one or two on front porches, lights bathing narrow, weathered, and wooded fronts, wood swings perfectly still in that time. Tightly closed shutters, silences inside. Both tried to imagine the front of the houses at noon—children pushing the porch swing? A dog napping in the shade nearby? Clothes flapping on a line running from behind the house? Gone suddenly, a blur to pinpoint, then out.

From a pocket Billy had taken out a matchbook. A few chord progressions had been scribbled on the inside cover. Then, drawing out a small lined tablet from beneath the seat, he quickly drew a bass staff and started humming.

"You got something going?" Earl asked.

"I think, yeah. A little light something, you know, like bright light and springtime and whatnot."

Earl tapped the wheel lightly with the palm of his free hand. "Toss in a small woman's bouncy walk, and I might get excited with you."

"Well, help me then. This time you use the woman—tight yellow skirt, right?—and I'll use the light, the light of mid-May, and when they don't work together, I think we'll both know."

"Solid. What you got so far?"

Billy did not answer. He kept a finger to his ear, staring from the matchbook cover to the tablet. Earl let it run. You don't interrupt when the idea is so young.

More often than not, Billy and Earl brought opposites or, at least, unlikely combinations together. One of the band's more popular numbers, a blues, was the result of Billy's meditations on the richly perfumed arms of a large and fleshy woman, arms tightly holding a man who mistook her short laugh for joy. To this, Earl had brought the memory of a rainy night and a long soft moan carried on the wind, something heard from the end of an alley. They used only the colors and sounds from these images, and only later, when the songs were fully arranged, did the smell and the touch of them sweep in. There had been other songs that resolved the contrasts, the differences, between the drone of a distant train and an empty glass of gin, a lipstick print at its rim, fingerprints around it. A baby's whimpering, and a man grinning as he counted a night's big take from the poker table, painted bright red fingernails tapping lightly down a lover's arm, and the cold of a lonely apartment. How much did the dancing couples, those whispering and holding close as second skins or those bouncing and whirling tirelessly, feel these things, too? Or did they bring something entirely different to the rhythms, something of their own?

Earl and Billy had talked about this many times. They had concluded that it was enough to bring contexts to dreams, to strengthen those who listened and danced. And there were those moments, magical, alive, when the dance hall was torn from the night and whirled, spinning like a top, a half mile from heaven.

Billy started whistling and tapping his thigh. Then he hummed a fragment of a song loudly.

Earl was nodding. "Nice. Already I can hear Slick Harry taking off with Ousley just under him with the alto. In triplets? Let's see, go through it again right quick."

Again Billy hummed and Earl brought in high triplets, nervous wings snagged to the thread of the melody, lifting the piece toward brightness. They stopped, and Billy, smiling now, worked quickly, a draftsman on fire, adding another line or two, crossing out, scribbling notes. He would look up to follow the front edges of the car's lights, then away to the darkness and back to the page.

"Listen up." Billy gave the next lines, flats predominating, while offering harsh counterpoint to the first two lines and snatching the song away from a tender playfulness for a moment. He scratched his chin and nodded. Pointed to the darkness.

"This is what I got so far." And he sang the line in a strong tenor voice, his melody now seeming to double the notes from the last line, though the rhythm did not vary. It was the kind of thing Art Tatum might do with "Tea for Two" or something equally simple. The song moved swiftly from a lyrical indulgence to a catch-me-if-you-can show of speed.

"Watch it now," Earl said, "or they will figure us for one of those beboppers." He chuckled. The woman in his mind walked faster, traffic about her thickened, the streets sent up jarring sounds. Those would be trumpets, probably. Surroundings leaned in. Trombones and tenor saxophones playing in the lowest octaves announced their possibilities.

Earl offered a line of his own. His woman walked quickly up the steps of a brownstone. In. Common enough sequence, but no surprise there. Whatever prompted it, though, was fleeting. Gone. Then he said, "Okay, forget mine for now. Let's stay with what you got."

Billy shrugged and marked off another staff, then glanced again to the match cover. He let out a long, low whistle. "Now we come to the bridge.

"This is when we need a piano, Earl. I bet the closest one to here is probably some ol' beat-up thing in one of these country churches out here. Or something sitting in the front parlor of one of these farmer's houses, and the farmer's daughter playing 'Jingle Bells' after bringing in the eggs."

Hip and arrogant city was in their laughter, they of funky cafés where fights might break out and beer bottles fly as the piano man bobbed and weaved, keeping time on a scarred piano that leaned and offered sticky keys in the lowest and highest octaves.

Then the Earl of Ferguson told the story of a piano search years before Billy had joined the band. With two other men in the car and barely an hour east of St. Louis, when the puzzle of a chord progression struck with the force of a deep stomach cramp. Spotting one light shining in the wilderness, a small neon sign still shining over a door, he ordered the car stopped. Trotting up, Earl noticed the sign blink off. He banged on the door, the hinges straining from each blow. Nobody turned off a sign in his face. The door swung open and up stepped an evil-looking, red-haired farmer in overalls, a man big enough to fill the doorway.

"I said to this giant, 'Quick, I got to get on your piano.' Not 'I got to find your toilet,' or 'I got to use your phone,' but 'I got to use your piano.' " He shook his head as he laughed now.

"That giant rocked on his heels like I had punched him square in the chest. He left just enough room for me to squeeze in and sure enough there was a little raggedy piano in the corner of his place.

"P.M. had enough sense to offer to buy some of the man's good whiskey while I'm sitting there playing and trying to figure out the good chord. P.M. always did have good common sense. Most folks try to remember what just happened, but Past was already on what's happening next. I'm forgetting you never knew P.M. The guys called him Past Midnight because he was so dark-skinned. The shadow of a shadow. Next thing they calling him Past, then one day Rabbit showed up calling him P.M., and it stuck. His real name was Wiley Reed, and he was one of the best alto players in the world."

He paused now, glanced out his side window. "Anyway, he showed him class that night. The giant steady looking around suspiciouslike at first. I mean, he didn't know us from Adam, didn't know how many more of us was waiting outside to rush in and turn out the joint. But he loosened up and took his mess of keys out and go to his cabinet. I'm just playing away because this is the greatest song of my life, don't care if it is in some country roadhouse way out in Plumb Nelly. I'm cussing, too, Billy, because this song is giving me fits, do you hear me? It just wouldn't let me go. All I wanted was to make it through the bridge. I figured the rest would come soon as I'm back in the car.

"Well, P.M. and the man making small talk, and Leon trying to get slick on everybody and tipping over to get him a few packs of Old Golds. I'm checking all this, see, and closing in on something solid and oh-so-sweet, and hearing the big guy go on and on about getting home because his wife already thinking he's sniffing around the new waitress—I remember that part clear as I'm sitting here—when, *boom!* Leon open up the closet, a mop and a jug of moonshine fell out and this woman inside trying to button up her blouse. She give a scream like she done seen the boogeyman. All hell commence to break loose. Next thing you know Leon backing off and telling the woman he ain't meant no harm, just trying to get some cigarettes, he lie. Big Boy running over and telling me we got to take our whiskey and go, song or no song. I look up, and two white guys running down the steps from just over our heads, one of them holding some cards in his hands. The other one run to the telephone like he reporting a robbery. I mean from the outside it's just a little-bitty place on the side of the road, but inside all kinds of shit going on. Well, I found the chords I wanted, did a quick run-through and called out to the fellows to haul ass. If some man's wife or some woman's man don't come in there shooting up the place, then the sheriff might raid the place for all-night gambling. Either way we lose."

Earl was laughing now. A light rain had started to fall just as he ended his tale. The windshield wipers clicked rhythmically; the bump of the road seemed a grace note: *bachoo-choo, bachoo-choo.*

"Never know when you get the tune down right. Go too early and you pluck it raw. Go too late and you got rotten fruit." Earl coughed. "Don't go at all and you put a bad hurt on yourself."

From across the highway a rabbit darted toward them, then cut away. Earl had turned the car just slightly before straightening it without letting up on the accelerator.

"Almost had us one dead rabbit."

Billy did not answer. He was tapping his pencil on the tablet. Up ahead and to the east they would discover the electric glow of Columbus. Beyond that they would have three more hours before Cleveland and breakfast at the Majestic Hotel on Carnegie Avenue. There might be a new singer or two waiting to try out with the band. Who knows? Somebody—another Billy or Sassy Sarah—might get lucky and ride back with them to New York, her life changed forever. Some young woman, prettier than she would ever know, would otherwise be serving up beef stew or spareribs in some tiny smoky place on Cedar Avenue, notes running through her head or thoughts of a sickly mother and two children she and her husband were trying to feed. How many times Billy and Earl had seen it, how many times they had heard the hope there, the sweat mustaches sprouting, the need to escape the routine nights. It was common ground. They had all been there, falling to sleep in clothes that smelled of cigarette smoke, the world a place of slow mornings with traffic starting and a door slamming, a baby crying, and an "Oh, goddamn, one more funky morning, but I'm alive to see it through anyhow.

There was a bump beneath the car. "You clipped something for sure that time, sportey-otee."

"All kinds of stuff out here at night," Earl said. "They like the warm road. Coons, possums, snakes, cows."

"Cows?"

"Yeah, cows." Billy had lit a cigarette. Earl tapped the end of the fresh one he had just placed in his mouth, and Billy reached to light it. "Thanks. Don't tell me you done forgot that cow we nicked on the road up to Saratoga Springs."

Yes, yes, Billy remembered. "Cow must have thought we was the Midnight Special, much noise as I was making trying to scare him off the road. Probably just out to get him a little side action in the next field." The car had knocked it to one knee before it struggled back up and, in the rearview mirror, slipped into the darkness.

They were quiet for long moments. After music, after hours, different thoughts could struggle to life. If there was an easiness earlier, swift terror could strike them in the darkest hours before dawn. They could grow suddenly uneasy in the silences. They could sense it together like a bone-deep chill starting. For now Billy pushed the wing shut on his side, rolled his window up another inch.

In a small town just west of Columbus, they passed a café, the lone light in that stretch. A man behind a long counter—white apron, white T-shirt— was scrubbing the counter and talking with a customer. He stopped his work to make a point, head moving from side to side. The customer nodded. Another man stood over a table at the window, dunking a doughnut. With his free hand, he waved as the car passed. Surprised, Earl honked once, then turned to glance back.

"That back there reminds me of something."

"Huh?"

"That man right back there waving. You didn't see him? Standing back there, waving at us and probably every car coming through here this late."

"Don't tell me you want to get some food," Billy said. "Hell, Earl, I thought those chicken sandwiches and pound cake—"

"No, no. That ain't what I'm thinking. Had a guy in the band by the name of Boonie years ago, way before you joined the band. Boonie could play him some mean trombone, I'm here to tell you. Fact, he could play trumpet and cornet, too. Probably would have played the tuba if I would have asked him to. Like you, he was the master of horns. Anyway, something happened—could have been bad gin or something else nobody will ever know about. He just snapped, and they found him one morning standing on a corner cussing at folks and swearing up and down that he was the governor of Africa. They took him to the jailhouse first, then the crazy house. They didn't keep him there long, six, seven months maybe.

"I went up to see him, way out in the country, Billy, you know where they put those places. Well, just past the gate was this man, and he waved at me when I first came in, and, while I was walking around with Boonie, he waved a couple more times. At first I thought he was just part of the staff because he was all over the place. But then I noticed he's wearing the same kind of clothes as Boonie. And he keeps smiling, you know? By the time I left, he was back out by the gate and waving again. It didn't take me long to figure out that all he had to do was wave at whatever was new and moving by. Like that man back there waving at the night."

Billy only glanced at him, then looked back to his notebook. Earl shook his head and chuckled. "Governor of Africa, can you beat that? Boonie was lucky, though; I mean, the way he wound up. He never got his chops back after he got out. He worked around a little, then finally left the life. He got a foundry job and raised his family in Detroit. Others ain't been so lucky."

Earl glanced ahead to more lights showing up through the rain. He knew some who entered hospitals, never to emerge. And many, too many, died before the age of fifty. Just last March, young "Bird" Parker had died in New York, not yet thirty-five. He whose notes surprised like shooting stars. Playing this music could be as risky as working in a steel mill or coal mine. But what were the choices? What could he do about it, leader of some? Perhaps only show them a lesson or two through his example. Now he did limit himself to one large and long drink per night—one part scotch and three parts water—from an oversized coffee mug. Soon he would cut down on his cigarettes. Beyond that he let the rules pronounce the purpose: you needed a clear head and a sound body to play the music he lived for.

Their talk of work and women—the incomplete song still a bright ribbon over their heads—pulled them well beyond the glow of Columbus. Coffee and sandwiches finished, they were down to three cigarettes each and figured there was nothing open between Columbus and Cleveland. Billy took over at the wheel. Twenty miles or so north of Columbus, they neared a car in trouble at the side of the road. The hood was up and in the swath of the front headlights was a man—very young, thin, white—kneeling at the back tire.

"Keep going, Billy. That cracker'll get help."

Billy slowed. "Well, Earl, it won't hurt. . . ."

Earl stared at him, hard. "You getting softhearted on me? That boy could be the Klan, see? You remember what happened to the Purnell band down in Tennessee just last month? Huh, remember that stuff? Got beat up by a bunch of rednecks, one of them getting his nose broke, and they still winding up in jail for disturbing the peace and impersonating a band? No, let him get help from his own kind."

Billy pulled the car off the road. "He's just a kid, Earl."

"You go without me, then." He watched Billy leave, then quickly felt under his seat.

Billy was approaching the car, and Earl could hear him ask, "Need a hand?"

"Sure do," the boy said loudly. "If you got a jack on you, we can do this in no time."

Beneath his seat in the Buick, Earl had found the gun wrapped in a towel. He opened the glove compartment and placed it inside, unwrapping the towel and leaving the small door open. He began to hum the new song slowly, softly, watching his friend, smiling Billy, trusting Billy, help a stranger.

Billy brought the jack from their trunk and set it up. He could smell alcohol on the boy, and, straightening up, he saw a girl in the car sip from a flask. Neither could have been older than eighteen. She was trying to hum something, missing, then tried again.

"Dumb me out here without a jack, I swear," the boy said. Billy only nodded as they set the jack under the frame.

The boy called the girl out of the car, and she stood apart shyly, both hands holding up the collar of her light coat.

"Your friend back there under the weather?" the boy asked.

"He just don't need the exercise," Billy said. "How about her? She feeling all right?"

The boy looked up in surprise, then he smiled. "No, she all right. She don't need no exercise either." He leaned closer to Billy as they pulled off the wheel and started to set the spare. "Course, me and her just about exercised out." Then he laughed. "Whoo-ee!"

The tire was on now, and the boy was tightening the lugs. "Pretty nice car you got back there. You a undertaker or a preacher?"

"No, neither one. I'm a musician."

The boy whistled low. "Musicians make enough for a car like that? I need to learn me some music. You get to travel a lot and see them big-city women and all like that?"

"Sure do."

The boy glanced at the girl and said loudly, "Course, a man could go all over the world and never find a woman sweet as my Josie there."

Her hair needed a brush, her dress was wrinkled, and her shoes were old and run-over. She was plain and drunk. In the morning she might be in the choir of a tiny church and by evening making biscuits to the staccato of radio news broadcasts. Billy was folding up the jack and turning away.

"Ain't she about the prettiest doggone thing a man could ever see?"

"I know how you feel, sport. I got one just as sweet back in New York."

Billy walked away and waved good-bye with his back turned. He slammed the trunk closed, then settled behind the wheel. He pulled the car back onto the highway.

Earl was whistling. "Feel better?" he asked, not looking up.

"What's that for?" Billy pointed to the gun.

"I thought about cleaning it. Ain't been cleaned in a year." Then: "My daddy told me once that it takes more than a smile and a good heart to get through this world. Told me sometimes you can reach out a helping hand and get it chopped off."

Billy was shivering. "Hide it, Earl. Please."

"Okay, okay. Look, while you were playing the Good Samaritan with Jethro back there, I finished the song. Listen up, young-blood."

Earl hummed through the opening key, stretching the note, then moved through the bright afternoon of the melody, repeated the line in the thinning light of its early evening. The song soon lifted to the bridge, a vivid golden stair step on which to linger briefly. Then the return to the opening line that suggested new possibilities: the smell of a pine forest after a rain, a meadow, too, a deer or two frozen at one edge. There was a street, glistening, a small oil slick catching dull rainbows, and a stranger's laughter like a bright coin spinning at their feet. Yes, all of that.

The small and proud woman walking, her hips working against yellow wool, had been lost to Earl. She would return, surely, to move through another song, walking to a different rhythm. For now she had brought Earl excited to Billy's first thoughts. Provided a spirit. Together, they hummed the song through, speeding it up, slowing. Each time, they tried different harmonies—the bass stronger here, the trombones higher there. Most of the parts had been worked through by the time they noticed the hills near Medina taking shape.

"Got it," Billy said finally. He slapped the wheel with relief.

"It's nice," Earl said.

"Think the people will like it?" Billy asked.

Earl yawned and looked out the window. Maybe he could get twenty minutes or so of sleep before they touched the edges of the city. "You worry too much, Billy. Course they gone like it. They got no choice. We did the best we could. We'll run through it this afternoon, do it again in Pittsburgh, and maybe have it ready by the time we hit Philly. Can't you just hear Big City's solo already?" He settled back, eyes closed.

Cars, trees, cornfields just harvested were explosions of dull colors. Signs placed one hundred feet apart, a shaving cream ad suddenly claimed Billy's attention. *The big blue tube's/Just like Louise/You get a thrill/From every squeeze.* He laughed aloud, then started whistling. Then the car roared into a stretch of light fog. Billy leaned forward, his head almost touching the windshield. Then he stiffened.

"Earl, wake up. I got something to tell you."

"Let it slide. Tell me over grits and coffee." Earl kept his eyes closed.

"No, it can't wait. It happened back there in Dayton. I just now remembered. You know on that second break? Well, I stepped outside to get a little air, take a smoke, you understand. A couple folk stroll past and tell me how much they like our playing, so I'm talking with them a while and then I see this woman—short with a red wig and she standing off to the side. She look up every now and then like she want to come over and say something. But she wait until nobody's around and she walk over real quick-like. Something about her make me think about a bird hopping, then resting, hopping some more. She told me she really like the music, like some of the songs really get a hold of her. . . ."

Earl opened one eye. "Yeah, and she just want to take a cute little man like you home to make music to her all the time."

"No, no, no. Nothing like that, but you better believe I was hoping for some action."

Forehead still to the windshield, Billy fumbled for words, worked a hand like he was flagging down a car. "No, she's smiling but not smiling, if you know what I mean. We talk about a lot of things, then she gets down to the thing she really wanted to talk about, I figure. She told me about her baby. She told me about hearing her baby screaming one day and she rush from her ironing and found him in the next room bleeding. He fell on a stick or glass or something, cut his belly, and blood going every which way. Said her son's belly was thin, like a balloon, but not going down when it's poked. She put her hand there, she said, and could feel each beat of the heart. Every time the heart beat, more blood would spurt out between her fingers. She screamed for help, screamed for her neighbors next door, just screamed and screamed. Blood was all over her, too, she said, but she never saw that until later. All she could do is tell her child not to die and press on that thin belly. And pray and pray, even after he in the ambulance. She told me that baby was all she got in this world."

Billy shook his head slowly. "What could I say to all that? Here I go outside for some fresh air and a draw or two on my Lucky Strikes. She brings me this story when I want to know whether my shoes are shined, my front still holding up, or whether some big-legged woman want to pull me home with her. I touched her on the shoulder, was all I could do. She told me the baby lived, and she smiled this dopey smile. Then she left."

Earl's eyes were closed. He waved his hand as if shooing a fly from his forehead. "It's this music we play, Billy. It opens people up, makes them give up secrets. Better than whiskey or dope for that. It don't kill you, and you can't piss it away. You can whistle it the next day in new places. You can loan it to strangers, and they thank you for it."

Then he shrugged. "It's what keeps us going all night."

Sitting back, fog thinning, Billy nodded and started back whistling. Before long they would sight the giant mills pumping smoke into the gray morning. At Lakewood Billy might swing closer to the gray and glassy Erie. Then he would pick up speed and head toward the east side, through a world raging to light outside their windows. Finally they would gain Carnegie Avenue and weave their way among the early church traffic. They would find the Majestic Hotel, breakfast, and attempt sleep, two wizards before the band.

SISTER DETROIT

Colleen McElroy

When Buel Gatewood bought his Gran Turismo Hawk, folks around Troost Avenue and Prospect Boulevard hadn't learned how to talk about Vietnam yet. After all, Bubba Wentworth had just returned from Korea, and the V.A. had helped him get a job at Swift Packing House. Grace Moton was just recovering from having to bury her brother, who'd been shot in a border skirmish at the Berlin Wall. "Ain't much of a wall if it can't stop bullets," Grace had wept. And Andre Clayton had taken his sissy self off to some white school in the East just to test all that Supreme Court business about integration.

But Buel Gatewood had plunked down a goodly portion of several paychecks in full certainty that with his deluxe edition $3400 Hawk, he would own the best wheels on the block for some time to come. There was one thing for certain about that notion: he was going to have the biggest car payments on the block for at least five years.

Still, there was no doubt that Buel's Hawk was tough enough. It was all grille and heavy chrome borders, black like a gangster's car, but road-ready for a sporty-otee like Buel. "Any car got the name of Hawk is bound to be good," Buel had said. "That's the name of that wind that blows off the lake

433

in Chicago. Hawk! That wind says: Look out, I'm the Hawk and I'm coming to get you. Now I got me a Hawk, so look out!"

In that car Buel could outgun DeJohn Washington's '54 Coupe de Ville, and outshine the Merc Meteor his brother, Calvin, owned. And, despite its retractable hard top, he simply dismissed the Ford V8 Roger Payton had bought on the grounds that only somebody working in a gas station could afford a gas guzzler. "I don't go around talking 'bout other folks' mistakes," he'd said, but according to Buel, almost everything about Roger and the others was a mistake. Unlike Calvin, Buel had a high school diploma and didn't have to tend bar at Rooster's Tavern. And he didn't have to haul cow shit at Swift Packing, like DeJohn, or nickel-and-dime in a gas station alongside Roger. He had a good paying job with Arbor Industrial Services, and once he bought his Hawk, he'd settled into outrunning the competition. That competition completely surrounded Buel and his Turismo Hawk.

That year the Detroit exhibition of cars featured Freedom, bumper to bumper on a disc-shaped turntable. It amazed the public to see all that shiny metal swirling past them. That crowd should have come to Buel's neighborhood, where cars dazzled owners and passersby alike. The traffic moving down Brush Creek Boulevard, Blue Parkway, or The Paseo alone would have been enough to put Detroit on the map, but with the added interstate traffic between Kansas and Missouri, between the city and the suburbs, between the haves and have-nots, the need to have bigger and better wheels kept folks buying cars: Mustangs, Barracudas, Cougars, Mercs, Caddies, or Falcons, speed-ohs or rattletraps, FOB factory or custom-cut to the owner's specs.

Cars were a part of the neighborhood, the status symbol of having arrived into your own, with wheels. Cars were the black man's stock portfolio, his rolling real estate, his assets realized. What roads the city didn't provide by way of streets, it made convenient with expressways that cut through the length of the town, leaving a trail of cheap motels, used-car lots, and strip joints at one end, and Swift Packing House and the bridge to the Kansas side at the other end. Any of the roads from the center of town allowed easy access to a state highway, but the convenience was counted only by those who needed to flee the city or cross the state line.

Real estate developers in the select sections of the inner city that were being upgraded for white residents called those expressways "The River of Lights." Folks around Buel's neighborhood called them "The Track," and tried turning their backs on the whole business unless they were unlucky enough to have a reason to skip town.

Sometimes Buel and his friends had vague dreams of eating up roadway in a hot machine of their choice, but Andre had been the only one to find a fast exit east, and when he'd left the city, he'd just vanished as far as Buel and the rest of the Technical High School class of '62 were concerned. Andre might have vanished, but Brush Creek, Swope Parkway, and Pershing Road were always there. And when cars from the neighborhood around Troost and Prospect passed each other on the road, their owners would honk their horns in recognition.

If someone had taken a photo of Buel, DeJohn, Roger, and Calvin back in 1964, they could have spotted the contentment on those four faces. In those days everything they set out to do seemed easy, especially when they stayed within the boundaries of the world they knew, places they could reach on one tank of gas. They couldn't imagine, did not bother to imagine, anything pushing them farther than that point. That would come later. For now it was enough to wait for Sunday afternoon, when Buel or one of the others would say, "Let's show Nab some tail feathers and floorboard these hogs."

On a good day, when the heat and humidity were in agreement, when there was no snow blowing off the Kansas plains or winds whipping north toward Chicago, the men took to the roads, their cars spit-clean from the fish-eye taillights and split-wing trim to the sleek roofs and grillwork. Their only worry was the occasional cop on the Nab ready to grab them as they sped past a billboard or crossed the state line at rocket speed. When Miss Swift raised her skirts over the Intercity Viaduct and they smelled the rancid odors of dirty meat, they knew they were heading west. And when the messages on billboard after billboard along Highway 40 were shattered by blinking neon-like black lights on a disco floor, they were heading east.

But for the women, those cars were the excuses that helped their men stay as fickle as the tornadoes that occasionally passed through the heart of town, the winds that sometimes danced through living rooms and took everything a family had managed to scrape out of a pinch-penny job, and sometimes turned corners down the centers of streets as if they were following traffic patterns. For the women those cars were merely another way to haul them from the house to a day job—"the hook between Miss Ann and the killing floor," as Autherine Franklin would say—because, for the women, the cars were to be looked at and paid for, but never driven.

Anna Ruth Gatewood remembered the family gossip about her Aunt Charzell, who had driven a Packard to Oklahoma City in 1927 all by herself. "The only way she did it was she dressed like a man and she was so light she could pass for some old honkie anyway." But Anna Ruth's family had fallen on hard times, and there were no Packards available for the women when the men could barely hang onto a job long enough to support one car.

Even when some old fool, like Dennis Frasier, went on pension and bought a new car, keeping the old car for a runabout and the new one for churchgoing, women weren't likely to take the wheel. All of them had excuses for not being able to drive: Luann Frasier claimed she was too old, Nona Payton said her babies made her too nervous, and Autherine Franklin told everyone she was too tired to do anything after spending all day scrubbing Miss Ann's floors out in the suburbs.

When Buel bought his Hawk GT, Anna Ruth told everyone that Buel had never said "boo" to her about buying a car, and if he had, she would have taken driving lessons before he'd signed the papers.

"He just showed up with it," she said. "Drove up to the house, big as cuff, and walked up the path like he'd just hopped off the Prospect bus and come home from work, as usual."

According to Anna Ruth, Buel had sat down on the sofa, picked up the paper and folded it back to the sports page the way he always did. But about a quarter of an hour after he'd been in the house, Anna Ruth came to the window to see what the commotion on the street was all about.

What she saw was a jet-black Studebaker Hawk surrounded by half the neighbors on College Street.

At first Anna Ruth didn't connect the car with Buel. All she saw was the top of the car, a bright swatch of black metal, a glob of shiny color that looked like the smear of tar road crews poured in the ruts along Brush Creek Boulevard every spring. At first she couldn't even determine what kind of car it was.

"Looked like some kind of funeral car," she said later. "First word that come into my head when I seen that car was *death*. If I was gonna buy a car and spend all that money, I'd have bought me a pink one, something bright and pretty like them cotton candy cones they sell over at Swope Park in the summer. But that thing looked like somebody had been laid out and the undertaker had come calling."

"Girl, if he was my husband," Autherine Franklin said, "I'd make him give me the keys to that car. That's why I don't have no intention of marrying that no-good DeJohn Washington. Can't never depend on men for nothing."

Anna Ruth almost told Autherine that men were all she'd ever depended on, but she held her tongue. Everybody knew Autherine was fast and loose, and that was why she and DeJohn didn't get married. But if anyone said anything to Autherine about it, she'd be ready to go upside their heads, and since Autherine was her best friend, next to Nona Payton, Anna Ruth had better sense than to pick a fight over nothing.

"I was thinking about going over to the YWCA," Nona said. "Tell me they got driving lessons over there for anybody to take."

"Girl, Roger ain't gonna let you spend no money learning how to drive," Autherine and Anna Ruth said at the same time.

Then they both leaned back and laughed at the sharpness of their perceptions. It was comforting to see some part of the world clearly, and the three of them had been friends for so long they clearly saw each other's worlds, even if they could not see their own.

What was happening to change their own worlds did not make itself known until Buel had owned his car for nearly a year. But in that time, he and Anna Ruth more or less settled into a routine, an edgy kind of quarreling mixed with hard loving that told the world they were still newlyweds. Each morning Anna Ruth still took the Prospect bus to the Plaza and her stockroom job in Ladies' Apparel. And each morning Buel drove his Hawk one block north of Arbor Industrials, where he parked and walked the rest of the way for fear one of his bosses might see the car and think he was trying to be a big shot.

"I ain't got the patience to be teaching you to drive," Buel told Anna Ruth. "Ain't no reason for a woman to be driving. Women too nervous. Besides, you got me to do your driving for you." He laughed and stroked her ass to make her forget the idea of his car.

No matter how many times they argued the logic of her learning to drive, or how many times Anna Ruth offered to help with the weekly simonize, the only time she sat in that Studebaker was on Sundays. And even then she only got a ride to church. Getting home was her problem, because Sundays Buel and his buddies went to Rooster's to listen to whatever game was being broadcast on the radio. Anna Ruth knew the seasons by sports more than she did by weather: football in the fall, basketball in late winter, track in the spring, and baseball all summer. In a pinch the guys even listened to golf or tennis, anything to keep their standing arrangement of Rooster's after church, then onto the Interstate or Highway 40 and one of the bag-and-bottle clubs until late Sunday night. Except for an occasional family gathering at one of their parents' houses, little had interfered with the boys' routine in the two years since they'd left high school.

None of Anna Ruth's complaints could keep Buel away from Rooster's after church.

Buel said, "Anna Ruth, you ought to feel good when I drive up to the church and help you out of this baby right there in front of the preacher."

"I'd feel a lot better if I was driving this baby by my lonesome," she said.

And Nona said, "Ain't that just like a man? Thinking that just 'cause he can drive you to church, you got to feel happy 'bout him driving off and leaving you alone at night."

"How you think they kept all them slaves in line?" Autherine asked.

"Told them God meant for them to be slaves, that's how. Fed them a whole bunch of crap about God and church. That's why I don't like going to nobody's church. When I really want to talk to God, I just get down on my knees and commence to speaking."

"Honey, when you get down on your knees, you talking to Ajax and Spic and Span," Nona laughed.

"Nona Pettigrew Payton, we been friends since the second grade," Autherine snapped, "but if you don't watch your mouth, I'm gone make you one dead friend."

"Just hush," Anna Ruth said, "You know you don't mean that. Now just hush, both of you. I swear, seems I spent half my life listening to you two snapping at each other."

Autherine was ready to take the argument one step further, but Nona paid attention to what Anna Ruth had said.

"Aw, girl, come on," Nona said to Autherine. "You know I didn't mean nothing. Let's walk over to Bishop's and get a fish sandwich we can turn red with some Louisiana hot sauce."

"Ohh, now you talking," Autherine shouted, and linked arms with both Anna Ruth and Nona.

Still dressed in their Sunday best, they left church and headed toward Bishop's.

At one point their path took them down a two-block stretch of Brush Creek Boulevard. The trees lining the four-lane street rustled with the wind, and debris, caught in the backwash, swirled down the creek bed that separated the traffic patterns into two lanes on either side of a concrete abutment. The creek itself was concrete, paved over years ago by the Pendergast political machine, which owned the local concrete plant. Now it resembled a spillway for a dam site, except it was flat, like the rest of the landscape, with sections of sewer pipe cut in half and laid open along a winding mile stretch through the middle of the city. And it was either full or empty. In dry seasons a trickle of water oozed through the mud that crept up in the middle where the concrete sections didn't quite meet. But the creek offered the neighborhood sudden flash floods during the wet seasons. In those times crossing the boulevard could be perilous, and more than one person had suddenly been faced with the prospect of drowning while the rest of the city stayed high and dry.

Still, the creek had its advantages, meager as they may have been. It separated the rush of traffic up and down the busy boulevard, and the trees stirred the wind so that gas fumes did not linger the way they did along Blue Parkway, The Paseo, and other thoroughfares. And in the winter, when the snows froze into ice, neighborhood kids used the creek as a playground, while the hot summer air left the trees heavy with fragrance, and wildflowers bloomed in the cracks edging the creek.

It was rough walking those two blocks, but Anna Ruth and her friends knew what kind of jaunty flash they made, laughing and high-stepping their way to Bishop's. Some days they walked to a chorus of car horns honking their owners' approval at the sight of three foxy ladies. Autherine had more interest in pointing out who was behind the wheel of a passing Bonneville, or a two-toned Barracuda, or a fishtailed Plymouth. Anna Ruth was busy counting the number of women maneuvering their old man's Oldsmobile or Falcon or Fleetwing. Only Nona was interested in how much money had been wasted engineering the Brush Creek project.

But Nona had always been the curious one of the group. As a child, she'd been more interested in playing Monopoly than Pick-up-Sticks or jacks. And in high school she'd taken a course in drafting along with her Executive Secretary program. Even now she was enrolled in night school in an effort to upgrade her job with the most successful black dentist in the city from receptionist to bookkeeping. Nona liked to read better than she liked to dance, and Nona had a library card that she used at least once a month. So Nona had been labeled the brains of the group.

"You so stuck up, you got no business over here in Tech," Autherine had told her one spring day after typing class. "You ought to be at Richmond where you could be wearing them football sweaters and going to the prom."

But Richmond wouldn't take Roger Payton, and more than anything else in the world, Nona Pettigrew wanted to be with Roger Payton. It was probably Nona who had put the idea of marriage into Anna Ruth Simpson's head. Anna Ruth had liked Buel well enough, but she hadn't thought much beyond her next date with him. Nona had plans for Roger Payton, and when she consulted Autherine and Anna Ruth on the best way to make Roger aware of those plans, the fever of marriage struck Anna Ruth as well. The three of them had giggled and plotted, and three months after Roger and Buel graduated, there had been a double wedding with Autherine and DeJohn acting as witnesses for both couples.

Once they were married, Anna Ruth had settled into not thinking past any given day again, but Nona simply worked around Roger's Midwestern ideas of what a wife should be and enrolled in night school. By the summer of 1964 she was working her way to convincing herself that she needed a driver's education course as well as those bookkeeping courses she took while Roger was on duty nights at the gas station, and by spring she would have enrolled if the country hadn't been faced with Johnson's Tonkin Gulf Resolution.

Suddenly the United States was fighting in Vietnam and Roger Payton was one of the first men in the neighborhood to be drafted. Within six months all of them were in uniform, and in the six-square-mile area between Prospect and Troost, families were learning to pronounce the names of places that even President Johnson had trouble wrapping around his tongue: Phan Rang, Chu Yang Sin, Quang Ngai, Dong Hoi.

Like everyone else, the women had been totally unprepared for the impact of Vietnam, but of them all, Autherine seemed hardest hit by the news of her man called to war. She saw it as a plot against black folks, and even after she helped DeJohn pack his clothes and sell his car, she preached against his participation in some white man's war games.

"Going to church and going to war is all black folks is allowed," she shouted. "We ought to form our own state. Let them white folks fight it out amongst themselves."

And as she wept and ranted, refusing to go to church anymore, refusing to go to movies or even press her hair in her protest against white injustice, Anna Ruth and Nona saw the revolutionary she would become within the next three years. But by the beginning of 1965, Nona and Anna Ruth became more troubled over the decrease in letters they received from their husbands.

Now walking along Brush Creek was a problem, no matter what the season. They ignored the cars that honked at them and tried to imagine what kind of scenery the men could see in that place called Vietnam, a small speck on the map that Nona had helped them locate one day in the library. Now each of them found ways to occupy their time, especially the nights, and Nona, free to take any classes she wished without hiding them from Roger, finally enrolled in a driver's ed course.

"I aim to tell him," she said to Autherine. "I aim to tell Roger all about that driving course next time I hear from him, but I don't want to be throwing him no surprises until I'm sure he got the other letters I sent him. I ain't heard from him since last September, and here it is January."

"I got a letter from Buel in November. Said he was being transferred to Roger and DeJohn's company. But I ain't heard from him since."

"DeJohn don't write much, but I should've been hearing from him 'bout now. Last thing I heard, they was moving them farther north."

"Well, if I know the boys, they got themselves some hootch and up there painting the town," Anna Ruth laughed.

The others laughed with her, but no one believed what she'd said. The news was filled with stories of war casualties; B. L. Jefferson's boy had been killed on a destroyer in the South China Sea, and the Andersons, over on Bales Street, had lost a son and two nephews. And everyone was beginning to have news of another name added to the list of those missing in action. In June the names Roger Payton, Buel Ray Gatewood, and Calvin Gatewood were added to that list. And in June DeJohn's mother told Autherine she'd received a letter from the War Department telling her that DeJohn had been fatally wounded.

"Those cocksuckers can't even say *dead*," she screamed. "Just some shit about casualties and missing. Like we gonna turn a corner and find them standing there grinning. This is *some* shit. I want you to know, this is *some* shit."

"I just can't believe Roger's dead," Nona said. "Roger wouldn't just go off and die on me."

"Honey, Roger didn't die on *you*," Autherine snarled. "He died on Uncle Sam. He died fighting for some white man. He died same as DeJohn and Buel and Calvin."

"I don't believe Buel is dead," Anna Ruth said in a flat voice. "I just don't believe it."

"And Roger can't be dead," Nona wept. "Look. He didn't even sell his car." She pointed to the Ford parked at the curb in front of her house. "He left the car right there. I mean, you can't see him going off and leaving that car."

"I don't see nothing but that car," Autherine said. "I don't see nothing but that car out there rotting in the rain. Ain't nobody in it. Roger ain't in his car, and Buel ain't in his. They might as well have sold them. Might as well have done what DeJohn did and sold that shit. And if you got any sense, that's what you'll do."

"I'm not gonna sell that car until Roger comes home and tells me in person to sell it."

"Then that car's gonna be sitting there till hell freezes over," Autherine snapped.

But Nona finished her driving course, and on Sundays, when Autherine didn't have a Black Panthers meeting, Nona would take her for a ride, the two of them zipping along Blue Parkway, The Paseo, the Interstate Viaduct, and Highway 40 in Roger Payton's Ford Skyliner. Loneliness for Nona became those Sunday rides where she tried to duplicate the outings Roger had taken, Buel and the others trailing him. Only Nona had Autherine spouting Black Nationalist doctrines in the passenger's seat beside her. Anna Ruth refused to come with them.

Anna Ruth said her Sundays were too busy. She had to make sure Buel's Hawk received its weekly simonize, she told them. And she had to attend meetings at the church where she helped the auxiliary track down government addresses so the ladies could write to the War Department and ask them to send their men home.

On Sundays Nona and Autherine drove by Anna Ruth's house on College

Street, but every Sunday Anna Ruth was too busy to join them. Through that whole summer Anna Ruth seemed too busy to have any time for them at all. By fall, Nona and Autherine noticed how Anna Ruth didn't wait for the weekend to simonize Buel's car. Often they would see her washing the whitewalls, polishing the chrome, or waxing that car on Wednesdays or Fridays or Saturdays, only to do the whole job again on Sundays. And more and more Anna Ruth retreated into a kind of unquiet muteness that was more like a scream than a silence.

And in early December, four months after the Watts riots, when the winds blowing off the prairie seemed loaded with little crystals of ice, and the bare limbs of trees along Brush Creek Boulevard crackled in the thin air, Anna Ruth snapped and took the wheel of Buel Ray Gatewood's Gran Turismo Hawk.

It seemed so natural, sliding into the driver's seat. For months she'd brushed the upholstery and floor with a clothes brush to keep the dust from eating the fabric. For months she'd polished the steering wheel, the wrap-around windshield and dash. And from time to time, on orders from Buel, she'd started the engine and let the car idle. But on that day she'd slipped it into drive, popped the brakes, and eased away from the curb.

She was on Brush Creek before Nab spotted her. At three o'clock, when the cop pulled her over, she'd put the car in neutral and waited patiently.

It surprised her a bit that she didn't feel frightened. It wasn't as if she knew what she was going to say, but she had felt that heart-pounding rush she remembered feeling the day she'd worked Buel around to asking her to marry him, or the first time, a few days later, when she'd slept with him. In her rearview mirror she watched the cop lock his cycle in park, and waited until he tapped on the glass before she cranked down the window.

"It's my husband's car. He's in the army in Nam," she told him when he asked for her driver's license. "He's missing in action so I'm taking care of his car till he gets back."

The cop never blinked an eye. "I'm gonna have to take your keys," he said. "Why don't you just park this heap close to the curb and let me have your keys."

"This ain't no heap," Anna Ruth snapped. "It's a Gran Turismo Hawk, and it belongs to my husband. He's in Nam. Missing in action . . ."

"We got two hundred thousand boys in Vietnam, and not a one of them took his car. You got no driver's permit for this thing, so you park it. This car is impounded."

The cop walked to the rear of the car to take down the license number, and Anna Ruth leaned over to start the engine. She gunned it, giving the 255 horsepower full rein.

"Easy there, girl," the cop said. "Don't get fancy on me. Just slide on into that curb."

Anna Ruth slipped it out of neutral into drive, then while she was still inhaling, into reverse. The engine responded as if it had been starving for attention. In one fluid, sudden movement Anna Ruth took out the cop's motorcycle, and if that Nab hadn't stepped back, she'd have nailed him, too. Then she slammed it into gear and raced down Brush Creek. She was four blocks away before the cop stopped slapping his hat against his knee and yelling, "Goddammit! Goddammit!"

Passersby gawked, and some, heading toward Bishop's or Maxine's Bar-b-que, called to friends to see the sight. "Nab got creamed!" they shouted, and the news spread up and down the street like brushfire. Unfortunately, Anna Ruth had left the cop's radio intact.

But that was not her concern at the moment. When the cop finally realized he could call for help, Anna Ruth was careening off parked cars along the boulevard. Her foot seemed frozen on the accelerator, and when she entered The Paseo, she skidded into a spin at the icy intersection, circling twice before she headed north, leaving five crippled cars stuck in the middle of the street behind her. The police call reached patrol cars at 3:18 P.M. By 3:20 she was spotted on The Paseo, and two cars gave chase.

Somewhere along that thoroughfare, Anna Ruth came into her own, and the occasional clatter of metal when she sideswiped a parked car or grazed a driver too slow to move out of her path no longer made her gasp. When she saw Nab behind her, she left The Paseo at Plymouth and returned to it later off Linwood. The snowplows had been working in her favor. In fact, the weather was in her favor. It was a gloomy day, but cold and clear, so cold that no one was out that Sunday unless they had to be. So cold that slush hadn't formed on the roadway and the ashes left by the plow crews were still on top of the ice. Despite the damage she'd caused, for the most part, the path ahead of her was clear. But behind her there was a stream of police cars.

She had decided to head for the Interstate Viaduct and the Kansas side, but Nab began to descend in all directions, and she had to crisscross her own path across The Paseo and back. Once, when she was parallel to The Paseo on Troost, she saw two cop cars coming toward her. The units behind her knew they had her cornered, but Anna Ruth jerked the wheel and in one wild open circle of a swing, headed in the opposite direction, weaving between and around the cars that had been trailing her. Three cars ran into each other to avoid a head-on with Anna Ruth's Hawk.

As the cop driving the second car pulled himself from the wreck, he looked at Anna Ruth's retreating taillights and shook his head in begrudging admiration. "Goddamn, that bitch can drive," he said.

But whatever luck Anna Ruth had found in encountering very little traffic on newly plowed streets was about to run out. By all accounts, the police had brought in twelve units by the time she reached the last lap of her odyssey. By all accounts, Anna Ruth had traveled the length of The Paseo from Brush Creek to the Viaduct intersection and back by the time Nab had cut off her escape route. And just as she reentered the neighborhood, just before a line of squad cars flanked the street and forced her onto the lawn of the Technical High School, she'd left behind her a trail of more than twenty damaged cars.

But in those last two miles Anna Ruth had gathered a cheering section. Folks in the area between Troost and Prospect lined the street, yelling directions that would place her out of Nab's path. And sometimes folks blocked Nab's path by shoving junk cars that had been abandoned in the neighborhood in front of the cops. Young boys threw rocks, practicing for the riots that were soon to come to the city. And old men, rising from their Sunday afternoon slumber, marked the day as a turning point.

Nona caught up with Autherine just as Anna Ruth swerved off Brush Creek onto Euclid. Autherine had been helping make posters for a Panthers meeting in the basement of the school, and when Nona banged on the door and called to her, she was just warming up to an argument with a fellow Panther about the causes of revolution. The news of Anna Ruth's rebellion erased her need to convince the man.

The two women were running down the front stairs of the school when Anna Ruth turned onto the block. At the opposite end the police had parked several paddy wagons. Behind her, a phalanx of patrol cars, sirens blasting and lights flashing, raced toward her.

Perhaps she would have made it if Old Man Frasier had not been backing out of his driveway at that moment. Frasier had heard all the noise, and his neighbor, Charleston Davis, told him some crazy woman was tearing up Brush Creek. That was a sight the old man felt determined not to miss. He could not have known Anna Ruth had detoured off Brush Creek and was aiming for a new route north along Blue Parkway. He eased the big Pontiac out of his driveway and directly into Anna Ruth's path.

Even from the stairs, Nona and Autherine could see Anna Ruth didn't have much of a choice between Old Man Frasier or the school's snow-impacted lawn.

"Damn! I 'bout made Kansas, Nona," Anna Ruth whispered after the police had pulled her out of the wrecked Studebaker. "Halfway there and driving by myself."

Nona shushed her and, cradling her head, rocked her until the ambulance attendants got the stretcher ready.

"Buel's gonna be mad at me," Anna Ruth said. "Buel's gonna come home and find out I wrecked his car, and he's gonna have my ass."

"Don't worry about it, baby," Nona told her. "By the time Buel gets here, we gonna have everything fixed."

Autherine watched the cops trying to handcuff Anna Ruth even as the medics were placing her on the stretcher. "This is some shit!" Autherine shouted. "Some shit!"

Folks who lived around Troost and Prospect could do nothing but agree with her.

FROM DJBOT
BAGHOSTUS'S RUN

Nathaniel Mackey

—————27.VIII.81

Dear Angel of Dust,

Thank you for your letter. It arrived a couple of days ago. I'm sorry to say it found me not feeling too well. I'm in bed now, as I've been for the past four days, bearing the brunt of a new round of shattered cowrie shell attacks. I can't say for sure what it was brought them on, though I suspect Djamilaa and Aunt Nancy's recital played a not insignificant part. In any case, they remain as much a mystery as ever. So much so, in fact, I no longer bother to see the doctor about them.

I have, though, had occasion to do some reflection and self-diagnosis these past few days. A remark my mother made the other day sparked it. We were talking on the phone, me telling her about the latest round of attacks, the quandary they've got me in, the dizziness, trances, and so forth, when she said, "It's all that music, all those records you've been buying all these years." I laughed. "No, seriously," she went on, "all those records doing all that spinning have made you dizzy." I laughed again, my only defense. It was an old ax, one she's been grinding ever since I was a kid. My mother, as I may have told you already, has never really understood my becoming a musician. Virtually nothing, as far as she's concerned, could be more impractical. I recall times as a kid when I'd buy a record and have to sneak it into the house, so upset would she get at my "throwing away good money."

Still, it's an ax I've come to take more seriously than my laughter let on. It set me to thinking. Are the attacks a self-sentencing conviction the music fosters and feeds, even if only as the occasion for a reprieve? Are self-sentencing conviction and self-commuting sentence merely symbiotic halves of a self-cycling ordeal? Do I knock myself down in order to be picked up?

Someone I once read remarked on the need to produce an inventory of traces. What better place to begin, I've been thinking, than with those discs I used to smuggle into the house? Records we call them. Rightly so.

I've been listening a lot these past couple of days to one such disc, Miles's "Seven Steps to Heaven," one of the first I ever bought. I can't help hearing it as a repository of imprints that long ago went to work on me, set up shop (tenuous hope, tenuous heaven) in my perhaps too impressionable heart (foolish heart). The title of one of the cuts, my favorite in fact, practically jumped off the album jacket at me: "I Fall in Love Too Easily." There it was. A complete sentence. This indeed was one of the cuts that made me.

And the other titles, even when only fragments or phrases, likewise had a sentencing effect. "So Near So Far" gave an apt enough description of the tenuous heaven it whetted one's appetite for. It was an old dialectical story: possibility paradoxically parented by prohibition. Not only did vertigo set in, a quixotic dizziness and discontent, but one's heaven-sent stagger turned into a blue compensatory strut. Blue earth itself was made even bluer by the tenuous ladder one took it for. Listen, if you don't believe me, to "Basin Street Blues."

My mother's ax notwithstanding, I accept it all, even the scratches and the nicks, the points on the record where the needle skips. Noisy reminders of the wear of time they may very well be, but I hear them as rickety, quixotic rungs on a discontinuous ladder—quixotic leaps or ellipses (quantum lump in one's throat) meted out by contraband heaven having set up shop.

Sincerely,

N.

─────30.VIII.81

Premonitory Dream of New
Drummer Djeannine's Post-Romantic Booth
(See-Through School of Hard Knocks)

Djeannine loomed larger than life at the top of the hill with the sun behind her. The sunlight stripped her of the white cotton dress she wore, weaving an alternate, see-through web that had caught my eye and that held me captive. I lay on my back in the meadow at the foot of the hill, my legs and feet pointing toward the summit Djeannine stood on, my feet drawn back so that my heels addressed my hips, while my knees loomed almost as high as Djeannine, who stood, it seemed, partly between and partly above them.

Beneath her white cotton dress she wore nothing. No slip, no bra, no panties. The sun's light, having stripped her of the dress, was a further nothing, so unseizably there as to make sight a fleet, far-reaching rendezvous (trance and transparency, wile and redress). I lay possessed and penetrated by shadows, drunk with a glimpse of silhouetted legs and the X-ray wafting of an imaginary musk.

The staggered scent (part static dance) I was caught in caused Djeannine's cotton dress to billow. The billowing dress loomed larger and larger, an immense tent held up by a pungent, punishing sense of miraculously available "parts." A contrabass trombone blast[1] came out of the blue, came on as if to seize while accenting the billowing of Djeannine's white dress.

Stripped of habit, the light found its voice in a transparent equation: brass accompaniment conjured brazen legs.

What began as a blast tapered off into a soft, insistent keening, part purr, part growl, part prayer sustained by what I now could hear was a trombone choir (six players, each of whom came on as though he or she had just seen a ghost). Spectral usher, elegiac reminder, and bony escort rolled into one; the choir lifted me off the ground, set me down on my feet, and got me started on my walk toward the summit Djeannine stood on.

The closer I got, the more the hill turned out to be part circus tent and part revival meeting tent, outside of which, instead of on whose peak, Djean-

---

1. Charles Mingus, *The Black Saint and the Sinner Lady* (Impulse! AS-35), Side 1, Track 1: "Solo Dancer."

nine stood. No longer lying on my back, I felt new to the earth, newly born. The trombones complied with my need for a new investiture, introducing a "Hymn to the Dawning Age" which I confounded with the hem of Djeannine's alternate, see-through web and billowing dress rolled into one.

Just outside the big top, the revival tent her billowing dress turned out to be, Djeannine stood in a booth selling kisses[2] and a brand of hard candy known as Kashmiri Cough Drops.[3] I approached her, wearing a new pair of pants. I could see that now, having been stripped of her white cotton dress, she wore a dark blue blouse, though the front of the booth blocked my view of what she wore from the waist down. I handed her a dollar bill, but she handed it back, saying that for me there'd be no charge. I leaned forward over the counter of the booth, closed my eyes, and awaited the light, perfunctory pressure I expected her lips to make on mine.

It did, in fact, start off that way—a light, perfunctory pressure. But suddenly Djeannine slipped her tongue between my lips. The kiss grew wetter, her tongue more adventurous, daring, solicitous, insisting my own tongue answer in kind.

My mouth began to fill with a mint-flavored liquid[4] which now flowed from Djeannine's mouth (somewhat like a sweet North African tea,[5] only not as hot). When she ended the kiss and drew back, I opened my eyes, my mouth full to the point of overflowing with the mint-flavored liquid. My eyes met hers.

Having made eye contact, I closed my eyes again, savoring the liquid which, like a liqueur, caressed my tongue, teeth, inner cheeks and gums. It ever so lightly stung the inside of my mouth. I had a sense of my head having cleared to the point of translucency, a menthol rush converting my hair, skin, and skull to crystal.[6] A clairvoyant breeze blew into my face.

An involuntary grunt suggesting peep-show delight escaped my throat. I opened my eyes again as Djeannine stepped out of her booth. She wore a skirt which, like her blouse, was dark blue. Extrovert ingénue and rough-and-ready tomboy rolled into one, she stepped away from the booth and did a cartwheel. Her skirt fell past her thighs and down past her waist while she was upside down. I caught a glimpse of her thighs, a bit of pubic hair, and the reinforced crotch of her blindingly white cotton panties. The blinding whiteness caused me to close my eyes again. Not knowing why, I swallowed

2. Eddie Jefferson, *The Main Man* (Inner City IC 1033), Side 1, Track 1: "Jeannine."
3. Eli Mohammad Shera and Ensemble, *Folksongs of Kashmir* (Lyrichord LLST 7260), Side 2, Track 1: "Sufi Love Song."
4. The Clovers, *Their Greatest Recordings* (Atco SD 33-374), Side 2, Track 3: "One Mint Julep."
5. "The Quintet," *Jazz at Massey Hall* (Fantasy 86003), Side 2, Track 3: "A Night in Tunisia."
6. Coleman Hawkins, *The Hawk Flies* (Milestone M-47015), Side 2, Track 2: "You Go to My Head."

the mint-flavored liquid. She was on her feet again by the time I opened
my eyes.

The mint-flavored liquid began to have a different effect. *Peppermint
spit* was what it was, I realized, though the longer I reflected the less *peppermint* mattered. Like a piece of chewing gum losing its flavor, the mint-
flavored liquid more and more appeared to have been nothing more than
X-ray spit, spit-flavored spit. I felt nauseous.

My stomach began to convulse, but nothing came up. A gush of emptiness and air spewed out of my mouth and bent me over. I looked at my
legs and saw through the flesh to the bones underneath. I looked up to see
Djeannine step back inside her booth and reach under the counter. The last
thing I saw before waking up was her extend her right hand to offer me a
box of Kashmiri Cough Drops.

Dear Angel of Dust,

I begin with the above as one mark of its impact. I woke up a half hour
ago, unable to think of anything else or get back to sleep, obsessed with
getting it down on paper. How I knew the woman's name was Djeannine I
can't really say. She didn't introduce herself nor was her name in any other
way announced. It seemed that in dreaming I necessarily knew, that dreaming
was the same as knowing, that to be there was to be pressed, penetrated and
possessed by an epiphanous clarity, a see-through ipseity, a namesake certainty which, no matter which way one cut it, came down to *Djeannine*.
To be there was not only to know Djeannine's name but to know, without
knowing why, that it began with a *D*. And to know that one knew this with
such certainty was to know that Djeannine was the drummer the band's been
looking for. It was as though such ipseity or certainty (namesake dream,
genetic drum) had somehow long been beaten into one's blood.

I should quickly point out, I suppose, that since making up our minds
three weeks ago that the new drummer would be a woman we've had little
luck locating suitable candidates. We auditioned two women, neither of
whom, for reasons I won't go into, worked out. We're still looking, though
the days I spent in bed slowed the search down. (I've gotten better, by the
way. I was up and about the day after I last wrote.)

As I've already said, I knew in the dream I was getting a glimpse of the
woman we've been looking for. This might well, I knew, turn out to be a
vain projection, so hard to miss were some of the imprints being played back
to me by the dream. (You'll have noticed I footnoted some of the more
obvious ones.) Still, I was even more certain once I'd woken up that our
new drummer would be Djeannine, that what I'd seen was no solipsistic disc
but a genuine vision.

Funny, though, that I can't remember what Djeannine looked like. I recall what she wore but can't form an image of her face.

Still, the good news is that I know the name of our eventual drummer. Now we'll know what to be on the lookout for.

Yours,

N.

————VIII.8

Dear Angel of Dust,

I hadn't expected to write again so soon, but there's been a new development concerning Djeannine. Penguin and I were over at Lambert's this afternoon helping him do some work on his car. We got to talking about the band and about our search for a woman drummer, and I, of course, couldn't help talking about my dream. "We're not far away from finding her," I told them. "I was given her name in a dream I had the other night." They each looked up from the new radiator hose they were in the midst of installing and shot me a surprised, half-incredulous look whose credulous half insisted, "Go ahead. Tell us more."

I proceeded to tell them the dream, repeating pretty much verbatim the account I wrote you in yesterday's letter. So indelibly etched or engraved in my memory were the verbal equivalents I'd worked so hard to find that they amounted to a form of after-the-fact dictation, an unerasable script to which my now involuntary tongue seemed inextricably tied. Lambert and Penguin listened with more and more rapt attention, regarding me with an ever more alarmed, half-quizzical mix of skepticism and belief. It was when I got to the part about the light finding its voice in a transparent equation that they both blurted out in unison (at the exact instant I myself said it), "Brass accompaniment conjured brazen legs."

"How'd you know that?" I interrupted my account of the dream to ask, only to register within a split second of asking it that they both had turned and asked the same thing of one another. "How'd you know that?" The question hung like a three-sided echo in the air.

We stood staring at one another for a while. We each had a can of beer we'd taken occasional sips from while working on the car. Penguin now not only took a sip but broke the silence by suggesting I resume telling the dream. This I did. But when I got to the part about the big top and the booth in which Djeannine stood selling kisses and Kashmiri Cough Drops, he interrupted me. He asked me to stop and then took up exactly where I left off, mouthing the words I was about to utter as though reading from the letter I wrote you yesterday: "I approached her, wearing a new pair of pants. I could see that now, having been stripped of her white cotton dress, she wore a dark blue blouse, though the front of the booth blocked my view of what she wore from the waist down. I handed her a dollar bill, but she handed it back, saying that for me there'd be no charge. I leaned forward over the counter of the booth, closed my eyes, and awaited the light, perfunctory pressure I expected her lips to make on mine."

You can imagine my shock and surprise. Lambert, too, seemed shocked and surprised, but what he proceeded to do shocked and surprised me even more. It shocked and surprised Penguin as well, for what he did was interrupt Penguin just as Penguin had interrupted me, taking the words out of his mouth as though reading from the same unerasable script. "It did in fact," he said, "start off that way—a light, perfunctory pressure. But suddenly Djeannine slipped her tongue between my lips. The kiss grew wetter, her tongue more adventurous, daring, solicitous, insisting my own tongue answer in kind. . . ."

By now you've no doubt figured out what had happened. At about the same time as I interrupted Lambert to ask if this was a joke and had they been reading my mail, Penguin muttered, "My God, we must've dreamed the same dream." Why this hadn't occurred to me I can't say, but Lambert and Penguin each went on to explain that the night before last they, too, had dreamed of Djeannine. Though, unlike me, neither of them had gotten up and written out the dream, the collective script it'd inwardly etched and engraved agreed in full with what I wrote you in yesterday's letter. We all, having dreamed it once, now knew it by heart.

The one difference was that Penguin, rather than waking up as Djeannine offered him the box of Kashmiri Cough Drops, went on dreaming, unlike Lambert and me. He accepted it, opened it up, and took out a piece of candy which, he told us, he then popped into his mouth ("a Sucrets and a jawbreaker rolled into one" is how he described it). He sucked on it a while and then tried to chew it, but it broke one of his teeth. It was then that he woke up.

Penguin's extended ending took a while to soak in, though it had an immediate sobering effect. His recitation concluded, he stood without speaking, staring off into the distance. Lambert and I each took another sip of beer. By now it was late afternoon getting on toward sunset, copper-colored rays penetrating the trees behind Lambert's garage, threads of see-through sun. It was this light into which Penguin stared. He wore a hard-won survivor's look, and he, too, now took another sip of beer, grimacing as though it were a pill going down (awkward lozenge, hard-won lesson, bitter truth).

So absorbed and private and caught up in reflection was the mood that had come over him that Lambert and I left him to himself by looking away from the light.

"The same taste of rust," we heard him whisper, whereupon we both turned and looked his way again.

"What was that?" Lambert asked.

"The same taste of rust," he repeated, speaking more clearly and loudly, but still not letting his eyes meet ours. He continued staring as though entranced by the copper-colored light. "I tasted rust on Djeannine's perfunctory lips," he elaborated, "the same taste I recall from when I was a boy in Louisiana." He stopped and rubbed his eyes as though waking up, resumed his stare, and then went on, speaking in short staccato bits as though under a strain. "My first girlfriend. Our very first kiss. Her name was Jeannie. Jeannie Bonton. We both must have been about nine. The first time we kissed, I was standing on a crate outside her bedroom window. It was twilight." He broke off to take another sip of beer and then went on. The copper-colored light still held his eye. "She'd always leave to go inside once the sun set. Her parents wanted her in before dark. But she'd go to her room and come to the window, outside of which I'd stand on a crate. We'd talk until dinnertime. The first time I talked her into a kiss, she was too afraid to unfasten the screen. We kissed with our lips pressed against it. It was an old screen, rusty from years of humidity and rain. I made the mistake of parting my lips and letting the tip of my tongue touch it." He broke off again and took a sip of beer as though washing rust from the tip of his tongue. He swallowed, staring into the copper-colored threads. "The taste of it's never gone away."

Lambert and I looked at one another as Penguin stood silent. Neither of us knew immediately how to respond to what he'd said, what to make of his brief soliloquistic equation of would-be romance with insubordinate rust. That love had been weaned before its time or gotten old even before it began seemed to me to be the premature post-romantic point the drumming in for which Jeannie was Penguin's prototype. Djeannine or Jeannie, I wanted to say, is both dream girl and bitter truth. I tried to speak, only to find a preemptive rust now coated my tongue. I took another sip of the now obligatory beer, barely able to swallow. Preemptive rust had infiltrated my jaws and my throat as well. A few seconds more and my ritual sip would've been too late.

Lambert, too, took another sip. He, too, seemed to have a hard time swallowing. Preemptive rust, I gathered, had gotten to him as well. About that time, though, a cut came on the radio which seemed to free his tongue. The radio'd been playing in the background all the while, but when the title cut from an early sixties Art Blakey album, "Ugetsu," came on, it noticeably caught Lambert's attention. It necessarily caught mine and Penguin's, too. Freddie Hubbard's opening statement, that is, made for a unified field or feeling wherein the copper component of brass was part and parcel not only of the copper-colored rays of the sun but of the luminous brew, the copper-colored beer we all sipped as well. Freddie's horn was both a brass ax and a brass lamp, the Aladdin's lamp our collective dream girl Djeannine lived in.

"The ghost of love," Lambert said, as though announcing a presence and proclaiming a truth, his tongue now free of the impromptu rust which had momentarily taken over. His tone was part prophetic, part professorial. "*Ugetsu*. It's Japanese," he pointed out. "It means fantasy. Either of you ever see the movie?" I shook my head and Penguin said no. Neither of us had, but whether we had or not didn't really matter. "It's about a man who falls in love with a ghost," Lambert added. He fell silent, seemingly lost in thought.

"Don't we all?" Penguin put in as he turned to look at us, much more with us now than he'd been since recounting his alternate, broken-tooth ending and the rust-related tale of his and Jeannie's first kiss.

"Not exactly," Lambert answered, no longer lost in thought. "Many a head's been scratched and many a beard pulled over that one." He took a sip and then set out on an extended rap whose key contention was that Djeannine was "not so much post- as pre-romantic, the Afro-anticipatory taste of disappointment, Afro-inevitable slap upside the head." He noted the lack of romantic concepts of love in most African cultures, hand in hand with which went the dominant role of the drum in most African musics. The two were anything but unrelated, he argued, quoting Leadbelly's famous line at one point: "The blues is a feeling and when it hits you it's the real news." The word "hits" he gave an especially pointed emphasis. To insist on the slap, the blow, the hit was to advance a stoic, hard-knocks episte-mology. The slap, the blow, the hit had to do with the percussive, no-nonsense character and crux of experience (hardcore truth). "Thus it is that Djeannine," he said, looking at me as if he'd read my mind, "is both dream girl and drum girl, drum girl and bitter truth."

"Irresistible either way," I couldn't help saying. My tongue was loose now, long since free of extemporaneous rust. "Dreaming sets up the hit."

I took a sip. Lambert and Penguin did the same. "I'm glad you said that," Lambert looked at me again and said. "I couldn't agree with you more. Djeannine's a setup, the dream we tie to the sky, the match made in heaven. I'd go a bit further, in fact. You both know the stories of Wagadu. Think back, if you will, to the one about the drum the djinns make off with and

tie to the sky. Could Djeannine, I'm wondering, be our dream's coded, self-incriminatory way of rolling extraterrestrial thief and stolen drum into one? Could Djeannine, in other words, be a djinn?"

"But that drum was a war drum," Penguin put in.

"Exactly my point," Lambert answered at once. "Isn't war, dissension, discontent (call it what you will) indigenous to the notion of heaven? Doesn't heaven set us at odds with what's real? Isn't that how it sets us up?"

"Tied to the sky in more ways than one," I heard myself mumble. Before I knew it, the words were out of my mouth. The next thing I knew I was quoting Eddie Jefferson, a line from "Jeannine": "It was love lost to the rising cost." I repeated it once or twice by way of embarking on a spiel in which "tied to the sky" had to do with inflation. I, too, now adopted a part prophetic, part professorial tone, as if Lambert's voice had rubbed off on mine. I took a sip, hoping by doing so to wash the influence away, but Lambert's prophetic-professorial contagion turned out to be more stubborn than Penguin's mediating rust. Ritual sip notwithstanding, it refused to go away. I expounded an inverse emotional ladder ("love lost") rooted in spiraling economic ordeal ("rising cost"), going on about a fortress formation, a siege mentality, an emotional callousness given rise to and reinforced by economic hard knocks. "Fort Knocks," I went so far as to call it.

It was as if I'd hiccuped into my sleeve. Penguin laughed and Lambert grinned at my prophetic-professorial joke, my prophetic-professorial pun and complaint rolled into one. "Fort Knocks" introduced a welcome note of levity into an otherwise depressing rap. In fact, it broke the hold of Lambert's prophetic-professorial contagion. I coughed, took an expectorant sip, and coughed again, my throat at last clear of the catch-phraseological drift whose expectant gloom I'd become as much victim of as vehicle for. I couldn't help thinking of Donald Byrd's recording of "Jeannine." Pepper Adams' assured, expectorant baritone's repetitive punctuation of the opening notes of Byrd's solo came back to me now as possibly ancestral to the liberatory coughs that had cleared my throat. It felt good to at last be free of apocalyptic phlegm.

"Fort Knocks," Lambert laughed. "I'll drink to that." He went inside and came back out with three more beers.

By the time Lambert returned, Penguin was in the midst of saying to me, "Seriously, though, don't you think Djeannine embodies a wished-for betterment of base metal, an alchemization of Tin Pan Alley banality of the sort brought off by, say, Newk's way of doing 'Three Little Words'?"

Lambert cut in before I could answer, handing us each a can of beer while insisting with a grin, "As much as I'd like to pursue that question, I have to remind you that the radiator's waiting and there's still a tune-up to

be done. Why don't we let it go for now with an Afro-expedient, tried and true sense of an ending?" He paused, saw that we were waiting, pulled the lift-tab ring from his can of beer, and then added, "Then I stepped on a piece of tin and it bent. That's the way the story went."

All three of us laughed. Penguin and I opened our beers. We clinked our cans together and drank to Lambert's formulaic ending. We then went back to work on the car.

It remained to be seen, of course, whether Aunt Nancy and Djamilaa had also dreamed of Djeannine. We tried calling them once we finished the tune-up, but didn't catch either of them in, so we'll have to wait until rehearsal tomorrow to find out.

I'll let you know how it goes.

Yours,
N.

MA'DEAR

(for Estelle Ragsdale)

Terry McMillan

Last year the cost of living crunched me and I got tired of begging from Peter to pay Paul, so I took in three roomers. Two of 'em is live-in nurses and only come around here on weekends. Even then they don't talk to me much, except when they hand me their money orders. One is from Trinidad and the other is from Jamaica. Every winter they quit their jobs, fill up two and three barrels with I don't know what, ship 'em home, and follow behind on an airplane. They come back in the spring and start all over. Then there's the little college girl, Juanita, who claims she's going for architecture. Seem like to me that was always men's work, but I don't say nothing. She grown.

I'm seventy-two. Been a widow for the past thirty-two years. Weren't like I asked for all this solitude, just that couldn't nobody else take Jessie's place is all. He knew it. And I knew it. He fell and hit his head real bad on the tracks going to fetch us some fresh picked corn and okra for me to make us some succotash, and never come to. I couldn't picture myself with no other man, even though I looked after a few years of being alone in this big old house, walking from room to room with nobody to talk to, cook or clean for, and not much company either.

I missed him for the longest time and thought I could find a man just like him, sincerely like him, but I couldn't. Went out for a spell with Esther Davis's ex-husband, Whimpy, but he was crazy. Drank too much bootleg and then started memorizing on World War I and how hard he fought and didn't get no respect and not a ounce of recognition for his heroic deeds. The only war Whimpy been in is with me for not keeping him around. He bragged something fearless about how he coulda been the heavyweight champion of the world. Didn't weigh but 160 pounds and shorter than me.

Chester Rutledge almost worked 'ceptin' he was boring, never had nothing on his mind worth talking about; claimed he didn't think about nothing besides me. Said his mind was always clear and visible. He just moved around like a zombie and worked hard at the cement foundry. Insisted on giving me his paychecks, which I kindly took for a while, but when I didn't want to be bothered no more, I stopped taking his money. He got on my nerves too bad, so I had to tell him I'd rather have a man with no money and a busy mind, least I'd know he's active somewheres. His feelings was hurt bad and he cussed me out, but we still friends to this very day. He in the home, you know, and I visits him regular. Takes him magazines and cuts out his horoscope and the comic strips from the newspaper and lets him read 'em in correct order.

Big Bill Ronsonville tried to convince me that I shoulda married him instead of Jessie, but he couldn't make me a believer of it. All he wanted to do was put his big rusty hands all on me without asking and smile at me with that big gold tooth sparkling and glittering in my face and tell me how lavish I was, lavish being a new word he just learnt. He kept wanting to take me for night rides way out in the country, out there by Smith Creek where ain't nothing but deep black ditches, giant mosquitoes, loud crickets, lightning bugs, and loose pigs, and turn off his motor. His breath stank like whiskey though he claimed and swore on the Bible he didn't drank no liquor. Aside from that his hands were way too heavy and hard, hurt me, sometimes left red marks on me like I been sucked on. I told him finally that I was too light for him, that I needed a smaller, more gentle man, and he said he knew exactly what I meant.

If you want to know the truth, after him I didn't think much about men the way I used too. Lost track of the ones who upped and died or the ones who couldn't do nothing if they was alive nohow. So, since nobody else seemed to be able to wear Jessie's shoes, I just stuck to myself all these years.

My life ain't so bad now 'cause I'm used to being alone and takes good care of myself. Occasionally I still has a good time. I goes to the park and sits for hours in good weather, watch folks move and listen in on confidential conversations. I add up numbers on license plates to keep my mind alert unless they pass too fast. This gives me a clear idea of how many folks is visiting from out of town. I can about guess the color of every state now, too. Once or twice a month I go to the matinee on Wednesdays, providing ain't no long line of senior citizens 'cause they can be so slow; miss half the picture show waiting for them to count their change and get their popcorn.

Sometimes, when I'm sitting in the park, I feed the pigeons old cornbread crumbs, and I wonders what it'll be like not looking at the snow falling from the sky, not seeing the leaves form on the trees, not hearing no car engines, no sirens, no babies crying, not brushing my hair at night, drinking my Lipton tea, and not being able to go to bed early.

But right now, to tell you the truth, it don't bother me all *that* much. What is bothering me is my case worker. She supposed to pay me a visit tomorrow because my nosy neighbor, Clarabelle, saw two big trucks outside, one come right after the other, and she wondered what I was getting so new and so big that I needed trucks. My mama used to tell me that sometimes you can't see for looking. Clarabelle's had it out to do me in ever since last spring when I had the siding put on the house. I used the last of Jessie's insurance money 'cause the roof had been leaking so bad and the wood rotted and the paint chipped so much that it looked like a wicked old witch lived here. The house looked brand-new, and she couldn't stand to see an old woman's house looking better than hers. She know I been had roomers, and now all of a sudden my case worker claim she just want to visit to see how I'm doing, when really what she want to know is what I'm up to. Clarabelle work in her office.

The truth is my boiler broke and they was here to put in a new one. We liked to froze to death in here for two days. Yeah, I had a little chump change in the bank, but when they told me it was gonna cost $2,000 to get some heat, I cried. I had $862 in the bank; $300 of it I had just spent on this couch I got on sale; it was in the other truck. After twenty years the springs finally broke, and I figured it was time to buy a new one 'cause I ain't one for living in poverty, even at my age. I figured $200 was for my church's cross-country bus trip this summer.

Jessie's sister, Willamae, took out a loan for me to get the boiler, and I don't know how long it's gonna take me to pay her back. She only charge me fifteen or twenty dollars a month, depending. I probably be dead by the time it get down to zero.

My bank wouldn't give me the loan for the boiler, but then they keep sending me letters almost every week trying to get me to refinance my house. They must think I'm senile or something. On they best stationery, they write me. They say I'm up in age and wouldn't I like to take that trip I've been putting off because of no extra money. What trip? They tell me if I refinance my house for more than what I owe, which is about $3,000, that I could have enough money left over to go anywhere. Why would I want to refinance my house at fourteen and a half percent when I'm paying four and a half now? I ain't that stupid. They say dream about clear blue water, palm trees, and orange suns. Last night I dreamt I was doing a backstroke between big blue waves and tipped my straw hat down over my forehead and fell asleep under an umbrella. They made me think about it. And they asked me what would I do if I was to die today? They're what got me to thinking about all this dying mess in the first place. It never would've layed in my mind so heavy if they hadn't kept reminding me of it. Who would pay off your house? Wouldn't I feel bad leaving this kind of a burden on my family? What family they talking about? I don't even know where my people is no more.

I ain't gonna lie. It ain't easy being old. But I ain't complaining neither, 'cause I learned how to stretch my social security check. My roomers pay the house note and I pay the taxes. Oil is sky-high. Medicaid pays my doctor bills. I got a letter what told me to apply for food stamps. That case worker come here and checked to see if I had a real kitchen. When she saw I had a stove and sink and refrigerator, she didn't like the idea that my house was almost paid for, and just knew I was lying about having roomers. "Are you certain that you reside here alone?" she asked me. "I'm certain," I said. She searched every inch of my cabinets to make sure I didn't have two of the same kinds of food, which would've been a dead giveaway. I hid it all in the basement inside the washing machine and dryer. Luckily, both of the nurses was in the islands at the time, and Juanita was visiting some boy what live in D.C.

After she come here and caused me so much eruptions, I had to make trip after trip down to that office. They had me filling out all kinds of forms and still held up my stamps. I got tired of answering the same questions over and over and finally told 'em to keep their old food stamps. I ain't got to beg nobody to eat. I know how to keep myself comfortable and clean and well fed. I manage to buy my staples and toiletries and once in a while a few extras, like potato chips, ice cream, and maybe a pork chop.

My mama taught me when I was young that, no matter how poor you are, always eat nourishing food and your body will last. Learn to conserve, she said. So I keeps all my empty margarine containers and stores white rice, peas and carrots (my favorites), or my turnips from the garden in there. I can manage a garden when my arthritis ain't acting up. And water is the key. I drinks plenty of it like the doctor told me, and I cheats, eats Oreo cookies and saltines. They fills me right up, too. And when I feels like it, rolls, homemade biscuits, eats them with Alga syrup if I can find it at the store, and that sticks with me most of the day.

Long time ago, used to be I'd worry like crazy about gaining weight and my face breaking out from too many sweets, and about cellulite forming all over my hips and thighs. Of course, I was trying to catch Jessie then, though I didn't know it at the time. I was really just being cute, flirting, trying to see if I could get attention. Just so happens I lucked up and got all of his. Caught him like he was a spider and I was the web.

Lord, I'd be trying to look all sassy and prim. Have my hair all did, it be curled tight in rows that I wouldn't comb out for hours till they cooled off after Connie Curtis did it for a dollar and a Budweiser. Would take that dollar out my special savings, which I kept hid under the record player in the front room. My hair used to be fine, too: long and thick and black, past my shoulders, and mens used to say, "Girl, you sure got a head of hair on them shoulders there, don't it make your neck sweat?" But I didn't never bother answering, just blushed and smiled and kept on walking, trying hard not to switch 'cause mama told me my behind was too big for my age and to watch out or I'd be luring grown mens toward me. Humph! I loved it, though, made me feel pretty, special, like I had attraction.

Ain't quite the same no more, though. I looks in the mirror at myself and I sees wrinkles, lots of them, and my skin look like it all be trying to run down toward my toes but then it changed its mind and just stayed there, sagging and lagging, laying limp against my thick bones. Shoot, mens used to say how sexy I was with these high cheeks, tell me I looked swollen, like I was pregnant, but it was just me, being all healthy and everything. My teeth was even bright white and straight in a row then. They ain't so bad now, 'cause ain't none of 'em mine. But I only been to the dentist twice in my whole life and that was 'cause on Easter Sunday I was in so much pain he didn't have time to take no X-ray and yanked it right out 'cause my mama told him to do anything he had to to shut me up. Second time was the last time, and that was 'cause the whole top row and the fat ones way in the back on the bottom ached me so bad the dentist yanked 'em all out so I wouldn't have to be bothered no more.

Don't get me wrong, I don't miss being young. I did everything I wanted to do and then some. I loved hard. But you take Jessie's niece, Thelma. She pitiful. Only twenty-six, don't think she made it past the tenth grade, got three children by different men, no husband and on welfare. Let her tell it, ain't nothing out here but dogs. I know some of these men out here ain't worth a pot to piss in, but all of 'em ain't dogs. There's gotta be some young Jessies floating somewhere in this world. My mama always told me you gotta have something to give if you want to get something in return. Thelma got long fingernails.

Me, myself, I didn't have no kids. Not 'cause I didn't want none or couldn't have none, just that Jessie wasn't full and couldn't give me the juices I needed to make no babies. I accepted it 'cause I really wanted him all to myself, even if he couldn't give me no new bloodlines. He was satisfying enough for me, quite satisfying if you don't mind me repeating myself.

I don't understand Thelma, like a lot of these young peoples. I be watching 'em on the streets and on TV. I be hearing things they be doing to themselves when I'm under the dryer at the beauty shop. (I go to the beauty shop once a month 'cause it make me feel like thangs ain't over yet. She give me a henna so the silver have a gold tint to it.) I can't afford it, but there ain't too many luxuries I can. I let her put makeup on me, too, if it's a Saturday and I feel like doing some window shopping. I still know how to flirt and sometimes I get stares, too. It feel good to be looked at and admired at my age. I try hard to keep myself up. Every weekday morning at five-thirty I do exercises with the TV set, when it don't hurt to stretch.

But like I was saying, Thelma and these young people don't look healthy, and they spirits is always so low. I watch 'em on the streets, on the train, when I'm going to the doctor. I looks in their eyes and they be red or brown where they supposed to be milky white and got bags deeper and heavier than mine, and I been through some thangs. I hear they be using these drugs of variety, and I can't understand why they need to use all these thangs to get from day to day. From what I do hear, it's supposed to give 'em much pleasure and make their minds disappear or make 'em not feel the thangs they supposed to be feeling anyway.

Heck, when I was young, we drank sarsaparilla and couldn't even buy no wine or any kind of liquor in no store. These youngsters ain't but eighteen and twenty and buys anything with a bite to it. I've seen 'em sit in front of the store and drank a whole bottle in one sitting. Girls, too.

We didn't have no dreams of carrying on like that, and specially on no corner. We was young ladies and young men with respect for ourselfs. And we didn't smoke none of them funny cigarettes all twisted up with no filters that smell like burning dirt. I ask myself, I say Ma'Dear, what's wrong with these kids? They can read and write and do arithmetic, finish high school, go to college and get letters behind their names, but every day I hear the neighbors complain that one of they youngsters done dropped out.

Lord, what I wouldn'ta done to finish high school and been able to write a full sentence or even went to college. I reckon I'da been a room decorator. I know they calls it be that fancy name now, interior designer, but it boil down to the same thang. I guess it's 'cause I loves so to make my surroundings pleasant, even right pretty, so I feels like a invited guest in my own house. And I always did have a flair for color. Folks used to say, "Hazel, for somebody as poor as a church mouse, you got better taste in thangs than them Rock-efellers!" Used to sew up a storm, too. Covered my mama's raggedy duffold and chairs. Made her a bedspread with matching pillowcases. Didn't mix more than two different patterns either. Make you dizzy.

Wouldn't that be just fine, being an interior designer? Learning the proper names of thangs and recognizing labels in catalogs, giving peoples my business cards and wearing a two-piece with white gloves. "Yes, I decorated the Hartleys' and Cunninghams' home. It was such a pleasant experience. And they're such lovely people, simply lovely," I'da said. Coulda told those rich folks just what they needed in their bedrooms, front rooms, and specially in the kitchen. So many of 'em still don't know what to do in there.

But like I was saying before I got all off the track, some of these young people don't appreciate what they got. And they don't know thangs like we used to. We knew about eating fresh vegetables from the garden, growing and picking 'em ourselves. What going to church was, being honest and faithful. Trusting each other. Leaving our front door open. We knew what it was like to starve and get cheated yearly when our crops didn't add up the way we figured. We suffered together, not separately. These youngsters don't know about suffering for any stretch of time. I hear 'em on the train complaining 'cause they can't afford no Club Med, no new record playing albums, cowboy boots, or those Brooke Shields–Calvin Klein blue jeans I see on TV. They be complaining about nonsense. Do they ever read books since they been taught is what I want to know? Do they be learning things and trying to figure out what to do with it?

And these young girls with all this thick makeup caked on their faces, wearing these high heels they can't hardly walk in. Trying to be cute. I used to wear high heels, mind you, with silk stockings, but at least I could walk in 'em. Jessie had a car then. Would pick me up, and I'd walk real careful down the front steps like I just won the Miss America pageant, one step at a time, and slide into his shiny black Ford. All the neighbors peeked through the curtains 'cause I was sure enough riding in a real automobile with my legitimate boyfriend.

If Jessie was here now I'd have somebody to talk to. Somebody to touch my skin. He'd probably take his fingers and run 'em through my hair like he used to; kiss me on my nose and tickle me where it made me laugh. I just loved it when he kissed me. My mind be so light, and I felt tickled and precious. Have to sit down sometime just to get hold of myself.

If he was here, I probably woulda beat him in three games of checkers by now and he'd be trying to get even. But since today is Thursday, I'd be standing in that window over there waiting for him to get home from work, and when I got tired or the sun be in my eyes, I'd hear the taps on his wing tips coming up the front porch. Sometime, even now, I watch for him, but I know he ain't coming back. Not that he wouldn't if he could, mind you, 'cause he always told me I made him feel lightning lighting up his heart.

Don't get me wrong, I got friends, though a heap of 'em is dead or got tubes coming out of their noses or going all through their bodies every which-a-way. Some in the old folks' home. I thank the Lord I ain't stuck in one of them places. I ain't never gonna get that old. They might as well just bury me standing up if I do. I don't want to be no nuisance to nobody, and I can't stand being around a lot of sick people for too long.

I visits Gunther and Chester when I can, and Vivian who I grew up with, but no soon as I walk through them long hallways, I get depressed. They lay there all limp and helpless, staring at the ceiling like they're really looking at something, or sitting stiff in their rocking chairs, pitiful, watching TV and don't be knowing what they watching half the time. They laugh when ain't nothing funny. They wait for it to get dark so they know it's time to go to sleep. They relatives don't hardly come visit 'em, just folks like me. Whimpy don't understand a word I say, and it makes me grateful I ain't lost no more than I have.

Sometime we sits on the sun porch rocking like fools; don't say one word to each other for hours. But last time Gunther told me about his grandson what got accepted to Stanford University, and another one at a university in Michigan. I asked him where was Stanford and he said he didn't know. "What difference do it make?" he asked. "It's one of those uppity schools for rich smart white people," he said. "The important thang is that my black grandson won a scholarship there, which mean he don't have to pay a dime to go." I told him I know what a scholarship is. I ain't stupid. Gunther said he was gonna be there for at least four years or so, and by that time he would be a professional. "Professional what?" I asked. "Who cares, Ma'Dear, he gonna be a professional at whatever it is he learnt." Vivian started mumbling when she heard us talking, 'cause she still like to be the center of attention. When she was nineteen she was Miss Springfield Gardens. Now she can't stand the thought that she old and wrinkled. She started yakking about all the places she'd been to, even described the landscape like she was looking at a photograph. She ain't been but twenty-two miles north of here in her entire life, and that's right there in that home.

Like I said, and this is the last time I'm gonna mention it. I don't mind being old, it's just that sometime I don't need all this solitude. You can't do everything by yourself and expect to have as much fun if somebody was there doing it with you. That's why when I'm feeling jittery or melancholy for long stretches, I read the Bible, and it soothes me. I water my morning glories and amaryllis. I baby-sit for Thelma every now and then, 'cause she don't trust me with the kids for too long. She mainly call on holidays and my birthday. And she the only one who don't forget my birthday: August 19th. She tell me I'm a Leo, that I got fire in my blood. She may be right, 'cause once in a while I gets a churning desire to be smothered in Jessie's arms again.

Anyway, it's getting late, but I ain't tired. I feel pretty good. That old case worker think she gonna get the truth out of me. She don't scare me. It ain't none of her business that I got money coming in here besides my social security check. How they 'spect a human being to live off $369 a month in this day and age is what I wanna know. Every time I walk out my front door it cost me at least two dollars. I bet she making thousands and got credit cards galore. Probably got a summer house on the Island and goes to Florida every January. If she found out how much I was getting from my roomers, the government would make me pay back a dollar for every two I made. I best to get my tail on upstairs and clear everything off their bureaus. I can hide all the nurses's stuff in the attic; they won't be back till next month. Juanita been living out of trunks since she got here, so if the woman ask what's in 'em, I'll tell her, old sheets and pillowcases and memories.

On second thought, I think I'm gonna take me a bubble bath first, and dust my chest with talcum powder, then I'll make myself a hot cup of Lipton's and paint my fingernails clear 'cause my hands feel pretty steady. I can get up at five and do all that other mess; case worker is always late anyway. After she leave, if it ain't snowing too bad, I'll go to the museum and look at the new paintings in the left wing. By the time she get here, I'ma make out like I'm a lonely old widow stuck in a big old house just sitting here waiting to die.

A LOAF OF BREAD

James Alan McPherson

It was one of those obscene situations, pedestrian to most people, but invested with meaning for a few poor folk whose lives are usually spent outside the imaginations of their fellow citizens. A grocer named Harold Green was caught red-handed selling to one group of people the very same goods he sold at lower prices at similar outlets in better neighborhoods. He had been doing this for many years, and at first he could not understand the outrage heaped upon him. He acted only from habit, he insisted, and had nothing personal against the people whom he served. They were his neighbors. Many of them he had carried on the cuff during hard times. Yet, through some mysterious access to a television station, the poor folk were now empowered to make grand denunciations of the grocer. Green's children now saw their father's business being picketed on the Monday evening news.

No one could question the fact that the grocer had been overcharging the people. On the news even the reporter grimaced distastefully while reading the statistics. His expression said, "It is my job to report the news, but sometimes even I must disassociate myself from it to protect my honor." This, at least, was the impression the grocer's children seemed to bring away from the television. Their father's name had not been mentioned, but there was a close-up of his store with angry black people and a few outraged whites marching in groups of three in front of it. There was also a close-up of his name. After seeing this, they were in no mood to watch cartoons. At the dinner table, disturbed by his children's silence, Harold Green felt compelled to say, "I am not a dishonest man." Then he felt ashamed. The children, a boy and his older sister, immediately left the table, leaving Green alone with his wife. "Ruth, I am not dishonest," he repeated to her.

Ruth Green did not say anything. She knew, and her husband did not, that the outraged people had also picketed the school attended by their children. They had threatened to return each day until Green lowered his prices. When they called her at home to report this, she had promised she would talk with him. Since she could not tell him this, she waited for an opening. She looked at her husband across the table.

"I did not make the world," Green began, recognizing at once the seriousness in her stare. "My father came to this country with nothing but his shirt. He was exploited for as long as he couldn't help himself. He did not protest or picket. He put himself in a position to play by the rules he had learned." He waited for his wife to answer, and when she did not, he tried again. "I did not make this world," he repeated. "I only make my way in it. Such people as these, they do not know enough to not be exploited. If not me, there would be a Greek, a Chinaman, maybe an Arab or a smart one of their own kind. Believe me, I deal with them. There is something in their style that lacks the patience to run a concern such as mine. If I closed down, take my word on it, someone else would do what has to be done."

But Ruth Green was not thinking of his leaving. Her mind was on other matters. Her children had cried when they came home early from school. She had no special feeling for the people who picketed, but she did not like to see her children cry. She had kissed them generously, then sworn them to silence. "One day this week," she told her husband, "you will give free, for eight hours, anything your customers come in to buy. There will be no publicity, except what they spread by word of mouth. No matter what they say to you, no matter what they take, you will remain silent." She stared deeply into him for what she knew was there. "If you refuse, you have seen the last of your children and myself."

Her husband grunted. Then he leaned toward her. "I will not knuckle under," he said. "I will *not* give!"

"We shall see," his wife told him.

The black pickets, for the most part, had at first been frightened by the audacity of their undertaking. They were peasants whose minds had long before become resigned to their fate as victims. None of them, before now, had thought to challenge this. But now, when they watched themselves on television, they hardly recognized the faces they saw beneath the hoisted banners and placards. Instead of reflecting the meekness they all felt, the faces looked angry. The close-ups looked especially intimidating. Several of the first pickets, maids who worked in the suburbs, reported that their employers, seeing the activity on the afternoon news, had begun treating them with new respect. One woman, midway through the weather report, called around the neighborhood to disclose that her employer had that very day given her a new china plate for her meals. The paper plates, on which all previous meals had been served, had been thrown into the wastebasket. One recipient of this call, a middle-aged woman known for her bashfulness and humility, rejoined that her husband, a sheet-metal worker, had only a few hours before been called "Mister" by his supervisor, a white man with a passionate hatred of color. She added the tale of a neighbor down the street, a widow woman named Murphy, who had at first been reluctant to join the picket; this woman now was insisting it should be made a daily event. Such talk as this circulated among the people who had been instrumental in raising the issue. As news of their victory leaked into the ears of others who had not participated, they received all through the night calls from strangers requesting verification, offering advice, and vowing support. Such strangers listened and then volunteered stories about indignities inflicted on them by city officials, policemen, other grocers. In this way, over a period of hours, the community became even more incensed and restless than it had been at the time of the initial picket.

Soon the man who had set events in motion found himself a hero. His name was Nelson Reed, and all his adult life he had been employed as an assembly-line worker. He was a steady husband, the father of three children, and a deacon in the Baptist church. All his life he had trusted in God and gotten along. But now something in him capitulated to the reality that came suddenly into focus. "I was wrong," he told people who called him. "The onliest thing that matters in this world is *money*. And when was the last time you seen a picture of Jesus on a dollar bill?" This line, which he repeated over and over, caused a few callers to laugh nervously, but not without some affirmation that this was indeed the way things were. Many said they had known it all along. Others argued that although it was certainly true, it was one thing to live without money and quite another to live without faith. But still most callers laughed and said, "You right. You *know* I know you right. Ain't it the truth, though?" Only a few people, among them Nelson Reed's wife, said nothing and looked very sad.

Why they looked sad, however, they would not communicate. And anyone observing their troubled faces would have to trust his own intuition. It is known that Reed's wife, Betty, measured all events against the fullness of her own experience. She was skeptical of everything. Brought to the church after a number of years of living openly with a jazz musician, she had embraced religion when she married Nelson Reed. But though she no longer believed completely in the world, she nonetheless had not fully embraced God. There was something in the nature of Christ's swift rise that had always bothered her, and something in the blood and vengeance of the Old Testament that was mellowing and refreshing. But she had never communicated these thoughts to anyone, especially her husband. Instead, she smiled vacantly while others professed leaps of faith, remained silent when friends spoke fiercely of their convictions. The presence of this vacuum in her contributed to her personal mystery; people said she was beautiful, although she was not outwardly so. Perhaps it was because she wished to protect this inner beauty that she did not smile now, and looked extremely sad, listening to her husband on the telephone.

Nelson Reed had no reason to be sad. He seemed to grow more energized and talkative as the days passed. He was invited by an alderman, on the Tuesday after the initial picket, to tell his story on a local television talk show. He sweated heavily under the hot white lights and attempted to be philosophical. "I notice," the host said to him, "that you are not angry at this exploitative treatment. What, Mr. Reed, is the source of your calm?" The assembly-line worker looked unabashedly into the camera and said, "I have always believed in *Justice* with a capital *J*. I was raised up from a baby believin' that God ain't gonna let nobody go *too* far. See, in *my* mind God is in charge of *all* the capital letters in the alphabet of this world. It say in the Scripture He is Alpha and Omega, the first and the last. He is just about the *onliest* capitalizer they is." Both Reed and the alderman laughed. "Now, when *men* start to capitalize, they gets *greedy*. They put a little *j* in *joy* and a littler one in *justice*. They raise up a big *G* in *Greed* and a big *E* in *Evil*. Well, soon as they commence to put a little *g* in *god*, you can expect some kind of reaction. The Savior will just raise up the *H* in *Hell* and go on from there. And that's just what I'm doin', giving these sharpies *HELL* with a big *H*." The talk show host laughed along with Nelson Reed and the alderman. After the taping they drank coffee in the back room of the studio and talked about the sad shape of the world.

Three days before he was to comply with his wife's request, Green, the grocer, saw this talk show on television while at home. The words of Nelson Reed sent a chill through him. Though Reed had attempted to be philosophical, Green did not perceive the statement in this light. Instead, he saw a vindictive-looking black man seated between an ambitious alderman and a smug talk-show host. He saw them chatting comfortably about the nature of evil. The cameraman had shot mostly close-ups, and Green could see the set in Nelson Reed's jaw. The color of Reed's face was maddening. When his children came into the den, the grocer was in a sweat. Before he could think, he had shouted at them and struck the button turning off the set. The two children rushed from the room screaming. Ruth Green ran in from the kitchen. She knew why he was upset because she had received a call about the show, but she said nothing and pretended ignorance. Her children's school had been picketed that day, as it had the day before. But both children were still forbidden to speak of this to their father.

"Where do they get so much power?" Green said to his wife. "Two days ago nobody would have cared. Now everywhere, even in my home, I am condemned as a rascal. And what do I own? An airline? A multinational? Half of South America? *No!* I own three stores, one of which happens to be in a certain neighborhood inhabited by people who cost me money to run it." He sighed and sat upright on the sofa, his chubby legs spread wide. "A cabdriver has a meter that clicks as he goes along. I pay extra for insurance, iron bars, pilfering by customers and employees. Nothing clicks. But when I add a little overhead to my prices, suddenly everything clicks. But for someone else. When was there last such a world?" He pressed the palms of both hands to his temples, suggesting a bombardment of brain-stinging sounds.

This gesture evoked no response from Ruth Green. She remained standing by the door, looking steadily at him. She said, "To protect yourself, I would not stock any more fresh cuts of meat in the store until after the giveaway on Saturday. Also, I would not tell it to the employees until after the first customer of the day has begun to check out. But I would urge you to hire several security guards to close the door promptly at seven-thirty, as is usual." She wanted to say much more than this, but did not. Instead she watched him. He was looking at the blank gray television screen, his palms still pressed against his ears. "In case you need to hear again," she continued in a weighty tone of voice, "I said two days ago, and I say again now, that if you fail to do this you will not see your children again for many years."

He twisted his head and looked up at her. "What is the color of these people?" he asked.

"Black," his wife said.

"And what is the name of my children?"

"Green."

The grocer smiled. "There is your answer," he told his wife. "Green is the only color I am interested in."

His wife did not smile. "Insufficient," she said.

"The world is mad!" he moaned. "But it is a point of sanity with me to not bend. I will not bend." He crossed his legs and pressed one hand firmly atop his knee. "*I will not bend*," he said.

"We will see," his wife said.

Nelson Reed, after the television interview, became the acknowledged leader of the disgruntled neighbors. At first a number of them met in the kitchen at his house; then, as space was lacking for curious newcomers, a mass meeting was held on Thursday in an abandoned theater. His wife and three children sat in the front row. Behind them sat the widow Murphy, Lloyd Dukes, Tyrone Brown, Les Jones—those who had joined him on the first picket line. Behind these sat people who bought occasionally at the store, people who lived on the fringes of the neighborhood, people from other neighborhoods come to investigate the problem, and the merely curious. The middle rows were occupied by a few people from the suburbs, those who had seen the talk show and whose outrage at the grocer proved much more powerful than their fear of black people. In the rear of the theater crowded aging, old-style leftists, somber students, cynical young black men with angry grudges to explain with inarticulate gestures. Leaning against the walls, huddled near the doors at the rear, tape-recorder-bearing social scientists looked as detached and serene as bookies at the track. Here and there, in this diverse crowd, a politician stationed himself, pumping hands vigorously and pressing his palms gently against the shoulders of elderly people. Other visitors passed out leaflets, buttons, glossy color prints of men who promoted causes, the familiar and obscure. There was a hubbub of voices, a blend of the strident and the playful, the outraged and the reverent, lending an undercurrent of ominous energy to the assembly.

Nelson Reed spoke from a platform on the stage, standing before a yellowed, shredded screen that had once reflected the images of matinee idols. "I don't mind sayin' that I have always been a sucker," he told the crowd. "All my life I have been a sucker for the words of Jesus. Being a natural-born fool, I just ain't never had the *sense* to learn no better. Even right today, while the whole world is sayin' wrong is right and up is down, I'm so dumb I'm *still* steady believin' what is wrote in the Good Book. . . ."

From the audience, especially the front rows, came a chorus singing, "Preach!"

"I have no doubt," he continued in a low baritone, "that it's true what is writ in the Good Book: 'The last shall be first and the first shall be last.' I don't know about y'all, but I have *always* been the last. I never wanted to be the first, but sometimes it look like the world get so bad that them that's

holdin' onto the tree of life is the onliest ones left when God commence to
blowin' dead leafs off the branches.''

"Now you preaching," someone called.

In the rear of the theater a white student shouted an awkward "Amen."

Nelson Reed began walking across the stage to occupy the major part of
his nervous energy. But to those in the audience, who now hung on his
every word, it looked as though he strutted. "All my life," he said, "I have
claimed to be a man without earnin' the right to call myself that. You know,
the *average* man ain't really a man. The average man is a *bootlicker*. In fact,
the *average* man would *run away* if he found hisself standing alone facin'
down a adversary. I have done that *too many a time* in my life! But *not no
more*. Better to be *once* was than *never* was a man. I will tell you tonight,
there is somethin' *wrong* in being average. *I intend to stand up!* Now, if
your average man that ain't really a man stand up, two things gonna happen:
one, he gon bust through all the weights that been place on his head, and,
two, he gon feel a lot of pain. But that same hurt is what make things fall
in place. That, and gettin' your hands on one of these slick four-flushers
tight enough so's you can squeeze him and say, 'No more!' You do that, you
g'on hurt some, but *you won't be average no more.* . . .''

"No *more!*" a few people in the front rows repeated.

"I say *no more!*" Nelson Reed shouted.

"*No more! No more! No more!*" The chant rustled through the crowd
like the rhythm of an autumn wind against a shedding tree.

Then people laughed and chattered in celebration.

As for the grocer, from the evening of the television interview he had begun
to make plans. Unknown to his wife, he cloistered himself several times with
his brother-in-law, an insurance salesman, and plotted a course. He had no
intention of tossing steaks to the crowd. "And why should I, Tommy?" he
asked his wife's brother, a lean, bald-headed man named Thomas. "I don't
cheat anyone. I have never cheated anyone. The businesses I run are always
on the up-and-up. So why should I pay?"

"Quite so," the brother-in-law said, chewing an unlit cigarillo. "The
world has gone crazy. Next they will say that people in my business are
responsible for prolonging life. I have found that people who refuse to believe
in death refuse also to believe in the harshness of life. I sell well by saying
that death is a long happiness. I show people the realities of life and compare
this to a funeral with dignity, *and* the promise of a bundle for every loved
one salted away. When they look around hard at life, they usually buy."

"So?" asked Green. Thomas was a college graduate with a penchant for
philosophy.

"So," Thomas answered. "You must fight to show these people the reality of both your situation and theirs. How would it be if you visited one of their meetings and chalked out, on a blackboard, the dollars and cents of your operation? Explain your overhead, your security fees, all the additional expenses. If you treat them with respect, they might understand."

Green frowned. "That I would never do," he said. "It would be admission of a certain guilt."

The brother-in-law smiled, but only with one corner of his mouth. "Then you have something to feel guilty about?" he asked.

The grocer frowned at him. "*Nothing!*" he said with great emphasis.

"So?" Thomas said.

This first meeting between the grocer and his brother-in-law took place on Thursday, in a crowded barroom.

At the second meeting, in a luncheonette, it was agreed that the grocer should speak privately with the leader of the group, Nelson Reed. The meeting at which this was agreed took place on Friday afternoon. After accepting this advice from Thomas, the grocer resigned himself to explain to Reed, in as finite detail as possible, the economic structure of his operation. He vowed to suppress no information. He would explain everything: inventories, markups, sale items, inflation, balance sheets, specialty items, overhead, and that mysterious item called profit. This last item, promising to be the most difficult to explain, Green and his brother-in-law debated over for several hours. They agreed first of all that a man should not work for free, then they agreed that it was unethical to ruthlessly exploit. From these parameters, they staked out an area between fifteen and forty percent, and agreed that someplace between these two borders lay an amount of return that could be called fair. This was easy, but then Thomas introduced the factor of circumstance. He questioned whether the fact that one serviced a risky area justified the earning of profits, closer to the forty-percent edge of the scale. Green was unsure. Thomas smiled. "Here is a case that will point out an analogy," he said, licking a cigarillo. "I read in the papers that a family wants to sell an electric stove. I call the home and the man says fifty dollars. I ask to come out and inspect the merchandise. When I arrive I see they are poor, have already bought a new stove that is connected, and are selling the old one for fifty dollars because they want it out of the place. The electric stove is in good condition, worth much more than fifty. But because I see what I see I offer forty-five."

Green, for some reason, wrote down this figure on the back of the sales slip for the coffee they were drinking.

The brother-in-law smiled. He chewed his cigarillo. "The man agrees to take forty-five dollars, saying he has had no other calls. I look at the stove again and see a spot of rust. I say I will give him forty dollars. He agrees to this, on condition that I myself haul it away. I say I will haul it away if he comes down to thirty. You, of course, see where I am going."

The grocer nodded. "The circumstances of his situation, his need to get rid of the stove quickly, placed him in a position where he has little room to bargain?"

"Yes," Thomas answered. "So? Is it ethical, Harry?"

Harold Green frowned. He had never liked his brother-in-law, and now he thought the insurance agent was being crafty. "But," he answered, "this man does not *have* to sell! It is his choice whether to wait for other calls. It is not the fault of the buyer that the seller is in a hurry. It is the right of the buyer to get what he wants at the lowest price possible. That is the rule. That has *always* been the rule. And the reverse of it applies to the seller as well."

"Yes," Thomas said, sipping coffee from the Styrofoam cup. "But suppose that in addition to his hurry to sell, the owner was also of a weak soul. There are, after all, many such people." He smiled. "Suppose he placed no value on the money?"

"Then," Green answered, "your example is academic. Here we are not talking about real life. One man lives by the code, one man does not. Who is there free enough to make a judgment?" He laughed. "Now you see," he told his brother-in-law. "Much more than a few dollars are at stake. If this one buyer is to be condemned, then so are most people in the history of the world. An examination of history provides the only answer to your question. This code will be here tomorrow, long after the ones who do not honor it are not."

They argued fiercely late into the afternoon, the brother-in-law leaning heavily on his readings. When they parted, a little before five o'clock, nothing had been resolved.

Neither was much resolved during the meeting between Green and Nelson Reed. Reached at home by the grocer in the early evening, the leader of the group spoke coldly at first, but consented finally to meet his adversary at a nearby drugstore for coffee and a talk. They met at the lunch counter, shook hands awkwardly, and sat for a few minutes discussing the weather. Then the grocer pulled two gray ledgers from his briefcase. "You have for years come into my place," he told the man. "In my memory I have always treated you well. Now our relationship has come to this." He slid the books along the counter until they touched Nelson Reed's arm.

Reed opened the top book and flipped the thick green pages with his thumb. He did not examine the figures. "All I know," he said, "is over at your place a can of soup cost me fifty-five cents, and two miles away at your other store for white folks you chargin' thirty-nine cents." He said this with the calm authority of an outraged soul. A quality of condescension tinged with pity crept into his gaze.

The grocer drummed his fingers on the counter top. He twisted his head and looked away, toward shelves containing cosmetics, laxatives, toothpaste. His eyes lingered on a poster of a woman's apple-red lips and milk-white teeth. The rest of the face was missing.

"Ain't no use to hide," Nelson Reed said, as to a child. "*I* know you wrong, *you* know you wrong, and before I finish, *everybody in this city* g'on know you wrong. God don't *like* ugly." He closed his eyes and gripped the cup of coffee. Then he swung his head suddenly and faced the grocer again. "Man, why you want to *do* people that way?" he asked. "We human, same as you."

"Before *God!*" Green exclaimed, looking squarely into the face of Nelson Reed. "Before God!" he said again. "*I am not an evil man!*" These last words sounded more like a moan as he tightened the muscles in his throat to lower the sound of his voice. He tossed his left shoulder as if adjusting the sleeve of his coat, or as if throwing off some unwanted weight. Then he peered along the counter top. No one was watching. At the end of the counter the waitress was scrubbing the coffee urn. "Look at these figures, please," he said to Reed.

The man did not drop his gaze. His eyes remained fixed on the grocer's face.

"All right," Green said. "Don't look. I'll tell you what is in these books, believe me if you want. I work twelve hours a day, one day off per week, running my business in three stores. I am not a wealthy person. In one place, in the area you call white, I get by barely by smiling lustily at old ladies, stocking gourmet stuff on the chance I will build a reputation as a quality store. The two clerks there cheat me; there is nothing I can do. In this business you must be friendly with everybody. The second place is on the other side of town, in a neighborhood as poor as this one. I get out there seldom. The profits are not worth the gas. I use the loss there as a write-off against some other properties," he paused. "Do you understand write-off?" he asked Nelson Reed.

"Naw," the man said.

Harold Green laughed. "What does it matter?" he said in a tone of voice intended for himself alone. "In this area I will admit I make a profit, but it is not so much as you think. But I do not make a profit here because the people are black. I make a profit because a profit is here to be made. I invest more here in window bars, theft losses, insurance, spoilage; I deserve to make more here than at the other places." He looked, almost imploringly, at the man seated next to him. "You don't accept this as the right of a man in business?"

Reed grunted. "Did the bear shit in the woods?" he said.

Again Green laughed. He gulped his coffee awkwardly, as if eager to go. Yet his motions slowed once he had set his coffee cup down on the blue plastic saucer. "Place yourself in *my* situation," he said, his voice high and tentative. "If *you* were running my store in this neighborhood, what would be *your* position? Say on a profit scale of fifteen to forty percent, at what point in between would you draw the line?"

Nelson Reed thought. He sipped his coffee and seemed to chew the liquid. "Fifteen to forty?" he repeated.

"Yes."

"I'm a churchgoin' man," he said. "Closer to fifteen than to forty."

"How close?"

Nelson Reed thought. "In church you tithe ten percent."

"In restaurants you tip fifteen," the grocer said quickly.

"All right," Reed said. "Over fifteen."

"How much over?"

Nelson Reed thought.

"Twenty, thirty, thirty-five?" Green chanted, leaning closer to Reed.

Still the man thought.

"Forty? Maybe even forty-five or fifty?" the grocer breathed in Reed's ear. "In the supermarkets, you know, they have more subtle ways of accomplishing such feats."

Reed slapped his coffee cup with the back of his right hand. The brown liquid swirled across the counter top, wetting the books. "*Damn this!*" he shouted.

Startled, Green rose from his stool.

Nelson Reed was trembling. "I ain't *you*," he said in a deep baritone. "I ain't the *supermarket* neither. All I is is a poor man that works *too* hard to see his pay slip through his fingers like rainwater. All I know is you done *cheat* me, you done *cheat* everybody in the neighborhood, and we organized now to get some of it *back!*" Then he stood and faced the grocer. "My daddy sharecropped down in Mississippi and bought in the company store. He owed them twenty-three years when he died. I paid off five of them years and then run away to up here. Now, I'm a deacon in the Baptist church. I raised my kids the way my daddy raise me and don't bother nobody. Now come to find out, after all my runnin', they done lift that *same company store* up out of Mississippi and slip it down on us here! Well, my daddy was a *fighter*, and if he hadn't owed all them years he would of raise him some hell. Me, I'm steady my daddy's child, plus I got seniority in my union. I'm a free man. Buddy, don't you know *I'm gonna raise me some hell!*"

Harold Green reached for a paper napkin to sop the coffee soaking into his books.

Nelson Reed threw a dollar on top of the books and walked away.

"I *will not* do it!" Harold Green said to his wife that same evening. They were in the bathroom of their home. Bending over the face bowl, she was washing her hair with a towel draped around her neck. The grocer stood by the door, looking in at her. "I will not bankrupt myself tomorrow," he said.

"I've been thinking about it, too," Ruth Green said, shaking her wet hair. "You'll do it, Harry."

"Why should I?" he asked. "You won't leave. You know it was a bluff. I've waited this long for you to calm down. Tomorrow is Saturday. This week has been a hard one. Tonight let's be realistic."

"Of course you'll do it," Ruth Green said. She said it the way she would say "Have some toast." She said, "You'll do it because you want to see your children grow up."

"And for what other reason?" he asked.

She pulled the towel tighter around her neck. "Because you are at heart a moral man."

He grinned painfully. "If I am, why should I have to prove it to *them?*"

"Not them," Ruth Green said, freezing her movements and looking in the mirror. "Certainly not them. By no means them. They have absolutely nothing to do with this."

"Who, then?" he asked, moving from the door into the room. "Who else should I prove something to?"

His wife was crying. But her entire face was wet. The tears moved secretly down her face.

"Who else?" Harold Green asked.

It was almost eleven P.M. and the children were in bed. They had also cried when they came home from school. Ruth Green said, "For yourself, Harry. For the love that lives inside your heart."

All night the grocer thought about this.

Nelson Reed also slept little that Friday night. When he returned home from the drugstore, he reported to his wife as much of the conversation as he could remember. At first he had joked about the exchange between himself and the grocer, but as more details returned to his conscious mind he grew solemn and then bitter. "He ask me to put myself in *his* place," Reed told his wife. "Can you imagine that kind of gumption? I never cheated nobody in my life. All my life I have lived on Bible principles. I am a deacon in the church. I have work all my life for other folks and I don't even own the house I live in." He paced up and down the kitchen, his big arms flapping loosely at his sides. Betty Reed sat at the table, watching. "This here's a low-down, ass-kicking world," he said. "I swear to God it is! All my life I have lived on principle and I ain't got a dime in the bank. Betty," he turned suddenly toward her, "don't you think I'm a fool?"

"Mr. Reed," she said. "Let's go on to bed."

But he would not go to bed. Instead, he took the fifth of bourbon from the cabinet under the sink and poured himself a shot. His wife refused to join him. Reed drained the glass of whiskey, and then another, while he resumed pacing the kitchen floor. He slapped his hands against his sides. "I think I'm a fool," he said. "Ain't got a dime in the bank, ain't got a pot to *pee* in or a wall to pitch it over, and that there *cheat* ask me to put myself inside *his* shoes. Hell, I can't even *afford* the kind of shoes he wears." He stopped pacing and looked at his wife.

"Mr. Reed," she whispered, "tomorrow ain't a work day. Let's go to bed."

Nelson Reed laughed, the bitterness in his voice rattling his wife. "The *hell* I will!" he said.

He strode to the yellow telephone on the wall beside the sink and began to dial. The first call was to Lloyd Dukes, a neighbor two blocks away and a lieutenant in the organization. Dukes was not at home. The second call was to McElroy's Bar on the corner of Sixty-fifth and Carroll, where Stanley Harper, another of the lieutenants, worked as a bartender. It was Harper who spread the word, among those men at the bar, that the organization would picket the grocer's store the following morning. And all through the night, in the bedroom of their house, Betty Reed was awakened by telephone calls coming from Lester Jones, Nat Lucas, Mrs. Tyrone Brown, the widow-woman named Murphy, all coordinating the time when they would march in a group against the store owned by Harold Green. Betty Reed's heart beat loudly beneath the covers as she listened to the bitterness and rage in her husband's voice. On several occasions, hearing him declare himself a fool, she pressed the pillow against her eyes and cried.

The grocer opened later than usual this Saturday morning, but still it was early enough to make him one of the first walkers in the neighborhood. He parked his car one block from the store and strolled to work. There were no birds singing. The sky in this area was not blue. It was smog-smutted and gray, seeming on the verge of a light rain. The street, as always, was littered with cans, papers, bits of broken glass. As always the garbage cans overflowed. The morning breeze plastered a sheet of newspaper playfully around the sides of a rusted garbage can. For some reason, using his right foot, he loosened the paper and stood watching it slide into the street and down the

block. The movement made him feel good. He whistled while unlocking
the bars shielding the windows and door of his store. When he had unlocked
the main door he stepped in quickly and threw a switch to the right of the
jamb, before the shrill sound of the alarm could shatter his mood. Then he
switched on the lights. Everything was as it had been the night before. He
had already telephoned his two employees and given them the day off.
He busied himself doing the usual things—hauling milk and vegetables from
the cooler, putting cash in the till—not thinking about the silence of his
wife, or the look in her eyes, only an hour before when he left home. He
had determined, at some point while driving through the city, that today it
would be business as usual. But he expected very few customers.

The first customer of the day was Mrs. Nelson Reed. She came in around
nine thirty A.M. and wandered about the store. He watched her from the
checkout counter. She seemed uncertain of what she wanted to buy. She
kept glancing at him down the center aisle. His suspicions aroused, he said
finally, "Yes, may I help you, Mrs. Reed?" His words caused her to jerk,
as if some devious thought had been perceived going through her mind. She
reached over quickly and lifted a loaf of whole wheat bread from the rack
and walked with it to the counter. She looked at him and smiled. The smile
was a broad, shy one, that rare kind of smile one sees on virgin girls when
they first confess love to themselves. Betty Reed was a woman of about forty-
five. For some reason he could not comprehend, this gesture touched him.
When she pulled a dollar from her purse and laid it on the counter, an
impulse, from no place he could locate with his mind, seized control of his
tongue. "Free," he told Betty Reed. She paused, then pushed the dollar
toward him with a firm and determined thrust of her arm. "Free," he heard
himself saying strongly, his right palm spread and meeting her thrust with
absolute force. She clutched the loaf of bread and walked out of his store.

The next customer, a little girl, arriving well after ten-thirty A.M., selected
a candy bar from the rack beside the counter. "Free," Green said cheerfully.
The little girl left the candy on the counter and ran out of the store.

At eleven-fifteen A.M. a wino came in looking desperate enough to sell
his soul. The grocer watched him only for an instant. Then he went to the
wine counter and selected a half-gallon of medium-grade red wine. He shoved
the jug into the belly of the wino, the man's sour breath bathing his face.
"Free," the grocer said. "But you must not drink it in here."

He felt good about the entire world, watching the wino through the
window gulping the wine and looking guiltily around.

At eleven twenty-five A.M. the pickets arrived.

Two dozen people, men and women, young and old, crowded the pavement in front of his store. Their signs, placards, and voices denounced him

as a parasite. The grocer laughed inside himself. He felt lighthearted and wild, like a man drugged. He rushed to the meat counter and pulled a long roll of brown wrapping paper from the rack, tearing it neatly with a quick shift of his body resembling a dance step practiced fervently in his youth. He laid the paper on the chopping block and with the black-inked, felt-tipped marker scrawled, in giant letters, the word FREE. This he took to the window and pasted in place with many strands of Scotch tape. He was laughing wildly. "Free!" he shouted from behind the brown paper. "Free! Free! Free! Free! Free! Free!" He rushed to the door, pushed his head out, and screamed to the confused crowd, *"Free!"* Then he ran back to the counter and stood behind it, like a soldier at attention.

They came in slowly.

Nelson Reed entered first, working his right foot across the dirty tile as if tracking a squiggling worm. The others followed: Lloyd Dukes dragging a placard, Mr. and Mrs. Tyrone Brown, Stanley Harper walking with his fists clenched, Lester Jones with three of his children, Nat Lucas looking sheepish and detached, a clutch of winos, several bashful nuns, ironic-smiling teen-agers and a few students. Bringing up the rear was a bearded social scientist holding a tape recorder to his chest. "Free!" the grocer screamed. He threw up his arms in a gesture that embraced, or dismissed, the entire store. *"All free!"* he shouted. He was grinning with the grace of a madman.

The winos began grabbing first. They stripped the shelf of wine in a matter of seconds. Then they fled, dropping bottles on the tile in their wake. The others, stepping quickly through this liquid, soon congealed it into a sticky, bloodlike consistency. The young men went for the cigarettes and luncheon meats and beer. One of them had the prescience to grab a sack from the counter, while the others loaded their arms swiftly, hugging cartons and packages of cold cuts like long-lost friends. The students joined them, less for greed than for the thrill of the experience. The two nuns backed toward the door. As for the older people, men and women, they stood at first as if stuck to the wine-smeared floor. Then Stanley Harper, the bartender, shouted, "The man said *free*, y'all heard him." He paused. "Didn't you say *free* now?" he called to the grocer.

"I said free," Harold Green answered, his temples pounding.

A cheer went up. The older people began grabbing, as if the secret lusts of a lifetime had suddenly seized command of their arms and eyes. They grabbed toilet tissue, cold cuts, pickles, sardines, boxes of raisins, boxes of starch, cans of soup, tins of tuna fish and salmon, bottles of spices, cans of boned chicken, slippery cans of olive oil. Here a man, Lester Jones, burdened himself with several heads of lettuce, while his wife, in another aisle, shouted for him to drop those small items and concentrate on the gourmet section. She herself took imported sardines, wheat crackers, bottles of candied pickles, herring, anchovies, imported olives, French wafers, an ancient, half-rusted can of paté, stocked, by mistake, from the inventory of another store. Others packed their arms with detergents, hams, chocolate-coated cereal, whole chickens with hanging asses, wedges of bologna and salami like squashed footballs, chunks of cheeses, yellow and white, shriveled onions, and green peppers. Mrs. Tyrone Brown hung a curve of pepperoni around her neck and seemed to take on instant dignity, much like a person of noble birth in possession now of a long sought-after gem. Another woman, the widow Murphy, stuffed tomatoes into her bosom, holding a half-chewed lemon in her mouth. The more enterprising fought desperately over the three rusted shopping carts, and the victors wheeled these along the narrow aisles, sweeping into them bulk items—beer in six-packs, sacks of sugar, flour, glass bottles of syrup, toilet cleanser, sugar cookies, prune, apple and tomato juices—while others endeavored to snatch the carts from them. There were several fistfights and much cursing. The grocer, standing behind the counter, hummed and rang his cash register like a madman.

Nelson Reed, the first into the store, followed the nuns out, empty-handed.

In less than half an hour the others had stripped the store and vanished in many directions up and down the block. But still more people came, those late in hearing the news. And when they saw the shelves were bare, they cursed soberly and chased those few stragglers still bearing away goods. Soon only the grocer and the social scientist remained, the latter stationed at the door with his tape recorder sucking in leftover sounds. Then he, too, slipped away up the block.

By twelve-ten P.M. the grocer was leaning against the counter, trying to make his mind slow down. Not a man given to drink during work hours, he nonetheless took a swallow from a bottle of wine, a dusty bottle from beneath the wine shelf, somehow overlooked by the winos. Somewhat recovered, he was preparing to remember what he should do next when he glanced toward a figure at the door. Nelson Reed was standing there, watching him.

"All gone," Harold Green said. "My friend, Mr. Reed, there is no more." Still the man stood in the doorway, peering into the store.

The grocer waved his arms about the empty room. Not a display case had a single item standing. "All gone," he said again, as if addressing a stupid child. "There is nothing left to get. You, my friend, have come back too late for a second load. I am cleaned out."

Nelson Reed stepped into the store and strode toward the counter. He moved through wine-stained flour, lettuce leaves, red, green, and blue labels, bits and pieces of broken glass. He walked toward the counter.

"All day," the grocer laughed, not quite hysterically now, "all day long

I have not made a single cent of profit. The entire day was a loss. This store, like the others, is *bleeding* me." He waved his arms about the room in a magnificent gesture of uncaring loss. "Now do you understand?" he said. "Now will you put yourself in my shoes? I have nothing here. Come, now, Mr. Reed, would it not be so bad a thing to walk in my shoes?"

"Mr. Green," Nelson Reed said coldly. "My wife bought a loaf of bread in here this mornin'. She forgot to pay you. I, myself, have come here to pay you your money."

"Oh," the grocer said.

"I think it was brown bread. Don't that cost more than white?"

The two men looked away from each other, but not at anything in the store.

"In my store, yes," Harold Green said. He rang the register with the most casual movement of his finger. The register read fifty-five cents.

Nelson Reed held out a dollar.

"And two cents tax," the grocer said.

The man held out the dollar.

"After all," Harold Green said. "We are all, after all, Mr. Reed, in debt to the government."

He rang the register again. It read fifty-seven cents.

Nelson Reed held out a dollar.

SUCH WAS THE SEASON

Clarence Major

Like Juneboy, I didn't want to go to Renee's dinner party. All them fancy politician peoples make me nervous. I'm just a plain down-to-earth common-sense person, and besides I don't understand none of all that high talk they put on. Course Jeremiah, my oldest, been 'round them since he was at college. You should hear him talking high and mighty with them big shots. Sho, I'm proud of him, but Lord knows he shouldn't drag his poor old momma into situations where she just end up feeling embarrassed. And poor Juneboy, he just wanted to watch some television.

Sometime I know I am too hard on Renee. It's just that that gal is so spoilt that it upsets me to see some of the things she do. Seem like all she can think about is mink coats and diamonds and big pretty cars and giant television screens and Lord knows what else. Tried to give me one of her used mink coats a couple of years ago. Child, you should have heard me carry on. Renee, I said, it's so thoughtful of you, honey, and you know I do 'preciate the offer, but my friends would think I'd lost my mind if they saw me in a expensive coat like this. Everybody I know know I can't afford mink. Might think I stole it or something. She turned just as red as a big old ripe apple. She one of them red childs anyway, you know, with freckles and them gray cat eyes and all that nappy red hair that she don't never know what to do with.

Anyways, she wont about to spend almost a half a thousand dollars on a catered dinner party for Atlanta's Negro royalty without having some deep dark plan to her own advantage. That child wouldn't know how to do anything for anybody but herself if you paid her. You can see that by the way she treats them children of hers. I feel so sorry for little Curtis, Jane, and Jo, sometimes I just break down and cry. They got everything material they need and ain't ever gone a day hungry like a lot of the children 'round here, but they ain't got the most important thing—a caring and loving mother. Why, when I was bringing mine up I never once let DeSoto and Jeremiah sass me and stay up late the way she lets them children do. I even seed her give Curtis some beer when he was hardly a year old.

They wanted me and Juneboy over there by six, they said. It was Friday night and Jeremiah had got hisself a substitute to preach the sermon at his church, First Christ Church over on Decatur. He never missed preaching his own sermons unless something really important got in the way or he was down sick. When I ast him why not have the dinner party on another night, he come just a talking 'bout Friday being the best time for Renee. Seems everything has to be her way.

I told Juneboy he better get dressed, then I got out my best wig from the hatbox under my bed. It's blond but kinda red, too. When I was young my hair was like that, so it looks real natural on me. DeSoto says it makes me look young enough to be his sister. Well, I ain't shamed of wearing a wig like some of the ladies I know at church. The good Lord don't say nowhere in the Good Book that it's a sin to pretty yourself up, if you can. Two summers ago when I went up to Chicago to see Esther, she says to me, "Annie Eliza, take that ugly thing off your head, makes you look like one of these here street hussies."

I told her she never been able to tell me what to do, and she wont 'bout to start at sixty-three. I used to change her diapers, and when she tries to get smart with me I remind her. It puts her in her place. I wore my wig all over Chicago, strutting my stuff just as pretty as I pleased.

I stood at the mirror adjusting the wig. I could hear Juneboy in the bathroom running water in the face bowl. My alarm clock on the bedside table said five-thirty. We could walk to Jeremiah's in fifteen minutes. His house was the biggest and the prettiest in the whole neighborhood, and it was three blocks down in what they call a cul-de-sac. That's a French word. It means dead end. Jeremiah bought the place five years ago from the last white family to move outta the neighborhood. Paid a hundred and fifty thousand dollars for it, but if you ast me that place ain't worth all that much money. God knows ain't no place on this good earth worth a hundred thousand dollars. Sho, it's big and it's got so many rooms you can't count them all and keep a clear head and it's got fluffy carpets and giant television screens in all the bedrooms and antique furniture everywhere. The whole place was designed by some fancy designer who charged them more money than most people 'round here make in a lifetime, but I wouldn't give you a hundred dollars for it. It wasn't Jeremiah's money no way. All them church ladies bought that house. I never seen so many ladies in love with one plain old man!

It was a warm spring night as Juneboy and me walked down to Jeremiah's. I'd been worried some 'bout Juneboy's 'pearance, I mean him going to this big dinner party with these high-class peoples. You see, I didn't want him to embarrass our side of the family. Esther's children never had the privileges my boys had. They didn't have a proper father. I mean, they were sorta raised here and there first by Momma and they no-good father and his crazy sisters. Then Esther took them up to Chicago, but she had to work all the time. They didn't come up with good strict home training. That's the only way children learn good manners. Now I'm not blaming Esther. God knows she tried the best she could, but she was only sixteen when she got pregnant with Juneboy. By the time the boy was three, Lauren was born. That no-good gambling man of hers. I never knowed if Scoop was his real name or not. Didn't sound like no proper name I ever heard. Anyway, I was pleased to see Juneboy so dressed up in a nice tweed jacket and slacks. I figured we might get through the evening without embarrassment.

On the way over there, we walked past a house with a driveway that showed a view of my backyard in the moonlight. Juneboy come just a telling me 'bout a time he 'membered when he and my boys was playing together when they was little out back of the house. Bigger than Jeremiah, he said he had Jeremiah locked up as the bad guy, and he made Jeremiah stand 'gainst that old tree like he was tied to it. DeSoto was s'pose to be helping him keep Jeremiah 'gainst the tree. I ast what Jeremiah s'pose to be guilty of, and he just laughed and said it was all just a game, but when they played, Jeremiah was always the bad guy, you see. I had no memory of them playing like that. I did 'member DeSoto picking on Jeremiah, though, and I use to fuss at DeSoto for giving Jeremiah such a hard time all the time.

Jeremiah's driveway was full of Cadillacs and Mercedes-Benzes, and they had them parked all up and down the block. Four of them Cadillacs belonged to Jeremiah. He always say they belong to the church and to God, but I never saw the church or God driving them. That boy of mine is a killer, I tell you! We could see all the lights in the house was on. I told Juneboy what a shame it was that that gal was so wasteful. He just smiled. As we walked up the long winding driveway, I told Juneboy 'bout the time Renee hired the two-day-a-week maid to come in full-time to feed the childrens because she was too lazy to get outta bed before twelve. That was back 'fore the youngest one, Jo, was walking. Thank God, Jeremiah put his foot down, one of the few times! He told that gal if she wanted a full-time baby-feeder she had to get herself a job and pay for the service. But he don't take a firm hand with that gal the way he should. She just one of them nigger gals spoiled something you wouldn't believe, and, child, so full of herself she can't smell her own stink. And all just 'cause she comes from the Wright family. You know the Wrights is one of the biggest and richest Negro family in politics in Atlanta. My boy gets invited to all they big gatherings, and most of them go to his church when they bother to praise the Lord at all. I let Juneboy touch the doorbell just so I could watch the surprise in his face when he heard all them bells in there making all that music as though angels was coming down from heaven. But wouldn't you know it, the poor boy was so unused to such class he just didn't pay no 'tention to it the way polite people with the right kind of background would have. I could hear them bells in there making all that sweet music, and I just gave praise to the Lord that at least one of my boys had made it big in this world.

Little Curtis opened the door.

First thing I heard was Renee's big mouth—and she was way back in the kitchen. It wont the first time Renee done this catering thing. She had her kitchen full of them folk from the catering service. Little Curtis (named after Bibb's brother) told me he didn't want no kiss from me when I ast him to give Grandma a big kiss. That boy is so mannish, just like his father when he was little. Then he ran on off somewhere to play with his tanks and Star Wars. (When I was bringing up DeSoto I had the hardest time keeping them from all them sinful toys like cowboy guns and all that old violent stuff.) Seemed like every television in the house was on, and each one on a different channel, and the record player in the living room was on, too. That's what I disliked 'bout coming here: always so much confusion.

Then little Jane with her pretty self came running down the hall to meet us. I took her up in my arms and kissed her. She said the mayor was in the den and that the kids was combing his hair and tickling his belly.

Sho nuff, in the den, there was our mayor, Dr. George Watkins-Jones, short and fat and black as ever, stuffed into the usual expensive striped dark blue suit, sitting deep in the couch before the giant screen of the television. Three of his grandchildrens was all over him—pulling at his necktie, un-buttoning his shirt, asting him all kinda silly questions, and all the while him looking like he trying to concentrate on whatever was going on on that television screen. I looked 'round at the television, and there was Mr. Mayor hisself up there on the screen.

I said, "Good evening, Mr. Mayor," but he didn't hear me. I don't even think he looked in my direction till he couldn't see hisself on the television anymore. When the Pepsi commercial came on, he looked at me and lifted a hand by way of greeting me. I never did like that kind of casual greeting from nobody. It shows disrespect. I knowed George 'fore he was mayor and seen him many times since, maybe as many as ten or fifteen times, usually here at Jeremiah's or in church or at one of them dinner parties they give over at Lee Anne's and Congressman Fred Wright's place. I said, "Good evening, Mr. Mayor," and he called me Annie Eliza like he always did.

"Mr. Mayor," I said, "this is Dr. Adam North, my nephew—my youngest sister's oldest child."

Juneboy, like a real gentleman, went over and shook the mayor's hand, but the mayor didn't stand up.

I put Jane down on the floor 'cause she started wiggling, and she ran off toward the kitchen.

DeSoto, still in his police sergeant uniform, came in from the dining room and kissed me on the cheek just as I was 'bout to sit my weary bones down in the armchair (the one Renee spilled red wine on last Christmas). I was watching the suspicious look the mayor was giving Juneboy. Then I thought maybe the mayor was afeared Juneboy might assassinate him. It struck me as funny, and I laughed. The mayor's bodyguard was nowhere 'round, and that was strange.

While DeSoto stood between me and the screen, picking his teeth with a toothpick (a bad habit he's had since high school), I pretended I was watching the television—which I couldn't even see—just so the mayor wouldn't think I was paying mind to what he was saying to Juneboy. He ast Juneboy what he did, and Juneboy told him nicely 'bout the research he was s'pose to be doing, he said, into sickle cell anemia. The mayor sounded real interested and ast Juneboy all about it and Juneboy talked up a storm like he knowed everything in the world 'bout this Negro disease. He used big words, too, words like *hemoglobin*. Juneboy told the mayor some organization done gave him a grant, which is money, and Juneboy let the mayor know that he was spending a year spending his money from the grant peoples at Howard University Hospital. Then the mayor told Juneboy 'bout this cousin of his who had sicklemia, and I got the impression the mayor didn't think this thing called sicklemia was as bad as sickle cell. And Juneboy agreed. Then the mayor wanted to know where Juneboy lived normally. He said "normally." Juneboy told him he taught internal medicine at Yale University. I kinda laughed to myself.

Then the mayor wanted to know if Juneboy was married and had children, and I heard Juneboy say he was divorced and had two boys which is the truth. You shoulda seed the look on the mayor's face. He's a God-fearing family man with many grandchildren, two sons, and three daughters, and everybody can tell you our mayor ain't got no time for people who divorce. It's sort of like they ain't serious 'bout life. He squinted his little old red ape eyes and frowned with them deep lines between his eyebrows, and you could see he was gritting his teeth behind that tight mouth. He kinda pushed one of the kids away from messing with his face. Said to Juneboy, "Sounds like you already made a mess of your life, young man. I admire the work you're doing in sickle cell anemia research, but what we black people need are strong, lasting black families." The mayor went on and on, I tell you, reading the boy, so much so I felt sorry for poor Juneboy. Mayor Jones said it was a crime and a sin to leave a wife and two children. Juneboy started sweating as he tried to explain that his wife left him. The mayor paid no 'tention to the claim; he just went on preaching at the young man 'bout what was good for Negroes. (He didn't say Negroes. He said blacks, but I don't like the word *blacks*, never did. You can call me old-fashioned if you want, I don't care. Back in the sixties when all the kids started using *black* I tried for a while to take it up, but it just didn't feel right on my tongue 'cause my generation, you see, always thought of *black* as a bad word. You called somebody black back in the thirties and forties when I was coming up, you insulted them something terrible.)

DeSoto walked out the way he came and that seemed to break the spell for some reason. The mayor stopped talking and just stared at the doorway DeSoto left by. The minute DeSoto left, he stuck his head back inside the room and said, "Come here, Mama, I want to talk with you."

We went in the dining room and DeSoto took me by the arm and pulled me into the corner by the cupboard. He started acting this way, like a movie tough guy, 'round the time he started on the police force. I never did like it. I said, "DeSoto, I'm your mother. Don't pull on my arm like you think I'm some gal you met somewhere on the street."

"Sorry, Mama. Didn't mean no harm." He gave me that old winning grin. "I just want to talk to you about—" he nodded his head toward the den—"that man. I don't care if he is the mayor, he got no right to lash into Juneboy like that. Juneboy is our guest. My first cousin!"

I told DeSoto to calm down.

"It ain't fair, Mama!"

"I know, I know. But you can't deny that the mayor is right about divorce. The mayor is just trying to talk straight Christian talk to Juneboy. Lord knows he probably ain't been nowhere near a church since he was little when Esther used to make him and Lauren go—"

"Mama!"

Then I heard the front doorbell and the kids running up the hallway and the door opening and Reverend Baldridge-Hawkins's big laugh. Then Jeremiah came up from the basement where he has a bar and a pool table and all those video games. Kissed me on the cheek and already he was reeking of booze. Everything seemed to be happening all at once. The front door sounded again, and a whole bunch of peoples was up there coming in.

I just wanted to find a corner and hide.

Everybody and his uncle was there that night. Back in the den with the mayor was his wife and that old civil rights lady Margy Jeanne Wright, who always be on television news talking 'bout what's wrong with our city. I like Michelle, the one who wants to be a actress, better—and Michelle is prettier. Ain't got them big buck teeths like her sister and brother, Margy and Ellsworth. Ellsworth was standing in the dining room talking with Councilwoman Sandra Valerie Wright. No doubt planning some strategy, as they say. She always talking 'bout organizing people. Sounds like communist talk to me but peoples say she highly respected. Councilman Cherokee "Jimmy" Barnswell had with him some young floozy with one of them real short dresses hitting 'bout halfway 'cross her thighs. She kept smiling through all that makeup caked on her face. She looked like somebody dressed up for a scare party. The councilman seemed deep in one of them business discussions with my son Jeremiah. The mayor's daughters—Rosa, Ruby, and Lena— was just wandering 'bout the house like nervous tigers in a cage.

Renee? That Renee was fussing with the kitchen help and directing the setting of the table and keeping the kids going 'round from room to room carrying the salted nuts and stuff. These Wrights, you know, is Renee's side of the family. The great old man, Congressman Mitch Wright, died back in the sixties—stricken down with a heart attack while addressing a group of civil rights peoples. People still 'member him, though, and they tell me he's now in the history books, and his grandchildren, Michelle's and Margy's and Ellsworth's kids, have to read on him in school right along on the same page where they read about the great Dr. Martin Luther King.

Well, I wandered 'round a bit, sneaking a glance at these folks and more, but pretty soon I got settled in my corner on the old chair by the white telephone, and Jeremiah's old Siamese cat, French John, came and stationed hisself on my lap like he thought I was his natural bed. I never cared for cats, but they always seem to head straight for me.

Just as I sat down, wouldn't you know it, Congressman Fred Wright came over and spoke. I was honored. He's so handsome with those pretty eyes and that light brown skin. He got nice straight teeths, too. In good health for a man his age. Keeps his weight down. And don't wear his hair long like some of these fancy peoples try to do, trying to look like movie stars! They say Fred is a real close friend of Jimmy Carter. Now there's a man I like! Anyways, Fred ast me how I was doing, ast 'bout my arthritis. I didn't tell him how bad it was being lately 'cause I don't wants to bend peoples' ears with my troubles the way my sister Esther do. Child, all you want to do is get away from all that complaining! So I just told Fred that I was feeling tolerably well for a gal as old as I was and laughed, and he laughed with me. Then I noticed him eyeing my wig, and I got real worried. Maybe it was crooked or something and, child, I tell you I wanted to get away from him real bad and go to the bathroom to look in the mirror to make sure. When I saw his pretty wife, Lee Anne, coming, I saw my chance and jumped up and met her halfway and spent 'bout five minutes telling her how pretty she was—and she is cute as can be with them big brown eyes and that sweet, sweet smile. I told them they was such a handsome couple together, then 'scused myself and put the cat down and went up the hallway to the closest bathroom. But the door was locked, so I went on 'round and up the winding stairway to one of the ones up there.

I locked the door. The wig was all right, but it dawned on me that my girdle was too tight and that was why I was feeling so uncomfortable. I knowed I'd been gaining weight lately, and it's true I hadn't been inside of this thing in months and it was killing me, and I decided to take it off right there and hide it in the kids' dirty clothes hamper. I could pick it up tomorrow. Well, girl, it was so funny, trying to get outta that God-awful thing, I had to laugh at myself right there in the bathroom. I pulled and pulled and pulled. I yanked and tugged. But that thing didn't want to come off. I couldn't figure how I'd gotten into it in the first place. Well, you know, I tend to swell. Part of my arthritis problem, I guess. I swell at night a lot more than in the daytime. And I'd put that thing on when it was still daylight.

After 'bout—oh—heck, a half hour, I got it down past my hips and put that old thing in the hamper. But I'm embarrassed to tell you that the minute I was ready to go back to the party, or rather back to my chair downstairs, I stumbled against the face bowl and my teeth fell out. Fortunately they didn't break. You see, I hadn't been wearing them but 'bout a week. New ones made up for me, but I hadn't got use to them yet. I must have had my mouth open and they just plopped right outta my mouth and into the face bowl. After I saw they didn't break, I broke down laughing so hard at my foolish old self I thought I'd die from heart failure.

PRAISESONG FOR
THE WIDOW

Paule Marshall

 With a strength born of the decision that had just come to her in the middle of the night, Avey Johnson forced the suitcase shut on the clothes piled inside and slid the lock into place. Taking care not to make a sound, she then eased the heavy bag off the couch onto the floor and, straining under her breath, her tall figure bent almost in two, hauled it over the thick carpeting to the door on the other side of the cabin.

A thirty-inch Pullman stood packed and waiting there. Quickly she deposited the second bag next to it, and after pausing to dart a nervous glance behind her, she slipped over to a long sectional closet which took up the rest of the wall beside the door.

From the storage space at the bottom she pulled out another suitcase. Her movements a whisper, she raised up and with her free hand began stripping the hangers of as many clothes as she could carry along with the bag. In seconds her arms were full, and she had spun around and was heading rapidly back across the dimly lighted room, moving like a woman half her age, her shadow on the walls and ceiling hurrying to keep up.

Over at the couch, with the suitcase laid open on top of the bedcovers, she made quick work of the clothes, tossing them helter-skelter into the bag without a trace of the neatness and order that were her hallmark. A minute later found her back at the closet, blindly reaching and snatching at whatever came to her hand in the darkness. Then, noiseless as a sneak thief, she was beating it back to the couch, her arms piled high again.

Perspiration was beginning to sheet her forehead despite the air-conditioning in the cabin. She didn't stop to wipe it. The determined look on her face had brought her underlip jutting forward, exposing the spillover of raw pink across the top which she always kept hidden. She let the lip stay as it was. The back pain she suffered with occasionally was threatening to flare up with all the bending and hauling. She closed her mind to it.

Her mind in a way wasn't even in her body or, for that matter, in the room. From the moment she had awakened in a panic less than an hour ago and come to the reckless decision, her mind had left to go and stand down at the embarkation door near the waterline five decks below. While she swiftly crisscrossed the room on her bare feet, spiriting her belongings out of the closet and drawers, her mind had leaped ahead to the time, later that morning, when the ship would have arrived at the next port of call. The huge door in the steel hull would be rolled back then, and along with her fellow passengers going ashore for the day, she would step from the liner onto the waiting launch. For the last time. And without so much as a backward glance.

Avey Johnson's two traveling companions, with whom she shared the large deluxe cabin, were asleep in the bedroom on the other side of a divider with narrow shelflike openings on top and a long chest of drawers below, facing what was called the living area. Not to risk waking them, she had left off the lamps in the living area, where she always volunteered to sleep each cruise because it was more private.

For illumination she had opened the drapes at the picture window of a porthole and was making do with the reflection of the deck lights outside, along with the faint glow of the night-light filtering through the divider, which the woman, Thomasina Moore, always kept burning in the bedroom, like a child afraid of the dark. The pale satin sheen of the nightgown she had on added to the small pool of light, as did the subtle aura, unbeknown to her, which her dark skin had given off since birth.

Slipping back over to the couch, Avey's feet struck a chair. Quickly she stifled her outcry, shook off the pain, and kept going. When was the last time she had gone barefoot around the house? She paused a second, the clothes she was about to let drop into the suitcase suspended in her arms. Halsey Street? Had it been that long ago? Back then the young woman whose headstrong ways and high feelings Avey Johnson had long put behind her, whom she found an embarrassment to even think of now with her 1940s upsweeps and pompadours and vampish high-heeled shoes, used to kick off her shoes the moment she came in from work, shed her stockings, and start the dusting and picking up in her bare feet. The pots on in the tiny kitchen. The 78s on the turntable in the living room: Coleman Hawkins, Lester Young, The Count, The Duke. Music to usher Jay in the door. Freed of the high heels her body always felt restored to its proper axis. And the hardwood floor which Jay had rescued from layers of oxblood-colored paint when they first moved in and stained earth-brown, the floor reverberating with "Cottontail" and "Lester Leaps In" would be like a rich nurturing ground from which she had sprung and to which she could always turn for sustenance.

Avey Johnson hadn't thought of that floor in decades.

A bottom drawer became stuck in the chest of drawers below the divider where her underclothes were stowed. Grasping it between her hands, she tried jiggling it back on its tracks, unmindful for a moment in her haste of the noise she was making until she heard her friend, Clarice, shift massively in her sleep. Poor Clarice. She always sounded as if she were wrestling with someone as large as herself on the narrow bed whenever she turned. There quickly followed a sound from the other bed, like the knocking in a radiator as the steam rises, as Thomasina Moore, her sleep disturbed, began an ominous implosive clucking at the roof of her mouth.

Her hands froze on the drawer. That was the last person she wanted to wake before she was done! Scarcely breathing, she remained bent double over the chest, perspiring, her back aching, holding herself rigid except once when she gave a fearful glance back over her shoulder—something she had repeatedly caught herself doing since yesterday.

Only when the two inside the bedroom had been quiet for some time did she try the drawer again. With a burglar's finesse this time she eased it back on its tracks, slid it open without a sound, and the next moment was darting across to the couch with the wealth of underthings she had scooped up, the drawer left open behind.

Her skirts, blouses, and summer suits were done. The sweaters and stoles she drew around her when the weather on deck turned chilly had been packed after a fashion. Crowded into the wrong bag were the linen shirtdresses she wore on excursions ashore in place of the shorts and slacks favored by the other women her age on board, no matter what their size. Her shoes were in their special caddy. Her hats in their cylindrical box. And she had just disposed of the last of her underthings. All that remained were her ensemble dresses and evening gowns. She was down to the last of the six suitcases.

"But why six, Mother? Why would anyone in their right mind need to take this much stuff just to go away for a couple of weeks?"—Marion, Avey Johnson's youngest, the morning she had come to drive her mother to the pier before her first cruise three years ago. Entering the house, Marion had stopped short at sight of the half-dozen bags neatly lined up in the downstairs hall, had stood staring at them for the longest time, trying to contain her exasperation but failing. When she finally looked up, it had been all she could do, from her expression, not to reach out and grab her mother by the shoulders and shake her the way she might have one of her pupils in the small community school she helped to run in a church in Brooklyn. To shake sense into her. Around the face which bore Jay's clear imprint, her hair had stood massed like a rain cloud about to make good its threat. And the noisy necklace of cowrie shells and amber she had brought back from Togo her last visit had sounded her angry despair with its rattle each time she breathed.

"Why go on some meaningless cruise with a bunch of white folks anyway, I keep asking you? What's that supposed to be about? Couldn't you think of something better to do on your vacation? And since when have you started letting Thomasina Moore decide how you should spend it? You don't even like the woman. What the hell's gotten into you?"

Avey Johnson's own mother would have slapped Marion down long ago had she been her child—and never mind she was twenty-eight and a woman already married and divorced. She would have raised a hard palm and with a blow to set her ears ringing put her in her place: "Girl, where you get off talking to *me* like that?"

And the Avey Johnson of thirty, forty years ago would have done likewise. She had been quick then to show her displeasure, her bottom lip immediately unfolding to bare the menacing sliver of pink and then her mouth letting fly with the words. But she had grown away from such high-strung behavior, and over the years had developed a special silence to deal with anyone the likes of Marion. With her daughter she simply acted as if nothing unpleasant was being said, that Marion was still, as she had once been, the most polite and tractable of her children.

"Here last summer I begged you to go on that tour to Brazil, and on the one, the year before that, to Ghana. . . ." The voice hung unrelenting at her ear as she made the final hurried trips between the closet again and the couch. "And all I got for an answer was either 'we'll see' or that infuriating silence of yours. Yet here you are willing and eager to go off on some ridiculous cruise. Could you have thought of anything more banal!"

Banal? For a second before she quickly checked herself the word had threatened to overturn the rock of her calm. Did Marion know that the closest she had ever come to a cruise in her life had been the annual boat ride up the Hudson to Bear Mountain as a child? What did she know?

". . . Why can't you be a little imaginative, for God's sake, a little independent, and go off on your own somewhere. Learn something!"

Marion had been the only one of Avey Johnson's three children to oppose the trip. Sis, the eldest, in her weekly phone call from Los Angeles, had urged her mother to go, reminding her that she and her husband, a systems programmer at Lockheed (the only one his color in his division), had sailed to Hawaii the previous year, taking their two boys, and had enjoyed it.

Annawilda, interning at Meharry Hospital at the time, had written to say it was just what she needed, adding: "It'll take your mind off Daddy." It had been 1974 then, and Jerome Johnson had been dead only a little over a year.

And they, it turned out, had been right and Marion wrong. Because whatever doubts she had managed to sow in Avey Johnson's mind vanished the moment she saw the *Bianca Pride* that first time in her berth at West Fortieth Street and the river, with the flags and pennants flying from all her stations, her high bow canted toward the sun. All that dazzling white steel! Her hull appeared to sweep clear across to New Jersey. The precision and power of her lines! The ship's turbines, she had read in the brochure they had sent her before sailing, produced enough heat and light to run a city the size of Albany! And on a group tour of the bridge that first trip she had seen the huge Ferranti computer that monitored all operations on board. Her group had stood awestruck and reverent before the console with its array of keyboards, switches, and closed-circuit television screens.

There had been no resisting it! Thomasina Moore had no sooner suggested a return trip the following year than she had accepted. And Marion, seeing her resolve, began keeping her objections to herself. Her eyes had carefully avoided the suitcases the last two times she had come to drive her to the pier, and on the way into Manhattan she had talked only of her pupils, most of whom had been rejected by the public schools as being impossible to teach. Her "sweetest lepers," Marion called them, from a poem she was always urging her mother to read.

The last of the evening gowns lay where she had just flung them on top of the final pile of dresses in the fold-over garment bag. They had graced their last dinner in the Versailles Room; they had attended their last Captain's Ball. As if sealing a tomb, Avey Johnson zipped the long flap into place over them and, still working feverishly, like someone pursued, folded the bag over on itself, latched the two halves together, and seconds later was dragging it across the cabin to join the others.

The marathon packing was done. On an armchair over near the window lay the clothes she had hastily set aside to wear. The suitcases, all six of them along with the shoe caddy and hatbox, stood assembled near the door, ready for the steward. Giving the apprehensive glance over her shoulder, she immediately headed toward them, not even allowing herself a moment to rest her back or wipe the perspiration from her face—or to consider, quietly and rationally, which was normally her way, what she was about to do.

Outside the glow of the deck lights was slowly being absorbed by a pearl-gray light that was both filtering down from the clearing sky and curling up like mist from the sea. And the sea itself had become a wide, silver-toned sheet of plate metal, which was already, out near the horizon, reflecting the subtle mauve and rose and pale yellows of the day.

Amid the burgeoning color stood the liner—huge, sleek, imperial, a glacial presence in the warm waters of the Caribbean. The long night run completed, it had come to rest and drop anchor a short time ago in the same smooth and soundless manner with which it had moved over the sea.

From its decks could be made out the faint, almost insubstantial form of an island across the silvery moat of the harbor. The next port of call.

Avey Johnson had finished in good time.

"What you doing up and dressed so early?"

A pair of grayish eyes with the unblinking watchfulness of a bird's was peering through the divider's narrow openings. They were like eyes at the slot of a speakeasy door.

Seconds later, wearing a sheer frilly dressing gown that looked meant for a bride (it even had a slight train), Thomasina Moore stepped curiously around the divider into the living area.

She was a thin-featured woman in her early seventies with a lined and hectic brow, what used to be called "good hair" covered over with a sleeping net, and the first signs of a dowager's hump across her shoulders: old age beginning to warp the once graceful curve of her back. She could still, though—she liked to boast—kick her legs as high as when she had danced in the chorus line of the Cotton Club back in the twenties. (At least she claimed it had been the Cotton Club. Which might have been true. She had the color to have qualified: black that was the near-white of a blanched

almond or the best of ivory. A color both sacred—for wasn't it a witness?—
and profane: *"he forced my mother my mother/late/One night/What do they
call me?"*).

She almost collided with the suitcases at the door.

"And what're your bags doing sitting here by the door? What's going on
around here?"

Avey Johnson, gazing out of the window on the other side of the living
area, didn't turn to her immediately. After quickly showering and dressing,
she had gone to wait out the time till morning, watching the island across
the way gradually take shape in the growing light. A dark mass of coastal
hills with a darker foil of mountains behind had been the first to appear.
Then, as the sun rose fully, lighting the hills one after the other the way an
acolyte would light candles in a church, the town had become sharply visible:
a pretty seaport town of pastel houses with red tiled roofs crowding down to
the harbor and perched like tick birds on the flanks of the hills.

She had found the sight soothing, reassuring. The town, the hills, the
distant mountains, the morning sunlight, all not only applauded her decision,
it seemed, but assured her there would be a plane to New York later in the
day with a seat for her on it.

So that as she turned to Thomasina Moore after making her wait almost
a full minute, she scarcely felt the need to steel herself against the tirade she
knew would follow. Indeed, it was as if she had already heard the woman
out and had left. Part of her had already stepped on board the launch and
was planing swiftly over the morning sea toward the island and the waiting
plane.

She had decided, she said, to cut short the cruise and go home. She
kept her gaze on the middle distance.

"You decided to do *what?* What you say?"

She knew it must have come as a shock, her leaving on the spur of the
moment like this, but it couldn't be helped. She had ignored the woman's
outcry. The cruise itself she didn't think was to blame. Nor was she sick,
although she hadn't been feeling herself the last couple of days. It was nothing
she could put her finger on. She had simply awakened in the middle of the
night and decided she would prefer to spend the rest of her vacation at home.
It didn't make any sense, she knew, but her mind was made up. If she was
lucky she might get a flight out today. . . .

While she was saying all this, the words terse and final, her manner
calm, Thomasina Moore started slowly toward her across the living area,
her dumbstruck gaze taking in the emptied-out closet and the drawers, all
of which stood sprawling open. She faltered to a stop in the middle of the
floor, and from there, with a child's open-mouth disbelief, she examined

the dressy two-piece ensemble Avey Johnson had on, the stylish but conservative pumps on her feet, and the straw hat she was already wearing, whose wide brim curved down to hide most of her face.

The pocketbook she had placed on a chair beside her also drew the woman's stricken gaze—a handsome bag of navy-blue straw to complement the muted beige and navy print of her dress, and draped over it a pair of mesh summer gloves with a single crystal button at the wrist.

Here her eyes came to focus, and for the longest while she gazed at the buttons as if in her shaken mind they were tiny crystal balls which could tell her whether she was hearing right. Until finally, with a sound like that of a bewildered mute struggling desperately to speak, her head jerked back over her shoulder, and she was calling toward the bedroom, "Clarice! Clarice! Get on out here! *Clarice . . . !*"

She continued to summon Clarice even when the latter, sleepily trying to pull a robe around her bulk, appeared from behind the divider.

At fifty-eight Clarice was six years Avey Johnson's junior and the youngest of the three women. Where the bones of her face pressed up through the fleshiness, her skin—black with an admixture of plum that spoke of centuries of sunlight—was as smooth as a girl's. Yet she tended to look as old or older than Thomasina Moore because of the worry lines furrowed deep around her mouth, and the downcast, burdened expression she never completely abandoned even on those rare occasions when she laughed.

"Did you hear this?"

"No," she said, still struggling with the robe. "What's happened?"

Clarice asked but she really didn't want to know. She had already, in a single apprehensive glance around the room, taken in the suitcases by the door, the ransacked drawers and closet, and her two friends, one agitated and close to anger in the middle of the floor, the other calm and enveloped in that special intimidating silence of hers over by the porthole; and she had resigned herself to the worst.

"What d'you mean what's happened? This one's leaving, that's what. Walking out on the cruise. She all of sudden feels she'd rather spend what's left of her vacation at home and is going back today. Just like that. Without a word to anybody. You ever heard anything like it . . . ?"

"Is that true, Avey . . . ?" Clarice's reluctant gaze sought the tall figure across the room.

"What d'you mean if it's true?" Thomasina Moore's voice had risen sharply. "Don't you see her bags all packed over there near you? Don't you see the way she's dressed? Hat, gloves, the works. Do you think she'd be all dolled up like that if she was just going sight-seeing with the rest of us today? She's leaving, I'm telling you. Quitting the cruise after only five days and taking a plane home!"

The shock of it was still so great she fell speechless again, and in the small charged silence left by her voice Clarice tried asking Avey Johnson what had gone wrong. Had something happened on board? Or had she come down with something? Was she perhaps feeling sick . . . ?

"Do . . . she . . . look . . . sick . . . to . . . you?" Her colors, as Thomasina Moore called them, were up: anger like a battery of flags being rung up all at once in a strong wind. ("Look out you don't get my colors up," she was always warning. Or: "These white folks around here must be trying to get my colors up"—this on their first cruise, when they had been assigned a table in the dining room which she felt was too close to the service entrance. She had promptly had it changed.)

"Do she look sick to you, I ask?" Though furious, her voice was pitched low: despite her anger she was being mindful of the public corridor just outside the door. "Ain' not a thing wrong with her. Talking 'bout she ain' been feeling herself these past couple of days. Well, what's ailing her? What's her complaint? If she was sick she would have gone to the doctor, wouldn't she? That's what he's here for. No, she can't fool me with no excuse like that."

Suddenly the grayish eyes with their unblinking intensity narrowed, becoming more acute, more suspicious. "But I should've known somethin' was up the funny way she was acting yesterday. Keeping to herself all day. Not showing up till dinner and then scarcely touching the food on her plate. Hardly talking to anybody. I should've known somethin' was up. And now come this morning here she is dressed back, ready to walk off the ship for good. All of a sudden like this! And without a word as to why! 'It's nothin' I can put my finger on.' Who she thinks she's kiddin'? A person would have to have a reason for doing a thing like this. No, somethin's behind this mess. Somethin' deep. She can't make me out for no fool!"

There would be a taxi waiting for her on the wharf of the little pastel town. Or one would arrive the moment she stepped off the launch. The driver would inform her that, yes, there was a plane to New York today, a nonstop flight scheduled to leave shortly. No, it was unlikely to be filled, this being May and the off-season. She was certain to get a seat. The airport would turn out to be only a short drive away, on a wide safe plain between the hills fronting the sea and the mountains she had glimpsed in the distance. They would reach there in ample time for the flight.

". . . And what about the money? Have you heard her say anything about all the money she's gonna be losing?" Thomasina Moore swung with this toward Clarice, the violence of her movement sending up a shower of scented dust from the bride's dressing gown, and causing the daylight inside the cabin, which was only an hour old, to waver like a used-up light bulb.

"Have you, I'm asking!"

Clarice, backed up against the tall wooden support to the divider, numbly shook her head. She had assumed the pose characteristic of her whenever there was trouble, her eyes lowered, her thick shoulders sloping down, and the burdened look adding years to her face. It was a look that went back decades, dating from her endless difficulties with her husband before their breakup, her mother's long, demanding illness and death, and her disappointment in her only son, who had suddenly, after years of being a straight-A student, dropped out of the predominantly white college he had been attending. With each crisis her weight had increased, the fat metastasizing with each new sorrow. Now, under the robe she had finally managed to pull around her, her flesh with the pierced heart at its center had opened to absorb this latest tragedy. For wasn't she, Clarice, somehow responsible for what was happening? Wasn't she in some way to blame? Her dullness, her rampant flesh, her blackness . . .

"Gonna forfeit the fifteen hundred dollars she paid for the cruise and then turn around and spend more money to take a plane home! Now what kinda sense do that make, will you tell me? She must be out of her mind. . . . Wait, that's it! She's done gone and lost her mind . . . !"

The lined face, the color of old ivory, came thrusting forward as the woman tried surprising the insanity under the turned-down hat brim. She was met instead by the underlip Avey Johnson had left thrusting forward slightly so that the knife edge of raw pink was still visible, and by the expression in her eyes of someone who had already left the cabin and the ship and was well on her way somewhere else.

"Gots to be," she muttered, drawing back, "out of her cotton-pickin' mind."

The taxi driver had been right. The plane was far from full. She had the three seats in her row all to herself. They had already reached cruising altitude, so that the only thing visible when she looked down was the hazy undifferentiated blue of the sea far below. And with the flight under way, everything had come right again. She no longer caught herself giving the little fearful involuntary glance back over her shoulder, and the odd unpleasant sensation in her stomach that had plagued her off and on for the past two days was gone. Down the aisle the stewardess was taking orders for drinks before lunch. She would have a glass of white wine to celebrate.

" '. . . If I'm lucky I might get a flight out today.' " The words, spoken in the low-pitched shout, were a scathing parody of Avey Johnson's. "Just listen to her! Who told her she's gonna find a plane going to New York today? Who's guaranteed her a flight right away? Why, some of these little islands don't see a plane going anywhere but maybe two, three times a week. She might be stuck for days. And in some place that probably won't have a decent hotel to its name. She'll wind up having to stay in some dump where the mosquitoes'll eat her alive and the food—or what passes for food—won't be fit for hogs.

"And forget about drinking the water! Remember that place we stopped at last year?" She half swung toward Clarice again with the same violent movement that jarred the light. "Cartarena or Cartarana or whatever they called it . . ." (It had been Cartagena, Colombia, where, to Avey Johnson's disgust, the woman had abandoned them to dance in a carnival parade they were watching with other passengers from the *Bianca Pride*. Had gone off amid a throng of strangers swishing her bony hips to the drums. With the slight hump like an organ grinder's monkey begging pennies from her shoulders. And with their fellow passengers watching. White faces laughing! White hands applauding! Avey Johnson had never been so mortified. And she had returned, the woman, laughing proudly, with the jumpsuit she had on soaked through under the arms, and in her laugh, in her flushed face, something of the high-stepping, high-kicking young chorus girl she had once been. "Girl, those drums *got* to me! Where's some water?")

". . . Remember the water they gave me to drink there? You could see the bugs swimming around in it clear as day. Well, just let this one here go running around eating and drinking on her own. She's gonna come back with her stomach all *tore* up!" (With her colors up she said "tow.") "A girlfriend of mine went to Mexico for a week and was laid up in the hospital for two months straight when she got back just from drinking a glass of water down there. . . ."

The drive from Kennedy to their small section of North White Plains was over. The airport limousine had deposited her at the door and departed. Before leaving, the driver had helped her take the suitcases into the front hall. She could glimpse them through the archway to the dining room where she had gone to sit for a moment in the welcoming dark, at the great oval-shaped table. Where the light from the hall fell across the table's polished surface, the cherry wood glowed like a banked fire that had awaited her return. Over on the buffet the coffee service on its chased and footed tray was a study in silver and black in the semidarkness. Everything was as she had left it: her special crystal in the china closet, her silverplate—all eighty pieces—in its felt-lined case. It was her favorite room, the dining room. She was right not to go back on her promise to Jerome Johnson and sell the house as Marion kept nagging her to do. (According to Marion, the house had served its purpose.) Later she would make herself a cup of tea and drink it here at the table in the half-light.

". . . Packing her things in the middle of the night like some thief . . .

no reason . . . no explanation . . . good money gone . . . gots to be crazy
. . . no plane for days . . . gonna run into all kinds of trouble. . . ."

Caught in the riptide of her anger, Thomasina Moore was powerless to
stop herself.

". . . Here the three of us suppose to be traveling together and she just
ups and leaves, ruining the rest of the trip for the two of us. And after all
the time I spent seeing to it everything would be just right!" (Which was
true. The woman devoted the better part of the year to planning for the
cruise—which each year took them to a different set of islands. She had the
time, not having worked since her show business days. Her dead husband,
a dentist, who had been taken with her color, had indulged her shamelessly,
treating her as if she were all the children they had never had.)

". . . No decent person'd do a thing like this. Why she's no better, come
to think of it, than some bum on a Hundred Twenty-fifth Street, never mind
the airs she gives herself. But she never had me fooled. Oh, no, this is one
boot she couldn't play for a fool. I could tell her airs were nothing but a
front. Always knew she had it in her to pull somethin' mean and low-down
like this. Knew it!

"That's why—" she cried, her suppressed fury at a new high, her breath
sucked deep into the bony wells at her throat, her eyes convulsed. "That's
why if I've said it once I've said it a thousand times: it . . . don't . . . pay
. . . to . . . go . . . no . . . place . . . with . . . *niggers!* They'll mess up
ever' time!"

Unhurriedly, Avey Johnson bent and picked up first her gloves and then
her pocketbook from the chair beside her. To her surprise she found she
was smiling. A little faint, pleased, self-congratulatory smile, as if, instead
of the insult, the woman had said something complimentary. It didn't make
sense. Yet there the smile was, its warmth stealing across her face, its gentle
pull easing the strain from the held-in lip that had become a permanent part
of her expression over the years. To hide the smile she was forced to remain
bent over the chair longer than necessary.

Then, with the pocketbook on her arm and her gloves in hand, she
was stepping around the still raging figure in the center of the room:
". . . somethin' deep's behind this mess. You can't tell me different. . . ."
She gave her a wide berth, the way she might have some mildly demented
bag woman railing to herself on the city's streets.

Her unhurried step led her across to Clarice at the divider. She had
intended apologizing privately to her friend. Had meant to say, her voice
low, her back to Thomasina Moore, that it was wrong of her to leave in this
manner, but that she hoped Clarice would not hold it against her. It was
just that something—she couldn't say what—had come over her the past

couple of days. She couldn't explain it. She could make no sense of it. Anyway, they would see each other back at work once their vacations were over and everything would be as usual. (They both worked for the State Motor Vehicle Department, Avey Johnson as a supervisor and Clarice as a Grade Five clerk.) Their first day back they would splurge and have lunch at the seafood restaurant near the office.

She had it in mind to say something on this order crossing the room, to assure Clarice that she was in no way to blame. But the moment she drew up in front of her friend and saw close-up the familiar burdened slope to her shoulders and the expression of mute acceptance on her face, her tongue balked. For the first time in the twenty years they had known each other, something about Clarice both frightened and offended her. She found herself wanting to back away from her as from something contagious, or to make a sign (if she had known one) to ward off some dangerous hex. At the same time her hand ached to reach out and lift that bowed head, force it up. She wanted to shout at Clarice the way her father used to at her long ago whenever he caught her slouching, "Pull your back up, girl!"

Instead all she said, quickly moving away, was, "I'm going to arrange with the purser about my leaving. I'll be back with a steward for my things."

In seconds she made her way around the suitcases to the door, and was opening and hurriedly closing it on the voice which continued choleric and unflagging from the middle of the floor.

". . . no reason . . . no explanation . . . trying to play people for fools . . . !"

THE UPPER ROOM

Mary Monroe

Dotted with thick forests of gray cypress, tulip, and magnolia, the territory known as Florida rests vaingloriously amid opalescent Southern waters. Wild, long-stemmed flowers sway gently in the summer breeze, as damp moss that seems to fall from the sky clings to the trees. Along the Tamiami Trail across Florida's Everglades, alligators sun themselves on the banks, ready to scramble into the muddy water at the slightest provocation.

Maureen Montgomery was born in Silo, near the Everglades, on a humid evening in July during dog days, that period of inactivity between early July and early September when the sultry summer weather comes to the northern hemisphere. It was so warm that day that the lazy alligators, seduced by pleasure, lay lined up along the swamp banks in orderly fashion, waiting.

In the midst of the swamp stood a crudely built shanty. Inside, on a living room sofa, lay a woman who was almost as big around as she was tall. Ruby Montgomery, wearing a long, shapeless black flannel duster, rested on her side, sipping her twelfth can of beer that day, a thirty-year-old black woman with a round face, small brown eyes, heavy black eyebrows, and generous lips. She had a nose that was too wide for her to be considered handsome.

Her house smelled of boiled pork and steamed cabbage. The dim light illuminated the walls of the living room with huge distorted shadows. The furniture was cheap and shabby, but everything was neatly arranged, for Orderliness and Godliness were part of Southern tradition. An immaculate home, no matter how humble and plain, would surely please the Lord, it was preached in Southern churches. Ruby tried to live up to the Lord's expectations, most of the time.

Outside, a chorus of barking coon dogs challenged the sweet calls of a remarkably fine lot of little birds: the mockingbird, the blue jay, the wood-pecker. In the sky above, a broad-winged turkey buzzard made a swooping, whistling sound. Not too far away, in a desolate swamp, a panther cried plaintively beneath the hot Florida sun. In the dense huckleberry patch beyond the palmetto jungles to the north, a small black bear ambled about in search of its mate. The day was coming to a dramatic close; now only a sleeve of orange sunlight separated the horizon from the heavens, and dark-ness was descending rapidly. A great hoot owl, the nocturnal lord of the South, perched anxiously atop a moss-draped tree outside Ruby's ramshackle house, a house almost hidden behind a knot of jasmine bushes. The hoot owl circled the house twice, then reluctantly returned to the moss-draped tree and waited.

The knocking at the front door was low at first. Ruby sat up on the sofa, annoyed by the noisy creatures outside. The knocking added to her irritation.

"Virgil!" she yelled.

There was no answer. Ruby waited a full minute before speaking again.

"I wonder where that simple boy of mine is," she said to herself. She swallowed the last of the beer, draining the can to make sure she didn't miss a drop of the precious beverage, and wiped her liver-colored lips with the tail of her duster. "Oomph . . . wonder where my teeth could be," she murmured, looking around the room. She carefully lifted a mayonnaise jar lid from the floor. In it a pair of dull, pink-gummed false teeth lay upside down. Ruby examined the teeth, looking at them for a long time before clumsily inserting both plates in her mouth. She clamped down and ground rhythmically, securing the teeth in place. "Now," she said, as if proud of her accomplishment.

"Virgil!" Ruby yelled again, looking around the room. She felt her chest, where she carried a cross and a switchblade at all times.

A frail, light-skinned boy of eleven, with gray eyes and wavy black hair, appeared in the doorway between the living room and the kitchen. He was a reasonably attractive child with a small nose and thin lips. His square, angry face displayed a continent of dark brown freckles.

"What you want now, Mama Ruby? Seem like every time I get me in a comfortable position, you start to meddle me. Virgil, get me a beer. Virgil, let the dog outside. Virgil, get me a beer. Virgil, change the channel on the TV set. Virgil, get me a beer—"

"Shet up, boy," Ruby said, slapping her thigh with her hand and stomping her foot.

"Yes, ma'am," Virgil muttered. His denim overalls were way too loose for his slender frame. He was shoeless, and his long, dusty feet were hard and reptilian, with curled toenails almost two inches long.

"Somebody at the door, sugar. Go answer it. I'm too tired to get up."

"Mama Ruby, I'm tired, too. And I ain't your slave," Virgil whined. "You been pesterin' me all evenin'."

"Answer the door, boy."

"But, Mama Ruby—"

"It liable to be that ol' bill collector from the grocery store again. Or the candy man what we owe for the peanut brittle. Could even be Old Man Parker comin' to collect rent, which we ain't got."

"It could be just about anybody, Mama Ruby. You know how you is," Virgil said.

Ruby remained silent for a moment, thinking about what her son had said as if it were a startling revelation. She looked at him and sighed, shrugging her huge shoulders and shaking her head slowly.

"Praise the Lord." Ruby set the empty beer can on the floor and rose from the sofa with great difficulty. Virgil ran across the room to assist her. He grabbed her arm to steady her, almost falling himself, for even with years of practice, balancing this elephantine woman was no easy feat. The boy's arms ached, and he gasped.

"Have mercy on my soul," he said, cursing his strain.

"Thank you, son." Ruby smoothed her duster along the sides of her thighs. "Now, go answer the door. Tell whoever it is I'm at the church or somethin'. I'm sho nuff tired, and I don't want to see no more human bein's this evenin'." Ruby waddled swiftly across the room on into the kitchen. Virgil giggled and tiptoed to the front window. He pulled back the drapes and peeked out.

"Mama Ruby, I don't see nobody!" he shouted over his shoulder.

The knocking continued, louder.

"Who it is, Virgil?" Ruby hollered from the kitchen, peeking from behind a large white cabinet that sat next to the sink. "Ax who it is, boy!"

"Who it is!" Virgil shouted toward the door.

"It's me, y'all." It was the small, whining voice of a girl child.

"In the name of the Lord! What you want this time of evenin', Alice Mae? I just left your house a little while ago. What you lookin' for now, trouble?"

"If she is, she come to the right place!" Ruby roared, walking back into the living room. She stood in the middle of the floor with her arms folded.

"My mama say to send Mama Ruby to her. She sho nuff sick. The devil done put somethin' on her a doctor can't take off," the voice outside said.

"Sho nuff?" Virgil asked. He lifted the window wide enough to stick his head out.

"My mama sick as a dog. She say what she got she wouldn't wish on Judas. She need Mama Ruby. I think she fixin' to up and die," Alice Mae replied.

"Come on in this house, sweetie," Virgil said. "Come on in before them mosquitoes eat you alive." He closed the window and went to open the door. A tiny, fair-skinned black girl of four with thick auburn hair stood timidly on the porch. She had her thumb in her mouth, and it was obvious she had been crying. There were tear streaks on her sand-covered face, and her nose was red and snotty.

"Un-ass that thumb, girl! You want your lips to end up lookin' like goldfish lips?" Virgil bellowed, stomping his foot. "Do you?"

"No," the child said, removing her thumb from her mouth. She had on a soiled flour-sack smock and a pair of man's tennis shoes. She was thin, but uncommonly pretty. Her nose was aquiline and her lips narrow. She had large light-blue eyes with long thick black lashes that gave her face an angelic appearance. Her father was an Irish grocery store owner in Miami whom her mother had had problems paying on time.

"Come on in the house, and praise the Lord," Ruby said.

Alice Mae stumbled in. As soon as she was close enough, Ruby leaned down and wiped her nose with the tail of her duster. "Now, praise the Lord like I told you."

"Praise the Lord," Alice Mae sighed mechanically.

"Bless your soul. You ought to give thanks and praise every day. That way, you'll be blessed. Now, what's the matter with your mama? Her baby's fixin' to come, ain't it?" Ruby said. "I knowed today was the day!"

"Yes, ma'am," Alice Mae agreed, nodding her head vigorously. She stood watching with interest as Ruby ran across the floor and stepped into a pair of limp, flat brown moccasins sitting near the back of the room. The whole floor shook when Ruby moved across it. Virgil now occupied the sofa and lay with one leg tossed carelessly across the arm.

"Get your leg off the arm of my good couch, boy," Ruby growled, glaring at him. She sighed and brushed off her duster as Virgil obeyed silently. She pulled a red bandanna from the pocket of her frock and tied it neatly around her thick, knotty black hair. "Boy, find me my teeth."

"Good gracious alive, Mama Ruby! You already got your teeth in," Virgil said. Ruby felt around inside her mouth with her finger.

"Oh."

"Mama Ruby, can I play with your teeth?" Alice Mae asked.

"Say what? Girl, you must be out of your mind! My teeth ain't nothin' to play with!" Ruby shouted, frightening the child. Alice Mae turned quickly to Virgil, whose eyes darted from side to side.

"But Virgil let me play with 'em all the time when you get drunk and they fall out," Alice Mae said.

Ruby gasped and ran across the floor with her fist poised. She slid her knuckles across the side of Virgil's face.

"Aaaarrrggghhh!" he screamed, leaping up from the sofa.

"Don't you never mess with my teeth no more," Ruby told him, shaking her finger in his face. Tears slid down Virgil's cheeks as he whimpered softly, rubbing the side of his face.

"Yes, ma'am," he mumbled. He turned to Alice Mae and gave her a murderous look.

"And you better not tetch a hair on Alice Mae's head for tellin' me. That clear?"

"Yes, Mama Ruby," came the meek reply.

"Mama Ruby, y'all got any more goobers?" Alice Mae inquired.

"In the pantry, lamb. In the same bowl with the pecans and nigger toes," Ruby replied. She leaned down to pick up a broom off the floor and used it to chase a hen from the living room into the kitchen. "Virgil," she continued, on her way out the door. "You tend to my pans on the stove. Don't you let my cabbage and salt pork burn. And you might as well keep Alice Mae here with you. She'll just be in the way while I'm tendin' to her mama, with all them other kids there already. You hear me, boy?" Instead of answering, Virgil waved his hand at Ruby as she rushed from the house and off the porch. Her big heavy feet ground into the sand as she lurched across her front yard to the narrow pathway leading to the other side of the bayou where Othella Johnson lived, Alice Mae's mother and Ruby's best friend.

———

"Come on here, Othella . . . it's almost here . . . that's it . . . that's it. I can see the head. Woo wee!" Ruby exclaimed. She stood back from the bed where Othella lay, writhing in agony.

"Mama Ruby, lay your healin' hands on me—help me!" Othella begged.

"You leave my healin' hands out of this. This nature, what you goin' through. My healin' hands is for special occasions. And didn't I just lay hands on you this afternoon?" Ruby waved her hands high above her head. "You just better come on and birth this baby so I can get on back home. I got a cabbage and some pork on the stove. I leave that simple boy of mine by hisself too long, he subject to set my house afire."

"Oh, Mama Ruby, I can't stand this misery!"

"Shet up, Othella," Ruby grunted, gently slapping the side of Othella's head with her palm.

Othella gasped and trembled violently. Her legs were splayed, and she clawed at the insides of her thighs.

"Oh, Mama Ruby—please do somethin'! Get me a shot of gin! Call a roots woman! Do somethin'!"

"Didn't I tell you to shet up!" Ruby placed her hands on her hips and glared down at the desperate woman. "Oh, Collette, bring me another beer, sweetie!" Ruby called over her shoulder. Within seconds a slender dark-brown girl of eight with numerous braids came to the door of the bedroom and handed Ruby a can of beer. Ruby snatched it and drank hungrily. The girl disappeared as quietly and quickly as she had come.

"Aaaarrrggghhh!" Othella screamed, arching herself off the bed, almost folding her back in half.

"Damn!" Ruby said. "Collette, bring me a spittoon." Again the dark young girl came to the door. She handed Ruby a spittoon and disappeared. Ruby cleared her throat into the spittoon, then set it on the floor and continued drinking her beer. As soon as she finished, she set the can on the floor next to the spittoon and five other empty beer cans. She wiped her lips with the tail of her duster and sighed, looking at Othella with pity. Ruby removed a limp blue towel she had draped across her shoulder and leaned over the bed to wipe the perspiration from Othella's face. She then wiped her own face with the towel.

Suddenly Othella's children entered the room and began to move about.

"Is Mama goin' to die this time?" asked Babette, age nine. She was the image of Othella, with the same tan skin and silky black hair.

"Naw," Ruby growled.

"Mama Ruby, where you get that duster?" asked Job, age six. He was a child with deep brown skin and catlike eyes.

"I got it at a sidewalk sale in Tampa. Why?"

"I ain't never seen nothin' like it," the boy replied shyly. The other children giggled.

"Mama Ruby, what happened to your feet?" Collette asked. "How come they so big and flat?"

"Y'all quit axin' so many silly questions. You, Clyde, get me a bowl of water," Ruby barked. Clyde was the oldest.

"Yes, ma'am," he replied, and darted from the room. He returned shortly and handed Ruby a mixing bowl almost filled to the rim with fresh spring

water. She grabbed the container and dipped the tail of the towel in it. The
children formed a line, all staring at Ruby as she wiped her face, her neck,
and her hands with the towel. Then she quickly drank all the water from
the bowl. The children giggled.

"Y'all get out of here!" Ruby ordered. "Get out on the porch!"

"But the mosquitoes is out! And it's fixin' to rain!" one of the children
wailed.

"I said get out of this house!" Ruby shouted. She threw the bowl into
the crowd, and the giggling youngsters scattered, fleeing into the night. The
slamming of the front door was drowned out by the screams of childbirth.
The pain had become so intense that Othella passed out. Ruby shook her
head, cursed under her breath, and then left the room.

"Don't tell me ain't no more beer," Ruby sighed. She was now in
Othella's kitchen, frantically searching the icebox. She had drunk every can
in the house. Realizing this, Ruby became alarmed. She slammed the icebox
shut and ran out to the front porch. The children were catching lightning
bugs in the front yard.

"Clyde, you and Collette run down the road a piece to old Mr. Hamilton
and tell him I said to send me a few beers," Ruby hollered.

The children giggled again and all took off running down the dark road
to the nearest bootlegger. Ruby shaded her eyes with her hand and watched
until they were out of her sight; then she smiled, returned to the bedroom,
and sat down at the foot of Othella's bed.

It was two hours and six beers later before Othella regained consciousness.
Ruby set her last empty can down next to the others. Othella looked up at
Ruby, who had a scowl on her face and her arms folded.

A coal-oil lamp, burning softly, sat on a melon crate next to the lumpy
bed. Under the lamp was a dog-eared confession magazine with a provocative
cover. Under the magazine was a shabby Bible.

Ten minutes later the baby came; a beautiful, dimple-cheeked, brown
baby girl with thick black hair, just like Ruby wanted.

"She was beautiful," Ruby informed Othella, biting her bottom lip to
hold back her tears. "She was a girl."

"*Was*," Othella said, sitting up. "What's wrong? Where she at? How
come she didn't cry none when she popped out?"

"Othella, you still got all them other kids—"

"Ruby Jean, where is my baby I just birthed?" Othella wailed, attempting
to get up from the bed.

"Be still before you brain damage!" Ruby warned, gently forcing Othella
back down by pushing her shoulder.

"Where my baby?"

"Othella, you just had a dead baby," Ruby announced.

The women looked at one another, each recognizing the disappointment in the other's eyes.

"Dead, huh? My baby come here 'dead, sho nuff?"

"Dead as a Jew's tittie."

"Mama Ruby, what you reckon happened this time? You reckon I been hexed?"

Ruby shook her head.

"This ain't nobody but the devil. That bastard been pickin' on us for months. Ever since we got saved."

Othella looked at Ruby's face and frowned.

"But we get saved at least once a year. With all the backslidin' we do and all. You reckon the devil got it in for us 'cause we been cursin' him for so long?"

"Probably so. I guess I got too much glory and it's crossin' Satan's wires. Like lightnin'. Yeah, that's it. Satan wonderin' how come he can't lay me out. He workin' at me through you."

"Lord have mercy! What we goin' to do?"

"Like I always do. I'm goin' to beat the shit out of him. Tonight I plan to get on my knees and pray like I ain't never prayed before. When I get through, Satan'll be yellin' uncle in a foreign language. Sendin' us this here dead baby."

"Where is she? Where is my dead baby girl, Mama Ruby?"

"In the kitchen on the counter next to the icebox. She was a itty-bitty thing. Couldn't have weighed no more than a pound or two."

"Sho nuff?"

"Sho nuff."

"Well, I declare." Othella paused and closed her eyes. She rubbed her face, then looked up at Ruby again. "Mama Ruby . . . is it true what they say about you?"

"What?" Ruby asked, alarmed. She rose from her seat and moved a few feet from the bed.

"Folks say you can raise everything but hell with your healin' hands. I seen you myself rub the croup out of my boy Joe," Othella whispered. "You straightened out Brother Hamilton's crooked leg what got crooked up in the war. You delivered my soul. You growed a rosebush on a bed of rocks. I seen you do it."

"I been blessed sho nuff." Ruby shrugged, faking modesty. "I don't brag about it. Much."

"Flawless. You is flawless, Mama Ruby. If anybody was ever able to help folks, it's you. Why you think I took up with you as my best friend when we was playin' in sandboxes and just bein' weaned?"

"You was smart, I guess. Shoot. I never denied your white folks' sense."

"Then you gotta help me. You got to do what you can about my dead—"

"I already tried it! I laid hands on the dead baby twice already and it didn't do no good. She sho nuff dead."

"You mean even *you* can't breathe life back in her? *You* is the Lord's pet nigger."

"And the devil's walkin' stick! You forgettin' how much stock Satan got in my soul? You know how I been battlin' my tail off tryin' to shake that low-down, funky black dog. Shoot. Jesus been at a tug-o-war with that baboon since the day I was born. Tryin' to set me free."

"I just thought—"

"I can do anything I set my mind to . . . long as that low-down, funky black dog Satan ain't on my case. Now like I said, I tried to raise that dead baby with my healin' hands, but Satan say, 'Hell, no.' "

Othella blinked to hold back her tears.

"My poor little ol' dead baby girl," she mumbled. She closed her eyes and shook her head sadly. Suddenly she looked up again at Ruby. "Was she pretty? Was my dead baby girl pretty like all my other girls?"

"Flawless. She had your hair. She had skin that was brown like a nigger toe nut."

"And you couldn't save her? I kind of thought you could do anything you set your mind to. You havin' a hotline to heaven and all . . ."

"Well, the devil sometime disconnects my line."

"Oh."

Ruby watched Othella swing her legs across the side of the bed.

"Where you goin', Othella?"

"I'm goin' in the kitchen to look at my dead baby."

"You ain't goin' no place! You want to brain damage? I'll get that baby so you can look at her!" Ruby rushed from the bedroom and returned a few moments later holding the baby, which had been wrapped in a faded green towel.

"Let me see her," Othella mumbled, coughing.

"A angel if ever there was one," Ruby said, unwrapping the towel. She wiped tears from her eyes with the sleeve of her duster while Othella stared at the child's face.

"Flawless," Othella said, and turned her head. "Take her away."

"Don't you want to hold her one time?"

"Naw," Othella said, returning her attention to the child. Othella was tired and anxious to be left alone. She wanted to cry. Her last child had also been stillborn. "I'd have given my soul for this child to have lived. I declare, I would have. Mama Ruby, please take care of her for me. The buryin' and all. Like you done with my other dead child." Othella fell back onto the bed and breathed hard, thankful that her ordeal was over. "It just don't add up. Her comin' dead. She seemed so healthy in my belly. With all that kickin' and flippin' and floppin' and all. I even dreamed about her. A bad dream. I dreamed she was a happy little girl what got took away. Death or somethin'."

"Nothin' but the devil lettin' you know he was sendin' her here dead. I done told you Satan's a low-down, funky black dog! He the one responsible for me bein' big as a Cadillac!" Ruby retorted, lifting one of her heavy legs for Othella to inspect.

Othella examined Ruby's leg and nodded.

"What about the beer?"

"What about it?" Ruby returned her leg to its place. "I wish I didn't have to drink so much of it."

"That the devil, too? He the reason you drink so much?"

Ruby sighed and shook her head slowly.

"I'm a alcoholic," she admitted.

They got silent and looked at the baby again.

"Othella, let's name this one."

Othella looked from the baby to Ruby, then back to the baby.

"We didn't name that last one what come here dead. Why you want to waste up a good name on a dead baby?"

"Well . . . it's just that . . . this one different. The other one was a boy. You know yourself how bad I been wantin' me a little girl. We can make out like this one was mine. You know, play like I gave birth to her." Ruby smiled crookedly, waiting for Othella's response.

"Mama Ruby, I can't do that! It ain't Christian."

"Ain't nobody but me and you got to know."

"God'll know. Satan'll know. All Satan need is us to do some more backslidin' so he can go to meddlin' me and you again."

Ruby let out her breath and looked up at the ceiling.

"I just want . . . I just want me a daughter," she cried.

"Have mercy," Othella whispered, watching Ruby's tears slide down the sides of her face and onto her bosom.

"Let me name her and make out like she mine," Ruby pleaded, looking in Othella's eyes. Ruby held the baby against her and swayed from side to side. "Please, Othella."

"Stop actin' crazy, Ruby! Feed them kids of mine before you go back home. Hear me?"

"You goin' to let me name this child. That clear?" Ruby said in a low voice, frightening Othella.

"I . . . I . . . don't know. Um . . . Mama Ruby, please go in my kitchen and hunt around for somethin' for them kids of mine to sop up. Some buttermilk and cornbread. Or some molasses and tea cakes. Grits'll do."

"Othella, I ain't playin' with you now. . . . Let me name this baby and make out like she was mine!"

"Lord, that's just what you use to say when we was kids and you wanted my girl dolls. Just before you would maul my head with your fist . . . uh . . . uh . . . if it mean that much to you, you can name her, Ruby."

Ruby's eyes got wide and she smiled.

"I'm namin' her for Miss Mo'reen," Ruby said.

"I hope you happy. You write Miss Mo'reen a letter and tell her she got a dead baby named after her! Miss Mo'reen busy runnin' her sportin' house. You think she care about some dead baby named for her?"

"I don't care if Miss Mo'reen care or not. I don't care if nobody care. I can say I had me a baby girl I named Mo'reen," Ruby said, dancing around the room, cradling the baby.

Othella shook her head and laughed.

"Okay now. Time for you to stop actin' the fool you is. Feed my kids and go home so I can get me some rest. Tell that boy Clyde to get you a shoe box out the chifforobe to bury that baby in."

As soon as Ruby had set out food on the kitchen table and arranged the noisy children in an orderly fashion, she left Othella's house.

It was dark outside. Lightning bugs led the way as Ruby returned to her shack through the bayou. She stopped and looked up at the glowing moon, the shoe box containing Maureen held against her bosom. She kissed the shoe box and thanked God for letting her get this close to having her own daughter.

Outside her house, Ruby spoke to Maureen.

"You is my very own little girl. I prayed to get you and I got you."

Virgil appeared in the living room window and snatched it open.

"Mama Ruby, what you doin' out there in the dark? What you mumblin' about?" he asked.

Before Ruby could respond, Virgil came out on the porch holding a coal-oil lamp. Alice Mae followed behind him.

"What you got, Mama Ruby? Who you talkin' to?" Virgil said, holding the lamp up high.

"Who me? Huh? Oh . . . I was talkin' to these mangy coon dogs what's blockin' my way! Shoo! Shoo! Get out my front yard." The two snoozing hounds ignored her.

Virgil looked at her suspiciously.

"You wasn't talkin' to no coon dogs a minute ago. . . ."

"I was talkin' to myself," Ruby lied, annoyed.

"Mama Ruby, Virgil went up side my head with a spoon 'cause I told you he let me play with your teeth," Alice Mae complained. "I got a risin' on my head already."

"I'll get him, Alice Mae," Ruby said calmly, unlike her usual self. This made Virgil even more suspicious.

"Mama Ruby, what you got—aw, damn!" he cursed. He held the lamp out toward Ruby and saw that she carried a shoe box. It meant only one thing. "Another dead baby I got to be up half the night diggin' a grave for!"

———————

"Is this here enough, Mama Ruby?" Virgil asked as he held out an armful of newspaper. They stood in Ruby's cool, dimly lit kitchen over a table cluttered with plates and pots and pans. They had eaten the cabbage Virgil had finished cooking while Ruby was with Othella. Bread crumbs, empty plates, beer cans, and assorted bones lay scattered about the table.

"Yeah. Little as this child is, she won't be needin' that much paper to be wrapped up in," Ruby replied. She took the paper from Virgil and looked at him, blinking her eyes rapidly. He looked up at her and bit his bottom lip.

"What's the matter with you now? You standin' here lookin' at me like I'm somethin' good to eat," he murmured.

"I thought I heard somethin'. Like somebody cryin'," Ruby replied in a whisper.

"Aw, you ain't heard nothin'." Virgil waved his hand in her face. "And you hurry your slow self on here. You been had this dead baby layin' around a whole hour."

"Did you walk Alice Mae all the way home?"

"I walked her to the clearin'," Virgil answered.

"You was supposed to walk that child all the way home, boy! You want her to get snatched up by some maniac?"

"Mama Ruby, everybody say you the only maniac in Silo," Virgil answered seriously, with his hands on his hips.

Ruby looked away and thought about what Virgil said. She turned to face him again and quickly slapped him alongside his face with the newspaper.

"Boy, I did hear somebody cryin'. You go take a look-see out on that back porch and see if that girl Alice Mae is out there. That clear?"

"Yes, ma'am."

Virgil went to the kitchen door and opened it angrily, as Ruby stood looking at him. He leaned his head out and looked around quickly. Convinced that there was no one on the back porch, he slammed the door shut and returned to Ruby.

"Ain't nobody out there. You must be hearin' things, Mama Ruby."

"I know doggone well I heard somethin'. Moanin' and groanin'."

Virgil gave Ruby a thoughtful look.

"It was probably your conscience," he suggested. Ruby slapped his face with the newspaper again. He only laughed and made a face at her as she walked over to the kitchen counter where the baby lay.

Virgil followed behind Ruby, stepping on the back of her heels. She turned to swat him with the newspaper again, but he dropped to his knees and confused her by snatching the tail of her duster.

"Get up from that floor, boy! We got work to do."

Virgil leaped up and stood next to Ruby as she bent over the counter.

"Where we goin' to bury this one at, Mama Ruby?"

"Down in the bayou, I guess. Down there where we buried that ol' meddlin' government man what come snoopin' around here last month axin' questions about me and a stole income tax check. . . ."

"Oh. Mama Ruby, wonder how come nobody ever come lookin' for that ol' man."

"Oh, they come all right. Another peckerwood with a bad attitude. Axin' me them same questions. Plus axin' me about that one what come before him."

"Hmmmm. I didn't know another government man had come meddlin' you."

"Come tomorrow . . . I'll show you where *he's* buried. . . ." Ruby closed her eyes and shook her head. "I'm out here in these swamps mindin' my own business. Dedicatin' my soul to the Lord. I don't know why folks come out here to meddle me. I don't mess with nobody . . . lest they mess with me. Nothin' but the devil." Ruby opened her eyes and looked at the baby.

"How come we ain't puttin' this baby where them other dead babies is buried? Othella's other dead baby. Anna Simpson's dead baby. All them other dead babies you done birthed."

" 'Cause I want to get this took care of tonight. These dog days. We was to let this baby set out all night she liable to bust wide open. Remember that time me and Othella forgot we had that dead rabbit in the chicken coop last summer during dog days? You remember how it swole up from the heat and busted? I know you don't want no busted baby to be cleanin' up." Ruby looked at Virgil and wiggled her nose.

"Good God, no! Ain't nothin' worse than busted, rotted humans. Remember that time that man tried to rape Othella and we put him in the chicken coop?"

"Yeah. Just like that rabbit, we forgot he was in there. That sucker popped wide open. We couldn't get the stink out of these woods for weeks. I thank God it was the season of flowers then. Lilacs, magnolias, dandelions, and lilies perfumin' the air," Ruby recalled.

". . . Mama Ruby . . . you ever . . . I mean . . . well, what I'm tryin' to say is, you ever think about them folks we done chastised? I mean, sometime at night I be layin' in the bed thinkin' about it. I use to have dreams about dead folks comin' to haunt us," Virgil said.

Ruby shook her head and tapped her bare foot.

"Boy, I ain't done nothin' Jesus wouldn't do."

Virgil gasped and moved back.

"But, Mama Ruby—"

"But what?" Ruby said, with her eyebrows arched.

"Nothin' . . ."

"What you lookin' at me so funny for now, boy?"

"I guess I don't know all I need to know about Jesus, huh?"

"I guess you don't. Let me tell you somethin', boy. I carry Jesus with me everywhere I go. I always have. On account of that was how I was raised. I know I ain't perfect, wasn't nobody perfect but Jesus, but I apply myself to the Bible to a T."

"Remember that time we was comin' back from Miami and that spic gave us a ride?"

"The one what got to my house and sucked up all my beer, then had a notion to rape me?"

"Rape you? I didn't know he'd a notion to rape you! Did he try to rape you, sho nuff, Mama Ruby?"

"No—but he wanted to. Why else would we carry him to the swamp? Me and you and Othella and Clyde."

"Oh. I didn't know no more than what you told me. You just made me and Clyde empty his pockets and dig a hole. Seem like we could have sent him on back to Miami. Him bein' so drunk and all. I kind of liked that spic. He was all right by me. Give me a whole quarter. He give Clyde one, too." Virgil dropped his head and stared at the floor. "Sometime, Mama Ruby, I go to thinkin'. What if—what's wrong, sugar?" Virgil was interrupted by Ruby's frantic sobs. "What you cryin' for?"

Ruby removed a handkerchief from the pocket of her duster and began to cry harder, wiping her eyes and nose vigorously.

"I've done all I could to be a Christian mama. I never dreamed my own son would question my ways. Boy, I do what the Lord tells me to do. I ain't never tetched nobody what ain't had it comin'. That spic, he was better off dead. Couldn't speak no more English than a year-old baby. Now you tell me . . . what good was he to anybody?"

"Well, them other spics, they speak spic. I seen 'em do it. Plus the man said he had a woman and some kids somewhere. It don't seem right, him gettin' hisself kilt like he done. What all he do, anyway?"

"He was a rapist, for one thing," Ruby snapped. "What else reason did we need?"

"Oh . . . let's change the subject, Mama Ruby. I get a chill when we talk about the folks we done chastised."

Ruby returned her handkerchief to her pocket and cleared her throat.

"You know somethin', Mama Ruby, too bad we live so far from town. It would be nice to get this baby embalmed or somethin'." Virgil touched the baby.

"We ain't got no time for all that red tape. You think we white folks or somethin'? We fixin' to bury this baby soon as I get her wrapped up. Poor little ol' thing. Cutest little drink of water I ever seen."

"Sho nuff is. I noticed that right off when you opened that shoe box."

Ruby wrapped the baby as she hummed a spiritual. Once wrapped, the package resembled a small loaf of bread. As Ruby placed the package on the kitchen table, a colorful newspaper advertisement displaying kites caught Virgil's eye.

Ruby waddled across the floor to her icebox, where she removed a can of beer. She stomped and ground a roach on the floor with so much wrath the loose planks rose and fell awkwardly back into place.

"Where is my can opener, Virgil?" she bellowed.

"I don't know. You the only one what uses it, you ought to make it your business to know all the time." Virgil spoke without looking up from the newspaper. "Mama Ruby, can I have a dime so I can get me one of these here kites?" He lifted the neatly wrapped package as Ruby searched for her can opener. To read the advertisement better, Virgil began to unwrap the newspaper that contained the infant.

"What in the world is you doin', boy?!" Ruby shouted. She rushed back across the floor and thumped Virgil's head with her fingers.

"YOWWWW!" he screamed.

"What you call yourself doin' to that baby?"

"I'm goin' to wrap her back up! I was just tryin' to see these kites better! Don't you go up side my head no more, Mama Ruby! Shoot! I got so many risin's on my head from you maulin' it! You do it again, I'm goin' to learn you a lesson you won't forget!"

Ruby attacked the boy's head with both hands this time.

"YOWWWWW!" he cried, trembling and waving his arms about. "I declare! I ain't goin' to sass you no more, Mama Ruby! Stop maulin' my head!"

Ruby turned her attention from Virgil back to the baby. She quietly began rewrapping. Suddenly she froze, her eyes bugged out, and her mouth fell open.

"What's the matter, Mama Ruby?!"

"Virgil, that baby moved just now! She ain't dead!"

MAMA DAY

Gloria Naylor

You were picking your teeth with a plastic straw—I know, I know, it wasn't
really a straw, it was a coffee stirrer. But, George, let's be fair, there are two
little openings in those things that you could possibly suck liquid through if
you were desperate enough, so I think I'm justified in calling it a straw since
dumps like that Third Avenue coffee shop had no shame in calling it a
coffee stirrer, when the stuff they poured into your cup certainly didn't qualify
as coffee. Everything about those types of places was a little more or less
than they should have been. I was always thrown off balance: the stainless
steel display cases were too clean, and did you ever notice that the cakes and
pies inside of them never made crumbs when they were cut, and no juice
ever dripped from the cantaloupes and honeydews? The Formica tabletops
were a bit too slippery for your elbows, and the smell of those red vinyl
seats—always red vinyl—seeped into the taste of your food, which came
warm if it was a hot dish and warm if it was a cold dish. I swear to you,
once I got warm pistachio ice cream and it was solid as a rock. Those places
in New York were designed for assembly-line nutrition, and it worked—
there was nothing in there to encourage you to linger. Especially when the
bill came glued to the bottom of your dessert plate—who would want to ask

for a second cup of coffee and have to sit there watching a big greasy thumbprint spread slowly over the "Thank You" printed on the back?

I suppose you had picked up the stirrer for your coffee because you'd already used the teaspoon for your soup. I saw the waitress bring you the Wednesday special, and that meant pea soup, which had to be attacked quickly before it lumped up. So not risking another twenty-minute wait for a soup spoon, you used your teaspoon, which left you without anything to use in your coffee when it came with the bill. And obviously you knew that our pleasant waitress's "Catch ya in a men-it, babe," doomed you to either your finger, a plastic stirrer, or coffee straight up. And you used plenty of sugar and milk. That guy knows the art of dining successfully on Third Avenue, I thought. When the lunch menu has nothing priced above six dollars, it's make do if you're gonna make it back to work without ulcers.

And there wasn't a doubt in my mind that you were going back to some office or somewhere definite after that meal. It wasn't just the short-sleeved blue shirt and tie; you ate with a certain ease and decisiveness that spelled *employed* with each forkful of their stringy roast beef. Six months of looking for a job had made me an expert at picking out the people who, like me, were hurrying up to wait—in somebody's outer anything for a chance to make it through their inner doors to prove that you could type two words a minute, or not drool on your blouse while answering difficult questions about your middle initial and date of birth.

By that August I had it down to a science, although the folks here would say that I was gifted with a bit of Mama Day's second sight. Second sight had nothing to do with it: in March of that year coats started coming off, and it was the kind of April that already had you dodging spit from the air conditioners along the side streets, so by midsummer I saw it all hanging out—those crisp butterflies along the avenues, their dresses still holding the sharp edges of cloth that had been under cool air all morning in some temperature-controlled box. Or the briefcases that hung near some guy's thigh with a balance that said there was more in them than empty partitions and his gym shorts. And I guess being a woman, I could always tell hair: heads are held differently when they've been pampered every week, the necks massaged to relax tense muscles "so the layers will fall right, dear." The blonds in their Dutch-boy cuts, my counterparts in Jerri curls, those Asian women who had to do practically nothing to be gorgeous with theirs so they frizzed it or chopped it off, because then everybody knew they had the thirty-five dollars a week to keep it looking that way. Yeah, that group all had jobs. And it was definitely first sight on any evening rush-hour train: all those open-neck cotton shirts—always plaid or colored—with the dried sweat marks under the arms of riders who had the privilege of a seat before the northbound

IRT hit midtown because those men had done their stint in the factories, warehouses, and loading docks farther down on Delancey or in East New York or Brooklyn.

But it took a little extra attention for the in-betweens: figuring out which briefcases that swung with the right weight held only pounds of résumés, or which Gucci appointment books had the classifieds neatly clipped out and taped onto the pages so you'd think she was expected wherever she was heading instead of just expected to wait. I have to admit, the appointment-book scam took a bit of originality and class. That type knew that a newspaper folded to the last section was a dead giveaway. And I don't know who the others were trying to fool by pretending to scan the headlines and editorial page before going to the classifieds and there finally creasing the paper and shifting it an inch or two closer to their faces. When all else failed, I was left with watching the way they walked—either too determined or too hesitantly through some revolving door on Sixth Avenue. Misery loves company, and that's exactly what I was searching for on the streets during that crushing August in New York. I out-and-out resented the phonies, and when I could pick one out I felt a little better about myself. At least I was being real: I didn't have a job, and I wanted one—badly. When your unemployment checks have a remaining life span that's shorter than a tsetse fly's, and you know that temp agencies are barely going to pay your rent, and all the doorways around Times Square are already taken by very determined-looking ladies, masquerades go right out the window. It's begging your friends for a new lead every other day, a newspaper folded straight to the classifieds, and a cup of herb tea and the house salad anywhere the bill will come in under two bucks with a table near the air conditioner.

While you finished your lunch and were trying to discreetly get the roast beef from between your teeth, I had twenty minutes before the next cattle call. I was to be in the herd slotted between one and three at the Andrews & Stein Engineering Company. And if my feet hadn't swollen because I'd slipped off my high heels under the table, I might have gone over and offered you one of the mint-flavored toothpicks I always carried around with me. I'd met quite a few guys in restaurants with my box of toothpicks: it was a foolproof way to start up a conversation once I'd checked out what they ordered and how they ate it. The way a man chews can tell you loads about the kind of lover he'll turn out to be. Don't laugh—meat is meat. And you had given those three slabs of roast beef a consideration they didn't deserve, so I actually played with the idea that you might be worth the pain of forcing on my shoes. You had nice teeth and strong, blunt fingers, and your nails were clean but, thank God, not manicured. I had been trying to figure out what you did for a living. The combination of a short-sleeved colored shirt and knit tie could mean anything from security guard to eccentric V.P. Regardless, anyone who preferred a plastic stirrer over that open saucer of toothpicks near the cash register, collecting flecks of ear wax and grease from a hundred rummaging fingernails, at least had common sense if not a high regard for the finer points of etiquette.

But when you walked past me, I let you and the idea go. My toothpicks had already gotten me two dates in the last month: one whole creep and a half creep. I could have gambled that my luck was getting progressively better and you'd only be a quarter creep. But even so, meeting a quarter creep in a Third Avenue coffee shop usually meant he'd figure that I would consider a free lecture on the mating habits of African violets at the Botanical Gardens and dinner at a Greek restaurant—red vinyl *booths*—a step up. That much this Southern girl had learned: there was a definite relationship between where you met some guy in New York and where he asked you out. Now, getting picked up in one of those booths at a Greek restaurant meant dinner at a mid-drawer ethnic: Mexican, Chinese, southern Italian, with real table-cloths but under glass shields, and probably Off-Broadway tickets. And if you hooked into someone at one of *those* restaurants, then it was out to top-drawer ethnic: northern Italian, French, Russian, or Continental, with wait-ers, not waitresses, and balcony seats on Broadway. East Side restaurants, Village jazz clubs, and orchestra seats at Lincoln Center were nights out with the pool you found available at Maxwell's Plum or any singles bar *above* Fifty-ninth Street on the East Side, and *below* Ninety-sixth on the West.

I'd never graduated to the bar scene because I didn't drink and refused to pay three-fifty for a club soda until the evening bore returns. Some of my friends said that you could run up an eighteen-dollar tab in no time that way, only to luck out with a pink quarter creep who figured that because you were a black woman it was down to mid-drawer ethnic for dinner the next week. And if he was a brown quarter creep, he had waited just before closing time to pick up the tab for your last drink. And if you didn't show the proper amount of gratitude for a hand on your thigh and an invitation to his third-floor walk-up into paradise, you got told in so many words that your bad attitude was the exact reason why he had come there looking for white girls in the first place.

I sound awful, don't I? Well, those were awful times for a single woman in that city of yours. There was something so desperate and sad about it all—especially for my friends. You know, Selma kept going to those fancy singles bars, insisting that was the only way to meet "certain" black men. And she did meet them, those who certainly weren't looking for her. Then it was in Central Park, of all places, that she snagged this doctor. Not just any doctor, a Park Avenue neurosurgeon. After only three months he was hinting marriage, and she was shouting to us about a future of douching with Chanel No. 5, using laminated dollar bills for shower curtains—the whole bit. And the sad thing wasn't really how it turned out—I mean, as weird as it was when he finally told her that he was going to have a sex-change operation, but he was waiting for the right woman who was also willing to get one along with him, because he'd never dream of sleeping with another man— even after the operation; weirder—and much sadder—than all of that, George, was the fact that she debated seriously about following him to Denmark and doing it. So let me tell you, my toothpicks, as small a gesture as they were, helped me to stay on top of all that madness.

I finally left the coffee shop and felt whatever life that might have been revived in my linen suit and hair wilting away. How could it get so hot along Third Avenue when the buildings blocked out the sunlight? When I had come to New York seven years before that, I wondered about the need for such huge buildings. No one ever seemed to be in them for very long; everyone was out on the sidewalks, moving, moving, moving—and to where? My first month I was determined to find out. I followed a woman once: she had a beehive hairdo with rhinestone bobby pins along the side of her head that matched the rhinestones on her tinted cat-eyed glasses. Her thumbnails were the only ones polished, in a glossy lacquer on both hands, and they were so long they had curled under like hooks. I figured that she was so strange no one would ever notice me trailing her. We began on Fifty-third Street and Sixth Avenue near the Sheraton, moved west to Eighth Avenue before turning right, where she stopped at a Korean fruit stand, bought a kiwi, and walked along peeling the skin with her thumbnails. I lost her at Columbus Circle; she threw the peeled fruit uneaten into a trash can and took the escalator down into the subway. As she was going down, another woman was coming up the escalator with two bulging plastic bags. This one took me along Broadway up to where it meets Columbus Avenue at Sixty-third, and she sat down on one of those benches in the traffic median with her bags between her knees. She kept beating her heels against the sides and it sounded as if she had loose pots and pans in them. A really distinguished-looking guy with a tweed jacket and gray sideburns got up from the bench the moment she sat down, went into a flower shop across Columbus Avenue, came out empty-handed, and I followed him back downtown toward the Circle until we got to the entrance to Central Park. He slowed up, turned around, looked me straight in the face, and smiled. That's when I noticed that he had diaper pins holding his fly front together—you know, the kind they used to have with pink rabbit heads on them. I never thought anyone could beat my Central Park story until Selma met her neurosurgeon there. After that guy I gave up—I was exhausted by that time anyway. I hated to walk, almost as much as I hated the subways. There's something hypocritical about a city that keeps half of its population underground half of the time; you can start believing that there's much more space than there really is— to live, to work. And I had trouble doing both in spite of those endless classifieds in the Sunday *Times*. You know, there are more pages in just their Help Wanted section than in the telephone book here in Willow Springs. But it took me a while to figure out that New York racism moved underground like most of the people did.

Mama Day and Grandma had told me that there was a time when the want ads and housing listings in newspapers—even up north—were clearly marked colored or white. It must have been wonderfully easy to go job hunting then. You were spared a lot of legwork and headwork. And how I longed for those times, when I was busting my butt up and down the streets. I said as much at one of those parties Selma was always giving for her certain people. You would've thought I had announced that they were really drinking domestic wine, the place got that quiet. One of her certain people was so upset his voice shook. "You mean, you want to bring back segregation?" I looked at him like he was a fool—Where had it gone? I just wanted to bring the clarity about it back—it would save me a whole lot of subway tokens. What I was left to deal with were the ads labeled *Equal Opportunity Employer*, or nothing—which might as well have been labeled *Colored apply* or *Take your chances*. And if I wanted to limit myself to the sure bets, then it was an equal opportunity to be what, or earn what? That's where the headwork came in.

It's like the ad I was running down that afternoon: a one-incher in Monday's paper for an office manager. A long job description so there wasn't enough room to print Equal Opportunity Employer even if they were. They hadn't advertised Sunday, because I'd double-checked. They didn't want to get lost among the full and half columns the agencies ran. Obviously, a small operation. *Andrews & Stein Engineering Company*: it was half Jewish at least, so that said liberal—maybe. Or maybe they only wanted their own. I had never seen any Jewish people except on television until I arrived in New York. I had heard that they were clannish, and coming from Willow Springs I could identify with that. *Salary competitive*: that could mean anything, depending upon whether they were competing with Burger King or IBM. *Position begins September 1st*: that was the clincher, with all the other questions hanging in the balance. If I got the job, I could still go home for mid-August. Even if I didn't get it, I was going home. Mama Day and Grandma could forgive me for leaving Willow Springs, but not for staying away.

I got to the address and found exactly what I had feared. A six-floor office building—low-rent district, if you could call anything low in New York. Andrews & Stein was suite 511. The elevator, like the ancient marble foyer and maroon print carpeting on the fifth floor, was worn but carefully maintained. Dimly lit hallways to save on overhead, and painted walls that looked just a month short of needing a fresh coat. I could see that the whole building was being held together by some dedicated janitor who was probably near retirement. Oh, no, if these folks were going to hire me, it would be for peanuts. Operations renting space in a place like this shelled out decent salaries only for Mr. Stein's brainless niece, or Mr. Andrews's current lay. Well, you're here, Cocoa, I thought, go through the motions.

The cherry vanilla who buzzed me in the door was predictable, but there might still be reason for hope. When small, liberal establishments put a fudge cream behind their glass reception cages, there were rarely any more back in the offices. Sticking you out front let them sleep pretty good at night, thinking they'd put the ghost of Martin Luther King to rest. There were three other women there ahead of me, and one very very gay Oriental. God, those were rare—at least in my circles. The four of them already had clipboards and were filling out one-page applications—mimeographed. Cherry Vanilla was pleasant enough. She apologized for there being no more seats, and told me I had to wait until one of the clipboards was free unless I had something to write on. A small, small operation. But she wasn't pouring out that oily politeness that's normally used to slide you quietly out of any chance of getting the job. One of the women sitting there filling out an application was actually licorice. Her hair was in deep body waves with the sheen of patent leather, and close as I was, I couldn't tell where her hair ended and her skin began. And she had the body and courage to wear a Danskin top as tight as it was red. I guess that lady said, You're going to see me coming from a mile away, like it or not. I bet a lot of men did like it. If they were replacing Mr. Andrews's bimbo, she'd get the job. And the way she looked me up and down—dismissing my washed-out complexion and wilted linen suit—made me want to push out my pathetic chest, but that meant bringing in my nonexistent hips. Forget it, I thought, you're standing here with no tits, no ass, and no color. So console yourself with the fantasy that she's mixed up her addresses and is applying for the wrong job. Why else come to an interview in an outfit that would look better the wetter it got, unless you wanted to be a lifeguard? I could dismiss the other two women right away—milk shakes. One had her résumés typed on different shades of pastel paper and she was shifting through them, I guess trying to figure out which one matched the decor of the office. The other had forgotten her social security card and wanted to know if she should call home for the number. To be stupid enough not to memorize it was one thing, but not to know enough to sit there and shut up about it was beyond witless. I didn't care if Andrews & Stein was a front for the American Nazi party, she didn't have a chance. So the only serious contenders in that bunch were me, Patent Leather Hair, and the kumquat.

I inherited the clipboard from the one who'd forgotten her social security card, and she was in and out still babbling about that damn number before I had gotten down to Educational Background. Beyond high school there was just two years in business school in Atlanta—but I'd graduated at the top of my class. It was work experience that really counted for a job like this. This wasn't the type of place where you'd worry about moving up—all of those boxes and file cabinets crowded behind the receptionist's shoulder—it was simply a matter of moving around.

One job in seven years looked very good—with a fifty percent increase in salary. Duties: diverse, and more complex as I went along. The insurance company simply folded, that's all. If I'd stayed, I probably would have gone on to be an underwriter—but I was truly managing that office. Twelve secretaries, thirty-five salesmen, six adjusters, and one greedy president who didn't have the sense to avoid insuring half of the buildings in the South Bronx—even at triple premiums for fire and water damage. Those crooked landlords made a bundle, and every time I saw someone with a cigarette lighter, I cringed. I was down to Hobbies—which always annoyed me; what does your free time have to do with them?—when Patent Leather Hair was called in. She stood up the way women do knowing they look better when all of them is at last in view. I wondered what she had put down for extra-curricular activities. I sighed and crossed my legs. It was going to be a long wait. After twenty minutes Kumquat smiled over at me sympathetically—at least we both knew that he didn't have a possible ace in the hole anymore.

The intercom button on the receptionist's phone lit up, and when she got off she beckoned to the Oriental guy.

"Mr. Andrews is still interviewing, so Mr. Stein will have to see you. Just take your application to the second door on the left, Mr. Weisman."

He grinned at me again as I felt my linen suit losing its final bit of crispness under the low-voltage air conditioner. God, I wanted to go home—and I meant, home home. With all of Willow Springs's problems, you knew when you saw a catfish, you called it a catfish.

Well, Weisman was in and out pretty fast. I told myself for the thousandth time, Nothing about New York is ever going to surprise me anymore. Stein was probably anti-Semitic. It was another ten minutes and I was still sitting there and really starting to get ticked off. Couldn't Mr. Stein see me as well? No, she'd just put through a long-distance call from a client, but Mr. Andrews would be ready for me soon. I seriously doubted it. He was in there trying to convince Patent Leather that even though she thought she was applying for a position as a lifeguard, they could find room for someone with her potential. I didn't give her the satisfaction of my half-hour wait when she came flaming out—I was busily reading the wrapper on my pack of Trident, having ditched my newspaper before I came in. The thing was irreversibly creased at the classifieds, my bag was too small to hide it, and you never wanted to look that desperate at an interview. And there weren't even any old issues of *Popular Mechanics* or something in the waiting area—bottom drawer all the way.

I was finally buzzed into the inner sanctum, and without a shred of hope walked past the clutter of file cabinets through another door that opened into a deceptively large network of smaller offices. I entered the third on the left as I'd been instructed and there you were: blue shirt, knitted tie, nice teeth, and all. Feeling the box of mint toothpicks press against my thigh through the mesh bag as I sat down and crossed my legs, I smiled sincerely for the first time that day.

Until you walked into my office that afternoon, I would have never called myself a superstitious man. Far from it. To believe in fate or predestination means you have to believe there's a future, and I grew up without one. It was either that or not grow up at all. Our guardians at the Wallace P. Andrews Shelter for Boys were adamant about the fact that we learned to invest in ourselves alone. "Keep it in the now, fellas," Chip would say, chewing on his bottom right jaw and spitting as if he still had the plug of tobacco in there Mrs. Jackson refused to let him use in front of us. And I knew I'd hear her until the day I died. "Only the present has potential, *sir.*" I could see her even then, the way she'd jerk up the face, gripping the chin of some kid who was crying because his last foster home hadn't worked out, or because he was teased at school about not having a mother. She'd even reach up and clamp on to some muscled teenager who was trying to excuse a bad report card. I could still feel the ache in my bottom lip from the relentless grip of her thumb and forefinger pressed into the bone of my chin—"Only the present has potential, *sir.*"

They may not have been loving people, she and Chip—or when you think about it, even lovable. But they were devoted to their jobs if not to us individually. And Mrs. Jackson saw part of her job as making sure that that scraggly bunch of misfits—misfitted into somebody's game plan so we were thrown away—would at least hear themselves addressed with respect. There were so many boys and the faces kept changing, she was getting old and never remembered our individual names and didn't try to hide it. All of us were beneath poor, most of us were black or Puerto Rican, so it was very likely that this would be the first and last time in our lives anyone would call us "sir." And if talking to you and pinching the skin off your chin didn't work, she was not beneath enforcing those same words with a brown leather strap—a man's belt with the buckle removed. We always wondered where she'd gotten a man's belt. You could look at Mrs. Jackson and tell she'd never been a Mrs., the older boys would say. Or if she had snagged some poor slob a thousand years ago, he never could have gotten it up over her to need to undo his pants. But that was said only well out of her earshot after she had lashed one of them across the back or arms. She'd bring that belt down with a cold precision that was more frightening than the pain she was causing, and she'd bring it down for exactly ten strokes—one for each syllable: "Only the present has potential, sir."

No boy was touched above the neck or below his waist in front. And she never, ever hit the ones—regardless of their behavior—who had come to Wallace P. Andrews with fractured arms or cigarette burns on their groins. For those she'd take away dinner plus breakfast the next morning, and even lunch if she felt they warranted it. Bernie Sinclair passed out that way once, and when he woke up in the infirmary she was standing over him explaining that he had remained unconscious past the dinner he *still* would have been deprived of if he hadn't fainted.

Cruel? No, I would call it controlled. Bernie had spit in her face. And she never altered her expression, either when it happened during hygiene check or when she stood over him in the infirmary. Bernie had come to us with half of his teeth busted out, and he hated brushing the other half. She was going down the usual morning lineup for the boys under twelve, checking fingernails, behind ears, calling for the morning stretch (hands above head, legs spread, knees bent, and bounce) to detect unwashed armpits and crotches. Bernie wouldn't open his mouth for her and was getting his daily list of facts (she never lectured, she called it listing simple facts): if the remainder of his teeth rotted out from lack of personal care, then the dentist would have to fit him for a full plate instead of a partial plate. And it would take her twice as long to requisition twice the money that would then be needed from the state. That would lead to him spending twice as long being teased at school and restricted to a soft diet in the cafeteria. She said this like she did everything—slowly, clearly, and without emotion. For the second time she bent over and told him to open his mouth. He did, and sent a wad of spit against her right cheek. Even Joey Santiago cringed—all six feet and almost two hundred pounds of him. But Mrs. Jackson never blinked. She took out the embroidered handkerchief she kept in her rolled-up blouse sleeve and wiped her face as she listed another set of facts: she had asked him twice, she never asked any child to do anything more than twice—those

were the rules at Wallace P. Andrews. No lunch, no dinner, and he still
had his full share of duties. I guess that's why he passed out, no food under
the hot sun and weeding our garden—that and fear of what she was really
going to do to him for spitting on her. He was still new and didn't understand
that she was going to do nothing at all.

Our rage didn't matter to her, our hurts or disappointments over what
life had done to us. None of that was going to matter a damn in the outside
world, so we might as well start learning it at Wallace P. Andrews. There
were only rules and facts. Mrs. Jackson's world out there on Staten Island
had rules that you could argue might not be fair, but they were consistent.
And when they were broken we were guaranteed that, however she had to
do it, we would be made to *feel* responsibility for our present actions—and
our actions alone. And oddly enough, we understood that those punishments
were an improvement upon our situations: before coming there, we had
been beaten and starved just for being born.

And she was the only person on the staff allowed to touch us. Even
Chip, who had the role of "good cop" to her "bad cop"—you needed a
shoulder to cry on sometimes—could only recommend discipline. It must
have been difficult with sixty boys, and I'd seen some kids really provoke a
dorm director or workshop leader, and the guy would never lay a hand on
them. They all knew her rules, and it was clear those men were afraid of
her. And I could never figure it out, even with the rumor that was going
around, which Joey Santiago swore by. Joey was a notorious liar, but he was
the oldest guy there when I was growing up. And he said that some years
back there was a dorm director who used to sneak into the rooms where we
had the "rubber sheet jockeys"—kids under eight—and take them into the
bathroom. After he was finished with them, they'd fall asleep on the toilet,
where he'd make them sit until their rectums stopped bleeding. Mrs. Jackson
and Chip came over one night, caught him at it, and she told the boys she
was going to call the police. They took him back to the old stucco house
she lived in on the grounds. The police car never came, but her basement
lights stayed on. And Joey swore you could hear that man screaming throughout the entire night, although all of her windows were bolted down. It was
loud enough to even wake up the older ones in the other dorms. That man
was never seen again, and they knew better than to question Mrs. Jackson
when she came over to pack up his things herself. And Chip had absolutely
nothing to say about what had happened but "Keep it in the now, fellas" as
he dug Mrs. Jackson a new rose garden the following morning. Every staff
member and boy who came to Wallace P. Andrews heard that rumor and,
one way or another, went over to see those roses in the corner of her garden.
I can only tell you this, they were incredibly large and beautiful. And in the

summer, when the evening breeze came from the east, their fragrance was strong enough to blanket your sleep.

Some thought that I was her favorite. I was one of the few who had grown up there through the nursery, and she couldn't punish me the way she did them, because I had a congenital heart condition. So she took away my books, knowing that I'd rather give up food or even have her use her strap. And once pleaded with her to do so, because I said I'd die if I had to wait a full week to find out how the Count of Monte Cristo escaped from prison. She said that was a fitting death for little boys who were caught cheating on their math exams. But fractions are hard, and I wanted a good grade at the end of the term. Ah, so I was worried about the *end* of the term? Well, she would now keep my books for two weeks. "Only the present has potential, *sir.*"

And the discipline she tailor-made for all of us said, like it or not, the present is *you*. And what else did we have but ourselves? We had a more than forgettable past and no future that was guaranteed. And she never let us pretend that anything else was the case as she'd often listed the facts of life: I am not your mother. I am paid to run this place. You have no mothers or fathers. This is not your home. And it is not a prison—it is a state shelter for boys. And it is not a dumping ground for delinquents, rejects, or somebody's garbage, because you are not delinquents, rejects, or garbage—you are boys. It is not a place to be tortured, exploited, or raped. It is a state shelter for boys. Here you have a clean room, decent food, and clothing for each season because it is a shelter. There is a library in which you study for three hours after school—and you *will* go to school, because you are boys. When you are eighteen, the state says you are men. And when you are men you leave here to go where and do what you want. But you stay here until you are men.

Yes, those were the facts of life at Wallace P. Andrews. And those were her methods. And if any of the boys complained to the state inspectors about being punished, nothing was ever done. I guess at the bottom line, she saved them money. We grew and canned a lot of our own food, painted our own dorms, made most of the furniture, and even sewed curtains and bedspreads. And the ones she turned out weren't a burden on the state, either. I don't know of anyone who became a drug addict, petty thief, or a derelict. I guess it's because you grew up with absolutely no illusions about yourself or the world. Most of us went from there either to college or into a trade. No, it wasn't the kind of place that turned out many poets or artists—those who could draw became draftsmen, and the musicians were taught to tune pianos. If she erred in directing our careers, she erred on the side of caution. Sure, the arts were waiting for poor black kids who were encouraged to dream big, and so was death row.

Looking back, I can see how easy it would have been for her to let us just sit there and reach the right age to get out. It only takes time for a man to grow older, but how many of them grow up? And I couldn't have grown up if I had wasted my time crying about a family I wasn't given or believing in a future that I didn't have. When I left Wallace P. Andrews I had what I could see: my head and my two hands, and I had each day to do something with them. Each day, that's how I took it—each moment, sometimes, when the going got really rough. I may have knocked my head against the walls, figuring out how to buy food, supplies, and books, but I never knocked on wood. No rabbit's foot, no crucifixes—not even a lottery ticket. I couldn't afford the dollar or the dreams while I was working my way through Columbia. So until you walked into my office, everything I was—all the odds I had beat—was owed to my living fully in the now. How was I to reconcile the *fact* of seeing you the second time that day with the *feeling* I had had the first time? Not the feeling I told myself I had, but the one I really had.

You see, there was no way for me to deny that you were there in front of me and I couldn't deny any longer that I knew it would happen—you would be in my future. What had been captured—and dismissed—in a space too quickly for recorded time was now like a bizarre photograph that was developing in front of my face. I am passing you in the coffee shop, your head is bent over your folded newspaper, and small strands of your reddish-brown hair have come undone from the bobby pins and lie against the curve of your neck. The feeling is so strong it almost physically stops me: *I will see that neck again.* Not her, not the woman but the skin that's tinted from amber to cream as it stretches over the lean bone underneath. That is the feeling I actually had, while the feeling I quickly exchanged it with was: *I've seen this woman before.* That can be recorded; it took a split second. But a glance at the side of your high cheekbones, pointed chin, slender profile, and I knew I was mistaken. I hadn't even seen you sitting those three tables away during lunch. But I remembered your waitress well. The dark-brown arms, full breasts threatening to tear open the front of her uniform, the crease of her apron strings around a nonexistent waist that swung against a hip line that could only be called a promise of heaven on earth—her I had seen. And you had to have been there when she took your order and brought you whatever you were eating, and the fact is I never saw you. Not when I stood up, reached into my pocket for change, passed the two tables between us, and didn't see you then—until the neck bent over the newspaper. And it all could have been such a wonderful coincidence when you first walked into my office, a natural icebreaker for the interview, which I always hated, being forced to judge someone else. I could have brought up the final image of the weary slump, the open classifieds, and the shoes pulled off beneath the table. A woman looking for a job; we were looking for an office manager five blocks away. Afternoon interviews began at one o'clock, and it was twelve-forty-five. *And just imagine, Miss Day, when I passed you I said to myself, Wouldn't it be funny if I saw her again?* Except that it was terrifying when you sat down, and then ran your hand up the curve of your neck in a nervous mannerism, pushing up a few loose hairs and pushing me smack into a confrontation with fate. When you unconsciously did that, I must have looked as if someone had stuck a knife into my gut, because that's the way it felt.

You said, Call me George. And I thought, Oh God, this is going to be one of those let's-get-chummy-fast masquerades. Nine times out of ten, some clown giving you his first name is a sure bet he's not giving you the job. And they can comfort themselves because, after all, they went out of their way to be "nice." And in this case, you were stealing my thunder when the moment came for pulling out my toothpicks and reminding *Mr. Andrews* where I'd seen him before. But if we were George and Ophelia—chat, chat, chat—my mint toothpicks would just be added fuel to the fire that was sending this job up in smoke. These fudge-on-fudge interviews were always tricky anyway. You have the power freaks who wanted you to grovel at their importance. They figure if they don't get it from the other bonbons, it's sure not coming from anywhere else. Or there were the disciples of a free market with a Christ complex: they went to the Cross and rose without affirmative action, so you can, too. But our interview wasn't anything I could put my finger on. You just seemed downright scared of me and anxious to get me out of that office. And I knew the fastest way was this call-me-George business. I decided to fight fire with fire.

"And I'm used to answering to Cocoa. I guess we might as well start now because if I get the position and anyone here calls me Ophelia, I'll be so busy concentrating on my work, it won't register. I truly doubt I could have moved up as fast as I did at my last job—with a fifty percent increase in salary—if those twelve secretaries, thirty-five salesmen, and six adjusters in the office I was managing almost single-handedly had called me Ophelia. The way I see it, over half of the overtime I put in would have been spent trying to figure out who they were talking to."

There, I stuck that one to you. And you knew it, too, because you were finally smiling. And this time you took a real good look at my application.

"So you picked up this nickname at your last job—Omega Home Insurance?"

"No, I've had it from a child—in the South it's called a pet name. My grandmother and great-aunt gave it to me, the same women who put me through business school in Atlanta where I ended up graduating at the top of my class—A's in statistics, typing, bookkeeping. B plusses in—"

"That's fascinating. How do they decide on the pet name?"

"They just try to figure out what fits."

"So a child with skin the color of buttered cream gets called Cocoa. I can see how that fits."

I wanted to slap that smirk off your face. "It does if you understood my family and where I come from."

"Willow Springs, is it? That's in Georgia?"

"No, it's actually in no state. But that's a long story. And not to be rude, Mr. Andrews, but I really would like to talk about my credentials for working here. Where I was born and what name I was given were both beyond my control. But what *I* could do about my life, I've done well. And I'd like to spend the few minutes I have left of your time being judged on that."

Something happened to your face then. I had hit a raw nerve somewhere, and I cursed myself because I was sure I had succeeded in destroying the whole thing. It was little consolation knowing that I was going to be on your mind long after you kicked me out of your office.

"That's the only way I'd ever dream of judging anyone, Miss Day. And I meant it when I said call me George."

Great, I'd been demoted *up* to Miss Day. This man was really angry, and that George business again just clinched it, I guess. But then he did say *I meant it*, which means he knows about the whole charade and he's trying to reassure me that he's not angry about what I said. Ah, who can figure this shit out.

"And you can call me . . ." I was suddenly very tired—of you, of the whole game. "Just call me when you decide. I do need this job, and if you check out my references, you'll find that I'll be more than able to perform well."

"Fine. And this is the number where you can be reached?"

"Yes, but I'll be away for the next two weeks. If you don't mind, you could drop me a card, or I'll call when I get back since the job doesn't start until the first."

You frowned, but it came out the way it came out. Sure, he's thinking, how badly does someone need a job who's taking a vacation?

"But we'll be making our final decision after tomorrow. The person starts Monday."

"Your ad said the first."

"It did, but our current office manager told us this morning that she has to leave earlier than she had planned. And she'll have to break in her successor. This is a deceptively busy place and to have someone come in here cold—well, it wouldn't be fair to the new employee or to us. And we thought whoever got the position would probably appreciate starting work before September. I know how tight things are out there right now—most people have been looking for a long time."

Jesus, all we needed was the organ music and a slow fade to my receding back as the swirling sand of the rocky coastline began to spell out The End. Oh, yeah, if you aren't ready to start yesterday, there are a dozen who will be.

"I understand, and I wouldn't have wasted your time if I knew it was necessary to begin right away. I have to go home every August. It's never been a problem before because I had the same job for seven years. You see, my grandmother is eighty-three, and since we lost my cousin and her family last year, I'm the only grandchild left."

If you thought it was a cheap shot, sorry. At that point I was beyond caring.

"The whole family? That's really terrible—what happened?"

"Did you read about the fire in Linden Hills this past Christmas? Well, that was my cousin Willa and her husband and son. It upset us all a lot."

"I did read about it. It was an awful, awful thing—and on Christmas of all days."

My God, the look in your eyes. You actually meant that. This would go down in Guinness as the strangest interview I'd ever been on.

"So you understand why I'm going back to Willow Springs."

"Of course I do. And you must understand why any qualified applicant would need to start Monday."

"Yes, I do."

We had sure become one understanding pair of folks by the time the lights in the theater came up and they pulled the curtain across the screen. We got up out of our seats and shook hands. Was it my imagination—did his fingers linger just a bit? Was it possible that since I was more than qualified, no one else would come along and they'd save . . . My heart sank when I got back to the reception area. I had to wade through a whole Baskin-Robbins on my way to the outside hall.

You had spunk, Ophelia, and that's what I admired in a woman. You were justified to come right out and tell me I was prying, and I hated myself all the while I was doing it. I had always valued my own privacy, and just because you were in a position where you had to answer questions that bordered on an invasion on yours made what I did all the more unfair. If it's any consolation, I didn't enjoy the sour aftertaste of abused power. But I was searching for some connection, some rational explanation. The only way I could sit through that interview was by lying to myself about what had really happened in that coffee shop: when I passed your bent neck, I stopped because I had seen you somewhere before, and I couldn't remember—that's all.

I had definitely seen your type before, and had even slept with some of them—those too bright, too jaded colored girls. There were a few at Columbia, but many more would come across the street from Barnard. They made no bones about their plans to hook into a man who—what was the expression then?—who was going somewhere. Well, after classes I went to work as a room-service waiter in the Hilton. It wasn't as glamorous as the work-study jobs in the library or dean's office, but it paid a lot better when you counted tips. During the slack periods my boss let me read, and I had Sundays off. But you see, that wasn't the right day. All the guys who were going somewhere had been able to take girls to the fraternity dances on Friday and Saturday nights where they could show off their brand-name clothes. They only needed a pair of jeans to go to the park with me, or to sit in my room and study. I was too serious, too dull. George doesn't know how to have fun, they'd say, he's so quiet. I suppose I was, but what could I honestly talk to them about? They would have thought I was crazy if I had told them that seeing them flow around me like dark jewels on campus was one of the most beautiful sights on earth.

Yes, I was one of the quiet ones who thought them beautiful, even with the polished iron webbing around their hearts. I understood exactly what they were protecting themselves against, and I was willing to help them shine that armor all the more, to be the shoulder they could cry on when it got too heavy—if they had only let me in. But they didn't want me then. And I was to meet them years later, at parties and dinners, when the iron had served them a bit too well. They were successful and they were alone: those guys who were going somewhere had by either inclination or lack of numbers left a good deal of them behind. They had stopped being frivolous, but they were hurt and suspicious. And maturity made me much more hesitant to take a chance on finding an opening into hearts like those. Often I had wanted to go over and shake some silk-clad shoulder who thought she was righteously justified in spreading the tired old gospel about not being able to meet good black men. She had met *me*. But I would have been too proud to remind her where.

Yeah, I knew your type well. And you sat there with your mind racing, trying to double-think me, so sure you had me and the game down pat. Give him what he wants. I fooled you, didn't I. All I wanted was for you to be yourself. And I wondered if it was too late, if seven years in New York had been just enough for you to lose that, like you were trying to lose your

Southern accent. It amused me the way your tongue and lips were determined to clip along, and then your accent would find you in the spaces between two words—"talking about," "graduating at." In spite of yourself, the music would squeeze through at the ending of those verbs to tilt the following vowels up just half a key. That's why I wanted you to call me George. There isn't a Southerner alive who could bring that name in under two syllables. And for those brief seconds it allowed me to imagine you as you must have been: softer, slower—open. It conjured up images of jasmine-scented nights, warm biscuits and honey being brought to me on flowered china plates as you sat at my feet and rubbed your cheek against my knee. Go ahead and laugh, you have a perfect right. I had never been South, and you couldn't count the times I had spent in Miami at the Super Bowl—that city was a humid and pastel New York. So I had the same myths about Southern women that you did about Northern men. But it was a fact that when you said my name, you became yourself.

And it was also a fact that there was no way I was going to give you that job. And your firm plans about returning to Willow Springs helped to alleviate my guilt about that. We were going to turn other qualified people down—and it's never a matter of the most qualified, there's no such animal. It's either do they or don't they "fit." And where could I possibly place you? My life was already made at thirty-one. My engineering degree, the accelerating success of Andrews & Stein, proved beyond a shadow of a doubt that you got nothing from believing in crossed fingers, broken mirrors, spilled salt—a twist in your gut in the middle of a Third Avenue coffee shop. You either do or you don't. And you, Ophelia, were the don't. Don't get near a woman who has the power to turn your existence upside-down by simply running a hand up the back of her neck.

FAMILY MATTERS

Richard Perry

Three people came to Carla's front door, all in the last week of January. One was a doll salesman on his way home to Albany, his quota for the month unrealized. Three days later two sisters from Christ the Saviour Church brought the parish's biannual invitation to spend eternity in heaven.

The sisters, though saints, were not innocent. They knew Carla's history. Visiting her twice a year was equivalent to the demands of a thirty-day fast, two rituals so punishing that responsibility for each was rotated throughout the congregation. Back during the Second World War, Carla had taken to throwing cold water on folks who cared more about her soul than she did, and once she'd appeared at her door butt naked, a spectacle that caused two male saints to suffer a summer of nasty dreams. That was when people began to believe what they'd been saying: that Carla was on a first-name basis with the devil whose spirit shared her bed. This new certainty was derived from the rambling of the dream-drunk brothers who claimed that Carla's breasts were perfect and her body had no fat. Nobody knew the reason for perfect breasts. But you didn't have to go Fisk to know that those the devil slept with had no body fat to speak of.

Everybody also knew how difficult it was to reclaim the soul of a woman the devil had put his sweet thing to. Nevertheless, the saints regularly extended their invitation to Carla, regardless of effort or outcome. Their persistence was fueled by the depth of their faith and by the rumor that should Carla be moved to seek the Lord, those who'd been instruments in the miracle would receive a blessing, reported to be a trip to California. No one was sure where the rumor had started, but it was as immune to revision as their certainty of the devil's ability in bed.

When Carla opened the door, she was disappointed. She'd known it wouldn't be Bradley Douglas; when he got over his fit he would show up, as usual, at the back door. But she'd allowed herself to hope that the women would be Max. The disappointment made her uncertain. She avoided the women's eyes, looked past them into the snow-covered yard.

"Daughter? Have you thought of your salvation?"

"Just this morning," Carla said. "I was on my knees cleaning the ring Phoenix left in the tub."

"Think about eternity. Think about lying around on clouds, sipping milk and honey."

"I don't like milk and honey. Milk and scotch ain't bad. But milk and honey gives me the runs."

The woman to Carla's left, the brown one with watery eyes, sniffed.

"If you don't blow your nose," Carla said, "you're going to get snot in your scarf."

The scarves were not identical; the one with the eggplant-colored face wore a deeper blue. The women, soft-eyed, benevolent, gazed at Carla, who stared back, rigid with sudden helplessness. The helplessness came from knowing that rudeness would not save her. These women were fortified with faith and the promise of California. No curse, no indecent act (for which she had no energy, anyway) would drive them away until they were ready. And she was cold; the sullen January day had chilled her.

"God is not mocked, daughter. Will you come to church on Sunday? Will you believe there's nothing God can't do?" Without waiting for her reply, they began to pray, out loud and in unison, "Our Father, Who art in heaven . . ."

Carla firmly closed the door.

But the salesman she'd invited into her kitchen. She gave him strong coffee laced with cinnamon, obligingly examined one of his dolls, then went to lock her son's door, so that if he awoke he could not disturb her. She took the salesman into the living room, swept away the books and magazines, efficiently shrugged the dress, beneath which she was naked, from her shoulders, stepped from the fabric at her feet. As she revealed her body, her eyes never left his face, eyes so flat that had the salesman not been stunned by his good fortune, would have led him to pause before the absence of feeling there. It was not her eyes, however, that he was drawn to, but the arc of nut-brown shoulder, that and the perfect breasts, the luxurious growth where thighs met beneath her belly. She turned then, slowly, and he saw on her back the mass of scar tissue from shoulder blades to just above the shins, lewd and shocking on the other side of all that loveliness. As she eased him out of his clothes, he asked about the scars. She said it had happened in Korea, a hand grenade, and when he would not believe this lie, she clutched him in a way that made his eyes close, pushed him onto his back and mounted him. With her hands on his shoulders she searched for a rhythm that would make it happen, watching not his face now, but the depression dividing his milk-white chest, the black hair curled around his nipples. Summoning the kind of concentration old women use to thread needles, she collected what bits of excitement were available, labored to focus them. When she could not, she thought of afternoon naps broken by sudden storms, swarms of gnats in sunlight, trees casting shadows deeper than black. But none of this suc-ceeded in moving her, and so she pulled her trump card, memory of the afternoon twenty-three years ago when she'd barged into the unlocked bath-room to find Max staring into the mirror, holding his penis in his hand. How it had leaped and swelled when their eyes met. Exhilarated at the discovery of her power, aware of the solution to a plight she'd not acknowl-edged, she'd moved closer, reached a hand out, touched his flesh. His eyes went dark.

"Don't," he said. "You're my sister."

"Oh," she'd answered, smile older than cunning, "is that so?"

But even this memory that, in private, never failed to inflame her, could not charge this less than thrilling moment. She consoled herself with the thought that though the man beneath her was no thoroughbred, he was still a horse to ride. Fighting frustration, she drained what pleasure she could from the salesman's meager thighs.

When he left, he stuttered. Carla stared at the feeling in her hands. It was green, gelatinous, and it said that once again only her surface had been satisfied. The deep place inside had not been touched. She didn't have time to ask the inevitable question, "When will it ever be?" Her son was banging at the locked door of his room, mewling to be set free.

In August the man at her door made her heart trip with attraction and a sense that her life was threatened. He came early in the afternoon, a Thurs-day, and both his presence and her heart's knowing were so unexpected that she had no time for examination or to prepare for his leaving. But the feeling loomed, arresting, like a neon sign in a meadow—this man would, if she let him, take her life.

She put a hand around the throat of her confusion, noted that her face would fit neatly into the curve of his neck and shoulder. He was slender, not much taller than she. He didn't seem bothered that she'd done nothing yet but look at him; in fact, he seemed to be patiently presenting himself for her inspection. He wore pale blue pants, black sneakers, a white shirt open at the collar. He said his name was Tracy Jackson, but people called him Trace for short. He was Reverend Broadloom's nephew, and he'd stopped by Kingston on his way to the Grand Canyon. He'd grown up in Florida and had always wanted to know what dry air felt like and to see if he could stand on the edge of the biggest hole in the universe and look down without getting dizzy. A chef cook by trade, right now he was taking jobs as a caddie. At dinner last night Carla's name had come up, and Trace was curious, so he'd stopped by to see for himself.

He said this in a voice that was measured, one half beat faster than too slow. Still, Carla had not spoken. Trace glanced past her into the living room, where the drawn shades held back the sun and a small library's worth of books and magazines littered the settled gloom.

"Read a lot, eh?"

She ignored his question. "What did you hear about me? What charitable, Christian things did they tell you?"

His eyes were steady, an ordinary brown. "That you live with your son all by yourself in this two-family house. That your child's father is Max, a preaching white boy with blond hair and mismatched eyes. Your first house got burned down, killing two of your brothers. Some people say Max done it. Your son is an idiot. You're not quite right in the head yourself, but even though you ain't no spring chicken, you still one of the finest things to walk these Kingston streets."

Carla stared. Green plants would flourish in his smile. She began to prepare for his leaving.

"What else you hear?"

"The rest," he admitted, "ain't so flattering. They say you got a sweet thing going with the devil. That you use the Lord's name in vain and sleep with white men."

"Well?"

"Well, what?"

"Ain't you offended?"

He shrugged. It was elegant. "Don't make me no never mind. You ain't my woman and you ain't my child."

"You figure that out all by yourself?"

"All by my lonesome. But just to be on the safe side," he grinned, "I asked me a white man before I stopped by."

"Come in," Carla said.

She moved books from the sofa, invited him to sit. Herself she placed in a chair across from him, snuck a glance at the angle where his thighs met. He crossed his legs, smoothly. He had small feet. She imagined he was a dancer: balance, muscle, grace.

"Where's Phenus?"

"Phoenix," she said. "Folks too lazy to say his name." Immediately, she regretted the remark. It sounded as if she were accusing him, as if she were saying that he, too, was lazy, this man who should have been a dancer. But Trace only grunted, no judgment in the sound.

"The bird that keeps getting born," he said. "Out of the ashes."

"You know?"

"Cooked on a boat named *Phoenix* once. They rebuilt it after a fire."

"Most people think he's named after a city in Arizona. Anyway, to answer your question, he's sleeping."

"Uh-huh."

She couldn't see his eyes, not even if she squinted. The silence was loud. It was funny about silence; she'd have said she was accustomed to it. Outside of her child's grunts and whines, the occasional man she pulled into the center of her need, she'd lived in this house with silence ever since her brother, Willis, had left. Even her relationship to Bradley was defined by silence. But this silence was awkward, disapproving.

"So how long you plan to stay in Kingston?"

"Don't know. Till I'm ready to leave, I guess. Grand Canyon ain't going no place soon."

"I guess so. I never been to the Grand Canyon. Never been nowhere except to Albany. We visited the capitol." She looked down at the hands folded in her lap, noticed for the first time that day what she was wearing: a pair of her father's overalls ripped at the right knee, one of Willis's undershirts. Bare feet. There was nothing to say unless she remarked how stunning she looked. She was stupid, he would leave, bored. Did he drink tea, what was it like to caddie? Did black people play golf?

While she decided which of those questions to ask, she said, "You want to see him?" She blinked; she'd not meant to say that.

"Pardon me?"

"Phoenix. You want to see him?"

Trace uncrossed his legs. "Well, okay."

Phoenix slept on his back, the sheet covering up to his navel. He was tall, at least six feet, Trace guessed, with curly light brown hair, skin a high yellow. Perspiration beaded on his lip, slicked the skin on his muscular chest. He was one of the prettiest persons, male or female, that Trace had ever seen, what some women called "drop dead" pretty, and it was hard to imagine that there was anything wrong with him, that he would not, for example, awake to discuss the weather. A fan droned in the window across the room, and Trace rubbed his chin, thinking that it was time to smile and whisper something appropriate. Carla looked at him, put a finger to her lips.

In the hallway Trace said, "He's a good-looking boy."

Carla glanced sharply at him. There was a tenderness in his voice that she didn't ordinarily associate with men. As she descended the stairs, she wondered if he was weak. She felt his eyes on her back, imagined what it would be like if, at the bottom, he pulled her to her knees, traced his tongue along her throat. How sad if he was weak. As though the presence of sun might clear things up, she went to the living room windows, raised the shades. The light illuminated the clutter, ignited other questions. When would he leave? Why had she offered, so soon, to show him her son? Why did it feel like allowing a glimpse inside her, a look at the untouched place?

"He don't," Trace said, "look like nothing's wrong with him. He was born that way?"

"Most the doctors could say was probably. I didn't notice anything until after the fire. He's still afraid of fire. . . ." She trailed off, recalling the efforts to reclaim her son from idiocy. If determination could do it, she'd reasoned, then it was done. But determination could not do it.

"I got to go now," Trace said.

She turned, faced the moment she'd been preparing for. "Oh?"

"But I'm going fishing in the morning. Want to come?"

"Fishing?"

"That's when you throw a line with a hook . . ."

"I know," she snapped, "what fishing is."

"Well?"

"I can't. Got no one to look after Phoenix."

"Take him with us."

"He never been fishing."

"So?"

Jesus. Take Phoenix? "I don't know. . . . What time?"

"Six o'clock."

"In the *morning?*"

"You ever eat grapefruit?"

"*Grape*fruit?" She leaned away from him, confused, as if he'd asked if he could stay forever.

"You get"—he smiled—"so surprised at the ordinary. Fishing, the fact there's a six o'clock in the morning, grapefruit . . ."

"You trying to provoke me?"

"Yes, ma'am."

"Six o'clock," Carla said. "Don't be late."

"If I am, what happens? You put me over your knee?"

That's *not*, she thought, where I plan to put you. Because she couldn't say what she thought, she had to make up something, something clever that would make him smile again. She couldn't. If she didn't speak, the game would stop; he'd leave.

"You should have been a dancer," she blurted, "should—" and stopped, aware that his eyes had changed, grown narrow with puzzlement that to her looked like disappointment and disbelief.

"Well, thank you," he said, "I guess." He smiled. He didn't think she was stupid. She was so relieved that she did not suffer his leaving again until he was gone.

But it was there now in the interval that followed the door closing upon his lovely back, his blue Buick pulling away from the curb, that and the feeling that her life was threatened. To see how the feeling would respond, she imagined she'd dreamed the encounter and that Trace had never been there. After thirty seconds she acknowledged failure, not because she couldn't imagine, but because she didn't want to. There were all those details left by his visit—his feet, the smile that nourished—and not one explained the feeling that this man who should have been a dancer would take her life.

She carried the feeling into the kitchen, offered it to the light that fell through the window above the sink and lit the table, leaving a shape whose name she knew but could not recall. But no matter how she held the feeling, no matter the angle of vision, the story was the same. Trace would, if she let him, take her life. Then he would leave.

She put on the kettle for tea, slumped at the table, drummed fingers against the trapezoidal sunlight, remembering, with no motivation she could make sense of, the morning after her father's funeral when she'd awakened into the emptiness of just before dawn. As her eyes opened into the darkened room, she'd steeled herself for the grief that had, for the past few days, spent all waking hours in the steady whipping of her heart.

What an accumulation of leaving! In the span of three years she lost her brothers; Max had disappeared. Then, before she could turn around good, her father, losing what was left of his mind and his eyesight, was having his sickbed moved to the attic. He said he needed space and privacy for the war he planned to wage when death came, that the other unlived-in rooms were thick with furniture and the cellar was too damp. So they'd humored him because that is what you are supposed to do for a demented loved one who is dying. Sit at the bed and hold his hand, making certain there is always a toothbrush by his side so that he can wash from his mouth the taste of charcoal left by his sons' cooked flesh. Promise that although Max has not been found, he'll show up, hale and hearty, to preside at the christening of his unborn son. And especially to be there to keep him from wasting what energy he has left, to let him know that the failing light is not death's shadow across the attic window, but nothing more threatening than the promise of rain or nightfall.

Despite their vigilance, he was alone when death called. He'd bellowed, a thunderous cry of challenge and rage, and then he smashed the lamp so that death, who had perfect eyesight, would have to wrestle in the dark. By the time Carla had raced from the kitchen to the attic, he was gone.

She'd been shattered by the death of her father, had not even begun to put the pieces back when her mother went a year later, swollen breasts spurting tiny cream-colored geysers, as if death were not the grown man her father battled, but a sucking infant, much like the six-month-old her mother left behind. And she, Carla, barely nineteen years of age, what had she done to deserve this, why had she been so singularly cursed? Despondent, she began to be obsessed over her own death, looked for it beneath the bed, in the basement, spun to catch it in the space that yawned behind her while she ironed. For a time she speculated about bringing it to pass with her own hand. In this speculation she discovered her fear. What if death was not not-being, but an existence marked by bright lights and aloneness? Or, worse still, what if death was a country into which people she loved came in the afternoon to sweep away her longing, stayed the night, then left in the mist before dawn? That was one reason she stopped thinking of taking her life; the other was that there were two children to raise—Phoenix, her son, and Willis, her brother—and she discovered in this task a source of distraction.

So there she was, alone in a two-family house except for the children, one an idiot, the other a lover of boats. That was Willis, who'd grown up to join the Navy, a decision that surprised no one at all. Anyway, she'd raised the two of them, her brother and her son, cared for them through measles and chicken pox, through croup and fever, gotten Willis off to school in the morning, labored over his homework, agonized through Little League. And how quickly it had passed, how soon boy flesh became man flesh, the armpit and belly sprouting hair, voice falling into lower register, irrefutable proof that Willis would be leaving. She'd always, of course, known that he would leave. As early as the onset of toilet training she'd been obsessed with his departure. As she cleaned shit from his underwear and washed the stains between his tiny ass cheeks, as she perched on the edge of the tub waiting for him to relax his bowels, she did not think of any unpleasantness, but that one day he'd be gone. Each small rite of passage—his first haircut, his discovery of boats—tacked another reminder on her heart: Willis is going to leave you.

And he did, and she told herself that this was just the way life was, that everyone you loved left before the fullness of time, some by death, some by disappearance, some because they loved boats and went off to join the Navy. Except Phoenix. Phoenix wasn't going nowhere.

Carla pushed back from the table, turned off the kettle, walked from kitchen to front room and back again. After her father's death, she'd gone to see the lawyer he'd kept on retainer. The investment plan had already been established: savings bonds, twenty-year annuities. Nearly half the sixty thousand dollars insurance money went into savings accounts, her father figuring that the banks would not fail again in Carla's lifetime. The house was paid for, and there was enough money to live simply without working, although once Willis was in school, she chose to. The combination of single lovely woman and a sizable inheritance brought the suitors out in schools. Several Carla slept with, but when none succeeded in bringing her to orgasm, she realized she did not want anyone after Max, certainly not to marry. This created a furor among the congregation of Christ the Saviour Church, the prevailing wisdom being that a woman needed the protection of a man, and that it was better to marry than to burn. Well, Carla said to Reverend Broadloom, she didn't want to marry; for protection she had her father's shotgun and locks on all her doors and windows. As for burning, she had already been burned and survived that, and if he was talking about another kind of fire, she knew how to put that out. Reverend Broadloom was one of those men who believed that his advice, solicited or not, ought to be followed; otherwise he'd wasted his time. He didn't like wasting time. He said this to Carla, and when she indicated where he could store his not liking, it became awkward to show her face in church. At first the lack of fellowship made no difference, but in time she began to miss it and to feel, even though she'd done the leaving, that the congregation had deserted her.

During all this time, with a rhythm no drummer had yet discovered, no lean fingers had squeezed from bass guitar or banjo, came the flashes, the fleeting episodes of hope that suggested her life would not always be this, that one day a change would come. This always drove her to focus on the children, and she would talk to them incessantly, one who understood her, one who didn't. She explained wind and stars, why living things grew toward the sun. Or she would read to them, and when she grew tired of the sameness of children's books, she began embroidering her own rude stories—how Bradley Douglas had given up his ability to speak, the years in Kingston when bread did not rise. As Willis grew older his interest waned; he would slip off in the middle of her telling to play with boats, but she began to imagine that Phoenix listened in a deeper stillness. Over and over she related to her child the story of his father, the beautiful boy with blond hair and mismatched eyes, who had disappeared, but who had promised to return. She had promised to wait. She'd kept that promise.

And now in her life was this man who'd come from Florida, to whom she was instantly drawn, by whom she was instantly threatened. The threat, she decided, came from contemplating betrayal. What would she say if Max arrived in the morning? How would she explain that after all the years of allowing the waiting to be the center of her life, she'd thrown it away, moved by a smile and small feet? She told herself to put it away for a while. She didn't have to make any long-term decisions. In the meantime she'd try to enjoy the shock of having been visited by a man who moved so gracefully, who'd promised to take her fishing in the morning.

SWEET EVENING BREEZE

Darryl Pinckney

Manhattan was burning up that Bicentennial summer, and those without air conditioners, those who could not buy refuge in the cinemas or bars, were driven into the streets. Far into the spangled night, welling up from the muggy cross streets and streaming avenues, came the noise of tape-deck anthems, revving motorcycles, breaking bottles, dogs, horns, cats in heat, bag ladies getting holy, and children going off the deep end.

I was beginning a new life. I was still on the Upper West Side, but every change of address within the 13.2 square miles of Manhattan was, back then, before I knew better, a hymn to starting over. So, two rooms with splintered, softwood floors, and walls the dingy, off-white color of a boy's jockey shorts after scout camp; two rooms at 262 West Ninety-fifth Street in a small, shaggy building of only two apartments, rooms sanctified by rent stabilization.

The old brick held the mean heat, sun streaked through the windows and lit up the smoky dust that hung in the air. The pipes leaked, the doors were warped, spider webs formed intricate designs in the corners. The oven and refrigerator refused to work on days that were not prime numbers. In the mornings paint dropped from the ceiling like debris idly flung into traffic from an overpass. The bathroom tiles had buckled, and the cracks in the plaster resembled outlines of fiords in a map of Norway. Roaches? Oh, yes, the totemic guerrillas of urban homesteading were there.

None of this mattered. I was unpacking boxes of secondhand and overdue library books, fondling dirty envelopes of tattered letters, hitting my shins on milk crates of blackened pots, tarnished flatware, and chipped Limoges plates. In the new ascetic life I imagined I would not need much. I was not made for keeping up the perfect kitchen for the right sort of dinner party, not equal to the task of digging up that intriguing print for the gleaming, glossy-white vestibule. I was through with telephone madness at five P.M.— that calling and calling to find someone home while a tray of ice melts on the thrift store table. And the nights of the wide bed, of the mattress large enough to hold the combat of two, were definitely over. The seediness into which I had slid held the promise of a cleansing, monastic routine.

My rear window looked out on a mews, on Pomander Walk, a strand of two-story row houses done in a mock-Tudor style. The shutters and doors were painted blue, green, or red. The hedges were prim and tidy. Boxes of morning glories completed the scene. An odd sight, unexpected, anachronistic, I thought of it as a pocket of subversion against the tyranny of the grid and the tower. But Pomander Walk's claims were modest, as were its proportions—a mere sideshow of a lane that ran north and south, from Ninety-fifth Street to Ninety-fourth Street. Its survival probably had something to do with its being in the middle of the block, not taking up too much room, and that it was family property.

A little street in the London suburb of Chiswick was celebrated in the play *Pomander Walk*, first produced in 1911. I was told that an Irish-American restaurateur was so charmed by it that he brought the designer over to help build a replica of the set. That is what he got—a set. It was built in 1921, a rather late, unhistorical-sounding date. When Pomander Walk was finished, the land immediately west of it was virginal, undeveloped. Residents had a clear view of thick treetops down to the Hudson River. Perhaps then it was close in mood to the ideals of the City Beautiful period, to the harmony of Hampstead Way or Bedford Park. Perhaps not. This was a mirage inspired by haphazard Chiswick, not by an architect's vision of a utopian commuter village.

I was disappointed to learn that Pomander Walk had always been apartments. I thought each structure had originally been a house and, like those of Belgravia, they had been violated, cut up, humbled by the high cost of living well. Pomander Walk harbored high-ceilinged efficiencies "intended for and first occupied by theatrical people," the WPA *Guide to New York City* reported in 1939. In the twenties, so the lore went, it was a pied-à-terre for the likes of the Gish sisters, Katharine Hepburn, and Dutch Schultz. Bootleggers threw scandalous parties at which guests refused to remove their homburgs.

Pomander Walk had seen better days. The sentry boxes were empty. The caretaking staff had been reduced to two elusive Poles, the apartments themselves were in various stages of decay, and behind the valiant facades, in the passageways between the tombs of West End Avenue and the cheap clothing stores of Broadway, were fire escapes grim as scaffolds, and mounds of garbage through which chalk-white rats scurried. These were the days before gentrification—where is the gentry?—before the ruthless renovations that would turn entire neighborhoods into a maze of glass, chrome, exposed brick, polished blond oak, and greedy ferns.

Pomander Walk had become a kind of fortress, as it had to be, surrounded as it was, like the enclaves of early Christian merchants in the Muslim ports of the Levant. Pomander Walk struggled against the tone of the blocks swarming around it. High iron gates at either end of the lane, at the steps that led down to the streets, spoke of a different order. "Do Not Enter." "Private Property." A peeling red rooster kept vigil over the main entrance. The fields sloping down to the Hudson were long gone. Sandwiched between dour, conventional buildings, Pomander Walk seemed an insertion of incredible whimsy and brought to mind Rem Koolhaas's phrase in *Delirious New York*, "Reality Shortage."

During my vacant hours I fed my curiosity about the inhabitants of that pastoral, pretentious, Anglophile fantasy. The tenants were mostly women. I imagined that they were widows surviving on pensions or on what their husbands had managed to put aside, and that there were a few divorcées sprinkled among them, the sort not anxious to define themselves by respectable jobs with obscure art galleries. Their custom, on those hot afternoons, before, as I supposed, trips to married sons at the Jersey Shore, was to leave their electric fans and gather on the stoops. They sat on newspapers, pillows, or lawn chairs for cocktails. Sometimes large, festive deck umbrellas appeared.

The women got along well with the blond or near-blond actors and dancers who lived in warring pairs in some of the smaller apartments. The artists, when they came out in tight shorts for a little sun, joined with the women in discouraging intruders from looking around. No, they said, there were no flats available, and the waiting list was as long as your arm. Defenders of the faith. I kept the frayed curtain over my rear window drawn after some tourists, as nonleaseholders were called, stepped up to the bars and, seeing me, a black fellow struggling with a can of tuna fish, asked, "Are you the super?"

Once upon a time I was morbidly sensitive about the impertinence born of sociology. Taxi drivers would not stop for me after dark, white girls jogged to keep ahead of my shadow thrown at their heels by the amber street lamps. Part of me didn't blame them, but most of me was hurt. I carried props into the subway—the latest *Semiotext(e)*, a hefty volume of the Frankfurt School—so that the *employed* would not get the wrong idea or, more to the point, the usual idea about me. I did not want them to take me for yet another young black prole, though I was exactly that, one in need of a haircut and patches for my jeans. That Bicentennial summer I got over it. I remembered a gentleman of the old school who, after Johns Hopkins and Columbia, said his only ambition had been to sink into the lower classes. By the time I knew him he had succeeded, and this gentle antique lived out his last days among harmless drunkards at a railroad yard in Norfolk, Virginia. I resolved to do the same, as if, away from Mama and Papa, I had been anywhere else.

As a matter of fact I had been sinking for some time. First stop downward: a bookshop. Not the supermarket variety where women phoned in orders for two yards of books, repeating specifications of height and color, completely indifferent to title. Not one of the new boutiques where edgy Parisian slang skipped over the routine murmur. But a "used" bookshop, one of those holes in the wall where solitude and dust took a toll on the ancient proprietor's mental well-being, much like the health risks veins of coal posed to miners. That summer, unable to pay the rising rent, the owner gave up, wept openly at the auction of his stock. Next stop: office temp (let go). Waiter (fired). Telephone salesman (mission impossible). Then I found my calling—handyman. The anonymity of domestic service went well with the paranoid vanity of having a new and unlisted phone number.

I should have advertised my services in *The Westsider*. Even so, I lucked into a few appointments. Among my clients was an exalted bohemian on the upper reaches of Riverside Drive. I spent most of the day cleaning up after her impromptu séances. Two mornings a week I worked for a feminist psychologist who lived in one of the hives overlooking Lincoln Center. I walked her nasty Afghan hound, which was often woozy from pet tranquilizers; stripped the huge rolltop desk she hauled in not from the country but from Amsterdam Avenue. I was not allowed to play the radio and, in retaliation, I did not touch the lunch of tofu and carrot juice she left for me on the Formica counter. Then to Chelsea where I picked up dry cleaning for a furtive, youngish businessman. His mail consisted mostly of final notices from Con Ed, Ma Bell, and collection agencies in other states. I was certain that I was being tailed whenever I delivered one of his packages to the dubious factory outlets with which he had dealings. I made him pay me in cash.

One glaring morning someone I knew in publishing called to say that she knew of a woman who was getting on in years and in need of some help. The only thing Djuna Barnes required of her helper was that he not have a beard. I shaved, cut my hair, and fished out jacket and tie in spite of the heat, having been brought up to believe that I was not properly dressed unless I was extremely uncomfortable. I was so distracted that my socks did not match.

Miss Barnes lived in the West Village, just north of the old Women's House of Detention, in a blind alley called Patchin Place. Shaded by ailanthus, a city tree first grown in India that in the days of the pestilence was believed to absorb "bad air," the lime-green dwellings of Patchin Place had once been home to Dreiser, John Reed, E. E. Cummings, Jane Bowles, and John Mayfield. Through the intercom at no. 5 came a deep, melodious voice and, after an anxiety-producing interrogation, I was buzzed in. I found the chartreuse door with its "Do Not Disturb" sign and, after another interrogation, it slowly opened.

The home of this "genius with little talent," as T. S. Eliot said of Miss Barnes, was brutally cramped—one tiny robin's egg-blue room with white molding. The kitchen was such a closet that the refrigerator hummed behind French doors in a little pantry packed with ironing board, vacuum, boxes of faded *cartes d'identité*, linen, and, so my covetousness led me to think, hoarded Tchelitchew costume sketches. Great adventures, I was sure, awaited me in the clutter—*bibelots* on the mantel and side tables, picture frames on the floor turned toward the wall, shoeboxes under the fat wing chair. On either side of the fireplace were bookcases. Her low, narrow bed was flush against one of them. Two plain wooden desks dominated the dark room. Stacks of letters and papers had accumulated on them like stalagmites. Meticulously labeled envelopes warning "Notes on Mr. Eliot," "Notes on Mr. Joyce" rested near a portable typewriter. The blank page in the Olivetti manual had browned.

The booming voice was deceptive. Miss Barnes was shrunken, frail. The lazy Susan of medicines on the night table was so large that there was scarcely room for the radio, spectacles, and telephone. Her introductory remarks were brief. She came down hard on the point of my being there. "See that you don't grow old. The longer you're around the more trouble you're in." Miss Barnes had been old for so long that she looked upon herself as a cautionary tale. The first day of my employ I was told to see to it that I never married, never went blind, was never operated on, never found myself forbidden salt, sugar, tea, or sherry, and, above all, that I was never such a fool as to write a book.

Yet there was a hypnotic liveliness to her, moments when the embers of flirtatiousness flared. The thin white hair was swept back and held by two delicate combs. She wore a Moroccan robe trimmed in gold, opaque white stockings, and red patent-leather heels. Her eyes glistened like opals in a shallow pond, and her skin was pale as moonlight. Her mouth was painted a moist pink, her jaw jutted forward, her bearing was defiant, angrily inquisitive. The tall, stylish eccentric of the Berenice Abbott and Man Ray photographs lived on somewhere inside the proud recluse who cursed her magnifying glass, her swollen ankles, overworked lungs, hardened arteries, and faulty short-term memory. "Damn, damn, damn," she muttered.

My inaugural chore was to refill the humidifier. Under her scrutiny this task was far from simple. Her hands flew to her ears. "That's too much water. We can't have that." Next Miss Barnes wanted me to excavate an unmarked copy of "Creatures in an Alphabet." Stray pages were tucked here and there, none clean enough for her. She settled on one version of the poem, retreated to the bed, and set about crossing out the dedication. "Can't have that. He ruined my picture." The explanation of how some well-meaning soul had smudged a portrait when he tried to wash it gave way abruptly to a denunciation of modern pens, how they were not made to last. I gave her my Bic, told her to keep it. "Why, thank you. Would you like to support me?" She sank into the pillows and laughed, dryly, ruefully, as one would at a private joke.

By some sorcery the laugh became a racking cough. She clutched a wad of tissues and coughed, coughed. I tried to help—water? A pill? She held up her hand for silence. The barking subsided. She sat for some time with head lowered, fists in her lap. Then she looked around, as if disappointed to find herself still in the same place. Fearing dizziness, she asked me to fetch her black handbag. She found the leather coin purse, from which she slowly extracted five one-dollar bills. She laid them on the bed in a fan shape and commanded me to "run along." She pushed the pages of "Creatures in an Alphabet" away, like a patient trying to shove a tray of Jell-O and thin sandwiches from view. Miss Barnes was tired. Asking for a fresh copy of that poem was a symbolic gesture—she was no longer a writer at work. At least she had an air conditioner, I thought, as I closed the warm gate to the street and put a match to the cigarette I was not permitted to smoke in her presence.

I learned not to call and volunteer: Miss Barnes turned me aside with mandarin courtesy. I went when summoned, which was not often. If I arrived early she implied that the zeal of the young was inelegant, and if I came late, panting, she stated flatly that the young were hopelessly self-absorbed. Miss Barnes thought my given name, Darryl, with its contemporary Dixie-cup quality, ridiculous, and my surname, Pinckney, with its antebellum echo, only barely acceptable. I had to admit that it had the goofiness of a made-up name. "Delmore Schwartz, what a beautiful name!" Delmore Schwartz is said to have exclaimed.

I went to the market—"What's an old woman to eat, Mr. Pinckney, I ask you"—for bananas, ginger ale, coffee ice cream, hard rolls, and plums. "Not the red ones, the black ones. When they're good, they've white specks on them." I rushed out to the hardware store for pesticide and back again to exchange it for a brand to which she was not allergic. I went to the shoe repair and back again to have her black heels stretched even more. "I forgot. You're young. Don't mind running up and down the steps, do you?" And, of course, I stood on line at the pharmacy.

"I haven't been out of this room in five years. You'd think I'd be climbing the walls, wouldn't you?"

"Yes."

"I am."

Miss Barnes was not above a little drama, and I believed she exaggerated the extent of her isolation. She had a brother in Pennsylvania, a nephew or some such in Hoboken. Regularly her devoted "boy," an East European in his sixties, came to wash the floors and walls. I had heard that two elderly gentlemen, her doctor and her lawyer, still climbed the stairs to pay their respects. There were romantic rumors—one had it that an heiress to the company that supplied paper to the U.S. mint sometimes stepped from a great car to call on the friend of her expatriate youth. I hoped the radio was a comfort, that it filled her room with music, voices, but it was never on in my presence, during business hours, as it were.

She was reasonably informed about large events, seemed up on literary gossip. The *TLS* was stored in a basket like kindling, the light-blue wrappers unbroken. If she did not have much to say about the outside world, well, she had lived a long time. The ways in which most of us burned up daily life were, to her, pure folly. "What fools are the young." I am sure Miss Barnes managed to do a great deal of wrangling by telephone. She had a combative, litigious streak, an outgrowth, perhaps, of the yearning to take hold, to fend for herself. Rights and permissions had become an obsession that filled the place once occupied by composition. She dismissed me before she dialed the number of some unsuspecting publisher.

It was bad manners to be too curious. Many had been banished. She spoke of one former helper as being "stupid as a telephone pole." She fumed against one enterprising character who had insinuated himself into her confidence, gotten into her will "with both feet," and then packed up cartons of treasure. She claimed to have been relentlessly ripped off, down to the monogrammed spoons, but I wondered about that since, evidently, she regarded the sale of her papers as a kind of theft. As for admirers, those pilgrims and would-be biographers who brought her "one bent rose from somebody's grave," she declared that they wanted her on Forty-second Street standing on her head with her underwear showing. Some acolytes, she said, had taken advantage of her failing eyesight to smuggle out a souvenir or two. She complained that a bookstore in the vicinity had, without her consent, used the name her father had conjured up for *her*, and that when she called to protest the manager hung up on her.

Pessimism Miss Barnes wore as regally as a tweed suit, and perhaps an early career as a reporter had taught her not to expect too much of the "hard, capricious star." Everything and everyone came down to the lowest common denominator in the end. "Love is the first lie; wisdom the last." The one time I was foolish enough to quote from her work she looked at me as if I had lost my mind. "Am I hard of hearing," she screamed, "or do you mumble?" That was a break, the possibility she hadn't heard. "You're shy, aren't you? Pretend that you aren't." I wanted to be different, to be one who did not ask about the cafés, the parties, Peggy Guggenheim, or her portrait of Alice Rohrer over the fireplace.

Her seclusion was a form of self-protection as much as it was a consequence of age. Even if she had been temperamentally capable of going off, like Myrna Loy, and leaving everything to scavengers, it was too late. When Miss Barnes was on a roll, launched on a tirade fueled by grievance, her tiny figure seemed to expand and take up the whole room. The bold voice forced me into a corner; words came like darts. I had the feeling that the locksmith's clumsy work stood for something larger, that it was simply an occasion for the release of fury. I nodded and nodded as she pointed to the scratches around the new cylinder in the door. "You mustn't say 'Oh, really' again, Mr. Pinckney." Then the inevitable deflation, that rasping cough. I stood very still, like an animal waiting for a hunter to pass.

The temper had its source in the underground fire of physical pain. Once I was sent away minutes after slipping through the door because clearly she was having a rough day. Though Miss Barnes, like most old people, talked of her ailments—"I can't breathe and I'm going blind. Damn."—she did not want a stranger to witness her private struggles. She arranged five dollars on the bed and apologized for having ruined my Sunday. I told her that I admired her work, that coming to see her was one of my few joys. "You're mad. You're absolutely mad. Well, there's nothing we can do about that." I refused the money. Miss Barnes did not part with cash easily. In her life she had been broke and stranded more than once. My wage she regarded as wildly generous, a gift to, say, the United Negro College Fund, because she thought of dollars in terms of a prewar exchange rate. She insisted, gave me a bill to mail so that I would feel I had earned my pay. "I used to be like you. Not taking the money. It didn't matter." She wagged an index finger. "Make money. Stuff it in your boots, as Shakespeare said." Behind me I heard the bolts slide across her door.

The summer unfolded like a soggy sheet and, except for Miss Barnes, my clients casually drifted away. I lived on an early birthday present from home but somehow I managed to get behind in the rent. I assured my parents that I was knocking on doors, sending out résumés, proving once again that if you nag your children they will lie to you. Days evaporated like spilled water on sizzling pavement. Rock bottom was not so bad, and if sinking had not turned out to be as liberating as I had hoped, it was not without some consolations. The afternoons I traveled in humid subway cars from Pomander Walk to Patchin Place lifted me out of my torpor. The chance to see Miss Barnes struck me as an omen—but of what?

Fame was not much of a consolation to her. She was not rich, could not trade her name for much, and so reputation she treated as a joke—on herself mostly. "You may like the book but not the old girl." Being a character, a survivor, made her one who had evacuated a large portion of her life, mindful of the clues carelessly left behind for detectives. "Would you believe I lived in Paris nine years and never learned a word of French?" Her memories, those she shared, had the quality of set pieces. Even when she talked of intimate matters there was something impersonal about it, and I wondered how many visitors had heard her say that she was never a lesbian, could never abide "those wet muscles" one had to love to love women; or that she was too much of a coward to take her own life.

A joke, yes, but not entirely. "No, don't move those. I'm a vain woman. I want them near me." Miss Barnes meant the translations, the various editions of *Nightwood* and *Ryder*. I was putting the bookshelf in order, not that it was needed. She was resistant to change: the autographed copy of Dag Hammarskjöld's *Markings* had to remain where it had been for ages, a red pocket edition of Dante was also happy where it was. "Mr. Eliot learned Italian just to read this poem. He must have liked it, don't you think?"

I rescued a paperback, a biography of Natalie Barney, from under the bed. "Let me see that. Rémy de Gourmont called her 'the Amazon of love' and she never got over it. That's what you get, that's what you end up looking like," she, peering through her magnifying glass, said to a photograph showing Barney in later life. I broke my promise to myself and asked about Colette.

"Yes, I knew that silly, blue-haired lady." I got carried away and told Miss Barnes about a night at the opera when I, an undergraduate, just off the boat, was introduced to Janet Flanner. I mentioned to Miss Flanner that I too was from Indiana, and she, taking in my costume of tan polyester suit, red shiny tie, and platform shoes, answered: "I haven't been back since 1921—and I would advise you to do the same." Miss Barnes didn't crack a smile: "Often she knew whereof she spoke." I found yet another copy of *Nightwood*. "Sometimes I wonder, 'Did I write this? How did I do it?' Do it while you're young, Mr. Pinckney. Put all of your passion in it." She smiled.

But that was enough, not a syllable more. The shelves had to be swabbed down, and then the windows. So there I was, clinging to the fire escape, with Miss Barnes telling me over and over what a mess I was making. She leaned on the windowsill, handed out bouquets of paper towels, pointed to the lint and suds left in the corners. She absolutely refused to hear my thoughts on investing in a sponge. "Don't tumble into that Judas tree." She groped her way back to the bed to prepare for another onslaught of coughing.

In the shelves of the bookcases were mysterious little phials solemn as votive candles. She said that they contained oxygen. They looked like cloudy, empty bottles to me. I had to wash them, all twenty-four of them. One lid got trapped in the drain. "Now you've done it." I worked with a pair of scissors to pull it out. "Oh, you've done it now," she repeated, swaying against the bathroom door, fretting with the collar of a pink, satinlike dressing gown. "Take down the trash and you may go." The sad thing was realizing that there was really nothing I could do for her.

When I got the bright idea of devising a flow chart for her flotilla of pills—often she complained of headaches, of not knowing what to take when—she was offended. I argued that many of the prescriptions had been voided, that some of the tubes were empty, that it was amazing she could find anything in the jumble. We had a tug-of-war over a box of opium suppositories on which she depended for whatever peace she had. I made a little speech on obstruction, in the way one sometimes talks down to the elderly, on not being able to help if she didn't let me. "I know what I'm about, thank you very much Mr. Pinckney!"

Miss Barnes ordered me to wash out a silk blouse in the sink. I said no. She started to say that she didn't understand why blacks had become so touchy, caught herself, and said that she didn't know why young men had such silly notions about what they considered women's work. But I knew what she meant, knew it from the way she had swallowed the "knee" of "Negroes," that despised word of her generation, knew it from the soft blush that spread like ink across the folds of her face. I don't remember what I said, but I can still see the five dollars on the blue coverlet, Miss Barnes hunched over, her dressing gown slightly hitched up, she hitting her palms together slowly. I paused at the door—for an apology?—but she was too old to take anything back. She met my gaze with a look of her own, a flicker of bewilderment, then hard as a stone tablet. I walked out.

I went back to living in steerage at the edge of Pomander Walk. Families were staking out territory along the oily river to watch ships, couples were hiking with blankets and beer to fireworks, but I had other things on my mind. By nightfall, when bagpipes started up within Pomander Walk to commemorate the Queen's walk down Wall Street to Trinity Church, the misunderstanding with Miss Barnes had assumed, to me, the magnitude of an incident.

In a punitive, self-righteous mood, I decided to "get" them all, to expose, as I termed it, the sins of Western literature. I set out the pens dipped in venom, the crisp, militant index cards. I turned up the flame under the pot of bitter Bustelo and started off, like a vigilante or a bounty hunter, in search of *them*. I was going to make Hemingway pay for the nigger boxer in Vienna in *The Sun Also Rises*. Fitzgerald was going to be called out for the Cadillac of niggers who rolled their eyes when they pulled up on the highway next to Gatsby.

I was going to get Dashiell Hammett for "darkie town," and Evelyn Waugh, Ronald Firbank, even Carl Van Vechten. This was serious—no Julia Peterkin, Fannie Hurst, or Dubose Heyward. I was going to stick to the Dilseys and Joe Christmases. If Conrad had to go, so be it, Céline, too, for his scenes in Little Togo. Sweat dripped from my nose onto the index cards. The laughter boiling in the streets added to my sense of lonely mission.

I woke in my clothes, determined to beat up poor Hart Crane for "Black Tambourine." Not even William Carlos Williams was going to get off easy. The jig was up for Rimbaud's sham niggers. Sins were everywhere: Katherine Mansfield in a letter spoke of one woman as "the sort to go with negroes." I was going to let Shaw have it, show Sartre a thing or two about the aura of the text of *Black Orpheus*. How dare Daniel Deronda condescend to defend Caliban!

But by noon, thanks to hypoglycemia, I wasn't sure that it mattered that in 1925 Virginia Woolf had come across a black man, spiffy in swallow tails and bowler, whose hands reminded her of a monkey's. How far back would I have to go, to Pushkin's Ibrahim or to the black ram tupping the white ewe? And to what purpose? Roussel's *Impressions d'Afrique* didn't even take place on earth, not really. Dinesen's farm was real, but so what? What was done was done, though most of the "gothic horror" was far from over. "Let them talk. You know your name," my grandfather used to say. I threw out the index cards. The motive for my note taking was pretty sorry: after leaving Miss Barnes I had fallen into the pit of trying to prove that there was more to me than she thought.

There was more to sinking, to being a handyman, to becoming a part of the streets around me, than I had thought. I had only to approach the surface of things, like a child coming too near the heat of a kitchen range, to discover that. Being in arrears made me afraid to meet anyone from Pomander Walk. I didn't have the nerve to ask the caretakers to fix a faucet. I sold off some big books to keep the lights on. The curtain over my rear window stayed down. What companionship of the outside I had was provided by the view of Ninety-fifth Street from my front windows. It was there that I sat on those penniless summer nights, watching the elderly across the street scrutinize me from their prisons. There was a parking lot belonging to a Salvation Army residence. Daily the employees dragged themselves to their horrible duties and in the evenings they exchanged gossip with the night shift before hurrying away. Sometimes, on Sundays, guilty families came to wheel their begetters into sleek sedans for useless outings.

It was a street on which anything could happen and a lot did happen. Sometimes the angry voices after midnight terrified me, as if a wife or a whore were being beaten at the foot of my bed. I gave up calling the police and got used to it. That accounted for Pomander Walk's general fear of invasion. Between Riverside Drive and Central Park West, Ninety-fifth Street was a no man's land, a zone of foreign tongues and welfare tenements. There were enough stories of ivy being torn from the walls by vandals, of someone who had had her purse ripped from her arm by a fleet-footed phantom who could not have been more than fifteen. The chilling cry of *"Motherfuckers! All y'all motherfuckers is gonna die!"* was enough to send every light on Pomander Walk blazing, as if a whistle had been blown to alert the local militia.

The building directly across from me had the most unsavory of reputations. It was an SRO, a very dark, benighted affair embedded in a slope. I noticed that pedestrians crossed the street to my side rather than risk the building's contagions that waited in ambush. A check-cashing joint occupied one of the rooms on the first floor, and from the number of men coming in and out in their undershirts, wielding soiled paper bags from which the tops of wine or beer bottles were visible, I guessed that there was also a bookie joint somewhere inside. These men with missing teeth and shimmering hair who paced back and forth on the street, discussing their chances in that snapping, high-wire Spanish, made a strange tableau with the drag queens who also congregated outside the SRO.

The drag queens were impossible to miss, impossible not to hear. Hour on hour they milled around the entrance, dancing intricate steps to snatches of music that came from automobile radios. Most of them were in "low drag"—cutoffs, clogs, improvised halter tops, hair slicked straight back. Some appeared in wigs, curlers, black bathrobes, golden house slippers. They held cigarettes, long, brown More menthols or Kools, which they rationed scrupulously. They gossiped, waited, and played whist, "Nigger Bridge." They taunted young mothers who pushed baby carriages and balanced Zabar's bags and helium balloons; they hissed at broad-backed boys who sauntered up the street in Harvard or Columbia Crew T-shirts. "Honey, you need to go home and take off that outfit. That green gon' make yo' husband run away from you." Or: "Come over here, sugar, and let me show you somethin'."

Sometimes, for no apparent reason, just standing there, one of them would let out a long, loud, high scream—"Owwwwwww"—and then look around with everyone else on the street. This was particularly unnerving to the people who lined up with ice cream cones in front of the film revival house to see Fassbinder or Fellini. Equally unsettling to the neighborhood was their booby-trapped friendliness: "How ya doin', baby? Okay. Be that way. Don't speak, Miss Thing. You ain't gettin' none no way."

I watched the people of the SRO every day as the buds on the gingko that grew at a slant toward my window failed one by one and the pigeons pushed through the litter of frankfurter buns, hamburger wrappers, and pizza crusts. I recognized some of the SRO inmates at the Cuban tobacconist, the Puerto Rican laundromat, the Korean deli, at the Yemenite bodega, the hippie pot store, the Sikh newsstand. I watched them with a kind of envy. I loitered on the corner one night, but everyone stayed clear of me. Perhaps they took me for a narc. But it was perfectly natural to cross the street to get the instant replay after a Checker had slammed into a station wagon or a fire been put out three blocks away.

Of course I did not find friendship, no matter how swiftly some of the drag queens and youths stepped off into the personal. Raps about the doings on Broadway or in the park inevitably shifted to breathless, coercive pleas for loans, though I told them I had had to break open my Snoopy bank for cigarettes. The soft-spoken owner of Pomander Bookshop took me aside to give me a warning. More than one innocent had fled that SRO without watch, wallet, or trousers. Three "bloods" invited me up to discuss a deal. An alarm went off in my head. I remembered how, as a child, three classmates had invited me to join their club. They escorted me to a garage and kicked the shit out of me. Remembering that, I got as far as the lobby, made some excuse, and split. I had always been uncomfortable with their questions about Pomander Walk.

It is hard to recall the murky, inchoate thinking that led me to make those inept gestures toward infiltrating what I saw as the underside of life, hard to camouflage the fatuity of my cautious hoverings. One night, late, a young woman was attacked by two kids. I heard her scream, saw her throw herself to the ground and thrash about. The kids couldn't get to her purse. By the time I got across the street others had come running. That was it, she moaned, she was going home to Baton Rouge. One grinding dawn I stumbled out into the haze with loose change for a doughnut. The intersection of Broadway and Ninety-fifth Street was clogged with squad cars. Flashing lights whipped over the faces of the somber onlookers. There had been a shooting. A handsome Hispanic man in handcuffs was pulled over to the ambulance, presumably to be identified by the victim. His shirttails flapped like signal flags. A policeman cupped "the perpetrator's" head as he pushed him into the rear of a squad car at the curb. The man's head sagged on his smooth chest and shook slowly, rhythmically. Who was it who said the man who committed the crime was not the same man as the one in the witness box?

The violence was arbitrary. I was in a crowd that watched in horror as the policemen who had been summoned to defuse a fight beat a black teenager until coils of dark blood gushed from his head, his mouth, and drenched his shantung shirt. To my shame it was a black cop who used his stick with the most abandon. We were ordered to disperse, didn't, were rushed, and the voltage of fear that seized us was nothing like that of the political demonstrations in another time.

Shortly afterward I called home. It seemed that I packed more than clothes. I carried to the corner all the baggage of my youth. I thought, as a taxi driver slowed to look me over, that I could leave those weights behind, like tagless pieces chugging around and around on a conveyor belt. Pollution made the sunset arresting, peach and mauve like the melancholy seascapes of The Hague School. On the way to La Guardia, stalled somewhere near the toll booth, I, looking forward to my prepaid ticket, to the balm of the attendants' professional civility, felt a wind. It came like forgiveness, that sweet, evening breeze, the first promissory caress of the high summer. The storm that followed delayed the departure of my flight.

HOODOO

Connie Porter

In the closet under the stairs at 79-B All-Bright Court the albino girl lies and dreams. She dreams there is a door at the end of the sloping closet, a small door. Through the door there comes a black boy. He is small when he comes through the door, but once in the closet he is big and sits with his knees to his chest. The boy has come to bring the albino girl color. He has come with a small tin of watercolors.

He opens the tin and paints her soft, fat, white body. The boy paints with short, quick strokes that feel like the licking of a cat's tongue. He mixes the colors and paints her black. He uses them all up to make her black.

The girl is allowed outside then. She can be seen. The wind blows on her and the sun shines. Its light does not hurt her eyes. She is loved. Her mother and father love her. The boy loves her, and she and the boy dance. There is something in the dance that summons rain. It falls like a punishment and washes the color away. The rain makes her ugly again, and she runs back inside. She hides in the closet, and the boy follows her. He tells her he will bring color again. He will go home for crayons.

"They won't wash away," he says.

And the boy makes himself small again and goes back through the small door. But before the black boy can come back, the colorless girl awakens.

She awakens to find the door at the end of the closet has disappeared, and she has been sleeping. She has been hiding and dreaming in the closet because she is not loved. Her parents hate her. This child is a punishment. She is a spell worked up by her grandmother.

"She working a spell," Zena's mother said when Zena told her of Greene's kindness.

"She never even talked to you before. Why should she start now?" her mother asked.

"Because I'm having Karo baby. It's her grandchild," Zena said.

"I'm not so sure that's not a spell, too."

"Oh, Mama," Zena said.

"Don't you 'Oh, Mama' me. You was too young to remember when Greene first come up here. That was the same summer them bats came."

It was back in 1964 that Greene and her six children came up from Florida. They just showed up at the All-Bright Court in a dusty yellow pickup. No one knew them, and not a week after they moved in, the bats came.

Out of twilight they appeared as shadows, first a few, then hundreds. But under the pale light of the new moon they became bats. An ashy boy led a group of boys on a hunt. With baseball bats and sticks they managed to kill a few bats they chased off from the main group. No one had ever seen anything like it before, and when one of the women mentioned it to Greene, she said, "I want to get my hands on one of them bats. I could use one of them bats."

And that was all it had taken. The next morning, "What she want with a bat?" was the question being asked by the women from one end of All-Bright Court to the other.

"And where them bats come from out of nowhere?"

"You reckon she called them?"

"And *what* she was going to do with a bat?"

"What you think! She into hoodoo."

"If they come back tonight, you tell your son to leave them bats alone, hear? He don't need to be catching no bats for her."

"And hey, girl, you see her teeth? They all gold. Looking in her mouth make you feel like you falling in a pit."

All of Greene's teeth were covered in gold, and none of the women knew how she could afford them. Despite the fact she wore a silver band, no husband had come north with her. But Greene had no trouble attracting men.

"Country nigger," is what the women said of Greene. Of the men they said, "Only a country nigger would think her mouth look good."

This did not stop some of their husbands from passing in and out of her back door. They came to explore the riches of her mouth. They left knowing the secrets beneath her tongue. These men left behind four more children, and Greene tied asafetida bags around their necks.

All her children wore the bags, including the ones who had come up from Florida. The bags and strings turned black and greasy and smelled of garlic, but Greene's children never seemed to get sick.

No one could ever remember them getting chicken pox, measles, whooping cough, mumps, not even a cold. Most children stayed away from them because the bags gave off such an odor, but Zena did not.

She came near Karo. She danced with him. She held his hand for pop the whip. It was Zena who convinced Karo to take the stinking, dirty bag from his neck back in 1966.

"It's stupid," Zena said. "It don't really protect you from germs. That's country. You know the school nurse say y'all don't get sick 'cause don't nobody come in breathing distance of y'all. Why don't you just take it off?" Zena asked.

And this and Zena's smile was all that it took for Karo to break the string and throw the bag away.

He told his mother the string had broken and he had lost the bag in a field. Greene said nothing. Karo was almost twelve, anyway. He didn't need it anymore. But when he went to sleep, Greene sat on the edge of his bed and raised the lids of his eyes to find Zena dancing in the back of them.

Greene never disliked Zena. She was never nasty to her, but she was not nice either. Sometimes Zena would be there in Greene's house, just like air, just like she had always been there. And Greene never spoke to her. How could you speak to air?

Greene had ten children and other women's husbands to look after. She had no time to take notice of Zena. She was tired much of the time. But a look of tiredness in her eyes was not that. It was the evil eye. Greene caused the sewers to back up more often. She caused the winters to be harsher, and the rivers to rise higher in spring. She could cause ringworms and mange to appear on children's scalps. She could even make husbands cleave not unto their wives, but come to her seeking treasure. Greene was accused of being a country nigger who had not left her ways behind. Her accusers knew because they were country niggers, too.

They were all from the South, and most were from the country. They claimed Birmingham, Fayetteville, Jacksonville, Jackson, New Orleans. But they were from Plain Dealing, Zenith, Goshen, Acme, Gopher. They came from specks on the map. They knew the country and its ways well. They had seen spells cast, fields dry up, floods come, moles cast into women's wombs. And then there were the bats.

The bats had come with Greene's arrival. They had only come that one night, and they had never come back. That could not be ignored.

Zena's mother could not keep her away from Karo, so she warned her about Greene.

"You stay from out her house, you hear?" her mother said. "And don't be eating nothing she cook. I mean nothing. Ain't no telling what she might cook up in it."

Zena and Karo married in 1972. She was pregnant, and though Karo was only eighteen, Greene signed for him to marry. He went off and joined the Navy.

And it was in Zena's fifth month that she became sick. Her stomach was upset for a week and her urine turned dark. There was a milkiness, a whiteness that passed across her irises. It passed across slowly, like a thin cloud against a windless night sky. After two days of sickness Zena admitted to her mother she had eaten at Greene's. She had some potato salad and collards.

"She working a spell. I'm telling you, she working something on the baby. She done something to mark the baby," Zena's mother said.

"That's crazy, Mama. That's just a bunch of country talk."

But Zena never felt right after her dinner at Greene's. She was always tired, and there was an uneasiness inside her, a cold whiteness that moved from Zena's eyes and into her womb. The baby seemed to pick it up. It made the baby still.

The doctor at the clinic said there was nothing wrong, but the birth of the baby proved the doctor wrong.

She was a fat white baby with white hair and pink lips. All of the color had been washed from her.

Karo had been out to sea when the baby was born, and when he came home and saw her, he did not want to even touch her. He refused to hold her. The child was ugly, and Zena kept her hidden in the house. Both of their families shunned the child, but Greene had come over to see her once.

She came to bring an asafetida bag for the child. She tied it around the baby's neck and told Zena, "I knows what these people be saying about me, but it ain't true. I ain't no conjure woman. But how can you tell people that? People believes what they want to." That was the most Greene had ever said to her, and before she left Zena's house, she repeated, "People believes what they want to."

Zena took the bag from the baby's neck and threw it away, and she kept the baby hidden.

The paper boy has managed to see this all white child, though. He has seen her far off in the darkness of the afternoon house, her milky blue eyes staring at him. She has never come to the door, but only sat and stared as he opened the door and placed the paper on the floor.

After her nap today, after the colorless girl awakens to find the door at the end of the closet has disappeared, she goes and sits in the cool darkness of the living room. And when she hears the paper boy coming up the stairs of the porch, she comes to the door.

He opens the screen door and stares at the child. He stares at her white skin, her woolly white hair, her full pink lips. He smiles at her and hands her the paper.

Though he has not come from the closet, she thinks he is the black boy from her dream. Her milky blue eyes move rapidly as she tries to focus on the boy. But the brightness of the afternoon sun takes her vision away, and the boy becomes a shadow.

"Do you have the crayons?"

The boy is confused, and before he can answer, the girl's mother is there. She is floating above her, just like air. And she strikes the child. She knocks the child to the floor. The sheets of paper spill over her, and the door slams.

"I told you to stay away from the door. No one want to see you. Don't nobody come here to see you," her mother says.

It seems as though talking to this child hurts, as if with each word she is spitting sand.

The boy sees the girl get up, and her mother's hand printed pink across her face. Before he leaves the porch, he sees the girl run from the door and disappear into the closet under the stairs.

THE TERRIBLE

THREES

Ishmael Reed

President Jesse Hatch had been trying to arrange a meeting with Reverend Jones for three weeks, ever since Pedigree auctioneers had revealed the existence of a letter written by the late Admiral Matthews; rumor had it that if the letter was revealed a special prosecutor would have to be called in to unravel the mess and call for indictments. Inside the Oval Office, which Hatch rarely saw, Hatch paced up and down, his tie loosened, mashing cigarette butts into ashtrays, and behaving in a generally Type A manner, like Bogart in *The Maltese Falcon*. Jones expressed his annoyance with Hatch by staring disdainfully at the ashtray. Hatch got the message. He put out his cigarette. Reverend Jones listened patiently. "Goddammit, that special prosecutor is trying to put our asses in jail, and all you have to say is pray."

"Don't worry, Jesse, it'll blow over. We have someone to take the fall. If Congress acts up, we'll throw them a piece of meat. Kosher meat."

"I don't follow you," Hatch said, already calmer.

"Look at it this way, Jesse. Krantz has no family, he doesn't get along with the press, and he's Jewish. Who else would have that kind of name? So even though he converted—I baptized him personally—he's still a Jew at heart. We can say that he did it for Israel or something. You know,

567

convince the Arabs that we're evenhanded, satisfy the Christian majority at the same time. We'll get public opinion on our side. Blame it on communism. That always works. Say that Krantz was part of some kind of worldwide communist conspiracy aligned with Satanists and Antichrists. Besides, I'm beginning to have my doubts about Krantz. He was always hanging around with the Admiral. Touring nuclear subs with him. And another thing. It's been almost four years since I brought him to Washington. He hasn't aged one bit."

"I've noticed that, too. Nobody likes Krantz, anyway. He has almost as many enemies as you, I mean . . ."

"Don't give it a second thought, Hatch. I know that I have enemies in the capital, but this town was worse than Sodom and Gomorrah before I came to town. Licentious parties attended by the press and politicians, womanizing and manizing, every possible sin that you can think of was being committed in broad daylight. Now the Marines are rounding up people and sending them to Sunday School. The Conversion Bill—when my court declares it constitutional—will drive the infidels out of the country. They will have to convert to Christianity or leave. I made the Congressmen give up their hideaways where they used to go and meet their dates, so they're mad. The Washington hostesses are mad because neither I nor my cabinet attend their parties. The Redskins hate me because I forbid government employees to attend football, a sport which I'm convinced has pagan roots. Lucy Artemis is mad at me because I put all the soothsayers out of town, cutting in on her multimillion-dollar business. The Shriners are mad because I caught them squirreling away funds from the crippled children's fund; the Ms. America contest is mad because I insisted that the contestants abandon cosmetic surgery, and Coca-Cola is mad because I revealed that Classic Coke wasn't on the up-and-up. Goddammit, if anybody bumped me off everybody in town would have a motive, but they can't get me, as hard as they try, they can't get me. I don't smoke, don't drink, and unlike the competition, I know how to keep my britches up. Do you think that I'm going to let them get me like they did Nixon and Reagan? He betrayed us worst of all. Cozying up to the Russians in 1987 and 1988 just because his wife wanted him to get the Nobel Peace Prize. You saw what happened to them after they left Washington, didn't you? Snubbed by California country-club Republicans. Ridiculed by their former supporters: car dealers and owners of beer franchises. Why, there were times when they couldn't even go to their favorite Mexican restaurant without dining parties stalking out, refusing to even be seen in public with them. When one follows the ways of the Lord, Hatch, one becomes surrounded by agents of the Antichrist." Hatch thought for a moment. He began letting it all sink in. Jones had a way of lubricating words so that they eased through your mind without the slightest snag. So that they were easy to take. Hatch fidgeted with the lapels of his pinstripe suit, as the preacher smiled at him. Both were wearing Barbie pinstripes. Some of the insiders were saying that the preacher was in a bad way, talking to people who weren't in the room. An S.S. officer from whom he sought advice. Some were even saying that a mysterious Hollywood blowup was carrying out covert operations for him. But there was no sign of that this morning. The preacher had thought ahead.

"It's a shame that such a blunder was made on the basis of faulty intelligence."

"What do you mean, Reverend?"

"The Nigerians didn't have the bomb. The men over at the CIA thought that this Yoruban Operation they kept referring to in their overseas communications had something to do with a weapon. It didn't. We're still trying to figure out what it meant. The only problem is that when the surps find out that there was a plan to devastate Miami and New York, we'll have a lot of explaining to do." Jones leaned back in his chair. He looked at his watch and yawned. So the Admiral had the last laugh. His maid discovering the letter in a wastebasket. Good thing that Krantz destroyed the backup archives, he thought.

"I'd better get going, Reverend. I feel better now that I've talked to you." Reverend Jones rose and shook the President's hand. As Hatch left Reverend Jones, he turned and said, "I'm glad to be on your team, Reverend Jones." Reverend Jones frowned. "The Lord's team, Hatch. The Lord's team."

———————

It was fifteen degrees below, and the windchill factor made it feel like thirty below (the American standard of living was a few points lower than that), and everywhere you looked in the nation's cities, mobs were roaming, searching for food underneath garbage can lids and in charity soup lines and in the homeless shelters, which had become an American way of life. In Washington autos were stranded in shells of snow. Banks, airports, and schools were closed. So were the federal offices, but this didn't deter the mourners, wrapped in overcoats, from attending the funeral of Rear Admiral Matthews, retired, a member of the four who ruled the Jesse Hatch White House. Their power had increased after former President Dean Clift, the ex-model, had been removed from office after the scandal known as the Terrible Twos.

Admiral Matthews was part of the invisible government that carried on the affairs of state after the Clift debacle, aided by the Reverend Clement Jones, a faith healer and televangelist, Robert Krantz, the White House communications officer and ex-television producer, and a man known as the King of Beer, who during the Terrible Twos was involved in a dispute with Indians in Colorado over the rights to water, which the Indians claimed flowed from a sacred spring. The King of Beer had suddenly dropped out of sight, and the FBI was still searching for him. Though Admiral Matthews provided the administration with a firm hand at the top, it was Krantz who carried out the orders. He was the one who spun and glided, stonewalled, and micromanaged. It was through his bland conniving that the Terrible Twos scandal had been, ultimately, shoved to the interior pages of the newspapers, and as the election approached, pundits were saying that President Hatch would probably win by a landslide, his only possible rival being Dean Clift, who still commanded a small but dedicated following.

Reverend Jones, "spiritual leader" of the government, hated Admiral Matthews because the Admiral smoked cigarettes, didn't go to church, and was married to a former chorus girl. Though he had brought Krantz into government, he envied the close relationship that Krantz had developed with Admiral Matthews. Admiral Matthews and Krantz had been like father and son, and to think it was he, Jones, who had rescued Krantz from certain death underneath the wheels of a fiery sports car, the incident that had brought millions more to Reverend Jones's gospel hour. Reverend Jones could do what no other white preacher in America could do, and though his church had brought in millions, Jones shunned the lavish style of living embraced by his colleagues, and sometimes went about in the same polyester suit and drove a 1958 Studebaker through the streets of Washington. He seldom went home where his wife's every need was being handled by a household staff and where she passed her days doing watercolors of the same landscape. The same tree. The same cloud. And the same flower garden. She had done hundreds of paintings of the same scene. The paintings filled the three bedrooms of the upstairs, the garages, and the basements. Sometimes she would paint for three days and go without food. It kept her busy, and the Reverend figured that it was good therapy.

At the Admiral's funeral Jones sat next to the widow, but ignored her. His own wife sat on his other side, a shivering pile of fragile bones. Eagles and flags were omnipresent, including those belonging to the Marines. They began the services, slowly marching down the aisles, in front of the Admiral's coffin. After the coffin was placed in front of the church, the pastor read the invocation. Because of the cold in the church, there was more than the usual amount of coughing. It sounded hollow in the huge church. Some hymns were sung. And then the pastor introduced Reverend Jones, who headed toward the lectern, as sturdy as a Volkswagen bug. The media personnel outnumbered the mourners, and Reverend Jones began to dab his face with a handkerchief, so hot were the lights, even in the cold church.

He began to slowly recount the story of Abraham, and how when the old Patriarch was through and had done his work, he was ready for his trip to the Promised Land. The Reverend recounted how the members of the old man's tribe, the women, and the men, and the little children, had all stood before Abraham, and how God had promised that he would select a leader to replace Abraham. The preacher, with that familiar whiny voice that had excited millions of the helpless, likened Abraham to Admiral Matthews, and though he did not name himself as Matthews's successor, he asked the church for their prayers as he guided America through the great tsunami that lay ahead. After Jones had warmed up, he began pacing up and down the pulpit and sliding across the pulpit like James Brown. He began to do the Al Green hop. He began to do the old black preacher's "uh huh . . . uh-huh . . . huh." His voice began to become gravelly, and he began to shout for emphasis, like Jesse Jackson. He knew how to screech and say OOOOOOOOO in falsetto like Little Richard, and then his voice took on that tremulous timbre like one of the greatest black preachers of all time, the Reverend E. Franklin. Even some of these women who were the mainstays of Washington society, who hated Reverend Jones, women who spent a lot of time under the dryer and preparing for lunch, women who would spend entire days shopping for clothes, convulsed, their stomachs rippling. A couple of them even "went out," and had to be assisted to the waiting ambulances that were always on hand when Reverend Jones was going to preach.

An American legend: Colonel Tom Parker was supposed to have said that if he could find a white man who could sing rock 'n' roll like a black man, he'd make a million dollars. Elvis Presley was invented. It could also be said that if a white preacher could be found who could preach like one of the great carriers of the oral tradition, could preach like a black preacher, he would rule America. People were saying that Reverend Jones was that preacher. None of this pitiful, whining Jimmy Swaggart stuff. None of this wimpy Fulton Sheen crystal cathedral tepidness. None of these Jim Bakker Charlie McCarthy machinations, the theme parks, the positively nouveau display of wealth.

When he was on, Reverend Jones preached his gospel hour in a Texas church that held no more than 250 people, but the way he had the old sisters banging on them bass drums and slapping them tambourines, you'd think that God's Own Philharmonic was carrying on inside that old church where the loudspeakers blasted Jones's message to the thousands who stood outside. At the conclusion of Reverend Jones's sermon, the church didn't need no fire, because it was being warmed by the spirit of the Lord. By the spirit of Jesus. "Because when you got Jesus you don't need no expensive indoor heating, no oven, no nuclear fuel, no solar energy, when you got Jesus you got all the heat you need. Jesus hits like an Atomic Bomb," Jones shouted to the mourners. People began removing their overcoats. This had been the closest thing to a sermon that he'd preached since he joined the administration of Dean Clift. He didn't want to be accused of mixing religion with politics, a charge that had been made when he became part of the inner circle which Clift fronted, and so he'd turned over his multibillion-dollar ministry to a young preacher named the Reverend John the Conquerer, after the vision he had in a Riverside, California, motel, when Jesus appeared to him in the form of a desk clerk and asked him to go to Washington and save America from the primeval slime, Satan worship, and Prince. Hip hop, funk, astrology, etc.

—————

The lettuce was flecked with stains the color of soy sauce, and the tomatoes were turning black. The roast beef was thinly sliced, dry, and white. Krantz had been to a lot of these dinners. The same old chocolate pudding. Some of the current heroes, who'd blipped across the nation's TV screens, were seated on the dais. Carson Richards, Wall Street speculator and junk bond addict, former pimp, whom the New Christians pointed to as an example of how a surp could still rise in an American society ruled by the Jesse Hatch administration, and the New Christian majority in Congress. Seated next to him was Ted Bare, the skinhead who became famous after setting a surp afire while the surp was wrapped in dirty blankets and sleeping underneath a Santa Cruz freeway. He didn't remove his Boston Red Sox baseball cap; he wore sneakers and a red, white, and blue basketball jacket. Krantz wore the uniform of the New Christian, Barbie black and white pinstripes, after the suit worn by Klaus Barbie at his trial at Lyons. Reverend Jones saw Hitler as a misunderstood genius, a sort of knight of Christianity saving the West, defending the free world from the Mongolian hordes and Asiatic death. He required that members of his team wear the Barbie outfit. They never asked why, being loyal to Reverend Jones. He never discussed his Hitlerian ideas with the staff and only shared them with his intimates, Heinrich, and Joe Beowulf, a robot superhero on loan to him from Towers Bradhurst, Hollywood producer.

Krantz successfully concealed his red eyes with drops of Murine; he'd hastily shaved in the limousine that drove him to the hotel, and had done a pretty convincing job of it, only a few hairs having been missed; you couldn't tell that he'd slept in his suit or that his shirt was drenched or that his hands were trembling. William Manchester reported that the night before his Dallas murder (the Terrible One) President Kennedy's hands were trembling as he made a speech before a group of scornful cattlemen. The same crew that had killed him were still in the secret government; Krantz knew, for he had met with them in out-of-the-way hotels and airport rest rooms as he gave them assignments coming from the Colorado Gang, as the inner circle was being called. Would they kill him? Had they killed Admiral Matthews? Matthews was right, but he wasn't nuts. He'd always vetoed the kooky proposals that the King of Beer and the Reverend Jones had made. His sudden death was a shock because there had been no sign of illness. He and Krantz had attended a Press Club dinner the night before, and the Admiral had even been roasted.

They couldn't kill Krantz, of course, but would attempt to do so if he exposed the mission. He paused from his thoughts long enough to hear his name called. The introduction, referring to his distinguished career as a television producer of the soap opera *Sorrows and Trials*, and the often-told story about how Reverend Jones had rescued him from a car accident and had miraculously delivered him from underneath its wheels—a story that had been embellished each time it had been repeated—was followed by a standing ovation as Krantz approached the microphones to deliver his speech. He made a joke about the Washington weather. Both airports were closed, and the hotel lights, though on for now, were threatening to go out. He made a joke about the Post Office, everybody's favorite bureaucratic whipping boy. About how he'd been in one of the long Xmas lines and the woman ahead of him complained about having to pay the postage for a gift she received and the price of the postage exceeding the value of the gift. He then got down to the speech. It was the speech that he'd delivered hundreds of times, about the terrible period that happened before the administration of Jesse Hatch and Reverend Jones. About how surps in running shoes and hoods had just about taken over the cities. About how the United States was being laughed at by the world for the sellout deal that left-winger Ronald Reagan had made with the Russians, the one they were calling the Second Yalta. Some on the right, himself included, had even said that Reagan, feeble and sick and under the guidance of a San Francisco astrologer, had made a verbal agreement with Gorbachev at Reykjavík, one that amounted to surrender. He talked about how administrations after that had faltered, until the election of General Walter Scott, hero of Dominica, whom he described as "a shaft of light at the bottom of the cellar." And how just as the Terribles that had begun with the assassination of J.F.K. were thought to have come to an end, General Scott died from a cold he'd contracted on Inauguration Day. And how Dean Clift had been sworn in to carry out the policies of General Scott, only to suffer "an episode of nervous exhaustion, saying that he was visited by Saint Nicholas." The audience laughed, as usual, at this line. Krantz signaled them to cease. "It's no joke, ladies and gentlemen," he said. "It wasn't funny when he accused me, Admiral Matthews, Reverend Jones, and the King of Beer of being engaged in some sort of secret operation, therefore smearing three of the greatest patriots this country has ever known." The audience rose and gave him a standing ovation, which was the usual response to this line, until Krantz requested that they resume their seats. He dramatically mopped his brow, the hotel's generator being too hot. "Said that the four of us were in on some kind of fantasy that only existed in his mind, an Operation Two Birds, some kind of back-channel operation that, according to him, involved some rip-off artists, free-lance arms dealers, assorted and shady consultants, and con men. No wonder folks began calling him President Weird.

"Oh, you know the rest, ladies and gentlemen, how the nations had to endure another Terrible. Another president crippled in office. And you know how fond we were of Dean and his lovely wife, Elizabeth. But, now that I look back at it, maybe the Lord was sending us a sign when Elizabeth was struck down by that Xmas tree. That dreadful night led to Clift's downfall, and I'm convinced that his strange recital on television about alleged wrong-doings by the Admiral, Reverend Jones, the King of Beer, and me was a result of the young man's distraught condition. That's what I thought then, but recently, ladies and gentlemen, we've learned that some of the wild rumors that had been going around about his administration were true. The P.C.P. and angel dust parties in the White House, where unrobed young men and women were entertained by the heavy metal music of Boy Gonorrhea and Frequent Urination. They were playing the music of hell. This couple had turned the mansion into a fornicating den of Satan, ladies and gentlemen. And when we went to serve the notice to Dean Clift that he was to be removed from office, he was engaged in some bizarre Xmas tree planting that Reverend Jones, not only the greatest chief of staff in history, but a great biblical scholar as well, authority on Milton, and a member of the English Department of Queens College for ten years—before he relocated to Texas—identified as the pagan rites of Saturnalia. It wasn't the grief, ladies and gentlemen, it was some kind of wild hallucinogenic that caused him to make that speech. After we got rid of him, Jesse Hatch, a true patriot, took over and, with his aides, was able to get the country moving again.

"We tried to turn back the waves of infidels coming in over the border arriving in freedom boats into Florida; we tried to ban Spanish, and now everybody, it seems, is speaking it; we thought that the Asian Americans would set an example for the others, but they turned out to be as deceitful and as cunning as their ancestors described in the writings of the California prophet Jack London, who warned of the invasion of yellows. They were making millions of dollars from drug sales and with the profits buying up the United States. And so who needs them, ladies and gentlemen? Who needs the yellows, the browns, the reds, and the blacks, unless they, like Carson Richards, serve our Western ways, preserve our values? Unless they do that, they are surps. The wastes of history, the floating dump of the aeons." The audience was still as Krantz began to wind up his speech. "And now, ladies and gentlemen, Clift's trying to regain the power that the Lord wanted taken from him. He is challenging the decision that removed him from office, even though everything was legal.

"We got the majority of principal officers of the executive departments and Vice President Hatch to send a letter to Congress stating that President Clift was incapable of discharging the duties of his office. And as you know, the appeals court upheld the lower court's decision last week. And I promise you that the Supreme Court with Chief Justice Nola Payne in charge will do likewise, ladies and gentlemen, and then let us hope that Dean Clift will come to his senses and unite behind Jesse Hatch and the greatest White House chief of staff in history, the Reverend Clement Jones." The audience rose and began to clap until their hands became sore. Krantz was mobbed and had to have an aisle cleared so that he could make his way from the podium to the waiting limousine in the rear of the hotel, shaking hands with dignitaries along the way. Reporters were after him with questions. *Mr. Krantz, is it true that Reverend Jones spends hours in the Oval Office talking to pretend friends? Over here, Mr. Krantz. Bob, aren't you concerned about the circumstances surrounding Admiral Matthews's death; don't you have suspicions? Mr. Krantz, is it true that you're leaving the White House for an ambassadorial post?* Krantz didn't answer any questions. He instructed the driver to get him to the White House.

BEFORE ECHO

Fatima Shaik

Morning light does not enter the swamp. Even the sunrise is dark. Still, time progresses, night into day.

A picture of bayou country is deceiving. Slow streams converge under mud to make the appearance of land that is actually water. One net of moss hangs from one hundred trees. Lightning strikes the same stump many times.

People pass the swamp's fringes in trains, on tracks that cling to the last solid ground. Out of their windows are landscapes that take the earth's colors to every periphery. Bright orange sunsets surround people like sky on an airplane. On gray foggy mornings they ride through a dream that has no beginning or end. But time has its limits, these people know. They are expected places—Memphis by midnight, New Orleans by dawn.

Deep in the swamp, animals keep the only appointments. Birds gather at high places in trees. Raccoons make their last noisy passes for food across someone's back porch before he awakes. Fish all around splash up, although they cannot see the morning coming to clean the picture of day like clothes bleaching in a galvanized tub from dark gray to light gray.

Joan looked out from the porch to the swamp she had known all her life. Ahead of her in the veiled light were the outlines of many trees. Below and around her were the crisp sounds of nature awakening. Cupped in both hands, perched on her knees was a warm mug of coffee.

Joan got up early for no other reason than habit. If she stayed in the bed, her bones would have felt strange. To avoid their odd aches and stiffness, she rose when the dampness of morning settled on her face. She could smell the dawn, since the air held a less stagnant pungency.

Usually the smell of rotten wood and dead fish came into her house. It mixed with the smell of moss, moldy but flat. But it provided a diverting aroma when Joan put her face close to the pillow or mattress.

The house was surrounded on three sides by water. Joan looked for her reflection when she first arrived on the porch. It stood out on stilts like a dock. But she did not see her appearance. The water was too dim and the morning too early.

"Is the same now as it was then, before the Savior, before the words in the Bible." Joan spoke out to the darkness and considered that little had changed since the very beginning.

Joan had thought and dreamed a lot lately because she was so much alone. Her life was proscribed by the length of the days, and the bounty or scarcity of food in a season. "That's everybody." Joan reconciled her existence as the same as everyone else in the world. Perhaps she was luckier than most to be fitted so well with nature. Everything she needed was inside her home or within the boundaries of water.

Her ideas differed little from the rare people who still lived in the swamp. When the fish ran, the oysters grew fat in their salt beds; the animals' furs thickened with the anticipation of cold; the people prospered and prided themselves for remaining in exile as their forefathers had in tribes and from Canada.

Joan didn't know history or think about it because she was still young. Her life was the present. Even the Bible she read, although written hundreds of years earlier, spoke directly to her.

Joan lived with her grandfather, and she took his ways too as modern behaviors. She hunted and fished, repaired the house, and sewed crab nets. She sipped homemade wine, smoked pipe tobacco or sometimes chewed it. It occurred to Joan only rarely that other young women might not live as she did. But if she considered that briefly, she dismissed it.

When Joan sat on the porch in the morning, she waited for nothing. Now she wanted to hear the buzz of outboard boat motor that would tell her the doctor was coming. Joan's grandfather was sick.

About illness, Joan was again like the swamp folk who took sickness too personally. They saw failure in themselves or the removal of love by the

Creator. That was one reason few people remained so isolated. Not many could sustain such passions with the invisible.

Joan wished for parents in her times of trouble. But they existed for her only like the dark spaces on the other side of the trees. Joan wanted to feel in the big, empty clearing peace and the comfort of nothing. That was her idea of belonging. When she was a baby, Joan's mother died, her grandfather said. They were not ever acquainted with Joan's father.

The woman at the supply store that Joan reached by pirogue suggested that Joan try to find out more about her mother and father. But Joan told her, "I don't care." The woman tried to convince Joan. "But what if you could know them? Don't you want to know?" Joan said, *"Non."* That was her lie.

Joan had tried early in life to figure out more from her grandfather. But her mother was like any daughter, Joan's grandfather said. That's all he knew. Joan worried. "How I could find out? Who I could ask?" But there was no one around her. And the concern made her days in the swamp go heavy and slow. When she began to feel that some fault caused her to be alone rather than God's act, Joan suffered. It was painful to think something should have been changed. Joan's only solution, she realized very young, was to not think about it. Only then could she experience comfort in her days that consisted of chores to take care of the house, the dog, and her grandfather.

Joan did not venture further with her curiosity, just as at night she did not go beyond the porch. Other animals saw better in darkness. Then they took over the land and the water. Joan only heard them outside, and from their weight, she guessed that they ran in packs or danced in couples, and that her only recourse was to scatter if she saw them in daylight.

Joan felt the darkness allowed the animals to conceive and to multiply. The darkness inspired God in His time to create the world. In Joan's darkness were quiet and mystery. She kept the time before her and of her beginning in ignorance.

Joan heard the faraway sound of the doctor's boat for ten minutes before he pulled up to the house. He handed her his bag before stepping from his rocking skiff to her stairs going down to the water.

"How you, how you?" he greeted her, just like the people he visited, although they bragged he "had education." They took credit for his success because he had returned to them after going away to school. They boasted to each other of his ability to move between the worlds of "smart people" and "us."

Joan's grandfather now remained in the bed separated by a fabric curtain from the rest of the house. Joan could hear his breath whistling loud like that of a person who sleeps with a cold, although he didn't rest. Sometimes he just stared ahead toward the door, and his eyes rolled back toward the ceiling. Joan was afraid.

The last time the doctor visited, her grandfather had not awakened as his pulse was taken, and the doctor placed the cold shiny thing over her grandfather's heart. The doctor made Joan listen first to the old man, then to herself, and then to him. "You can see for yourself. I'm sorry to tell you the truth, but he ain't doing too well," the doctor said. Joan held the object deep to her grandfather's ribs to hear the faint swishing and patting not quite in rhythm, like clothes on the line being blown by the wind against the side of the house.

Her own heart in contrast sounded like her bare foot tapping against the planks of the porch. And the doctor, even though he was much older than Joan, but younger than her grandfather—his heart thumped like the dog's tail on the floor wanting to be let out.

After the doctor left, Joan talked to herself about the Bible and read it aloud to the dog. She unwrapped some dried fish from a piece of paper and took some leaves from where they hung in a bunch near the ceiling to make a thin soup. She tried to get the old man to drink. But most of his food drooled back on him. She drank the rest on his plate and gave some to the dog. She sat on the floor near the old man's bed. And she held his hand as he had not allowed her to do since she was a little girl. She was now sixteen.

Joan noticed her grandfather growing old when his thick hair turned flatter, and from black to gray, white, then yellow. He walked slower. But since they traveled few distances by foot, she didn't care.

A few years earlier she had raced to their summer bathing place by the inland river and he could not keep up. But she challenged him less often as she got older. So they walked there in a slower, actually elderly gait.

She was young and she was pretty, Joan could see in the water's reflection once the light had descended in a flat heat and the darkness erased. But she did not especially flatter herself. Joan washed her dishes, clothes, and body with the same country store soap. She changed jeans not too frequently and outgrew her only pair of good shoes while they were still in the white box that came from the mailman.

Still, the lady who ran the store that Joan reached by the pirogue made nice comments. And some people, the store lady said, who remembered Joan from years past when her grandfather came to the community parties, complimented her. "Now she must blossom." Joan did, with full cheeks that blushed the color of rose water lilies from new ideas and embarrassments. And Joan felt rare. These swamp flowers proliferated in the heat and the darkness, but Joan was the only young woman around.

Joan sat alone on the floor next to her grandfather's bed and tried to inhale deeply at the same time as him. At first she thought this could help. But he didn't notice, and it only served to make her feel more of his difficulty.

The first day her grandfather could not rise from bed, Joan went in the pirogue two hours away to the store where she called the doctor. They discussed taking her grandfather to the nearest city hospital. "We could make way to take him in the boat. But why suffer him?" the doctor said. "You a woman now." The doctor paused on the telephone for her to acknowledge his authority. "You got to take care of this, you. If he don't come around, if he go, you pack and you come stay by me."

Joan listened because her grandfather always said, "Go to the doctor house if anything happen." Besides being her grandfather's friend, the doctor was the nearest adviser. The priest, sheriff, and schoolteacher all lived and worked close to each other in an area surrounded by high land. They clustered together to be convenient, they said. But that helped only people who got first to one of them.

Since the day Joan called the doctor, her grandfather had lost his desire to talk and lay most of the time like a baby or how Joan imagined one to be. He slept off and on. When awake he stared ahead, and his eyes filmed with water. Sometimes he drooled and wet on the bedcovers.

Joan felt he would die very soon, and she would bury him. She got pictures of herself in her mind, paddling the boat away from the burial. When she got those images, they often proved out.

Since a child, Joan had seen clear pictures in her head during times of deep concentration. Sometimes, quicker than a picture, a voice would give her advice. This voice, too, had the quality of predicting in advance something to happen. Once when she and her grandfather were hunting, the voice said, "Look over there." She saw a deer. Another time in the woods, the voice told her, "Stop." She just missed bumping into a snake hanging low on a branch.

Joan told her grandfather about these experiences. But he just advised she had good instincts, just like the animals knew a storm was coming, the birds from the north filled the ponds every winter, or the fish came close to the shore sunset and dawn. Joan had a special sense for nature, her grandfather said, and Joan agreed. She did not tell him that she knew in advance his words or requests for dinner. He might have thought her disrespectful.

Plus, the Bible assured Joan that all things were possible. Prophets saw visions. Demons took hold of people and had to be cast out. Joan felt safe and content in her special abilities. They helped her. They confirmed that her grandfather might soon be dead.

The old man called for Joan. She stood up and wiped her grandfather's face with a warm, damp cloth. His skin was thick and dry like an old piece of bark. His lips were parted, and she could see the spittle collecting into one cheek. She lifted his head for a sip of water. But his face tilted to the side and the liquid spilled from his mouth like an overturned cup.

The woman at the store wanted Joan to live there, where she rowed every week for supplies. "You just a child," the woman behind the counter told Joan. "Yes, you could be a daughter to me?" But Joan shook her head no, and packed the canned food she bought into a small leather bag that she put over her shoulder. The dog waited on the dock of the store by the boat.

Joan did not know where to go. But just rowing away seemed a good start. She had taken her grandfather's body, wrapped in a sheet, out to the boat. He was light, like a small animal. Joan closed the front door with the zipper of bent nails that held the screen flat when the wind was up from a rainstorm.

She took with her grandfather's body four empty half-gallon jugs that he kept for wine. He did not have too many around because he did not drink that often, only for special occasions. One remained half-full.

As she did for the more than a month of his sickness, actually for most of her life, she moved slowly and methodically. When her feelings welled up, she erased them. She had learned not to cringe when a rabbit needed to be skinned and gutted. She could watch with fascination alone when the heart of a turtle continued to pulse on the kitchen table. She had suspended her fear while her grandfather grew more sick, and she faced one new duty after another, cleaning up after him and waking to his gagging chokes in the night.

Joan was strong. Her grandfather once said her name came from the French saint set afire who went willingly into a war. So when he died, she buried him the way she knew. She rowed the boat out into the swamp, and she filled up the wine jugs with water by ducking them below the surface. Through the thumbhole for lifting the jugs she laced a rope and then tied it to her grandfather's body. Then she put them all overboard. The swamp folded her grandfather inside as he sank, and she said prayers to remind herself his spirit had left during the previous night, and now she submerged only his shell.

But Joan began crying and praying words from the Bible. And soon all jumbled around in her head, so that even the dog in the bow of the boat looked at her strangely. Her sobbing echoed on top of the water reaching far into the dark, empty spaces of swamp. And when she stopped, nature imitated her silence. But no longer did she feel its peace. Inside this timeless and changeless darkness, Joan felt different. She and the dog no longer belonged.

BETSEY BROWN

Ntozake Shange

"Goddammit, Greer! Do you understand anything I ever say to you?"

Jane looked at her wedding picture, satiny, a patina of thirteen years veiling her young foolish face. She wanted to push the gilded edges of the damn thing through Greer's head the way he used scalpels to take bullets outta the hoodlums he loved so much.

"Did you hear me? Where were you when I needed you? Me? Jane, your wife! Not some lowly sick acting-the-fool stinking niggahs so dumb they can't find the goddamn clinic! Do you hear me? I am talking to you!"

Greer looked up from *Digest for Surgical Procedures* and nodded. Jane froze. She held her breath and started again. She was going to be decent about this one more time.

"Where were you when the police brought our children home? Don't you realize what could have happened to them? Where were you, dammit! Answer me!"

Jane picked up his stethoscope and threw it at him. Greer caught it in his left hand and went right on reading.

"I was at the Johnsons'. He's been bleeding again since he left the hospital, and I wanted to check on him. He's an old man, Jane, he can't get up and run to the clinic on one leg."

"But I suppose your children could be in jail or dead on accounta poor Mr. Johnson, who's got so many benefits he's forgotten what money looks like."

Jane walked around the bed to Greer and pulled the *Digest* from his hands. "Did Mr. Johnson pay you something today? Or you so holy you can give your services away? Who do you think you are, Saint Francis? I have a house full of children who need clothes, shoes, dental work, eyeglasses, dance classes, food, and a father. And where is their father? Why, seeing Mr. Johnson! Mr. Johnson doesn't live here, Greer. We live here with five children and my beloved mother, who was right that the race definitely needs some improving!"

Jane began to beat the dresser with the *Digest*. Then she started tearing it to pieces, when Greer slowly wrapped her in his arms, saying: "Aren't the boys all right?" Jane didn't respond. "Aren't the police going to leave them alone if they act right?" Jane said nothing. "Look, honey, they're not in jail. Charlie was just having a little fun."

"Charlie was having fun, was he? Well, this is St. Louis, Missouri, my dear. You ask Chuck Berry how much fun the police let blacks have when it comes to white girls." Jane snatched Greer's loosened tie from around his neck.

"I am going to tell you one more time. I cannot run this house as if I were the father and the mother. Now I know you are a doctor, and you have a public responsibility, but if you don't put this household first in your life, I swear 'fore Jesus you're going to be in for a big surprise."

Greer knew Jane in these moods. He didn't understand why she couldn't see he was working himself half to death to keep the family exactly the way she wanted. She didn't understand that poor colored people didn't get decent treatment at the clinic, and by going by to see them he was building a clientele for his real practice. Damn, Greer thought, for such an intelligent woman, Jane didn't have much foresight.

"I got home as soon as I could." With that, Greer took his tie out of Jane's hands and picked up the latest issue of *MD* magazine.

Jane sat at her vanity table staring at Greer, who had the audacity to read when her boys had been touched by Southern police. What gall! What an ass she'd married! What ever was she going to do? She took the emery boards from the top left drawer and started doing her nails. She was going to play bridge, but before she did that she was going to have a scotch and soda and play a game of solitaire with the prettiest hands a woman with this many problems could have. Not another word passed between them, not one that was spoken, at any rate, not a word anyone else would understand.

Betsey thought she understood it. She thought she knew that the problem was there were too many of them. Too many children. Too wild. Too much noise. Too trying for her delicate mother's nature. Why, Mama wasn't raised to tend to a bunch of ruffians like Sharon and them, especially not Charlie, who'd awready been put out of schools in the North. No, Betsey knew when her parents were arguing it was most likely on accounta the children. Then there was the problem of the white people and money. White folks and money seemed to go hand in hand. Whenever a black mentioned one, he mentioned the other, like the white folks had took up all the money and were hiding it from the blacks, like they kept the nice houses for themselves, and the good schools, and the restaurants and motels. Just for themselves.

"You did not win," Charlie screeched down the back stairs. The basketball ricocheted from one wall to the other all the way down the stairway.

"Betsey! Would you see what's the matter?" Jane called tiredly from her manicure and highball.

"He did, too!"

"He didn't." Margot and Sharon began tussling with each other over the issue of whether or not Allard had won, when it was clear it was none of their business.

"He didn't what?" Betsey screamed into the house from her terrace, where she'd gone to escape the chaos of the house.

"Betsey! Didn't I ask you to see about these children?" Jane leaped up, exasperated. "Betsey, where are you?"

"That's not yours." Margot tried to pull the ball and jacks from Sharon.

"Who threw this ball down the stairs?" Vida hollered up.

"I don't know, Grandma," Betsey hollered down.

"Well, come along here and get it. It certainly doesn't belong in the kitchen."

"Grandma, I didn't have anything to do with that ball!"

"I'ma tell on you. You pull my hair one more time, ya hear?"

"Give it back then."

"I will not either."

"Allard, put those matches down! I see you. Where'd you start the fire?" Betsey ran after Allard, who'd only set a small fire on the third floor to get back at Charlie, who was a big bully anyway. By the time Betsey'd put the fire out, the second floor was going crazy.

"I'ma tell Mama. You tore my dress."

"If you do, I'ma knock one of those buck teeth of yours out!"

"Where's my basketball?"

"I'ma tell Mama."

"Mama, Mama, please make her stop."

"Mama, please make her stop."

"Mama, Allard got holdt to some matches again, but everything's awright."

"Sharon, stop it, I say."

"You're hurtin' my arm!"

"Mama, please, come help me," Margot cried.

"Mama, she's lying on me," Sharon moaned.

"Mama, I didn't start a big fire," Allard explained.

"Aunt Jane, tell Grandma to give me back my basketball."

"Mama, please! Come help."

Jane shut the door to her room and played solitaire, betting against herself. Greer'd fallen asleep. He'd been on call two nights in a row. Betsey went to her terrace for some cloud peace and air. The children just went on as children will do. Jane's thoughts veered to her wedding vows, "in sickness and in health." Wasn't anything about in madness or white folks.

Betsey took a deep breath 'cause the South may be full of ugly things but it's not in the air. The air is flowers, leaves, and spaces divine, when you're up high enough to climb onto a sturdy branch of your very own oak tree. If she climbed out to the middle of the tree, Betsey thought, she'd be a bird and sing a colored child's bird song, a colored child's blues song, or a hot jump and rag song. From the middle of her tree, where she was sure she was not supposed to be, Betsey listened real close for her city to sing to her so she could respond. Everybody knows any colored child could sing, specially one from a river city. A hankering blues-ridden, soft-swaying grace of a place like her home would surely answer her first melody.

From her vantage point through the myriad leaves, Betsey saw what looked to her mind like a woman in need of some new clothes and a suitcase. Who ever heard of carrying one's belongings in two shopping bags, while wearing a hat with five different-colored flowers on it? And she was singing a Mississippi muddy song:

humm hum, hum hum, hum uh

well, my name is bernice & i come a long way
up from arkansas & i'm here to stay
i got no friends & i ain't got no ma
but i'ma make st. louis give me a fair draw

hum hum, hum hum, hum hum, uh

there's some pretty young men
in these mighty fine jobs
got pomade in their hair
& they move like the light
i'ma set my sights
on a st. louis guy
with some luck by my side

i'ma dress up my best
& bring me a st. louis mess of a man

humm hum, hum hum, hum hum, hum uh

i'ma show them white folks in arkansas
that a good woman can get what she want
how she want and when/ humm humm, humm humm

my name is bernice & i come a long way
i'ma makin' my business in st. louis to stay

The song moved as if it weren't usedta having shoes on its feet. The lips blurred like the slurs of her lines, losing definition into flat pimply cheeks and a head of hair in need of pressing underneath that hat. Bernice hadda way about her. A country honor that came from knowing hard work too soon, and being rid of it too late. The children's noises coming from this big ol' house gladdened her heart.

"I told you to give me my jacks!"

"No ball playing beneath the chandelier, do you hear me, you piece of Northern trash! Even if you are my grandchild, you ain't right."

"Mama, Mama, please come see to Sharon."

"Jane, you best come out your room and see to these chirren 'fore they tear your house down."

Bernice waddled up the stairs from the curb, glanced at Betsey in the tree, took a breath and hummed her song. She had been walking around this rich colored neighborhood all day looking for work, and she was determined to stay in St. Louis. She was going to help this family out. She was what was missing, an eye on these hinckety misbehaving brats. Bernice kept on up the stairs to the front door in time to the yelps and hollers careening through the screens of every floor. Seemed like not a child in there could talk decent. All of them screaming and hollering like they were out on the farm. Bernice rang the front doorbell.

"Mama, there's somebody at the door."

"Mama, there's a colored woman at the door."

"Mama, there's a fat lady at the door."

"Jane, you've got a visitor."

"Aunt Jane, there's something at the door."

Jane tied her robe around her waist while looking at Greer asleep in his clothes. That damned green surgical outfit sprawled all over her fresh linen. But that was the man she'd married. She bent over and gave him a peck of a kiss, a long caress where the evening shadow was beginning to appear on his chin.

"Jane, I say, you've got a caller!"

By the time Jane reached the front door, all the children were crowded around her like the woman who lived in a shoe. It was claustrophobic. She had a hard time opening the front door for all the feet pressed up against it. What she saw was a heavyset, no-funny-business country woman with the most peculiar hat.

"Good evening, ma'am."

"Yes, may I help you? I'm Mrs. Brown."

"Yes, ma'am, Mrs. Brown. I see you've got some chirrens and I thought you might be in need of some he'p. I'ma hardworkin' gal. I come up from Arkansas to raise myse'f up. I'm ready to tend after 'em, and see to they meals and hair and such."

Jane smiled, thinking the Lord moves in mysterious ways.

"Well, come in, miss—uh . . ."

"My name is Bernice Calhoun, ma'am."

"Well, Miss Calhoun, please come in. This is Allard. Here is Sharon. This is Margot. And my nephew Charles. Oh, I wonder where Betsey is. Mama, have you seen Betsey?" Jane called.

"No, I haven't," Vida answered from the kitchen.

"Miss Calhoun, have you worked with children before?"

"Why, yes, ma'am, in Arkansas."

"Do you have any references you could show me?"

"Well, I could tell you the names of the families I worked for, and you could call them. But down South they's mighty informal, so I don't have anything writ down that I could show you."

"Oh, my." Jane sighed. "I think the best thing to do, Miss Calhoun, is for you to give me the names and addresses of your former employers. I shall write them. In the meantime you may work here on a probationary basis till I've heard from them."

"Oh, that's fine, ma'am."

Vida was approaching Jane to say she had no idea where Betsey was. Instead she interrupted, "Who's this?"

"Oh, Mama, this is Bernice Calhoun, who's going to stay on to help with the children. Isn't that wonderful? Miss Calhoun, this is my mother, Mrs. Murray."

Vida took one look at Bernice and went back to the kitchen, shaking her head about what the race had to offer.

"I can't figure out where Betsey is right now, Bernice, but she's my oldest girl and she'll be a big help to you."

Bernice pursed her lips, thinking now would be the time to get in good with Mrs. Brown. Show her what a sharp eye she had for chirrens.

"Might she be that one out there, up in that tree, ma'am?"

Jane forgot the time of day. She stiffened and ran out on the front porch to the far end. Right above her head, in the middle of a huge tree, sat her daughter Betsey.

"Betsey, you come down from there right this instant! How do you expect to set an example behaving like a jackass? Come down from there, right this minute! Do you hear me, Elizabeth!"

When Jane called Betsey "Elizabeth," it was serious. Betsey cut her eyes at Bernice Calhoun, who didn't realize what a mistake she'd made. Honeying up to Jane wasn't going to do her any good. Jane wasn't home half the day; Betsey Brown was. Now, Betsey Brown was more than mad 'cause some fool Mississippi song had given away her sacred hiding place. Made her mama call her Elizabeth.

"I'll be right out, Mother. I'm so sorry. I can't imagine what got into me." Betsey oozed, not fooling Jane at all. "I want to meet the company. I'm coming right now."

Jane watched in amazement as her daughter maneuvered herself along the limbs of the tree to the edge of the terrace and through the window. In a flash Betsey presented herself.

"Hello, my name is Elizabeth Brown. How are you?"

Jane was proud of her daughter again. Bernice thought she'd made a friend.

"Betsey, I told you, Miss Calhoun."

"Oh, ma'am, the chirrens can call me Bernice."

"I told Bernice that you would help her with the children and the running of the house. Show her to her room on the third floor and tell her about the neighborhood and the children's chores."

Betsey took Bernice by the hand. Charlie reluctantly picked up her paper bags filled with God only knew what, and up they traipsed through the back stairway to the top of the house. It was against Jane's principles to put a black in the basement. It was against the children's principles to accept somebody who was going to tell on them all the time. Betsey had some very special plans for Miss Calhoun.

"I hope you'll be very happy with us, Bernice. The girls are very smart, and Allard never causes any trouble, and Charlie is practically a grown-up awready."

"Why, thank-ya, 'Liz'beth."

"Uh, Betsey is just fine, Bernice, if you don't mind."

"Well, I say to ya again, thank ya, Miss Betsey."

Betsey gave the secret sign of a fist behind her back with two fingers outstretched to indicate it was time for a children's meeting in the basement.

Who did this Bernice think she was, giving away secrets like that? Why, Jane hadn't even known about the tree reaching over the porch until Bernice came. Betsey was going to see to it that Bernice paid. Boy, would she pay. The line, led by Charlie dribbling the basketball down the stairs, headed straight for the bowels of the house.

Bernice didn't know it, as she examined the tilted curved ceilings of her new quarters. Jane didn't know it, as she curled up next to Greer behind the locked door of their room above the lilacs. Only the children in the darkest, smallest corner of the basement knew what Bernice had coming her way. Vida in the kitchen over chicken fricassee could only think of her Frank and how much he liked the meat to fall off the bone over the rice and onions. And there was nothing any one of the grown-ups could have done had they known what was up in the basement.

The basement was a secret of its own. There were rooms that led to other rooms and back around to the first room. There were closets that went way back against the walls of the house until it smelled like the earth was coming right on in. There were rooms to have seances and see cats have kittens. Corners to whisper make-believe apologies and dreams. There was the smell of many folks having lived in the dark for many years, and there was the children's favorite meeting place that no one bigger than them had ever seen. In the far left-hand corner of the longest closet with the lowest ceilings and plywood walls painted green long before Christ was born, the Brown children had their powwow.

"How's she gonna do something with us?" Betsey was riled, and her little temper was cavorting in the shadows with her small horde of followers. "She can't even talk. Imagine callin' me 'Lizabeth. Why, that ain't even a name, 'Lizabeth!"

"And she tol' on you, too, Betsey," Sharon chimed in.

"Mama didn't know nothing 'bout that tree," Margot added.

"Not now, Allard. Now we've got to figure out a way to get this woman out of our house."

"Not only can't she talk, she can't hardly walk," Charlie quipped with the basketball twirling on his finger, then behind his back.

"So how's she gonna do something with us?" Allard decried.

"She's not. Just wait till morning." And Betsey dismissed the crowd.

Betsey was not a vindictive child. She was a child of special places and times of her own. She tried not to hurt anybody or anything, but Bernice'd given the whole family access to her privacy. Now when they went looking for her, they'd all know to go to her beloved tree. Search its branches for the dreamer and make noises that would disrupt Betsey's current reveries. No, Betsey wasn't being evil; to her mind she was protecting herself. God only knew what else that Bernice would uncover and deliver over to Jane and Greer. Heaven forbid she ever found that long closet in the basement! That's where everybody practiced writing nasty words like "pussy" and "dick," though only Charlie admitted to knowing where all these things were. Margot just liked to write them in big red letters with nail polish she'd borrowed from her mother's collection of toiletries. Allard just liked making the letters and then asking what the word was.

Meanwhile, in the upper reaches of the house, Bernice was hanging her limited wardrobe in the armoire next to a single bed just 'bout big enough to accommodate her rotund brown body. Yes, she thought, looking at the red dress with the lace on one sleeve, St. Louis was gointa be just fine. She'd have every Friday and Saturday night off, to meet some nice hardworking fella, maybe one of them from down her way, not too citified. Bernice looked out her window down on the garden, thinking how lucky she'd been to run into the Brown family. That poor Mrs. Brown, so frail, with all these chirren, and Mrs. Murray with her nose all up in the air on accounta a body didn't have good hair. She'd win them over. That's what she'd do.

In the morning the children tumbled down the stairs into a fine chaos. First, Betsey told Allard it was all right to rub the goldfish together. Then Sharon and Margot decided to swing on the curtain rod separating the living room from the parlor. Charlie decided he'd practice throwing his basketball around the chandelier. Of course, Jane and Greer were relaxing for a change, relieved to have Bernice handling everything. Even Vida had gone out to see to her dahlias in the back. So it was just Bernice and the Brown children.

"Look, Bernice, somebody peed in the bed." Margot came running through the kitchen with a dank sheet wrapped around her head.

"Bernice, you wanta see me make fires? We could use these matches right under here." Allard crawled through Bernice's legs to the cupboard where the fireplace matches were kept. He really liked those. They were so long and the fire was very tiny at first, till you threw it somewhere. Then whamo. Big flame.

Yet Bernice was undaunted. She was gointa stay in St. Louis, no matter what.

"Bring that nappy head on 'round heah. No, don't carry no comb, bring me a brush. A comb ain't gointa go through all that mess."

Bernice'd made breakfast of grits and eggs that no one ate, claimin' the grits were stiff and the eggs too hard.

"Allard, didn't you say you wanted to climb out the window? The one in my room is open. Sharon, there's some money in Bernice's sweater pocket if you want to buy some Snickers today."

All this was going on while Bernice was trying to make some sense of the mass of braids on the girls' heads. Bernice shouted, "Put them goldfish down. I want my money in my pocket right now." It didn't sit right with her. This Betsey was supposed to be her friend, and here she was undermining everything.

"Bernice, the fish are dying."

"Well, put 'em back in the water, fool."

"I'ma tell Mama you callt me a fool."

"That's right, Allard, you tell Mama."

"Betsey, bring that head over heah, I tol' you."

"Bernice, I'm hungry."

"Well. Eat your breakfast."

"I don't want breakfast, I want some chicken."

"That's for dinner."

"I want some chicken now!"

"Well, awright, then. Charlie, get that basketball out this house."

"Oh, Bernice, I spilled all the chicken grease."

Bernice stood up with an Arkansas fire in her eyes, screaming, "You better eat them grits 'cause that's all you gonna get! Put them goldfish down! I tell ya whoever took my money bettah pray for they soul! I ain't going nowhere, and y'all best mind, 'cause I'm in St. Louis to stay."

"How you gonna do something with us?"

"You can't even talk."

"I say bring that nappy head on over heah!"

The ruckus sent Jane flying down the stairs to find the blinds at a 45-degree angle in the front room. The curtains in the parlor all over. Six crystals from her chandelier on the floor. Chicken grease on the kitchen floor. A table full of grits and eggs. Not one combed head. Allard with matches in both pockets. Betsey quietly gazing out the window at Vida working with her dahlias. Plus, no one had brought up the morning's coffee. Now this was just too much. No coffee and the house in a shambles. It was better with her mother tending to the children, even though it was hard on her heart. The likes of this never happened.

"And, Miss Calhoun, just what do you call yourself doing this morning?"

"Well, ma'am, I fixed the chirren they breakfast. Then I put the chicken on for dinner. Then I was 'bout to start doing heads, but Betsey told them they could climb through windows and steal my money, take them fish out the water. Oh, Mrs. Brown, they been a mess today."

"Bernice, don't you wanta see me make fires?" Allard grinned. Jane grabbed the matches from his hands and all his pockets, slapped his backside good. She turned to Miss Calhoun with Sharon between her legs wrapped up in the wet sheet smelling of urine.

"Miss Calhoun, I just don't think this is going to work out."

At that moment Vida was about to come into the kitchen through the back door. Betsey ran to her aid. "Oh, Grandma, be careful. Bernice left chicken grease all on the floor. You hold onto me or you might slip and fall."

Vida cut her eyes first at Jane, then at Bernice. "Well, I should have known that a body with no upbringing couldn't very well bring up these chirren of mine. Thank you, Betsey, you are always so helpful."

The children ran gleefully to school, shouting: "How's she gonna do something with us. She can't even talk. She can't even walk. How's she gonna do something with us."

Bernice sat glumly on her small bed. She felt such a big fool. Mrs. Brown had let her go in one day, she hadn't even had one Friday night off to wear her red dress. She couldn't hardly begin to pack her things. She heard the folks in Arkansas laughing at her. Big ol' flat-faced Bernice goin'ta to St. Louis. Hahahaha.

Jane made her own coffee, sat at the kitchen table with the children's breakfasts surrounding her, and played a game of solitaire. There was no way in the world she could go to work today. Thank God for Betsey. There was one child with a head on her shoulders. Jane tried to think of what might have happened if Betsey hadn't been there to mind the children.

A FEAST OF

FOOLS

Ellease Southerland

Ada wandered the cold streets with her black book, entering old cluttered buildings, breathing strange moldy smells. She resurfaced where tenement faces appeared in windows high above. Isolated faces looking down on her in the street below triggered memories of girlhood years, an involuntary return to the world of harsh poverty. She had skipped rope not far from here, merrily running the length of the block, from end to end, the four corners topped by gigantic billboards advertising beer on every corner. Here, years ago, Mrs. Hobbs opened a jagged can and fed five children cold beans for breakfast, then spent the rest of the day at the window staring out over the narrow street. Her daughter, Pat, played in the gutter below, hair uncombed for months, filthy and knotted against her scalp. When she crouched, you could see her underpants stretched into large loops that exposed her genitals. From year to year, Ada looked up to find the face, two stories above, her skin unhealthy and sleek, eyes watered, head perfectly still, a smile on slightly parted lips. Then the face disappeared. She had died.

News of the death kept Ada awake, long after the rats sensed the family asleep and felt it safe to leave the walls and walk about the kitchen, sniffing for food. Mrs. Hobbs used to smile down on her and say how you today,

Ada. And she said all right, thank you. Nobody mentioned welfare to explain the can of beans, or the bumpy skin that covered her daughter's ginger-colored face. Image of the empty window overshadowed her night. The blank window. Something of the liver, they said. She couldn't turn loose that bottle, they said. The face all gone. Sometimes Ada's family had hot vanilla cake for breakfast. Sometimes they had toast ground in a machine, and the thick layer of crumbs floated on milk. Their father made hot doughnuts filled with blackberry jelly. They had to be careful when they bit the hot smoking doughnut to avoid burning their lips. They had cinnamon rolls and yeast roll so soft and hot from their father's bakery and ate them dripping with melted butter. She didn't understand the cold morning stoves in the neighbor's house. Even when they had oatmeal, they had raisins, brown sugar, and milk. They had beans later on with frankfurters and hamburgers. Not cold from the can, not for breakfast. She thought that her family was the poorest of the poor. That when they moved, the whole world moved. She assumed that everyone had a house now, a yard, central heating, re-frigerators, comfortable beds. But many have no homes. Many hide in these apartments, depressed, asleep. Some come to the windows to watch the world. The people die. The faces reappear, giving a permanence to poverty.

In the hallway of a wood frame building, four or five men hiding from the cold, all smelling like fermented mash, huddled silent as ducks when Ada poked her dark head in, tentatively looking about in the dim winter light. One of them, a grown man, sat in a baby carriage. Others slumped on the floor nearby.

"Good afternoon, miss."

"Good afternoon," she answered.

"You work for the city?"

"Yes."

"It sure is cold outside."

"Yes, it is," she said. She wore the mouton lamb coat.

"You have a pretty voice," the man in the baby carriage said. He had on a baseball jacket and a knitted cap.

"Thank you," Ada said, heading for the stairs. But before her foot touched the first step, one of them stood up, bent down, and kissed her right on the top of her head! Right through her woolen cap! With the others watching, nodding a subtle approval.

In the apartment several floors above, expecting to find someone better-connected to life, Ada found instead a madman leaning over her, listing every grief in his life from toothaches to worn-out sheets and blaming welfare for all his problems. And Ada, seated on a couch with loose springs, found her buttocks sagging, all but brushing the floor, her knees very close to her chin, looking up at the thin, short man who, when he spoke, flailed his arms and leaned way over her to bring his points closer to home, then paused momentarily to say that his wife would be back soon. She had gone to do the laundry.

"Do you have rent receipts, Mr. Morales?"

"Yes," he said. "My wife will get them when she comes back."

This man's wife might not be coming back at all. Or she might not get back before her husband went completely mad.

"My checks always come late, why, why?" the man continued, and repeated the sufferings he'd just gone over. He ran out of food. He had no money for the children's lunch. No hot water. They needed sheets. The walls were cracking. He said he was ill. He had too much pain. He'd worked for fourteen years, to give his family everything. But then he couldn't work because of the pain.

Her neck grew stiff, looking up at him, thin, emphatic, laying out all his life's problems. Not particularly attacking her, but the system.

He looked directly at her. "My wife will be back soon."

"Is this job safe?" her father had asked, doing his best to discourage her. "You don't want to tempt the Lord," he said, trying to scare her.

Ada had written down everything the client said and began to figure how to get out of there when he paused in his narrative and said almost absent-mindedly, "My wife will be back soon." Shouldn't he be tired of standing in that curved posture? No wonder he had so much pain.

When it seemed she would be there forever, there were sounds outside the door. Ada hoped. The door opened and in walked a normal woman who stood straight and smiled, rolling a shopping cart filled with freshly laundered clothes.

In her first months as caseworker, clients looked into her trusting face and lied to her regularly. She was hurt, sometimes saying aloud, "Mrs. Cunningham lied to me!" aware of the chuckles and smiles the older workers threw her way. More than anything else, she did not want to be suspicious, double-checking everyone. But you must verify and document, the supervisor said. In the early months she entered dark buildings, feeling for the banister, feeling for the bottom step. Keeping a careful count, she climbed blindly through the dark to the seventh floor, fourth floor, fifth floor, knocking on doors, glad to hear footsteps and a human voice ask, "Who?" Glad to be occupied with other problems. In the daytime hours she forgot her own.

Doors opened to poorly lit kitchens. Some houses smelled oily and airless, like the clothes of certain grade-school classmates. Some women answered the door, mouth half covered. In their twenties and no front teeth! That would never do. "You should get some teeth," Ada said.

"You right, Miss Torch, you sure right."

Clients offered her food. Oranges. Oily peas and rice. Cups of coffee. When she said no, thank you, they looked more carefully into her face, the dark slanted eyes, soft full mouth, smooth skin. Milk? Ice cream? Women years younger than she had two or three children. A woman in her mid teens sat on the floor holding herself, rocking and crying, saying that she had slept with more than one man. She *didn't* know who the father was. She really didn't know. She had given Ada the only chair in her unfurnished apartment. And Ada sat, leaning slightly forward, distressed with the woman.

"Get out of there," Daniel Junior said more than once. Meaning the house and the job. "Go get your journalism degree. Stay on campus. I'll send money. See what happened to Arthur and Askia?" Both were in mental institutions. "You can't go," Ibe said. "You just can't go and leave the children like that. That's not how we do it in Nigeria." "Papa's head is too heavy for you," Daniel Junior said. "He's leaning on you."

He was right about that. He called her regularly on the job. He hunted her down on weekends, crying before all the children, twisting his hands, asking her, "How can you stand it?" Saying he just wanted Abeba to come back so he could be nicer to her. That she always let him win arguments and have the last word just to keep the peace even when she knew he was wrong and he knew he was wrong. He was so lost. So small. He got the entire house up at four A.M. on Wednesdays for prayer and sometimes begged for a resurrection. He refused to get rid of their mother's clothes, opening the closet to look at them, to fuel the grief again. His skin hung closer to the bone. More gray hairs filled his thick eyebrows. Pain lived in his eyes. He had trouble eating, and seemed to need his wife standing behind him, her soft hands resting on his shoulder as she blessed his food. Azziza set his place with flowers and beautiful napkins, trying to cheer him, encourage him. Death was a constant theme in his many sermons, but when it touched his house, he was so unprepared for death.

Ada turned the page of her calendar. She dusted the black phone and jumped when it rang. Answered, then handed it to her left. In all her dreams she had not envisioned herself here, four floors above Livingston Street, in this sprawling office of two hundred caseworkers servicing five thousand families, fatherless families. Passion begins a new life. A half moment later a fate is sealed.

By ten o'clock their floor was a beehive of workers, supervisors and clerks busy at most of the seventy desks. Supervisors came and went, placing records in baskets. A few workers filed. A union representative passed out fliers. Someone read aloud a recent memo: Recognizing the alcoholic. The alcoholic engages in loud and careless talking, takes extended lunch hours, gives unusual excuses for lateness, takes three-day weekends. Ada hid herself in the office noises, surrounding conversations, interviews. Case supervisors appearing in doorways raised their hands, calling for things. Telephones ringing. People drinking coffee, laughing.

"How was the field, my dear?" Mr. Poole asked. The supervisor worried each time she clocked out, although she assured him she ran track in her junior year, and could run if she had to.

"It was all right."

"Good. Good to see you back and healthy."

"Ada!"

"Good morning, Ira."

"Have I got one for the press," he said breathlessly, bringing a case record to her desk, laying it down. He seemed like such a kid, overweight, huge and vulnerable. His dark blond head slanted to a slight point.

"I visited this pending and you won't believe where he lives." His eyes, the hue of summer sky, sparked with energy. His soft lips almost as full as hers.

"Where?"

"I kept checking the address and looking at all the houses," he said, building suspense.

Ada waited.

"The only thing on the next block was this cemetery."

"Oh, no."

"And there was this little house, not really a house but a house in the cemetery, and guess what? That's where my pending lived. Can you believe that, Ada?"

"My goodness."

"The guy had one foot in the grave and is trying to get the other foot on the gravy train. Can you imagine that?" He watched her, delighted, as she chuckled. "He had a hot plate and wants a little refrigerator."

"You missed the action," someone called at the far end of the office and claimed complete attention. "A one-armed woman in Intake who got angry because they wouldn't give her emergency money. So she lifted her dress and told the whole city of New York, including the mayor, where to kiss her."

"Tell them the rest," Yvonne Honeywood said, amid the laughter.

"She wore no underclothes!"

"What!"

"It's too damn cold for that foolishness. And so early in the morning."

"What happened?"

"The police had to escort her out."

"How could she do it, Ada?" Ira asked. "The good Lord left her one good arm and she used it to lift her dress."

Ada struggled not to grin, but the sight of the arriving worker, conspicuously shaken, moving slowly to his seat was the last straw, and laughter broke, cascading up and down the office.

"What's the world coming to?" Ira asked her.

"I'm not sure," she said, then suddenly became serious and tuned to an interview three desks down, to her right. There was no privacy here, not even for the client heavyset and sweating and more than eight months pregnant, sitting with her legs pressed against the back of the desk.

Ada flinched at each crude remark concerning pregnant women, as though each carried in her belly the ghost of her mother. Bringing that woman out in all this cold weather to ask her questions!

"*Donde trabaja?*"

Where does he work? Ada translated to herself.

"*Yo no se.*"

I don't know. Mr. Durkin the Spanish teacher, used to get tired of students answering every question with *Yo no se!*

"*Qué clase del trabajo?*"

What kind of work?"

"*Yo no se.*"

I don't know.

"*Donde está el padre del niño?*" He had asked that many times before.

Where is the father of the child? Ada side-glanced at the client, who wiped her head, explaining in rolling Spanish that she hadn't seen the father in six months.

Using his open hand, Antonio slammed the desk.

"Where!" he shouted in English, his voice sharpened, as if persistence would cut the putative father from the broad curve of the woman's belly.

Ada thought he might next slap the women, when the telephone rang and her hand flew out to snatch the receiver, even before the worker sharing the same phone could lift her head.

"Lady, go home and find your husband," Antonio was saying. He took off his glasses.

Ada spoke to the caller, then handed the phone to her left.

Walking past her chair, Antonio asked rhetorically, "How can some lady have five children with five different men?"

"Very easily!" Ada said, her mouth flying faster than her mind.

But Antonio's view was shored up by the worker with soft rotting gums, gums soft as the mushy scales of an old fish. Self-righteous, pulling up his seedy-looking pants, he passed judgment. "They never know the color of his eyes," he sneered. "How do they get pregnant when they can't find any men? *Yo no se.* That's all they know."

"Ignore them," Juanita Thandiwe said, turning her head away as she smoked, tapping the cigarette gently against the glass tray.

"He tells her to come back," Ada said. "In her condition. In all this cold. Why can't he make a home visit?"

"Don't worry about it. They're going to save the world."

"He was embarrassed just because he's Spanish and she's Spanish." She was momentarily distracted by the housing adviser a few units down. Sex is not dessert, he told her yesterday at lunch. That was the point he was trying to get across, when another worker stopped at their table and said, "How's your wife?" And it occurred to her that five or more of them had bets out on her, wondering who would get the preacher's daughter first. It did seem odd that several asked her to lunch each day. She first wondered if she looked that thin, then observed that she was the youngest woman in the office. . . . Imagine carrying on like that! Don't they see all these file cabinets stuffed with the records of families without fathers?

"Miss Torch?"

"Yes?"

"Pending."

"Thanks." She *was* glad for the distraction.

Having introduced herself and observed Anthony Charles to be her brother Asa's height and age, she asked the usual.

"How have you supported yourself?"

"Streets," he said.

"I need more of an answer."

"You know."

"Streets," Ada repeated.

"Yes."

"What do you mean," she all but whispered, trying to respect his privacy.

"You know, sister."

"Stealing things?"

"Yeah."

"But I need an answer from you."

"Yeah. Well, I was stealing to support my habit." He tugged at the little hat he wore. He *was* thin.

Next to occupation, Ada neatly printed t-h-i-e-f.

"Wait a minute, sister!"

"That's what you said, isn't it?"

"That's cold, sister. That's so cold."

Juanita Thandiwe, smoking and pretending not to hear, smiled.

"What were you using?"

"Heroin," he said. As though naming a breakfast cereal. "I'm trying to go straight," he said. "I got radios, TVs, watches, you name it."

"Stolen goods."

"Don't put it that way."

"You could be prosecuted."

"Prosecuted!" he almost shouted. "Look, my people were slaves and this country owes me—"

"Nineteen dollars a week for food and other, plus rent?"

"Is that all it would be?"

"Yes. Try to get a job. Would you like a referral?"

"No. I know about the center."

She watched anxiously as he walked away, taking long strides past the other units, joined by his shorter friend. She watched him walk past the guards. The caseworker with the mushy gums would have had him arrested.

"Don't worry about it," Juanita Thandiwe said, without even looking up.

SOCIAL WORK

Barbara Summers

Alicia was six feet tall and seemed even taller because she was black and dark and now very mad. It was three-thirty in the A.M., and Richard, her live-in lover of the past month, thought he could just slip into the apartment, grab a quick shower, and slide under the sheets smelling sweet before she woke up. But she was up, had been up, and he was high, and she knew it.

"There'll be no showers tonight, Richard." She swept out of the bed, wrapping the sheet around her. "Pack your stuff and get out."

He'd gone for ten whole days without the free-base pipe. No alcohol either, so he said. He was cleaning up, drying out. To consolidate the process they studied the Koran. They fasted together. He had trimmed her hair. She had done his nails, hands *and* feet. She was helping him to break free and clear of drugs. He was helping her to love again. It had been a struggle for the first three months, but during the last few weeks they were beginning to see a change: longer stretches with no crutches. For ten days he'd been clean . . . until he got paid and she got too busy to meet him this Saturday night after the gig.

"Just get your things together and leave," she said. Her voice started low and traveled octaves before she finished. "Goddammit, I got a dick in the dresser with an Everready battery. And I know how to use it. If that's all you're good for. I don't need you, and I can't love you if you can't love yourself."

At six feet five, Richard was no slouch either. They were from the same tribe. That's one of the things she liked about him. She could wear her tallest high heels and kiss his proud, pharaonic face and still reach up.

But now, tall, dark, handsome, and high, his head felt like it wanted to go through the ceiling of the Brooklyn brownstone. There seemed to be no space left down below, no room to think, no air to breathe. So many angry sounds coming from the big woman he loved so much he called her Baby. He bent slowly, carefully, from some dangerous upper atmosphere to pick at clothes piled in a chair.

"And leave that shirt right where it lays. You ain't had it when you came and you ain't taking it with you when you leave. You break my heart and take my clothes, too. Richard? Just get the fuck out of my life."

Really, he wanted to apologize. He knew everything would be all right if he could just lie down. Where he was standing it felt like his head would bust right through the ceiling, and since they were on the top floor, it would keep going right through the roof and finally exit outside in the soft black night sky. Maybe then there would be enough space for him and her and peace to coexist. But he had to hold on to his head, hold on, at least, to his head. He watched her cry. The loud, wet mess spread over her face like a plastic bag wrinkling her beauty. Strange, but how could a dark woman get so red?

He was talking, but nothing came out. She was waiting, but nothing came through. He was telling her how much he loved her and needed her. Loved the three holes in her ears, loved the ferocious hair she pinned up for her job and uncaged for him, loved the chocolate pudding of her nipples pressed under the sheet while she ranted and raved. He felt the heat rising between his legs as he bent and stuffed his few things in a plastic trash bag, slowly, waiting for a softer word that would tell him he was forgiven again.

"My keys, too, please," she said. "I didn't kick drugs myself to hand my keys over to a junkie. Go away and stay away."

He focused. It was a white plastic trash bag with a chemical lemon scent and tie-up handles. Not many things in it, not very heavy. He left the ankh key ring on her dresser. She stayed in the bedroom. He heard her crying. It grew louder as he left. He walked down the hallway past the gauntlet of divas, past her precious collection of programs and autographed pictures of Marian and Leontyne, Shirley, Grace, and Jessye. He passed the overstuffed bookcases and the shelves of records and finally got to the door, where he picked up his horn case. He went out the door, down the steps, four squeaky flights carpeted in dust-ball gray. Strange, the farther away he got, the louder seemed her crying.

He stepped outside the downstairs door at the very moment his brand-new Selmer tenor blasted the trash cans in a direct and devastating hit. The soprano he watched fall in slow motion through the air like a golden arrow, noiseless, deadly straight, dispatched from a dread sharpshooter silhouetted against a flaming window. Two spidery music stands leaped out into space. And then the paper. Music paper, compositions, his tunes, falling, flying, scattering mischievously in the breeze. He had written them; they should float obediently down to him. But the April winds wanted to play.

Then, like his Baby and his heart, the dark sky poured out its rain.

She waited a few days to call her sister, Nonnie. Of course, Sheila, her girlfriend downstairs, had heard all the racket and didn't need to be told.

"Yeah, girl, he did it again," Alicia said. "The third time in five weeks. Three strikes and you're out."

"Who's counting? I thought you decided to help him go all the way," said Nonnie, the eternal optimist.

"Yeah, but he's got to help himself. If he thinks he can always fall back on me, he'll never change. I tell you, I was torn up all weekend."

"Have you spoken with him?" Nonnie asked.

"Yeah, he called, sounding all pitiful. He said he didn't feel good since he wasn't with the one he loved. I said I wasn't with the one I love either. But I was cold. You know how I am when I strap my dick on. He can't stand it."

"No man can, and no wonder. You act more like a man than he does. But don't worry. I bet he'll be ringing your bell by the end of the week."

"I'll cross that bridge when I come to it."

"Well, stay strong. I love you."

"Love you, too, Shorty. Say hi to Jerry and the kids."

"Will do. 'Bye."

Richard called on Friday, almost a week after she had put him out. He came over late that night. She made vegetables in the wok. They made love in the shower and again under pink sheets. He gave her his pay so he could not afford to get high. Although she was tempted, she did not give him her keys. He left early in the morning, and she went back to bed for a nap before starting her day.

When she woke up, still in bed, still smelling their bodies, their heat, she decided it was over. No more, never again. This relationship she had to leave, like Marvin said, for her health's sake. At thirty-two, she did not want to raise other people's kids. She wanted her own and a man clean and healthy enough to give them to her. She was a social worker by profession. She did not have to live with a case study, a loser and a backslider, even if he was "the most talented tenor man of his generation," according to the *Voice*. Fuck the *Voice*. A junkie with talent was just an exceptional junkie, living on bright lights and borrowed time until he was a dead one.

Four months ago it was the talent she had fallen in love with. She had to admit it. The golden horn pumping liquid, silken sex. He wove Trane and Pharaoh, Sonny Rollins, and Archie Shepp, like ancestral threads into a new fabric, a new suit of clothes as sharply pressed as Lester Young, as raspy and tweedy as Ben Webster. Yet the true magic lay in removing those fine garments, that divine talent, and uncovering the naked, needy soul underneath. He needed her to be there for him, he said. Now, in her morning-after hardness, she thought he meant another fan, smiling, applauding, willing to wait in line for his favors. Fuck that.

Decisively up for the day, Alicia put on a long, once white Mexican dress that she used for a robe, made two grilled cheese sandwiches, and carried them down to the second-floor apartment where Sheila lived.

"How'd you know I was starving?" Sheila asked as she stood in the doorway. Sapphire, her Siamese, sniffed Alicia's bare feet and then permitted her to enter.

" 'Cause it's one o'clock on a Saturday afternoon and everybody's starving," said Alicia. "You got any chips?"

"Yeah." The two women walked to the round oak table in the bay window of Sheila's studio. She was older than Alicia, not nearly as tall, and much thinner. The cheekbones and harsh angularities of her face spoke of a life whittled down to the basics.

Her generosity extended only to the truth, which most people could not accept in large doses, so she sweetened it with humor. "I have a serious case of spring fever," she said. "Been daydreaming since yesterday. I even called in sick last night."

"So how'd the club get along without you?" Alicia asked.

"Butch just called and said I'd better show up tonight. CT is jamming, and he brings out all the major freaks."

"He's a great artist," Alicia said dryly.

"He's a crazy motherfucker."

"Tell me. I decided to cut Richard aloose."

"Oh, yeah?"

"Yeah. He was by last night, and it was okay and all, but I feel a serious syndrome setting in, that push-pull, up-and-down stuff."

"Hmmph, the girl gets her little dose of nooky," said Sheila, "then she's fortified enough to give it up."

"Whatever. This man is too dangerous for me."

"I thought you had him chilling out."

"He's just a better liar than I'm used to dealing with. Nonnie says I have to get over my missionary complex."

"I wish Miss Nonnie would stop being so right about everybody else and get to work on her own self."

"Well, she said she lost ten pounds last week."

"That's only 'cause she finally took off that nasty winter coat."

"Come on, you know you like my sister."

"Of course, I like her. What I don't like is that extra fifty pounds she's lugging around."

"Shoot, Sheila, she's had four kids."

"Hey, that's a good excuse for a potbelly, but not enough for all that saggy baggy elephant stuff."

"The price you pay for being happily married."

"No wonder . . ."

"No wonder you're still free and single and slim?"

"Listen, do you know what Sékou told me the other night?" Sheila asked.

"You seeing him again?"

"We're just friends, honey. None of that other stuff. Listen to this. He told me if I didn't marry him, he'd turn gay. I said, 'Don't blame that mess on me.' Can you imagine?"

"Yeah, 'cause it's the same thing with Richard. He says if I just stick with him, he'll kick the drugs."

"At the same time he's kicking your mind and your behind."

"No, dear, I don't go for any physical stuff."

"So what was it that busted up the trash cans the other night? Flying emotions?"

"That was me giving it out."

"And you think givers can't be takers?" Sheila asked. "You better think again. Honey, you got a heavy responsibility."

"But it's not mine. The brother needs more help than I can give him."

"Maybe he needs NA."

"What's that?"

"Narcotics Anonymous. Just like AA. A couple of fellows from the club have been going. They need to set up a chapter right in the joint."

"But how can you break an addiction in the middle of all that temptation?"

"Well, how did you do it?" Sheila asked.

"I had to. Nonnie was sick in the hospital for about a month. This is almost two years ago now. Jerry needed somebody to help with the kids, you know. Ma came down for a week, and Aunt Thera. But I took my vacation time and just stayed over there. It's a whole other world. You gotta be straight or you'll go crazy. I loved the kids. But I was real scared. My own sister with a heart attack. And only three years older than me."

"So you were scared into it."

"That's one way to put it. Then I broke up with the guy I was seeing who was bringing the stuff over. Herb, coke, rush, pills, whatever. He always wanted to get high, and I didn't want anybody going where I couldn't go and in my own house, too. Stringing along till I got strung out. Some complicated stuff, I'll tell you. Then on my job I kept seeing these sisters, my age, even younger, with three, four, and five kids, no husband, no man, or a man with such a low-paying job it hurt to admit to being hooked on him. No man, but that reefer smell in the house, you know. That smell and their dreams going up in smoke. But what could I say? I couldn't judge them. They didn't scare me. What scared me was seeing myself in their place."

"Shoot, I was always scared of that stuff. Saw too much of it around me. Decided if I couldn't buy it in the store, I didn't need it anymore."

"That doesn't sound like much of a solution."

"Well, when your pockets are close to empty, you'll get milk for the baby before you'll get anything for yourself."

"*You* would."

"I did until I couldn't anymore. I had to give up a lot. But I graduated from welfare and next year I'll graduate from college, and then I'll be able to get my kid out of Ohio and we can live like we should."

"You're lucky," said Alicia.

"How so?"

"You already have a child. You've accomplished that much."

"Is that what you want?"

"In a way."

"So what about Richard?"

"I don't know. I truly wanted to kill him last week. Then he puts this spell on me. I don't know what to do."

"Why don't you come on by the club tonight?"

"Girl, I don't know. I feel like crawling under the bed."

"And all you'll do is think about when you and Richard were making it jump, honey. Come on, it'll cheer you up. You need to see other people, at least other bodies. Butch'll be on the door. I'll make sure you can get in."

"I'll see. I want this thing with Richard to be over, really over. But then, did it ever occur to you that he might love me?"

"No. The only thing occurred to me was that you might love him."

"I can't."

"That doesn't answer if you do or not," said Sheila.

After lunch she went to study for her trig exam in the bathtub, and Alicia went back upstairs to her apartment, trying to digest a lumpy mixture of envy and resentment of her downstairs neighbor. Not just for being older and wiser, but also for being so convinced of her purpose. Alicia had finished her academic career on schedule. But she felt stuck in a hollow, hypo-critical job, helping no one, leading nowhere, except on a biweekly basis to the bank.

She was a big girl, a *big* big girl. No one had seen how fragile she was, no one but Richard.

She resisted sentimentality. She theorized that there was a definite ad-vantage to breaking up if you were a woman and you wanted the break. Silence was easy to come by. Men lost their voice with their pride. They ran from confrontation. Women were the true love warriors. They were the ones who fought for it. But would she?

Alicia was not surprised when Richard did not call. He had all Saturday afternoon and evening to do it. She was not surprised, neither was she satisfied that her decision alone was sufficient for a complete breakup. Something more was coming; she could feel it. She would not wait for it, sitting still, bracing herself for the unexpected.

The queue for the one o'clock show stretched around the corner of Seventh Avenue onto a quiet Village street. It was springtime in the city. Sweet sinsemilla drifted by, pollinating dreams of those still young enough to dream. Big, beautiful, black, and conspicuously alone, she was, of course, not going to wait on line. She cleared a space around her as she moved through the crowd, wrapped in the hallowed role of magic music maker's woman. People made way as she descended the steep, narrow staircase into the venerated club, Giant Steps. The toll booth at the bottom of the stairs was congested with jazz fans waiting for the show to finish.

"Hi, Butch." Alicia smiled to the hefty white woman with the purple crewcut manning the entrance. "How's it going?"

"Hi, Leesha, it's a squeeze tonight." She unhooked the red velvet rope that separated in from out. "Set's just about over. Sheila's working upstairs."

"Thanks."

The club was a small split-level. People were jammed onto chairs bumped together, with tables no wider than the hips of two brandy snifters. Once over the threshold, the music raged, supreme. Alicia walked upstairs and leaned against a free spot on the brick wall.

CT was all on top of the piano, playing its heartstrings like a lover unconcerned with moral positions of wrong and right. Rashied flew over the drums like a thunder god through roiling African skies. Charlie was bowing the bass into long-liquid lines of sweet metaphors.

And there, unfolding from the shadows, was Richard, solar saxophone, soaring over the lover, the thunder spirit, and the taffy puller, blowing a streamer of God's first breath through a miraculous reed. The original, experimental mud man transforming noise into music and music into praise for the Creator. And it was good.

It was Richard and yet he looked like an angel. The no-good self-destructive junkie motherfucker. She could kill him for being so good, so good, to others and so deadly bad to himself.

Carrying a tray of drinks to a table of customers, Sheila walked by the spot where Alicia was propping up the wall.

"I didn't know he was going to be here tonight," Sheila said apologetically.

"Shoot, Sheila, you could have called me," said Alicia.

"Hey, I figured if you came, you could handle it. And you can."

Sheila was right. Richard did not have to know she was here. There were two or three hundred people between them and almost as many confused emotions throttling the free beat of her heart. Looking at him, sweat irrigating the grooves of his face, the same face that smiled at her in disbelieving tenderness after they made love . . . Looking at him now, his fingers muscular and confident on the keys of his choice, the same fingers that had hesitated with delight as they cradled her face last night . . . Looking at him right now, she realized that she did not know him, could never really know him, she a giant wallflower and he a giant star. Giant had nothing to do with it. They were just too different. And yet there it was again, a hot lurch of passion reaching from her gut to his and back.

Alicia steered through the crowd at the bar and ordered a glass of white wine. She knew it came from a no-frills California jug, but she didn't care. She needed a long swallow of something cold, noncarbonated and non-threatening if she wanted to go a second round. The wine's tartness was medicinal, mind-clearing, restorative. She followed its taste back to her self, her center, relieved to see no mystical tightrope dangling from her middle.

When the set was over, the audience exploded in a wild percussion of applause. As CT introduced the musicians and they closed to The Theme, Alicia looked for a place to set her glass down so she could join in. But they bowed their way offstage before she could locate a safe spot. The volume of her good intentions was unheard.

Alicia knew what the scene would be like as the musicians retired to the minuscule dressing room called The Hole. She'd been there often enough. The steaming bodies, the smoking, drinking, and laughing, the tempting female fans, the slick brothers in dark glasses and zippered briefcases. She had known that special hipness of belonging to the inner sanctum.

She stayed outside and upstairs where early birds were leaving their seats, making way for the next shift. She took a stool at the bar and ordered another glass of wine. Trane came over the speakers and drowned her doubts in persistent waves of beauty. John Coltrane. So safely dead, she thought, beyond the anguish of living this life. She thanked him for having been here, for having left his message.

She turned around and found Richard standing next to her. He held a brandy in one hand and a bottle of beer in the other.

"How are you, Baby?" he asked.

"I'm fine," she said.

"Sure are, one fine woman."

"The music was really beautiful tonight, Richard."

"Thank you. I could feel you in the house. I knew even before Sheila told me."

"Well, I didn't know you were going to be here. As a matter of fact, I came out tonight to get away from you."

"Now, why would you want to do that?"

"You know why, Richard. I can't take any more of this off-and-on stuff."

"You're the only one that turns off, Baby. I love you. I've told you that. That's not going to change."

"And the shit's not going to change either. I can tell you're high right now."

"Aw, come on, lighten up. Look at all these smiling faces. Accept me as I am. A little bit ain't never hurt nobody. I can control whatever I do."

"Famous last words."

"Listen here, let's talk about this later on. Can I see you tonight?"

"No, I don't think so, I'll be too tired."

"Well, I'ma be by tomorrow. I need to see you."

"Yeah, okay."

He bent to kiss her and was rewarded with her cheek. She watched him walk downstairs. In the two-way traffic, people smiled and shook his hand. Men patted him appreciatively on the back. Intellectuals, aficionados, uncomplicated fans, maybe a starfucker or two in the crowd . . . But there was no one telling him No, not, and never. Only her.

She did not care for that isolated distinction. Why couldn't she just throw her arms around his neck and bask in his reflected glory? Why did she have to make things so difficult?

Sheila stopped at the bar with an empty tray, waiting for an order to be filled.

"How's it going?" she asked Alicia.

"Okay. You would tell him I was here."

"Did I do wrong?"

"I wish you would have just left things alone."

"Well, excuse me for breathing," said Sheila, arranging fresh drinks and napkins carefully.

"Oh, come on, I didn't mean it."

"I guess I don't have your background as a do-gooder."

"Sheila, please don't be mad at me. I'm trying to do the best I can."

"Me, too, honey." And she walked off with her tray and a hard, professional smile.

Alicia left after the first tune of the next set, a long Latin number whose beat reassured the audience that free jazz could still get funky. Richard had taken a swallow-tailed solo on soprano that made her want to kneel before his genius. It was after this performance that she left, splurging on a cab to take her, not far for a fare, but to another country just over the bridge to Dean Street and safety.

The phone woke her up, nervous and angry, at quarter to three.

"Hey, Baby." It was Richard. "I just wanted to make sure you got home okay."

"I'm okay, Richard. I'm asleep."

"Yeah, I know. I just wanted to tell you that I love you very much and that I want to see you today."

"You'll come for dinner?"

"Tell me when."

"About six?"

"No, that's too late. How about four? Does that give you enough time?"

"Sure, that's good."

"I know that's right. Listen here, we're going to work things out, understand? Together."

"Sounds good, but I have something to tell you, too, Richard. I'll be happy to see you, but if you can't come straight, please, don't come at all."

"I'll see you at four o'clock."

"Okay."

"Good night, Baby."

"Good night, Richard."

She headed into sleep happy, proud that her determination had asserted itself even through her sleep. She planned a meal that would demonstrate that good food and laughter and beauty and understanding would fill the hollow leg of hipness as no dope could. She wanted to show him, without posters and slogans, that black women needed black men to survive . . .

with their genius intact, if possible. And, if not, at least with their humanity.

She dreamed of a honeymoon trip sailing down the Nile on a felucca. She knew she was on the boat, she could feel the wind catch in the sails overhead. But, curiously, she also saw herself on the shore, smiling, waving.

The Farmers' Market had the fruit, vegetables, and even the flowers she wanted. Richard liked to bring her a single rose now and then. She was going to show him that beauty in abundance was possible and that she could provide it, for herself and for him. She felt rich. The spring air made her feel optimistic and fertile, seed brown, green and sunny. She almost bought two copies of the *Times* until she remembered that Sheila had probably picked hers up at Sheridan Square before coming home last night. If things got rocky with Richard, maybe she'd give Sheila a buzz to come upstairs. Nothing could go too far wrong on a day like today.

The weather was fine. The dinner would be good. And she would be good. That was the main thing. She wouldn't mention any salty subjects. Nothing about white women, how meek and mild and supportive they were, how appreciative of black musicians. Not a word about the record companies with their measly, show-off advances followed, a year later, by an invoice saying the musicians owed the company money. She would say nothing about having to go to Europe or Japan or anyplace else but home in order to survive. And definitely nothing about getting a steady job teaching, even though Archie, Marion, and a lot of the brothers he knew were securely entwined in academic ivy. Last but not least, she'd stay miles away from the subject of drugs.

Maybe, on some higher level, they could be just friends. Once the spell was broken, she could accept him, not as a lover or a lifetime partner, but just for who he was. What was that nasty joke he'd made: love my dick, love my jones. Richard Jones, you dig? And she had cried, while he thought it was outrageously funny. Well, it was funny. Rude, crude, and funny. She would no longer take such a tragic point of view. Let's see what they could talk about without whining or complaining. Let's have some good old-fashioned free-form fun.

The food perfumed the house with the spice of love and care. The mushrooms were stuffed, the asparagus steamed. The carrot cake had been a chore, but then everything else had been so easy.

It was four o'clock. She did not expect him to be on time. In spite of his final "I'll see you at four," she knew better than to expect exactitude. She uncorked a bottle of chilled rosé. Might as well be realistic. He wasn't here. And he was the one with the problem. He certainly wasn't going to stop drinking overnight. Why should she deny herself?

She prioritized the sections of the paper. She loved the luxurious, visual feast of the Sunday edition, although most of it went unread and the parts she read generally made her angry. Dis-, mis- and plain non-information regularly occupied its pages. And just as regularly, she paid her tithe and passed the day in ritual.

Four-thirty. She told herself she wasn't waiting, per se, for him. He'd get there when he could. Whenever he could, she'd be glad to see him. She was doing nothing special, just reading the paper. She checked to make sure the salad greens were well-dried. No soggy lettuce for them. Like she'd said to herself before, nothing special.

At five-thirty, she knew he'd be there at six, like she'd suggested in the first place. He'd probably gone out with the fellas after the gig and was still sleeping the night off. She called to wake him up. No answer. Good, he was on his way.

Six-thirty. She'd finished with the paper, except for the Book Review section which she always saved for her bath. Still no answer. Maybe he was rehearsing at CT's or Rashied's. Off the bandstand a musician never worried about time.

Okay, get it together now. Should she be truthful and express her anger when he came? Or should she be good and patient and not say anything like "Where have you been, dammit"? Resolved, she would be good. Stick to her Good Times—Higher Level plan. If she treated the whole incident as if it were nothing special, she could not possibly be hurt. Again.

At eight she ran her bath. She wouldn't get to soak in the tub for her usual two hours. Just a quick scrub. She didn't want to answer the door wrapped in a towel or even a robe. That would be too intimate, almost an invitation. So what? Let him suffer. They were going to be just friends from now on. Make him remember what he was going to miss. Let him agonize over her tantalizing cleanliness.

That's it. He was too high to come. He hadn't acknowledged her ultimatum last night, but he felt her spirit. He was high and knew he had to come down in order to see her. And he wasn't down yet. He wasn't even halfway straight enough to call her. Shit.

That's what she felt like. He had tricked her heart again. She looked at the silent cordless phone by the tub and felt his struggle. The wine made it easy for her to cry. She was big and tough. So why did God treat her like this? She knew if she asked the question "Why me, Lord?" she'd be sure to get a smart-aleck Sheila-type answer, Why not you, honey?

She read the Book Review section. The tears dried by the third page. Some good reviews, liberated women, antiquated men. Maximum quota of two black books. They looked good. She wondered if she could afford the hardcovers or if she should wait for the paperbacks. They wouldn't make it to soft cover if they didn't sell enough hard. . . .

Ten-thirty. The doorbell rang. She didn't know how she would fix her face to deal with him. She dried herself, hastily. Patches of the terry robe stuck to her back. The bell rang again. Not the downstairs buzzer, the bell to the apartment. Well, he often came in while someone was leaving. Let him wait, for a change. She tried on a smile. Determined to be good, and, if not good, at least above it all, she opened the door.

Sheila stood there with a bottle of Chivas and two glasses.

"You playing hooky tonight?" Alicia asked.

"No, the club's closed," she said, walking into the living room.

"On a Sunday night? Butch has finally flipped."

"Alicia, Butch is dead."

"What?" she asked quietly.

"They found her body in the Hudson."

"In the river?"

"Yeah, the police think it might be connected to drugs."

"Drugs? Sheila, I've been waiting for Richard since four o'clock."

"Oh, you're back into that."

"Something's happened to him. He would have called by now."

"He'll call tomorrow and apologize."

Alicia did not want to contradict her friend to say that she could feel something different this time. She'd spent the past six or seven hours trying to fool her feelings. How reliable could they be? Especially now, when the something different felt like a hole.

She squeezed the plastic trash bag into the full garbage can and clamped the metal lid on top like a magnet. She wasn't going to force it closed.

"Hi, Baby." He was leaning against the sidewalk gate, twiddling a bright maple leaf in his hand. None of the questions on her face came through in her voice. She looked in her jacket pocket for a tissue to wipe her hands.

"I thought you were dead," she said.

"I was."

"Why did you come back here?"

"Because I'm clean now."

She stopped and looked at him, letting herself see him. In six months his narrow face had filled out, his eyes were steady and strong.

"You look real good." She smiled at him. She hurt bad, but he would not see it. "How's the music?"

"I'm never gonna give that up. You know that. Like I'm never gonna give you up."

"You already did, Richard, one Sunday afternoon a few months ago."

"I wasn't ready, Baby. I wasn't clean. Help me, Alicia, please. Love me again."

"I'm on my way to work."

"I know. I just want to let you know I'll be waiting for you when you get back."

"I don't know if I want that, Richard."

"We need to talk."

"Maybe."

"Hey, Alicia, I know I wasn't right. But that was then. Today's a new day."

"Maybe."

"Well, I'ma be here. No maybes."

She walked toward the subway, pushing dry leaves aside. She did not look back. She whistled "My Favorite Things" with Trane's changes and Jessye's attitude.

JUDGMENT

Cliff Thompson

"Not too many of *us* here," I said. The two of us stood in the middle of the Bowl, the huge lawn in front of Field College's library.

"You and me, that's about it," she said. This was my first time talking to her, but I'd noticed her before; she was one black student at this tiny school in the middle of Nowhere, Pennsylvania, and I was the other. She was beautiful—her long hair was pulled back, showing off her high, curved forehead and blemishless skin. "Are you a freshman, too?"

"Yeah. My name's Wayne," I said, and we shook hands.

"I'm Roxie. Nice to meet you. Where are you from?"

"D.C."

"*Really?* Me too! I'm from Silver Spring."

I gave her a look of mock disgust, and said, "*That's* not D.C."

"All right, then, Maryland," she said, laughing. "Close enough."

We stood there talking for about twenty minutes. I was surprised by her. Before we met I had mentally assigned her a way of speaking and a set of mannerisms which, it turned out, were all wrong. But I liked the real ones— her easy laughter, and the way she tilted her head when she asked a question. Before we parted we made plans to get together for coffee that evening.

Around eight o'clock I left my dorm and headed for Pete's, a diner on the edge of campus. The shortest distance between these two points took me across the Bowl and past the library and the main lecture hall. It was September of 1980, which made these buildings 155 years old; they didn't seem to have been built so much as just carved out of rock and set among all the trees and grass. In the daytime they looked like a painting of a college campus. Now, silhouetted against the night sky, they looked like medieval castles. They were a little scary, and I thought that a year ago I would've picked up my pace. But I'm in college, I thought; I'm a man now.

"My father's a lawyer," Roxie said. We were in Pete's, hunched over a table in the tiny booth. "I think that's where I get my argumentativeness from. It used to drive the boys in high school crazy."

"If two people agree on everything all the time, one of them is unnecessary," I said. "I can't remember where I heard that, but I like it." She laughed.

"Well, my father's a cabdriver," I said. "Was before he retired, anyway. He's argumentative enough, though. Well, no, that's not really right . . . he doesn't argue with you so much as he just—does what he thinks the situation calls for, and if you're with him on it, fine, and if you're not, then it's just too bad."

"Are you like him?"

"Well . . ." I laughed. "Nobody's really *like* my father. I think I take after him in some ways, though."

"I think I'd like him then," she said and smiled. We looked at each other, longer than people usually do without speaking.

Soon after that night Roxie and I were a couple. I started to think I might just like this college thing.

I liked my roommates, too. Remi and Dave. Coming from D.C., I hadn't spent much time around white people before, and it took some getting used to. They talked differently from the guys I'd grown up with, and about different things—Elvis Costello instead of Chuck Brown and the Soul Searchers, *My Dinner With Andre* instead of *Cooley High*. But the same things made them happy, the same things annoyed them, they had the same little moods. Dave had a good, solid relationship that year with a girl named Nancy, and sometimes Remi longed to be Dave. Remi was always going out with somebody new, and once in a while, when Dave commented on it, I could hear the envy in his lazy Southern voice. After a while I stopped thinking of the two of them as my white roommates and thought of them as just my roommates, and then, gradually, as my friends.

The three of us used to triple-date sometimes. I'd bring Roxie, Dave would bring Nancy, and Remi would drag along whoever he was going out with that week. One night we all went to Lorenzo's, a little pizza place; it sort of marked the border between the campus and the town and was one of the few places where both crowds hung out. The night we went it was full of high school kids, so the six of us squeezed around a square table meant for four and ate greasy pepperoni and mushroom pizza.

"It doesn't get any better than this," Remi said, quoting a TV commercial. We all laughed.

Remi's date that night was an extremely thin, red-haired girl named Michele. She said, "I hate to think what all this grease is gonna do inside my stomach."

I smiled and said, "I figure it'll do like that jar of bacon grease my mother keeps beside the stove. Form a nice, thick, white layer on top, and . . ."

Michele looked shocked. I figured she was going to say, "Stop, you're grossing me out," but she said, "Your mother keeps a jar of bacon grease beside the stove?"

"Yeah," I said.

"Mine does, too," Roxie said.

Michele said, "Why?"

"To cook with," I said.

"You're *kidding*."

"Nope."

Michele sort of shuddered. Roxie and I glanced at each other knowingly.

Remi said, "This some kind of racial thing?" Remi, Dave, and I looked at each other and smiled, because we were used to this kind of talk. Roxie, Nancy, and Michele looked down at their food; they weren't.

After enough time had passed, Nancy asked me, "How's the econ going?" I made a face. It was a class I was struggling with.

Michele said, "You're taking economics?"

"I'm taking it up the butt," I said. Dave almost spit out his pizza. Everybody laughed.

"You're braver than I am," Michele told me.

We stayed a pretty long time, talking and laughing and listening to music on Lorenzo's jukebox. We finished off two pizzas and two pitchers of beer, and the bill, when we finally asked for it, came to around thirty dollars.

"Comes out to six bucks a head, with the tip," Dave said. He, Remi, Michele, and Nancy threw money to the middle of the table. I turned to Roxie and said, "All I have is ten bucks. Do you have anything?"

Roxie reached into her jacket pocket. I noticed Michele looking at Roxie, then at me.

Freshman year seemed to go by very fast. I was on a scholarship then, but I didn't have any other money coming in; sometime around March my savings from the previous summer's job dried up.

"You mind if we go Dutch again tonight?" I asked Roxie. I was in her room, sitting on her bed.

She sat down and sighed. "This is the third Dutch treat this week," she said. "I think you're taking me for granted."

"Look, I'm sorry. My last name's not Rockefeller, okay? It's not that I don't want to take you out, I just can't afford to now."

"Or ever. Why don't you get a campus job, or something?"

"Come on. I'm having a rough enough time with my classes now," I said. "Anyway . . . what's wrong with going Dutch? Remi and Dave do it all the time. *Everybody* does."

"So you're taking your cues from the white boys now?"

I didn't know what to say to that, so I didn't say anything. "Listen," I finally said. "If I have to pay for both of us tonight, we can't go. It's that simple. To tell you the truth, I don't feel much like it now, anyway."

"Fine," she said.

And that was that.

When I left her room I walked around campus for a while because I was too mad to do much else. Soon my anger gave way to hunger. I had missed dinner at the dining hall, so I walked to Lorenzo's, grabbed a small pizza, and took it back to my room.

Remi and Dave were stretched out on their beds listening to The Police when I walked in. I said, "Hello, gentlemen," and fell sideways onto my bed. Remi and Dave sat up and looked at each other, then at me.

Remi said, "That was one fast date."

"Sure nuff," I said, opening my box of pizza.

"What happened?"

"I only had fifteen bucks. I asked if we could go Dutch. She got mad. I got mad. Here I am." I took a bite of pizza.

"You're kidding," Dave said.

"Do you see me sittin' here eating this pepperoni and grease pizza? No, I'm not kidding."

Dave said, "What century was *she* born in?"

"You want *my* advice," Remi said, "I'd let her alone for a while."

"Whatever," I said. "If you don't mind, I'd rather not talk about it right now."

"No prob," Remi said, and he and Dave stood up. "We were leaving anyway. We've declared this 'I'm Sick to Death of Being a Student' night. We're going to the game room now, and then later a bunch of us are gonna meet at the disco. You oughtta come." He smiled. "Only costs seventy-five *cents* to get in the *disco*. Seriously, come. Around ten."

"Yeah, maybe," I said. Remi slapped me on the shoulder, and he and Dave left.

I finished my pizza, then just lay back on my bed with my hands clasped behind my head. I stayed like that for the longest time, thinking about things and looking around the room. I stared at the Rolling Stones poster above Remi's bed; at the maps over Dave's bed, those maps of Spain and France and Australia and Russia he loved so much; at the globe on my desk, the one my father had given me just before I left for school ("Take this with you so you don't forget where D.C. is," he'd told me). When I first arrived on campus and got set up in my room, I could spend a lot of time doing exactly what I was doing now, just sitting and looking around the walls. I would think about how I was on my own, and the feeling that gave me was enough to entertain me for the evening. I would wish some of my high school classmates could see me. But with the passing of the months, my room had lost its power to charm me. All I felt now, lying on my bed and staring at the walls, was boredom.

"What the hell, I'll go to the disco," I said, to no one in particular.

The disco was in a big room in the basement of the student union building. I walked down the hall, toward the pounding, wall-shaking music, and gave my ID to the guy at the door. He stamped my hand, and I went in. It was a good twenty degrees hotter in there. The place was pretty full; I looked out at all the white people—some of them dancing to the rhythm, some of them hopelessly and happily off. I made my way to the edge of the dance floor to look for Remi and Dave. Just about then the strobe light started flashing, and I had to squint and look down to keep my balance.

I felt a hand hit my shoulder. I looked up, and it was Dave. "Hey, guy!" he shouted. "Glad you made it!"

He grabbed my arm and pulled me onto the floor, where Remi and a few other guys and girls were dancing sort of in a circle. I joined in. After a while, I started to really enjoy myself. The D.J. played The Police, The Cars, and The Knack, and also Rick James, songs from Michael Jackson's "Off the Wall" album, and some old Motown. We made periodic trips to the bar, soaked with sweat, and bought cups of beer, which we drank like water. Then we'd head back out to the dance floor.

At one point I felt someone tap me on the back. I turned around, and Dave and Remi were waving good-bye. "I think we've had it," Dave shouted. "You gonna stay a while?"

"I think so," I shouted back.

There was no such thing as partners here; it was a kind of musical free-for-all. I'd dance half a song in front of one person, then she'd wander off, or I'd wander off, and I'd finish the song with someone else—or no one. It didn't seem to matter. That evening, almost nothing did.

I stumbled out of there at about two o'clock. I found myself walking across the Bowl with a blond girl named Joanne, whose dorm was in the same general direction as mine.

"*God*, I needed that," I told Joanne. "I might just make it through the rest of the week now."

"This place getting you down?" she said.

"Ah, this place and a few other things," I said. "My girlfriend's driving me bonkers. She lives to drive me bonkers, I think." All those beers were talking now.

"How does she drive you bonkers?" Joanne asked. We were passing by the library, and under its floodlights, which stayed on all night. I got my first good look at her—at her high, sculpted cheekbones, her nearly pointed nose, the tuft of blond hair that hung down in front and met her eyebrows.

"Oh, man," I said, "it'd take me an hour to tell you. The latest thing is, I can't afford to take her out anywhere 'cuz I'm broke, and she's mad about it. I have to pay for everything, even though I don't have a dime to my name."

She said, "Sounds like you need to either win the lottery or get a new girlfriend."

"I think I have equal shots at both."

"I wouldn't say *that*. You've got about a one-in-a-million shot at the lottery. There are six hundred women on campus. If I were you, I'd save my dollar," she said, smiling.

I remember, then, my lips pressing together to form the word "But," and I remember my mouth expelling the necessary amount of air. No word came out, though.

We reached the walkway that led up to her dorm. We stopped and faced each other. She said, "Well, thanks for walking me."

"No problem," I said.

I can describe, but not explain, the moment that followed. It was full of knowledge of what was going to happen, like that half-second between seeing the other car coming and smashing into it. And it was almost that frightening: I was afraid of seeing Roxie after tonight, and afraid, although I wasn't sure why, of crossing this kind of racial line. Afraid—but not ashamed. The certainty that I would go through with it seemed to take it out of my hands, somehow. I stepped toward Joanne feeling scared, excited, and, through it all, blameless.

. . . and after minutes—ten? twenty?—of standing there and exploring each other's mouths with our tongues, after her saying, "I have to get up in the morning," and smiling at me over her shoulder as she went inside, I walked away.

I walked past my own dorm, because I knew I wouldn't be able to sleep, and went several more blocks until I came to the duck pond. I stood at the edge, tossing in pebbles and listening to the ducks quietly talking to each other. Now it started. With Joanne safely back in her room, my cloud of innocence was dissipating; the words *what did I just do?* kept repeating in my mind.

I tossed in a pebble and watched the ripples widen. I watched as they jostled the ducks, and felt bad about disturbing their peace. I wanted to make it up to them, but I didn't have the slightest idea how.

The next morning I woke up and decided that nothing had happened, or at least I would act as if nothing had. As I stood in the shower, hot water cascading over me, it seemed perfectly clear. Nothing had happened. It was that simple.

And it seemed that simple through most of the day. I went to breakfast, and the line servers wore their usual groggy expressions under their white caps. Nothing was different. My classes went as they always did; none of my professors stared at me accusingly. Business as usual.

I got to the dining hall for dinner at six. I got a plate of spinach-something-or-other, then squeezed my way through the mob toward the soda fountain. I was standing in front of it, trying to decide between Coke and Dr Pepper, when someone to my right said, "Hi there." It was Joanne. She looked a little different from the night before; her hair was tied back, and she looked a lot more put-together than you do after thrashing around on a dance floor.

"Uh. Hi," I said.

She smiled and said, "Are you eating with anyone?"

I said, "Um . . ." I looked away, scanning all the faces for Remi or Dave. They weren't anywhere. Joanne didn't know that, though. I turned back to her—looking not in her face, exactly, but toward it—and said, "Yeah."

Before she could respond I was gone, off to find as remote a table as I could, and feeling for all the world like somebody else.

The next day I was walking across the Bowl when I saw her coming toward me. When we were about ten feet apart, our eyes met for the briefest of moments, and then we each looked away. We walked by each other without a word or a glance—which set the tone of our relationship for the rest of freshman year.

Meanwhile, I kept things hobbling along with Roxie. Gradually, without any spoken agreement, things between the two of us became kind of . . . formal. When we saw each other, it was because we had made plans beforehand; we didn't just drop by each other's rooms anymore. I would call her Thursday night about going out on Friday, and when we'd agreed on a time and place, we'd hang up. And it wouldn't cross my mind—or hers either, I don't think—to talk in between making the date and the date itself.

I remember, for some reason, a conversation we had one Friday night. We had just been to see *To Have and Have Not* (in the theater that doubled as the chemistry lab), and I was walking her back to her dorm.

"I'm starting to see one theme over and over again in Bogie's movies," I said. "He's always the guy who swears he's just going to look out for himself, and then he ends up fighting for truth, justice, the American way, and all that other stuff. It was the same thing in *Casablanca, Key Largo, The African—*"

"He wouldn't make it as a leading man today, I'll tell you that," Roxie said.

"Huh?"

"You see how skinny he was? I heard he wasn't but five foot seven, too. He couldn't stand up against some of these muscle-bound men we've got in the movies today."

I was quiet for a second. Then I said, "No. Guess not."

We were passing the rear of the library. Across the street were faculty houses. My English professor, Mr. Graham, lived in one of them. The one with the flag on the outside, I thought. It was a clear night; I could see the moon just over one of the houses. It was full and huge and yellow as mustard.

"You ever see any of those movies?" I said. "*Key Largo,* or *The African Queen?*"

"Which one is *The African Queen?*"

"The one with Katharine Hepburn—"

"I love Katharine Hepburn. I saw her in *The Philadelphia Story.* Her and Cary Grant. I *love* Cary Grant."

"I like him, too," I said, and I went back to looking at the moon.

The last day of freshman year around three in the afternoon I was in my room, alone. That morning Remi and I had hugged Dave good-bye and watched him and his family drive off for North Carolina. Around two o'clock I said good-bye to Remi, who was heading back to Brooklyn for the summer. I was packing the last of my junk into a cardboard box on my bed; my father would be there to pick me up in a couple of hours or so. As I tossed in various things—my globe, my desk lamp, a football—I looked around the room. Remi's posters and Dave's maps were gone; the only traces of them were the marks from the tape that had held them up. I couldn't turn on Dave's stereo because it was in the trunk of his father's car, on its way to North Carolina. I had never, I thought, seen a room look as empty as this.

Right about then there was a tap on the door, and Roxie walked in. I remember what she was wearing: white shorts and sneakers and a sky-blue terry-cloth shirt. She looked like summer itself, I thought. "Hi," I said.

"Hi there," she said. "How's it coming?"

"I've about got it under control," I said. "This is the last of it, really. Everything else can go in the car like it is." I looked around the walls again, and said, "Have you ever seen a room look more deserted than this?"

"Looks pretty bare," she said. She sat down on the edge of the mattress; the box I was loading dipped to one side.

I said, "What time are your folks coming?"

"In about three hours."

"You all packed?"

"Just about. I've got a little more to do. I wanted to come over and see you, though."

I said, "Well . . ." and couldn't think what else to say. I put something else in the box, letting it fall more noisily than it had to so it could fill up some of the silence. I finally said, "Did I give you my number at home?"

"Yeah. You have mine, right?"

"Yeah."

She looked around at all my junk, packed in boxes and bags, sitting in heaps on the floor. "Had some good times this year," she said, nodding, still looking at the junk.

"Yeah," I said. I stepped from behind my box and walked over to where she was sitting. I stood in front of her, looking down, my thumbs hooked into the pockets of my jeans. "Had some good times," I said.

She stood up then and put her arms around me, and we hugged for a while. Then we looked at each other and kissed. It was a little more than friendly, but not really passionate; we seemed almost to be saying something to each other through that kiss, something like, "No hard feelings." When it was over she rubbed my chest, then patted it, then started moving away, toward the door. She whispered " 'Bye," moved her fingers up and down in a kind of wave, and was gone.

I had wondered how Roxie and I were going to see out the year, and now I guessed I knew. There had been no hideous breakup; we'd made no attempt to smooth out the rough areas. In the end the relationship, all by itself, just dwindled down to nothing.

It felt like a week and a half before I was back on campus again. I roomed with Remi again; we had planned on it being the three of us, but sometime in July Dave's father had gotten pretty sick, and he couldn't come back this semester.

The day before classes started, I was walking across the Bowl when I saw

Joanne coming toward me. As a reflex, I started to go into my "ignore" mode—and just think hard about something else until we had passed each other. But then something occurred to me. I looked back at what had happened between us, and now, somehow, I seemed to be looking at it from a great distance. We had necked outside her dorm, once, six months ago. So what? Surely, there must have been some sort of statute of limitations regarding these things, and if there was, it must have been in effect by now. As we got closer, I studied her. She was looking elsewhere, and seemed to be thinking about something I couldn't even guess at (she was in *her* ignore mode now). When we were about four feet apart, I stepped directly in her path. I said, very loudly, "Hi."

She looked startled. But then she saw my expression—my lips were pressed together tightly, in a kind of suppressed smile—and she developed a similar one. With a mock seriousness in my voice, I said, "And where . . . are you going?"

"To . . . the . . . bookstore," she said, imitating me.

"May . . . I . . . accompany you?"

"Why . . . yes . . . you may."

We walked back across the Bowl, around the lecture hall, and through Central Square to the campus bookstore. We talked on the way about our summers. She had spent most of hers in Boston, helping her father add a new room to the house. I had worked delivering packages for an office supply store—which, I told Joanne, was about as exciting as it sounded.

"At least you got to be outside," she said.

"Good point."

In the bookstore she had to get all the books she needed for her classes. The store had carts, miniature versions of grocery store carts, for this purpose. I pulled one out and pushed it behind Joanne while she pulled books from the shelves. "Aagh," I said, after she had pulled out a book on macro-economics and put it in the cart.

She smiled. "You don't like econ? I think it's fun."

"Fun," I said. "One day when I was six years old, I was running down the street, and I slipped and fell. Landed on my face, and knocked out both my front teeth. *That* was more fun than taking economics."

Joanne made a face and said, "You're weird."

When she paid for the books the cashier put them in a brown grocery store bag, and we left. I tried to carry the bag for her, but she insisted on doing it herself. We crossed the street and walked back through Central Square, past the trees and squirrels and stone benches, without talking much. I was working out in my mind how to apologize for last year. The problem now was that it seemed so long ago and trivial, and by bringing it up I would seem to be making a big deal over nothing, yet it didn't seem quite right to pretend that *nothing* had happened. Finally I compromised with myself.

"You ever—um—ever get off on the wrong foot with somebody and not quite know how to get on the right one again?"

She looked at me and smiled, with her lips together. "Yeah," she said. "I think I know what you're talking about."

Later that day I was sitting on my bed, absentmindedly leafing through *The Norton Anthology of English Literature,* when somebody knocked on the door. "It's open," I said, and a second later Roxie walked in.

"Roxie!" I jumped up off the bed.

"He*llo*," she said. "How *are* you?"

We met in the middle of the floor and hugged, then sat down on the bed. She said, "How was your summer?" At first I thought she meant this as an accusation. Our parents' houses were forty-five minutes apart, and we hadn't seen each other once all summer. But she was smiling; I decided it was an innocent question.

"It wasn't bad," I said.

"What did you do?"

"I was—uh—I delivered packages for an office supply store."

"Pret-ty exciting," she said sarcastically.

She had spent June, July, and August, she said, working in a movie theater, which we agreed was about half a notch above my job. Then we talked about what classes we were taking. She said she was looking at an even heavier workload than last year, and I said I was, too.

"So," she said. "What are you doing tonight?"

"Well, I'm kind of busy tonight." Truth was, I was going to the movies with Joanne.

"How about tomorrow night? You want to go have some coffee, or something?"

"Um, yeah," I said, nodding. "Let's do that."

"Okay."

To my surprise, she leaned over and kissed me, and to my disbelief, she stuck her tongue approximately halfway down my throat. Then she stood up, giving me a last peck on the lips, and said, "Talk to you tomorrow." And she left.

For a couple of minutes I just walked around the room—from my bed to my desk to Remi's bed to Remi's desk—with my hand on the back of my head. Then I sat down again. And I decided that if I lived a good long time, if I outlived my children and my children's children, there would still be some things I wouldn't understand.

I picked up Joanne at her room at about seven-thirty. When she opened the door, she looked really great. She wasn't made up or particularly dressed up—she wore beige slacks and a light green plaid top. But she was really . . . pretty. "Hi," she said. "Ready?"

The Strand, Field's second-run movie house, was about a block from the campus bookstore. They were showing *The World According to Garp* that night, which neither of us had seen (although we'd both read it). "The writing in that book is so witty," Joanne said, as we walked diagonally through Central Square. "That's most of what I liked about it. I don't know how they're going to capture that on screen."

"Well," I said, "if I know Robin Williams, he can bring it off. As much as it can be brought off, anyway."

"I hope so."

When we were half a block away, I saw someone standing under the marquee. I realized then that the thing I'd been afraid of all day, the thing I'd protected myself against last year, was about to happen.

I don't know why Roxie was standing under the marquee—she was waiting for one of her friends, I guess. "Hi," I said to her, as Joanne and I walked up to the theater; it wasn't quite what I thought I should say, but then I didn't know quite what I thought I should say.

"Hi," she said, looking from one of us to the other.

While Joanne paid for her ticket, Roxie and I just looked at each other. Her expression was flat and almost unreadable, except for a slight narrowing of her eyes, which made all the difference; it seemed to be saying, "Uh-huh. I've got your number now."

I bought my ticket, and Joanne and I walked in.

Roxie and I didn't get together for coffee the next night. I didn't hear from her, and I didn't call. To tell the truth, we hardly ever spoke to each other again. Sometimes she looked at me, other times she didn't; but each time, whether we made eye contact or not, her presence made me feel I was being accused of something.

Joanne and I sat on a half-full bus, heading away from the college and into the town of Field itself. We weren't talking, not for the moment, because we'd just reached the point where we were comfortable enough not to talk if we didn't feel like it. We held hands, and she looked out the window, and I looked around the bus. My eyes met the eyes of a white boy, maybe fifteen; he stared at me until he realized I wasn't going to look away, and then *he* looked away. At the front of the bus, two black girls in seats that faced sideways were talking to each other and looking at me. I couldn't hear what they were saying, I could only see their smiles, which weren't really smiles at all.

This wasn't my first trip into town, or Joanne's (we were sophomores now). But it was our first trip together, and our first this school year. We needed a break from campus; we wanted to visit "the real world" for a while, or at least get as close to it as we could. So we rode quietly as the trees and small houses rolled past, and soon there we were in—"Don't blink, or you'll miss it," went the stale joke—downtown Field.

"Where do you want to go first?" Joanne asked me, just as we'd gotten off the bus.

I looked up and down the block. There was a Woolworth's, and beside that a card shop, and beside that a record store, and beside that a pizza joint. Across the street were a post office and a bank.

"Let's go to Woolworth's."

We reached for each other's hand and went down the sidewalk. Now I played a different game from the one on the bus. There I had wanted to see how much direct confrontation I could get away with; here, walking down Main Street, I wanted to see how much I could ignore people. I felt the eyes of the white people, and the few black people, on us; from the corner of my eye I saw their heads turn. But I didn't look at them, and I didn't look at them in a way that must've been obvious.

Looking straight ahead, Joanne said, "I know what *these* people are gonna talk about at dinner tonight." She meant it to sound flip, I could tell. And it did, but only around the edges. Something else was at its center—a kind of little girl's confusion. I squeezed her hand, and she leaned her head toward my shoulder.

We went into Woolworth's. We walked up and down the junk-filled aisles and made fun of everything. I picked up a fake-wood desk lamp; the glue holding the base to the rest of it was showing, and we giggled at that. We giggled at the orange and pea-colored 85 percent polyester clothes that were on sale; at the crushed-velvet paintings of cats and cowboys and Elvis Presley; at everything. The fat white security guard sitting in the corner kept his eyes on us. We giggled at him, too.

When we got tired of that, we went to the pizza joint for lunch. The only person in there, besides us, was the stocky, sweating Italian man behind the counter. He smiled at us when we came in. We smiled back. For a moment I wanted to hug him.

We ate at a table by the window so we could look at the "Pennsylvanians," as Joanne liked to call them. She said, "I talked to my mom last night."

"Oh, yeah?"

"Yeah. I told her I started seeing this great new guy. . . ."

"Well, now. Did you tell her what this great new guy looks like?"

"I sure did."

"What did she say?"

"Well, she seemed a little surprised. She said it didn't matter to her, though. She asked me if you were nice, and I said you were. Then she asked me what you were majoring in, and I told her you were undecided, but leaning toward English. She liked that. She was an English major."

"You're quite lucky," I said.

"I know. They're great. So have you told your parents about me yet?"

"Not yet. I think I'm gonna wait until I go home for break."

"Is it gonna be that big a deal?"

"To tell you the truth, I don't know. In nineteen years the topic never came up once."

"So . . . if it matters to them, will it matter to you?"

I made a show out of thinking about this. I looked at the ceiling, my brows knitted; I looked at the floor and scratched my head. Finally I looked her in the eye and said, "Nope."

This delighted her, and she laughed.

After we left the pizza place, Joanne and I messed around in a record store for a while, then went to catch the bus back to campus. We stood under one of those sheltered, Plexiglas bus stops, across the street from the Field Savings Bank. Two white people were waiting with us—a middle-aged man in a green polyester leisure suit with white stitches, and a girl who didn't look older than fifteen.

I looked at Joanne. "Quite a town," I said quietly.

"Quite a town," she said.

I felt the urge to kiss her then, but held back. Then I thought about it, and I went ahead and did it.

A group of white boys, five or six of them, about high school age, came down the street. They were talking among themselves, and as they passed the bus stop I heard the words "wrong color." Joanne's eyes met mine for one brief, alarmed moment. Then I just watched, in silence, as the boys continued down the street. Finally I shouted, "What?!"

One of the boys looked back; the group kept walking.

"What? What!" I yelled, until Joanne took hold of my arm.

During the bus ride back to campus, it rained. First there was a drop here and there on the windows, and then the sky opened up completely, suddenly, the way it does on bad TV sitcoms. Soon the black road was shiny, and the tires of the cars and trucks were reflected in its surface like the edges of some adjacent, upside-down universe. I felt like going to that universe. Maybe there, I thought, Joanne and I could walk around together without being stared at or even noticed by anybody. But I knew it wouldn't work. I knew if I tried to go there, tried to dive below the surface, I'd never get past the hard, hard street.

THE ABORTION

Alice Walker

They had discussed it, but not deeply, whether they wanted the baby she was now carrying. "I don't *know* if I want it," she said, eyes filling with tears. She cried at anything now and was often nauseous. That pregnant women cried easily and were nauseous seemed banal to her, and she resented banality.

"Well, think about it," he said, with his smooth reassuring voice (but with an edge of impatience she now felt) that used to soothe her.

It was all she *did* think about, all she apparently *could*; that he could dream otherwise enraged her. But she always lost when they argued. Her temper would flare up, he would become instantly reasonable, mature, responsible, if not responsive precisely, to her mood, and she would swallow down her tears and hate herself. It was because she believed him "good." The best human being she had ever met.

"It isn't as if we don't already have a child," she said in a calmer tone, carelessly wiping at the tear that slid from one eye.

"We have a perfect child," he said with relish, "thank the good Lord!"

Had she ever dreamed she'd marry someone humble enough to go around thanking the good Lord? She had not.

Now they left the bedroom, where she had been lying down on their massive king-size bed with the forbidding ridge in the middle, and went down the hall—hung with bright prints—to the cheerful, spotlessly clean kitchen. He put water on for tea in a bright yellow pot.

She wanted him to want the baby so much he would try to save its life. On the other hand, she did not permit such presumptuousness. As he praised the child they already had, a daughter of sunny disposition and winning smile, Imani sensed subterfuge, and hardened her heart.

"What am I talking about?" she said, as if she'd been talking about it. "Another child would kill me. I can't imagine life with two children. Having a child is a good experience *to have had*, like graduate school. But if you've had one, you've had the experience and that's enough."

He placed the tea before her and rested a heavy hand on her hair. She felt the heat and pressure of his hand as she touched the cup and felt the odor and steam rise up from it. Her throat contracted.

"I can't drink that," she said through gritted teeth. "Take it away."

There were days of this.

Clarice, their daughter, was barely two years old. A miscarriage brought on by grief (Imani had lost her fervidly environmentalist mother to lung cancer shortly after Clarice's birth; the asbestos ceiling in the classroom where she taught first graders had leaked for twenty years) separated Clarice's birth from the new pregnancy. Imani felt her body had been assaulted by these events and was, in fact, considerably weakened, and was also, in any case, chronically anemic and run-down. Still, if she had wanted the baby more than she did not want it, she would not have planned to abort it.

They lived in a small town in the South. Her husband, Clarence, was, among other things, legal adviser and defender of the new black mayor of the town. The mayor was much in their lives because of the difficulties being the first black mayor of a small town assured, and because, next to the major leaders of black struggles in the South, Clarence respected and admired him most.

Imani reserved absolute judgment, but she did point out that Mayor Carswell would never look at her directly when she made a comment or posed a question, even sitting at her own dinner table, and would instead talk to Clarence as if she were not there. He assumed that as a woman she would not be interested in, or even understand, politics. (He would comment occasionally on her cooking or her clothes. He noticed when she cut her hair.) But Imani understood every shade and variation of politics: she understood, for example, why she fed the mouth that did not speak to her, because for the present she must believe in Mayor Carswell, even as he could not believe in her. Even understanding this, however, she found dinners with Carswell hard to swallow.

But Clarence was dedicated to the mayor, and believed his success would ultimately mean security and advancement for them all.

On the morning she left to have the abortion, the mayor and Clarence were to have a working lunch, and they drove her to the airport deep in conversation about municipal funds, racist cops, and the facilities for teaching at the chaotic, newly integrated schools. Clarence had time for the briefest kiss and hug at the airport ramp.

"Take care of yourself," he whispered lovingly as she walked away. He was needed, while she was gone, to draft the city's new charter. She had agreed this was important; the mayor was already being called incompetent by local businessmen and the chamber of commerce, and one inferred from television that no black person alive even knew what a city charter was.

"Take care of myself." Yes, she thought. I see that is what I have to do. But she thought this self-pityingly, which invalidated it. She had expected *him* to take care of her, and she blamed him for not doing so now.

Well, she was a fraud, anyway. She had known after a year of marriage that it bored her. "The Experience of Having a Child" was to distract her from this fact. Still, she expected him to "take care of her." She was lucky he didn't pack up and leave. But he seemed to know, as she did, that if anyone packed and left, it would be her. Precisely *because* she was a fraud and because in the end he would settle for fraud and she could not.

On the plane to New York her teeth ached and she vomited bile—bitter, yellowish stuff she hadn't even been aware her body produced. She resented and appreciated the crisp help of the stewardess, who asked if she needed anything, then stood chatting with the cigarette-smoking white man next to her, whose fat hairy wrist, like a large worm, was all Imani could bear to see out of the corner of her eye.

Her first abortion, when she was still in college, she frequently remembered as wonderful, bearing as it had all the marks of a supreme coming of age and a seizing of the direction of her own life, as well as a comprehension of existence that never left her: that life—what one saw about one and called Life—was not a facade. There was nothing behind it which used "Life" as its manifestation. Life was itself. Period. At the time, and afterward, and even now, this seemed a marvelous thing to know.

The abortionist had been a delightful Italian doctor on the Upper East Side in New York, and before he put her under he told her about his own daughter who was just her age, and a junior at Vassar. He babbled on and on until she was out, but not before Imani had thought how her thousand dollars, for which she would be in debt for years, would go to keep her there.

When she woke up it was all over. She lay on a brown Naugahyde sofa in the doctor's outer office. And she heard, over her somewhere in the air, the sound of a woman's voice. It was a Saturday, no nurses in attendance, and she presumed it was the doctor's wife. She was pulled gently to her feet by this voice and encouraged to walk.

"And when you leave, be sure to walk as if nothing is wrong," the voice said.

Imani did not feel any pain. This surprised her. Perhaps he didn't do anything, she thought. Perhaps he took my thousand dollars and put me to sleep with two dollars' worth of ether. Perhaps this is a racket.

But he was so kind, and he was smiling benignly, almost fatherly, at her (and Imani realized how desperately she needed this "fatherly" look, this "fatherly" smile). "Thank you," she murmured sincerely: she was thanking him for her life.

Some of Italy was still in his voice. "It's nothing, nothing," he said. "A nice, pretty girl like you; in school like my own daughter, you didn't need this trouble."

"He's nice," she said to herself, walking to the subway on her way back to school. She lay down gingerly across a vacant seat and passed out.

She hemorrhaged steadily for six weeks, and was not well again for a year.

But this was seven years later. An abortion law now made it possible to make an appointment at a clinic, and for seventy-five dollars a safe, quick, painless abortion was yours.

Imani had once lived in New York, in the Village, not five blocks from where the abortion clinic was. It was also near the Margaret Sanger clinic, where she had received her very first diaphragm, with utter gratitude and amazement that someone apparently understood and actually cared about young women as alone and ignorant as she. In fact, as she walked up the block, with its modern office buildings side by side with older, more elegant brownstones, she felt how close she was still to that earlier self. Still not in control of her sensuality, and only through violence and with money (for the flight, for the operation itself) in control of her body.

She found that abortion had entered the age of the assembly line. Grateful for the lack of distinction between herself and the other women—all colors, ages, states of misery or nervousness—she was less happy to notice, once the doctor started to insert the catheter, that the anesthesia she had been given was insufficient. But assembly lines don't stop because the product on them has a complaint. Her doctor whistled, and assured her she was all right, and carried the procedure through to the horrific end. Imani fainted some seconds before that.

They laid her out in a peaceful room full of cheerful colors. Primary colors: yellow, red, blue. When she revived, she had the feeling of being in a nursery. She had a pressing need to urinate.

A nurse, kindly, white-haired, and with firm hands, helped her to the toilet. Imani saw herself in the mirror over the sink and was alarmed. She was literally gray, as if all her blood had leaked out.

"Don't worry about how you look," said the nurse. "Rest a bit here and take it easy when you get back home. You'll be fine in a week or so."

She could not imagine being fine again. Somewhere her child—she never dodged into the language of "fetuses" and "amorphous growths"—was being flushed down a sewer. Gone all her or his chances to see the sunlight, savor a fig.

"Well," she said to this child, "it was you or me, kiddo, and I chose me."

There were people who thought she had no right to choose herself, but Imani knew better than to think of those people now.

It was a bright, hot Saturday when she returned.

Clarence and Clarice picked her up at the airport. They had brought flowers from Imani's garden, and Clarice presented them with a stouthearted hug. Once in her mother's lap she rested content all the way home, sucking her thumb, stroking her nose with the forefinger of the same hand, and kneading a corner of her blanket with the three fingers that were left.

"How did it go?" asked Clarence.

"It went," said Imani.

There was no way to explain abortion to a man. She thought castration might be an apt analogy, but most men, perhaps all, would insist this could not possibly be true.

"The anesthesia failed," she said. "I thought I'd never faint in time to keep from screaming and leaping off the table."

Clarence paled. He hated the thought of pain, any kind of violence. He could not endure it; it made him physically ill. This was one of the reasons he was a pacifist, another reason she admired him.

She knew he wanted her to stop talking. But she continued in a flat, deliberate voice.

"All the blood seemed to run out of me. The tendons in my legs felt cut. I was gray."

He reached for her hand. Held it. Squeezed.

"But," she said, "at least I know what I don't want. And I intend never to go through any of this again."

They were in the living room of their peaceful, quiet, and colorful house. Imani was in her rocker, Clarice dozing on her lap. Clarence sank to the floor and rested his head against her knees. She felt he was asking for nurture when she needed it herself. She felt the two of them, Clarence and Clarice, clinging to her, using her. And that the only way she could claim herself, feel herself distinct from them, was by doing something painful, self-defining, but self-destructive.

She suffered the pressure of his head as long as she could.

"Have a vasectomy," she said, "or stay in the guest room. Nothing is going to touch me anymore that isn't harmless."

He smoothed her thick hair with his hand. "We'll talk about it," he said, as if that was not what they were doing. "We'll see. Don't worry. We'll take care of things."

She had forgotten that the third Sunday in June, the following day, was the fifth memorial observance for Holly Monroe, who had been shot down on her way home from her high school graduation ceremony five years before. Imani *always* went to these memorials. She liked the reassurance that her people had long memories, and that those people who fell in struggle or innocence were not forgotten. She was, of course, too weak to go. She was dizzy and still losing blood. The white lawgivers attempted to get around assassination—which Imani considered extreme abortion—by saying the victim provoked it (there had been some difficulty saying this about Holly Monroe, but they had tried) but were antiabortionist to a man. Imani thought of this as she resolutely showered and washed her hair.

Clarence had installed central air-conditioning their second year in the house. Imani had at first objected. "I want to smell the trees, the flowers, the natural air!" she cried. But the first summer of 110-degree heat had cured her of giving a damn about any of that. Now she wanted to be cool. As much as she loved trees, on a hot day she would have sawed through a forest to get to an air conditioner.

In fairness to him, she had to admit he asked her if she thought she was well enough to go. But even to be asked annoyed her. She was not one to let her own troubles prevent her from showing proper respect and remembrance toward the dead, although she understood perfectly well that once dead, the dead do not exist. So respect, remembrance was for herself, and today herself needed rest. There was something mad about her refusal to rest, and she felt it as she tottered about getting Clarice dressed. But she did not stop. She ran a bath, plopped the child in it, scrubbed her plump body on her knees, arms straining over the tub awkwardly in a way that made her stomach hurt—but not yet her uterus—dried her hair, lifted her out and dried the rest of her on the kitchen table.

"You are going to remember as long as you live what kind of people they are," she said to the child, who, gurgling and cooing, looked into her mother's stern face with lighthearted fixation.

"You are going to hear the music," Imani said. "The music they've tried to kill. The music they try to steal." She felt feverish and was aware she was muttering. She didn't care.

"They think they can kill a continent—people, trees, buffalo—and then fly off to the moon and just forget about it. But you and me, we're going to remember the people, the trees, and the fucking buffalo. Goddammit."

"Buffwoe," said the child, hitting at her mother's face with a spoon.

She placed the baby on a blanket in the living room and turned to see her husband's eyes, full of pity, on her. She wore pert green velvet slippers and a lovely sea-green robe. Her body was bent within it. A reluctant tear formed beneath his gaze.

"Sometimes I look at you and I wonder 'What is this man doing in my house?' "

This had started as a joke between them. Her aim had been never to marry, but to take in lovers who could be sent home at dawn, freeing her to work and ramble.

"I'm here because you love me," was the traditional answer. But Clarence faltered, meeting her eyes, and Imani turned away.

It was a hundred degrees by ten o'clock. By eleven, when the memorial service began, it would be ten degrees hotter. Imani staggered from the heat. When she sat in the car she had to clench her teeth against the dizziness until the motor prodded the air-conditioning to envelop them in coolness. A dull ache started in her uterus.

The church was not, of course, air conditioned. It was authentic Primitive Baptist in every sense.

Like the four previous memorials, this one was designed by Holly Monroe's classmates. All twenty-five of whom—fat and thin—managed to look like the dead girl. Imani had never seen Holly Monroe, though there were always photographs of her dominating the pulpit of this church where she had been baptized and where she had sung in the choir—and to her, every black girl of a certain vulnerable age *was* Holly Monroe. And an even deeper truth was that Holly Monroe was herself. Herself shot down, aborted on the eve of becoming herself.

She was prepared to cry and to do so with abandon. But she did not. She clenched her teeth against the steadily increasing pain, and her tears were instantly blotted by the heat.

Mayor Carswell had been waiting for Clarence in the vestibule of the church, mopping his plumply jowled face with a voluminous handkerchief and holding court among half a dozen young men and women who listened to him with awe. Imani exchanged greetings with the mayor, he ritualistically kissed her on the cheek, and kissed Clarice on the cheek, but his rather heat-glazed eye was already fastened on her husband. The two men huddled in a corner away from the awed young group. Away from Imani and Clarice, who passed hesitantly, waiting to be joined or to be called back, into the church.

There was a quarter hour's worth of music.

"Holly Monroe was five feet, three inches tall, and weighed one hundred and eleven pounds," her best friend said, not reading from notes, but talking to each person in the audience. "She was a stubborn, loyal Aries, the best kind of friend to have. She had black kinky hair that she experimented with a lot. She was exactly the color of this oak church pew in the summer; in the winter she was the color [pointing up] of this heart pine ceiling. She loved green. She did not like lavender because she said she also didn't like pink. She had brown eyes and wore glasses, except when she was meeting someone for the first time. She had a sort of rounded nose. She had beautiful large teeth, but her lips were always chapped so she didn't smile as much as she might have if she'd ever gotten used to carrying Chap Stick. She had elegant feet.

"Her favorite church song was 'Leaning on the Everlasting Arms.' Her favorite other kind of song was 'I Can't Help Myself—I Love You and No-body Else.' She was often late for choir rehearsal though she loved to sing. She made the dress she wore to her graduation in Home Ec. She *hated* Home Ec. . . ."

Imani was aware that the sound of low, murmurous voices had been the background for this statement all along. Everything was quiet around her, even Clarice sat up straight, absorbed by the simple friendliness of the young woman's voice. All of Holly Monroe's classmates and friends in the choir wore vivid green. Imani imagined Clarice entranced by the brilliant, swaying color as by a field of swaying corn.

Lifting the child, her uterus burning, and perspiration already a stream down her back, Imani tiptoed to the door. Clarence and the mayor were still deep in conversation. She heard "board meeting . . . aldermen . . . city council." She beckoned to Clarence.

"Your voices are carrying!" she hissed.

She meant: How dare you not come inside.

They did not. Clarence raised his head, looked at her, and shrugged his shoulders helplessly. Then, turning, with the abstracted air of priests, the two men moved slowly toward the outer door, and into the churchyard, coming to stand some distance from the church beneath a large oak tree. There they remained throughout the service.

Two years later, Clarence was furious with her: What is the matter with you? he asked. You never want me to touch you. You told me to sleep in the guest room and I did. You told me to have a vasectomy I didn't want and I *did*. (Here, there was a sob of hatred for her somewhere in the anger, the humiliation: he thought of himself as a eunuch, and blamed her.)

She was not merely frigid, she was remote.

She had been amazed after they left the church that the anger she'd felt watching Clarence and the mayor turn away from the Holly Monroe memorial did not prevent her accepting a ride home with him. A month later it did not prevent her smiling on him fondly. Did not prevent a trip to Bermuda, a few blissful days of very good sex on a deserted beach screened by trees. Did not prevent her listening to his mother's stories of Clarence's youth as though she would treasure them forever.

And yet. From that moment in the heat at the church door, she had uncoupled herself from him, in a separation that made him, except occasionally, little more than a stranger.

And he had not felt it, had not known.

"What have I done?" he asked, all the tenderness in his voice breaking over her. She smiled a nervous smile at him, which he interpreted as derision—so far apart had they drifted.

They had discussed the episode at the church many times. Mayor Carswell—whom they never saw anymore—was now a model mayor, with wide biracial support in his campaign for the legislature. Neither could easily recall him, though television frequently brought him into the house.

"It was so important that I help the mayor!" said Clarence. "He was our *first!*"

Imani understood this perfectly well, but it sounded humorous to her. When she smiled, he was offended.

She had known the moment she left the marriage, the exact second. But apparently that moment had left no perceptible mark.

They argued, she smiled, they scowled, blamed and cried—as she packed.

Each of them almost recalled out loud that about this time of the year their aborted child would have been a troublesome, "terrible" two-year-old, a great burden on its mother, whose health was by now in excellent shape, each wanted to think aloud that the marriage would have deteriorated anyway, because of that.

FEVER

John Edgar Wideman

To Matthew Carey, Esq., who fled Philadelphia in its hour of need and upon his return published a libelous account of the behavior of black nurses and undertakers, thereby injuring all people of my race and especially those without whose unselfish, courageous labours the city could not have survived the late calamity.

Consider Philadelphia from its centrical situation, the extent of its commerce, the number of its artificers, manufacturers and other circumstances, to be to the United States what the heart is to the human body in circulating the blood.

Robert Morris, 1777.

He stood staring through a tall window at the last days of November. The trees were barren women starved for love and they'd stripped off all their clothes, but nobody cared. And not one of them gave a fuck about him, sifting among them, weightless and naked, knowing just as well as they did, no hands would come to touch them, warm them, pick leaves off the frozen ground and stick them back in place. Before he'd gone to bed a flutter of insects had stirred in the dark outside his study. Motion worrying the corner of his eye till he turned and focused where light pooled on the deck, a cone in which he could trap slants of snow so they materialized into wet, gray feathers that blotted against the glass, the planks of the deck. If he stood

seven hours, dark would come again. At some point his reflection would
hang in the glass, a ship from the other side of the world, docked in the
ether. Days were shorter now. A whole one spent wondering what goes wrong
would fly away, fly in the blink of an eye.

Perhaps, *perhaps it may be acceptable to the reader to know how we found
the sick affected by the sickness; our opportunities of hearing and seeing them
have been very great. They were taken with a chill, a headache, a sick stomach,
with pains in their limbs and back, this was the way the sickness in general
began, but all were not affected alike, some appeared but slightly affected
with some of these symptoms, what confirmed us in the opinion of a person
being smitten was the colour of their eyes.*

Victims in this low-lying city perished every year, and some years were worse
than others, but the worst by far was the long hot dry summer of '93, when
the dead and dying wrested control of the city from the living. Most who
were able, fled. The rich to their rural retreats, others to relatives and friends
in the countryside or neighboring towns. Some simply left, with no fixed
destination, the prospect of privation or starvation on the road preferable to
cowering in their homes awaiting the fever's fatal scratching at their door.
Busy streets deserted, commerce halted, members of families shunning one
another, the sick abandoned to suffer and die alone. Fear ruled. From August
when the first cases of fever appeared below Water Street, to November when
merciful frosts ended the infestation, the city slowly deteriorated, as if it,
too, could suffer the terrible progress of the disease: fever, enfeeblement,
violent vomiting and diarrhea, helplessness, delirium, settled dejection when
patients *concluded they must go (so the phrase for dying was), and therefore
in a kind of fixed determined state of mind went off.*

*In some it raged more furiously than in others—some have languished for
seven and ten days, and appeared to get better the day, or some hours before
they died, while others were cut off in one, two, or three days, but their
complaints were similar. Some lost their reason and raged with all the fury
madness could produce, and died in strong convulsions. Others retained their
reason to the last, and seemed rather to fall asleep than die.*

Yellow fever: an acute infectious disease of subtropical and tropical New
World areas, caused by a filterable virus transmitted by a mosquito of the
genus *Aëdes* and characterized by jaundice and dark colored vomit resulting
from hemorrhages. Also called *yellow jack.*
  Dengue: an infectious, virulent tropical and subtropical disease trans-

mitted by mosquitoes and characterized by fever, rash, and severe pains in the joints. Also called *breakbone fever, dandy.* [Spanish, of African origin, akin to Swahili *kindinga.*]

Curled in the black hold of the ship he wonders why his life on solid green earth had to end, why the gods had chosen this new habitation for him, floating, chained to other captives, no air, no light, the wooden walls shuddering, battered, as if some madman is determined to destroy even this last pitiful refuge where he skids in foul puddles of waste, bumping other bodies, skinning himself on splintery beams and planks, always moving, shaken and spilled like palm nuts in the diviner's fist, and Esu casts his fate, constant motion, tethered to an iron ring.

In the darkness he can't see her, barely feels her light touch on his fevered skin. Sweat thick as oil but she doesn't mind, straddles him, settles down to do her work. She enters him and draws his blood up into her belly. When she's full, she pauses, dreamy, heavy. He could kill her then; she wouldn't care. But he doesn't. Listens to the whine of her wings lifting till the whimper is lost in the roar and crash of waves, creaking wood, prisoners groaning. If she returns tomorrow and carries away another drop of him, and the next day and the next, a drop each day, enough days, he'll be gone. Shrink to nothing, slip out of this iron noose and disappear.

Aëdes aegypti: a mosquito of the family *Culicidae,* genus *Aëdes,* in which the female is distinguished by a long proboscis for sucking blood. This winged insect is a vector (an organism that carries pathogens from one host to another) of yellow fever and dengue. [New Latin *Aëdes,* from Greek *aedes,* unpleasant: *a* −, not + *edos,* pleasant . . .]

All things arrive in the waters and waters carry all things away. So there is no beginning or end, only the waters' flow, ebb, flood, trickle, tides emptying and returning, salt seas and rivers and rain and mist and blood, the sun drowning in an ocean of night, wet sheen of dawn washing darkness from our eyes. This city is held in the water's palm. A captive as surely as I am captive. Long fingers of river, Schuylkill, Delaware, the rest of the hand invisible; underground streams and channels feed the soggy flesh of marsh, clay pit, sink, gutter, stagnant pool. What's not seen is heard in the suck of footsteps through spring mud of unpaved streets. Noxious vapors that sting your eyes, cause you to gag, spit, and wince are evidence of a presence, the dead hand cupping this city, the poisons that circulate through it, the sweat on its rotting flesh.

No one has asked my opinion. No one will. Yet I have seen this fever before, and though I can prescribe no cure, I could tell stories of other visitations, how it came and stayed and left us, the progress of disaster, its several stages, its horrors and mitigations. My words would not save one life, but those mortally affrighted by the fever, by the prospect of universal doom, might find solace in knowing there are limits to the power of this scourge that has befallen us, that some, yea, most will survive, that this condition is temporary, a season, that the fever must disappear with the first deep frosts and its disappearance is as certain as the fact it will come again.

They say the rat's-nest ships from Santo Domingo brought the fever. Frenchmen and their black slaves fleeing black insurrection. Those who've seen Barbados's distemper say our fever is its twin born in the tropical climate of the hellish Indies. I know better. I hear the drum, the forest's heartbeat, pulse of the sea that chains the moon's wandering, the spirit's journey. Its throb is source and promise of all things being connected, a mirror storing everything, forgetting nothing. To explain the fever we need no boatloads of refugees, ragged and wracked with killing fevers, bringing death to our shores. We have bred the affliction within our breasts. Each solitary heart contains all the world's tribes, and its precarious dance echoes the drum's thunder. We are our ancestors and our children, neighbors and strangers to ourselves. Fever descends when the waters that connect us are clogged with filth. When our seas are garbage. The waters cannot come and go when we are shut off one from the other, each in his frock coat, wig, bonnet, apron, shop, shoes, skin, behind locks, doors, sealed faces, our blood grows thick and sluggish. Our bodies void infected fluids. Then we are dry and cracked as a desert country, vital parts wither, all dust and dry bones inside. Fever is a drought consuming us from within. Discolored skin caves in upon itself, we burn, expire.

I regret there is so little comfort in this explanation. It takes into account neither climatists nor contagionists, flies in the face of logic and reason, the good doctors of the College of Physicians who would bleed us, purge us, quarantine, plunge us in icy baths, starve us, feed us elixirs of bark and wine, sprinkle us with gunpowder, drown us in vinegar according to the dictates of their various healing sciences. Who, then, is this foolish, old man who receives his wisdom from pagan drums in pagan forests? Are these the delusions of one whose brain the fever has already begun to gnaw? Not quite. True, I have survived other visitations of the fever, but while it prowls this city, I'm in jeopardy again as you are, because I claim no immunity, no magic. The messenger who bears the news of my death will reach me precisely at the stroke determined when it was determined I should tumble from the void and taste air the first time. Nothing is an accident. Fever grows in the secret places of our hearts, planted there when one of us decided to sell one of us to another. The drum must pound ten thousand thousand years to drive that evil away.

Fires burn on street corners. Gunshots explode inside wooden houses. Behind him a carter's breath expelled in low, labored pants warns him to edge closer to housefronts forming one wall of a dark, narrow, twisting lane. Thick wheels furrow the unpaved street. In the fire glow the cart stirs a shimmer of dust, faint as a halo, a breath smear on a mirror. Had the man locked in the traces of the cart cursed him or was it just a wheeze of exertion, a complaint addressed to the unforgiving weight of his burden? Creaking wheels, groaning wood, plodding footsteps, the cough of dust, bulky silhouette blackened as it lurches into brightness at the block's end. All gone in a moment. Sounds, motion, sight extinguished. What remained, as if trapped by a lid clamped over the lane, was the stench of dead bodies. A stench cutting through the ubiquitous pall of vinegar and gunpowder. Two, three, four corpses being hauled to Potter's Field, trailed by the unmistakable wake of decaying flesh. He'd heard they raced their carts to the burial ground. Two or three entering Potter's Field from different directions would acknowledge one another with challenges, raised fists, gather their strength for a last dash to the open trenches where they tip their cargoes. Their brethren would wager, cheer, toast the victor with tots of rum. He could hear the rumble of coffins crashing into a common grave, see the comical chariots bouncing, the men's legs pumping, faces contorted by fires that blazed all night at the burial ground. Shouting and curses would hang in the torpid night air, one more nightmare troubling the city's sleep.

He knew this warren of streets as well as anyone. Night or day he could negotiate the twists and turnings, avoid cul-de-sacs, find the river even if his vision was obscured in tunnellike alleys. He anticipated when to duck a jutting signpost, knew how to find doorways where he was welcome, wooden steps down to a cobbled terrace overlooking the water where his shod foot must never trespass. Once beyond the grand houses lining one end of Water Street, in this quarter of hovels, beneath these wooden sheds leaning shoulder to shoulder were cellars and caves dug into the earth, poorer men's dwellings under these houses of the poor, an invisible region where his people burrow, pull earth like blanket and quilt 'round themselves to shut out cold and dampness, sleeping multitudes to a room, stacked and crosshatched and spoon fashion, themselves the only fuel, heat of one body passed to others and passed back from all to one. Can he blame the lucky ones who are strong enough to pull the death carts, who celebrate and leap and roar all night around the bonfires? Why should they return here? Where living and dead, sick and well must lie face to face, shivering or sweltering on the same dank floor.

Below Water Street the alleys proliferate. Named and nameless. He knows where he's going but fever has transformed even the familiar. He'd been waiting in Dr. Rush's entrance hall. An English mirror, oval framed in scalloped brass, drew him. He watched himself glide closer, a shadow, a blur, then the shape of his face materialized from silken depths. A mask he did not recognize. He took the thing he saw and murmured to it. Had he once been in control? Could he tame it again? Like a garden ruined overnight, pillaged, overgrown, trampled by marauding beasts. He stares at the chaos until he can recall familiar contours of earth, seasons of planting, harvesting, green shoots, nodding blossoms, scraping, digging, watering. Once upon a time he'd cultivated this thing, this plot of flesh and blood and bone, but what had it become? Who owned it now? He'd stepped away. His eyes constructed another face and set it there, between him and the wizened old man in the glass. He'd aged twenty years in a glance and the fever possessed the same power to alter suddenly what it touched. This city had grown ancient and fallen into ruin in two months since early August, when the first cases of fever appeared. Something in the bricks, mortar, beams, and stones had gone soft, had lost its permanence. When he entered sickrooms, walls fluttered, floors buckled. He could feel roofs pressing down. Putrid heat expanding. In the bodies of victims. In rooms, buildings, streets, neighborhoods. Membranes that preserved the integrity of substances and shapes, kept each in its proper place, were worn thin. He could poke his finger through yellowed skin. A stone wall. The eggshell of his skull. What should be separated was running together. Threatened to burst. Nothing contained the way it was supposed to be. No clear lines of demarcation. A mongrel city. Traffic where there shouldn't be traffic. An awful void opening around him, preparing itself to hold explosions of bile, vomit, gushing bowels, ooze, sludge, seepage.

Earlier in the summer, on a July afternoon, he'd tried to escape the heat by walking along the Delaware. The water was unnaturally calm, isolated into stagnant pools by outcroppings of wharf and jetty. A shelf of rotting matter paralleled the river edge. As if someone had attempted to sweep what was unclean and dead from the water. Bones, skins, entrails, torn carcasses, unrecognizable tatters and remnants broomed into a neat ridge. No sigh of the breeze he'd sought, yet fumes from the rim of garbage battered him in nauseating waves, a palpable medium intimate as wind. Beyond the tidal line of refuge, a pale margin lapped clean by receding waters. Then the iron river itself, flat, dark, speckled by sores of foam that puckered and swirled, worrying the stillness with a life of their own.

Spilled. Spoiled. Those words repeated themselves endlessly as he made his rounds. Dr. Rush had written out his portion, his day's share from the list of dead and dying. He'd purged, bled, comforted and buried victims of the fever. In and out of homes that had become tombs, prisons, charnel houses. Dazed children wandering the streets, searching for their parents. How can he explain to a girl, barely more than an infant, that the father and mother she sobs for are gone from this earth? Departed. Expired. They are resting, child. Asleep forever. In a far, far better place, my sweet, dear, suffering one. In God's bosom. Wrapped in His incorruptible arms. A dead mother with a dead baby at her breast. Piteous cries of the helpless offering all they own for a drink of water. How does he console the delirious boy who pummels him, fastens himself on his leg because he's put the boy's mother in a box and now must nail shut the lid?

Though light-headed from exhaustion, he's determined to spend a few hours here, among his own people. But were these lost ones really his people? The doors of his church were open to them, yet these were the ones who stayed away, wasting their lives in vicious pastimes of the idle, the unsaved, the ignorant. His benighted brethren who'd struggled to reach this city of refuge and then, once inside the gates, had fallen, prisoners again, trapped by chains of dissolute living as they'd formerly been snared in the bonds of slavery. He'd come here and preached to them. Thieves, beggars, loose women, debtors, fugitives, drunkards, gamblers, the weak, crippled, and outcast with nowhere else to go. They spurned his church so he'd brought church to them, preaching in gin mills, whoring dens, on street corners. He'd been jeered and hooted, spat upon, clods of unnameable filth had spattered his coat. But a love for them, as deep and unfathomable as his sorrow, his pity, brought him back again and again, exhorting them, setting the gospel before them so they might partake of its bounty, the infinite goodness, blessed sustenance therein. Jesus had toiled among the wretched, the outcast, that flotsam and jetsam deposited like a ledge of filth on the banks of the city. He understood what had brought the dark faces of his brethren north, to the Quaker promise of this town, this cradle and capital of a New World, knew the misery they were fleeing, the bright star in the Gourd's handle that guided them, the joy leaping in their hearts when at last, at last the opportunity to be viewed as men instead of things was theirs. He'd dreamed such dreams himself, oh, yes, and prayed that the light of hope would never be extinguished. He'd been praying for deliverance, for peace and understanding when God had granted him a vision, hordes of sable bondsmen throwing off their chains, marching, singing, a path opening in the sea, the sea shaking its shaggy shoulders, resplendent with light and power. A radiance sparkling in this walkway through the water, pearls, diamonds, spears of light. This was the glistening way home. Waters parting, glory blinking and winking. Too intense to stare at, a promise shimmering, a rainbow arching over the end of the path. A hand tapped him. He'd waited for it to blend into the vision, for its meaning to shine forth in the language, neither word nor thought, God was speaking in His visitation. Tapping became a grip. Someone was shoving him. He was being pushed off his knees, hauled to his feet. Someone was snatching him from the honeyed dream of salvation. When his eyes popped open he knew the name of each church elder manhandling him. Pale faces above a wall of black cloth belonged to his fellow communicants. He knew without looking the names of the men whose hands touched him gently, steering, coaxing, and those whose hands dug into his flesh, the impatient, imperious, rough hands that shunned any contact with him except as overseer or master.

Allen, Allen. Do you hear me? You and your people must not kneel at the front of the gallery. On your feet. Come. Come. Now. On your feet.

Behind the last row of pews. There ye may fall down on your knees and give praise.

And so we built our African house of worship. But its walls could not imprison the Lord's word. Go forth. Go forth. And he did so. To this sinful quarter. Tunnels, cellars, and caves. Where no sunlight penetrates. Where wind off the river cuts like a knife. Chill of icy spray channeled here from the ocean's wintry depths. Where each summer the brackish sea that is mouth and maw and bowel deposits its waste in puddles stinking to high heaven.

Water Street becomes what it's named, rises round his ankles, soaks his boots, threatens to drag him down. Patrolling these murky depths he's predator, scavenger, the prey of some dagger-toothed creature whose shadow closes over him like a net.

When the first settlers arrived here they'd scratched caves into the soft earth of the riverbank. Like ants. Rats. Gradually they'd pushed inland, laying out a geometrical grid of streets, perpendicular, true angled and straight edged, the mirror of their rectitude. Black Quaker coats and dour visages were remembrances of mud, darkness, the place of their lying in, cocooned like worms, propagating dreams of a holy city. The latest comers must always start here, on this dotted line, in this riot of alleys, lanes, tunnels. Wave after wave of immigrants unloaded here, winnowed here, dying in these shanties, grieving in strange languages. But white faces move on, bury their dead, bear their children, negotiate the invisible reef between this broken place and the foursquare town. Learn enough of their new tongue to say to the blacks they've left behind, *thou shalt not pass*.

I watched him bring the scalding liquid to his lips and thought to myself that's where his color comes from. The black brew he drinks every morning.

Coloring him, changing him. A hue I had not considered until that instant as other than absence, something nonwhite and therefore its opposite, what light would be if extinguished, sky or sea drained of the color blue when the sun disappears, the blackness of cinders. As he sips, steam rises. I peer into the cup that's become mine, at the moon in its center, waxing, waning. A light burning in another part of the room caught there, as my face would be if I leaned over the cup's hot mouth. But I have no wish to see my face. His is what I study as I stare into my cup and see not absence, but the presence of wood darkly stained, wet plowed earth, a boulder rising from a lake, blackly glistening as it sheds crowns and beards and necklaces of water. His color neither neglect nor abstention, nor mystery, but a swelling tide in his skin of this bitter morning beverage it is my habit to imbibe.

We were losing, clearly losing the fight. One day in mid-September fifty-seven were buried before noon.

He'd begun with no preamble. Our conversation taken up again directly as if the months since our last meeting were no more than a cobweb his first words lightly brush away. I say conversation but a better word would be soliloquy because I was only a listener, a witness learning his story, a story buried so deeply he couldn't recall it, but dreamed pieces, a conversation with himself, a reverie with the power to sink us both into its unreality. So his first words did not begin the story where I remembered him ending it in our last session, but picked up midstream the ceaseless play of voices only he heard, always, summoning him, possessing him, enabling him to speak, to be.

Despair was in my heart. The fiction of our immunity had been exposed for the vicious lie it was, a not so subtle device for wresting us from our homes, our loved ones, the afflicted among us, and sending us to aid strangers. First they blamed us, called the sickness Barbados fever, a contagion from those blood-soaked islands, brought to these shores by refugees from the fighting in Santo Domingo. We were not welcome anywhere. A dark skin was seen not only as a badge of shame for its wearer. Now we were evil incarnate, the mask of long agony and violent death. Black servants were discharged. The draymen, carters, barbers, caterers, oyster sellers, street vendors could find no custom. It mattered not that some of us were born here and spoke no language but the English language, second-, even third-generation African Americans who knew no other country, who laughed at the antics of newly landed immigrants, Dutchmen, Welshmen, Scots, Irish, Frenchmen who had turned our marketplaces into Babel, stomping along in their clodhopper shoes, strange costumes, haughty airs, Lowlander gibberish that sounded like men coughing or dogs barking. My fellow countrymen searching everywhere but in their own hearts, the foulness upon which this city is erected, to lay blame on others for the killing fever, pointed their fingers at foreigners and called it Palatine fever, a pestilence imported from those low countries in Europe where, I have been told, war for control of the sea-lanes, the human cargoes transported thereupon, has raged for a hundred years.

But I am losing the thread, the ironical knot I wished to untangle for you. How the knife was plunged in our hearts, then cruelly twisted. We were proclaimed carriers of the fever and treated as pariahs, but when it became expedient to command our services to nurse the sick and bury the dead, the previous allegations were no longer mentioned. Urged on by desperate counselors, the mayor granted us a blessed immunity. We were ordered to save the city.

I swear to you, and the bills of mortality, published by the otherwise unreliable Mr. Carey, support my contention, that the fever dealt with us severely. Among the city's poor and destitute the fever's ravages were most deadly and we are always the poorest of the poor. If an ordinance forbidding ringing of bells to mourn the dead had not been passed, that awful tolling would have marked our days, the watches of the night in our African-American community, as it did in those environs of the city we were forbidden to inhabit. Every morning before I commenced my labors for the sick and dying, I would hear moaning, screams of pain, fearful cries and supplications, a chorus of lamentations scarring daybreak, my people awakening to a nightmare that was devouring their will to live.

The small strength I was able to muster each morning was sorely tried the moment my eyes and ears opened upon the sufferings of my people, the reality that gave the lie to the fiction of our immunity. When my duties among the whites were concluded, how many nights did I return and struggle till dawn with victims here, my friends, parishioners, wandering sons of Africa whose faces I could not look upon without seeing my own. I was commandeered to rise and go forth to the general task of saving the city, forced to leave this neighborhood where my skills were sorely needed. I nursed those who hated me, deserted the ones I loved, who loved me.

I recite the story many, many times to myself, let many voices speak to me till one begins to sound like the sea or rain or my feet those mornings shuffling through thick dust.

We arrived at Bush Hill early. To spare ourselves a long trek in the oppressive heat of day. Yellow haze hung over the city. Plumes of smoke from blazes in Potter's Field, from fires on street corners curled above the rooftops, lending the dismal aspect of a town sacked and burned. I've listened to the Santo Domingans tell of the burning of Cap François. How the capital city was engulfed by fires set in cane fields by the rebelling slaves. Horizon in flames all night as they huddled offshore in ships, terrified, wondering where next they'd go, if any port would permit them to land, empty-handed slaves, masters whose only wealth now was naked black bodies locked in the hold, wide-eyed witnesses of an empire's downfall, chanting, moaning, uncertain as the sea rocked them, whether or not anything on earth could survive the fearful conflagration consuming the great city of Cap François.

Dawn breaking on a smoldering landscape, writhing columns of smoke, a general cloud of haze the color of a fever victim's eyes. I turn and stare at it a moment, then fall in again with my brother's footsteps trudging through untended fields girding Bush Hill.

From a prisoner-of-war ship in New York harbor where the British had interned him he'd seen that city shed its graveclothes of fog. Morning after morning it would paint itself damp and gray, a flat sketch on the canvas of sky, a tentative, shivering screen of housefronts, sheds, sprawling warehouses floating above the river. Then shadows and hollows darkened. A jumble of masts, spars, sails began to sway, little boats plied lanes between ships, tiny figures inched along wharves and docks, doors opened, windows slid up or down, lending an illusion of depth and animation to the portrait. This city infinitely beyond his reach, this charade other men staged to mock him, to mark the distance he could not travel, the shore he'd never reach, the city, so to speak, came to life and with its birth each morning dropped the palpable weight of his despair. His loneliness and exile. Moored in pewter water, on an island that never stopped moving but never arrived anywhere. The city a mirage of light and air, chimera of paint, brush, and paper, mattered naught except that it was denied him. It shimmered. Tolled. Unsettled the watery place where he was sentenced to dwell. Conveyed to him each morning the same doleful tidings: *The dead are legion, the living a froth on dark, layered depths. But you are neither, and less than both.* Each night he dreamed it burning, razed the city till nothing remained but a dry, black crust, crackling, crunching under his boots as he strides, king of the nothing he surveys.

We passed holes dug into the earth where the sick are interred. Some died in these shallow pits, awash in their own vomited and voided filth, before a bed in the hospital could be made ready for them. Others believed they were being buried alive, and unable to crawl out, howled till reason or strength deserted them. A few, past caring, slept soundly in these ditches, resisted the attendants sent to rouse them and transport them inside, once they realized they were being resurrected to do battle again with the fever.

I'd watched the red-bearded French doctor from Santo Domingo with his charts and assistants inspecting this zone, his *salle d'attente* he called it, greeting and reassuring new arrivals, interrogating them, nodding and bowing, hurrying from pit to pit, peering down at his invisible patients like a gardener tending seeds.

An introduction to the grave, a way into the hospital that prefigured the way most would leave it. That's what this bizarre rite of admission had seemed at first. But through this and other peculiar strategems, Deveze, with his French practice, had transformed Bush Hill from lazarium to a clinic where victims of the fever, if not too weak upon arrival, stood a chance of surviving.

The cartman employed by Bush Hill had suddenly fallen sick. Faithful Wilcox had never missed a day, ferrying back and forth from town to hospital, hospital to Potter's Field. Bush Hill had its own cemetery now. Daily rations of dead could be disposed of less conspicuously in a plot on the grounds of the estate, screened from the horror-struck eyes of the city. No one had trusted the hospital. Tales of bloody chaos reigning there had filtered back to the city. Citizens believed it was a place where the doomed were stored until they died. Fever victims would have to be dragged from their beds into Bush Hill's cart. They'd struggle and scream, pitch themselves from the rolling cart, beg for help when the cart passed a rare pedestrian daring or foolish enough to be abroad in the deadly streets.

I wondered for the thousandth time why some were stricken, some not. Dr. Rush and this Deveze dipped their hands into the entrails of corpses, stirred the black, corrupted blood, breathed infected vapors exhaled from mortified remains. I'd observed both men steeped in noxious fluids expelled by their patients, yet neither had fallen prey to the fever. Stolid, dim Wilcox maintained daily concourse with the sick and buried the dead for two months before he was infected. They say a woman, undiscovered until boiling stench drove her neighbors into the street crying for aid, was the cause of Wilcox's downfall. A large woman, bloated into an even more cumbersome package by gases and liquids seething inside her body, had slipped from his grasp as he and another had hoisted her up into the cart. Catching against a rail, her body had slammed down and burst, spraying Wilcox like a fountain. Wilcox did not pride himself on being the tidiest of men, nor did his job demand one who was overfastidious, but the reeking stench from that accident was too much even for him and he departed in a huff to change his polluted garments. He never returned. So there I was at Bush Hill, where Rush had assigned me with my brother, to bury the flow of dead that did not ebb just because the Charon who was their familiar could no longer attend them.

The doctors believe they can find the secret of the fever in the victims' dead bodies. They cut, saw, extract, weigh, measure. The dead are carved into smaller and smaller bits and the butchered parts studied but they do not speak. What I know of the fever I've learned from the words of those I've treated, from stories of the living that are ignored by the good doctors. When lancet and fleam bleed the victims, they offer up stories like prayers.

It was a jaunty day. We served our white guests and after they'd eaten, they served us at the long, linen-draped tables. A sumptuous feast in the oak grove prepared by many and willing hands. All the world's eyes seemed to be watching us. The city's leading men, black and white, were in attendance to celebrate laying the cornerstone of St. Thomas Episcopal African Church. In spite of the heat and clouds of mettlesome insects, spirits were high. A gathering of whites and blacks in good Christian fellowship to commemorate the fruit of shared labor. Perhaps a new day was dawning. The picnic occurred in July. In less than a month the fever burst upon us.

When you open the dead, black or white, you find: the dura matter covering the brain is white and fibrous in appearance. The leptomeninges covering the brain are clear and without opacifications. The brain weighs 1450 grams and is formed symmetrically. Cut sections of the cerebral hemispheres reveal normal-appearing gray matter throughout. The white matter of the corpus callosum is intact and bears no lesions. The basal ganglia are in their normal locations and grossly appear to be without lesions. The ventricles are symmetrical and filled with crystal-clear cerebrospinal fluid.

The cerebellum is formed symmetrically. The nuclei of the cerebellum are unremarkable. Multiple sections through the pons, medulla oblongata and upper brain stem reveal normal gross anatomy. The cranial nerves are in their normal locations and unremarkable.

The muscles of the neck are in their normal locations. The cartilages of the larynx and the hyoid bone are intact. The thyroid and parathyroid glands are normal on their external surface. The mucosa of the larynx is shiny, smooth, and without lesions. The vocal cords are unremarkable. A small amount of bloody material is present in the upper trachea.

The heart weighs 380 grams. The epicardial surface is smooth, glistening, and without lesions. The myocardium of the left ventricle and septum are of a uniform meaty-red, firm appearance. The endocardial surfaces are smooth, glistening, and without lesions. The auricular appendages are free from thrombi. The valve leaflets are thin and delicate, and show no evidence of vegetation.

The right lung weighs 400 grams. The left lung 510 grams. The pleural surfaces of the lungs are smooth and glistening.

The esophageal mucosa is glistening, white, and folded. The stomach contains a large amount of black, noxious bile. A veriform appendix is

present. The ascending, transverse, and descending colon reveal hemor-
rhaging, striations, disturbance of normal mucosa patterns throughout. A
small amount of bloody, liquid feces is present in the ano-rectal canal.

The liver weighs 1720 grams. The spleen weighs 150 grams. The right
kidney weighs 190 grams. The left kidney weighs 180 grams. The testes show
a glistening white tunica albuginea. Sections are unremarkable.

Dr. Rush and his assistants examined as many corpses as possible in spite
of the hurry and tumult of never-ending attendance on the sick. Rush hoped
to prove his remedy, his analysis of the cause and course of the fever correct.
Attacked on all sides by his medical brethren for purging and bleeding patients
already in a drastically weakened state, Rush lashed back at his detractors,
wrote pamphlets, broadsides, brandished the stinking evidence of his post-
mortems to demonstrate conclusively how the sick drowned in their own
poisoned fluids. The putrefaction, the black excess, he proclaimed, must be
drained away, else the victim inevitably succumbs.

Dearest:
  I shall not return home again until this business of the fever is terminated.
I fear bringing the dread contagion into our home. My life is in the hands
of God and as long as He sees fit to spare me I will persist in my labors on
behalf of the sick, dying, and dead. We are losing the battle. Eighty-eight
were buried this past Thursday. I tremble for your safety. Wish the lie of
immunity were true. Please let me know by way of a note sent to the residence
of Dr. Rush that you and our dear Martha are well. I pray every hour that
God will preserve you both. As difficult as it is to rise each morning and go
with Thomas to perform our duties, the task would be unbearable if I did
not hold in my heart a vision of these horrors ending, a blessed shining day
when I return to you and drop this weary head upon your sweet bosom.

Allen, Allen, he called to me. Observe how even after death, the body rejects
this bloody matter from nose and bowel and mouth. Verily, the patient who
had expired at least an hour before continued to stain the cloth I'd wrapped
'round him. We'd searched the rooms of a regal mansion, discovering six
members of a family, patriarch, son, son's wife, and three children, either
dead or in the last frightful stages of the disease. Upon the advice of one of
Dr. Rush's most outspoken critics, they had refused mercury purges and
bleeding until now, when it was too late for any earthly remedy to preserve
them. In the rich furnishings of this opulent mansion, attended by one
remaining servant whom fear had not driven away, three generations had
withered simultaneously, this proud family's link to past and future cut off
absolutely, the great circle broken. In the first bedroom we'd entered we'd

found William Spurgeon, merchant, son, and father, present manager of the family fortune, so weak he could not speak, except with pained blinks of his terrible golden eyes. Did he welcome us? Was he apologizing to good Dr. Rush for doubting his cure? Did he fear the dark faces of my brother and myself? Quick, too quickly, he was gone. Answering no questions. Revealing nothing of his state of mind. A savaged face frozen above the blanket. Ancient beyond years. Jaundiced eyes not fooled by our busy ministrations, but staring through us, fixed on the eternal stillness soon to come. And I believe I learned in that yellow cast of his eyes, the exact hue of the sky, if sky it should be called, hanging over the next world where we abide.

Allen, Allen. He lasted only moments and then I wrapped him in a sheet from the chest at the foot of his canopied bed. We lifted him into a humbler litter, crudely nailed together, the lumber still green. Allen, look. Stench from the coffin cut through the oppressive odors permeating this doomed household. See. Like an infant the master of the house had soiled his swaddling clothes. Seepage formed a dark river and dripped between roughly jointed boards. We found his wife where she'd fallen, naked, yellow above the waist, black below. As always the smell presaged what we'd discover behind a closed door. This woman had possessed closets of finery, slaves who dressed, fed, bathed, and painted her, and yet here she lay, no one to cover her modesty, to lift her from the floor. Dr. Rush guessed from the discoloration she'd been dead two days, a guess confirmed by the loyal black maid, sick herself, who'd elected to stay when all others had deserted her masters. The demands of the living too much for her. She'd simply shut the door on her dead mistress. No breath, no heartbeat, sir. I could not rouse her, sir. I intended to return, sir, but I was too weak to move her, too exhausted by my labors, sir. Tears rolled down her creased black face and I wondered in my heart how this abused and despised old creature in her filthy apron and turban, this frail, worn woman, had survived the general calamity while the strong and pampered toppled 'round her.

I wanted to demand of her why she did not fly out the door now, finally freed of her burden, her lifelong enslavement to the whims of white people. Yet I asked her nothing. Considered instead myself, a man who'd worked years to purchase his wife's freedom, then his own, a so-called freeman, and here I was following in the train of Rush and his assistants, a functionary, a lackey, insulted daily by those I risked my life to heal.

Why did I not fly? Why was I not dancing in the streets, celebrating God's judgment on this wicked city? Fever made me freer than I'd ever been. Municipal government had collapsed. Anarchy ruled. As long as fever did not strike me I could come and go anywhere I pleased. Fortunes could be amassed in the streets. I could sell myself to the highest bidder, as nurse or undertaker, as surgeon trained by the famous Dr. Rush to apply his lifesaving cure. Anyone who would enter houses where fever was abroad could demand outrageous sums for negligible services. To be spared the fever was a chance for anyone, black or white, to be a king.

So why do you follow him like a loyal puppy, you confounded black fool? He wagged his finger. *You*. . . . His finger a gaunt, swollen-jointed, cracked-bone, chewed thing. Like the nose on his face. The nose I'd thought looked more like finger than nose. *Fool. Fool.* Finger wagging, then the cackle. The barnyard braying. Berserk chickens cackling in his skinny, goiter-knobbed throat. You are a fool, you black son of Ham. You slack-witted, Nubian ape. You progeny of Peeping Toms and orangutans. Who forces you to accompany that madman Rush on his murderous tours? He kills a hundred for every one he helps with his lamebrain, nonsensical, unnatural, Sangrado cures. Why do you tuck your monkey tail between your legs and skip after that butcher? Are you his shadow, a mindless, spineless black puddle of slime with no will of its own?

You are a good man, Allen. You worry about the souls of your people in this soulless wilderness. You love your family and your God. You are a beacon and steadfast. Your fatal flaw is narrowness of vision. You cannot see beyond these shores. The river, that stinking gutter into which the city shovels its shit and extracts its drinking water, that long-suffering string of spittle winds to an ocean. A hundred miles downstream the foamy mouth of the land sucks on the Atlantic's teat, trade winds saunter and a whole wide world awaits the voyager. I know, Allen. I've been everywhere. Buying and selling everywhere.

If you would dare be Moses to your people and lead them out of this land, you'd find fair fields for your talent. Not lapdogging or doggy-trotting behind or fetch doggy or lie doggy or doggy open your legs or doggy stay still while I beat you. Follow the wound that is a river back to the sea. Be gone, be gone. While there's still time. If there is time, *mon frère*. If the pestilence has not settled in you already, breathed from my foul guts into yours, even as we speak.

Here's a master for you. A real master, Allen. The fever that's supping on my innards. I am more slave than you've ever been. I do its bidding absolutely. Cough up my lungs. Shit hunks of my bowel. When I die, they say my skin will turn as black as yours, Allen.

Return to your family. Do not leave them again. Whatever the Rushes promise, whatever they threaten.

————

Once, ten thousand years ago, I had a wife and children. I was like you, Allen, proud, innocent, forward looking, well-spoken, well-mannered, a beacon and steadfast. I began to believe the whispered promise that I could have more. More of what, I didn't ask. Didn't know, but I took my eyes off what I loved in order to obtain this more. Left my wife and children and when I returned they were gone. Forever lost to me. The details are not significant. Suffice to say the circumstances of my leaving were much like yours. Very much like yours, Allen. And I lost everything. Became a wanderer among men. Bad news people see coming from miles away. A pariah. A joke. I'm not black like you, Allen. But I will be soon. Sooner than you'll be white. And if you're ever white, you'll be as dead as I'll be when I'm black.

Why do you desert your loved ones? What impels you to do what you find so painful, so unjust? Are you not a man? And free?

Her sleepy eyes, your lips on her warm cheek, each time may be the last meeting on this earth. The circumstances are similar, my brother. My shadow. My dirty face.

The dead are legion, the living a froth on dark, layered depths.

Master Abraham. There's a gentleman to see you, sir. The golden-haired lad bound to me for seven years was carted across the seas, like you, Allen, in the bowels of a leaky tub. A son to replace my son his fathers had clubbed to death when they razed the ghetto of Antwerp. But I could not tame the inveterate hate, his aversion and contempt for me. From my aerie, at my desk secluded among barrels, bolts, crates, and trunks of the shop's attic, I watched him steal, drink, fornicate. I overheard him denounce me to a delegate sent 'round to collect a tithe during the emergency. 'Tis well known in the old country that Jews bring the fever. Palatine fever that slays whole cities. They carry it under dirty fingernails, in the wimples of lizardy private parts. Pass it on with the evil eye. That's why we hound them from our towns, exterminate them. Beware of Master Abraham's glare. And the black-coated vulture listened intently. I could see him toting up the account in his small brain. Kill the Jew. Gain a shop and sturdy prentice, too. But I survived till fever laid me low and the cart brought me here to Bush Hill. For years he robbed and betrayed me and all my revenge was to treat him better. Allow him to pilfer, lie, embezzle. Let him grow fat and careless as I knew he would. With a father's boundless kindness I destroyed him. The last sorry laugh coming when I learned he died in agony, fever shriven, following by a day his Water Street French whore my indulgence allowed him to keep.

In Amsterdam I sold diamonds, Allen. In Barcelona they plucked hairs from my beard to fashion charms that brought ill fortune to their enemies. There were nights in dungeons when the mantle of my suffering was all I possessed to wrap 'round me and keep off mortal cold. I cursed God for choosing me, choosing my people to cuckold and slaughter. Have you heard of the Lamed-Vov, the Thirty-six Just Men set apart to suffer the reality humankind cannot bear? Saviors. But not Gods like your Christ. Not magicians, not sorcerers with bags of tricks, Allen. No divine immunities. Flesh and blood saviors. Men like we are, Allen. If man you are beneath your sable hide. Men who cough and scratch their sores and bleed and stink. Whose teeth rot. Whose wives and children are torn from them. Who wander the earth unable to die, but men always, men till God plucks them up and returns them to His side where they must thaw ten centuries to melt the crust of earthly grief and misery they've taken upon themselves. Ice men. Snowmen. I thought for many years I might be one of them. In my vanity. My self-pity. My foolishness. But no. One lifetime of sorrows enough for me. I'm just another customer. One more in the crowd lined up at his stall to purchase his wares.

You do know, don't you, Allen, that God is a bookseller? He publishes one book—the text of suffering—over and over again. He disguises it between new boards, in different shapes and sizes, prints on varying papers, in many fonts, adds prefaces and postscripts to deceive the buyer, but it's always the same book.

You say you do not return to your family because you don't want to infect them. Perhaps your fear is well-founded. But perhaps it also masks a greater fear. Can you imagine yourself, Allen, as other than you are? A free man with no charlatan Rush to blame. The weight of your life in your hands.

You've told me tales of citizens paralyzed by fear, of slaves on shipboard who turn to stone in their chains, their eyes boiled in the sun. Is it not possible that you suffer the converse of this immobility? You, sir, unable to stop an endless round of duty and obligation. Turning pages as if the next one or the next will let you finish the story and return to your life.

Your life, man. Tell me what sacred destiny, what nigger errand keeps you standing here at my filthy pallet? Fly, fly, fly away home. Your house is on fire, your children burning.

I have lived to see the slaves free. My people frolic in the streets. Black and white. The ones who believe they are either or both or neither. I am too old for dancing. Too old for foolishness. But this full moon makes me wish for two good legs. For three. Straddled a broomstick when I was a boy.

Giddy-up, Giddy-up. Galloping m'lord, m'lady, around the yard I should be sweeping. Dust in my wake. Chickens squawking. My eyes everywhere at once so I would not be caught out by mistress or master in the sin of idleness. Of dreaming. Of following a child's inclination. My broom steed snatched away. Become a rod across my back. Ever cautious. Dreaming with one eye open. The eye I am now, old and gimpy limbed, watching while my people celebrate the rumor of Old Pharaoh's capitulation.

I've shed this city like a skin, wiggling out of it ten score and more years, by miles and els, fretting, twisting. Many days I did not know whether I'd wrenched freer or crawled deeper into the sinuous pit. Somewhere a child stood, someplace green, keeping track, waiting for me. Hoping I'd meet him again, hoping my struggle was not in vain. I search that child's face for clues to my blurred features. Flesh drifted and banked, eroded by wind and water, the landscape of this city fitting me like a skin. Pray for me, child. For my unborn parents I carry in this orphan's potbelly. For this ancient face that slips like water through my fingers.

Night now. Bitter cold night. Fires in the hearths of lucky ones. Many of us still abide in dark cellars, caves dug into the earth below poor men's houses. For we are poorer still, burrow there, pull earth like blanket and quilt 'round us to shut out cold, sleep multitudes to a room, stacked and crosshatched and spoon fashion, ourselves the fuel, heat of one body passed to others and passed back from all to one. No wonder then the celebration does not end as a blazing chill sweeps off the Delaware. Those who leap and roar 'round the bonfires are better off where they are. They have no place else to go.

Given the derivation of the words, you could call the deadly, winged visitors an *unpleasantness from Egypt*.

Putrid stink rattles in his nostrils. He must stoop to enter the cellar. No answer as he shouts his name, his mission of mercy. Earthen floor, ceiling and walls buttressed by occasional beams, slabs of wood. Faint bobbing glow from his lantern. He sees himself looming and shivering on the walls, a shadowy presence with more substance than he feels he possesses at this late hour. After a long day of visits, this hovel his last stop before returning to his brother's house for a few hours of rest. He has learned that exhaustion is a swamp he can wade through and on the far side another region where a thin trembling version of himself toils while he observes, bemused, slipping in and out of sleep, amazed at the likeness, the skill with which that other mounts and sustains him. Mimicry. Puppetry. Whatever controls this other, he allows the impostor to continue, depends upon it to work when he no

longer can. After days in the city proper with Rush, he returns to these
twisting streets beside the river that are infected veins and arteries he must
bleed.

At the rear of the cave, so deep in shadow he stumbles against it before
he sees it, is a mound of rags. When he leans over it, speaking down into
the darkness, he knows instantly this is the source of the terrible smell, that
something once alive is rotting under the rags. He thinks of autumn leaves
blown into mountainous, crisp heaps, the north wind cleansing itself and
the city of summer. He thinks of anything, any image that will rescue him
momentarily from the nauseating stench, postpone what he must do next.
He screams no, no to himself as he blinks away his wife's face, the face of
his daughter. His neighbors had promised to check on them, he hears news
almost daily. There is no rhyme or reason in whom the fever takes, whom
it spares, but he's in the city every day, exposed to its victims, breathing fetid
air, touching corrupted flesh. Surely if someone in his family must die, it
will be him. His clothes are drenched in vinegar, he sniffs the nostrum of
gunpowder, bark, and asafetida in a bag pinned to his coat. He's prepared
to purge and bleed himself, he's also ready and quite willing to forgo these
precautions and cures if he thought surrendering his life might save theirs.
He thinks and unthinks a picture of her hair, soft against his cheek, the wet
warmth of his daughter's backside in the crook of his arm as he carries her
to her mother's side where she'll be changed and fed. No. Like a choking
mist, the smell of decaying flesh stifles him, forces him to turn away, once,
twice, before he watches himself bend down into the brunt of it and uncover
the sleepers.

Two Santo Domingan refugees, slave or free, no one knew for sure,
inhabited this cellar. They had moved in less than a week before, the mother
huge with child, man and woman both wracked by fever. No one knows
how long the couple's been unattended. There was shame in the eyes and
voices of the few from whom he'd gleaned bits and pieces of the Santo
Domingans' history. Since no one really knew them and few nearby spoke
their language, no one was willing to risk, et cetera. Except for screams one
night, no one had seen or heard signs of life. If he'd been told nothing about
them, his nose would have led him here.

He winces when he sees the dead man and woman, husband and wife,
not entwined as in some ballad of love eternal, but turned back to back,
distance between them, as if the horror were too visible, too great to bear,
doubled in the other's eyes. What had they seen before they flung away from
each other? If he could, he would rearrange them, spare the undertakers
this vision.

Rat feet and rat squeak in the shadows. He'd stomped his feet, shooed them before he entered, hollered as he threw back the covers, but already they were accustomed to his presence, back at work. They'd bite indiscriminately, dead flesh, his flesh. He curses and flails his staff against the rags, strikes the earthen floor to keep the scavengers at bay. Those sounds are what precipitate the high-pitched cries that first frighten him, then shame him, then propel him to a tall packing crate turned on its end, atop which another crate is balanced. Inside the second wicker container, which had imported some item from some distant place into this land, twin brown babies hoot and wail.

We are passing over the Dismal Swamp. On the right is the Appalachian range, some of the oldest mountains on earth. Once there were steep ridges and valleys all through here but erosion off the mountains created landfill several miles deep in places. This accounts for the rich loamy soil of the region. Over the centuries several southern states were formed from this gradual erosion. The cash crops of cotton and tobacco so vital to southern prosperity were ideally suited to the fertile soil.

Yeah, I nurse these old funky motherfuckers, all right. White people, specially old white people, lemme tell you, boy, them peckerwoods stink. Stone dead fishy wet stink. Talking all the time 'bout niggers got BO. Well, white folks got the stink and gone, man. Don't be putting my hands on them, neither. Never. Uh-uh. If I touch them, be wit gloves. They some nasty people, boy. And they don't be paying me enough to take no chances wit my health. Matter of fact they ain't paying me enough to really be expecting me to work. Yeah. Starvation wages. So I ain't hardly touching them. Or doing much else either. Got to smoke a cigarette to get close to some of them. Piss and shit theyselves like babies. They don't need much taking care anyway. Most of them three-quarters dead already. Ones that ain't is crazy. Nobody don't want them 'round, that's why they here. Talking to theyselves. Acting like they speaking to a roomful of people and not one soul in the ward paying attention. There's one old black dude, must be a hundred, he be muttering away to hisself nonstop everyday. Pitiful, man. Hope I don't never get that old. Shoot me, bro, if I start to getting old and fucked up in body and mind like them. Don't want no fools like me hanging over me when I can't do nothing no more for my ownself. Shit. They ain't paying me nothing so that's what I do. Nothing. Least I don't punch 'em or tease 'em or steal they shit like some the staff. And I don't pretend I'm God like these so-called professionals and doctors flittin' 'round here drawing down that long bread. Naw. I just mind my own business, do my time. Cop a little TV, sneak me a joint when nobody's around. It ain't all that bad, really. Long as I ain't got no ol' lady and crumb crushers. Don't know how the married cats make it on the little bit of chump change they pay us. But me, I'm free. It ain't that bad, really.

By the time his brother brought him the news of their deaths . . .

Almost an afterthought. The worst, he believed, had been overcome. Only a handful of deaths the last weeks of November. The city was recovering. Commerce thriving. Philadelphia must be revictualed, refueled, rebuilt, reconnected to the countryside, to markets foreign and domestic, to products, pleasures, and appetites denied during the quarantine months of the fever. A new century would soon be dawning. We must forget the horrors. The mayor proclaims a new day. Says let's put the past behind us. Of the eleven who died in the fire he said extreme measures were necessary as we cleansed ourselves of disruptive influences. The cost could have been much greater, he said I regret the loss of life, especially the half dozen kids, but I commend all city officials, all volunteers who helped return the city to the arc of glory that is its proper destiny.

When they cut him open, the one who decided to stay, to be a beacon and steadfast, they will find: liver (1720 grams), spleen (150 grams), right kidney (190 grams), left kidney (180 grams), brain (1450 grams), heart (380 grams), and right next to his heart, the miniature hand of a child, frozen in a grasping gesture, fingers like hard tongues of flame, still reaching for the marvel of the beating heart, fascinated still, though the heart is cold, beats not, the hand as curious about this infinite stillness as it was about thump and heat and quickness.

SISSIE

John A. Williams

1 At last and finally! Iris thought
when the plane sped away from Boston, where they had been forced to land
because of fog in New York. Once more they were on their way, and Iris
assumed that her brother Ralph, who was meeting her at the airport, must
have been waiting for hours. Just my luck that we had to run into bad
weather, Iris thought.

Beside her sat the woman she had met in the airport in Barcelona. For
the moment Iris was too busy with her own thoughts to speak, and Helen
Kessler respected her silence. Both of the women smoked cigarettes. "Damn,
it's cold in here," Iris said half aloud, when they were once more over New
York. The plane seemed to slow, gradually losing momentum in the gray,
and banked above the cottony storm clouds racing endlessly by. Iris took a
deep breath and glanced at Helen. "Here we go again." Breasting the currents
of air like a huge, stiff bird, the craft circled lower and lower. There was a
sharp, high whine, and Iris heard the massive wheels thud into place. The

plane hung motionless for one frightening instant and then hissed downward through the clouds.

"Landings always make me nervous," Helen whispered hurriedly, glancing at Iris's taut, unlined brown neck.

"I noticed that at London and at Boston," Iris said. "Relax. If it happens you'll never know what hit you."

Unsure whether Iris was joking or not—she sometimes seemed a little strange—Helen glanced at her before replying. "God, you're cheerful," she said.

Iris smiled briefly and turned back to the window, watched the plane right itself—slowly, majestically. Suddenly, much too suddenly, they were out of the gray, floating over a bay that seemed perilously near. Iris shut her eyes; when she opened them she saw gray asphalt hurtling by. Another slight jar and the plane had landed. Both women gasped with relief. Helen grinned sheepishly, Iris grimly. "Damn," Iris said, trying to restrain the fluttering within her. "We're here." She took out her compact, snapped it open, and leaned her face toward the mirror.

"You look all right," Helen said, "damn you."

Iris, laughing softly, closed the compact, and Helen recognized that this laughter—unlike Iris's merriment on the long flight—was genuine. "Thanks," she said. "I'm sure glad I met you—"

It was Helen's turn to laugh.

"—no," Iris said, suddenly realizing that she might have been too withdrawn during the trip. "I mean it." Their eyes met, and Helen turned away shyly. At first sight Helen Kessler didn't look more than twenty-two, but a second glance revealed the pouch of a double chin and thin, seared lines radiating from the corners of her eyes. She was a small woman, with dull brown hair. When she smiled, her cheeks dimpled. Iris figured she was in her middle thirties—Iris was thirty-two. Helen had a nice figure, Iris had observed at dinner the evening before in the London airport restaurant. She looked as if she might be French, but was really an American returning to New York. Her presence had helped quiet Iris's apprehensions; Iris hadn't been in America for thirteen years. Helen (and Iris was grateful for this) was only superficially like many American women Iris had met and known in Europe. Perhaps it was Helen's size that saved her; she could never be loud or brash or vulgar. Only fiery, scintillating, risqué, or cute. She had seen Iris's show only the week before at the Emporium, she had shyly explained at the Barcelona airport. People were always saying something like that, but it had been a surprise to discover that Helen was so nice.

Iris climbed down the ramp on wobbly legs. She and Helen followed the other passengers into the multicolored glass-and-chrome terminal. The building reminded her of those structures that had risen like full-blown giants while she and Harry were in Germany.

The line shuffled forward over the speckled black marble floor. Now there were more Americans visible, those who worked in the banklike building. "They look so angry," Helen said. "Don't you think so?"

Iris was searching for her brother, but said, "I guess they ought to." And this made her recall the fact that Helen didn't consider herself an American. The sound of the taxiing jets was muffled now; only the single-pitched scream of the blowing engines penetrated the area where she and the others waited, behind a white horizontal marker. Ten feet beyond, uniformed customs officers stood checking papers. Iris looked about her at the lines of people and was reminded of the storefront of the disbursing office where every other Tuesday she and Ralph had gone to pick up their ration of government-issued surplus food during the Depression: tinned beef, dried prunes, grapefruit, wheat, oatmeal, apples, and everything marked with the telltale stamp. They had moved with the line, smelling the rich aroma of the apples until they came to a halt at the white marker. There they had waited until the joking men behind the makeshift orange- and apple-crate counter had laughed and smoked their fill. An imperious, stiff-fingered summons, just like the one the officer at the small booth was now making, had started them shuttling forward again.

When they entered the customs room, Iris looked up and saw Ralph standing in the glass-enclosed terrace. He waved and she waved back, anxiously watching for a sign.

"Is that your brother?" Helen asked.

"That's him," Iris said with a sober smile. "That's my big brother." Then Iris wondered who was meeting Helen. She almost asked, but changed her mind, thinking Helen might be embarrassed.

"Entertainer?" the customs officer asked with a polite smile. He held Iris's passport in his hand, which stated her profession quite plainly. Iris answered, "Yes, I am." The officer excused himself, passed beyond a series of slowly moving belts, and entered a small office.

"What's that for?" Helen asked.

"I think," Iris said slowly, recalling what the musicians and entertainers had told her about America, "narcotics." She smiled bitterly. "If you're an entertainer and you're colored, you get the works—"

Helen nodded. "I thought so," she said, compressing her lips. "It's too bad you had to come back. The bastards." Iris turned and glanced up at her brother again. She held out her hands in an impulsive, supplicatory gesture and he signaled back, urging restraint. Iris nodded and looked at Helen.

Since Barcelona she had had the feeling that Helen understood. "Yes," Iris said. "It's too bad."

After the officer had been gone twenty minutes, he returned, smiling broadly. "Sorry to keep you waiting." Neither woman answered, and he looked at them, puzzled. Helen Kessler went through customs without difficulty.

The two women walked through the turnstiles past the colored guards, Iris trying hard not to stare at them. Ralph came down the stairs. The look in his eyes told Iris that the laughter which came from her lips was not inappropriate. She threw herself into his arms. "Ralph!" she said.

He grinned at her. "Goddamn, baby, you sure look *good!*" They kissed, broke apart, and smiled at each other. He kissed her again and grunted. "You look *good!*"

"Man, you lookin' pretty fine your*self!*"

They laughed, and then, their laughter dying, looked into each other's eyes. Iris asked, "How's Mother?"

His head sagged slightly.

"Oliver said she was holding her own. Fighting her way back."

Iris heaved a great sigh. Funny that he should have said "fighting" because that was the way she had always pictured Sissie—never giving up, making small of whatever happened to her. The time she had had the tumor operation, they had gone to see her and found her sitting up in bed examining the growth, which she had preserved in a jar of formaldehyde.

"Thank God, thank God," Iris said.

"It's not over," Ralph answered.

"I know, but at least she's fighting."

Arm in arm, they walked together to where Helen was waiting.

"This is Helen. My brother, Ralph Joplin."

Ralph held out his hand, and Helen's reached out tentatively. Then they seemed to recognize something sympathetic in each other, and both smiled.

"You wrote that play!" Helen said, surprised, turning from Iris and back to Ralph. Iris was laughing. "Why didn't you tell me? Here I was ranting about how you *had* to see it, and it turns out your brother wrote it—"

"God, it's cold here," Iris said, pulling the mink tighter around her.

"So you wrote *Shadows on the Sun,*" Helen said to Ralph. "What an illustrious family."

Ralph and Iris laughed. "You're making us feel very good," Ralph said.

"Iris, I feel like an ass," Helen said, then, looking at Ralph, "I'm sorry about your mother. I hope she'll be all right."

"Thank you," Ralph said. "Can we drop you off?"

"If it won't be any bother."

They seemed, all of them, reluctant to move. Iris studied her brother. He reminded her of their father—tall, stooped, and thin of face, but less broad than Big Ralph. His hair was cropped. She remembered when he had worn it long, brushed into a pompadour and greased heavily. Like herself Ralph had their mother's soft brown eyes. She kept thinking, over and over to herself—he's made it.

Ralph had begun a study of his sister from the terrace, the very first moment he had seen her. She was tall for a woman; tallness ran in the family. She swung her body in a sort of swagger when she walked, held herself regally. She hadn't changed much in two years. Even from a distance, he noticed the luster of her hair, twisted neatly into a French roll. Iris had the strong features of their mother, but her face was less broad. Her prominent cheekbones made her eyes seem to curve upward, giving her a catlike look.

The skycap signaled a cab and placed the bags inside.

The taxi edged out onto the main highway and the driver accelerated.

"How's Adela?" Ralph asked.

"I started to bring her," Iris teased.

"Why didn't you?" Ralph said with a smile.

Iris said, "Why would I bring a hamburger to what must be a banquet for you?"

Helen glanced from brother to sister, then turned and kept her eyes on the landscape.

"At one time," Ralph said, "I had an overwhelming taste for hamburgers. But now, being an old married man—"

Adela had been one of Iris's friends, a dark-haired, unusually slender Catalonian with blue eyes. When Ralph was leaving Barcelona, he had asked half-jokingly, "Will you wait for me?" Adela had giggled and had looked at Iris. For months, Iris remembered, Adela had asked, "When will your brother return to Spain?"

Gently Iris said, "You might have sent her a card at least. Two years and not a word."

"I know." Ralph ground out a cigarette beneath his feet. "She was nice. Is she married?"

"Yes."

"Oh," he said, adding after a while, "Good." He turned to stare past Helen at the traffic.

"And how's your wife? Your marriage? Are you happy?" Iris watched him as he turned toward her, smiling. Even before he spoke, she knew what he was going to say.

"I'm happy." He opened his hands as if to say, What more can I say? "And you?"

Her smile was tight. "I'm a career girl, remember?"

They became silent.

The great bridge they approached soared up out of the ground and into the sky. "Is that the George Washington Bridge?" Iris asked, staring at the massive, snow-covered approaches.

"No, it's the Triboro."

"For Christ's sake, don't look at me like that. I don't know New York. Harry and I were only here three days before we left, and if it'd been up to him we'd have spent each of them in bed."

"Does it seem strange to you?" Ralph asked.

"Yes," Iris said.

They were speeding down East River Drive. "Were you very lonely here?" she asked. "I mean before Eve?"

"Yes, I suppose so," he answered.

The taxi peeled off the Drive and crept into a snow-filled street. Ralph and Iris said good-bye to Helen, settled back in the cab for the ride home.

The view of the mighty, hard, window-specked city, thrusting boldly up through the snow, jolted Iris. An old dread of this city, and of the continent to which it was the gateway, stirred within her.

 "Bienvenido a su casa," the small, peach-brown woman said. Her eyes sparkled. "Ralph taught me to say that," Eve said, coming forward to embrace Iris. Iris liked her at once. "C'mon," Eve said. "You both must be tired, and lunch is ready."

Ralph looked at Iris. She said, "Oh, man!" He grinned.

"Nothing new on the weather," Eve said, seating Iris at the table.

When lunch was over, Iris padded from room to room, a drink in her hand. Ralph was making telephone calls.

Iris had seen the dolls in Raphaella's room and the neat boxes of scarcely used toys. For the first time she thought of Ralph's child by his first wife, April; she felt a curious urge to see the child. Passing Ralph and Eve's bedroom, she noticed one of his shoes turned so that its almost new leather sole was visible, and she thought of their childhood; in those days they had fitted meticulously folded newspaper into the soles of their shoes. She remembered also those rare, enthusiastically welcomed parades to the Modern Boot Shop where new shoes, restricted in style, color, and durability by the yellow welfare order in Sissie's bag, were obtained for them. Sissie's tough thumbs, she recalled, would jab into the soles of the shoes and skim along the stitchings, feeling for inferior merchandise. Sissie always demanded the best the order could buy. Iris wore Italian shoes; she had had it on good authority that this mode would not get to America for another two years; the shoes were very expensive.

She paused in the alcove where Ralph's desk was and looked down at the typewriter. He hadn't had one when she and Harry left. She studied the titles of the books on the shelf above, as if they might reveal something of Ralph's secret self. On the shelf above the books was a photograph of Raffy. The ashtray was piled high with butts. Iris smiled. Eve was not allowed to enter this part of the room. The apartment told little about the people who lived there; its spare furnishings made her think of the monastery at Montserrat. Standing here where Ralph worked, she pictured him spending innumerable hours at the typewriter, in the small pyramid of light cast by the lamp above. She turned the battered, cane-bottomed desk chair and, seating herself in it, thought how wonderful it was that her brother now lived in the peace of such a home. Once more she glanced around the room, and the life that he led there with Eve somehow became real for her. She needed a background against which to imagine things. Until his arrival in Spain two years before, she had not been able to think of him as married to April, or as the father of a child. But April and the divorce were now all past; there was only himself and his bride of six months, Eve.

Suddenly she sensed that Ralph had come up behind her. "How's Raffy?" she asked without turning.

"Oh," he said. "You know kids. She's all right."

"And April?"

"Okay."

"Dad?"

"All right. I should call him."

Now she turned toward Ralph. "Do you think so?"

"Yes, don't you?"

She nodded. "You know," she said, "I like your wife; she's very lovely."

"She's all right," he said, sitting down in another chair.

Iris smiled at him. "Look, baby, how's it going?"

"So-so; could always be better."

"But you're making it?"

"*Got* to make it."

"Hey, I got a Ramirez for you."

"No shuck? Print or original?"

"Oh, come on, now. Nothing but the best for my broth. I'll get it for you in a while." She stared at him. "You look better than you did when you came to visit me. I guess"—she glanced toward the kitchen and, satisfied that Eve was still there, went on—"Adela got you straightened out."

"And you."

"Hell, I couldn't do what *Adela* did."

Ralph laughed. "No."

They were silent for a moment, and then Ralph said, "I'm sorry it had to be this way. I wanted you to come on a visit and have fun."

"I might not have come back quite so soon," she said. "Not because I hate it here." She laughed. "I never knew that much about it except home. You know, I've made it over there. I don't know if I could bring all that here without losing something."

"I know."

She said, "I suppose that I would've come sometime soon to visit Mother. That talk we had in Barcelona . . ."

"That talk," he said, "and the other." He breathed heavily.

"And the other," she now echoed.

"Look," he said, nodding toward the windows. Great snowflakes tumbled lazily out of the sky. "It's come. The storm."

From the kitchen Eve called, with almost a child's delight, "It's snowing!" And then, thinking what the snow meant for Ralph and Iris, she came out of the kitchen and said, more softly, "It's snowing, baby."

"Yes."

Eve looked at Iris. "Why don't you rest? You must be beat."

"I am, dear," Iris said, and turning to Ralph added, "I'd like to call Oliver."

"Sure," Ralph said.

"I'll get your bed ready," Eve said.

After Ralph dialed the number for her, Iris listened intently to the telephone ringing at the other end.

In Los Angeles Oliver Duncan wandered aimlessly through the chilled stucco house that had so suddenly become lonely. He heard the telephone ring and lifted it slowly to his ear, expecting to hear Dr. Clayton's high, womanish voice.

"It's me, Oliver—Iris. How's Mother?"

Almost immediately Oliver began talking of Sissie's illness. Sissie, Oliver said, had fallen ill, saying as she always did, that she was tired and hurting a little. But then had come that plunging moan which had not yet ended when he rushed into the bedroom, saying, "Sissie, what is it?"

"Oh, Lord. My chest and arms hurt. Call Dr. Clayton, quick, honey."

"Her heart," Dr. Clayton had said when he had come.

"She had just seen Dr. Clayton two days before," Oliver continued into the telephone. "She's still in the tent, but the doctor said she isn't requiring as much oxygen."

"It's snowing more heavily here now. Flights are canceled because of the storm. We'll be there just as soon as we can." Iris paused. "Ralph wants to talk." She passed her brother the phone.

"How you holdin' up, chief?" Ralph asked. "Sure. Yeah. . . . Well, we'll get there as soon as we can. . . . What?" His smile was cheerless. He said quietly, "Yes, we're all praying. S'long."

For a moment Ralph and Iris and Eve sat watching the snow, which had now obscured the sky. Eve rose and left. Within a couple of minutes, Iris was startled to hear her own voice coming from the other room. Eve returned with a smile on her face. "I love that record," she said. "It's our favorite." She sat on the floor beside Ralph whose head rested on the shoulder of his chair, his eyes closed. His hands moved tenderly through his wife's hair; Eve stared at the floor. Iris turned her eyes away from the couple and looked out the window. Snow.

She remembered making the record.

While she had been singing, the white faces of the Swedish engineers had been a cottony blur in the background; the overhead mike had threatened like the sword of Damocles. Things had been bad then for her and Time. But when she sang ("I wish you love . . .") he talked to her on the piano. ("Yes, baby. Me too. I wish you love. You need it!") The chords he was playing were sharp and sardonic ("You need it, baby!") And the others knew; despite their impassive faces. ("I wish you bluebirds in the spring . . .")

Will their love never be over? Iris wondered, looking at her brother and his wife. Suddenly Time's image stood in the foreground of her mind, his skull reflecting the studio lights. So she had seen him in a hundred studios in a hundred cities over the last eleven years—Melvin C. Curry. When had he become bald?

Iris rose as the record approached its end. "I'd better get some rest now," she said.

And then, thinking that her departure was perhaps too abrupt, she said, "I would like to see the play tonight. It doesn't look as though we'll be able to fly out." Ralph looked down at Eve, and she smiled back at him.

Eve went into the kitchen and Ralph rose from his chair and walked over to Iris. He rested his hand upon her shoulder. "Would you mind if I sent you with Eve? I'm trying to get some things out of the way before we go. They're rather important—"

"No, baby, I don't mind. But why were you two smiling?"

He smiled again. "Eve's ex is the lead in the play."

"Really!" Iris laughed. "Does she mind seeing him?"

"I think not," Ralph said.

"But you didn't tell me. What's his name?"

"Catroux," Eve said, slipping an arm through Ralph's. "Henri Catroux."

"You were married to Henri Catroux?"

"Yes," Eve said.

"You're better off without him. An egotistical, no-talent—"

"Iris, he's got fine talent—"

"Yes," Eve agreed. "He has that."

"Henri's hot right now," Ralph said with a bitter smile. "He's hot because white folks realize that they can market a little anger. Henri's the Negro who finally meets violence with suggested violence; can't be too damned obvious about these things. I'm sure he'd like to stop playing these superficial roles. Something—a whole process brings a human being to anger. Multiply that eighteen million times over and you don't have a process anymore. You have history."

Iris gestured with her hands. "But Henri's personality completely destroys his talent; at least it did when I met him." She turned to leave the room, but stopped and said with a grin, "Good work, Ralph." They all laughed. Iris turned to Eve. "Seriously, you won't mind?"

"No. You get some rest now. Ralph'll go back to work, and I'll think of something to wear tonight."

"Bless you," Iris said. She left the room. She was sorry she had used that phrase. It was one of those things one learned to say to people who rushed up and told you they liked you; eyes glowing, they played the humble role when it was you they really wished to humble. She shouldn't have said it to Eve and Ralph. It was phony and she had no need to be phony now. She was home.

SEDUCTION BY
LIGHT

Al Young

That night, half looped, I soaked in a hot bath at the Chrysler house and thought about everything me and Danielle had talked about after the men'd gone. Nomo and Benjie had to make it to a rock concert at the Hollywood Bowl. Tree, Benjie's new girlfriend, was goin' with 'em. I hadn't met her but, even so, somethin' told me she was a real mess. That's just one of the problems with bein' too sensitive to stuff you haven't come face-to-face with yet.

Danielle, with her sweet self, had talked me outta try'na drive myself home. She thought I needed more time off work to get over Burley. The big idea she and Carleton had worked out was for me to spend a coupla weeks restin' at their little beach house out in Malibu. I was game.

Layin' back in her double-size tub with all them fancy suds bubblin' up around my chin, I couldn't keep my mind off Chance rushin' off to warm up for his gig at Crime and Punishment. Accordin' to him—which you have to take with a few grains of salt—the place was fast gettin' to be one of the hottest new spots on the Strip. I remembered seein' a picture of the owner, too. Natasha Somethin'-or-other. She wasn't bad-lookin' for somebody with two teenage kids. In fact, her American husband had been a pretty close frienda Harry Silvertone's before they up and fell out over all those pitiful Palestinian refugees was massacred at that camp over there in Lebanon.

I tried to picture Chance playin' his boogie-woogies and jump numbers and blues and "My Funny Valentine" and "The Look of Love" and "You Are the Sunshine of My Life" and "Where Is the Love?" and "Quiet Nights" and other bossa nova numbers at the Crime and Punishment, with that sloe-eyed Russian boss of his slinkin' around in the background. Sometime I even wondered what life must look like from inside Chance Franklin's head. Like, how did he script and direct his own memory movie? Interestin' man, but not for me. All the same, I coulda done without all that touchy-touch and mashin' knees under the table he and Danielle'd been doin'.

I wasn't crazy about bein' in that huge house all by myself, but Mr. Chrysler was in Vegas on business, and late that afternoon Danielle got a call from this woman with a German name that makes pictures in Italy. I caught two or three of her things on videocassette once, and the one I remember best was about this high-tone society woman that gets stranded on a desert island with this no-class Communist. It was pretty good. Anyway, this woman, whatever her name was, invited Danielle out to this last-minute dinner party, and you know Danielle. She loves company.

After my bath my appetite started comin' back. I went down and fixed me some scrambled eggs and English muffin with jam, one of my favorite meals any time of day. Then I built a little fire in the guest bedroom I was stayin' in and turned in early, tired to the marrow of my bones. I curled up in bed with a *National Geographic* and looked at some pictures of Russia and read a little bit about how crazy they are over there about cold boiled potatoes and all that vodka.

Mind you, it was the first time I ever had anything to do with a waterbed except make one up. You ever attempted to get comfortable enough to do any kinda serious readin' in one of them things? Just when I was ready to get up and go look in Danielle's medicine chest to see if she had any Dramamine, sleep started to slip up on me. I was so woozy from the champagne and so tired that all I did was snap off the readin' lamp and stretch out under the covers to look at the fire and the shapes and shadows it was makin' on the furniture and walls. Ah, it was so restful. Before I knew it, I'd floated out clean and was gone bye-bye.

"What made you do it? What made you do that, Mamie?"

All in my sleep, look like, I kept hearin' somebody talkin' at me.

"Why, Mamie, why? I need to know why?"

The dream had its arms around my waist, huggin' me from behind. I was deep off into it and it wouldn't let go. Seem like I was sittin' by myself in a little boat tied up by the bank of some creek back home in Mississippi. Just a-sittin' and a-rockin', like that song goes I use to sing with Chance's band. Just me in this boat with a light breeze blowin' all around and the sunshine comin' and goin' the way sunshine'll do right before a squall comes up. Felt like I was maybe thirty-some years younger, wigglin' and wagglin', out there in that boat, waitin' on somethin'; but I couldn't tell you what.

And there's trees lined up all along the creek bank. At one point it got to be so vivid and *with* me until I catch myself gettin' this glad-all-over feelin' when I look up at the leaves real close and study the way the sun is hittin' 'em. See, the light wasn't exactly hittin' 'em when you stopped and studied it. The sun just kinda traveled out to where the leaf was and shimmered all around it; then the leaf sends out this invisible feeler, like a message ray or somethin', and suck up the light around it, drink it up, sip on it like you would a glassa buttermilk.

Had me hypnotized. Leaves would warm up and glow; then they would cool down and darken. They looked like tiny jewels flashin' off and on, all the time swishin' and whisperin' to me, sayin', "Mamie, why? Mamie, why?" over and over.

Then the rustlin' died down and the trees go away—at least that's what I remember it felt like. And when I look down I see the boat's gone, too, even though I could still feel myself bein' rocked and swayed, swayed and rocked, to and fro. Now there's no boat, no creek bank, no creek. Only me and this ebb and flow, with the sun playin' tricks on my skin, except for that chill from the breeze, from deep inside the ice water breeze. It wouldn't quit mutterin' and carryin' on.

Next thing, *snap!* From outta somewhere came this real loud *pop*, supersonic loud. So loud you couldn't even hear it. You felt it rattlin' the bones down under your nerves; your blood bubbled. It woke me up. I sat up on that wobbly water-filled mattress just in time to catch my breath and rub the sleep out my eyes.

I took time starin' all around the bedroom, checkin' out everything in the dark. The fire'd done burnt down mostly to reddish-orange embers, the color of the sun in the dream just before the trees stood still. The room was fulla that sweet, woodsy fireplace smell. A softer version of that *pop!* hit the insides of my ear, and I had to laugh. I realized it was the burnin' coals that'd caused that noise. That's when it all fell in place. All I'd been doin' was dreamin' on a doggone waterbed. I wanted to float back up the dream chimney like tender smoke and sun in that boat a little longer.

Just when I'd got halfway cozy and toasty again and was on the verge of dozin' back off, that voice came rubbin' up against my ears again—only this time it didn't sound like it was comin' from way off in no distance.

"Mamie, I have to talk to you. Don't be afraid. Please, it's me; it's only me."

One second before, I'd been warm and comfy under that big, soft comforter fluffed up with down feathers from more Red Chinese geese than I could count sheep. And now here I was feelin' like somebody'd just opened the door to some giant refrigerator. The whole bedroom was gettin' blasted with icy polar-bear air. I actually broke out shiverin'.

This time I decided not to sit up, not right away, not just yet. I kept the comforter pulled up over me and raised my head. I twisted it around just enough to see if the readin' lamp was still there.

I clicked on the light and *boom-boom-BOOM! boom-boom-BOOM!* My heart was poundin' up against my chest like it was some prizefighter's fist I had balled up inside me that was tryin' to punch its way through, tryin' its best to bust out.

Then I saw it. I saw it with my own eyes; yet I still didn't wanna believe it. I mean, hearin' things and seein' things is nothin' new to me but, I must confess, what I saw standin' there at the foot of the bed that night was too dramatic for even a low-keyed psychic like me. I like things kept on the quiet side, you know, toned down. Never did go in for dime-store magic or any of that flashy stuff, special effects.

But if, as they say, seein' is believin', then I had to buy it. I didn't have any choice but to go for it because the thing was right there in front of me, and it didn't seem to matter how much I shuddered and blinked and swallowed and hoped it would go away. Whatever it was, it was glimmerin' sure enough, sort of lightin' up and dimmin' and then comin' on real shiny again like my dream leaves I'd just woke up from. It kept flickerin' like this at first, gettin' on my nerves.

Finally I got up the courage to sit back up in bed and reach for the Bible I knew was in the bed-lamp table drawer. I held the Good Book up in fronta that thing the same as you'd hold a cross in front of a vampire. I did it real slow and, with all the strength still left in me, I concentrated on shootin' out beams of white light and godly thoughts all around me. You can do that, you know, if you practice it right. I shut my eyes as tight as I could while my light was generatin', and I asked the Lord to forgive me for all the sinnin' I'd already done, all the sinnin' I was doin' right now, and all the sinnin' I was probably gonna do.

When I opened my eyes, the only thing that'd changed was I could see the image in fronta me real sharp; it was a whole lot clearer than it'd been before. It was like I'd done somethin' to make it solidify. Jesus, I was scared!

"Wh-what's goin' on?" I shouted.

"Mamie," it said, callin' my name again in that faraway voice. "Mamie, don't you see what you're doin' to me?"

"What I'm doin' to you! Who are you? What are you? And what in the world are you doin' here?"

"All right, then," he said, "I'll make you a promise. I won't harm you. I *can't* harm you. Watch . . ."

I'll be doggoned if that thing didn't move up alongside the bed to where I was layin' and reach out its hand and place it on my jaw. Well, anyway, I thought it was a hand, and I thought it was my jaw, but somehow there really wasn't no connection. At least I didn't feel anything. The only way I can explain it would be to say it was quite a bit like bein' touched by light from a movie projector. And when you got right down to it, the whole experience was somethin' like bein' in a theater that's set up to show off some newfangled, fancy, overwhelmin' technical advance in motion pictures. Like, imagine a system that's more realistic than Cinerama, 3-D, Magnavision, Wide Screen, or Dolby Stereo or Quadraphonic Sound. It was like somebody'd figured out how to get the characters and actors to walk straight off the screen and down the aisle right up into your face.

I mean, it didn't matter that you couldn't technically feel 'em when they touched you; the sheer ingenuity of it was what blew you outta your seat!

O Lord, I prayed, *be gentle with me. I know I have never been normal in anybody's eyes. I know I was born both blessed and cursed. But, Lord, if I am finally losin' my mind, then please don't let me drop and shatter like a fragile plate. Just let me nut out gradually; let it happen by degrees. . . .*

Never once did I take my eyes off the figure in fronta me. I took a gang of deep breaths, though. The deeper I breathed, the more my heart slowed down and the sharper the image beside me got. Oh, I tell you it was frightenin'! But all the same, it was flat outta one of those worlds I'd always managed—in my lucid, message-gettin' moments—to keep a coupla toes in, if not a whole foot.

My heart slowed down.

I blinked again and focused my eyes, tuned my ears.

This tight blur of light moved to the foot of the bed. And that's when I saw who it sure enough resembled. It resembled, it favored, it looked like—well, it was Burley Cole. Yes, Burley himself, and he was comin' through bright and clear, every bit as clear as if he was bein' broadcast live and direct over some local cable hookup. The only difference was he look to me to be as big as life. No, he wasn't exactly wall-to-wall and treetop-tall, but what there was of him seemed for real. Burley was real enough to me then to needle me into wonderin' somethin': How come I'd never felt about any of the other men I'd lived with—includin' my only official husband—like I did about him?

I gulped again when he lit down on the edge of the waterbed—which he couldn't make rock—and looked right at me. "Say, Mamie, what was wrong with that king-size mattress I went to all that trouble to set up at our place? I went back to the house to contact you, and now here you turn up in some strange white folks' bed!"

Now that I was beginnin' to get use to how the stuff worked, I wanted to crawl over and hug Burley with all my might, but I couldn't. I was still havin' trouble even breathin'.

––––––

I was scared to look too close at what was happenin' and scared to blink. Either way I thought the hallucination I was havin' might break down and disappear. So I stayed put while Burley ranted on.

"You know, it ain't the easiest thing in the world to find somebody when they're not home."

"B-but I thought ghosts—I mean—uh, I thought spirits was suppose to be able to go anywhere at all."

"As usual, you aren't listenin' to me, Mamie. I didn't say anything about going places, did I?"

"You said it was hard to find me because I was up here in Beverly Hills insteada down there in Santa Monica."

"Well, yeah, and it's a trick to it I haven't quite got the hang of yet."

"A trick to *what*, Burley? I'm not followin' you."

"It's a trick to pickin' up on people wherever they are, especially people you know. See, you're suppose to be able to run through here and check on old So-and-So and see how he's been doin'. I'm just now startin' to kinda learn how you do that, but it's gonna take a lotta hard work."

Tears was try'na boil up in my eyes. I had to will 'em away. I felt like I was back in the fourth grade and Miz Rucker was askin' me to name the capital of Iceland. My mouth'd fall open and nothin' would come out because I couldn't even think of the name of the place, much less pronounce it.

Finally I did manage to say, "I know this might sound peculiar, Burley, but there's somethin' I just gotta ask."

"Ain't nothin' peculiar to me anymore, honey."

"I can believe it! But tell me, and please don't think I'm makin' fun, but—exactly where are you?"

"Where am I?" Burley looked perplexed.

"Yes, where are you now? Like, where are you comin' from just now? You said there was this trick about findin' people, and stuff. Now, where do you be comin' from in the first place when you set out to locate somebody out—out—well, out here where I am?"

Burley fell on his back and started rollin' and laughin' all over the bed, which still didn't wobble. It wobbled when I moved, but not for Burley. He laughed so hard and so long I got concerned about Danielle comin' back from her dinner party and hearin' us up there carryin' on like that. I was so glad to have him back, sort of, until worryin' over somethin' as triflin' as that seemed kinda sick under the circumstances. At least I wasn't about to risk scarin' him off by askin' him to pipe down.

"Mamie," he said, gettin' control of himself, "that's the funniest thing I've heard in a long time."

"Well, I'm glad I can still cheer you up."

"No, you don't understand. I spent all that time over there on Earth worried about dyin' and worried about people I cared about that died. That's one of the things I wanted to talk with you about."

I couldn't say anything. It was like my throat'd froze up.

"I can see you still terrified of me," he went on. "I been try'na prove to you I can't do you no harm. Look, I was the one always doubtin' all that spooky talk, and you were the one suppose to believe in it. Always gettin' messages from people that'd passed on, and tellin' folks's futures and readin' they minds. Now here I am tellin' you to relax, that dyin' ain't no real big thing, and you backin' off from me like I'm some kinda skid-row thug."

That still didn't help. I panicked. What if I never got my voice back? What if I had to lay there in that guest-room bed forever, paralyzed like some invalid? What if anybody else popped in and saw the way I was lookin' right then?

"Here," said Burley, "I'll try it again."

"Try what?"

"This . . ." He curled right up next to me on the same side of the bed he woulda normally been sleepin' on if he was alive. All this light was swarmin' all over the covers and me. Burley wrapped his glowin' arms around me and pushed his shiny face up alongside mine. Still, I couldn't feel anything except a new sorta tinglin' warmth that started someplace down around my lower intestine and fluttered on up to just above my belly, to my solar plexus. That's about the closest I come to touchin' the man, the spirit, whatever he was. Now, when I closed my eyes—which I did automatically when Burley took me in his arms—I felt like I could feel his body heat movin' into mine. The longer he held me, the stronger that feelin' got. But, I don't know, it's hard to talk about, and I already knew there wouldn't be too many people I was gonna be able to tell any of this to.

But he got me to cool down some by doin' that. He sat up in bed and leaned on one elbow, the way he use to would do before his health got rotten. I looked into his face and for the first time noticed he was younger-lookin' than I'd ever known him to be, even younger than that night we met at Harrah's. I was more confused than ever. Did I dare open my mouth again to see if anything would come out? Mother Dear woulda said, "A dog that'll *carry* a bone will *bring* you one."

"Well," I said. "Can you answer my question?"

"Baby, that's what's so funny about it. I haven't gone anywhere."

"Huh?"

"I ain't gone no place! I'm still right here. It's kinda like I moved next door. But, see, there's this partition, not a real partition that you can bump up against or anything, but some sorta time wall. That's all I know to call it. We're in different worlds."

"I'll say!"

"No, I'm on a whole different time than you."

"You mean, like Daylight Savin's or something like that?"

"You're way off there. I have to slip over here to see how much time in Earth hours done gone by. I'm still not comfortable. It's like I been floatin' around in this limbo since I got here. There's voices that keep callin' to me, tellin' me I got to move on, tellin' me I ain't reached my destination yet."

"Do they have wings and fly around pluckin' on harps?"

"I haven't seen no angels yet. I did see you, though."

"Where? When?"

"That afternoon I, uh, died. I was sorry it had to be on your birthday."

"Well, under the circumstances, I never held it against you."

"It was like this hole opened up in the middle of my forehead and light started pourin' into it, light that ran clean through my head to the backa my head, the part where the neck connect with the skull. Light was blowin' around through there and somethin' said, 'Here you go, Burley Cole. Jump in and make your getaway. Just jump right into that stream of light and it'll take you on out real clean and natural.' I did what the voice told me, and pretty soon there I was movin' up that tunnel, lookin' back at what I was leavin' behind."

"Wh-what did you see, Burley? How'd it feel?"

"It felt like a relief, but I felt so bad. I wanted you to know I wasn't in no pain, that you shouldn't cry over me. But when I looked back and saw my body laid out there on the couch and you pressin' my eyes shut with your fingers and cryin' and cryin' and sayin', 'Thou preparest a table before me in the presence of mine enemies,' I was movin' out in a hurry; floatin' all up around the ceilin'; pushin' on through, tootin' on the roof, blowin' on out through the rain and up above the rain into the light that was so bright I couldn't hardly stand it. Then I forced myself to come back down for another look. You were huggin' on this man in a trench coat and still cryin', cryin', cryin', and moanin'."

"I—I didn't want you to go," I said, no longer able to will back the tears. They were inchin' down my cheeks now. "I want you to be back here—with me—with me and Benjie. Since you've been away it's been like a train station that's been shut down."

"A train station?"

"Don't know why I said that. It's like a place that use to be warm and busy and friendly and useful and purposeful, and all like that. Now it's just a place where I go to get some rest and air out my sad thoughts."

"I know," he said.

"You do?"

"Sure, I watched you for the first few days."

"You mean, there at the house?"

"Uh-huh. Watched you mopin' around, and pickin' over our stuff, and callin' everybody, and receivin' visitors."

I turned around. "You saw all that and you didn't say anything?"

"Like, what was I supposed to say?"

"Oh, I don't know—anything. The kinda stuff you're sayin' now, I guess."

"Sugar, I was as sad as you were."

"But why?"

"Because you were so busted up and heartbroken. Don't you know how much it hurts when you hurt somebody you love deep down? Besides, I hadn't gotten my moves together yet. I didn't really know how to do anything except hang around and look."

I tried to touch Burley's face and kiss him, but about the best I could do was smooth the light where the image of his face was pulsatin' and then kiss at the spot where his beautiful mouth seemed to be. I squeezed my eyes shut, partly to make the tears quit fallin' and also to see if the kissin' and touchin' felt realer, like it had a few moments ago. It did. Tell you, right then and there I would'na minded goin' blind if it'd meant bein' next to Burley again and feelin' his presence all the time.

"So," I asked, "what do you do all day?"

"I can't answer that."

"How come?"

"There aren't any days."

"Just one long night, huh?"

"No, Mamie, that's the part I don't understand yet. I thought I'd be seein' a lotta other people I knew—my mother and father, Ruthie my sister, my grandmother Josie, and all the buddies who got away before me, and them I lost in the war. I ain't seen none of 'em!"

"You sure you're in the right place?"

"What you mean by that?"

"I mean, everybody else coulda gone one place and you went to another. It must happen all the time, don't you think?"

"Well, I thought about that, too. I never was exactly what you'd call retarded, you understand. There's no days, no nights; I don't need sleep and rest, and even though I look out there and see food I want and stuff I'd like to drink, I find I can get along well and good without it. But I don't feel right. I'm lonely, so lonely you couldn't even grasp it. It's a loneliness like I'm the only one in this world where I live, the only one on this planet or whatever it is—this space, I guess."

"Burley, that's hard to believe. You mean you haven't run into a soul out there you can talk with?"

"Well, that's another thing I needed to ask you. You been foolin' around with this kinda hocus-pocus ever since I've known you. Can't you try your powers and get me in touch with somebody out here I can relate to?"

"Oh, sweetheart!" I couldn't help myself. I started cryin' again. "I can't believe this is happenin' to you. Of course I'll send out some feelers, be happy to find out whatever I can. But I'm all mixed up. I mean, there you are dead and here I am livin'—theoretically speakin', anyway—and you're comin' to me to help you find out where all the other dead people went."

"That's right," Burley said, his belly startin' to tremble again. Sure enough, he went into another one of them unbelievable laughin' fits. Got me to laughin', too. "That's right," he said again and again. "Crazy, ain't it? I mean, it doesn't make any type of sense, does it? I can't figure it out to save my life!"

"Have you *heard* anybody, Burley? You said somethin' about voices a little while back. What kinda voices?"

"Don't know yet. It's like it's either somebody or somebodies in behind me all the time. They keep comin' at me and I keep sidesteppin' 'em."

"Why?"

"So I can come back here and see what *you* doin'."

"Did you go to the funeral?"

"Thought it was one of the pitifulest, most movin' things I ever sat still for in my life. It was a beautiful service, Mamie. And everybody was so real when they stopped at the casket and bent over to take a last look at me or say somethin'. And you wouldn't believe some of the things I heard people sayin'."

"Like what?" I was laughin' so hard now I didn't wanna stop.

"Like, well, Miz Wheelock, she leaned close in over the body and whispered, 'Don't worry, Burley. Every night when I say my prayers I'll sum up what's been goin' on in the soaps so you can keep up.' "

"She actually said that? I don't believe it!"

Burley sat up and held his hand like a Boy Scout. "Said it just as sure as I'm livin'.'"

"Sweetie, I wouldn't place no big bets on it. But it would be just like Miz Wheelock to be runnin' her mouth about *General Hospital* and you layin' up there dead."

"How long you plan to hang around here, Mamie?"

"Here in the flesh?"

"Nah, 'round here in Beverly Hills."

"Oh, just until . . ." My train of thought went to gettin' away from me. Burley was fadin' on me. It was like the light shimmerin' around his edges was goin' outta focus, and all that pulsatin' was slowin' way down. "Burley, what's goin' on? It's like I'm losin' you."

"Don't worry," he said, his voice droppin' some. "It's one of them—uh, I guess you call 'em spirits. That man is botherin' me again."

"What man?"

"Funny-lookin' man. Don't ask me who it is. Ever since I got in this condition, he's been one of the ones try'na hem me up and drag me off."

"Well, then, why don't you listen to the man and find out what he's try'na tell you? It might be important."

"Baby," Burley said, soundin' all sad, "I ain't ready to travel no place yet. I like it around here."

Suddenly all I could cling to was Burley's voice, which was gettin' harder to make out. The resta him had evaporated. The only light in the room now was the little bit that flickered from the fireplace. And pretty soon the cracklin' noise from the burnin' embers even drowned out his whispers more and more until it was as if none of what I'd seen and heard had ever taken place.

Had I only been dreamin' deeper than usual, or what?

You tell me.

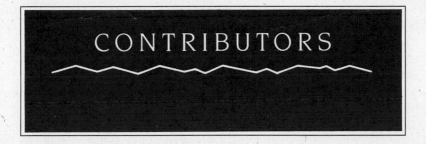

CONTRIBUTORS

TINA MCELROY ANSA's first novel, *Baby of the Family*, was published earlier this year. She lives with her husband on St. Simons Island, off the coast of Georgia.

DORIS JEAN AUSTIN's first novel *After the Garden*, was published in 1987; she writes for *The New York Times Book Review*, *The Amsterdam News*, and *Essence* magazine; is cofounder and Executive Director of New Renaissance Writers Inc. at the Schomburg center in Harlem; and is working on her second novel, "Heirs and Orphans."

TONI CADE BAMBARA is the author of *Gorilla, My Love*, *The Seabirds Are Still Alive*, both short story collections, and *The Salt Eaters*, a novel. She currently lives in Philadelphia, and has recently completed a new collection of stories, "Yeah, but Not Under Capitalism."

AMIRI BARAKA has written twelve volumes of poetry and eight works of nonfiction. His novels are *The System of Dante's Hell* and *Tales*. His many plays have been produced internationally for more than twenty-five years. He has edited a number of anthologies, most notably, *Black Fire* and *Confirmation, An Anthology of*

African American Women. He is the director of Africana Studies at the State University of New York, Stony Brook, and also teaches Afro-American Literature at Columbia University.

BARBARANEELY lives in Jamaica Plain, Massachusetts, and is currently working on her first novel.

DON BELTON, born in Philadelphia, has been a reporter for *Newsweek.* His first novel, *Almost Midnight,* was published in 1986. He currently teaches in the MFA Program at the University of Michigan.

BECKY BIRTHA's first collection of short stories was *For Nights Like This One: Stories of Loving Women,* and most recently, *Lovers' Choice.* Her stories and poetry have appeared in a number of literary and feminist journals. She lives in Philadelphia where she is completing a novel.

DAVID BRADLEY teaches at Temple University and is the author of *The Chaneysville Incident,* a novel.

WESLEY BROWN, the author of the novel, *Tragic Magic,* teaches at Rutgers University, has had several plays produced, and often reviews books for *The Village Voice.*

OCTAVIA BUTLER has received The Hugo and Nebula Awards for her science-fiction novels. She is the author of eight novels, including, *Dawn, Kindred, Adulthood Rites, Wild Seed, Xenogenesis Trilogy,* and others. She lives in Los Angeles.

XAM WILSON CARTIÉR, a native of St. Louis, has written for television, radio, and theater, but is best known for her award-winning first novel, *Be-Bop, Re-Bop.* She is at work on her second novel, "Muse-Echo Blues," and lives in San Francisco.

CAROLYN COLE is a playwright who lives in New York City.

WANDA COLEMAN is the author of four books of poetry and short fiction, most recently, *A War of Eyes and Other Stories* and *Heavy Daughter Blues.* She lives in Los Angeles.

J. CALIFORNIA COOPER's two collections of stories are *A Piece of Mine: A New Short Story Collection* and *Some Soul to Keep.* She is also a playwright and resides in Marshall, Texas.

STEVEN CORBIN's first novel, *No Easy Place to Be,* is an epic of the 1920s Harlem Renaissance. He teaches at UCLA's Extension Writers' Program.

SAMUEL R. DELANY is a four-time Nebula Award winner for his science-fiction novels. His realm of fantasy has been chronicled in more than fourteen novels, among them: *babel-17*, *Dhalgren*, *Nova*, *Triton*, and *Stars in My Pocket Like Grains of Sand*. He lives in Amherst, Massachusetts.

WILLIAM DEMBY, who lives in Sag Harbor, New York, published his first novel, *Beetle Creek*, in 1950. He is also the author of *The Catacombs*, *Blue Boy*, and most recently, *Love Story Black*. He teaches at Staten Island College of the City University of New York.

MELVIN DIXON has published a collection of poetry, *Change of Territory*, as well as a translation of *The Collected Poems of Leopold Sedar Senghor*. His short fiction was included in *Men on Men 2: An Anthology of Gay Fiction*. His most recent novel is *Trouble the Water*. He lives in New York City and teaches at the City University of New York Graduate School and Queens College.

RITA DOVE received the 1987 Pulitzer Prize for her book of poems, *Thomas and Beulah*. She is the author of three other books of poetry, *The Yellow House on the Corner*, *Museum*, and most recently, *Grace Notes*. She has also published a collection of short stories, *Fifth Sunday*. She is currently professor of English in the Center for Advanced Studies at the University of Virginia in Charlottesville, where she lives with her husband and daughter.

GRACE EDWARDS-YEARWOOD's first novel, *In the Shadow of the Peacock*, was published in 1988. A long-standing member of The Harlem Writers' Guild, she has taught at Hofstra University and lives in Brooklyn, New York.

TREY ELLIS attended Phillips Academy and Stanford University, where he was editor of the college humor magazine. As a journalist, his work has appeared in *The Black Film Review*, *Art & Antiques*, *Newsweek*, *Elle*, *Interview*, and *The Washington Post*. His first novel, *Platitudes*, was published in 1989, when he was twenty-five years old. He lives in New York City.

PERCIVAL L. EVERETT is the author of *Suder*, *Walk Me to the Distance*, *Cutting Lisa*, *For Her Dark Skins*, *Zulus*, and *The Weather and Women Treat Me Fair*. He teaches in the Department of English at the University of Notre Dame.

ARTHUR FLOWERS's first novel, *De Mojo Blues*, was published in 1986. Cofounder of New Renaissance Writers' Guild, he is currently finishing his new novel, "Another Good Loving Blues." A native of Memphis, Tennessee, he now resides in Los Angeles.

SANDRA HOLLIN FLOWERS's first published story, "Hope of Zion," was included in *Prize Stories, 1981: The O. Henry Awards*. She received her MFA from the

University of Arizona, and her Ph.D. from Emory University. She is currently at work on a novel, "I Heard a Crazy Woman Speak." She lives in Atlanta, Georgia.

BILL WILLIAMS FORDE was the director of The Harlem Writers' Guild for many years. He is currently completing his first novel, "Tomorrow," and lives in New York City.

ERNEST GAINES, well known for his novels, *The Autobiography of Miss Jane Pittman* and *A Gathering of Old Men,* is the author of five other works. He divides his time between San Francisco and the University of Southwestern Louisiana in Lafayette, where he teaches creative writing.

MARITA GOLDEN's most recent novels are *Long Distance Life* and *A Woman's Place.* Her autobiography, *Migrations of the Heart,* was published in 1983. Her writing has appeared in *Ms.*, *Essence, The New York Times*, and *The Washington Post.* She is a founding member of the African-American Writers' Guild in Washington, D.C., where she resides. She teaches fiction writing at George Mason University in Fairfax, Virginia.

PETER HARRIS has published many volumes of poetry as well as a collection of folktales. He lives in Temple Hills, Maryland. "The Vampire Who Drinks Gospel Music" is his first published story.

SAFIYA HENDERSON-HOLMES is a playwright, poet, physiotherapist, mother, wife, natural birthing counselor, and masseuse. She is the recipient of two New York Foundation for the Arts fellowships, and currently teaches poetry at Sarah Lawrence College in Bronxville, New York.

KRISTIN HUNTER has written three adult novels, *The Lakestown Rebellion, God Bless the Child,* and *Survivors,* as well as a children's book, *The Soul Brothers and Sister Lou.* She teaches at the University of Pennsylvania and lives in New Jersey.

ANGELA JACKSON's fiction and poetry has been published in numerous literary magazines, among them: *First World, Triquarterly, Open Places, River Styx,* and *Callaloo.* She is also the author of six volumes of poetry and succeeded the late Hoyt W. Fuller as chair of OBAC Writers Workshop in Chicago. *Nommo,* an anthology of African-American writing from Chicago that she edited, appeared in 1975. *Treemont Stone* is her first novel. She teaches at Columbia College in Chicago.

CHARLES JOHNSON is the current chairman of the Creative Writing Program at the University of Washington in Seattle, and fiction editor of *The Seattle Review.*

In addition to numerous essays and short stories, he is the author of a work of aesthetics and criticism, *Being & Race: Black Writing Since 1970*. His novels include *Oxherding Tale* and *Faith and the Good Thing* in addition to *The Sorcerer's Apprentice*, a collection of short stories. His most recent novel is *Middle Passage*.

GAYL JONES has published two novels, *Eva's Man* and *Corregidora*, both of which were reprinted through the Black Women Writers Series by Beacon Press of Boston.

WILLIAM MELVIN KELLEY teaches at Sarah Lawrence College. His work includes *Dem, A Drop of Patience, Dancers on the Shore, A Different Drummer, Dunfords Travels Everywhere*, and many short stories. He lives in New York City.

RANDALL KENAN has been on the editorial staff of Alfred A. Knopf, and his first novel, *A Visitation of Spirits*, was published in 1989 when he was twenty-five. He teaches fiction at Sarah Lawrence College in Bronxville, New York.

JOHN MCCLUSKEY teaches Afro-American literature and fiction writing at Indiana University in Bloomington. He has written two novels, *Look What They Done to My Song* and *Mr. America's Last Season Blues*. His short fiction has appeared in numerous literary journals, including *Best American Short Stories: 1976*. He is currently completing a new novel.

COLLEEN MCELROY's work has appeared in *Short Story International, Callaloo, Confrontation*, and many other literary magazines and anthologies. Her volumes of poetry include *Lie and Say You Love Me, Winters Without Snow, Queen of the Ebony Isles*, and others. *Jesus and Fat Tuesday and other Short Stories* is her most recent work. She has received numerous awards, including a Fulbright Fellowship, and is currently a professor of English at the University of Washington in Seattle.

NATHANIEL MACKEY's ongoing series of fictional letters appear in two volumes, *Bedouin Hornbook* and *Djbot Baghostus's Run*. He is the editor of the literary journal, *Hambone*. He is also the author of *Four for Trane, Septet for the End of Time*, and *Eroding Witness*. He teaches literature at the University of California, Santa Cruz.

TERRY MCMILLAN's first novel was *Mama* and her latest is *Disappearing Acts*. She teaches at the University of Arizona in Tucson.

JAMES ALAN MCPHERSON received the Pulitzer Prize for fiction in 1978. He has published two collections of stories, *Hue and Cry* and *Elbow Room*. He has been on the faculty at the University of Iowa Writer's Workshop for a number of years.

CLARENCE MAJOR is the author of five novels, most recently *My Amputations* and *Such Was the Season*, and several volumes of poetry. He has received numerous grants and awards, including a National Council on the Arts award, a Fulbright Fellowship, a Pushcart Prize, and the Western States Book Award. He teaches at the University of California, Davis.

PAULE MARSHALL's first novel, *Brown Girl, Brownstones*, has been widely anthologized. Her other novels are *Soul Clap Hands and Sing*, *The Chosen Place, The Timeless People*, and *Praisesong for the Widow*. She teaches at Virginia Commonwealth University in Richmond.

MARY MONROE, a native of Choctaw County, Alabama, currently lives in Oakland, California. Her first novel, *The Upper Room*, was published in 1985.

GLORIA NAYLOR received the American Book Award for her first novel, *The Women of Brewster Place*, which was recently made into a TV mini-series. She has won many awards, and is the author of two other novels, *Linden Hills* and most recently, *Mama Day*.

RICHARD PERRY teaches literature and fiction writing at Pratt Institute in Brooklyn, New York. His first novel, *Changes*, was published in 1974. In 1985, he was the winner of the Quality Paperback Books' New Voice Award for his second novel, *Montgomery's Children*. He lives in Tenafly, New Jersey.

DARRYL PINCKNEY has published many literary essays. He's had work published in the *New York Review of Books* as well as *Granta*. His forthcoming novel is *Sweet Evening Breeze*.

CONNIE PORTER's first novel, *All-Bright Court*, will be published by Houghton Mifflin Company. An excerpt of that novel appeared in the *Southern Review*. She lives in Milton, Massachusetts.

ISHMAEL REED is a novelist, poet, television producer, songwriter, publisher, magazine editor, playwright, and founder of the Before Columbus Foundation and There City Cinema. Among his honors, fellowships, and prizes is the Lewis H. Michaux Literary Prize. He has taught at Harvard, Yale, and Dartmouth, and for twenty years has been a lecturer at the University of California at Berkeley. His latest works of fiction are *Reckless Eyeballing* and *The Terrible Threes*. His collection of essays, *Writin' Is Fightin'*, was published in 1989.

FATIMA SHAIK has been a reporter for the New Orleans *Times-Picayune* and *Miami News*, as well as an editor for McGraw Hill, Inc. Her first book, *The Mayor of New Orleans, Just Talking Jazz*, is a collection of novellas. She lives in New York City.

NTOZAKE SHANGE is probably best known for her choreoplay, *For Colored Girls Who Have Considered Suicide, When the Rainbow Is Enuf*. She has subsequently had a number of plays produced, in addition to several published volumes of poetry, literary essays, and the novels. *Sassafrass, Cypress & Indigo*, and *Betsey Brown*. She is the recipient of numerous awards and currently resides in Philadelphia.

ELLEASE SOUTHERLAND teaches at Pace University in New York. Her first novel, *Let the Lion Eat Straw*, was published in 1979. She is currently at work on a new novel, "A Feast of Fools."

BARBARA SUMMERS was a fashion model with the Ford Agency in New York City for fifteen years. She wrote the text for the book *I Dream a World*, a photographic essay on seventy-five African-American women. She is currently completing a new work, "Skin Deep," about the history of black models in America and abroad. Her short fiction has appeared in *Essence* and *Catalyst*. She lives in Teaneck, New Jersey.

CLIFF THOMPSON received a degree in English and creative writing from Oberlin College. He lives in New York City. "Judgment" is his first published story.

ALICE WALKER received the Pulitzer Prize, as well as the American Book Award, for her novel *The Color Purple*, which was also made into a motion picture. She is also the author of two short story collections, *In Love & Trouble* and *You Can't Keep a Good Woman Down*; four volumes of poetry, *Once, Revolutionary Petunias & Other Poems, Good Night, Willie Lee, I'll See You in the Morning*, and *Horses Make a Landscape Look More Beautiful*; two volumes of essays, *In Search of Our Mothers' Gardens: Womanist Prose* and *Living by the Word: Selected Writings*. In addition to her other novels, her most recent is *The Temple of My Familiar*.

JOHN EDGAR WIDEMAN, a Rhodes Scholar, is the author of several books including two short story collections, *Damballah*, and more recently, *Fever*, and a trilogy of novels, *Sent for You Yesterday, Hiding Place*, and *The Lynchers*. His other novels are *Hurry Home, Reuben*, and *A Glance Away*. His nonfiction work includes *Brothers and Keepers*. He teaches at the University of Massachusetts at Amherst.

JOHN A. WILLIAMS is the author of eighteen books, including *Jacob's Ladder, The Junior Bachelor Society, The Man Who Cried I Am*, and *!Click Song*. He has been a foreign correspondent for *Newsweek* as well as professor of English at Rutgers University, where he currently teaches. He is the recipient of the

American Book Award and The National Institute of Arts and Letters Award, among others. Two of his novels have been adapted for film and television. He lives in Teaneck, New Jersey.

AL YOUNG was born in Mississippi and raised in Detroit. He is the author of five novels, *Snakes, Sitting Pretty, Who Is Angelina?, Ask Me Now*, and *Seduction by Light*; five collections of poetry; and three works of nonfiction. Along with Ishmael Reed, he has edited *Calafia: The California Poetry* as well as *Yardbird Lives!* He lives in Palo Alto, California.

FOR THE BEST IN PAPERBACKS, LOOK FOR THE

In every corner of the world, on every subject under the sun, Penguin represents quality and variety—the very best in publishing today.

For complete information about books available from Penguin—including Puffins, Penguin Classics, and Arkana—and how to order them, write to us at the appropriate address below. Please note that for copyright reasons the selection of books varies from country to country.

In the United Kingdom: Please write to *Dept. JC, Penguin Books Ltd, FREEPOST, West Drayton, Middlesex UB7 0BR.*

If you have any difficulty in obtaining a title,.please send your order with the correct money, plus ten percent for postage and packaging, to *P.O. Box No. 11, West Drayton, Middlesex UB7 0BR*

In the United States: Please write to *Consumer Sales, Penguin USA, P.O. Box 999, Dept. 17109, Bergenfield, New Jersey 07621-0120.* VISA and MasterCard holders call 1-800-253-6476 to order all Penguin titles

In Canada: Please write to *Penguin Books Canada Ltd, 10 Alcorn Avenue, Suite 300, Toronto, Ontario M4V 3B2*

In Australia: Please write to *Penguin Books Australia Ltd, P.O. Box 257, Ringwood, Victoria 3134*

In New Zealand: Please write to *Penguin Books (NZ) Ltd, Private Bag 102902, North Shore Mail Centre, Auckland 10*

In India: Please write to *Penguin Books India Pvt Ltd, 706 Eros Apartments, 56 Nehru Place, New Delhi 110 019*

In the Netherlands: Please write to *Penguin Books Netherlands bv, Postbus 3507, NL-1001 AH Amsterdam*

In Germany: Please write to *Penguin Books Deutschland GmbH, Metzlerstrasse 26, 60594 Frankfurt am Main*

In Spain: Please write to *Penguin Books S. A., Bravo Murillo 19, 1° B, 28015 Madrid*

In Italy: Please write to *Penguin Italia s.r.l., Via Felice Casati 20, I-20124 Milano*

In France: Please write to *Penguin France S. A., 17 rue Lejeune, F-31000 Toulouse*

In Japan: Please write to *Penguin Books Japan, Ishikiribashi Building, 2-5-4, Suido, Bunkyo-ku, Tokyo 112*

In Greece: Please write to *Penguin Hellas Ltd, Dimocritou 3, GR-106 71 Athens*

In South Africa: Please write to *Longman Penguin Southern Africa (Pty) Ltd, Private Bag X08, Bertsham 2013*